CLARE FRANCIS

Clare Francis is the author of seven internationally bestselling thrillers: *Night Sky*, *Red Crystal*, *Wolf Winter*, *Requiem*, *Deceit*, *Betrayal* and *A Dark Devotion*. She has also written three non-fiction books about her voyages across the oceans of the world.

Also by Clare Francis in Pan Books

Thrillers
Night Sky
Red Crystal
Wolf Winter
Requiem

Crime
Deceit
Betrayal
A Dark Devotion

Non-fiction
Come Hell or High Water
Come Wind or Weather
The Commanding Sea

CLARE FRANCIS

DECEIT

and

BETRAYAL

PAN BOOKS

First published 2001 by Pan Books
an imprint of Macmillan Publishers Ltd
25 Eccleston Place, London SW1W 9NF
Basingstoke and Oxford
Associated companies throughout the world
www.macmillan.com

ISBN 0 330 48938 0

A CIP catalogue record for this book is available from
the British Library.

Phototypeset by Intype, London
Printed and bound in Great Britain by
Mackays of Chatham plc, Chatham, Kent

DECEIT

For James

ONE

The organ booms out its summons, a single ragged chord. The reverberations are quelled by the rustle of people rising, the clearing of throats, the reopening of service sheets. I am late getting to my feet and Josh, who has jumped up with transparent and unashamed haste, turns questioningly, his mouth puckered in a look of mild impatience. Josh, our nine-year-old. Not mine alone, not yet; still ours. Though Harry has been dead almost three months I can't bring myself to think of Josh as fatherless. It seems too final somehow.

The last hymn. I am relieved. I shouldn't be, I suppose, but the service has been rather long, there have been no less than three eulogies, some of which, though well meant, did not seem to have much to do with the Harry I knew. And I am tired, so tired. My legs are leaden, my brain heavy.

At the same time I am aware of the morning having rushed by with bewildering speed. I wish I could rewind it and start again. From the moment I woke the children and we sat down to our silent breakfast, my mind has steadfastly refused to involve itself in the day's proceedings. It is part of my blocking out process. Even after so long I think I am still in a state of disbelief, and the seamless succession of prayers, addresses and hymns have passed in a dream, as if I were watching through a dark screen.

I am acutely aware that I should be making the most of this ceremony, that it provides an unrepeatable chance for me and the children to come to terms with Harry's death; yet for me at least the opportunity has largely been missed. The only sensation I can identify with any certainty is emptiness; that, and a dread tightness in my stomach, which, after all this time, has grown so familiar as to be almost unnoticeable.

We launch into the second verse. Katie, on my left, is standing very close. Her hand holds mine, as it has from the beginning of the service. Her touch, which is cool and firm and permits no wavering, gives me immeasurable support, and I know that she is drawing as much strength, if not more, from mine. Stand or fall, we are together.

Katie is not Harry's daughter, though for much of her young life she would have liked to be. Katie, now fifteen, is the daughter of my early marriage to a musician who faded from her life – and mine – many years ago. He was last heard of living in a beach commune in Mexico. Thus to all intents and purposes Katie has lost not one but two fathers, a double blow that she, with her anxious and fragile nature, isn't well equipped to deal with. She has taken Harry's death badly. For a time I thought she would never come to terms with it. If it hadn't been for our seven weeks in California, I think maybe she never would.

She is stronger now, but not so strong that I dare glance at her in case one or the other of us should betray an emotion that we would rather keep to ourselves. This is not, anyway, an occasion for sadness. It is, I remind myself, a time for thanksgiving. For Harry's life.

The choir bursts into soaring harmony. They are really

2

very good, this choir, some fine voices among them. I find my place on the sheet and mouth the refrain, 'O hear us when we cry to Thee, For those in peril on the sea.' This hymn, like everything else in the service, has been chosen by Harry's sister Anne. The selection was left to her partly because I have not been around to deal with such things, partly because Anne desperately wanted the job of organising the service. She too has taken Harry's death badly.

This hymn was an obvious, not to say inevitable, choice – Harry was lost at sea – but it is such an emotive piece that I find myself wishing it might have been left out. But I mustn't quibble; Anne has taken enormous pains over the arrangements. The flowers, enormous sprays of them, are spectacular, the service sheet beautifully printed, the turn-out strong – Anne has, I know, contacted great numbers of people by phone and letter in case they missed the newspaper announcement.

The final verse at last. A suppressed sob comes from close by. It is Anne, standing on the other side of Josh. She is fumbling with a handkerchief, she buries her nose in it. Beyond the trembling feathers of her hat, her husband Charles blinks uncertainly and, catching my eye, flashes me a glance of mild alarm. I give him a reassuring look. His mouth twitches in a grateful smile which does not quite conceal his discomfort. A product of Eton, hunting fields and Cirencester Agricultural College, Charles is more at ease with farming accounts than emotional crises.

As we sing the final lines something shifts inside me, the darkness moves aside, and I am at last able to focus on Harry, on the image of him that I want to keep, the Harry who gave me many years of contentment, who gave me Josh, who, during Katie's young years, gave her the father-figure she longed for; who was never, despite his

3

inadequacies and inconsistencies, the failure he feared himself to be.

These thoughts, coming so abruptly, threaten to tip me over an emotional drop that I instinctively avoid. Hastily I look down at Josh's shining hair. Taking after me, he is tall for his age, already approaching my shoulder. As he raises his head, I catch his profile, with its ski-jump nose, full mouth and long lashes. Never an ardent singer he has finally dropped all pretence at mouthing the words, and is staring at something high above the altar. His expression is one of duty and resignation that has long worn thin. I feel a stab of love for him, this strange child of mine, so contained, so extraordinarily unconcerned. He has an acceptance of events that baffles and impresses me in turns.

We kneel, the priest incants the commendation and blessing, there is a hush and I say my last prayers for Harry, gripping Katie's hand more tightly as I do so. I was never much of a one for prayer before, but I have prayed regularly since Harry's death. Hypocritical, I suppose, but the need is strong. I pray for the Harry that I loved. For the Harry that I loved and cared for to the best of my ability, that I supported in his many ventures, that I wish so very much were still alive.

We stand up. I risk a glance at Katie. Her mouth is firmly set, her eyes expressionless. Only her nostrils betray a rapid breathing. She catches my stare. Our eyes exchange enquiries and receive reassurances – a glance that says we are both all right this far. I reach for Josh's hand and prepare for the moment I dread, the walk down the wide aisle through the banks of faces.

But as I gather my things, Anne reaches past Josh to touch my arm and indicate that I must wait. I realise: I have forgotten the item that has been tacked onto the end of the programme, the item so dear to Anne's heart.

From the back of the church, a lone bugle rings out. The last post. I tried to persuade Anne to change her mind about this, I tried gently and diplomatically, and now I wish I had tried a little harder. In his days in the Parachute Regiment Harry served in the Falklands War, but he said he never got involved in any real battles, and it certainly wasn't a time he remembered with any great pride or pleasure. This didn't stop him from acquiring a war hero tag, drummed up by his supporters to bolster his election campaign. It was an embellishment that became over-played to the point of embarrassment, even for Harry. I felt that this service was not the moment to perpetuate the idea, that it would have been a good opportunity to play it down. But it seemed I was the only member of the family to think so, or at least the only one prepared to voice concern about it. Yet I am not good at fighting my corner, not in family matters which risk upset and resentment anyway, and when Anne mounted an emotionally charged defence I gave way.

The bugle call has a reputation for bringing tears to the driest eye. I realise that Katie, having managed reasonably well so far, has finally run into trouble. She has dropped her head, her mouth is skewed, she is frowning fiercely. I give her hand a rough shake. 'Almost there,' I whisper hoarsely. She shows no sign of hearing, and I cajole her. 'Hold on, baby. Hold on.'

The sound of the bugle dies away, the clergy start to progress out of the church. It's over at last.

I look up to see Jack gliding to a halt in front of Katie. Jack used to be Harry's business partner. He is also a godfather to Josh. I realise that he is intending to escort us to the church door. I am reluctant, I hold back. For this particular journey I would prefer that the children and I walked alone.

But Jack isn't someone who is easily deterred and I, as much as anyone, seem incapable of deterring him. Even here in the subdued atmosphere of the church he seems to overwhelm me and with an inevitability that dismays me I let him take my elbow.

We begin to walk. I force myself to meet the numerous eyes, even to smile, and am suddenly glad that I have made the effort, for though people stare – forced by tradition to wait for my departure they have little choice – the stares are warm and kind. There are so many people. And so many I had not expected to see, people from my past, neighbours from Suffolk, parents of Katie and Josh's school friends. I am deeply touched.

In the porch an usher is opening the heavy church doors. The London air flows in, heavy and hot with traffic fumes. I pause just short of the doors and turn, gathering the children on either side, ready for the line-up and ritual handshaking. Before I can stop myself I look questioningly to Jack, as if seeking his approval for this move.

Taking this as his due, he grips my arm lightly and narrows his eyes in a look that contains the appropriate mixture of understanding and solidarity. 'All right?' His voice is rough with sympathy. 'You did so well, Ellen. *So* well.' I suppose he means that I produced no tears, no embarrassments, no behaviour that could be judged to be anything less than immaculate.

Remembering the children, he adds emphatically, 'You *all* did well. Your father would have been proud of you.' He throws an avuncular smile at Katie, who, having no time for Jack, doggedly avoids his gaze. Undaunted, Jack runs a hand playfully over Josh's head.

I notice how beautifully dressed Jack is in a lightweight suit that must have come from Savile Row, how beneath the concerned expression he has a barely suppressed exuberance. But then, despite the business interests they still had in common, the recession never seemed to touch Jack as it did Harry. I recognise this inner light as the glow of success. Some new conquest, no doubt. Financial or female, it is hard to tell with Jack. Quietly, as soon as his attention is elsewhere, I disengage my arm.

'I'll give you people's names as they come to you,' Jack says, surveying the advancing line with a glint of relish.

'Thank you.'

'You know Reynolds is here? And Draycott.'

'Reynolds?'

He gives an awkward laugh, as if I have cracked a dubious joke. 'The party chairman,' he says firmly.

I was only checking. And Draycott, I remember, is a junior minister of health. Ever since I let Harry down by confusing a minister of the environment with a Labour back-bencher, thus mixing not only party – a heinous enough crime – but rank too, I have gone to great pains to make sure I have the names and jobs right. Harry, who always felt humiliation keenly, did not let me forget my gaffe for weeks afterwards.

The effort of preparing myself for this final test must show in my face because Jack says in his most soothing voice, 'I'll keep you briefed, don't worry.'

I smile my gratitude, which is real enough.

He squeezes my arm again. 'Sure you're all right?'

'Oh yes. Really.' I give a half-smile to prove it.

He leans close. 'Good girl. Knew you would be,' he says with a glance that is all largesse and pride. The role of family stalwart is one he seems to enjoy.

Anne and Charles approach. Jack, who has the remark for every occasion, says to Anne, 'A beautiful service. Congratulations.'

But Anne has her sights on me. She hisses over Katie's head in a not-so-low whisper, 'What about the children, Ellen? Shouldn't we get them to the hotel? They'll have had enough. Bound to. Haven't you, darlings? *Must* have had enough. You'll be longing for your lunch, I know you will. They've got meringues at the hotel, Josh. *And* chocolate cake.' Anne, childless herself, prides herself on her rapport with children, a conviction based on the belief that children are only happy when filled with rich food. Anne herself has perhaps never passed this stage in her own development, for at forty-three she is by any standards large and has never to anyone's knowledge tried to diet.

Aware of the danger of giving offence – always a risk with Anne – I say lightly, 'It's good of you, Anne, but I think they'd really prefer to stay. For the time being anyway.'

Anne gives me a look of irritation and bafflement, as if I am being unreasonable. In fact we have discussed this several times. I have told her from the beginning that it is my intention to keep the children with me at this stage of the proceedings. I have explained how I want them to meet their father's friends and acquaintances, to hear at first hand all the nice things they will say about him, so that they will see him through other people's eyes as well as their own.

Anne gives way, if only because of the crush of people building up behind her. Most of the family are already grouped on the far side of the porch – my father on a rare visit from Cornwall, wearing the expression of abandonment and defencelessness that he acquired long before Mother's death four years ago; my mother-in-law Diana, mother to Harry and Anne, glaring fiercely into the sunlight; and the faithful Margaret, Harry's secretary, keeper of birthdays and anniversaries, organiser of impossible schedules, who, although she is not strictly family, is treated as such by us all.

Jack, expansive and commanding, very much in his element, begins to announce people: an MP who shared a cramped office with Harry during Harry's all too brief spell in Parliament; the health minister, his presence apparently wrenched from the teeth of a busy schedule; business associates of Harry's, many of them unknown to me, courteous men with firm handshakes and evasive smiles who murmur gruff words to the children.

I check on Katie. We agreed that she could change her mind about this right up until the last minute, could go back to the hotel if she wished, but she seems to be doing all right. By way of confirmation she gives a careless glance that drifts past me and over the gathering. Josh, as usual, is taking things in his stride. Fidgeting, pulling impatient faces, impervious as ever.

Suffolk people now. The women kiss and hug me and look on me with worried eyes. They want to know what they can do now that I'm back, how they can help out. They make me swear to call them. They tell the children that their friends have missed them and are looking forward to seeing them again. The men kiss me a little more sedately and echo their wives, a nodding chorus. Anything they can do, anything at all.

Then Molly, who gives me a hug that almost robs me of breath. Molly is my closest friend. Irrepressible – some might say impossible – she works for a half-way house project for young offenders which she bamboozled me into raising money for.

9

'Oh, Ellen!' she cries, and when she pulls back her eyes are bright and fierce. 'God, you're thin!'

I make a face.

'You're back now?'

'I'm back.'

'Staying put?'

'Oh yes.'

'When am I going to see you?'

'Well . . . soon.'

'Soon!' she exclaims, refusing to interpret this as a rebuff. 'How soon? Tomorrow?'

I gesture possible difficulties. 'I don't know yet. I'll have to see . . .'

She gives me a look that is both disappointed and questioning. 'Why didn't you call?' she whispers harshly. 'Before you left?'

I shake my head. I can't begin to explain.

'I waited. I would have done anything, *anything*.'

I touch her hand. 'I know.'

She gives me another all-enveloping hug that drives her sleeve hard into my eye and makes me blink. I hug her back, but a little more hesitantly. The children apart, I love and trust Molly more than anyone else in the world, but just at the moment my equilibrium is too fragile to survive too much tender inspection and unconditional support.

Molly moves on reluctantly, her mouth pursed in a mixture of affection and rebuke.

A tall man of perhaps fifty stands before me. His stiff bearing, the cut of his double-breasted suit, the tap of his metal-tipped heels on the flagstones declare his military status well before Jack introduces him as Harry's CO, a colonel whose name as usual I do not catch. This is the first time I have met anyone from Harry's Falklands days.

I was never sure why this should be, why Harry, unlike most men of his background, of the well-connected officer class, failed to keep in touch with his regimental comrades. I assumed Harry's world had diverged too much from theirs, that business and politics left him too little time for the niceties of the past. But if I used to feel mild curiosity about this it is largely gone, and today is not anyway the time to satisfy it. I accept the colonel's formal words, his immaculately expressed regrets. His grey unblinking eyes are cool and unreadable, though not, I think, unsympathetic. I wonder how well he knew Harry.

A small bow and the colonel turns away.

More Suffolk people – the local builder, who spent the best part of a year renovating Pennygate; Jill Hooper, who cleans the house and looks after Josh when I am away; and Maurice, our gardener. I tell them how much I appreciate their coming all this way.

I find myself greeting a man with sideburns and a stern well-weathered face who, since Jack has got side-tracked, is forced to introduce himself. He has a Suffolk accent, an indistinct manner of speaking. It takes me a moment to grasp that he is attached to the coastguard service, and a further moment to understand that it was he who organised the search for Harry. To compensate for my initial blankness, I lurch into excessive thanks. I thank him for coming, I thank him for instigating what was, I feel sure, an extremely thorough search, I thank him for doing all he could. This effusiveness only serves to darken his expression. He shakes his head, he will not have it. From his point of view I suppose he judges the whole thing a professional failure, a blot on his record. The yacht not found. Nor the body. I assure him I do not blame him in the slightest for what I euphemistically call 'the way things

11

have worked out'. I am sure no one could have done more. He shrugs grudgingly. We stumble on for a few moments, then I grip his hand once again and, grateful to be released, he is gone.

The line keeps coming. I did not realise that Harry and I knew so many people. I have difficulty in remembering what I have just said and to whom. Falling back on my long months as a candidate's wife, I confine myself to a resolute smile and repeated thanks.

The stream of faces and outstretched hands begins to dwindle at last. Not an instant too soon. My legs are starting to go. The stress affects me this way, a sudden draining of energy from the limbs, a leaden sensation in the muscles. In California, where every trial of existence is confronted and analysed into submission, Katie and I went on a stress management course. Remembering our lessons, I concentrate on my breathing, I force the tension from my shoulders, I make a conscious effort to calm myself.

John Barrow, the local Conservative Association agent, has been hanging back and finally approaches. He wears his habitually lugubrious expression which gives him the air of being sorely tried. By his standards, I suppose he is. I don't think he ever really liked Harry, far less his candidature. Harry was acutely aware that, following his failure to win the seat in the 1987 election, Barrow secretly tried to oust him. Barrow had considered the seat to be winnable and blamed Harry for its loss. Even when the seat unexpectedly fell vacant almost four years later – the Liberal incumbent died of a heart attack – and Harry won the by-election by a narrow margin, Barrow was less than euphoric. Harry, who had an almost obsessive need to know what people were saying about him, discovered that Barrow was already expressing doubts about Harry's ability to hang on to the seat at the forthcoming general election. Barrow put Harry's by-election win down to the short-term publicity Harry had gained from organising a concert in aid of Rumanian orphans. The concern certainly got publicity – Harry managed to persuade two chart-topping pop groups and an Oscar-winning actress to take part – but Harry didn't figure much in the photocalls and I don't think it boosted his profile as much as Barrow thought it did.

Barrow's concerns about Harry's long-terms prospects were well-founded. In the 1992 general election, which came just five months after Harry entered Parliament, his constituents, bucking the national trend, voted Harry out.

Barrow shakes my hand and says the service was very good and that he is pleased at how many people have been able to come. He means, considering it has taken place in London. Like him, I would have preferred the service to have been held closer to home, in Woodbridge or, at a stretch, Ipswich. But Anne would not hear of it. The MPs and ministers by whom she sets such store would never travel that far from Westminster; and a service in London does, I realise, have a certain cachet.

'I feel you should know – we're selecting a new candidate. We've got a shortlist,' says Barrow in a confidential voice. He watches me closely and I realise he is concerned at how I will react to this news. 'We left it a while,' he adds. 'But after so long . . . well, we hoped it wouldn't be unacceptable to go ahead.' Wouldn't be unacceptable. To me, I suppose. Did he think I was going to be offended? Did he think I wanted the candidature left empty?

'Oh no, of course not. You must go ahead. I know Ha—' Oddly, I still stumble over Harry's name when talking to

13

people I don't know well. 'I'm sure Harry would have approved.' Then I add, more for something to say than out of any real interest, 'You've got some promising people lined up?'

'I think so.' From the way his eyes spark I would guess that he already has a strong candidate.

Katie pulls at my hand. She wants to go. And Josh, who has been gently and insistently prodding my leg for some minutes, has also reached the limits of his nine-year-old endurance. Margaret, who, as Harry's secretary for almost ten years, has perfected the art of appearing on cue, catches my signal and comes to scoop them up. Without meeting my eye Katie says, 'See you later, Mum,' and strides off with Josh in tow. As they're swallowed up by the dusty sunlight I feel a small pang. Whatever you do for your children, however much love and support you give them, you can't entirely protect them, they still have to face great chunks of life on their own.

'The final selection won't be till the end of the month,' Barrow says. 'Perhaps you might be able to come along then, to meet the new candidate? Nice if you could give your blessing. Pass on the torch, so to speak. People would appreciate that.'

The thought of a public event, of photographers and chattering party faithful fills me with dread, but for a moment I can't think of how to refuse. 'Well—'

'There's no hurry.'

'It's hard to plan. I—'

'Say no more.' Barrow attempts a rare smile which pulls his heavy face in directions it is not accustomed to go. Whatever he felt about Harry's abilities as a candidate, he has always been more than kind to me. 'We'll talk about it again, nearer the time.' He begins to move away then pauses, as if considering the wisdom of what he is about to say. Finally he says, 'You might want to know – I'd like it to be Crawley.'

'Crawley?' I am momentarily confused. Crawley is Jack. I repeat with a laugh, 'Crawley?'

Barrow confirms – it is Jack. And suddenly I understand what has given Jack his aura of suppressed excitement. He has in his sights a prize which for him will be as great a conquest as money or women. Jack has put himself up for Harry's candidature.

On the far side of the porch Jack is standing with some men I do not know. He is looking intent, his arms crossed, his well-defined features creased with concentration. Even as I watch, he goes into rapid and animated speech accompanied by strong precise gestures. The man of the moment.

Politics are, of course, an obvious step for him. If I had thought about it, which in the trauma of the last months I certainly have not, I might have seen this coming. Of striking appearance, exuding success of the most obvious kind, possessed of a persuasive and charming manner, he is ideal material for the candidature. With Barrow's support, I imagine he will almost certainly get it.

'You did know?' Barrow asks hesitantly, and from his expression I guess that someone – presumably Jack – was meant to have told me.

I make light of it. 'It's taking me time to catch up.' I show by my expression that I really don't mind not having been told, which in truth I don't. Harry's political career was only important to me while it was important to him. Now that he is dead I have no interest in the candidature, and if I feel anything at all it is relief at no longer having to live up to the standards of being a politician's wife. The days when I earnestly mugged up on local history and social issues and wore suitable clothes already seem blessedly remote.

Barrow interprets my indifference as approval for Jack's candidature. At least he looks pleased, though if he imagines my opinion counts for anything, I think he's mistaken.

Barrow, seeing that someone else is waiting to speak to me, makes way for a young man who I recognise but can't immediately place. My expression must give me away because the young man hastily announces himself as Tim Schwartz. I have him now. He is the director of the Rumanian orphans charity that Harry's concert raised all the money for. I met him once at a pre-concert reception, then again in the scrum of the concert itself. He is an earnest and rather severe young man with small unusually round eyes, like the watchful eyes of a small animal. He has the air of someone who is permanently irritated. I imagine that he is extremely able. I apologise for my lapse.

He dismisses this with a quick lift of his mouth, and fixes me with his odd gaze. 'Mrs Richmond, I'm sorry to bother you about this. But I was wondering, did you get my letter?'

'I've only just got back from America,' I explain. 'I haven't had a chance to look at anything yet, I'm afraid.'

He narrows his thin mouth and looks decidedly put out.

'I'll be getting down to the mail soon,' I offer. 'Next week . . .'

But his eyes are absorbed, as if he is already on to the next thought. 'I was wondering – I'm coming your way on Sunday. Would it be possible – could I drop by? It would only be for half an hour.'

I smile vaguely as I try to work out how I can put him

16

off. I have been back just two days, but the weekend already seems precious to me, a breathing space. I murmur, 'Sunday's rather difficult, I'm afraid.'

'It would only be half an hour,' he repeats, forcing an unconvincing smile that vanishes as rapidly as it came. 'It is rather urgent,' he adds with a tinge of impatience. 'It's the concert accounts, you see. We can't get moving on anything, not until they're sorted out . . .' He trails off, frowning, as if it is really too complex for him to explain or for me to understand.

'If it's about the concert I'm not sure I'll be able to help,' I say. 'I didn't have much to do with the organisation or anything, I'm afraid.'

'Maybe not, but I've tried your husband's advisers, I've tried them several times and . . .' He gestures the hopelessness of this avenue. 'Look – would Monday be better?'

'My husband's advisers?'

'Your solicitor – Leonard Braithwaite? And Gillespie at your accountants.'

'Oh. And they can't help?'

'They say not.'

'Well, then—'

'You're the only person who might be able to, you see.'

This argument is altogether too neat for me, and in my tiredness I can't find a way past it. 'Oh.'

'Monday then?'

'Monday?' I echo tautly. 'I'm not sure. I've so much . . .'

'I would appreciate it. It's really very important.'

I have the feeling that whatever argument I put up he will outmanoeuvre me. 'Well . . .' I say wearily and realise that I have drifted into agreement, and that I will have to commit myself to a time. We settle on noon. Immediately Tim Schwartz has gone I wish I had put him off until later in the week. Monday will be fraught enough as it is, with the post to face and all the other problems that I know are lying in wait for me.

For a moment no one notices that I am alone. I push my head back against the tightness in my shoulders, I knead a muscle in my neck, I think ahead to tonight when I will be home again, to when Anne and the rest of the family will have left and I won't have to make this effort any more. It's strange, but in California I dreaded the thought of being home again, of having to face the house alone. I thought it would bring Harry's death back, that it would make me relive it all, but as soon as we got back on Wednesday and I walked into the house, I knew it was going to be all right. The anticipation had been far worse than the event.

'Ellen!'

It is Charles, who takes me by the elbow and leads me towards the light. 'Got to look after you!' he states gravely. 'Must be absolutely worn out, poor old thing.'

Anne, who has been talking to one of the clergy, hurries forward. 'Absolutely!' she declares firmly, apropos of what I'm not quite sure, since she cannot have heard what Charles said. Signalling her farewells to the clergyman, she takes my other side and with Charles guides me through the doors. I am not so unsteady that I need this support, but I don't want to risk upsetting anyone by refusing it.

Emerging into the glare I see my father standing uncertainly at the top of the steps. With suitable explanations I unfasten myself and go across to him. Anne calls after me, 'Tell your father he's expected for lunch, won't you?'

Pa shuffles his feet at my approach and looks away. He is finding this whole episode difficult. Even when I was a child we never quite knew how to establish communications. We are so very different, he and I. Often when he looks at me I think he is amazed that we should be related at all. I am tall and fair, he of medium height and, before he went grey and thin on top, strikingly dark. He does not follow politics; I do not follow the sports results. After Mother died, it was a job to find common ground. We do our best. I phone him once a week, and we diligently go through our list of common interests: the children, our health, the state of our gardens.

His mouth forms into what is intended to be a smile but is closer to a grimace. I can see that he is longing to get away. Lunch can only be an ordeal for him. Also, though he has not actually said so, I think he has a woman friend down in Cornwall, someone he will want to be getting back to. And why not? He is still a robust man, a good catch for a lonely woman. I am pleased for him.

'No need to stay, Pa. Why don't you get an early train?'

He begins to protest, but not so strongly that I cannot win him over.

'Well – don't suppose I'll be much use,' he says finally.

'No, Pa.'

'And the food – you know.' Father is a plain-food man and does not hold with the sort of French restaurant where Anne and Charles have arranged for us to eat.

I put an arm round his neck and kiss him. He pecks my cheek awkwardly and pulls firmly back, anxious to be on his way now that it is all settled. He raises his hand in the direction of Harry's family, a wave so insignificant that there is little risk of it being noticed. He starts down the steps and turns to look back at me, but if he was going to say anything more he decides against it and with a last stab at a smile he continues down to the street. I watch him hail a cab and climb in. I wave but he does not look back.

Anne arrives breathlessly at my side. 'He's gone! Did he have to go?' She is put out, as she always is when her plans are upset. 'What will he do for lunch?'

'I think he wasn't very hungry. He had to get back. He sent his apologies.'

She gives me an odd look, as if she blames me for encouraging him to slip away, before gripping my arm again. Charles takes up station on my other side, giving my hand a small squeeze, and we prepare to start off again.

Jack, easing himself away from the last remaining mourners, takes charge of Diana, who seems far more in need of support than I. Diana has withered visibly since Harry's death. Her shoulders are stooped, her skin is grey and hangs loosely about her jaw, her dress flows voluminously over skeletal bones. She looks far older than her sixty-six years. The loss of a son is of course a terrible burden for any mother to bear, even Diana, who, despite her physical frailties and her drinking, has always given the impression of immense strength.

The sun is bright and we are half-way down the steps before I spot two photographers who seem to have come from nowhere. For an irrational moment and before I see the absurdity of the idea, I wonder if Anne has laid them on as one lays on photographers for a wedding.

'A bit much,' Charles mutters darkly, as close to anger as he ever gets. 'A bit unnecessary.'

I, too, wonder why they have come. Harry was not an MP for very long. He was not especially rich or powerful. There was nothing particularly newsworthy about him. Except the way he died, perhaps.

Anne has her chin up, showing a courageous face. I keep my eyes down, my face blank. I do not want anyone to read anything into my expression, or to see things that are not there.

Anne and Charles guide me towards a chauffeur driven car, one of the three that Jack has laid on for the day.

A man is waiting to intercept us. Coming so soon after the photographers my first thought is that he must be a reporter. I prepare to pass quickly by, but Anne and Charles slow down, we come face to face.

I realise my mistake: the man is a mourner, well-dressed, wearing a black tie and holding a service sheet. I half recognise him from the line-up, one of the many faces I did not know.

'Richard Moreland,' he said immediately, as if he wouldn't expect me to remember. 'I knew Harry from the Falklands.'

'Richard Moreland!' exclaims Anne, as if she knows the name. 'Well!' She clasps his hand. 'How very good of you to come. How very kind! You and Harry – well, my goodness!' She laughs her gracious laugh which after the trials of the day has become a little high-pitched.

Moreland smiles politely and brings his eyes back to mine. 'I just wanted to say that I'm staying not far from you, and if there's anything at all I can do . . .'

'That's very kind.'

Anne beams into Moreland's face. 'It's so nice to meet one of Harry's army friends,' she says in her nervous rapid speech. 'He hardly talked about his army days, you know, hardly at all. He wasn't one to dwell on the past – too much going on, of course, with Parliament and so on. But what a pleasure to meet you! A friend of Harry's from the Falklands, Charles! Did you hear that? It must have been amazing. I mean – the experience.'

Moreland's eyes glint slightly, his mouth tightens a little. He murmurs a perfunctory reply and says quietly to me, 'I'm just on the other side of the river, near Waldringfield. Perhaps I could come by one day?'

'Well . . . I . . .'

'When you've a moment,' he adds quickly. 'I'll phone, of course – if I may.'

Trapped, I gesture agreement.

The rituals we go through, the things we say. How many people have said that they will be coming to see me? I can't begin to count. Thirty? Forty? I hope they don't all mean it. Or if they do, that they will be easily dissuaded. All I really want is to be alone with Josh and with Katie when she's home from school, and for the three of us to be left to get on with things in our own way. I don't want endless reminiscences, long overblown talks of a golden past.

Richard Moreland, however, gives the impression of being quietly determined and I rather suspect he will not be put off.

'It was all Harry ever wanted,' Anne declares, 'the Paras. Because of Father, of course. You were in action together?'

'Not exactly. I was a Royal Marine, you see,' he says in his calm voice.

'Ohhh.' Anne draws the sound out while she adjusts to this news. 'But you and Harry—?' She regains momentum. 'Harry certainly mentioned your name. I remember it clearly. Aren't you—?' She smiles coyly, inviting revelations.

The heat closes in around me, the sun is very bright. I blink hard against the light. Perhaps I look unsteady because the next moment Moreland takes my arm and asks me if I'm all right. He opens the car door and, while Anne fusses in the background, he helps me inside.

I sink into the seat. On the pavement there is a flurry of discussion while Anne decides on who is to go in which car. I close my eyes for a second. When I reopen them Moreland is crouching in the still-open door.

'All right?' he repeats in that soft voice.

'I'm very tired.' Why I should tell him that, I'm not sure. He says gravely, 'Be careful, won't you.'

Careful? I nod vaguely.

He watches me for a moment. No, studies me, as if fixing an idea of me in his mind.

'I'll call you tomorrow then,' he says. He rises, only to reappear in the frame of the open door. 'By the way – does your boy like fishing? I thought I might go out some time. Perhaps he'd be interested?'

Interested? I'm not sure. When it comes to fishing Josh is rather fussy.

Moreland says diplomatically, 'Well, one of these days. If he feels like it.' He smiles again, a gentle smile, and closes the door. As he walks away he stops to talk to Leonard Braithwaite, my solicitor. They seem to know each other. Leonard smiles a lot. They shake hands as they part.

'That Richard Moreland,' Anne says, settling into the front seat. 'I'm *sure* Harry mentioned him. Isn't he a cousin of the Fenimores? I remember Harry saying he'd met a cousin of the Fenimores.'

'You're thinking of the Moore-Ingham chap,' Charles replies.

'Oh!' Anne makes a small exclamation of annoyance. 'Well! How confusing!'

I withdraw and, as always in my quiet moments, think of the children. I worry most about Katie, who was born with uncertainty and apprehension etched into her heart, who seemed to survive the trials of life by the narrowest of margins. As a baby she clung to me, at the mercy of the slightest trauma, and any confidence she has felt in the outside world has been achieved only by an effort of will.

My vision of our future tends to fluctuate. Sometimes it seems to stretch out before us, smooth and steady, so that we progress across it with hardly a ripple. At other times – usually in the night – it is grim and threatening and mountainous with difficulties and I feel sure we are going to founder. At these times I am stabbed by fear so violent that it shakes me awake in the darkness. But the more intense the fears, the more I try to conquer them.

We have come so far, we have survived so much. As I keep reminding myself, all we have to do now is hold on.

TWO

'Drop me by the gates!' Katie says suddenly, her voice high and brittle. I glance at her in surprise. She was all right a moment ago.

'But your stuff,' I reply faintly. 'How are you going to get it to the house?' I am thinking of the size of the school grounds, of the distance from the gates to Katie's house. 'And I told Mrs Anderson I'd go in and see her.'

Katie doesn't answer. She is staring ahead, her mouth pulled into a hard line, her gaze determinedly avoiding mine. I can't guess why she has made this abrupt decision. Perhaps, afflicted by teenage embarrassment, she does not want her friends to catch sight of me. Perhaps she is dreading her friends' sympathy and wants to face them alone.

I understand all this, but at the same time I can't help fretting over the practicalities. I sent her main trunk over yesterday but she still has two heavy bags and a CD-player to carry. Yet I'm too emotional to argue about it. I can only think that soon we will be separated, soon we will go through the lunatic ritual of parting. After so many weeks together, after all we have been through, I can hardly bear to think about it.

The gates come into sight. I do not approve of this place. Oh, it's pretty enough. The white stucco dormitory

25

buildings are dotted among smooth lawns, colourful rose beds and woodland. According to the prospectus the school boasts an unusual number of sports facilities including an Olympic-size pool and I've forgotten how many tennis courts. And the academic results, so everyone keeps telling me, are good. The staff expect Katie to win a place at a decent university in three years' time.

But I can't approve. Here parents give up their children to strangers for weeks on end and, unlike me, seem to do it gladly. You are told it does your child no harm, that things like unconditional love and physical contact and parental support will not be missed. I can't buy this. Boarding schools, it seems to me, are a peculiarly British madness, an inexplicable relic of Dickensian times that should have gone the same way as child labour and other primitive practices.

I used to say that I would never send the children away, no matter what, and I would say it with enough passion to belie my easygoing image. At first Harry argued for Josh to board. He himself had been sent away at seven and, like many who had survived the system, he believed it had done him more good than he'd realised at the time – in his case, with his problematic relationship with his mother, even I had to admit he may have been right. Also, though he never said so openly, I think he believed the old myth that an all-male school would make a better man of Josh, that I, as an unashamedly loving mother, was in danger of undermining Josh's masculinity. I used to challenge him about this in a light-hearted way – which was the only way with Harry – but he would simply laugh it off. In the end I got so upset that Harry relented and agreed to day school, at least until Josh was thirteen.

With Katie it was different. There was never any question of her going away. When Harry and I married, Katie was five and, it has to be said, at her most difficult and demanding. But Harry, who had taken on his role as surrogate father with some qualms, showed a tolerance that touched and delighted me. He appreciated Katie's overwhelming need for security and a home life.

This of course was long before Katie made up her mind. I see the same stubbornness in her expression now.

I draw up just inside the gates. 'I could drop you here and take your stuff up to the house,' I offer. 'Put everything inside the door . . .'

Katie sighs harshly and exclaims, 'No point!' Her anger has always been volcanic, even as a small child. It is a trait she hates passionately and has tried very hard to control.

'Okay,' I say reasonably. 'Why don't you go ahead with your stuff and I'll wait here for a while, until you're inside. Then I'll pop in and see Mrs Anderson.'

'No!' She is trembling visibly, near lift-off.

I leave it a moment before saying quietly, 'Do you want to talk about it?'

She turns away to look out of the window. My question has made her pause, as I'd hoped it would. While in California I went to an excellent therapist, a man with the unpromising name of Bob Block. After a time Katie agreed to see him too and, though she found the idea of talking to a stranger quite hard, she soon warmed to him and her sessions seemed to help her at least as much as mine helped me. Bob's favourite prompt was: 'Do you want to talk about it?'

Suddenly we're through the storm. The tension slips from Katie's body. She grimaces and rocks her head. 'Sorry, Mum.'

I grasp her arm. For a while neither of us speaks. 'It's

27

been a long day,' I say eventually. This is true in every sense. Lunch started and finished late and we got caught in the Friday afternoon jam out of London, then, just twenty minutes from home, we met an accident on the Ipswich bypass. The journey, which normally takes two and a quarter hours, took well over three. It was very hot, the three of us spoke only to complain, Josh got a headache.

But Katie, always her own harshest critic, is not prepared to forgive herself her momentary loss of control. She shakes her head in self-disgust.

I try to jolly her along. 'Josh got fairly ratty,' I point out. 'And Anne was absolutely exhausted.'

A humph of disapproval. 'Anne was drunk.'

'Oh,' I say. 'Was she?'

'She drank almost as much as Granny.' Katie is a bit of a puritan; she notices these things. She doesn't like excessive drinking in the family, nor any other kind of immoderate behaviour. 'And she stuffed herself. She had *three* lots of profiteroles.'

'Good God, did she? Oh well, you know how she is. She hates waste.'

Katie looks cross with me for making her smile, and we sit in companionable silence for a time, contemplating Anne and the profiteroles. The air is much cooler here than in the city, and there is the shimmer of a breeze in the heavy-leafed oaks.

'So . . .' I say at last.

'Take me to the house. Please. Sorry.'

I give her a quick kiss, which is just about permissible under the rules. No hugs, no farewell scenes allowed. This was agreed two days ago. This doesn't prevent me from feeling a fresh stab of impending loss as we drive slowly

28

through the grounds and draw up in front of Oakwood, Katie's house.

Katie fairly leaps out. She throws open the boot and I hear a bag thudding onto the ground. She bobs down at the window, fans out her fingers in a brief goodbye, and turns quickly away.

I watch her struggle towards the entrance, tottering under the weight of her CD-player and overstuffed bags. In the doorway she turns and throws me a brief almost garish smile, which I return as best I can. 'See you soon,' I mouth at her through the windscreen.

This smile of hers is a good sign, a declaration of her intention to get on with life and make a success of school. It was Bob Block who proposed that she and I should segment our lives, should create set times for work, for amusement, for deliberate and studied grief. I hope Katie has decided that school will be about work and laughter, that whatever anxiety and guilt remains, she will keep it for me and Pennygate. I want Katie to be happy and carefree, though this has always been difficult for her to achieve, even before life came and knocked her sideways.

Mrs Anderson, the housemistress, has a businesslike compassion that gets us quickly through the condolences, which I always find difficult, and on to Katie's welfare. We discuss how Katie is going to make up the schooling she's missed without feeling she is under pressure. We discuss the number of weekends she will come home. We agree that Katie should decide this for herself, that she should come out as often as she wishes. Mrs Anderson does not think it would be a good idea for her to come out mid-week, although, as the school is only fifteen minutes from Pennygate, it would be easy for her to do so. I have immediate visions of Katie getting into a state on a Tuesday night and having nobody to turn to. I know that I am probably worrying too much, that Katie is probably more resilient than I give her credit for. At the same time she is so easily knocked off-balance by the smaller obstacles of life that I cannot imagine she won't have some difficult moments.

In the end we compromise. We agree that Katie will be able to call me at any time from the relative privacy of Mrs Anderson's rooms.

I can do no more. To keep my mind off Katie, to suppress the heat behind my eyes, I drive back to Pennygate unusually fast. Fast by my standards, anyway. The local drivers and the narrow roads in this part of Suffolk frightened me into submission many years ago and I have long driven with care, though for some reason Anne has persuaded herself that I drive recklessly, and often recounts cautionary tales of fatal accidents for my benefit. It is part of her image of me, an image that is all artistic unreliability and lack of common sense, and bears very little relation to the person I am now. I think her idea of me stems from my art student days when I earned money singing blues with a semi-professional band that toured the universities; a brief enough era, God only knows, but one which to Anne appears sufficiently exotic to have fixed itself indelibly in her mind.

Pennygate stands at the end of a mile-long drive which passes through the Pennygate Estate. Most of the estate was sold to the neighbouring landowners in the sixties, and Harry sold the last few fields when we bought the house four years ago. Now only the drive and the fifteen acres immediately around the house remain.

I love the drive. It starts at a tiny gatehouse, long unoccupied, and carries on in a straight chestnut-lined avenue across broad fields towards the undulations and hidden dips that mark the banks of the unseen river. Turning to run parallel to the river, it follows the high ground through groves of pine and beech and mixed woodland. The track has a poor surface and has to be taken slowly – the recession hit us before we had time to repair it – but I rather like it that way. It gives me time to notice the seasons, to appreciate the loveliness of the place.

In my absence it has become full summer. The chestnuts under which I pass, the grass and the nearby woodland have turned a uniform shade of green. In the fields the crops are up – wheat, barley, rye, I'm never sure which. Far away across the river a field of vivid rape-seed blinks through the trees.

As a town person I took to country life with unexpected enthusiasm – unexpected even to me. Nothing I had read or seen, none of my occasional country weekends had prepared me for the extent of my conversion. Friends said I had become more countrified than the locals, and I suppose I had. I liked village life, I liked knowing everyone, I enjoyed making cakes for the fête and collecting for the church fund. The very parochialism of the life gave me a sense of security and ease. The life; and of course my marriage to Harry.

When Harry and I were first married – ten years ago this February – we lived on the outskirts of the village at the edge of the heath, where I would take Katie for walks. In those early days Harry and I would sometimes go for walks too, though he preferred to drive down to the river and walk along the marsh paths in the direction of the sea.

It was on one of those early river walks that Harry first pointed Pennygate out to me. We must have been quite far downriver because you can only see Pennygate from a distance, perched as it is quite high up and screened by trees from below. He said it was the best house on the river. There are few enough houses on the river – by a miraculous combination of private ownership and protection schemes the river, despite being a couple of hours from London, is almost completely undeveloped – but he was right. Pennygate, though it will never win prizes for architectural beauty, has by far the best view.

With hindsight I can see that Harry already had a gleam in his eye when he said this, that he had already set his sights on the house, but it was not in his nature to reveal his most private ambitions, even to me, not, at any rate, until they were within an inch of attainment. The one thing that he feared more than failure itself was the idea of having to admit it to anyone. Even with me, who was never less than supportive – or tried very hard to be – he found it hard to discuss his ambitions. At the beginning I used to feel rather hurt at this lack of trust. I tried to prise his plans gently out of him, to open up some sort of dialogue, but after a while I began to appreciate just how difficult this was for him, how paper-thin was his confidence, how for him the prospect of failure was almost like dying, and I learnt to suppress my curiosity, hard though it sometimes was.

After almost a mile the beech wood, which has never seemed taller, blots out the light, and then I am taking the last bend and ahead of me lie the four cottages which mark the boundary of the estate and the beginning of our land. Harry tried to persuade the landowners to sell us one of these cottages to house the staff we were planning to hire, but money got short and we never did acquire anything so grand as a permanent housekeeper.

Jill Hooper, who with her farm-worker husband occupies the second cottage and comes to clean for me three mornings a week, is standing in her gateway. She has changed the blue suit she wore at the service for her usual T-shirt and floral skirt. She waves heartily then lets her hand fall abruptly, as if uncertain as to the appropriateness of such a cheery gesture. Suddenly she waves again, signalling me to stop. She calls, 'Shall I have Josh for tea? I've got a lovely shepherd's pie in the oven.'

I thank her, I say Josh is fine and could not anyway eat another thing for hours. Waving, I drive on. I am lucky to have Jill. Not the most thorough cleaner in the world – even I who am far from fussy can't help noticing the dust she has missed – she is nevertheless immensely kind-hearted and will always look after Josh at short notice.

Pennygate is fifty yards on, hidden from the cottages by the high walls of the kitchen garden and the trees lining the circular sweep of the drive.

Margaret's car is parked in front of the house, alongside Anne and Charles's, and the stately blue Volvo of Leonard, our solicitor. I am relieved to see there is no sign of Jack's BMW. I park further to one side than normal. As I get out I notice that a drain-pipe beside a first-floor bathroom at the side of the house has been leaking, discolouring the Suffolk-pink rendering with streaks of brown. I suppose I will have to get it seen to, though I can't feel much enthusiasm. While I have always appreciated the wonderful location of the place, the large airy rooms on the garden side looking down to the river, I have never really loved the house itself. I am not absolutely sure why. Perhaps because, with seven bedrooms, it is too large to make me feel comfortable. Perhaps because I had no say in choosing it. Perhaps because we never found the happiness here that we had known at Heath End.

The house was built in the twenties, solidly. On this side it is at its plainest, the windows too small, the walls of the kitchen extensions too angular, the trees too close, so that, by contrast with the garden side, it seems dark and damp.

I slip in by the kitchen door and go straight up the back stairs to Josh's room. It is empty, which doesn't entirely surprise me. Josh may have looked exhausted when we got back from London, but he has extraordinary powers of recovery. Even as Katie and I left for the school he was edging towards the garden. He'll be in one of his hide-outs by now, or shooting home-made arrows at trees.

I stand for a moment in front of his desk with its pile of Disneyland memorabilia which will probably find its way onto the walls between the Batman stickers and posters of whale flukes rising high out of the sea. We went to Disneyland twice, but the second time wasn't a success. I hadn't appreciated how homesick Josh was, how impatient he was to return to his outdoor life. I had been devoting so much time to Katie that I think Josh often felt bored, even a little neglected.

Now we're back I'll be lucky to see him except at meal times. Sometimes I get uneasy when he's gone a long time, but he knows the rules, to stay in the grounds and never go down to the river unaccompanied. I have always worried about the children being near water. Also, though we own the land all the way down to the river, there's a public footpath which follows the bank and brings all kinds of strangers, especially in summer.

I go silently up the corridor to my bedroom. My half-unpacked bags still lie on the floor. In the dressing-room a light has been left on, illuminating Harry's suits where they hang in an orderly row. I notice that several of his shirts have been hung on the wrong rail and absently rearrange them. I stare at the suits. They will have to be disposed of. The thought touches me with quiet dread, but I decide it is a job best done sooner rather than later, perhaps as early as next week if I can find the time. They can go into the next sale in aid of the church fund, where they should raise a few pounds for the roof.

As I touch the cloth I catch the scent of Harry, a subdued blend of cologne and indefinable male odour which I recognise instantly. After all that's happened, it is this that finally unlocks the emotions of the day. No unreality now, just the enormity of what has happened. I lean against the shelving and cry silent tears that carve hot trails down my cheeks. I am not sure what I am feeling. I am never sure what I am feeling. Pain. Bewilderment. Rage.

Small darts of despair, too. But since despair is not something I allow into my repertoire of emotions, I quickly pad into the bathroom and scoop cold water onto my face until the heat is gone.

I glance in the mirror. I suppose I look the same, but I don't feel it. There is no avoiding my eyes, in which I see not only the person I used to be – someone increasingly, bafflingly remote – but also, looming ever larger, this strange new person I have become. This person has qualities I never realised I had, qualities which I do not particularly like but which I know I must hold on to with grim determination. If I ever lose sight of this, if I feel myself faltering, I only have to remember the children.

Instantly my mind flies to Katie and something lurches inside me. I do not dare to think of how much I am missing her already.

I splash more cold water over my eyes, then hot water, as hot as I can bear. Briskly I dry my face and brush my hair. I go and stand at the bedroom window, a moment of quiet before going down to the family.

I notice the lawn has patches of yellow; Charles told me yesterday there has been a shortage of rain. The formal garden, which is to the left and protected by a high wall from the frost-laden winter easterlies, does not seem too badly affected. If anything the roses look more abundant than usual. To the right the band of shrubs, oaks and wind-bent pines which conceal the track down to the quay is as dense as ever.

Ahead, the long expanse of lawn stretches out to a hidden ditch – I can never bring myself to call it a ha-ha – and beyond, a broad field that falls slowly away to the river where it meanders round in front of the house. The field is soft with some half-grown cereal which glows a limy yellow in the afternoon sun. The river, curving elegantly into the distance, is palest blue. In its middle reaches near Waldringfield several white-hulled yachts form dots of brightness.

When I first saw this view – the day that Harry finally announced he had bought the house – I was confused and dazzled by it. The way the river winds through the marshes as far as the eye can see – which on a clear day is the whole seven miles to the open sea – the way woods slope down to the marshes, the way the garden is so carefully designed to frame the scene: it is almost too perfect. After four years I am still in awe of it. Sometimes I feel it was intended for someone else altogether, and that I am here by accident.

Anne's voice drifts up from the terrace. I realise my absence will be holding things up. Making my way downstairs, I can't pretend I don't have to brace myself a little to meet Harry's family.

The drawing-room is a room that Harry encouraged

me to have interior-designed in English chintz, a style that in the end proved a little too crisp and cool to make it congenial. But Harry was pleased with it, and I never said I was anything less than happy with the result.

Diana is sitting in a chair by the window, silhouetted by the brilliance of the sunlit garden. Margaret is opposite her, perched on the large footstool. As I come in, Margaret catches my eye and raises her eyebrows slightly, a signal that things could be easier. With my mother-in-law things are rarely easy. Diana has a large drink in her hand – gin or vodka, she switches between the two – and it won't be her first of the evening, although Margaret will doubtless have tried to water them down. Diana has been a widow for almost forty years and a drinker of great resourcefulness and determination for perhaps thirty-five, although, since this is something the family discuss with emotion rather than detachment, the exact time scale is hard to establish.

At lunch Diana put away enough for two large men, but on this day of all days no one was going to try and stop her, least of all me. Even now she shows few signs of her prodigious intake; her control, while it lasts, is formidable.

She frowns, sucking in her cheeks. This is her look of displeasure, the one that would have Harry leaping out of his seat with agitation even before she spoke.

'There you are! Thought you might have gone off again!'

'Off?' I say.

'Off. *Off*. To America or wherever.'

Half-smiling, I shake my head.

She grunts, 'You were away long enough,' and there is a wobble of resentment in her voice.

'Well – seven weeks. But it was worth it.' This, I realise,

might be misinterpreted and I add, 'I mean, it was good for the children. They needed to get away.'

'Needed to get away?' She exaggerates the words. 'We could all do with getting away!' She lifts her glass and takes a long gulp, fuelling her pique. 'You should have been here! Then Anne wouldn't have made such a hash of the service. All that nonsense about a pop concert, for heaven's sake! Who wants to be remembered for a pop concert?'

'Well, it was quite something, raising all that money.'

She waves this aside. 'You should have been here, Ellen! You should have put a stop to it!' She fixes me with a droopy stare.

So I am not to be forgiven for going away. Anne has already let me know her views on my absence and the considerable inconvenience it has caused her. With Diana I think it is rather different. I suspect Diana is punishing me because I wasn't around to look after her. For all the hoops she put Harry through, for all the trials she has subjected the rest of us to, I have always felt a certain sympathy for her, and, grasping this, she has always made the most of it. Under her prickly veneer which she has maintained with such vigour over the years, she is rather a forlorn and unhappy person.

'But it was a fine service,' I say. 'Anne put an enormous amount of work into it.'

'She was just trying to make an impression for Charles. Trying to get him noticed!'

There must be a logic in this but I am too tired to guess what it might be. 'Oh?'

'Politics, politics! Got it all the way back in the car. They thought I was asleep, but I heard!'

I look to Margaret for help. Margaret, who is usually

the most direct of people, tucks her chin down to reduce the impact of her words. 'Charles is shortlisted for the candidature.'

I absorb this slowly. I thought Charles had given up all ideas of politics after an unsuccessful attempt to get selected for the next-door constituency eight years ago.

So many aspiring politicians in and around my family. Jack. And now Charles. 'Well. How splendid.' I take a long breath and get to my feet. 'I think I'll go and make some tea.'

'Just had tea!' Diana declares, as if this might keep me.

The kitchen is cool and quiet. This, more than any other room, is where I feel at home. It is furnished with pine that I found at country sales: a dresser whose shelves I have filled with blue china; wall units faced with old wooden shutters remade to size; a large Victorian table that has to be scrubbed hard to remove each spot of grease. Beyond, there is a lobby leading to a larder and a pantry. Late last autumn when I had thoughts of picking up my career again, I cleared out the pantry and made a small studio. I bought an expensive draughtsman's easel and a complete set of new materials. I worked on a few designs for a fund-raising poster for Molly's half-way house project, but they never seemed much good and when we couldn't get anyone to sponsor the cost of the printing I put them on one side.

I put the kettle on, find a tea-bag and perch on a stool while the water boils. I contemplate this wave of political activity that has grown up in my absence and feel profoundly grateful that I will not have to be a part of it. Political life was always an effort for me. The manœuvrings and the gossip and the backbiting never excited me as they did Harry. I didn't look forward to the evenings at the

Conservative Club or the socialising with the party faithful. I hope I never let these feelings show – I tried very hard not to – and if Harry guessed how I felt he never commented on it. He merely assumed he could rely on me, which he could.

Thinking about it, Anne would make a good candidate's wife. She has the ambition and drive. I am not so sure about Charles himself though. I don't think he has the aggression, what Harry used to call the nail-down mentality, and he has never struck me as a natural speaker.

The quiet on this side of the house is almost total. On the wall in front of me is the pinboard where I keep the household lists, school calendars and details of local events. It has not been touched since I went away. The household diary, the one where I scribble the family engagements, is still showing the week of 12th April, Easter Monday, the week we left for California. I take it down and leaf slowly back until I reach Friday, 26th March. There is nothing to show what happened, to mark the day in any special way. Two days earlier, on the Wednesday, I see that Josh went to a birthday party. It seems a long time ago now. And on the Thursday the engineer came to fix the washing machine. On the Friday itself there is a cryptic 'Load boat'. Then a line through the weekend, and written large: 'H & J take boat to the Hamble'. I forget now what excuse Jack gave for ducking out – a business meeting, something he couldn't get out of. It is his favourite escape clause: something I just can't get out of. But then I don't think he was ever that keen on the trip anyway. A coastal passage is not really Jack's thing. Too time-consuming, too little going on. If he sails at all, it is to take an adrenalin-charged rush around the buoys followed by a gin and tonic at the clubhouse.

There is more. On the line that divides the Friday and Saturday my handwriting says: 'Josh to Jill's. Ellen: supper at Molly's.' Then, on Saturday: 'Katie out?'

Slowly I tear the page out, followed by all the preceding ones. And all the ones leading up to the present week. I'm not sure why I am doing this, but I tear them neatly into two pieces then four.

'There you are!' says Anne, sweeping through the door. She comes as far as the sink. 'I had no idea you were back!' She looks rather cross with me.

I drop the scraps of paper in the bin. 'I was talking to Diana.'

'We've all been waiting.' She can't entirely hide the exasperation in her voice. 'Leonard too.'

'I'm sorry,' I smile quickly. 'I had to see Katie's house-mistress.'

'Yes, well . . . There's an awful lot to sort out here, you know. We've had to make a lot of decisions while you were away. Letters, bills, staff . . . *Mother*. It's been an awful job.'

'I do appreciate it, really.'

She blinks rapidly, not entirely mollified.

'I would like to say, Anne – thank you for the service. I know how much work you put into it. It was lovely.'

'Oh.' She's not sure how to take this, not sure if I'm just trying to humour her. For some reason, I have always managed to baffle Anne, to send her confusing signals. 'Well, I thought it was the least we could do,' she states with great dignity.

'And so many people.'

'Oh, you thought so? Really? Well, I was quite pleased, I must say. People are so busy nowadays. But most came – most people Harry would have wanted anyway.'

41

The people Harry would have wanted. Yes, I suppose they were. Harry knew many people, but his favourites were either successful types who had a buzz about them and made him feel alive, which he liked more than anything else, or, by complete contrast, very ordinary people, like the locals he used to meet occasionally at the village pub on Sunday evenings, the sort who, according to Harry, kept him in touch with reality. I think they also made him feel good because they reminded him of how much he had achieved.

For some reason, I also think of the people who were not there, the people that Harry fell out with over the years – early business associates, political allies, friends from the past. Harry could be abrasive under pressure; he did not keep his friends easily.

Anne's face creases into a grimace of anguish. 'I still can't believe he's gone, you know. There are whole times when I just . . .' She makes a despairing gesture. 'It's the not *knowing*. I wish – I wish they would *find* him! I really can't bear it! Having him out there – just *out* there somewhere. It's *awful*!'

I pour the hot water and keep pressing the tea-bag with a spoon until the liquid is almost black.

Anne sniffs fiercely. 'We haven't let them give up, you know!'

I hesitate for an instant before pulling a stool out from under the counter and offering it to her. 'Haven't let who give up?' I ask.

She perches on the stool grudgingly as if she doesn't really mean to stay. 'The coastguard!'

I must look blank or alarmed, or both, because she explains loudly, as if I might be having trouble hearing, 'Give up the *search*. They would have given up – oh, weeks ago. But we weren't having any of that! No, Charles got hold of some Felixstowe fishermen. Got them to chart the tides and everything, to say where the yacht was most likely to have gone down. Took the chart along to the coastguard. Otherwise they'd have been quite happy just to sit back and wait, you know. They kept saying it was bound to turn up sooner or later. I mean!'

My heart knocks once against my ribs. 'The boat?'

She blinks at the crassness of my question. 'Yes – the *boat*.' Her face folds into an expression of pain. 'Though they don't say anything about Harry, they don't say ...' She presses the back of her fist to her lips, she takes a deep breath.

I extract the tea-bag and squeeze it harshly. My throat is dry, I long to drink, but when I take a sip the tea scorches my tongue. 'Why do they think it's likely to turn up?' I ask.

Anne shrugs impatiently. 'Oh, I don't know. Something to do with the fishing boats – I don't know. *Anyway*, the point is they're having a proper look. *That's* the important thing!'

I stir the tea repeatedly in an effort to cool it down. When I don't respond, Anne is driven to repeat testily, 'They really would have given up, you know!'

'Yes, I see. I hadn't realised.' I try not to think of the yacht, but I see it lying there on the sea floor, I imagine its white hull reflecting light dimly back to the surface.

But why are they bound to find it? So much sea, such a small boat. I don't understand.

And why do they want to keep looking for it? After all this time I had assumed they would have given up. In fact, I had convinced myself. Forgetting how hot the tea is, I take a gulp and burn my throat.

Anne has returned to an earlier theme. 'There's been *so*

much to sort out,' she sighs. 'Honestly! The staff weren't getting paid – did you realise? And Mother's allowance, the bank stopped it – just like that, if you please. *We've* been paying it ever since – quite happy to, of course – but that's not the point.' Anne finds it impossible to talk calmly about money. Harry was the same. Their father, who lived in some style while he was alive, left heavy debts and Diana had a struggle to meet the school fees. There wasn't enough for skiing trips and expensive treats, and even thirty years later Harry still smarted at the memory of not being able to keep up with his schoolfriends.

'I hadn't realised you'd done so much,' I say. 'Thank you.'

'Well, someone had to!' The sharpness of her tone leaves me in no doubt that I have been derelict in my duty. 'You left so soon! So quickly! As if – well, as if you'd given up hope!'

'It was almost three weeks, Anne.'

'Just over two, I think, Ellen.'

I am not going to be drawn into an argument that is unlikely to achieve anything but bad feeling. 'I would have gone mad if I'd stayed,' I explain with sudden candour. 'And the children – I wanted to get them away.'

'Well, it's one thing to go away, and quite another to go just like that! At two days' notice, leaving everything in a mess! And as for the children – well, I would have thought it was very unsettling for them, being away from their friends in a strange place.'

I don't have the energy to defend myself. I shrug in mild apology. 'I did what I thought was right at the time.' I stand up. 'And now, forgive me, but if Leonard's waiting . . .'

Conflict passes over Anne's face. She doesn't like her flow being cut short, not when she is still brimming with things to say. She busies herself with a fresh handkerchief. I cross the distance between us and hold out my hands. My time away, my sessions with Bob Black, have only reinforced my belief that life is too short for resentments and petty grievances.

After a moment's hesitation – I think I have taken her by surprise – Anne brings her arms up and we embrace clumsily. Her cheek is warm and soft, her well-cushioned back rigid under its corsetry.

Charles has appeared in the doorway. Reading the emotional temperature, his face loops into a lazy smile. He, like me, prefers a life without discord. I decide, not for the first time, that he is a nice man, certainly too nice for politics.

I shake my head at him as I approach. 'I'm told you're going to throw yourself to the wolves.'

'What? Oh, that.' He attempts a solemn expression. 'It's not settled yet. Not too late to pull out. What do you think? I wanted to talk to you about it.'

'Me? Why me?'

'Well, I thought— You don't mind then?'

'Why should I?' I grasped his arm. 'Good luck to you.'

From behind, Anne says hurriedly, 'We were going to tell you, weren't we, Charles? We thought it would be wonderful to keep the seat in the family.' Much taken by the idea, her voice quivers, her eyes moisten. 'Make it into a bit of a tradition. Carry on Harry's work.'

I look back at Charles. He meets my eye. It might be my imagination, but I think there is a trace of sheepishness in his good-natured smile.

Anne leads the way into the hall. I touch Charles's arm and we fall behind. 'Anne tells me you went to see the coastguard,' I say as soon as she is out of earshot.

He stops, his expression both forthright and uneasy, as though he is worried about upsetting me. I give him my most unemotional expression.

'We felt they could be doing more, Ellen,' he says gruffly.

'And are they?'

He folds his arms and frowns at his feet. 'Well, they've agreed to focus things a bit more. Look at the most likely area.'

'They're searching then?'

He shakes his head grimly. 'No resources, I'm afraid. And they say the area is too wide anyway.'

I feel a rush of relief.

'No,' Charles continues in his stately manner, 'they rely on the local fishermen to keep a look-out for things that snag their nets or show up on their sonar, that kind of thing. But they do say that small vessels often get found that way, by the fishermen. Surprisingly often, in fact.'

The anxiety returns, and it must show in my face because Charles says worriedly, 'Now that's why I didn't tell you before, you see. I didn't want to raise your hopes.'

Raise my hopes? I find myself looking at him in open bewilderment before glancing away. 'Where's this new area then?'

'Oh, along the route south, as before. But also a bit to one side, to allow for the tides. We're not sure the coast-guard took the tides properly into account before, you see. Well, the inshore fishermen didn't think so anyway.'

'A bit to one side?'

He nods, thinking this is all the answer I need.

'Where exactly?' I ask lightly.

'Oh, west a bit,' he says. 'Inside the Gunfleet Sand. The tide sets in there, you see, in towards the mouth of the Thames. *If* Harry hadn't allowed for that, *if* the yacht had drifted . . . d'you see?'

I absorb this slowly. 'I see.'

He takes another reading of my face. Reaching awkwardly for my hand, he grasps it unhappily and says, 'Please don't hope for too much, Ellen.'

I put on my most robust look. 'No, I won't. But thanks. For taking the trouble.'

He smiles his bashful smile. 'The least I could do.' He releases my hand and pushes his shoulders back and looks suddenly much brighter.

Anne reappears and summons us impatiently to the drawing-room, where she is trying to persuade a haughty and belligerent Diana that it is time to go home. It takes the combined efforts of us all to persuade her into the car.

Before climbing into the driving seat, Charles gives me a brisk embrace. 'I don't think you should be here on your own,' he says with a frown.

I have Josh, I tell him. I'll be all right. In fact I'm not at all sure I will be all right, but I have learnt that at times like these, times when I am feeling unsettled, I am better off on my own, that indeed it is the only situation in which I feel safe.

As the car draws away Diana puts her face to the window and pulls a face at me, a face that says I have let her down. I give her a wave.

Margaret comes back into the house with me. She is certain there must be something she can do. She, like Charles, worries about leaving me alone, but I tell her to go home, that I will be fine and that I will see her on Monday when we tackle the paperwork. I have looked into the study and seen the neat piles of letters and bills waiting on Harry's desk, beautifully ordered and marked.

'You're sure?' asks Margaret, who can't bear the idea of leaving any task undone. Normally Margaret is based at Harry's office in Ipswich. She came to him nine years ago when he and Jack set up Ainswick Properties and started their first project, a shop and office development down by Ipswich station. She was newly divorced then after a long and, I think, difficult marriage. She must be in her mid-fifties now, a wiry, agile woman of great energy and common sense who is a devil at golf and was for several years women's county champion.

'No, you go home.' I pause, trying to grasp a half-remembered thought, the echo of some conversation from earlier in this endless day. Finally it comes back. 'The Rumanian orphans concert, Margaret. Do we have anything on it? I don't know – records, files?'

'There's a bit,' she says. 'Mainly fund-raising and correspondence. The files are at the office. Do you want me to bring them over?'

'No. Well, I don't think so. It's just that the charity director is keen to see me for some reason. He's coming on Monday.'

'Tim Schwartz? But that's ridiculous,' Margaret declares. 'He's already been on to me. He's already been in touch with Mr Gillespie. I'll have a word with him. He shouldn't be bothering you, and certainly not when you've only just got back. That's very naughty.'

'He said he'd tried Gillespie but had no luck.'

'Well, there you are! Even less reason to bother *you*. I'll put him off, shall I?'

I almost say yes, but the memory of Schwartz's insistent manner holds me back. 'Did he say what he wanted when he spoke to you?'

'Not really.' Immediately Margaret indicates that this is not strictly true. 'What he *asked* for were details of the banking arrangements for the concert. But when I gave them to him he said it wasn't enough. He needed access

48

to the invoices. That was when I put him in touch with Mr Gillespie.'

'Invoices?' I repeat, trying to maintain interest.

'I don't think we ever saw any,' says Margaret. 'Not that I remember. The bookkeeping was done by someone attached to the charity. *If* we had invoices they'd have been in the accounts file that I sent to Mr Gillespie some time ago.' Instantly she is concerned that she might have done the wrong thing. 'I can check with Mr Gillespie, if you like.'

Gillespie was Harry's accountant, and now, I suppose, he must be mine. I have met him only twice and what I remember of him is somewhat daunting. I shake my head.

'I'll put Mr Schwartz off then, shall I?'

I am tempted, but if I don't see Tim Schwartz then I'm not sure who will, and I don't think he'll take kindly to being palmed off. Also, if there's any problem that involves Harry, anything that needs sorting out, then I feel I should know about it. While I was away I made this decision to face up to situations, however difficult or unpleasant they might be, something I hadn't always managed to achieve in the past.

'No, I'll see him. It'll be better to see him.'

As she gets into her car, Margaret says, 'Why don't I check with Mr Gillespie anyway, just so we're clear on who's got what?'

I would have preferred to avoid even this small fuss but I can't think of a reason not to agree.

Before joining Leonard, waiting patiently in the drawing-room, I go outside and call half-heartedly for Josh.

The garden is overwhelming, the air warm and heavy with the scent of pine and grass, the lawn streaked with long golden light. An insect buzzes idly past, and floating up from the river comes the reedy call of a marsh bird.

I feel a sudden relief at being home, an unexpected gratitude at being returned to this small corner of the world, which, through some miracle, seems to continue as before, altered but unchanged. I thought it would be far harder coming back, that I'd find it agonising to see the river again, to sleep in our bed, to see and touch Harry's clothes. But I am stronger than I realise. I think I always have been.

I call again, but if Josh hears me he doesn't reply, and after a time I go back inside. Crossing the hall, I step lightly past the drawing-room door and enter the passage that leads to Harry's study. The walls are decorated with assorted hunting prints and antique maps of Suffolk, and, half-way along, a large framed nautical chart. This too is a bit of an antique. The markings are faint, intricate and closely packed and, in the poor light, it is a moment or two before I manage to find the Gunfleet Sand, which appears to be a long shoal radiating outwards from the mouth of the Thames. Comparing it to Harry's planned route, I see that it lies well off to the left as you look at the chart.

If they have to focus their attention anywhere, I suppose this is as good a place as any.

But I wish they would leave Harry in peace. The thought of them finding him gives me actual physical pain. All it could possibly achieve is heartache for the children and me. No one seems to have thought of that. Probably because no one has asked me. I should speak out; there is nothing to stop me. But I would have to argue long and hard, and I'm not sure I could do it convincingly.

THREE

The drawing-room is bright after the gloom of the passage. Leonard is sitting in an armchair on the far side of the flower-filled hearth. He pulls his tall frame hastily out of the chair. 'Ellen.' He pats my hand with light fluttering strokes, as if I am made of something more fragile than flesh and bone. His pepper-and-salt eyebrows, which protrude like porcupine quills, are pulled together in a frown. 'You must be *very* tired. We could easily leave this until another day, you know.' He releases my hand abruptly, as if he has already held it too long.

'I'd rather not.'

'It'd be *no* trouble to come back over the weekend. *Any* time at all.'

'I'd rather go ahead. If you don't mind.' I realise the news isn't going to be good – there have been hints and meaningful pauses from the family – and now it has got to the point where I would prefer to know the worst.

Leonard hovers a moment. 'You *are* taking care of yourself, Ellen? You've got someone in the house tonight? You shouldn't be alone, you know. Can't Molly stay with you?'

There is something about me – my appearance, my manner, I'm not sure what – that has always made people feel they must worry about me, people like Leonard and

Charles and Molly anyway. And with Harry's death their concern has been given full rein.

'Leonard,' I almost laugh, 'I'm all right.'

He stares at me, not entirely convinced, then gives a resigned nod.

We sit down. Leonard pulls his briefcase onto his lap and extracts a batch of papers from a folder. 'I'll start with the *legal situation*, if that's all right. Everything else rather *stems* from that.' Leonard, who must be nearer sixty than fifty, comes from the old breed of solicitor, the kind who cares for you from cradle to grave. Harry took him on soon after we married. The choice rather surprised me. Harry's other advisers – his accountants, financial consultants, corporate lawyers – were always young and assertive. But it was probably Leonard's very staidness, the very solidity of his values that recommended him to Harry.

'Since we last spoke, things have become a *little* clearer,' Leonard begins carefully. 'But I'm afraid that, generally speaking, the situation is rather – *difficult*, Ellen.' He pulls his cadaverous face into a regretful expression. 'As you know, the will is relatively straightforward, and under *normal* circumstances probate would be granted within months. But as things stand – well, I'm afraid we can't hope to have it proved for some *considerable* time—'

'The will,' I interrupt tentatively. 'I'm sorry – you wouldn't go through it for me?'

'What, the *terms*, you mean?'

'Yes.'

'Oh . . .' He is reluctant. I think he was keen to get the bad news over with and I have put him off his stride. 'Very well,' he says hesitantly. 'Is it one or two things you're not clear about, Ellen, or . . .?'

'Well, I think . . . just the basics, really.'

He gives me a sharp look, alive with sudden apprehension. 'But you *have* seen the will?'

'Well . . . not actually seen it, no.'

He tries again, gently. 'But you saw it some time ago?'

'Harry told me about it.'

'Oh!' Leonard's sense of propriety is offended. 'I thought— You said on the *phone*—'

I apologise. I explain that I was not at my brightest during that conversation which, if I remember correctly, took place at the unpromising hour of six a.m. just two days after the children and I arrived in California. I was awake, as it happened, but groggy with sleeping pills and whatever else I was taking at the time.

'Well, if Harry told you . . .' Leonard says, somewhat mollified.

When Josh was born Harry told me that if anything should happen to him we would be taken care of. He took a certain pride in being able to provide for us, something which, by his reckoning, his father had singularly failed to do for him. He told me there would be a trust fund but did not go into detail. He was never a person to reveal more than he chose to. Secrecy came naturally to him, a form of self-preservation that he had learnt in his troubled childhood.

It was two years ago that Harry mentioned he was setting up a special trust fund for Katie. I was proud, grateful, touched. Generally I don't believe inherited money does young people many favours, but for someone as insecure as Kate it would be a blessing, something to give her some much needed independence. Typically, Harry did not tell me how much was involved and, just as typically, I did not ask.

It wasn't until a few weeks before Harry died, when the

extent of his troubles was becoming clear even to me, that I thought about Katie's trust again, anxious in case Harry should change his mind about it. I went so far as to ask an accountant I met at a constituency gathering how trust funds operated. He assured me that a trust could not be dissolved once it was set up.

Leonard draws back his lips. 'It'll take some time to go through it.'

'Just the main points. That's all.'

Rallying, Leonard says in a brisk voice, 'Right.' He extracts a document from another of the folders on his lap.

'As I think I told you, Harry's last will is dated just after Josh's birth, with two codicils added to cover a few minor points. The essence of it is *this* . . . the bulk of the estate is to be formed into a *trust*, with myself and Jack Crawley as trustees. Diana will be one of the beneficiaries of this trust during her *lifetime*.' He gives me a quick glance to see if I am with him so far. 'As you know, Harry set up various annuities for her over the years, but under the terms of the will, she will receive an *income* from the trust, to replace her present allowance. The income is determined by various calculations. Er . . . Did you want the details?'

I shake my head.

'Well, once Diana is taken care of, then the trust will be for the *exclusive* benefit of *you*, as Harry's widow, and the *children* of the marriage – that is, Joshua. Now, so far as the administration of the trust goes, the trustees will have *wide* discretionary powers—'

The implications of what he is saying dawn slowly and strike me with sudden weight. 'But Katie—' I interrupt. 'What about Katie?' At the far end of the sofa the telephone starts to ring. I stare at Leonard. 'I thought – I thought there was a trust for Katie.'

Distracted, Leonard glances towards the telephone.

I say again, 'I thought there was a trust.'

My anxiety sends him back to his notes, though he must be aware of the answer. I am conscious of my heart beating away long seconds marked by the rhythmic warbling of the phone. 'A trust. Yes, *yes*,' he says in his deliberate voice, drawing out a paper. 'Thirty thousand pounds. But it was a gift in Harry's lifetime, you see. So it doesn't appear in the will. No *need* to have it in the will.' He gives a smile that was probably intended to reassure me but comes out as a grimace.

'I see,' I say uncertainly. I should be relieved – I am – but this doesn't stop a small knot of uneasiness collecting in my stomach. The phone rings on.

'Er . . .?' Leonard glances at the phone, longing to see it answered.

Suddenly I realise it might be Katie. I get to the receiver in time to hear the line buzzing emptily.

I return to my seat. I look at Leonard and grapple with an old suspicion that has resurfaced abruptly.

I ask, 'Katie's trust – when was it set up?'

'What? Oh . . .' He takes another look at his piece of paper. 'Er . . . Yes, two years ago. Almost exactly. *June*.'

'And before that?'

Leonard's head comes forward, he peers at me like an ancient bird. 'I'm sorry?'

'Before Harry set up the trust, what were the arrangements for Katie?'

'Well . . .' He blinks at me, suddenly a little wary. He waves a hand. 'Well, I could check back, *of course*. But Ellen dear' – he gives me his most benign smile – 'for the moment it might be best to press on. Otherwise we won't get through it all, and I don't want to keep you too late.'

'I only wanted to know . . . I just wanted to be clear . . .

There was no particular provision for Katie? Before?'

He stares at me. 'Well . . . no.' Hurriedly he leans forward and, resting his elbows on his knees, gestures reassurance with the spread of his long hands. 'But Ellen, don't take that to mean— Well, don't imagine that Harry intended Katie to be badly off. Not for a moment. In fact *quite* the opposite. This little trust was just a bonus for her, an *extra*. No, he assumed there'd be *plenty* in the main trust, that you would be so well provided for that you'd be able to support Katie *amply. Amply.*'

I nod slowly. 'I see. Thank you.'

Leonard searches my face. He says urgently, 'But listen, I would *not* get too concerned about all this if I were you, Ellen. Not at this stage. You see . . .' He proceeds awkwardly, 'When everything is finally *valued*, when all the calls on the estate are met, we might well find that everything is rather *different* . . .' He comes to a halt, pushing out his lip. 'Well, perhaps we'd better come on to that later. I will need to explain it in some *detail*.'

He is laying the ground for this bad news of his.

'I see,' I say. 'Go on.'

He peers at me anxiously. 'You're sure?'

I manage a smile. 'Sure.'

Leonard finds his place. 'The trust, as I say, is allowed considerable *flexibility*. The trustees will have discretion to provide either *capital* or *income* . . .'

I hardly hear him. I am still thinking of Katie's inheritance. Why nothing for her in the will? How could Harry have been so unfair? When Harry and I married he said he would do his best for Katie. He always spoke of her as his daughter, he encouraged her to call him Daddy. After Josh was born he talked about 'the children'. I had always assumed he wouldn't differentiate between them. I had always assumed – what an irony – that he loved her equally.

I digest this, I let it settle. It is not so very hard. Really, this is just one more small hurt in a long line of hurts that Harry dealt me in the last few months. As I absorb it, it begins to take on the colour of an older and more familiar emotion, one that I felt last autumn at the start of what was the most painful time for Harry and me. This emotion is a blend of misery and bafflement, and now it reopens like an old wound.

I became aware of silence, of Leonard watching me. 'I'm sorry, Leonard, I . . .'

He is half-way to his feet. 'Can I get you something? Water? Coffee?'

'No. You are sweet, but I'm fine.'

'You look completely worn out.'

I shake my head, I give a crooked grin. 'Honestly.'

'Do you want me to run over that last bit again?'

'No, no. Go on. Please.'

But something must have shown in my face because, after a moment's hesitation, Leonard brings himself to say, 'Did you think Katie would be getting a share of the main trust? Is that it?'

I spread my palms wide. A sudden heat pricks my eyes. I suppress it rapidly. What does it matter what I thought?

'It's not important now,' I say brightly, hoping he hasn't noticed the unsteadiness in my voice, the shine in my eyes. Whatever happens, I don't want to draw attention to how I feel about Harry's behaviour on this.

For a moment I think Leonard is going to say more but, reading my expression, he settles slowly back into his seat, though not without the occasional troubled glance in my direction.

'Now *probate* . . .' he says in a tired voice. 'Perhaps I should explain a few of the problems we're likely to encounter in obtaining probate. The main obstacle, as you might imagine, is the lack of a *death* certificate. Normally, in circumstances where – well—'

I help him along. 'Where there's no body.'

His mouth jerks up at the corners, a sort of nervous reflex. 'Er – *yes*. Where there's no *direct* evidence of death . . . then the statutory period for presumption of death is *seven* years. Now we wouldn't expect to have to wait *that* long, of course. Not in this case. The seven year rule is really designed for people who just up and off. You know, walk out of the door and are never seen again. No, in this sort of case, where there are *special* circumstances, one can apply for leave to swear to the death *within* the statutory period. But having said that, I have to warn you – it can be a long drawn-out process. There are certain *conditions* which have to be met. Even then it's up to the court, and they may not grant leave for some time, not until they're *absolutely* satisfied.' He crinkles up his eyes, he sucks in his breath. 'It could take years.'

I hadn't imagined that any of the legalities would be simple. At the same time I had rather hoped they could be cleared up in a matter of months rather than years. 'These conditions, what sort of thing . . .?'

'Well, they're designed for quite *different* circumstances, of course.' Seeing that I am not to be denied the detail, he assembles his fingers and counts them off slowly. 'First, nothing must be *heard* from the deceased, not by anyone who would normally expect to hear from him. Second, nothing must be *seen* of him – again by anyone who would normally expect to see him. And lastly, and I would imagine most importantly, the *circumstances* of the pre-

58

sumed death have to be taken into account. These would have to be sufficient to establish in the court's mind that death was very much *more* likely to have occurred than *not*.'

'But these circumstances, our circumstances – aren't they enough?'

He is not going to commit himself. 'It's really a matter for the experts, Ellen. They're coming back to me shortly. It's taken some time to assemble all the, er – appropriate information.'

'Appropriate information?' I echo mildly. 'The weather, you mean? The people who saw him. That ship.'

'The weather – yes, that must count for *something*, of course. But the sightings – well, they're not so sure. You see, it's not a matter of establishing whether or not Harry *left*. There's absolutely no doubt about that. So whether the yacht that fellow at Waldringfield saw going down the river was actually *Minerva* or some other yacht is slightly by the way. And the crew of the coaster, they couldn't actually identify the yacht they saw that night. But as I say, it's all rather *academic*, because we know that Harry and the yacht left the river. There's no doubt about that. D'you see?'

I give a tiny nod. 'What about the dory, then?'

'Well, yes, that *does* mean something, of course it does. But again . . .' He creases up his face regretfully. 'It's not quite *enough*.'

'But . . .' I give a small laugh of incredulity. 'It was found drifting. I mean, it wouldn't be drifting if something hadn't happened.'

Leonard draws a long breath. 'N-o-o,' he says in the tone of a parent humouring a child.

'I don't see . . .'

'I'm sorry?'

'Why isn't it important?'

'Because, umm . . .' He swivels a hand and claws the fingers slowly into his palm. 'Because, you see, in *theory*, the dinghy – the dory, you call it – could simply have come *loose*. Drifted away from the yacht without Harry realising it. It doesn't follow that the yacht itself got into trouble. D'you see?'

I am trying very hard to see. I look out of the window for a moment. 'What about *Minerva* being missing?' I ask, disliking the sarcasm in my voice. 'Isn't that significant either?'

'Ah! Well, that's significant, of *course*. Very. But from the soundings I've taken—' His face twitches at the unfortunate choice of words and he gestures apology before hurrying on. 'From what I can *glean*, it would be much more – well, *useful* if it were actually *found*. That would be the most powerful *evidence* of all, d'you see?'

I say abruptly, 'You mean, otherwise it could be assumed that Harry was half-way down the Atlantic, heading for South America!'

'No, no.' He attempts a dismissive laugh that doesn't quite come off. 'No—'

'Well, why else would they be so keen to find it?' The peevish edge is back in my voice. 'I mean, he was seen leaving the river. The weather was foul. He only had food for a couple of days. What else would he be doing but sailing for South America?'

Leonard looks vaguely alarmed. I don't think he has seen me in an abrasive mood before. 'I can assure you that no one's ever mentioned *anything* like that. Not for one moment, Ellen. No, it's simply a question of the weight of evidence.'

I sigh heavily. I know I shouldn't let this get to me, I know I am achieving nothing but anxiety and grief for myself, but I can't seem to prevent it.

Leonard explains patiently, 'Evidence can take *time* to—' He pulls himself up hastily, on the point, I guess, of saying to surface. 'To *turn up*,' he states carefully. 'The court really can't afford to be hasty. There have been cases . . . Well, you can imagine.'

'I don't want it to drag on . . .'

What I really mean is that I don't want Harry's life subjected to constant re-examination, though I don't say that.

Leonard makes a sympathetic face. 'No. I suppose we *could* try to apply for leave straight away . . .' He doesn't sound confident.

We are silent for a time. The garden has turned a rich gold in the evening sun. A vision leaps into my mind, one that I normally manage to keep at a tolerable distance. It catches me unawares, arriving by a side door that I have failed to defend. For a moment it overwhelms my imagination. I see Harry's body. It is lying in icy water, deep in the North Sea. I wish there were no detail, but the image is merciless. His eyes are open, his skin is grey and swollen, his body is rocked to and fro by the current. It is an image so ghastly that I cannot think it for very long without feeling I will go mad.

Leonard stirs. 'Um . . . Shall I go on or . . .?'

I get to my feet and go to the drinks tray. 'Do you want anything, Leonard?' He shakes his head. I am no drinker; the occasional glass of white wine is usually my limit. But I have a need for something to take me through the rest of the conversation. I stare indecisively at the bottles and finally pour myself a small brandy. I take a sip and wait for the unfamiliar warmth to fire my stomach before returning slowly to my seat.

'Sorry, Leonard. Do go on.'

He draws a breath to get himself going again. 'Until the death certificate is issued—' The phone interrupts. He looks at me plaintively. I go and answer it. It is Molly. She says she tried to call five minutes ago.

'Now listen,' she says in her no-nonsense voice, 'shall I come over? Have you eaten? You're not on your own, are you?'

I fend her off, though it's not easy.

'You may think you're doing fine, my love,' she says, 'but you *can't* be doing fine. And why can't I come over? Won't you at least bring Josh to lunch tomorrow?'

I promise I'll think about lunch and let her know in the morning. I would promise anything at the moment.

Leonard, who has picked up the gist of this conversation, looks approving as I sink back into my seat. 'Good to get out and about,' he says firmly. Like most people he seems to think solitude is the worst possible thing, that activity is the only effective antidote to bereavement. It would be useless to explain that I feel much stronger on my own than with other people.

Leonard resumes his troubled expression. 'Until the death certificate is issued there are going to be certain *difficulties*, I'm afraid. Particularly – well, *mainly* on the money front. For the time being you can continue to sign cheques on your *joint* account, there's no problem there. And the deposit account that feeds it still has *some* funds.'

'Anne said something about people not being paid.'

He makes a dismissive gesture. 'That was just the fools at the bank. For some reason known only to themselves they froze the deposit account. I soon pointed out their

62

error.' This he says with heavy irony. 'Harry had an automatic top-up arrangement. They had *no* authority to stop it.' He pauses delicately. 'But I have to mention . . . the funds in the deposit account *are* getting low. Just over five thousand, to be precise. Er – would you be having any calls against this in the next few weeks? Calls of any *size*?'

I presume he means bills from California. I try to think. Some will have come through already – the rent of the house in La Jolla, the airline tickets, the hire car. But some will still be in the pipeline – Bob Block's fees from my last few visits, the cost of the week we took in Yosemite Park.

'It depends what you mean by size.'

He nods sagely, as if this was an answer.

I ask, 'And when the five thousand's gone?'

His eyes slide away, he contorts his mouth inward. Even before he speaks, he has told me everything I need to know.

'That bad?' I give a dry laugh.

'There *are* assets, Ellen. A portfolio of stocks and shares. A life insurance policy. Something to be claimed for the loss of the yacht. And of course Harry's holding in Ainswick Properties. But the shares – well, they're in *Harry's* name, you see, and—'

'Couldn't I borrow against them or something?'

'In theory, *maybe*. But so far as I can tell at the moment – from what Gillespie says – well . . .' He sighs. 'The assets seem to be heavily encumbered.'

Encumbered. A strange archaic word. But I understand it well enough.

Leonard continues ponderously. 'I had a long meeting with Gillespie – now what I'm going to tell you is *totally* confidential, Ellen; he said to impress on you that it *really* mustn't go beyond the three of us – but apparently Ainswick has two major *creditors*, and one of them – a Middle

63

Eastern bank – called in its loan straight away, within a *week* of Harry's death. Very hasty, but that's the way these people are, I'm afraid. And the financial climate being what it is . . .' He gestures gloom.

'Ainswick couldn't pay?'

He shakes his head in agreement. 'The recession . . . A cash shortage . . . I don't think there're many property companies that could satisfy a sudden demand for cash in today's climate.' He fixes me with a sorrowful gaze. 'It seems Harry put up a large proportion of his *personal* portfolio as a guarantee – almost seventy-five per cent, Gillespie estimates – and, well . . . The bank has gone and *cashed* the shares.'

I chew on my lip, I raise my eyebrows. Leonard takes this as some sort of technical query and adds hastily, 'Oh, nothing illegal about it. Nothing *improper*. No, the bank was fully entitled apparently.' He frowns at his hands for a moment. 'Gillespie is holding the other bank off, but he tells me that negotiations are fairly *critical*. They're holding all Harry's remaining securities as a guarantee, along with an interest in Ainswick's most valuable property. Somewhere in London, I believe.'

'Shoreditch,' I murmur. 'An office block in Shoreditch.'

'Oh, is it? Gillespie didn't say. But anyway everything depends on the sale of this building apparently. According to Gillespie the whole thing is, er . . . fairly *critical* . . .' He peers at me unhappily from under his substantial eyebrows. He wants to make sure that I have read this message correctly, that I have understood that Ainswick may go under. 'I'm sorry, Ellen. I'm really sorry.'

I take my time. I let this settle over me gently.

I knew that Ainswick was in trouble. I had guessed long ago, months before Harry finally, angrily, admitted to it.

It wasn't a great feat of deduction. The bitter disappointment that Harry felt at losing his parliamentary seat was considerable – we lived through some black weeks – but even that couldn't account for the stress that he showed later last summer. While success made him calm and controlled, pressure made him hyperactive. As the recession bit deeper he spent less and less time at home, he propelled himself into a spiral of meetings, the few times he was home he drove nowhere – or maybe somewhere – late at night, he woke early to scribble in his study, as if by throwing time and energy at his problems he could simply wear them down.

Once I dared suggest that he might achieve more by slowing down a little. But Harry disliked even the mildest criticism, especially from me. Not because I wielded it often – quite the opposite – but because, I realise, it was in his relationship with me that he felt most vulnerable.

So there will be virtually no money, not from the estate anyway. I feel oddly unmoved. Maybe because there are many worse things that could happen, maybe because I can't believe I will be left entirely destitute. And because there's still the life insurance policy to be discussed.

'And Katie's trust?'

'Ah, *that's* unaffected. D'you see what I mean now, about things turning out rather differently? About the intentions of the will not meaning a great deal?'

I feel a small satisfaction at this unexpected turn. Nothing for me and Josh, something for Katie: there's a sort of justice in there somewhere. Thirty thousand was not a great deal by Harry's standards of course, but it's quite a bit by mine.

I dwell on this thought for a moment before asking, 'What about the house?'

'It's in *joint* names,' Leonard explains carefully, 'which means it can't be sold yet. But it *might* be possible to raise a further mortgage on it.' He puts a suitable note of caution into his voice. 'The existing mortgages and liens are quite large, of course. But it might be possible to *extend* them. So Gillespie says, anyway.'

I knew from something Harry said soon after he bought Pennygate that there was a mortgage, but I never gave it much thought until Leonard called me in California. I was sitting in my swimsuit in the air-conditioned cool of the La Jolla apartment, I remember, clutching the receiver – slippery with sun oil – to my shoulder, watching the children swimming in the communal pool under the harsh sun, when Leonard said that the debts against the house – two mortgages and a charge registered by a bank – totalled almost three hundred thousand.

'Of course,' Leonard says now, as he said then, 'the house is worth at least seventy or eighty thousand more. As long as prices stand up.'

But prices are not standing up, so the newspapers keep saying, and I can see that, by the time the house is finally sold, there may not be much left after interest payments.

'The insurance pay-out on the yacht should fetch fifty thousand or so – *eventually*. I've spoken to the insurance people. They're basically sympathetic, but because there's no actual wreck as yet . . . Well, I think it might be a *year* before terms are agreed.'

There is a pause. I wonder why Leonard does not return to the life policy. I know it is very substantial.

As if reading my mind, his face brightens a little. 'There *is* the life insurance, of course,' he says. 'It could be worth quite a bit – *eventually*. No claim can be made, of course, until the death certificate is issued. Even then it might be a while before they pay out. Insurance companies aren't exactly *forthcoming* in these circumstances.'

'How much is it worth?' I ask.

'In death benefit, you mean? Rather than cashing-in value?'

'Yes.'

'Five hundred and forty thousand.'

This is an enormous amount to me. I feel a surge of optimism. It will be more than enough for what I have in mind.

'And it would come straight to me, the money? Not into any trust?'

'Straight to you.'

I'd rather hoped as much.

'What about for now?' I ask. 'Couldn't I borrow against it?'

His brightness dims. 'It's back to the difficulty of establishing death. The whole thing's too uncertain, you see, from a potential *lender's* point of view.'

'Uncertain? But . . . they'll have to pay out, surely. Whatever happens.'

'Ah . . .' Leonard goes carefully again. '*We* may know that, Ellen. But to the insurers, you see, the facts will be looking *less* than conclusive. They will be forced to keep their minds open to *every* possibility you could ever imagine.' He gives an odd chuckle.

'Ah.' I nod sagely. 'You mean—?'

'Well – they have to consider things like suicide.' In his anxiety to make light of this he almost laughs. 'Intentional disappearance. That sort of thing. *Mad*, I know. But they're bureaucrats, that's the way they see things.'

'I see. And suicide would—?'

'I'm sorry?'

'It would affect things?'

'Oh yes. It would make the policy void.'

I knew this. Everyone knows this, whether they have life insurance or not. But I want to get everything absolutely clear, I want every question answered, every detail in place so that I can feel fully prepared.

'I was wondering ... assets. You've nothing of your *own*?' Leonard asks diffidently. 'No savings?'

I shake my head. I started my marriage with an old car, a tiny rented flat, and about a thousand in the bank. As a graphic designer in a small advertising agency, as a mother who believed in buying the best possible childcare, I was lucky to have that much.

Leonard leans forward again, hands latched over the front of his briefcase. 'Now you're *not* to worry, Ellen,' he says, forcing a note of cheer into his voice. 'Gillespie and I will go through the options. We'll arrange the best possible financial plan for you.'

'It doesn't sound as though there's a lot to arrange.'

He looks blank.

'Not a lot of money,' I explain with a sort of laugh.

But Leonard is beyond jokes, however feeble. 'There will be something left,' he says earnestly. 'It's just a question of finding the most cost-effective way of tiding you over. Until we can apply for the death certificate. Until that building sells.'

'Of course.' I grin at him.

He clicks his briefcase closed and regards me solemnly. 'I'm not sure I should have burdened you with all this.'

I drain the last of my brandy and stand up. 'For heaven's sake, Leonard!' I say half in exasperation, half in affection. 'What else were you going to do!'

My brittle tone seems to catch him by surprise. I think Leonard has always had this rather old-fashioned image of me as the quiet wife.

I walk with him towards the door. I pause. 'What about Jack? Is he having problems too?'

Leonard looks puzzled. 'Problems? I don't think so.'

'Isn't he affected by Ainswick?'

Leonard follows me thoughtfully into the hall. 'I don't think so. He severed all connection some time ago. I'll check. But . . .' He puts on his doubtful expression. 'I'm pretty sure.'

I knew that in their business life Jack and Harry had been going increasingly separate ways for some time, that Jack had other companies and other directorships. Yet for some reason I imagined that Jack had maintained an interest in Ainswick. In retrospect I see that this was naive of me. Jack, who has a rodent's instinct for doomed situations, would be far too canny to stay with a sinking ship.

Leonard chatters as we walk to his car: the service, how honoured and proud I must feel, the number of people who came, the great esteem they all felt for Harry.

We reach the car. Leonard slides his briefcase onto the back seat. He grasps me by the shoulders. 'Ellen *dear.*' He plants a paternal kiss on my forehead. 'You will take care? You will see people? If you want us to have Josh at all, we'd be delighted . . .' Leonard has a nice wife somewhere, a dedicated grandmother who rarely emerges except to go to church.

'He'll be going back to school after the weekend.'

'Well, if in the meantime . . . My nephew goes fishing most Sundays. If Josh wanted to go I'm sure it could be arranged.'

The talk of fishing reminds me of Richard Moreland

crouching in the open door of the car. I ask Leonard if he knows him.

'Oh yes!' Approval brightens Leonard's face. 'Nice chap! Friend of the Dartingtons. Renting their cottage at Waldringfield.'

The Dartingtons are a family who live on the other side of Woodbridge. They are substantial landowners, effortlessly and unobtrusively upper class, people who Anne and Charles count triumphantly among their friends. The father is a retired admiral and former ADC to one of the royal family, while two of the three sons are, if I remember, currently serving in the Navy. In this community it is more than enough to know that someone is a friend of people like the Dartingtons.

'But you know Moreland, surely?' Leonard blinks at me. 'I thought you must know him! He served in the Falklands with Harry.'

'No.'

'Oh . . .' A momentary adjustment and he brightens again. 'But you met this morning? Someone introduced you? Such an *immensely* nice man.'

I kiss him on the cheek. 'Goodbye, Leonard. And thank you.'

He drives a few yards before halting and thrusting his head out of the window. 'You're sure you'll be all right?'

I reassure him several times, and he is gone at last.

I go back into the house. My first thought is: no Katie, and my heart squeezes painfully. I shut the door and am struck by the absolute stillness of the place. Even when Harry wasn't here he used to leave a sort of energy behind him, a sense that things were about to happen, which they usually were. He was constantly asking me to put on goodwill events for the constituency, drinks parties for local worthies, dinner parties for the more influential. It took some time, but I like to think I became an efficient hostess.

It is almost half past nine, high time Josh appeared, if only for food. I go to the boot room to find some walking shoes. The footwear is arranged in racks. Most of it is Harry's: waders for salmon fishing – a short-lived interest this, Scotland was too far, the sport too static; brogues for pheasant shooting, a sport he returned to spasmodically in the winter; tennis shoes, almost new; squash shoes, unworn. When it came to hobbies Harry was a man of sudden enthusiasms, but as he lacked the time to improve his skills and could not bear to be less than proficient at whatever he did, his interest was apt to wane almost as rapidly as it had sprung up. Sailing, though it took me a long while to realise it, was the one exception.

I circle the lawn, calling Josh's name. I let myself out through the side gate and start down the track towards the river. Many times in the last weeks I have tried to picture this moment, tried to imagine how I would feel taking the path again after all this time. Oddly, I feel little. Just a tightness in my throat, a lightness in my stomach.

The sky is fading. Under the long arch of trees the light is already deep with shadows. I call Josh again. His hide-out is somewhere ahead. I am not sure of its exact location – I have never been invited to inspect it. A crow caws above. An outboard hums on the river.

Emerging from the vault of trees, I reach the point beyond which Josh is not permitted to go unaccompanied, and call again.

I wait, I listen. Finally I walk on towards the river. The track levels off and passes briefly between pastures inhabited by black-faced sheep before falling once more to the flatness of the river-bank and a copse of oak, haw-thorn and birch. The copse encircles a clearing of tussock grass and patches of flinty sand. On the far side of the clearing is the quay, an ancient stone-built structure some twelve feet wide protruding thirty or forty feet into the river, matted with couch grass and guarded by a tall stand of pines. Beside the quay is an equally ancient slipway, crumbling and uneven.

I don't resist the memories. I see *Minerva* as she was that day, tied up alongside, her silvery spars bare of sails, her decks cluttered with rope and sail-bags. I see Harry lifting boxes of provisions over the rails onto the deck, I see the darkening sky, the curtains of rain. The memory is clear, but oddly bearable for all that, probably because I have been here in my mind so many times before.

I see Harry's expression under the hood of his water-proofs, the grim determination that pushed his face into a mass of lines, and I wonder if he was ever really happy, even in the early years of our marriage. He tried very hard to be; he applied himself to marriage as he applied him-self to most things, with close attention. But there was a part of himself he could never risk, a sort of inner shame that held him back. He knew I loved him, I used to tell him often enough, but he could never quite accept this outpouring of affection, which to him was too uncon-ditional. He found it hard to understand why I didn't judge him as harshly as he judged himself. In those days, of course, I had no reason to.

I know the dory isn't here any more, I know it's being stored at the boatyard at Waldringfield, but this doesn't stop me from glancing down to where it used to lie tied up to the quay. At low tide it was unusable, squatting on the slipway at a drunken angle, but at anything above half tide Harry would jump into it, fire the outboard and, paying token obedience to the speed limit, race off to the pub at Waldringfield.

Tonight the tide is low, and the river winds sluggishly through the mud flats, looking as though it has no depth to it at all. A small boat makes its way upstream under outboard. On the far bank a group of walkers strides in single file along the embankment that straddles the marshes. A mile or so downstream, by the boatyard on the opposite shore, yachts are tightly clustered around the visitors' moorings. It is high season and the start of the weekend; by tomorrow the river, regarded as one of the prettiest on this coast, will be noisy with boats and shouting people.

The last time I came down here was with the senior police officer, Dawson, to show him the quay, to point out the mooring, to tell him what little I could. It was Thursday, I remember, five days after Harry disappeared, and cold, the river wind-blown and deserted.

I remember the day for another reason. It was the day that I realised I must get myself and the children away from Pennygate as soon as possible, that with so many pressures if we stayed any longer we would be in danger of falling apart. Self-control is an oddly treacherous thing. The instant you think you have mastered it, it deserts you, suddenly and without warning. It had almost happened once. I lived in dread of it happening again.

Climbing back up the track, I call for Josh with increasing frustration. As I pause for breath half-way up, his voice comes from close behind. 'Mum.'

I give a great start and jerk my head round. 'Where have you been?' I cry in fear and anger.

His lips pucker, he frowns.

I look around and see that we are just within the boundary of his permitted territory. I let my breath out slowly. 'Didn't you hear me?' I say weakly.

He shakes his head.

'I thought . . .' I gesture helplessly. 'I thought you were down at the river.'

Another shake of the head, more rapid.

'Sorry,' I sigh. 'Sorry.'

Josh contorts his mouth, a small peace offering. Feeling a rush of emotion, I put an arm round his shoulders and squeeze him to me.

'Supper?'

He greets the idea without much interest. We start up the hill.

'Long day,' I remark. I know he is tired, I sense he is not particularly keen to talk, but I am anxious to re-establish communications after the disruptions of the last few days. 'Had a good time?' I ask.

He lifts his shoulders high in another of these shrugs he uses as a substitute for conversation. Noticing that his clothes are still relatively clean, I wonder what he has been doing all this time. 'The hide-out okay?'

He pushes out his lip in partial agreement.

I trawl for questions. 'So what's new?'

'Someone's been there.'

'Where?'

'In the woods.'

'Oh? What – camping?'

He nods. 'In the bushes.'

My mind leaps to unsavoury thoughts of tramps and child molesters. 'You didn't see anyone?'

He shakes his head. 'The signs were pretty ancient.'

The signs. This is part of Josh's outdoor survival language which covers a range of expertise I don't pretend to grasp. But ancient I understand all right. 'This someone wasn't using your hide-out?'

He frowns at the stupidity of my question, from which I gather that his hide-out is so well concealed as to be undiscoverable.

The track steepens. We climb slowly through the darkening woods. Josh kicks at stones.

'Shall we get a schoolfriend over tomorrow?' I say brightly. 'Dan or someone?' Josh always resists these attempts to get him together with boys of his own age. He enjoys the days he spends with Dan, but he is just as happy on his own, if not more so. This time, however, I intend to push the idea. Josh will be going back to school on Monday and seeing Dan will ease his passage. 'I might be able to arrange for Dan's dad to take you fishing.'

He says matter-of-factly, 'Richard's taking me.'

'Richard? Richard who?'

He looks puzzled that I do not know. 'Dad's friend,' he explains.

'Ah.' Visions of the face framed by the open car door. 'You mean, Richard Moreland?'

'He was in the Marines.'

'Yes. Yes, I . . . heard. When did he ask you?'

This forces Josh to think. He has never been good with time. 'Umm . . . Teatime. About.'

'When I was taking Katie back?'

'Yup.'

'But – did he phone?'

'No. I saw him.'

'Where?'

'He came up here.'

'Did he now?' I say defensively. 'I thought I told you never to talk to strangers.'

Josh thinks about this for a moment. 'But he came and talked to me this morning. With Uncle Leonard.'

'What – at the service?'

He nods.

'Oh.' We walk on. 'I didn't realise. Oh. Well . . . we'll see.'

'He said he'd phone you.'

I hear the hope in his voice. Josh loves fishing more than almost anything else. And after spending so many weeks cooped up with Katie and me in what was inevitably a charged atmosphere, a trip in male company can only do him good.

'All right,' I say. 'But I'll need to know there are things like life-jackets and food, and where you're going, and when you're due back.' I try not to fuss over Josh but really I'm a born worrier.

We pass through the gate into the garden. A bird sings overhead, an astonishingly rich sound. I stand for a moment under the heavy trees, looking for it. When I glance round Josh has almost disappeared.

'Hey!'

He turns.

I catch up with him and give him an impulsive hug. 'Good to be home, eh?'

He does not push me away, but he does not hug me back either. He has been broadcasting this faint remoteness ever since his father died. I am never sure if it is part of his coping mechanism, or whether he is punishing me for some crime. I drop my arms. 'Well,' I say, filling my voice with cheer. 'What do you fancy? Pizza? Baked beans?'

In the dusk his expression has reverted to its usual breezy unconcern. 'Not hungry.'

He knows this ploy has no chance and as we turn for

the house I am already telling him that unless he feels strongly about it he is going to get baked beans.

A dark figure emerges from the shadows of the conservatory. My heart gives a small bump, I come stiffly to a halt. For a split second I seem to see Harry.

'There you are,' calls Jack, striding across the lawn towards us. 'I was beginning to think you'd vanished. *Hello*, Josh. How's the fishing?' He grips Josh's shoulder and gives him the benefit of his broadest smile. 'How about you taking me out one day? Catch a few bass, hmm? You'll have to tell me what's what, of course. Never could get bait to stay on the hook.' He laughs and drops his voice conspiratorially. 'Just the two of us, eh? And a few beers. 'Well—' He slides a theatrical glance in my direction. 'Coke, then. Now, listen, old chap, would you give me a minute with your mum?' He winks and, gripping Josh's shoulder, turns him deftly towards the house.

I suppress a faint resentment. It is partly the way Jack has arrived without warning, partly his use of this blatant and practised charm which, directed at a child, seems vaguely offensive.

I say more sharply than I mean to, 'No.' Then, aware that I have sounded unreasonable, I add, 'I really can't talk now, Jack. I've got to make supper.'

I start after Josh.

'Ellen. *Ellen*.' Jack has my elbow. He slows me down. 'Hold on, hold on. It won't take a minute.' His tone suggests that I am being childish. 'Ellen.' His voice become soft, coaxing.

I hesitate. I half turn. I say in all honesty, 'I'm very tired, Jack. Perhaps another time. If you wouldn't mind.'

He moves in front of me, very close. This is a way of his, to come so close that you are forced to tilt your head

77

back or look away. He reaches up and pushes a strand of hair away from my eye. 'Poor love, you *are* in a state.'

I draw back. 'I'm not in a state.' This is not strictly true – I am near my limits – but I am not about to admit this to Jack, who likes to feel that he has a disturbing effect on all women. 'It's just that I've had enough for one day.'

'*Ellen.*' He spreads his hands wide, looking misunderstood. 'I only came to find out if you needed anything. Any help. I know the situation is – well, far from easy. Leonard's kept me in touch. But I just wanted you to know that *whatever* happens, Ellen, *whatever* support you need – I'm here.' There is intimacy and compassion in his voice. Jack can do almost anything with his voice. It is rich and dark, like an actor's.

'Thank you. That's very kind. I do appreciate it.' I wonder just how much Jack knows about my financial situation.

'Ellen!' His tone is half-injured, half-amused. 'You seem cross with me. *Are* you?' He ducks his head to read my expression in the half-light.

If I try to answer this I will only get embroiled in ever decreasing explanations, in a sort of word game which, with Jack, will be impossible to win. I shake my head and turn for the house.

Jack walks at my side, watching me. 'You know, it isn't just because I *have* to be involved – as a trustee and all that. It's because' – his voice swoops low and soft – 'I *want* to help. Because I *care*.' He lets the thought hang in the air, gaining significance. He can't stop himself drawing closer, brushing his fingers across my hand. Physical contact with the opposite sex is a compulsion with Jack. 'I can't bear to think of you trying to get through this on your own, you know.'

'I've got Leonard.'

'Yes . . . Of course.' He makes Leonard sound like a decidedly mixed blessing. 'But Leonard can't do everything.' He strides ahead to put a restraining hand on the open door of the conservatory.

He leaves me too little room and as I turn sideways to pass through he catches me softly by the shoulder. 'Ellen – you're not cross with me, are you? *Are* you?' He tips me a self-mocking grin.

Drained, I sink back against the door frame. I sigh, 'Jack . . .'

'I'd be most upset if you were. You're very special to me, Ellen. Very special indeed.' His voice has acquired a rough edge, as if he is fighting some deep emotion. This is the trouble with Jack; he can make any statement sound plausible.

Yet I cannot take him seriously. For Jack, the moment is everything, and once it has passed he is easily distracted. I am not, anyway, his sort. Jack goes for super-confident, highly packaged women, the kind that proclaim a man's status like an expensive car.

I mumble that I am not cross with him, not in the least. Then, disentangling myself gently but unequivocally, I make for the kitchen.

The last time Jack offered to take care of me, it did not end well. Remembering it now, I feel an echo of mortification. He had caught me at my lowest ebb, one evening last November, soon after the truth of Harry's behaviour had been brought home to me in the most inescapable way. I was not so adept at hiding my feelings then. I let misery undermine my judgement. It only needed Jack to slip his arm round my shoulder for me to cry wretchedly, to discharge great bursts of despair. Such was my anguish

79

that I almost – so nearly – revealed my most bitter, most secret emotions to him.

Jack wasn't the best person to turn to, of course. I should have known this. I should have realised that he would instinctively offer the only sort of comfort that had any meaning for him. But when his mouth, which had been resting on my hair, travelled down my cheek and brushed my lips, I was held by inertia and surprise, like a mindless sixteen-year-old. I doubted my interpretation of what was happening. It wasn't until his hand arrived on my breast and squeezed it gently that I reacted. And, having delayed, I over-reacted. I was seized by a strange anger which probably had more to do with my feelings towards Harry than Jack. I did something I never knew I was capable of, although even as my hand flew out it seemed to travel in slow motion and I watched it with fascination, as if I might yet pull it back. I pushed my hand into his face and thrust it away from me, a hard shove. His head arced back, he caught himself just before he fell off the chair. I don't know which of us was more surprised by this show of force. Jack exclaimed, 'Christ!' over and over again and glared at me and muttered something, I think it was, 'So it's like that, is it?' Then, beginning to recover himself, his expression changed to one of grim amusement. 'I think you misunderstood me a little there,' he breathed. He even managed a thin laugh. Then he said ingenuously, 'Just trying to help,' and rested his fingers lightly on my hand: the misunderstood child asking forgiveness.

It was a long time ago now; it has no importance. I go quickly into the kitchen, flick on the lights and pull a can of baked beans out of the cupboard.

Jack strolls in behind me. 'Now, the first thing is to get you *settled* financially.' His voice has taken on a note of casual authority. 'The legal situation – Leonard has explained it all, has he?' He catches my nod. 'Well, it's obviously going to take time to sort out. Nothing we can do to hurry it up. So I've arranged with Gillespie for you to have something to tide you over. Call it a loan. But you're to have it for as long as you need it.' He leans against the counter and flourishes a hand. 'Just as long as you need it.'

I finish pouring the beans into a pan. 'It's very kind of you. I'm very touched. Very. And I'll certainly bear it in mind. But hopefully it won't be necessary.'

He takes this as an understandable show of reluctance, a necessary prelude to my accepting the money. He cajoles me gently to accept it straight away, finally he lets the subject drop, but with the knowing look of someone who is convinced I will see the light eventually.

He watches me saw bread into ragged slices. 'You could have done without Ainswick, too.'

I grunt non-committally.

'Leonard told you, did he?'

I give a vague shrug.

'There's still a chance, of course. If a buyer can be found for that damned Shoreditch property.'

'I thought you weren't involved in Ainswick any more.'

He picks up a piece of fallen crust and examines it for a moment before propelling it neatly into his mouth. 'I'm not,' he says with a heavy sigh, as if it were a great sadness to him.

The bread is too thick for the toaster and I have to manœuvre it down into the slot. 'I never knew – why did you leave?'

'What?' He seems a little surprised that I should ask. 'I suppose because Harry's ideas didn't mesh with mine any more,' he says at last. 'Partly that, and partly . . .' He chews pensively. 'Because Harry thought I'd done him a bad deal.'

'And had you?'

He looks suitably offended at my question then ignores it. 'The point is, he *thought* I had. I took a no-hope proposition off Ainswick's books when it needed some cash. Gave a bloody good price for it too. Probably twice what it was worth. Scrubland with no planning, and no prospects of getting it either. Then two years ago, right out of the blue, damn me if the planners don't suddenly reverse their policy and zone it for low-cost housing.' He makes an extravagant gesture of disbelief. 'Harry decided I must have had wind of it. God, if only I had – I'd have bought up more land.' He raises an eyebrow. 'Anyway if anyone should have got wind of it, it was Harry. He was the one with friends in the right places, not me.'

It seems to me that Jack, like Harry, always made it his business to know the people who might be useful to him, but I let it pass.

The toaster pops. I extricate the slices and drop them onto a plate. 'If you don't mind, Jack . . . I want to give Josh his supper.'

He draws himself elegantly away from the counter. 'Of course.' In one continuous movement he comes closer and drops a hand onto my neck. 'But we'll talk again soon, eh? You *will* let me take care of that money, won't you? Mmm?'

He smiles the lazy low-lidded smile he keeps for all women who are not old or hopelessly plain. His fingers stir against my skin. I move away, touching a distancing hand against his chest. I feel him stiffen. It is the hand: he has not forgiven me for pushing him away all those months ago.

'You can be very hard on people, Ellen.'

I shrug wordlessly.

'You were very hard on Harry,' he comments coldly.

'Was I?'

'All that business . . . you took it far too seriously, you know.'

The beans are sizzling. I reach for the switch and turn the gas off.

'You made it into something it wasn't,' Jack goes on. 'She was nothing, just a . . .' He wheels a hand, searching for the word.

'A younger, prettier, smarter version?' I attempt an ironic laugh which comes out wrong, almost like a gasp.

'It was just an *affair*, Ellen. It would never have come to anything. He would never have left you.'

This is Jack's view of adultery – just an affair. But then he has never been married, he has never seen it from the other side. 'I never thought he was going to leave me,' I say in a resentful manner which I instantly regret.

'Come on, Ellen,' Jack argues in a soft unyielding tone. 'You watched him like a hawk. You were obsessed. God – you could have cut the atmosphere with a knife. Even the best men stray, Ellen, but it's not the end of the world, you know.'

I cannot deal with this discussion. My breath is band-tight in my chest. I am desperate to be alone. 'Jack, please . . .'

He shakes his head sadly, as if I am a lost cause. When he kisses me goodbye he has a patriarchal smile, and, though I am not crying, he brushes my cheeks lightly with his thumbs as if to wipe away tears.

As he lets himself out I stare sightlessly at the over-cooked beans and think about Caroline Palmer.

*

FOUR

The phone pulls me out of a dark sleep. I open my eyes, half frightened that it will be night and that the nightmares are still to come. But grey light fills the room and I absorb the familiar shapes, the well-remembered pattern of the partly drawn curtains with something close to relief. For better or worse, I am home.

Rolling over, I reach for the phone. It is Molly. She wants to know if she has woken me.

The bedside clock says it is just before eleven. I try to remember when I finally fell asleep. Four or so. 'No,' I say. 'I was just getting up.'

'What about lunch?' She tempts me with favourite things, smoked salmon, artichokes, strawberries. 'And there's the most adorable puppy next door that Josh can play with.'

'Molly, I'd love to, but—'

'Ellen! I want to hear about America, I want to hear about *you*.'

'I've got to wait for Josh to get back from his fishing.'

'Come on your own then! Come on!'

'He's due back at lunchtime.'

Unabashed, Molly regroups. 'Who are these people he's gone with? Can't they keep him for a while? Or I could bring lunch over, a picnic.'

'Molly – I'm not sure. Can I call you later?'

'When?' she growls.

'As soon as I'm up?'

'Ellen . . .' she sighs. 'You know – I'm not at all sure what to do with you.'

'Oh, I'm all right.'

'Are you? I worry about you. I have this silly idea that you're bottling things up, that you're making yourself ill. I've never seen anyone so thin, Ellen. I couldn't believe it when I saw you yesterday. You haven't developed a *thing* about food, have you? You're not feeling guilty or something stupid? Everyone feels guilty when someone dies, you know. You're not tormenting yourself, are you?'

This is Molly's way, everything up front, nothing left unsaid. It is one of the reasons I am so fond of her. 'No,' I say carefully, 'it's not like that, Molly.'

'It's not— You don't blame yourself over that stupid business? That woman?'

I never told Molly about my troubles with Harry. I didn't have to. Being a person who misses little, she soon guessed that something was wrong. At first she contained her curiosity – though with obvious effort – and gave me silent unquestioning support, but then, as my unhappiness deepened, she began to ask questions. The other-woman scenario was almost the first thing she suggested. This surprised and grieved me; I hadn't realised people saw Harry as such an obvious candidate for adultery. I didn't bother to contradict her. There wasn't much point. At the same time I wouldn't talk about it. I didn't dare. With Molly, I was afraid I would say too much.

'I don't blame anyone, Molly. Really.' Even as I say it my heart tightens, I feel the old unsteadiness in my stomach. 'You'll call me straight back then?' Her voice has a lurking reproach. She is preparing herself for the fact that I will put her off again.

I find Josh's note on the kitchen table, anchored by the salt grinder. The writing is uneven, the spelling erratic, there are capitals in odd places. I can imagine him labouring over what for him is an exceptionally long message.

'We are trying other side of Waldringfield' – this misspelt and amended – 'and Kirton Creek. Have life-jacket and food. Back at lunchtime with fish.'

The assurance of this last statement is characteristic of Josh, who, whatever his failings at school, does not lack confidence out of doors. Reading the message again, I realise that, left to his own devices, he would never have provided half this information. Moreland must have stood over him, telling him what to write.

A bowl stands in the sink, whiskers of Josh's favourite cereal floating on the milk. Next to it is a plate dotted with crumbs and smears of butter, and a glass with a tidemark of orange juice, testaments to a proper breakfast.

On my way back I find another note, one that has been posted through the front door. It comes from two of my Heath End neighbours and directs me to the kitchen door where I find a cardboard box containing two quiches, an apple pie, a large bag of tomatoes, a selection of soft fruit, cream, two bottles of wine, a fruit cake, and a parcel of five or six gingerbread men. The gingerbread men have been made with the loving care of young hands that have rolled the mixture rather too thin in places and have pressed the button eyes too hard into the face, so that the sides of the head have ballooned out. There is a card for Katie, Josh and me, sent with 'tons of love' from the mothers and many carefully wrought kisses from the children.

My gratitude is touched with apprehension. What will these people expect of me? Brave widow, grieving wife. I'm not sure I can manage either role.

As I load the perishables into the fridge, I think of Katie. Her absence is like a constant ache, lurking just below my consciousness. We have become so close over the last months that we are almost like those twins you read about, hardly needing to voice our thoughts to each other. Quite apart from loving her in a passionately maternal way, I admire her so much. She is such a fine person, so generous, so brave, so easily wounded. So bad at being alone. And that is how I think of her now, among her noisy schoolmates – alone. I long to talk to her, but she has classes at this time on a Saturday morning and I won't be able to reach her until one-thirty.

I put off my call to Molly until I have had a shower and dressed and got a stiff coffee inside me. Even then I have to brace myself to tell her that lunch of any sort is going to be too difficult. Only half-jokingly, she accuses me of trying to avoid her. I placate her by asking her to lunch on Monday.

It is twelve. If I'm lucky I might have an hour before Josh comes back. The study is on the north side of the house, facing the vegetable garden. Harry always wanted a study like this, imposing, heavyweight, with tall ornamental bookshelves, bottle-green brocade curtains, silk wall hangings to match, and a wide mahogany knee-hole desk. In all but the brightest weather, however, the room is gloomy, and today it is positively dark. I turn on the concealed lighting, and splashes of light spring across the ceiling and the rows of reference books, the copies of *Hansard*, and the Victorian hunting scenes on either side of the window.

A table and office chair have been brought in and placed to the left of the door, facing a wall of books. Typewriter and paper stand on the table, ready for Margaret to start work on Monday.

The surface of Harry's desk is covered with sorted, clipped and weighted stacks of letters and papers, and I have to slide some to one side before I can place the desk lamp at the front where it will shine down into the drawers as I open them.

I have been through the desk once before, about three days before I left for America. I removed everything I thought Leonard might need, everything of an official or vaguely legal nature – Harry's birth certificate, passport, insurance certificates. The financial papers – share transactions and bank statements and so on – I gave to Margaret.

I go through what is left. Foreign money; travel and hotel guides; bills scored with a single ink-stroke and the date of payment; medical insurance leaflets; brochures for garden machinery, conservatories and solar heating; theatre and music programmes – though Harry went to this sort of thing out of duty rather than enjoyment. For him theatre was far less dramatic than real life, while classical music simply passed him by.

In a bottom drawer there is a box of unmounted snapshots from Harry's school and army days. He used to keep them in a battered old trunk at Heath End. When we were first married I had to persuade him to show them to me. He wasn't very keen. For some reason the past irritated – or bored – him, it was hard to know which.

There is a picture from a skiing trip – a grinning Harry standing outside a Verbier chalet in a group of young people vying with each other to strike the silliest pose; then a more formal group taken on an army climbing expedition in the barren hills of what looks like Scotland – a serious Harry here, stiff and grimly determined, scowling as he often did when he had his personal barriers up; then a shot of Harry with three fellow guests at a wedding reception. The party was held in Berkshire in a flapping marquee on a wind-blown Saturday in September 1982. I know exactly how it was, because it was here that Harry and I met. We were introduced by a former flatmate of mine and later that day, when seven or eight of us went on to dinner at an Indonesian restaurant off the Brompton Road, Harry and I were squashed next to each other at the cramped table.

I felt no instantaneous attraction for Harry. Rather, a sort of awe. It was hard not to be impressed by him. He was striking in a robust sort of way, broad-shouldered and athletic, exuding an overwhelming well-being with his lightly tanned skin, his clear eyes, his barely suppressed energy. Quick, sharp, poised effortlessly on the leading edge of the conversation, he was an exhilarating if daunting dinner companion. Rather than air my ignorance and my altogether slower wit, I kept my contributions to a minimum. It didn't worry me that I wasn't making an impression; I didn't think I was Harry's type. I didn't appreciate that for Harry it was my very lack of competitiveness, my relatively placid nature which were my greatest assets. Later he told me he came to a decision about me almost straight away. He couldn't say why. I suppose it was a sort of blind recognition. I think I made him feel safe.

By then my marriage had been over for two years and I was ripe for Harry's steady, almost circumspect, courtship. Not that I was immediately convinced. It took me some time to begin to appreciate the qualities that he took care to keep well hidden – an underlying vulnerability, an absurd generosity – and to realise that the things he most needed from me, trust and emotional security, were the very things that I could supply in abundance. He needed me and, for me, being needed is very close to love.

Now, looking at Harry as I first saw him, dressed in his wedding regalia, I remember the weeks and months after our own marriage, the feeling of unreserved happiness, of pride, and I wonder when the next great turning point came – when he stopped needing me. The awful thing is, I don't know, and I realise now that I probably never will. But at some point he slipped away from me into a dark world of his own. I can't help being haunted by the thought that I missed the signs, that he sent warnings which I chose not to read, that if only I hadn't been so wrapped up in the children and the satisfactions of my existence I might have realised something was wrong. When I'm being kind to myself I tell myself that times were difficult, that he was in such a stressed state that it would have been impossible for me to identify his separate preoccupations and obsessions. This thought, when I can keep any sort of hold on it, eases my guilt a little.

I glance through the remaining pictures. School, foreign holidays, army, an earlier skiing trip. In the drawer above are bunches of letters held together with elastic bands. Most date from the late seventies when Harry was posted to Germany and Northern Ireland. Several come from his girlfriend of the time, a bouncy girl called Susie whom I met some years ago. The letters are boisterous and devoid of intimacy.

The remaining drawers yield nothing, though even now I am not absolutely sure what I am looking for. A note perhaps. A letter. Some clue as to Harry's state of mind in the week before he died. A copy of the will, some sort of explanation as to why Katie was to be left so little. Anything, really, that might throw some light on those last six months, on what made Harry do what he did. I want so much to be rid of my anger, I want so much to understand.

I also want to be able to destroy anything before anyone else should find it.

I go round the desk and check the back for hidden compartments that I know perfectly well are not there. I search the cupboards that support the tall piers of bookshelves. Completing the circle, I sink back into the chair and open the centre drawer again. There are airline vouchers, Eurocheques, old pocket diaries from two and three years back, an abandoned address book. I flick through the diaries, but the entries, some in Margaret's neat hand, some in Harry's scrawl, have the innocent rhythm of happy days. The pocket address book, overfilled and well thumbed, is not dated, but is, I think, quite recent, last used perhaps eighteen months ago. I cannot help looking for Caroline Palmer's name, though I'm pretty sure Harry didn't know her at that time. I find nothing under either P or C.

At the back of the book, on an unprinted flysheet, Harry has printed several lists of numbers in his distinctive boxy handwriting. Credit card numbers identified by their prefixes: Amex, Visa, M/card. And what look like bank account numbers, prefixed by such abbreviations as P/A and D/A – personal account, deposit account.

I put the book to one side. While Harry was alive I only looked in this drawer twice, three times at the most, and that was when he phoned and asked me to see if he'd left his cheque-book behind. Once he had forgotten his keys. They aren't here now, I notice. There are only desk keys, spare outhouse keys, and, hidden at the back, one or two keys to the gun cabinet.

The phone rings. I feel a dart of hope that it will be Katie until I see it's barely half past twelve. Anne greets me in a taut voice. Closing the drawer, I hunch down over the desk, my elbows anchored in the gaps between the stacks of paper, while she recounts the full difficulties of having Diana to stay for the night, how she complained about her supper, how, having refused to go to bed, she fell asleep in her chair.

I make sympathetic noises. I suggest that maybe Diana was upset by the service and the talk of Charles's candidature and will feel calmer in a couple of days. Anne is not so sure. Listening as best I can, murmuring appropriately, my eyes stray to the papers by my right elbow, to one of Harry's credit card statements that Margaret has marked 'paid'. It is for March. I notice that Harry did not stint himself, even though we were under financial strain. The bill totals over five hundred pounds. There are charges for petrol and other mundane things, but also for goods from Turnbull and Asser – shirts presumably – and meals in London restaurants – a couple of fashionable places with prices to match, and two that I have never heard of with more modest prices. I wonder if it was Caroline Palmer that Harry took to these cheaper restaurants where presumably there was less chance of being recognised.

I wonder what Caroline Palmer is doing nowadays, I wonder if she is grieving for Harry. Somehow, I don't think so.

Anne's tone has changed. She has put on her petitioning voice, brusque and defensive. She says that Diana is due to return home to her cottage after the weekend, but that she is not at all sure it is safe to leave her alone for long, that someone will need keep an eye on her, but that it will be difficult for she herself or Charles to manage this every day while Charles is busy preparing for the selection proceedings.

I take up my cue. 'I'll look in,' I say, 'whenever I can.'

'Well, *if* you don't mind. We've had to deal with it all, you know. While you've been away.'

'Yes. Of course.'

There is a silence through which she conveys her considerable dissatisfaction with me.

'So . . .' she says at last. 'How did it go with Leonard?'

I tell her Leonard is sorting everything out. Then, in an attempt to restore family harmony, for which, it seems, I am to be held responsible, I recount the problems stemming from the lack of a death certificate and ask Anne's advice about the house, and whether she thinks I should try to let it. She warms a little to this appeal to her wisdom, she says she thinks I should stay put for the moment. By the time we ring off we have managed to re-establish some feeling of mutual support. It is always like this with Anne and me: shaky bridges in constant need of rebuilding.

I stare at the desk. I remember Harry's keys. I remember that somewhere on the bunch there should be a key to the one place that I haven't yet searched.

Harry kept two sets of keys; the spares should be in the house somewhere. I start for the stairs, then, reminded of another key, in need of maximum reassurance, I divert into the kitchen and feel inside the right-hand door of the old pine dresser that takes up most of the end wall. The second key to the gun cabinet is in its usual place, on a hook hidden behind the frame.

The phone again. I stop in the doorway, reluctant and indecisive. When the ringing finally stops, I cross the kitchen and switch on the answering machine.

The hall table – large and Jacobean, and something I suspect Harry paid far too much for – is very tidy. Some newly delivered country and sporting magazines stand in a pile next to a stupendous flower arrangement, a bowl of white roses, presented by a neighbour. The various hats Harry liked to scatter over the table have been removed, probably to the coat cupboard. The silver tray holds a neat stack of cards and circulars.

Harry sometimes left keys here but more often than not he kept them in his dressing-room. But when I go upstairs and look in the china bowl on top of the chest of drawers where he would drop them with a loud clink I find nothing but a few brass coins.

In the bedroom the phone rings again. I start slightly, I don't know why. The answering machine stifles the sound at the fourth ring.

In the top right-hand drawer of the chest are folded handkerchiefs, a dress tie, some unloved cufflinks relegated from the leather box in front of the mirror. Moving the handkerchiefs aside, I search the drawer. Though I have been to this chest countless times in the past to put clean linen away, this act, more than any other since I returned, makes me feel uncomfortable, like an intruder. I am struck by the irrational illusion that Harry is close by, that he has been gone only five minutes, that he will step round the door at any moment and demand to know what I am doing. Old guilt, new guilt. In the general well of remorse, it's hard to separate them.

There are no keys in here.

A door bangs downstairs, light feet run into the hall. My heart gives a small thump, I pull my hand back, I close the drawer.

'Mum!' Josh cries. 'Mum!'

I draw a slow breath. 'Here,' I call. 'Upstairs.'

Without thought, I pull open the left-hand drawer and glance quickly inside. Socks arranged in rank according to colour and thickness, a legacy of Harry's army days. And at the front, for anyone to see, the keys.

'Mum!' Josh arrives panting. 'We've got the fire going! It's already good and hot. And we've got tons of mullet. They're really hard to catch usually, but we've got a whole lot.' He gasps, '*Five*.'

'Five!' I look impressed. I slip the keys into my pocket. 'The fire's not ready yet. It's got to die down a bit.'

'Is there anything you need?' I make for the stairs. 'Bread or anything?'

'Oh no!'

'Nothing at all?'

'Richard's got everything.' He races past me to drape the top half of his body over the banister rail and slide rapidly down into the hall.

'What about ketchup?'

He snakes round the newel-post and drops onto the floor. 'Umm ... I don't think so.' There is doubt in his voice. Ketchup is Josh's great weakness. I raise a questioning eyebrow at him.

'No,' he says, with abrupt decision.

I nod wisely. Ketchup wouldn't perhaps be appropriate in the wild. I lead the way into the kitchen. 'Coke, then?'

'We've got lemonade.'

'You have everything then.' I lean against the kitchen table and regard my son with an upwelling of satisfaction and sudden optimism. I would love to reach out and touch him, but in this mannish self-sufficient mood of his I do not think he will take kindly to such an open display of affection. 'So ...?' I say. 'What can I do for you?'

'Oh!' exclaims Josh, remembering why he has come. 'There's enough for you. I mean, if you want to have some.'

'Well, thank you.' I give a slight bow. 'But wouldn't you rather have it all to yourselves?'

'There's too much.' He shuffles his feet.

I chew thoughtfully on my lip. 'But would you *like* me to come?'

'*Course!*' He rounds his eyes in rebuke, then spoils it by averting his gaze, which sends me a more confused message. 'Richard said—' He pauses, beset by some inner debate. The words, when they finally come, are delivered with a frown. 'He said to ask you nicely so you'd be sure to come.'

'Ah . . .' I nod gravely. 'In that case . . .' I accept, won over not so much by Josh's manner, beguiling though it is in a backhanded way, but by my desire to earn back that part of his approval which I sense I have lost.

I tell Josh I'll be down in twenty minutes or so. The phone rings. My eyes dart to the clock. Five past one. I turn up the answering machine, hoping for Katie, and hear Jack's sinuous voice. I turn the volume down again. When I look back Josh is gone.

I wait another five minutes, sitting at the counter with a second cup of coffee. In my mind's eye, I see Katie leaving the dining hall and walking towards her house. I try not to impose an expression on her face because, in my present mood, I know I will paint it dark and lost.

The phone is answered by a senior girl and I have to hang on for what seems a long time while she finds Katie.

'Mum?' Katie's voice has a lift to it. She tells me she is fine, that everyone is letting her get on with things, not paying her special attention – well, not so much that she can't deal with it.

I listen for shades of false cheer, for signs that she is

putting on a front for my benefit, that underneath it all she is struggling, but if there's anything to be heard in her voice it's relief.

'I'm so pleased, darling,' I say. 'That's wonderful.' I cannot help adding, 'But you will phone, won't you? If you need to talk?'

'I will, Mum. Don't worry. *Please*.'

'Okay. I promise!' I laugh to help the moment along. 'So . . . what's the news?'

She takes me through a change of teachers, a girl she liked who has had to leave because her parents can no longer pay the fees.

I say I am sorry about her friend. Then, in my brightest tone, I start to talk about what we will do next Saturday afternoon when she comes out for the weekend.

'Mum—' Her voice takes an uncertain swoop. 'I'm not so sure . . .'

'About what, honey?'

A whisper. 'Coming home.'

I take my time. 'Oh. I see.'

'Mum, you know I want to see you more than anything, you know I'm longing to see you, but . . .' Her voice is so faint I can hardly hear it.

I wait. I don't want to rush her. 'But what, darling?' I ask at last.

'I just . . .' A pause. 'I've got so much work, and . . .' She sighs. She takes a moment to sort it out in her mind. 'I can't deal with it just at the moment.'

I stare unseeing at the pinboard in front of me. 'I understand.'

'I'd feel so low, Mum.'

'Yes, darling,' I say. 'In that case it'd be a bad idea.' Against all reason, tears prick the back of my eyes.

'You don't mind, Mummy?'

'No! Of course not! No!' I give another laugh to persuade her that this is true. 'But I can't bear not to see you
at all, darling.'

'Course not.'

'Shall we have tea then? Go to that ridiculous place
with the cream buns? Or Sunday lunch. With Molly perhaps. You know she'd love to see us. She keeps asking—'
Aware that I am burbling on, I halt abruptly.

'That'd be lovely, Mum.'

I send a smile into the phone, as if this could be transmitted in some way. 'Katie,' I venture, 'you will say, won't
you, if . . . even for a moment . . .'

'Yes, Mum. Promise.'

'I just need to know you're okay.'

'I'm okay.'

We are silent for a moment.

'Love you, Mum.'

'I love you too, darling.'

I tell her that I am going to leave the answering machine
on for the time being, and that to be sure of reaching me
she should use what used to be Harry's line, the one he
kept for business and political calls. I start to remind her
of the number, but she has it off by heart. As I ring off, I
tell her once again that I love her.

I'm going to be late. I throw a bottle of wine, plastic
glasses, napkins, fruit and – unthinkingly – ketchup into
a basket, and make my way past the boot room to the
side door. There is no trace of yesterday's sun; the heat
already belongs to another world. The clouds are low and
heavy, there is a strong wind bounding up from the river.
My blood must have grown thin in America because as I
set off down the track I feel chilled almost immediately. In
no mood to turn back, I press on, walking faster.

As the track flattens out by the ribbon of pasture, I see streaks of smoke, torn from the tree-tops by the wind. I picture the man and boy tending the fire, and am struck by a powerful sense of *déjà vu*. It is a trick of memory, I realise, a confusion with a time soon after we moved here, when Harry brought Josh down to the quay to cook sausages on an open fire. In the summers that followed they often talked of doing it again but, what with Harry's campaigning and increasingly hectic business activities, they never quite managed it. Josh had to make do with humble barbecues, organised – and, more often than not, overcooked – by me at the house.

The two figures are crouched on the far side of the clearing, by an ancient fallen tree. Even at this distance I realise that the camp-fire is an impressive affair, encircled by stones, with a spit of impaled fish supported by crutches of forked branches, like some diagram in a Scout manual.

Moreland looks round, as if he has been expecting me at this precise moment, and, rising, comes to meet me. In old jeans and a sweater he looks leaner than before, and a little shorter, though he must be five foot ten. At five-nine, I am perhaps more aware of people's height than most women. We shake hands. He offers a cheerful smile, an open gaze. I am reminded of his frank appraisal of me as I sat in the car yesterday, and my impression – rightly or wrongly – that I had passed muster.

'You found the note this morning,' he says easily, reaching out to take my basket.

'Oh yes.' We begin to walk towards the fire. 'I was most honoured. It was the longest communication I've ever had from Josh.'

Moreland's mouth creases down, he looks across at me. Seeing that I have long since guessed how the note came about, he gives a sudden laugh that illuminates his face. 'Well . . . any prompting was purely accidental.'

'It's really most kind of you to go to all this trouble.'

'No trouble.' He seems surprised that I should think it was. 'I've enjoyed it. Josh's quite a character. And it's good to get out on the river.'

'You fish a lot?'

'Now and then—'

Josh calls loudly for us to hurry, that the meal is cooked. He shows me to the best – indeed, the only – seat, a sturdy branch protruding from the massive trunk of the fallen tree. He presents me with a whole fish accompanied by two slices of raggedly carved bread, served on a child's plastic plate of violent purple. His own plate is an equally turbulent puce.

Catching my expression, Moreland says, 'A little bright, aren't they? But the cottage is rather limited for picnic gear. It was either these or a set of bone china with dragons and fire-eaters on it.'

Josh raises his head and laughs, a sound that takes me by surprise. 'Dragons and fire-eaters!' he exclaims and laughs again. Moreland grins back and I wonder if he has made up the dragons and fire-eaters for Josh's benefit.

'You're staying in the Dartingtons' place?' I ask Moreland, revealing my limited knowledge of him.

'For the moment. But they want it back in a month. Then I'll have to find somewhere else. And I'm afraid' – he directs a rueful face towards Josh – 'a new place is unlikely to come with boats.'

He has brought wine, I notice. It stands ready opened, the cork pushed back into the neck as a temporary stopper. And two wine glasses – proper glass, not plastic.

'You're here for long?' I ask.

'Most of the summer – well, I hope so. Apart from a few trips to Saudi. I'm working on a project for them.' He pours the wine and hands me a glass. 'Patrol boats. Being built in Ipswich.'

'You're a boatbuilder?'

'What?' He examines the thought for an instant and laughs softly. 'No. Oh, that I were! No, I'm . . . well . . .' He shrugs self-deprecatingly. 'Just a glorified overseer, really.'

Josh is hovering impatiently. '*Mummy.*' He pushes at my plate, anxious for me to sample the fruits of his labours.

I accept Moreland's offer to fillet my fish. He uses a long thin-bladed knife which must be exceptionally sharp because it scythes effortlessly through the flesh, leaving hardly anything on the bone. He slips the fillets onto my plate with a deft movement. Watching him, I get the impression he is expert in all such practical things.

We eat like three seasoned campers, sitting around the open fire. I am not too proud to use a fork. Josh, rejecting such refinements, kneels in front of his meal and stabs at it with a short knife, then, when he thinks no one is looking, resorts to his fingers. Moreland, sitting cross-legged, fillets his fish and, laying it on the bread, constructs a giant sandwich. As he bites into it he drops a wink at Josh.

We talk of fishing and expeditions. We discuss survival techniques, how you find food in unlikely places, how you collect water in the desert. Or rather, Moreland and Josh pass these ideas back and forth while I pick at my fish. Moreland has a way of talking to Josh – of asking questions, of deferring to him – that has Josh discharging thoughts and ideas at a rate I rarely see nowadays. Occasionally Moreland glances at me with the ghost of a smile, a blink of the eyes, as if to reassure me that I am not excluded.

Moreland has a strong face, with blunt features and close-cropped brown hair that would probably be wavy if it were left to grow. His eyes, dark and wide-set, give an impression of self-possession, of preoccupation, but his smile gives a rather different message, of kindness and accessibility. It is a confusing face, hard to read. I wonder, not for the first time, why he is here.

He and Josh start to talk about sailing. I try to communicate some interest, then give up. Harry may have developed an infatuation with the water but it never transferred itself to me, and I maintained a strictly supportive role, as cabin cleaner, buyer of provisions, and – very occasionally, if Harry promised not to take us beyond the mouth of the river – inept and uncertain crew.

I drift with the moment. The wine, light and crisp, stills my brain. The wind hardly reaches into this corner of the clearing. I am no longer cold, I feel oddly safe.

Josh, abandoning the rest of his fish, which is now inextricably mashed up with the bones, departs with a bucket to obtain washing-up water from the end of the quay.

Moreland pours me another glass. He tells me what a fine service it was yesterday. 'It must have been a strain, though.'

'It was rather hot,' I agree. 'And there were so many people.' I examine the fire for a moment. 'How did you meet Harry?' I ask.

He hesitates for the tiniest instant, but it is enough to make me feel I am about to get a modified version of the truth.

'We met in pitch darkness,' he says lightly. 'In a bog. We

102

gave each other a terrible fright. Neither of us realised the other was there.'

'This was in the Falklands?'

He nods.

I try to imagine Harry and Moreland in this Falkland bog, in fear of the enemy, but the picture refuses to form, if only because it doesn't mesh with the little I gleaned from Harry. All Harry told me was that one of his men was badly injured by a sniper, and getting him to the medics delayed his unit so much that they missed much of the fighting.

'You knew him well?' I ask.

'No. Not then, anyway. We met again a couple of years ago, of course, over the Saudi deal.' I smile ignorance and he explains, 'The yard here' – he points a hand in the general direction of Ipswich – 'was tendering for the patrol boat order against several places in Europe. They needed all the help they could get. Harry persuaded the government to get behind it, got things going on the diplomatic front.' He gives a slow nod of acknowledgement. 'And very effective he was too, so they say.'

This does not surprise me. Harry loved manœuvring people and situations towards a goal, enjoyed using his power as an MP. Most of all, of course, he loved being at the centre of things.

'And then,' Moreland continues in a voice that is oddly diffident, 'he did me a great favour once.'

I do not doubt this either. Harry was a firm believer in the bestowing and collecting of favours; it was the currency by which he operated. If I am at all surprised, it is that Moreland should have been the beneficiary of Harry's largesse. As an overseer of boatbuilding projects, I would not have thought Moreland particularly influential.

I do not ask what this favour might have been. In the way of favours traded between men, I imagine it is something that Moreland would rather not discuss.

'Harry never talked about the Falklands,' I say reminiscently. 'Nor about the Paras, either. I don't think—' I pause, examining the remark for disloyalty. 'I don't think he ever really enjoyed soldiering.'

Moreland opens his mouth to speak, then changes his mind. Finally he says with a shrug, 'Well, it's a fairly dubious way to earn a living, isn't it, even at the best of times.'

'Dubious?' An odd word.

'Oh, I don't mean dishonourable.' He chuckles drily. 'I mean that you join up because – in my case anyway – your father was in the Marines, and his father before him, and in your eighteen-year-old innocence you think it'd be a good idea to do a few years' service, have a few years of stretching yourself in very well-defined directions.'

'And then you go to war.'

'Yes, strange that. You get to think you'll never do any real fighting and then suddenly there you are. It's the real thing.' His eyes veer towards the fire. He says with a grunt of disdain, 'People being killed. Friends. Nobody really warns you how you're going to feel about that.' His face tautens. His eyes swing back to mine.

I glance quickly away. I stare at the ashes. I'm not sure I am in the right state of mind for this sort of discussion. When I glance back, it is to find Moreland watching me.

'I think Harry was rather like you,' I remark. 'I think he joined because of his father. I mean, if one's looking for reasons. Losing his father so young, there was a sort of inevitability. A psychiatrist would probably say so, anyway.'

Moreland nods pensively, though I have the feeling that his thoughts, whatever they may be, are directed less at Harry than at me.

Josh comes into view, staggering under the weight of a slopping bucket. Moreland, catching my flicker of amusement, follows my gaze and, jumping to his feet, hails him. 'Easier to take the plates to the bucket, Josh.' Collecting the plates, Moreland scoops the bones into the embers and, shooting a quick smile in my direction, goes to meet Josh, who, having lowered the bucket to the ground, is resting athlete-style, bent forward, hands braced on knees.

I am on a downward slide from the wine, sleepy, mildly befuddled, pleasantly detached. As Moreland demonstrates dish-washing techniques to Josh, I get off my wooden perch and stretch out on the grass, eyes closed. It would be easy to doze but if I do I know I'll have trouble sleeping tonight, and it is the nights I've come to dread.

After a time I hear feet approaching and the sound of someone dropping onto the ground not far away.

'I trust Josh is going to maintain this sudden enthusiasm for washing up,' I murmur.

'Ahhh.' Moreland draws the sound out into a small laugh. 'I've done my best to encourage him.'

'Funny how men are perfectly capable of these things when it suits them.' I soften my voice to show there is no rancour in this.

'Ha! Now there's a statement that a man answers at his peril!' But his voice is warm; he enjoys this sort of debate. 'But you're right. Of course you're right. Guilty as charged. *Most* men, anyway. Naturally I am a glowing exception. But in our general defence, I must say that we used to be encouraged – still are, really – by, dare I say it, women, who make us feel unwelcome and incompetent in the kitchen.'

'No man in my life has ever been made to feel unwelcome in the kitchen,' I say.

He laughs, but a little awkwardly, and I sense Harry's presence, a shadow that falls across the conversation.

Then, as if in reply to some question, Moreland says, 'But he'll be all right, Josh. He'll be fine, you know. He's got . . .' He hums as he searches for the word. '*Passion*. Real enthusiasm.'

I ponder this compliment. Passion is not something that I would immediately consider in relation to Josh – or many other children for that matter – but in a sense Moreland is right; it is a good and positive thing to possess. Unless it is powerful and dark, like Harry's.

Moreland continues in what I realise is a single chain of thought, 'But you . . .' He is unusually hesitant. '. . . Well, I imagine things are not going to be so easy for you.' He adds quickly, 'I mean, legally. Financially.'

I open my eyes a fraction. The clouds bulge darkly overhead. 'Well, no. I don't think these things ever are.'

'I had a friend once . . . Her father was lost at sea. The family had a terrible job sorting it out.' I turn my head. He is sitting with his arms resting on his knees, squinting sideways at me. I sense an element of preparation in this, that he has guided the conversation towards this point. He goes on, 'The first lawyers got it wrong and wasted two years. The family ended up having to sell their house. I just wondered . . .' The slight awkwardness again, which seems uncharacteristic of him. 'You're all right for advice, are you? I know you've got Leonard. But what about experts? Has he managed to find the right people for you?'

It occurs to me that I could take this as an intrusion, that Moreland is overstepping the marks of our new acquaintance, but for some reason his interest does not bother me, perhaps because it is purely practical – about the only sort of interest I can deal with – and clearly well-meant.

'I think so.'

He nods eagerly. 'And the money side? Who's . . .?'

'Harry's accountant, Gillespie. He's meant to be good, so they say. Well – *sharp*. Which probably amounts to the same thing.'

Moreland seems content with this; he nods anyway. I pull myself up into a sitting position and yawn and stretch my arms, though my drowsiness has quite gone.

'I was wondering . . .' Moreland begins with an abrupt, frowning smile. 'I hope you don't mind my asking . . . but I'd be interested to know . . . what the weather was like that day? The day Harry set out. Here in the river. Was it misty?'

It is strange how the unease can fade, almost without my realising it, only to rush back with an unpleasant little lurch. I wonder why he wants to know. The question must show in my face because Moreland says, 'It's just that someone said it was foggy, someone else said it was quite clear. I've sailed off this coast. I was curious. Academic interest. But look, it doesn't matter if . . .'

I shrug, 'I don't mind.' I nearly say: It helps to talk about it. I look across the clearing to where Josh labours over his dishes, to the track just the other side of him and, beyond, to the trees, which, tormented by the wind, writhe and shiver continuously. 'Early on it was quite like this, but even windier. Harry thought of cancelling the trip. He phoned the weather people. But they told him the wind was going to drop and by mid-morning it did. In fact by noon, when Harry brought *Minerva* into the quay, there was hardly any wind at all. He was relieved. He didn't feel too confident in a blow. Not singlehanded anyway. Then, as we were loading up, the rain started. A steady downpour. Then – yes, I suppose you couldn't see very far.' The memory is vivid, a vision of the boat disappearing into an indistinct wall of grey until I could see nothing but the brilliant orange of Harry's waterproofs, a small blob of colour suspended as if in space. 'When the rain eased it was misty. But I wouldn't have said it was foggy. It might have got foggy in the evening, of course – I don't know. I'd gone out by then. I was the other side of Wood-bridge. It certainly wasn't foggy there.'

Moreland absorbs this slowly. 'Harry didn't go straight off?'

I am miles away. 'What?' I say, coming back with an effort. 'Oh no. He went to the mooring to wait for the tide. It wasn't right for going south, not till later. He'd worked it out – he had all the tide-tables. He was aiming to leave at five or six – something like that. But he couldn't wait at the quay, you see. *Minerva* had a deep keel. There wasn't enough water for her except at high tide. He had to take her out to the mooring as soon as we'd finished loading. He was going to spend the afternoon doing jobs on the boat then potter down to the end of the river and wait the last half hour there.'

'You don't know when he left?'

'No. By the time I got back from dinner it was too dark to go and check. But he was seen going down river by someone at Waldringfield at about five. Then a coaster saw a yacht through the mist or fog or whatever it was, later that evening.'

'Ah.' He nods slowly. 'No one else saw him?'

'I don't think so.'

'And he was aiming for the Hamble River?'

'Yes. But not in one go. He was going to stop on the way. He wasn't sure where. He was going to wait until he got tired, and then put in somewhere. Ramsgate, Brighton. He wasn't sure. Originally he was going with a friend – Jack Crawley – but Jack couldn't make it.'

Moreland contemplates the ground for a moment. 'He couldn't find anyone else?'

'Oh, he *could* have, but . . .'

Moreland waits silently. Eventually he murmurs, 'He wanted to go singlehanded?'

I spread my palms in bafflement. 'It was a challenge, I suppose. Something he'd never done before – a long passage, I mean, on his own. I think it frightened him rigid. But then,' I comment almost to myself, 'that was part of the attraction. At least I think so.' How do I explain? How do I explain this person, my husband, who walled off enormous areas of himself, who did not himself know what drove him?

'He hadn't sailed much before?' The softness of Moreland's voice does not conceal its attentiveness.

'Hardly at all, no. He was brought up not far from here – just north of Woodbridge – but he never sailed as a child. It was the quay that got him going – I mean, the fact that it came with the house. He didn't like to waste it. And then he was offered a good deal on *Minerva* and that was that. He had to learn everything from scratch. He bought books, got one of the lads from the local yard to teach him the rudiments, went racing a bit. Then, when *Minerva* came back from the yard, after she'd been refitted, he used to take friends out with him, people who knew the river – it's quite dangerous out by the entrance, the sandbanks shift—'

Moreland nods to show that he knows about the hazards of the bar. 'You never went with him?'

'Me? Oh no. Well – now and then, when he promised to keep in the river. And once or twice further out, when it was very calm. But I didn't enjoy it, I'm afraid. The water terrifies me.' I laugh at myself. 'Pathetic, really.'

'Not at all.' He says this in a kindly abstract way, although, having been a Royal Marine, he must find my lack of spirit quite alien.

'He took Josh sometimes,' I say, 'but Josh got bored. *Minerva* went too fast to catch fish.'

Moreland grins briefly. I notice that his eyes are more hazel than brown, and that when he smiles they lose all their pensiveness and glint with vitality.

We fall into an easy silence. Josh is still at the bucket. He has elongated the sleeve of his sweatshirt to cover his hand and form a dish-cloth with which to rub the plates. Drying, I hope vaguely, rather than washing.

'They think he must have been run down in the night,' I say, feeling compelled to complete the story, as much for myself as for Moreland. 'A ship that never saw him, never realised what had happened.'

Moreland looks towards some distant horizon then back at me, his face creased with renewed seriousness. 'It happens,' he murmurs.

In the silence that follows I picture the scene as Moreland must be seeing it, the small yacht, the ship bearing down on it in the dark, the lone figure failing to keep a proper watch, asleep perhaps, slouched over in the cockpit; then, with no warning, the cataclysmic impact.

'One thing . . .' Moreland asks almost casually. 'Why did Harry decide to take the dory, do you know?'

I am surprised at how well informed he is. 'The dory . . .?'

110

'It just seemed . . . Well, it's not really the sort of boat one would normally take on a long passage,' he explains with care. 'Impossible to stow on deck – impossible even to lift out of the water – and large and heavy to tow behind. It would have slowed him down a lot, and in any sort of sea, well . . . it could have filled up, broken loose – all sorts of things. He didn't have an inflatable? Something he could stow on deck?'

Leonard must have told him, I realise. Or – yes, of course – the lads at the boatyard in Waldringfield, the regulars in the pub. All the details of *Minerva*'s disappearance would have been thoroughly chewed over, country style.

I take my time. 'We had an inflatable, yes. A Zodiac. But he left it behind. It's in the garage, I think.'

'I see.' He still looks puzzled. He is on the point of asking something else when I point towards Josh, jogging towards us with the clanking bucket dancing lightly from one hand. Arriving, he pulls the cutlery from the bucket, gives it a last-minute polish on the much abused sleeve-end and holds it up for Moreland's inspection.

I hadn't realised how late it was. Kneeling, I sit back on my heels. 'Well . . .' I say with finality. 'It's been very nice.'

Moreland takes his cue. 'Thank you for lending me Josh for the morning.' He offers a hand and pulls me to my feet.

I look to where Josh is packing the lurid plastic plates into a rucksack. 'He seems to have enjoyed himself.'

'Well, perhaps I could take him again, while I still have the use of a boat. If that's all right?'

Instinctively I pause to weigh the idea, as I weigh every decision and response nowadays. 'Yes, of course.'

Moreland closes his rucksack and picks up my basket. With Josh in the lead, we start across the clearing.

'Harry was planning to cruise the South Coast, was

he?' Moreland asks quietly, as if our conversation hadn't been interrupted.

I walk on for a moment. 'He was going to base the boat in the Hamble for the summer,' I say. 'Use it as a hopping off point for gastronomic weekends in France.' I remember Harry telling me this. He had paused in the doorway of the kitchen on his way to the study. I remember his obvious irritation at being forced into this lie. He knew that I was aware of his real reason for taking the boat to a place far from home yet convenient for London. We both knew he was going to use it for his sessions with Caroline Palmer. I chose not to say anything. I had decided long before never to say anything.

Now I faithfully recount Harry's version. I recount his lie. Like most lies I have to tell nowadays, I manage it with conviction.

Later, when Moreland has been gone for some time and Josh is playing with his Game Boy and there is no one else about, I wander into the garden, making a slow circle that takes me round the perimeter of the lawn, through the wind-buffeted rose garden, past the glass-houses and lines of vegetables, and out into the drive by the door set into the high wall. Coming to the outbuildings, I pass the double garage that houses Harry's Mercedes and my far from shiny estate car and stop at the small single garage that we use for storage. Going in by the side door, I flick on the light and look straight into the far corner. Next to the surplus furniture and sundry yacht gear and the four-horse outboard motor, I see the Zodiac inflatable, exactly where Maurice, our gardener, left it.

The Zodiac has been incompletely deflated and inexpertly folded. Maurice offered to pack it away for me, and in my weariness that day I was quick to accept. From the look of it he didn't find the job easy. The folds are too bulky for the tall green bag and the boat bulges out from the top like a sluggish sea creature emerging from a pod. The grey rubberised fabric still has a smear of what at a distance looks like a pale wash of paint but which on closer examination is in fact encrusted mud that has dried into a craze of fine cracks.

The mud dried the same way on my skin, I remember. There were patches of it all over my upper arms and shins when I woke, confused and stiff, from that first exhausted sleep. The mud had smeared the sheets as well, and was stuck to my clothes in thick grey scabs. I scrubbed myself under the shower, I pulled the sheets off the bed, I put on some clean clothes before I went in search of Maurice to ask for help in bringing the Zodiac up from the quay.

I can see how strange the choice of the dory must look to Moreland. The dory is a wide, flat-bottomed dinghy with a powerful outboard. I can understand how it must bother him that Harry didn't choose to take the inflatable. But then Moreland is well versed in these things and Harry wasn't.

I should have mentioned that, I should have made it clear that Harry often made mistakes. Like misreading charts and going aground. Like getting ropes around the propeller.

I should have mentioned it. If the opportunity arises, I will.

I close the door behind me, wishing that I wasn't beset by so many well-meaning people. Moreland probably thinks he is being helpful in some way, just as Charles and Anne and Leonard are driven by the firm conviction that they are acting in my best interests. That is the irony. And there is little I can do to stop them.

*

FIVE

'Forgive me, but in your letter you said you were having difficulty in getting hold of the concert accounts,' I say to Tim Schwartz. 'And now – unless I'm getting this wrong – you're saying that you've got them after all.'

Schwartz sits stiffly on the edge of a cane chair, his arms resting on his knees, his narrow head framed by a weeping fig which, in my long absence, has lost most of its leaves. He sucks in his cheeks slightly, he regards me with an unyielding stare. I get the feeling that my slow grasp of the situation is a trial to him.

'What the auditors have,' he says in his tight voice, 'are the ledgers, the entries, that sort of thing. What they're missing is the necessary information to . . .' He gives a small gesture of what might be irritation. '. . . well, *interpret* the accounts.'

I pick up his letter from the table beside me. It is dated some weeks ago. I have read it several times since Margaret unearthed it from the waiting mail first thing this morning.

Glancing through it again now, I find that Tim Schwartz is no more precise on paper than he is in person. *Information relating to the concert accounts . . .*

'This information,' I ask. 'Could you perhaps be a bit more definite? It would help to know what to look for.'

'Well—' He gives a tense shrug. 'Anything, really. Correspondence, invoices, contracts, agreements . . .'

'I see.' The sun breaks through the heavy cloud and bathes the conservatory in a sudden burst of light. We blink at each other, re-establishing contact.

'The problem, Mrs Richmond,' he says abruptly, 'is that everything has come to a complete standstill. All our work, all our planning. Not a single child is benefiting or is likely to benefit until . . .' He breaks off and draws in his lips. 'You see, as things stand, the auditors can't pass the accounts for the concert – for ROC, which was the company set up especially for the concert. And while there are no accounts, the money's locked into the system. The charity can't receive the profits, not a penny. And to say we're desperate for the money . . .' He splays a hand and rolls his eyes.

I nod slowly. I explain cautiously, 'Well, after what you told me on Friday, we did have another look. Margaret – my husband's secretary – went through everything again over the weekend. She didn't find very much, I'm afraid. She doesn't think so anyway. Just some correspondence. But she's made up a list of the senders' names and the subject matter of each letter, just in case.' I take Margaret's neatly typed sheet from the seat next to me and hand it to him.

The spark that glimmers in Schwartz's eyes soon fades as he skims the page. 'I don't think . . .' He scans it again and shakes his head. 'No.' He gives a weary sigh. 'Nothing.' He hands it back.

Maybe it is the speed with which he reaches this conclusion, maybe it is his palpable gloom, but I have the feeling that he knows exactly what he is looking for and has at this very moment despaired of finding it. I also have the feeling that he thinks Harry is in some way to blame for these papers having gone missing. This realisation lodges uncomfortably in my mind. Part of me would like to retreat, to leave Schwartz and his problem to other people, as I used to leave everything that was at all difficult to Harry and his staff. But I promised myself some weeks ago that I would not run from anything, however trivial, however troublesome.

'Mr Schwartz— Tim—' I signal my uncertainty with an awkward laugh. 'You know, when . . . when you lose someone . . . When something terrible happens to you and your family . . . Well, people are very kind. Astonishingly kind. In fact I've been overwhelmed. So many letters. Such wonderful messages. And I know – I appreciate – how very difficult it is for them. I mean, lifting the phone, finding the right things to say . . .' Tim Schwartz is listening with the wary attention of someone who fears gratuitous and embarrassing confidences. I press on, 'But sometimes in their efforts to spare you pain, friends – people – can be almost too kind. They try to keep things from you. They mean well, of course – *of course* – but it doesn't actually help. Quite the opposite. You just end up getting surprises you'd rather not have.'

I don't need to go on; he has understood me very well. 'I did give the details to your accountant,' he says virtuously.

Since my return Gillespie has been conspicuous by his silence, a lapse – very probably innocent – into which I now read some significance. This, and Schwartz's wariness, revive my determination to hear more, and I press him for the details.

He contemplates the floor crossly for a moment. He does not want to get embroiled in further explanations

116

and difficulties. But when he brings his flat gaze back to mine I can see that, tedious though it is for him, he has decided to humour me. 'A major invoice seems to have gone astray,' he says briskly, as if, having made his decision, he is now in a hurry to get the information off his chest. 'It was – well, in theory, it *should* have been sent in by a company called Mountbay. They received a large cheque, at any rate. Though what services they provided to the concert, we have no idea. Anyway, this invoice is missing. Also, some of the other invoices from this Mountbay company, the ones that we *do* have, are inadequate for auditing purposes. They don't say anything about what Mountbay did or supplied. The auditors have looked into it, but as far as they can tell the company doesn't operate in the audio or stage equipment line – no one's ever heard of it anyway. And it didn't handle any of the artists who appeared. The auditors can't find any contract, any agreement – *nothing* to tell them what the company was about.' He stops abruptly and looks darkly away.

'So . . .' I pick up my question carefully. I do not want to look any more ignorant than I need to. 'Mountbay was paid by you—'

'Not by us,' he corrects me. 'Not by the charity. By The Rumanian Orphans Concert Limited – ROC. We thought it was safer to make it a separate limited company.' Struck by the irony of this, he gives a bitter laugh.

'By ROC. But surely—' I cast around for ideas. 'The people at Mountbay, can't they help? There must be someone there who remembers what they supplied to the concert.'

Schwartz leans back in his seat. He explains distantly, 'It's an offshore company, based in Guernsey. With nominee shareholders. There are no staff.'

'Oh.' I don't quite understand how a company can have no staff. 'Aren't there owners, people who would know?'

'The whole point of having nominee shareholders, so I'm told, is that no one ever gets to find out who the owners are.' His tone contrives to suggest that I should interpret this in a sinister way.

A movement catches my eye. Maurice is trudging across the lawn, a heavy bag of fertiliser or peat or something similar in his arms. 'Is there much involved?' I ask. 'Much money?'

'You could say that!' declares Schwartz. 'Over three hundred thousand pounds.'

Always such massive quantities of money. I find it hard to relate to them. Harry's debts, the mortgage, Ainswick; nothing with less than a long series of noughts on the end.

Maurice stops in front of a flower bed and lowers the bag. He contemplates the bed for a moment then turns away and starts back across the lawn. How much does he get paid? I try to remember, and wonder how much longer I can afford to keep him.

Finally I face the question that I will have to ask Schwartz sooner or later. With a small ache of foreboding, I say, 'Why did you think the invoice might be here?'

'Because your husband was the only person who dealt with Mountbay, Mrs Richmond. Who knew anything about them. Well, let's put it this way – we can't find anyone else who did! And' – his eyes fasten on mine – 'it was your husband who signed the cheques that went out to Mountbay, and took them for countersignature.' His tone, his stare are loaded with some meaning he wants me to read.

My God, Harry, what is this?

I search for something to say. 'This person who countersigned, what about him?'

118

Schwartz's eyes register a bleak amusement. 'It was our oldest trustee, Sir John Elphon.' He explains drily, 'Sir John is not a great detail man.'

There is a silence, we sit for a moment contemplating our different and common problems, then Tim Schwartz gets abruptly to his feet.

Rising more slowly, I try not to look as though I am staring down at him, though he is considerably shorter than I am. 'We'll take another look,' I say. 'Just in case.'

He gestures pessimism at this thought then pauses, hovering on the point of some disclosure. Righteousness finally overcomes reticence, and he says, 'I have to say that if things aren't resolved, if Mountbay doesn't have a proper claim to all this money they received, then there's going to have to be an investigation.'

I frown, I say sorrowfully, 'I see.'

To make sure I am left in no doubt as to the outcome, he adds, 'And the auditors seem to think that your husband will be held responsible.'

'But my husband is dead, Mr Schwartz.'

'Yes.' He gives a tiny sigh of forbearance, as though he is labouring under difficult circumstances. 'But if the auditors are unable to pass the accounts – which seems likely – then they will have to say *why*. They will have to allocate responsibility.' He adds brusquely, 'I'm sorry.'

I take him to the door. He tucks his briefcase high under his arm and surveys the drive with a frown.

'When you say Harry was responsible,' I say, 'you mean that he should have taken more care?'

'Mrs Richmond . . .' he gasps, momentarily at a loss. 'Your husband knew exactly what he was doing! He removed that money. He knew all about Mountbay. He—' Pulling up short, Schwartz looks away and glares angrily at the trees.

119

Unease pulls at my stomach. 'You're saying . . . terrible things, Mr Schwartz.'

He makes a token gesture of regret.

'Surely . . . there must be some way to avoid anything—' I want to say *public*.

'Well, the auditors won't wait for ever,' Schwartz exclaims with a bark of indignation. 'And nor, I have to say, will *we*! We've been banking on that money. It's getting to the point where the next shipment is going to have to be postponed. Medical supplies for the kids. Meant to be leaving in two weeks. It's them who're going to suffer, Mrs Richmond. The *kids*.' His glare is fired by moral outrage.

'How long before the auditors . . .?'

Calming himself a little, he says, 'No more than a couple of weeks.'

As soon as he is gone I take refuge in the kitchen and make a strong coffee. I sit at the counter, my head in my hands. I concentrate on my breathing. I fight down an impulse towards alarm and self-pity. I take my time. If I have learnt nothing else, it is that to have any hope of gaining control of myself and events around me, I have to think problems through slowly, at my own pace.

Those heavy glances of Schwartz's, those insinuations that he meant me to read, I read them now, I reject them, I re-examine them. Schwartz thinks not only that Harry was involved with Mountbay, but that this involvement was dishonourable. He thinks that Harry transferred the money for some motives of his own. This idea scares me, yet I am not sure how much weight I should attach to it.

But what worries me even more is that, whatever led to this business, whether or not Harry was at all negligent, enormous damage will be done if it gets out. Any investigation, however small, will look very bad for Harry. At best it will imply incompetence and high-handedness, at the worst, dishonesty. And the taint of dishonesty, however unjustly earned, would undo everything that I have fought so hard to achieve for the children. The loss of their father is hard enough for them to bear, but at least tragedy is straightforward and honourable, even, in some people's eyes, romantic. Dishonesty, though, is impossible to live down.

And money that belonged to a charity! Money that was bound for of all people – orphans!

God, Harry.

The coffee charges my blood. I have wild ideas – to rally Harry's friends in some way; to approach the charity auditors and explain to them – what? The ideas collapse. I feel muddled and anxious again.

I can't help wondering: did Harry realise this was coming down on him? Was this the last terrible problem that drove him over the edge?

I remember the last weekend before he died. I remember finding him at three in the morning in the drawing-room, lying on a sofa in semi-darkness. The light from the hall illuminated the glass of whisky which he held loosely on his stomach. As I came in he opened his eyes. I think he had been waiting for me. He gave a sardonic smile which seemed to contain all the resentment that I seemed to engender in him at the time and, though I see it only now, to contain, also, glimmers of despair. And maybe, if I'm really going to torture myself, I can also see in that derisive expression a cry for help.

There was no hope of my reading this or any other message, of course; by that time I was too bound up in his betrayal, which still loomed grotesquely, still produced such bewilderment and deep feelings of failure in me that, even after all those months, I couldn't see beyond it. I couldn't see beyond Harry's unwillingness to confront the issue, beyond his refusal to explain himself to me and acknowledge the damage and pain he was causing us. We were two immovable objects, trapped in mutual bafflement and guilt, our communications reduced to a series of set pieces.

We started one then.

'Just checking?' His tone was mocking, his voice thick with drink or tiredness or both.

I stood there, feeling useless. Then, as so often before, I tried diversion. 'I thought maybe we'd all go out for lunch tomorrow.'

But he wasn't going to be deflected that easily. 'Where d'you think I'd be, mmm?' he asked in a tone that was altogether more dangerous.

I could not answer this.

Turning his head to see me better, he demanded, 'Well?'

I sank wearily onto a chair.

He blew dismissively through his lips and murmured, 'Christ. Such faith, such faith.'

'I couldn't sleep, that was all.'

'Must be difficult with one eye open.' He snorted with feeble amusement.

The remark struck home, just as he intended it to. I couldn't help watching him. I did it all the time. When he disappeared at odd times I felt such a gnawing anxiety that I couldn't concentrate on anything until I had established where he was and what he was doing. When he was in the house, I had to know precisely where. It had, I suppose, become an obsession.

'Lunch,' he murmured. 'That's allowed, is it?'

'Katie and Josh would love it.' I tried to keep a light note to my voice, something that would leave the conversational door open.

A long pause, and he murmured, 'Too much work.'

'Oh? What a pity.' I wanted to sound reasonable, or at least understanding. 'Well – tea, then? At home, I mean. I could make a cake.' God, I thought, to such depths of subterfuge am I driven.

Harry gave me a strange unfocused stare, as if he was looking beyond me to some half-formed future that excluded me. Eventually he turned away and closed his eyes.

I waited but he never replied.

I was struck then by the realisation that despite all my hopes, despite all my efforts to bring us together again as a family, we were not going to make it. Simply, Harry's determination to make us fail was greater than mine to succeed, and I wasn't sure I could hold out against him any more. Until then, the possibility of us falling apart as a family had been unthinkable, a last and remote resort. But in the long silence of that dreary night I finally faced the fact that it might happen. Faced it – and could not bear it. The thought made me ill. I was wrenched by a sense of loss and outrage.

I spoke his name. I got up and knelt on the floor at his side.

His eyes stayed closed. His lips tightened.

The ghosts of countless failed conversations hung over me. I struggled for something new to say. But it was no good. All I could find was: 'I just want to understand. I just want to . . . understand.' I heard the emotion wobbling ignobly in my voice. I knew I was doing everything wrong. By this time he resented me touching him, but that didn't stop me from reaching out and putting a hand on his arm. His tension was tangible, like an electric charge.

'Come to bed,' I said. My voice sounded thin and pathetic in my ears. 'Why don't you . . .?' How I had the courage to say this I'm not sure, not when my confidence in this department was at rock-bottom, not when we hadn't slept together for weeks, not when I had long agonised over the thought that it might have been some failure of mine that had first started all our troubles.

I suppose it was simply that this age-old move was the only one I had left. But even as I made my clumsy offering I was tense with dread and hopelessness.

Harry opened his eyes and stared at the ceiling. He didn't say anything, he let me wait – he made me wait. Then he turned his bleary gaze slowly on mine, and gave me a narrow look of such bitterness and disgust that I surged with humiliation. It seemed to me that he had done this with the simple aim of hurting me. My throat swelled, my pulse beat violently in my head, my stomach filled with violence. I had never known real rage before, but I felt it then, a hot tide of resentment and fury that shot me blindly forward. I thought of everything he was doing to hurt our family, of the selfishness, and the damage. I thought of Katie. I forgot he was in the grip of what was really a sickness, I forgot the terrible strains he was under. I felt so angry at what he had reduced me to, at this unbearable sense of powerlessness, that for the first time in my life I wanted to strike out. I wanted to hurt him back, as he had hurt me. I wanted, for a moment, to kill him.

The moment passed, I'm not sure how. Somehow I held on to my rage and struggled to my feet and got away. But something terrible had happened in that moment, some Rubicon had been crossed. Both of us had glimpsed the depths we were capable of descending to.

The ragged tapping of the typewriter ceases as I open the study door. Margaret twists in her chair. 'Well?'

'Well,' I say with a shrug, 'nothing, really. The file – your list – didn't interest him.'

I sit down at Harry's desk. Margaret has explained how the paperwork is sorted. Directly in front of me are the typed letters awaiting my signature; to the right the letters that I will have to answer by hand – no dent in this pile yet; also the paid bills and a number of unpaid invoices with queries; to the left, documents and forms, most of them with yellow stickers bearing memos in Margaret's neat script. There is also a list of answering-machine messages from the weekend – about fifteen – and another six or seven calls taken by Margaret this morning.

Looking at all this, I feel engulfed again.

I pull the nearest pile towards me and stare unseeing at the first letter. I am still thinking of Schwartz.

'Margaret, do we have Harry's address books? His diaries?'

'The desk diaries are at the office,' she says in her measured voice. 'But I've got an address book here. And this year's pocket diary.'

I lean back from Harry's desk and, opening the centre drawer, pull out the old pocket diaries and hand them to her. 'I wondered – could you look through them for me? See if you can find anything about a company called Mountbay. It's based in Guernsey, I think.'

'Oh, but . . .' She hesitates. 'I've already looked. Mr Gillespie asked me to.' She adds quickly, 'We didn't find anything.'

I stare out through the window at the vegetable garden, at the glass-houses which lean against the vine-covered perimeter wall and, rising high above them, the tall beech wood beyond. I notice that the glass-houses have been whitewashed against the sun.

I half turn back to Margaret. 'What about meetings?'

'I'm sorry?'

'Did Harry have any meetings with people who – I don't know – could have had anything to do with this Mountbay company?'

'I can look.' Her tone betrays her doubts. 'I'm not sure if I'll find anything. He was a bit vague sometimes.' Harry was rarely vague. I think this is her way of saying he could be secretive.

'Well,' I say ponderously, 'what about people who weren't with any particular company then? Any meeting you can't place. I just thought, maybe . . . '

'Yes. Yes, I understand.' She sounds marginally more optimistic.

I wonder how Harry entered his appointments with Caroline Palmer. Presumably he wouldn't have used her name openly. Just her initials, perhaps. Or a code name. I wonder how much Margaret knew about this. She is a perceptive woman, she has a way of identifying people's foibles, of gently mocking their vanities. It's hard to believe that she could have been totally unaware of Harry's activities.

'I'd be most grateful,' I say. 'Then at least we can say we tried.'

She would like me to explain this, she would like to know what we're trying for, but she checks herself and turns back to her work.

I read the first of the letters that Margaret has composed for me – to the Inland Revenue, informing them of my changed circumstances – and put my best signature at the bottom. I begin to fold the letter, but Margaret calls, 'I'll do that!'

There are letters to the Department of Social Security,

to banks, insurance companies, building societies. I sign the rest of these letters without reading them.

I skip over the personal letters, which I cannot face just at the moment, and alight uncertainly on a pile of official-looking forms. A transfer form from the bank. Some sort of release form from Leonard's firm. And renewal forms. Do I want to renew our family subscription to the local sailing club? Do I want to renew the service contract on the house security system? Or the one on Harry's personal computer? My instinct is to rid myself of everything that I have no use for. I have modest dreams that encompass no service contracts, no staff, just a small cottage, a functional car, and enough money to ensure the children's security.

A claim form from a marine insurance company, presumably for the yacht. The stick-on note from Margaret asks me to sign it on the last page where marked, saying that Leonard will fill in the details.

Then, a household insurance form. In the claim box various items have been typed in. Clothing, cash, camera. And: Cellphone handset.

Margaret misses nothing.

'Margaret . . .'

She twists round and sees the claim form in my hand. 'Yes?'

'The mobile phone. It's definitely gone, is it?'

'Well, I rather assumed so. Mr Richmond always took it with him on the yacht, I think, didn't he? Oh, and there was the bill,' she adds rapidly. 'It showed several calls that Friday evening.'

'Yes . . . Could I see it – the bill?'

'It's at the office. I could bring it in tomorrow.'

'Thanks. I'd just be . . .' I gesture uncertainty. '. . . interested to see.'

'Of course!' Margaret exclaims in a voice of deep understanding. 'Of course. I'll bring it in.'

Thanking her, I sign the claim and, putting it aside, go to the next form. At first I think I'm misreading it, but no, it's an application for a firearms certificate, issued by the Suffolk Constabulary, itemising two shotguns.

I am puzzled. Harry's licence was only renewed last autumn, some time in October. I remember the police coming round to inspect the guns and check the security arrangements. When they'd finished their work Harry sat them down with some coffee – his offer of whisky was politely refused – and told them how scandalously underfunded he believed the Force to be and how he had fought hard in Parliament to get things improved.

I am baffled as to why the licence should need renewing again so soon. I am also bemused to see that the form is made out in my name.

At the top Margaret has attached a note on a yellow sticker. *Police will need to make inspection. Have suggested 8th.*

'Margaret, I'm sorry to bother you again.'

The typing ceases. 'No problem.'

'This firearms thing – I don't understand. We've already got a licence.'

'Oh yes, but it's in Mr Richmond's name, and since I thought you'd probably want to get rid of the guns I took it on myself to arrange the transfer. I do hope that was all right? They should be worth quite a bit. Four thousand or so. Well, that's what I've been told. The police explained the transfer to me. They said this was the best way. A bureaucratic thing. Any dealer'll take them, so long as they have the licence and proof of identity.'

'I see.' I study the form again. The eighth is tomorrow. I can't face the police so soon. 'Can we put them off?'

'Of course. Easily. But no need for you to be bothered. I could show them all the arrangements, the locker and so on. I was intending to do it anyway. They'd probably only need you for a signature.'

I duck my head into my hands and give my face a savage rub. 'No . . . Thanks all the same. I'll do it.'

'Are you sure?'

I tell her I'm sure.

'When would you like them to come then?'

'Not tomorrow. I won't be here tomorrow. Some other time.'

'Next week?'

'No, I think—' I stare out at the sky. I have a brief desire to be in the open, walking over the heath with Katie as we used to in the old days. 'No, let's get it over with. This week.'

The phone rings. Margaret crosses swiftly behind me to answer it. Capping the mouthpiece, she announces Leonard.

I take the phone.

'A bit of *good* news,' Leonard declares. 'Some money's come in. I thought I'd let you know straight away. It should be in your account by the end of the week. Ten *thousand*. Better, as they say, than a kick in the head.' He makes a wheezing sound that is something like a chuckle.

'Come in?' I echo vaguely. 'Where from?'

'From? Oh . . . a business loan. Something Harry set up some years ago. It came due this week.'

With the firearms certificate still in front of me I am finding it hard to focus on this, far less to identify what is bothering me about the news. 'And it's coming to me?'

'Yes!' he says triumphantly.

129

'Who from?'

'A business associate of Harry's.'

I hesitate. I don't want to seem ungrateful, but at the same time I have to ask, 'This individual, Leonard, is it – would I know him?'

A pause. I can imagine Leonard's expression of forbearance. He is thinking: why does she have to be difficult? 'Ellen . . . The thing is – I can't actually *say*. It was a confidential arrangement. One of those things . . . Nothing *sinister*, I assure you.' He gives his wheeze-like chuckle again.

I bristle. 'It's from Jack, isn't it?'

'What? No. Why should it be from Jack?'

'If it's from Jack I can't take it.'

'Ellen, I assure you it's not from Jack.'

I do not believe him. The whole thing bears Jack's stamp – a cosy little arrangement between men, the assumption that I would accept this unlikely story without question, that I wouldn't notice the astonishingly convenient timing of this magic money. I can imagine the two men congratulating themselves on their harmless little subterfuge.

But they have caught me at a sensitive time.

'I can't accept it, Leonard. I'm sorry. Not unless I know who it's from.'

'*Ellen*. I assure you this is the *genuine* repayment of a *genuine* loan. I guarantee it.'

'I don't want it,' I repeat stubbornly.

I imagine Leonard blinking in puzzlement, sighing inaudibly beyond the mouthpiece.

'Leonard? Please understand . . .'

'Well, I'm trying to. But you're wrong, you know.'

I feel a flicker of doubt, but I can't very well concede now.

I change the subject. 'While you're on . . .'

'Yes?'

I tell him that Tim Schwartz came to see me today.

'Oh, did he? Oh. *Oh*. I'm sorry about that. I'm sorry he's *bothered* you. You should have told me.'

Aware that Margaret has stopped typing, I drop my voice a little. 'What's it about, Leonard?'

'Gillespie would be the best person to talk to about that, Ellen.'

'But is it serious? He made it sound serious.'

'*Serious?* I can't hear you. Did you say *serious*? In what way?'

'Well . . .' I cup my hand round the phone. I hate having to say this, even to Leonard. 'He seems to think they're going to blame Harry for the accounts not being right.'

Leonard makes calming noises. 'Oh, no, no. I don't think so. No. *Gillespie* doesn't think there's a problem. He seems quite happy.'

In the hall the doorbell sounds. I swing round. Margaret is already getting up to answer it.

'But, Leonard,' I say as the door closes behind her, 'it's not just the accounts themselves, it's some money that Harry was responsible for. It seems that it might be' – I choose the most neutral word I can find – 'unaccounted for.'

A short silence. 'That *can't* be right.' Leonard has put on his most paternalistic tone. 'I'm sure that's not right, Ellen.'

I knead my forehead ferociously. For some reason Leonard's simple faith causes me fresh darts of anxiety.

'Leonard, would you do something for me?'

'Well – if I can.'

'If it wouldn't be too much trouble, would you look into this company that Tim Schwartz seems worried about? It's

131

called Mountbay. And he said it was based in Guernsey.'

'*Guernsey* . . .' He pulls in his breath doubtfully. 'A different legal system, Ellen. I'm not sure . . . A bit outside my scope.'

I am easily defeated by such arguments. 'Oh,' I say weakly.

'And really, Gillespie would be better placed.'

Gillespie, it seems, is best placed to know most things. It is I who feel badly placed to ask him.

Before ringing off, Leonard makes me promise to reconsider the issue of the returned loan. I promise, and even as I do so I think he is right and that I must be mad to consider turning down this money. Pride is all very well, but only when you can afford it.

The doorbell will have been Molly, arriving for the lunch I have not even begun to prepare. I linger at the desk a while longer. Finally, without enthusiasm, I reach for a pad to scribble a note to Margaret, asking her to arrange a meeting with Gillespie in London tomorrow.

I find Molly in the hall, chattering to Margaret. She greets me with an exclamation of joy and gives me one of her all-enveloping hugs.

'I'm taking you out!' she declares.

I make only token resistance. One of the delights of knowing Molly is her enthusiasm for bursts of indulgence.

She talks exuberantly as she drives, one hand on the wheel, the other weaving explanatory patterns in the air. She gives me news from the Project, stories of two protégés who have managed against the odds to land jobs, tales of several past residents – and one present – who have reoffended. She recounts their misdemeanours with the feigned scorn and cheerful resignation of someone who has learnt to live with frequent disappointment. She mocks their efforts at crime and condemns their fecklessness at being caught, as if she could do a lot better herself, which, given the many tales she has heard, she probably could. 'Stupid boy! Went for a Mercedes at a house up a long drive with an insomniac owner! Got collared before he reached the motorway. I ask you! When there're dozens of Cortinas on the Chantery Estate just begging to be had, and half of them nicked anyway! Really – what can you do?' She throws back her head and laughs her explosive belly laugh, which frequently turns heads in public places.

Molly is quite a bit older than me, I forget by how much – sixteen years perhaps – but sometimes I think she is younger. She has never lost her enthusiasm for people or life. And this despite ten years of loving a man she cheerfully called 'the rat', who, when he finally left his wife to move in with her, got cancer and died. Two years ago, when going through what she called her mid-life apex, she took up with a twenty-three-year-old bricklayer. She treated him as if he was lucky to have her which, by any reasonable standards, he was. He adored her in a startled bovine sort of way but the affair faded last autumn. 'Lovely but wearing,' Molly declared. She pleaded a need for independence, but I think he simply bored her.

Molly makes no concessions to time or fashion. Her dark hair, now salted with grey, grows in a vast uncontrolled cloud like something from a Beardsley picture. She wears seventies radical – ethnic, flowing; or else her own version of eighties casual – jeans and hugging T-shirts with scanty patterned waistcoats. In the last few years her beam has broadened, her bosom burgeoned, but she carries her weight unrepentantly. With her olive skin, oval eyes and chinking jewellery, she has the look of a stage gypsy.

For our lunch she has chosen a new Thai restaurant in

Woodbridge. Austere in correct nineties style, it is a blur of white walls, grey floor-tiles and white table-cloths relieved only by a splattering of single red carnations at each table, like specks of blood. As we glance indecisively down the packed menu, Molly gets onto the heated subject of the second half-way house which she has been trying to set up for as long as I have known her. It was Molly who, meeting me for the first time at a mayoral inauguration dinner, cornered me and, during an exhilarating and bemusing ten minutes, talked me into heading the fund-raising committee. We managed to raise three-quarters of the money by last September. The trustees approved the purchase of two adjacent properties for conversion into a fifteen-bedroom centre, but now there appears to be a problem with the planning department.

'It's this great toad Meacher,' Molly announces with narrow eyes. 'The chairman of the planning committee. I know he's blocking it. His minions mumble about fire regulations and access and all that stuff, but it's just excuses. It's Meacher himself – he's on the take. *That's* the real problem!' She pauses to make sure I have hoisted this in, that I am not showing disbelief at what might seem like a rather wild claim. 'I reckon he's been nobbled by the not-in-my-backyard mafia, led by the local builder who – wouldn't you believe it? – lives round the corner from our building. A neighbourhood lad-made-good – you know the sort – gold cufflinks, a house tarted up to within an inch of its life, a Mitsubishi Shogun in the drive.' She blows out her lips with disdain. 'Anyway him and Meacher are as thick as two banknotes in a bookie's pocket. We haven't a hope, not without an *in*.' She raises a finger. 'Could have done with Harry batting for us.'

'I'm not sure he knew Meacher,' I say. 'He never mentioned the name.'

She raises an eyebrow. 'Well, Jack knows him all right.' When I don't respond, she continues, 'I mean, Jack got permission for this development out by the bypass, didn't he?' She holds up her hands as if to pre-empt me. 'Oh, I'm not saying Jack bought his way in. God forbid! What I'm saying is' – she narrows her eyes theatrically – 'clout carries a lot of weight!'

The waiter hovers for the order but Molly asks for more time.

'If Jack knows him,' I suggest tentatively, 'couldn't he put in a word?'

'You mean, I should ask him?' Molly drops her chin and shoots me a look that tells me I should know better. 'I think not,' she says forcefully. She and Jack have never got on. She has never been able to resist discomfiting him, something he finds hard to forgive in a woman, and, though he makes attempts to laugh off her well-honed verbal shots, his smiles are decidedly stiff-lipped.

I can see where this is leading. I sigh inwardly. 'Molly, I would ask him myself. But I can't. Not at the moment.'

She reaches across the table and grabs my hand. 'No, no, my love, I didn't mean you to! No! Would I throw you to that lion? No – that wasn't what I meant! No . . .' She swings back in her seat and waves airily, her eyes sparking. 'No, I'm doing my own nobbling! Taming my own councillor. Bribing him with long lingering evenings over coffee and biscuits in the Project kitchen.' She drops a slow wink. 'Putty in my hands.'

Laughing, I shake my head.

'Food!' She thrusts the menu under my nose.

Indecisive, I let the waiter choose for me. I would have been happy with a single glass of wine but Molly orders a bottle. 'My treat,' she says.

I did not get round to eating any breakfast and the wine

is sharp on my stomach. I sip cautiously. I catch Molly watching me.

'Friends should never give advice,' she states with something approaching solemnity, 'friends should only ever listen. So what am I going to do?' She makes a show of leaning her arms on the table in an overtly interfering manner that is designed to disarm me. 'I'm going to say that I think you look terrible, that you're ludicrously thin, and that you should go and see someone.'

'Molly.' I smile. 'And who should I go and see?'

'A therapist. Someone to help you through all this.'

'I saw a therapist in America.'

She absorbs this. 'Well, perhaps you should go and see another one here.'

'I'm all right, Molly.'

'I haven't finished yet,' she says firmly as if I have tried to stop her. '*Normally* I think that what they say about not making any major decisions for at least six months after something like this happens is absolutely right. But not for *you*, not in *this* situation. I think you should leave that house as soon as possible, like instantly. I think you should move away. *That's* what I think.'

'But I don't want to move away.' I tell her about my plans, how I want a cottage in the village, a job that will fit around the children's school hours, but how it will take time because of the legal difficulties.

'But why stay in the village? Claustrophobic.'

'Well . . . the children. They have their friends here.'

'But what about you?'

'I have my friends here too.'

She clicks her tongue. 'You worry too much about the children!' She frowns at me, she would like to pursue this further, but we are interrupted by the arrival of the food.

136

'How was your weekend?' she asks brightly.

'Saturday was good,' I answer with equal brightness, as if we are in the business of cheering each other up. 'Josh caught some fish. We had a barbecue. Yesterday . . .' I indicate it was a little more mixed, which indeed it was. I sat down to reply to some letters first thing, only to find that I couldn't bring myself to trip out the ritual platitudes – the solemn thanks, the brave but understated acceptance of Harry's loss, the plucky little end note about how well the children were coping. The words jammed in my craw, I simply couldn't put them down, and when Josh thundered down for breakfast I broke off with relief. After the long night perhaps I overdid my welcome – I scooped him up and bear-hugged him and blew noisy kisses into his neck – but he soon wriggled free. If this little rebuff hadn't been so blithely and innocently delivered I might have thought he was punishing me again. I planned to spend the whole morning with him; we did some painting and played a bit of ping-pong. But it wasn't long before he slipped away into the garden. When I tracked him down, he announced that he was watching a bird's nest and needed to be alone. I felt a small pang. Then, hardening my heart, I got on with my day. When all is said and done, I am good at hardening my heart.

I say to Molly, 'I miss Katie so much. It's awful.'

An odd look comes over Molly's face. 'Katie'll be all right, you know. If you'll let her.'

I cannot entirely hide the dart of resentment I feel at this remark. Katie is not a subject on which I take criticism easily, even from Molly. I manage an uneasy half smile. 'I don't think I've . . . *hindered* her in any way.'

'Of course not, love, of course not,' Molly says a little too quickly. 'I'm just saying that she needs space. She needs to breathe. She's fifteen. She's almost grown up.'

'Molly—' I shrug my incomprehension. 'Since when haven't I given her space?'

'Since . . . well – last Christmas.'

I put my fork down very slowly and stare at my plate for a moment. The wine has made me emotional. 'I don't think that's true, Molly.'

'It was when things got bad with Harry. I noticed straight away. You sort of took refuge in Katie. I mean, nothing wrong with that, love. *Nothing*. It was just that I think it was a little too much for her. She sort of took on a hunted look.' She gives a pained sigh. 'God, I'm saying this all wrong . . . Bugger it, my sweet – *sorry*.' She reaches for my hand again. 'What I mean is, I love you both and I just think that . . .' She screws up her face into an expression of remorse.

'That Katie needs her space,' I echo flatly.

'Well – yes.'

I give an ambiguous shrug, as if I might be conceding the point, and after a moment we move self-consciously on to other things.

Molly chides me for not eating. 'What are you trying to do, darling! Give yourself anorexia? Get deficient in all your minerals? *Then* you'll really get depressed!'

Still trying to lighten the mood, she moves on again, entertaining me with a story of a bald and rotund Project trustee who has got caught out in a mundane sexual indiscretion.

I respond, I laugh, I am as thankful as ever to have Molly as a friend. But her remarks about Katie linger, a grain of discord that rubs at our affection. There was a similar wariness between us last autumn when my problems with Harry became too painful for me to discuss with her. She didn't say so, but I knew she was offended by my unwillingness to confide in her.

She chatters as she drives me home, but she is subdued, preoccupied. Drawing up in front of the house, she turns off the engine and says in a rush, 'Listen, you're not blaming yourself about Harry, are you, sweetie? If so, you really mustn't, you know!'

I laugh awkwardly. 'No.'

She stares at me fiercely, then looks away to the trees. 'He wasn't the easiest of men. Christ, I wouldn't have lasted five minutes with him!' Her eyes dart back. 'Sometimes I thought you were an absolute saint.'

She has never said this before. I rather wish she wasn't saying it now. 'He took good care of me, Molly.'

She makes a doubtful face. 'Yes, well – in his own fashion, I suppose.'

'He did,' I insist, feeling oddly distressed. 'And he was never unkind, Molly. I mean, he never *meant* to be unkind. He was just . . . unhappy about himself sometimes.'

Molly takes a long breath. 'Yes.'

'And he loved me,' I state solemnly. 'He always loved me.'

'So much that he hit you?' she says with sudden heat.

I look at her in astonishment. 'What? Where on earth did you get that idea?'

She makes a face that is both apologetic and knowing.

'He never hit me,' I say with quiet vehemence. 'Never!'

She says a small 'Oh.' Then: 'Sorry, darling, I didn't mean to upset you.'

'But it's not true.'

'No, of course,' she says placatingly.

'Why did you think it was?' I say, hearing my voice rise, wishing I had not drunk all that wine.

'Well . . .' She puts on a show of reluctance. 'It was hard *not* to notice.'

'Notice what?'

She won't say.

'*What?*' I insist.

'The bruises,' she says at last.

'You mean – on my arms? The time I fell in the boat? I told you – I fell. On the side of the cockpit.'

She nods slowly, as if bowing to the rules of some game which require the maximum denial on both sides. Then, switching mood, she says breezily, 'Well, anyway!'

But I can't leave it alone. 'Molly, he never hit me,' I repeat doggedly. 'I fell.'

'Okay, darling. Okay.' But I sense a lingering doubt.

Frustrated, close to anger, I turn away, I grope for the door.

Molly cries, 'Oh, honey! I can't bear it!' She won't let me go. 'I do love you!' she says. 'I do so want everything to be all right for you!'

She throws an arm round my neck and pulls me into an awkward hug. She says she is sorry. She says that of course she believes me, that she had just got this stupid idea, that it was silly. The more she tries to persuade me the more certain I am that she doesn't believe me, and I feel inexpressibly weary.

She walks with me to the door. She gets me talking about the week ahead, about the people I have to see.

'The police?' she says, hearing about the gun licence. She is silent for a moment. 'Look, before I forget, just to let you know . . . They came to see me after you'd gone away.' There is a note of rehearsal in her offhand tone. 'They were just checking up. You know.'

'Oh?'

'It was just routine, darling, like in the movies. They asked about the night Harry left – disappeared. They were perfectly happy. I told them that you came at six, we had supper together and you left about eleven-thirty.'

'Eleven-thirty?' I echoed quietly. 'Why did you say that?'

'Because. Well, it seemed a normal sort of time to leave.'

I stare at her. 'You didn't have to say that.' I am still absorbing the fact that the police thought it necessary to check up on me.

'Well, I wasn't going to tell them things they didn't need to know, was I?' retorts Molly.

I look at the shimmering trees, I hear an indistinct sound rising from the river, a whistle, a call. 'You should have told them the truth,' I say. The truth was that Katie phoned at about eight-thirty, in a bit of a state, and I went to see her. 'It wouldn't have mattered.'

'None of their business,' declares Molly.

I stand in the open door for some time after she has gone. Did the police think I was trying to hide something? Is that why they checked up on me? Worrying thoughts leap into my mind – that they know Harry was bankrupt, that Tim Schwartz has told them about the missing charity money, that – my heart sinks – they think Harry committed suicide and I am covering up in some way.

It takes me a moment to remind myself that this visit of theirs happened many weeks ago and that they have not been back since.

I have an hour left before I need to collect Josh from school. Margaret is still hard at work. She has drafted several more letters to officials and government departments, letters that I wouldn't have known how to begin. They are beautifully written, with authority and clarity. As I glance over them I remind myself that I mustn't get too accustomed to being looked after in this way. Margaret, like Maurice, is a luxury I cannot really afford.

She reports that she has fixed a meeting with Gillespie for eleven tomorrow at his office in the City. Also, that she has searched Harry's pocket diaries and found nothing. There are one or two entries she wants to check more thoroughly with Jane Furlow, who was Harry's parliamentary secretary during his time as an MP, but she is pretty sure there are no names or meetings that cannot be accounted for. She looks me straight in the eye as she says this, and I wonder if perhaps she didn't know about Caroline Palmer after all.

She guides me through a few pages from last year's diary. Her own entries are clear, Harry's less so but still decipherable. I query a few. Barber, tailor, business associate: Margaret knows them all.

Some of the evenings when he was in London have single pencil lines drawn through them, sometimes two in a week.

'And these?'

'To be kept free.'

'You mean . . .?'

'For meetings Mr Richmond arranged personally. Informal meetings.'

So that was how he did it.

I glance up at Margaret, but she is leafing studiously through the pages again. Suddenly I feel certain she knew about Caroline Palmer. Guessed, at least. Maybe she closed her mind out of loyalty, an unwitting collaborator. Maybe she thought a man like Harry was bound to have affairs and that it was of no great importance.

'So . . . nothing about the concert?' I sigh.

She shakes her head. 'I checked, but I remembered most

of the meetings anyway. Nearly all of them were with the promotion company. The rest with artists' agents, PR companies – that sort of thing.' She regards me solemnly.

'Thank you, Margaret.' What else did I expect? Part of me is relieved at failing to unearth anything disturbing, part of me feels a twinge of unease because, whatever we find or do not find here, the Mountbay situation is not going to go away.

While Margaret resumes her typing, I take another desultory look through the diaries and the office address book. The address book has nothing that could be Caroline Palmer under either P or C. But then, he probably knew her number by heart.

Remembering the obsolete address book I found on Saturday, I pull it out of the drawer and riffle through to the back and look at the lists of account numbers again. I debate whether to bother Margaret with them. Finally I take them over to her.

'Credit cards,' she agrees. She studies the second list. 'And these, yes, bank accounts. This one' – she points to the first, marked P/A – 'is Mr Richmond's personal account at Barclays in Woodbridge.' Her finger travels down. 'This is your joint account. Well, let's just make sure.' She refers to a memo card in her Filofax. 'Yes, your joint account. And this – the D/A – is the deposit account at Woodbridge. And these two, they're the Ainswick number one and number two accounts.' She lingers over a shorter number at the end of the list, which has no prefix or abbreviation. 'I don't know this one,' she says. She stares at it intently as if her gaze might force it to yield some information, then goes on to the bottom of the page, where a number stands on its own, prefixed by the letters 'S & M'. 'Nor this one, although I think it might be a building society account. The S & M sounds like a building society, doesn't it? But I'm not sure. I have no record of it. Though . . .' She pulls in her chin with concentration. '. . . I did see a statement once – well, just the heading. It was from S and something. It could have been S & M. I just glimpsed it, a financial statement. Some time ago.' I think she is trying to tell me she wasn't actually prying.

She is about to say more when the phone rings.

It is Josh's school. Instantly disorientated, thinking that time must somehow have evaporated and that I am late in picking Josh up, I look at my watch. Three-thirty. Or has it stopped?

The headmistress's voice is crisp and matter-of-fact as she tells me they cannot find Josh.

Something lurches heavily against my chest, a knocking dread that belongs to my worst imaginings.

He was there at lunchtime, she continues in her unemotional way, and in the playground during playtime. One of the children saw him just before double art at one forty-five, taking his overall from his peg. He was not missed until the art teacher counted heads for a project.

And Josh loves art. I stare blankly into the garden.

She informs me that the staff are still searching and have not lost hope of finding him in the grounds. The gardener, who has been working near the gates all day, has not seen him pass through. She has called the police because it is school policy to do so, but her tone suggests that she thinks this step will prove excessive.

I say I am on my way. Ringing off, I gather a measure of control, I suppress my imaginings because I know this is the only way I will get through the next few minutes. I hear myself giving Margaret the bare facts in a calm voice. She follows me to the door. She offers to drive me, but I ask her if she'd be so kind as to stay by the phone. She hands me my car keys and opens the door.

A strange car is standing in the drive. A man in a grey suit is getting out. My first thought is that the police have got here very quickly, that they are going to tell me something awful about Josh. The scene freezes, I feel an instant disconnection. Then I see that the car is small and dirty and the man is on his own. He turns and, above the city clothes, I recognise Moreland.

A fleeting relief, a momentary impatience at myself, and I hurry towards my car. Moreland calls to me, a soft hail of surprise. Signalling impossibilities, I wave him towards Margaret. Driving off I glimpse him still watching me before he turns towards Margaret.

St Edmund's is fifteen minutes away, on the edge of Woodbridge. During the journey I try to put myself into Josh's head. I try to imagine what would make him walk out. He seemed to be looking forward to getting back to school. Or was he? There are never any certainties with Josh. Immediately I start blaming myself. Missing the signs. Again.

Turning into the gates I do not see any gardener, and for the first time I notice how insecure the grounds are: low fences at the perimeter with rows of narrow gardens beyond, and lines of semi-detached houses with miserly windows and frilly net curtains that bob up in the centre, like watching eyes. Inside the grounds, shrubberies, out-buildings, playing fields: not so many places for a small boy to hide.

The headmistress sees me coming and meets me at the front door. Mrs Rothsay, a young self-contained forty. She shakes her head to indicate a lack of news then ushers me into her room where I stand uneasily, like a child awaiting interview. The police are searching, Mrs Rothsay says. So are three of the staff. Everything possible is being done. In the meantime, may she ask me about Josh?

My instinct is to be gone, to be out searching, but when she invites me to sit I sink meekly onto a small wooden chair that inhabits the wide open spaces beyond her desk.

How was Josh's behaviour over the last few days? she asks. Did he appear disturbed?

'He seemed all right,' I answer humbly.

'No signs of stress?'

'No.' But I am beginning to doubt my own judgement. 'Well, I don't think so. Not that I could see.'

'Was he worried about school?'

I shake my head numbly, remembering that I never actually asked him.

Mrs Rothsay regards me with sympathy. 'Would he make his way straight home, do you think?'

This question defeats me. Under the power of Mrs Rothsay's gaze, I rise and go to the window. Cars are creeping sedately into the drive, rocking over the sleeping policemen, as parents arrive to collect their children. I have a sudden yearning for the days when I had nothing more to absorb me than the school run.

Where would Josh go? 'I don't know,' I say. In voicing this, I see beyond the house to the woods. I see Josh in the clearing by the quay, stoking the open fire, glancing to Moreland with an expression of earnest contentment on his face.

I turn back. 'May I use the phone?'

I phone home. Margaret tells me that there is no news, that Moreland has gone out in search of Josh. She is not sure where he has gone exactly; down to the river, she thinks. Anyway, he has left his car.

146

I offer Mrs Rothsay a stumbled explanation and leave. In the drive the buzz of conversation fades, the mothers, standing in clusters, stare at me with droop-eyed pity. Two friends, Ruth and Mary, descend on me with fussy concern and fierce avowals of help. Mary announces that she has already despatched her husband to join the search. Other parents, they tell me, are organising themselves into search parties. Ruth takes my arm and guides me to my car. It takes all my meagre powers of persuasion to convince her that I am safe to drive back on my own.

Slamming the door, gunning the ignition, I run the gauntlet of concerned faces and speed for home. A heavy lorry and a school bus slow my progress along the main road, but once onto the estate I racket down the length of the drive, the potholes sending booming ricochets against the suspension. More cars have appeared in front of the house – a white police car with an orange stripe, and, unbelievably, Anne's estate car – how did she know? But the car I am looking for, Moreland's, is still there, parked untidily in the middle of the sweep. The sight of the muddy Golf, once black, a long way from new, fills me with a wild unreasoned confidence. I carry on past the house and, unlatching the cattle gate, swing it open and drive down the track to the river.

A solitary crow stalks the quay and rises languorously at my approach. The river, grey and swollen with fast-running tide, ripples furtively. The air is still. There is no one in sight except two fishermen on the opposite bank sitting immobile behind their rods.

I stand in the open and bellow a loud hello. The trees throw back a bleak silence. I start along the footpath that runs the length of the river-bank in the direction of Woodbridge. My shoes, smooth-soled and narrow-heeled, slip on the muddy surface. I am driven by the certainty that Moreland guessed right, that Josh would head for the river and that this is the way he would have come – this way or over the fields, through the wheat. No – not over the top. No. It has always been the river for Josh.

I try to calculate how far Moreland would have got by now, at what point he would converge with Josh. It never occurs to me that he might have given up. I see him searching in a systematic and knowledgeable way, I see him using an almost mystical skill that he has gained from his service days.

I slip and almost fall. I move onto tussock grass in search of more grip but my soles slide just as uselessly. I stop for a moment, getting my breath back. There is nothing ahead. Nothing but the narrow path meandering along the top of the embankment, the long bend of the river with its wide plateaux of marsh and bog intersected by tiny dried-out waterways. And, at the edge of the marsh, clearly visible at this state of the tide, the patch of mud where I found the Zodiac.

Starting off again, I can't help looking for signs of that day, of my blundering progress through the glutinous mud, as if something of my struggle to reach the boat might still be visible after all these weeks. But though each step took me up to my knees and the sucking mud tipped me over at least twice and the marks I left must have looked like those of a floundering animal, there's nothing left now. The mud flat is as smooth as burnished rock.

I catch the muffled sound of a car coming down the track behind me. When the engine note floats clear of the woods, I take a backward glance. It looks like – it can only be – the black Golf. I stop, bewildered.

A figure climbs out – Moreland – and, with a sharp

148

wave, runs towards me. He runs easily, lightly, his shirt ballooning out behind him.

Suddenly I know that Josh is safe, I know by the way Moreland is running, I know even before his voice carries across to me 'Found!' Before he repeats it in case I have not heard.

I start towards him, slither again, shoot my arms out to keep my balance.

'He's fine, *fine*,' Moreland calls as he covers the last few yards.

We come to a halt in front of each other. 'No harm done,' Moreland pants.

I nod wordlessly.

Perhaps in my relief I look angry because he adds, 'There was no reason. He can't say why. I honestly don't think he realised.' He grips my shoulder and gives me a smile that seems to contain understanding of everything that I am feeling.

'Where did you—?' I ask.

'Up by the old ferry. He'd crossed the road at the round-about and was coming along the river.'

'But when—?'

'We'd just got home when you rushed past.'

I bow my head, I give a long sigh. 'Well, thank you,' I say simply. 'Thank you.'

We stand for a while, his grip firm on my arm.

I give a feeble laugh and look up at him. 'These things . . . they give you a shock.'

He nods slowly. 'Yes.'

'I didn't realise he was . . . I thought . . .' But I can't express it.

'I'm sure he'll be fine. He *is* fine. But maybe . . .' He shrugs to show it's just an idea. 'Coming back after so long, the service . . . perhaps it brought everything home to him. And then it must have been a bit of a shock, having to go back to school.'

'And he didn't say anything?'

'No.' I sense a slight hesitation in his answer, but if he was going to say more he thinks better of it and we start back along the path. My soles slither on the mud and he takes me by the hand, he holds me firmly so I can't fall, and I think what a luxury it is to have someone to lean on, even for so brief a time.

SIX

It's quite a time since I came to Shoreditch. Seven – no, eight months ago. It was October, a Wednesday. I remember it in some detail, though I would rather I didn't. Dense rain had brought an early darkness, the trains out of Liverpool Street had been halted after a bomb scare, and I needed somewhere to wait. The cab driver overshot the building and squealed to a halt three doors down. He offered to reverse back but it looked dangerous in the rain and traffic, and I told him not to bother. My umbrella, one of those tiny collapsable jobs, saved my head and shoulders, but not my legs or shoes which were quickly soaked by the bouncing spray. Reaching the door, I couldn't raise the security guard and had to let myself in through the side door with the keys. I had my own keys then.

Now, as the cab draws up, I step out into harsh sunlight with Harry's keys ready in my hand. Three years after refurbishment, the five-storey building still reflects a confident sheen, the tinted windows mirror-sharp, the cladding gleaming palely. But the pavement in front of the grand post-modern doorway is uneven and marked with those strange black streaks and blobs that afflict the less salubrious London streets, while the hotchpotch of neighbouring buildings, long abandoned by the boom which so nearly reached them, have sunk into apathy and shabby disrepair.

An agent's sign has been fixed over the doorway offering fifty thousand square feet of air-conditioned office space at ten pounds per square foot. A previous offer of twelve pounds has been ostentatiously cancelled out with a red cross. A poster affixed to the inside of the glass doors and illustrated with the profile of a fierce Alsatian announces the name of a security company.

When Harry bought the building it was renamed Richmond House and the letters etched into the stone lintel over the door. There was a naming ceremony. It was at this party that I got my first inkling of the gamble Harry was taking with this project when someone – a prospective tenant, I suppose – not realising who I was, remarked baldly that the building was a street too far. Too far from the City proper.

The side door has locks at ground and eye level. Going through Harry's keys I pick the right one first time. Inside, the air is heavy with stagnant London heat, overlaid by a faint chemical tang. There are no signs of security guards. I avoid the lift and take the stairs to the fourth floor. The flat, described in the sales brochure as a director's *pied-à-terre* or dining/overnight suite, was interior-decorated and furnished as a sales lure. But when the building was still unlet after several months, after Harry, having lost his seat, could no longer justify a separate flat near the Commons, he began to use it himself.

The door to the flat is made of panelled mahogany which has been varnished to an excessive and rather garish shine. Standing in front of it, facing my blurred and distorted reflection, I remember when I last stood here, bedraggled and cold, looking forward to getting inside and taking off my wet shoes and grabbing the early news before trying for another train. I was rather pleased at having got myself this far, at not letting the terrorists or whoever it was at Liverpool Street get the better of me.

Entering the carpeted hall now, I close the door softly behind me and listen to the silence.

By chance I also closed the door softly that other time, although I wasn't expecting to hear anything. Bending down to flip off my shoes, the sound took me by surprise. I stood very still, faintly puzzled, faintly alarmed. Awareness came slowly and unevenly, in disconnected darts. First the sound itself – a rustle, the brush of fabric, very muffled. Then the direction – from beyond the bedroom door which was slightly ajar and showing a sliver of dull light. My first reaction was to retreat hastily in embarrassment. I thought I must have blundered into a situation where the flat was being used by someone else – I still had a fragment of naivety then.

But I didn't retreat. I didn't even move. I listened, my senses reaching out across the hallway. There was rustling again, then a creak, and another creak. Irregular creaks but gaining a sort of rhythm. I knew that rhythm; everyone knows that rhythm.

A sharp ache pulled at my chest. I tried not to think of Harry, but once the idea lodged in my mind it wouldn't go away. I felt a foreboding, matched only by my need to see into the room, a compulsion which drove me slowly but doggedly across the hall.

The door was open only a little way and I had to push it further to see the bed. Strange how at moments like that you think of something, anything, which does not involve the reality of what is in front of you. I thought that I had never seen people making love from this angle before, feet

153

on. In fact I had never watched anyone making love from any angle whatsoever, though if you go to films nowadays it's easy to imagine that you have.

The bedcovers were off. The woman – she didn't have a name then – had her legs arched high over Harry's back. Her feet traced circles in the air as she rolled and swayed to Harry's rhythm. Harry's buttocks looked broad and white and oddly shapeless as they flexed and pumped. I tried to persuade myself that for all its familiarity this straining body might after all belong to someone else – such shimmers of hope – but even as I thought it Harry raised his head a little as if to look into the woman's face and I saw the distinctive shape of his head, the hair that curled down behind his ears, his quarter profile.

I didn't move for what must have been several seconds. Violent sensations rushed at me, vivid, immensely confusing. My throat seized with shame, I was crippled by the sort of withering humiliation that I had not felt since childhood. Strangely, or perhaps not so strangely, the one thing I did not feel was jealousy.

It was the ragged grunts of pleasure-pain from Harry and the series of harsher cries from the woman that brought me to life again. That, and a certain brutality in their actions which made me want to shrink away. As I backed silently into the hall and pulled the door softly to, a long raw sound followed me; I couldn't make out whose. Then a deep laugh: hers.

I stood just inside the hall, my limbs locked with tension and shame. I thought wretched tormenting thoughts, some self-punishing, most riddled with half-focused anger. I wondered how many other dark obsessions Harry had been harbouring, what else he thought about in those secret compulsive moments of his.

Or was this simply an escape valve for him? Was this his way of keeping some sort of control over his life?

I clung to this idea. I kept some sort of a hold on it as I crept over to my shoes and pulled them hastily on and, suddenly desperate to be gone, let myself quietly out.

The place is silent now, the only sound the subdued murmurs of the city from beyond the heavy glazing. I notice that a fine layer of dust sits over the reproduction Regency table and that the carpet is flecked with lint.

I push open the door of the bedroom. Whatever emotions I felt that day have long since faded. If I feel anything at all it's indifference. The hanging rails are empty, the drawers also. There is a used tissue in the bedside table, a few pennies, a grocery receipt. A half-empty box of tissues lies under the bed.

A perfunctory look around the bathroom, which contains a packet of disposable razors and a tube of shampoo that has lost its cap, and then into the main room which is furnished in candy stripes, co-ordinated florals and contrasting blinds, like a display window in a fabric shop. Only two drawers here, both empty. I look behind the colour-matched prints that hang at precise intervals around the walls, but there is no safe. Nor, as far as I can tell, is there one of those cunning devices set into the floor or power points. In the kitchen the fridge contains a carton of coagulated milk and a can of beer. Jars of instant coffee and Coffeemate, both almost empty, sit in the cupboard.

The place is like a hotel suite, bland and anonymous. I don't know why I thought I would find anything here. I had the idea that Harry used the place regularly, but perhaps he went to Caroline Palmer's. I used to phone sometimes, but if Harry was here he didn't answer.

Those phone calls – what an effort it took me to make

them. I would sit at Pennygate in the long evenings, trying to hold on to the idea that things weren't irretrievable, that all it needed was for Harry and me to talk. But sometimes the silence and the loneliness would get to me. Then, hating myself, wishing I could stop myself, I would reach for the phone.

There's nothing here. At least, no evidence of Caroline Palmer's presence, which is the important thing. No papers either, though I'm not too sure what I was hoping to find. An invoice, I suppose. A file of accounts.

But I feel better for having come. And safer.

I take a last look in some unlikely places – the top of the kitchen cabinets, the back of the cleaning cupboard. Mindful of my grandmother who kept her jewellery in the back of the oven during the Blitz, I peer into the microwave and fan oven.

Leaving, I close the door stealthily, as if by habit, with no more than a click.

Gillespie's office is a twenty-minute walk away in the City proper. If the recession has bitten deeply into the financial world you wouldn't know it from the polished buildings, the glossy fascias of the banks, and the purposeful manner of the sleek young people who criss-cross the streets.

I arrive fifteen minutes early. I am left to wait until eleven precisely, when a secretary with glowing blonde hair and a confident stride ushers me into a conference room with no windows, a ceiling of harsh lights and wallpaper that plays tricks on your eyes. The long table is set with a dozen or so blotters, overlaid with writing pads and shop-new pencils. After some thought I choose a place half-way along the table, facing the door. As I sit down Gillespie enters.

156

'Mrs Richmond.'

He offers a thin hand. Reaching for it, I spill my hand-bag to the floor. Wishing I hadn't chosen this moment to look quite so inept, I duck to retrieve the contents.

As I re-emerge the secretary appears with coffee, though I have not asked for any.

Gillespie has taken a seat opposite me and placed a slim file on the table in front of him. 'I'm sorry I wasn't able to come to the service,' he says. 'An unavoidable crisis.' He regards me with a flat gaze. He is a slim, sleek man in his thirties with a narrow head and sharp features, slicked-back mousy hair and very white skin. His eyes are expressionless and unusually pale, almost without colour. 'I trust you received my letter? Of condolence?'

I don't remember seeing it, but I nod anyway.

'Now, how can I help you?' he asks. He sits erect, his hands laced loosely together on the table. 'I'm afraid your financial restructuring proposal isn't quite complete yet. We're waiting for a few final negotiations. I hope to have something to show you next week.'

I'm not sure what to make of this easy confidence. 'There's not going to be a problem then?'

'Oh, I think we'll be able to arrange something.'

'Leonard gave me the impression there wasn't much left.'

His eyebrows lift a fraction. 'There were large debts, certainly, but in the long term there should be sufficient assets for you to settle reasonably comfortably. The life insurance and so on.'

I dare to ask, 'And in the short term?'

'It's a question of finding satisfactory collateral and negotiating the best terms.'

'You mean, I'll have to borrow?'

The heavy lids droop in confirmation. 'Though I understand from Jack Crawley that he's willing to help out?' Reading the hesitation in my face, he continues, 'It would ease things considerably. Finding sufficient guarantees for the bank is proving something of a problem.' When I don't respond, he explains, 'The estate doesn't have many assets to borrow against, you see.'

'I see,' I echo slowly, thinking of Jack.

Gillespie's eyes flicker down towards his watch. 'So. How can I help you?'

'Oh . . . I just had a few questions . . .' I made a list of them on the train, to be sure I didn't forget anything, which can happen to me quite easily when I'm on uncertain ground.

While I extricate the list from the confusion of my bag, I ask about Ainswick, about how it's going.

'Well, as I think you'll appreciate by now, things are tough.' He has a flat hard-edged voice. 'There's no interest in the Shoreditch building. None. Well, we had one offer, but it was a complete flyer.'

My incomprehension must show in my face because he explains, 'Someone trying to pick up a desperation bargain. A derisory offer.'

I take this in, but slowly. 'So people realise Ainswick's in difficulties?' I ask tentatively.

'Everyone's in trouble. Everyone's getting stupid offers. Making bad deals or holding off until the market improves. The problem with Ainswick is that it can't hold off.'

I nod, as if I had understood this all along. 'I'm just trying to get things clear,' I explain. 'This offer, what would happen if Ainswick accepted it?'

He looks down at his hands. 'It would be a waste of time. The cash raised wouldn't cover the company's liabilities, and without further realisable assets it would have to go into liquidation. More coffee?'

I have barely touched the first cup. 'Thank you, no.' I take a sip to make up for lost time. 'But – forgive me – isn't there a risk that Ainswick will be in trouble anyway? I mean, if the building stays unsold?' I speak slowly to reduce the chances of sounding foolish. 'Wouldn't some sort of sale be better than none?'

A flicker of what might be amusement crosses Gillespie's face. 'It doesn't quite work that way. The directors have a duty to sell at a fair market price. This isn't by any stretch of the imagination a fair market price.'

I ask more cautiously, 'And these people won't increase their price?'

'It was a take-it-or-leave-it offer. No, the best thing is to hold off as long as we can and *hope* for a genuine buyer.'

'The chances aren't good then?'

For a moment I think he has not heard, then I realise that the low-lidded, down-turned expression he has taken on, the spreading of the palm just above the table, are his answer. I interpret this to mean there is no chance, or so little as makes no difference.

I give a false laugh. It is an old habit of mine, to try to ease difficult moments along in this way. It comes from having a mother who used silence as a weapon of attrition. 'Pretty hopeless then?' I say, making a face.

He squeezes his lips together by way of reply. His lips are thin and dry. He seems to be losing interest.

I might have left it there, but something about Gillespie's laconic manner rekindles my determination not to be put off.

I study my list. 'Who are the directors of Ainswick now?' I ask.

He blinks slowly. 'Myself. And, more recently,

Raymond Kerr. He has experience in marketing difficult properties.'

I ask studiously, 'And the estate agents – they're doing everything they can, are they?' Like everyone else I have heard stories about the offhandedness and general incompetence of estate agents, though most of these tales probably stemmed from before the recession.

Gillespie tilts his head a little and frowns, as if this is tantamount to questioning his judgement. 'Most certainly. They're a top firm. Extremely capable.'

The next question is probably naive but I ask it anyway. 'And the price – it's realistic?'

'Absolutely.' His tone is torpid, his eyes severe. 'But you must understand that twenty per cent of office space nationwide – on the fringes of the City more like thirty per cent – is unlet. We're still deep in recession. It's a buyer's market.'

'I see.' I read out the next question word for word. 'How long can Ainswick survive if Shoreditch doesn't sell?'

He takes a long breath. 'I think we might be able to *squeeze* four months. Which is a great deal longer than we deserve.' I don't ask why we're undeserving of this extra time; I don't want to hear about all the things that Harry should or shouldn't have done.

There are more questions I should probably ask, but Gillespie flusters me and I can't seem to pin them down.

I move on. I explain about the account numbers I found in Harry's old address book, how Margaret can't place two of them. I pass him the sheet that Margaret typed out for me.

Gillespie gives the numbers a perfunctory glance before tucking the paper into the file in front of him. 'I'll check,' he says.

This is all too abrupt for me. I lean forward, I make a smiling gesture towards the file. 'But what about those initials – S & M. Aren't they something? We thought a building society perhaps.'

He turns an ear, as if he hasn't quite caught what I'm saying. 'A building society? No . . . I don't believe so.'

'A bank, then?'

'I'll see if I can find out.'

I stare at him, not sure whether I am being palmed off. 'But what about the other number?'

'I'm sorry?' He opens his hand and cranes his head in a practised display of incomprehension.

'I thought perhaps . . . you might recognise it?'

Languidly, he slips Margaret's paper from his file and takes another look. 'A number,' he says in the exaggerated tones of someone who is being forced to explain the obvious, 'could be almost anything. It could be a balance, a payment, a reference. One has no way of knowing . . .' He lifts his shoulders elegantly.

'But it could be an account number?'

'It could be. Of course.'

'You don't have a record of Harry's accounts?'

'An accountant only knows what his client chooses to tell him, Mrs Richmond,' he says piously. 'But may I suggest' – he gives a patronising little smile – 'that you don't live in any great hope of finding undiscovered accounts filled with money.'

I regard him for a moment, the narrow face, the pale eyes. 'I'm not expecting anything like that, Mr Gillespie.'

'Fine,' he says, still with a hint of condescension. 'Fine.'

Letting this pass, I stare at the next heading on my list. 'The Rumanian concert,' I begin with a small sigh. 'Tim Schwartz came to see me. He asked about this company,

161

Mountbay. It supplied something – he isn't sure what – to the concert. He said the invoices had gone astray—'

'Schwartz has been on to me about that,' Gillespie cuts in smoothly. 'I've already told him I can't help.'

'Margaret thought you might have some accounts.'

'I wasn't in charge of the accounts.'

'But there were some figures she sent you?'

'They weren't accounts.'

I wonder if he is being unhelpful, or whether he just appears that way. 'The papers you *do* have, they don't shed any light on the thing?'

'No.'

I look away. The wallpaper, the latest thing in geometric black lines on grey zigzags, strobes violently. Blinking, I come back to Gillespie's level gaze. 'Tim Schwartz seems to think . . .' I hesitate. Though Gillespie is meant to be on my side, though I'm meant to be able to confide in him, I cannot get rid of the feeling that his interests don't entirely coincide with mine. But who else am I going to ask? I plunge forward. 'He thinks that Harry can be held legally responsible in some way.'

'Nonsense.'

'Well . . . he seems to think that the auditors will pick Harry out, that it'll look bad, as if he'd done it intentionally—'

'Done what? Schwartz doesn't know what he's talking about,' Gillespie says with emphasis. 'His own people did the bookkeeping, for heaven's sake.'

'Oh.' I can't judge the significance of this. 'You mean . . . ?'

'If there was a problem, they should have spotted it.'

'So . . . Harry can't be held responsible?' I'd love to believe this is true.

He flips a hand dismissively, sparking with sudden annoyance. 'Listen, these charity people have made good money out of the concert, something over a million. They shouldn't be whingeing.'

I venture, 'But Schwartz says the auditors won't sign the books – or whatever it is they have to do. And the charity can't get hold of any of the money.'

'Not your problem.' He bites the words off crisply, with satisfaction; someone who enjoys combative situations.

I venture, 'Wouldn't it – don't you think it might be an idea to get a second opinion?'

'What? Legal advice, you mean?' He takes a breath, he leans forward, he slides his elbows onto the table, he fixes me with his gaze. 'Listen, Mrs Richmond, the charity is *not* going to make a fuss, believe me. Not at the end of the day. It's not in their interests to do so. They'll distance themselves from the concert, maybe. They'll disown whoever they want to disown. But not publicly. You see, they can't get away from the fact that they themselves were meant to be keeping the books. If something's gone wrong with the accounts it's the trustees as a whole who must be held responsible. They can't try to pin it on the first convenient scapegoat.' He gives a derisory grunt. 'They want that million too badly. A million, I might add, that they would never have got otherwise. Believe me, they'll get the auditors to sign some sort of modified accounts, they'll get it through their committee somehow. They'll take the million and be very glad of it, which indeed they should be. It really *isn't* in their interests to make a fuss.'

I feel as though something is creeping over my skin. Gillespie's cynicism perhaps.

'But as far as you're concerned, the important thing is to do nothing,' he says. 'Be polite, whatever. But ignore them. Do nothing. They'll go away eventually. Just say that you're very sorry but you can't help.'

I gaze at him for several seconds. I want to say: *You mean, do as you're doing?* But I don't say that; I don't say anything. Slowly I gather my things.

Gillespie gets to his feet. 'You see the point?' he asks.

I take a moment to answer. I say, 'Yes.'

He almost looks pleased with me. I don't think he expected me to be so quick on the uptake.

He takes me to the lift. We talk about the weather.

I think I am gone from his mind even before the doors close.

I catch the 12.48 with half a minute to spare. Closing my eyes for what I mean to be a short doze, I sleep heavily most of the way home. I wake when the train judders to a halt somewhere outside Ipswich, my head twisted uncomfortably against the window, my mouth hanging inelegantly open for what, judging by the dryness of my tongue, must have been some time. I feel exhausted and refreshed at the same time. I probably had three hours' sleep last night. It was ten before Anne and Charles finally left, and for a long time afterwards I lay on the bed next to Josh's, listening to his soft breathing, occasionally raising my head to catch the outline of his head, going over things endlessly in my mind.

My thoughts hardly need direction, such well-worn grooves do they follow. Episodes rerun themselves in minute detail. And when I feel more than usually baffled by the past I switch to the present. I assess how I am doing. I try to see how my actions might appear to others, how I can incur even less attention than I hope I do already. I measure situations, I gauge dangers.

Round and round. I am very good at going round and round.

Now, to add to everything else, I have Josh to worry about.

I pick up the car from the station and, though it's far too early, drive straight to St Edmund's and wait in a quiet corner of the car park in the vague hope of going unnoticed by the other parents. This, I should have realised, is too much to wish for. Ruth, who is also early, finds me immediately, followed by two or three other mothers, who treat me with a sympathy that is warm but also scrutinising. They say their own children have given them dreadful moments. They say they are immensely relieved that Josh came to no harm. I tell them I am too. I make light of it. I say Josh was finding school a bit of a shock after lying on a beach for so long. By the time Josh finally emerges ten minutes late, I am desperate to be gone.

He kisses my cheek in a half-hearted way. He seems tired. At any rate he is not in a mood to talk. Once I have unwound a bit, I start to chatter about what we might do at the weekend, about sport, about the films that are showing in Ipswich. I don't talk about yesterday. I don't feel it would be helpful to ask him why he ran away. The experience will have been quite traumatic enough, finding the police waiting at home, realising the alarm he had caused, having Anne besiege him with a battery of dire warnings and tearful pleadings never to frighten her like that again. Besides, I have never believed in harping on about the children's mistakes. Life is tough enough already.

I don't appreciate the depth of Josh's mood until we're into the drive and half-way down the long straight that leads into the shadows of the beech wood, just moments from home. Then I catch something in his profile that makes me look again and ask if there's something the matter.

He doesn't answer.

'What is it, honey? Tell me.'

His lower lip pushes out, a battle rages across his features, then he says in a thin voice, 'I'd like to go to another school. Please.' It comes out fully formed, as if he has been rehearsing it in his mind.

'Darling . . .' I look at him so hard and so long that I nearly drive into the rough. Swinging back, hitting a hole that makes the car lurch, I say with sudden heat, 'Are the other children saying things? Are they bullying you? Is that it?'

He shakes his head bleakly.

'Darling, you don't have to put up with it, you know. You really don't! These kids, they just don't know what they're saying . . .'

He shakes his head more vehemently and, clamping his mouth tight shut, bunching up his eyes, he turns away to stare out of the window. This makes me think I'm on the right track.

We are there at last. I come up to the house too fast and brake in a cascade of gravel. Turning off the engine, I make myself wait for a second or two before saying softly: 'Honey, you know how kids are. Stupid. They're probably just jealous of all the attention you're getting. In fact, I would say that was definitely what it was about. Wouldn't you? I mean, you having had all this time off. And then yesterday. And well – everything.'

Josh looks down at his lap, he picks at the hem of his shorts. He shakes his head with world weariness, as if he knew I was bound to misunderstand.

I wait while he winds himself up to speak.

'I want to go somewhere else. Away.'

'Away? What do you mean away?'

But I know what he means, and knowing it, I am already shrinking inside.

He can't seem to come out and say it, so I say it for him. 'You mean, board? Go to boarding school?'

He nods, avoiding my eye.

I give a short laugh. 'But darling, that's not going to solve anything. I'll go and see Mrs Rothsay. I'll—'

'*Mum.*' He glares at me, his face taut with exasperation and anxiety. 'There's nothing wrong with school!' he almost shouts. 'I want to go somewhere else, that's all.' He drops his head again.

I gaze at him, fighting down the hurt. It is a while before I say, 'But why, darling? You have to tell me why.'

He pulls at the long thread that has prised loose from his shorts. He hunts for the words, almost speaks, hesitates again, and finally says in a voice that has almost faded away, 'It'd be more fun, that's all.'

More fun. This takes me aback. Fun. It's not a word that has come into my vocabulary too often recently. It's not something I have considered in relation to Josh's future – or Katie's, for that matter. I've thought a great deal about the importance of being together, of supporting each other while we find our feet. But fun? I suppose he has a point. Neither Katie nor I have exactly been a barrel of laughs in the last two months.

'Well . . . okay. I mean . . . we'll talk about it, darling.'

He tips me a look that contains more than a little scepticism and I feel bound to add: 'I promise I'll – *we'll* think about it, okay? It's a big thing to decide just like that.' I make a terrible stab at humour. 'Not trying to get away from your old mum, are you?'

This is unfair, the sort of question that comes uncomfortably close to the kind of emotional blackmail

167

that I dreaded in my own mother. The moment it's out of my mouth I wish it unsaid. But before I can retreat, Josh gives a fierce shake of his head and, gathering his satchel, jumps out of the car and heads for the kitchen door.

I climb out wearily, wondering where I have gone wrong.

The gibbering of TV cartoons comes from the sitting-room. As I start to make Josh his favourite Marmite and cucumber sandwiches Margaret comes in, hunting for tea.

I tell her the meeting with Gillespie went reasonably well. I don't offer any detail.

She tells me that she might have had some success with tracking down the S & M in Harry's old address book. 'There's a company called Simmonds Mitchell,' she says. 'They used to have an "and" between their names, but now they're just plain Simmonds Mitchell. It may not be the *only* S & M around, of course – or rather SM – but it's the only one I can find in London that's even half likely, and I've searched the whole of the S section in the business directory.'

I pour some juice for Josh. 'Who are they?'

'Commodity brokers.'

'Oh,' I say as if I know what this means. But I'm talking to Margaret and I don't have to pretend. 'I've heard of commodity brokers,' I tell her, 'I've always been impressed by people who are commodity brokers, but I don't think I've ever had the slightest idea what they do.'

'I think they're like stockbrokers,' she laughs, 'except that they buy and sell commodities instead of shares. Wheat, sugar, corn, tea – that sort of thing.'

Balancing the sandwiches and juice in one hand, I take

them through to Josh. He is sitting on the floor just feet from the TV. Knowing I don't like him to sit so close, he slithers backwards, eyes still firmly on the screen, and taking his tea, mumbles his thanks. I linger for a moment, looking down at the spindly child-legs that extend from the bright shorts, more knee joints and angular bones than muscle, at his ski-jump nose, at his rounded cheeks filled hamster-like with food; I look, and confusions bunch uncomfortably in my chest. So familiar, this child of mine; and so mystifying. Why boarding school? Why this wish to escape? Have the two of us lost some vital thread? Does he feel I have failed him in some way?

I can't begin to grasp the beginnings of an answer.

'I think what happens is that people trade against the future prices of commodities,' Margaret says as I come back into the kitchen. 'Like they think sugar will go up so they buy some and sell it at a profit a few months later. Simmonds Mitchell act as brokers and take a commission.'

'So people would have accounts there?'

'I checked.' She holds up a hand hastily. 'Oh, I didn't say who I was. I wasn't specific. I just asked them if their account numbers ran to six or seven digits. They said six.'

'And that—'

'Tallies.'

We wander down the passage to the study.

'Would it work like a bank account?' I say this almost to myself, since I don't really expect Margaret to have an answer.

'Well, I know Mr Richmond used to leave the proceeds from share sales with his stockbrokers while he decided what to buy next. Perhaps it was the same with these people.'

Coming into the study, I remember Gillespie's narrow

white face and the way he glanced dismissively over the sheet of account numbers. 'And is it a big company?'

'I don't know, it was hard to gauge, but the entry in the directory is in large print, and its address is right in the middle of the City.'

Probably large then; probably important. Gillespie must have heard of it. I wonder why he couldn't take a guess at the initials.

'I've got the Cellphone bill for you.' Margaret lifts it momentarily off the desk. 'And there are quite a few messages.' Since I haven't called anyone back since the weekend, the new messages have only served to lengthen the list. My father. Neighbours wondering if Josh would like to come over. Distant relations on Harry's side. Molly. Leonard. Jack, who has called twice since Saturday, the last time only a couple of hours ago to say that he will come and see me tomorrow 'if it would be convenient'.

'I said it was unlikely,' Margaret declares. 'I could ring him if you like, and put him off.' Although Margaret enjoys a brisk relationship with Jack, liberally peppered with banter, she has no illusions about him and her patience with his perennial charm has worn thin.

'What did he want?'

'Didn't say.'

'When's he thinking of coming?'

'Ten. But I made a lot of unlikely noises because I fixed the police for eleven' – she points to the message on the pad – 'and I thought it wouldn't leave you enough time to get anything done.'

'The gun inspection?'

'I could still put them off.'

I say, 'No.' Then, feeling I have to explain: 'I'd rather get them out of the way.'

'Of course. And Mr Crawley?'

'I'd like to get him out of the way too.'

Margaret sniggers. 'Wouldn't we all.'

A movement in the garden catches my eye. It is Maurice, carrying a laden trug out of the glass-house.

Watching him tramping towards the rose garden, I murmur, 'That policeman who came round when Harry died . . .'

'Dawson.'

'Dawson. Has he been in touch? Did he come back?'

'No, not since . . .' She thinks for a moment. 'Oooh, since just after you'd gone to America.'

'After?'

'Just a few days. A week maybe.'

'Here?'

'Oh no. He came to the office.'

Maurice passes out of sight. I turn back to Margaret. 'What did he want?'

'Oh, nothing really. He just asked a few standard questions. Well, I imagine they were standard.'

I wait for her to tell me.

Her eyes flick away, she says in a determinedly offhand manner, 'He just wanted to know what had happened in the weeks before Mr Richmond died. If Mr Richmond had any particular worries – that sort of thing. I said that like everyone else in the recession he had a few problems, but nothing that he couldn't deal with.'

'No . . . that's absolutely right. Thank you, Margaret.'

She looks quietly relieved at having passed this test.

'Oh, and Richard Moreland was hoping to see you.' She slides a message slip across the desk. 'He wondered if you were free for a short time tomorrow evening. Something he was coming to ask you yesterday when Josh went missing.'

Moreland. I am grateful for what he did yesterday, very

grateful. But his attention worries me in some unidentifiable way.

'He didn't say what it was?'

'No. He just left his number.'

I take the slip of paper and place it on top of the message pad.

Margaret gathers her things. At the door she gives me a small self-conscious hug. She has never done this before. I don't know why she should choose this moment to feel sorry for me. I smile as best I can, to show her I'm all right.

I get Josh to bed early and read him a long story, which I animate with actorish voices and exaggerated actions. He is not fooled, of course. He can see that I am pulling out all the stops, that with these risible antics I am trying to re-establish my standing as a worthy and entertaining companion. When he thinks I'm not looking he steals the occasional glances at me, now and again his mouth twitches in the direction of a smile, but for the most part he stares idly into space, pulling his face into ever more varied contortions.

As we hug good-night I sense in the perfunctory clutch of his arms a tinge of reproach because I have not yet met my promise to bring up the subject of boarding school.

I go downstairs in a forlorn mood, feeling that in some unavoidable way I have lost the battle of the boarding school even before it has begun. If his mind is made up and I force him to stay home, he will only resent me for it.

I take a plate of bread and cheese to the study and sit dejectedly at the desk. I pull the Cellphone bill towards me. It covers the month of March and runs to three full pages. About a hundred calls in all, each itemised. I go immediately to the end of the list, to 26 March, the day that Harry died. He made several calls – six, I count – all of them after midday, all, therefore, from the boat. His last call was timed at 23.50, to the house. Earlier there was a call to Katie, or rather to the Oakwood House staff number, which is the only one parents can call in on. Going back through the other calls, I look for numbers I don't know, I look for numbers I know well. There is nothing I don't expect to find.

I fold the bill and place it in the centre drawer of the desk.

Moreland's number faces me from the message pad. As I dial I wonder briefly what he does in the evenings. Whether he goes to the pub, or out to dinner with people like the Dartingtons, or swaps sailing stories around the yacht club bar. I place him everywhere, and nowhere.

He answers straight away. 'How are you?'

'I'm all right.'

'And Josh?'

'I don't really know.' Which is the truth, though I hadn't meant to say it. 'He's got it into his head that he wants to go to boarding school.'

'Ah. Not a good idea?'

'I'm trying to keep an open mind. I'm trying to—' My throat seizes, I dry up.

Filling the silence, Moreland says, 'Perhaps he'll forget about it in a few days.'

'Perhaps.' But I say it without conviction.

It occurs to me that Moreland would be a good person to talk to Josh. His opinion, being male, neutral and greatly respected, is likely to carry more weight than mine. At the same time I'm wary of involving him more deeply in our affairs. It is partly my lingering confusion about his motives, partly an instinct to keep him at a manageable distance.

I compromise. 'You were sent away at eight, weren't

173

you? You should explain the minus side to him,' I say, tying him down to a limited role. 'Tell him how homesick he'll get, how the other boys'll bully him if he cries, how they'll force him into becoming a regular-issue public schoolboy, all male bonding and locked-in English emotions and suppressed anger—' I halt, aware of the harshness in my voice.

Moreland gives a soft laugh. 'I could warn him, of course. But these places are much better than they used to be, Ellen.'

Old emotions barrel down on me. 'They still produce people who're unhappy with their feelings,' I say with sudden heat, 'who bottle things up, who, after their parents have dumped them there, never really trust or relate to anyone ever again. Who learn to live on two levels, to hide things, to deny their real emotions—' I break off.

'We're not all as bad as that, I hope!'

'Maybe not. But it can never be right. Not at eight! They're just babies at eight.'

'Ah, now that's another argument altogether.'

'It certainly is!'

I'm glad when he lets it go and says after a short silence, 'I'll do what I can, Ellen.'

I exhale slowly. 'Margaret said you wanted to see me about something?'

'Would you mind? It won't take long. Shall I come over tomorrow evening?'

'No,' I say immediately, calculating that I can make a duty call to Diana on the way. 'No. I'll come to you.'

We fix on eight.

I answer three more letters of condolence. If I had qualms about what to say, they seem to have faded, and I pitch my reply in the sort of brave understatement and widowly fortitude that is expected of me. By the end of the third letter I have polished one or two phrases until they have something of a ring to them. The more poignant the words, the less they seem to relate to me or Harry, though writing 'We will miss him very much' still fills my throat with sadness.

I put my pen down and watch the darkness creep out from beneath the thick canopy of beech trees. I am beginning to miss my talks with Bob Block; I miss his robust guidance, his benign good sense, his refusal to register the slightest shock. I try to imagine what he would tell me now. To take one day at a time? To start to put the past behind me and get on with my life? But how, Bob? How can I take one day at a time when each day brings new and disturbing shifts? How can I get on with my life when the past blocks every turn?

It is eleven a.m. California time. Bob will be with a client and, even if he calls me back, he's unlikely to have more than a minute or so to spare. A letter would, anyway, be better. The writing will be cathartic; I might not even need to send it.

I've never learnt to use Harry's personal computer, and Margaret's electronic typewriter, which has come from the office, has complicated things like memories and deletion systems that I don't understand. In the end I fetch my comfortable old portable from its home on a high shelf in the utility room.

I set it up, dusty and battered, on the shiny surface of Harry's desk, and search for paper. The desk drawers contain nothing but a few sheets of Ainswick stationery, and some notepaper headed 'Harry Richmond' in grey 24-point Times Europa Bold. I designed the letterhead, my only direct contribution to Harry's business. The rest of the stationery is kept in one of the cupboards that support the long line of bookshelves. Inside, on the top shelf, are boxes of printed paper in various styles, with a sample of its contents fixed to the lid. Below are the headed cards and compliments slips. And on the bottom shelf the plain A4, three boxes of it, from which I draw five or six sheets.

I wind a sheet into the machine. I sit and look at the last streaks of colour in the sky, I think about turning on more lights, I consider what I will say to Bob Block. Then, following some instinct to leave no corner of Harry's world unexplored, I go back to the plain A4 and riffle through each box in turn. The sheets fan past my fingers, blank and innocent.

I move to the boxes of printed stationery and go through each one: the two-thirds A4 headed 'Pennygate', the full size A4 of the same, the cards, the compliments slips, the 'Harry Richmond' paper in two different sizes. The box whose lid announces 'Ainswick Properties Ltd' (in scarlet 30-point Medici Script) contains a collection of different paper sizes, envelopes and compliments slips culminating, at the bottom, in full A4. I lift the block of A4 and let it ripple past my thumb, *Ainswick . . . Ainswick . . .* in a flickering lantern show of red print.

The streak of black disturbs the flow of scarlet like a flaw in a jewel. Even as I go back and draw out the sheet, I know what I will see. Ever since Tim Schwartz's visit I have been glimpsing this in some recess of my imagination.

I sink back on my heels and read in black 36-point Century Old Style: *Mountbay (Guernsey) Ltd.*

SEVEN

'Simmonds Mitchell.' A female voice, professionally uplifting.

To my annoyance I stumble, I explain myself awkwardly.

'Do you want billing or broking?'

I hesitate. I say I'm not sure. 'I want the person who deals with individual accounts. In general. Someone who . . .'

'One moment.'

Clicks on the line, then a brisk male voice against the drone of what I take to be the broking floor. 'Alan Bicknall.'

'I wanted to ask about an account.'

'Who do you normally deal with?'

'I don't know.'

'You don't have an account with us?'

'Well, I have a number.'

'Which is?'

I give him the number from Harry's address book with the sinking feeling that I am about to be found out. But he doesn't round on me. After a pause, he merely informs me that the broker isn't at his desk at present. Can he take a message?

I leave my name and number, wondering whether the absent broker will work out who I am, whether he will return the call.

I sink back in my seat with a fleeting sense of achievement. At least I have made the call, and for me that is something.

Outside, the garden is suffused with a thin troubled light beneath a mackerel sky. A wind has sprung up, bending the poplars into a silvery blur. Earlier, just after dawn, I went for a walk in the woods. The mist was tangled around the branches like wreaths of smoke. The air was filled with bird-song and hushed animal sounds. The loveliness made me sad. I concentrated on my breathing – slowly from the diaphragm: one of Bob Block's six so-called 'Paths to Progress' – and tried to come to terms with some uncomfortable truths. This was more difficult than the breathing. There was the realisation that Molly believes that Harry beat me, and that whatever I say she is not going to change her mind. Then there is Josh, who, it would appear, no longer wants to live with me. And finally it seems that my husband was involved in some shady dealing, possibly to the extent of knowingly removing money from a charity. Knowingly. But fraudulently too? In law I rather suspect there is no difference. Harry was many things – and a few things that some people found hard to take – but I can't believe he would have done something quite so cold-hearted. And something which carried such a very high risk of being found out.

When he started in politics he was scrupulous about avoiding situations that might compromise him in any way. He always repaid his personal debts. Once he insisted on driving back five miles to sort out a matter of some mistaken change.

He would have been highly sensitive to any risks, he would have been extremely wary.

But we had money then; perhaps that was the difference. Perhaps he simply got desperate.

Finally – and looming ever larger as I circled the woodland – I knew I had to brace myself for the visit from the police, something which filled me with quiet dread.

My walk lasted for the best part of an hour. Returning at six-thirty, I finished the letter to Bob Block. I told him everything – from the beginning I always told him everything. I reported on Katie and Josh. I went through the Mountbay business, Katie's legacy, the debts, the legal delays. I also told him how at the strangest moments I missed Harry dreadfully. The completed letter ran to four double-sided pages.

Then I wrote two drafts of a letter that I wasn't at all sure about sending, and which I put on one side while I got Josh his breakfast and drove him to school.

I take the drafts out again now. Though still undecided about the wisdom of it, I thread a sheet of the house notepaper into the portable and begin a fair copy. I had thought of addressing it to 'The Director, Mountbay (Guernsey) Ltd', but now I leave the company name on its own. The address, taken from the letterhead, is a Guernsey post office box number.

Dear Sirs, I write to make enquiries following the death of my husband, Harry Richmond. I wish to know if my late husband was associated with your company, and if so in what capacity. I would also be very grateful for information concerning any dealings your company may have had with the concert in aid of The Rumanian Orphans Appeal that my husband helped organise eighteen months ago. After some thought, I add: I would be extremely

179

grateful for any information of any nature that you are able to give me.

I sign it (Mrs) E. Richmond. As I start on the envelope, I hear Margaret's footsteps in the passage and slide the Mountbay notepaper into a drawer.

'Good morning,' Margaret calls brightly, passing the desk and putting her bag on a chair. She does a double take on the portable. 'Wow! What a machine!'

I pull the unfinished envelope out of the roller. 'It was my mother's.' I scoop up the typed letter and drafts and, keeping their faces towards me, clip them together with the envelope.

Margaret glances at the bundle. 'Did you want something posted?'

I look blank for a moment. 'Oh no . . . I need to have another look at it. I . . . It's not right yet.' Without thinking I open the drawer containing the Mountbay paper and slip the bundle on top. The Mountbay paper is lying face up and in the instant before it is covered I am aware of Margaret's eyes flicking down towards the letterhead.

I close the drawer rather more forcefully than I mean to, and make a surprised face at the noise. I wonder at my instinct for concealment; I wonder at my belief in the need for it. This, after all, is Margaret, who is not going to broadcast anything detrimental about Harry.

Margaret clasps her hands together and says gaily, 'Well, how about breakfast? Toast? Juice?'

'Just coffee, please.'

She tilts her head with gentle disapproval. She thinks I am letting myself go. She may be right. If I am gaining weight it's very little. And though I have always been a neat person, I can't have spent more than five minutes on my appearance this morning. I pulled my hair back into a band, I threw on jeans and a loose T-shirt. I am wearing old trainers, and without makeup my eyes tend to fade away and my skin to look washed out.

But whatever comment Margaret is about to make, the phone cuts her short. She scoops it up before I have begun to reach for it. She asks who is calling and, raising her eyebrows at me in a mixture of surprise and enquiry, announces Mr Noakes of Simmonds Mitchell.

'Mrs Richmond? Brian Noakes here. What can I do for you?' It is a chirpy voice with a cockney accent.

I begin, 'It's about an account . . .'

'And your client number?'

I read it out, aware that Margaret is getting to her feet and leaving the room.

'Just getting it up on my screen,' says Brian Noakes. 'There . . . How can I help?'

'I was wondering . . . is it possible to tell me the balance in the account?'

His voice changes. 'We haven't dealt before, have we, Mrs Richmond? I would normally speak to—?'

'My husband.'

'He isn't available?'

'My husband died in March.'

A tactful pause, and he says, 'Yes, of course. I was sorry to hear about it, Mrs Richmond. My condolences.'

'I was wondering what the balance was. We're trying to trace everything, you see.'

'Ummm.' He is consulting something, or considering. 'I can tell you that all right, Mrs Richmond. It's nil.'

'Ah.' I hadn't expected much else.

'Sorry not to be able to help more.' He sounds polite but pressed.

'Can I ask – has there been much money in the account in the past?'

'Ummm.' I imagine him scrolling back through the file.

181

'No recent dealing, Mrs Richmond. In fact nothing for almost a year.'

'I see. And then?'

'A sale of fifteen thousand pounds. A buy of ten. Before that ... a buy of five thousand. Then ... nothing back another six months.'

I expect him to ring off, but he says, 'Your husband – I read about it. I'm truly sorry.'

'Thanks.'

'Anything more I can do, please don't hesitate to call again.'

He sounds nice. 'Thank you.'

Ringing off, I draw a line through Simmonds Mitchell on my list. Disconsolately, I pull out the address book and flick through to the last page. All the numbers are accounted for now bar the one without prefix or identification at the end of the list of bank account numbers. This is a six-digit number. All the bank account numbers were eight-digit. The only other six-digit number belonged to the Simmonds Mitchell account.

I should have thought of that. I should have mentioned it.

I put the idea to one side, then change my mind and redial Simmonds Mitchell.

'I'm so sorry to bother you again,' I say when I get through to Brian Noakes. I explain about the unclaimed number. 'I'm sure it's nothing to do with you, but I thought I'd just check.'

'Hang on a mo.' A pause. 'Yes, that's one of ours.'

He's startled me. 'I'm sorry?'

'I dealt with your husband on that account.'

Now I'm simply confused. 'I don't understand.'

'It was another account of ours – a company account.'

182

But I need it spelt out for me. 'And the person you dealt with was my husband?'

'That's right.'

'Can you . . .' I am groping. '. . . tell me which company?'

'I can't really say anything about that, Mrs Richmond. You see, while I can tell you about a personal account that's in the family, so to speak, company accounts are confidential.'

'Not even the name?'

He groans with suitable regret. 'No. Sorry.'

'*Nothing?*' Taking his silence as something less than a refusal, I plead gently, 'I do realise your position, but if there was anything at all . . . You see, everything was left in rather a mess. It's going to take months to sort out. It would help so much, Mr Noakes.'

He gives a deep sigh. 'Well, I don't suppose I'd be giving too much away by telling you that the balance in this account is also nil.'

'Was any money put through recently?'

'Now I really can't tell you that, Mrs Richmond, much as I would like to.'

'Just an idea?'

'Brokers have had the chop for less, Mrs Richmond.'

'I wouldn't pass it on to anyone, I promise.'

'They could have my guts for garters.' But he is softening. His voice takes a conspiratorial swoop. 'What can I say?' In the pause that follows I see him tapping at his keyboard. 'There was regular trading over – let me see – most of the last year.'

'When you say regular . . .?'

'Regular. Every week or so.'

'How much?'

'Mrs Richmond,' he sucks in his breath as if I were causing him pain. '*Please*.'

'Were they large amounts?'

'You could say so.'

'And what happened to the money?'

'Happened?' There is something in his tone, a briskness, that warns me of what is coming next. 'Had to call for the margins. Yes . . .'

'Meaning?'

'Losses . . .' I can see him scrolling back through the screen again. 'Yes,' he says firmly. 'No good news at all, I'm afraid.'

'Forgive me, I want to be clear – all the money was lost?'

'That's about the size of it, Mrs Richmond.'

It's a moment before I remember to thank him.

'It was a pleasure, Mrs Richmond.'

For some minutes I sit staring into the garden.

How much was it, I wonder? And where did it come from? Ainswick money or charity money? If it is all gone I suppose it doesn't make any difference.

Rousing myself at last, I see that Jack is due at any moment. Jack is not someone I can face without a strong coffee, not when I am going to have to swallow my pride and ask him for money, and I pad down the corridor in search of Margaret and the percolator.

I hear the voices before I reach the kitchen; they stop as I open the door. Margaret looks at me with an over-bright expression that is slightly contrite, Jack with an instantaneous smile.

'Ellen!' Jack advances, arms outstretched, face creased up with pleasure, and grasps me in a fluid embrace. This is his you're-so-special embrace, which I am not so foolish as to imagine is reserved exclusively for me. He smells

184

newly scrubbed; a blend of mouthwash and eau-de-Cologne. He pulls back, holding me by the shoulders, and shakes his head. 'I really don't know,' he tuts with fond exasperation. 'I really don't know.'

Letting this pass, I make for the coffee, which Margaret is pouring into oversized cups. A spray of hastily arranged red roses sits in a vase beside the percolator. It is typical of Jack to have brought the one flower that my garden produces in abundance, typical of him to have brought roses, and red ones at that, which must by any standards be inappropriate. I begin to wonder what he wants from me.

He drapes himself over the counter and eyes me with a proprietorial air. He is wearing an immaculate grey suit with an unusually sober shirt in plain white, and a business tie. His shiny dark hair, which he has long worn rakishly over the forehead, is now shorter and combed back. The politically correct Jack, attuned to his new image.

'We were saying how thin you were,' he announces boldly. This is a way of his, to disarm you with his frankness.

Margaret, picking up her cup, winces slightly and throws me a look of denial and apology.

Jack rearranges his long limbs onto a stool. 'I was thinking that I should take you to that new restaurant at Aldeburgh.' Pleased with this idea, he surveys the room, awaiting our approval.

The phone rings and Margaret hurries away to answer it.

Instinctively seeking distance from Jack, I cross the kitchen and sit at the breakfast table. Jack twists on his stool to face me. 'So . . . How's it going?' He drops his voice intimately. 'I mean, *really*?'

'I'm managing.'

The distance does not suit him. He slides from his seat and brings his cup to the table. 'Mmm,' he grunts, drawing out a chair. 'I'm not sure about that.' He sprawls in the chair, holding the cup against his chest, fixing me with a languid gaze. 'You don't have to do this on your own, you know, Ellen. Friends are there to be used. They enjoy helping.'

'People are being very kind,' I say evasively. I describe just how kind, telling him of all the things that Leonard is doing for me, of all the neighbours' offers of help.

He drains his cup, pushes it onto the table and glances towards his watch. Realising how this might be interpreted, he seeks to camouflage the gesture by continuing the movement into a smooth adjustment of his cuff. Catching my look, seeing he has been caught out, he gives a grin of complicity, a blast of sparkling charm, as if to say: Would I be in a hurry to leave you?

I suppress a small smile.

Jack leans across the table, his eyes lizard-like, and lays his hand over mine. Immediately I want to pull away. It's not the touching that disturbs me – I love being touched – it's the way Jack turns the most basic contact into an understanding.

'Am I so terrible?' he chuckles, not expecting an answer from this ancient gambit which he has been using for as long as I can remember. 'All I ever needed,' he declares, 'was a good woman.'

'You've been going through good women all your life, Jack.'

He is delighted at my response. 'But what did they do to me? They threw me out!' This, too, is an old refrain, a blatant untruth delivered with a well-practised blend of regret and satisfaction.

'How's the candidacy going?' I remove my hand to pick up my coffee.

'Ah.' Instantly serious, he twists in his seat and, hooking an arm over the back of the chair, says in an altogether crisper tone, 'Well the favourite appears to be this Mrs Emma Reeves. With four children, for heaven's sake!' He shakes his head, in amazement or disapproval or both. 'Anyway, she's got this incredibly *correct* track record. You know – years sacrificed to hopeless seats, years canvassing tirelessly through the most deprived inner cities, years making brilliant speeches at the party conference. And now – lo! She is seeking her reward. A winnable seat on a cushy patch. Needless to say, she's also *tipped for great things . . .*' He slides me a sardonic glance. 'They always are, aren't they? She's getting a lot of push from Central Office – unofficial of *course*. But' – he raises a long index finger – 'all this correctness isn't going to count for as much as she may think. Barrow says the committee don't really want a star, they want someone who's going to do a good job for the constituency. Well, I mean—!' He flips a hand over, as if the point is self-evident. 'She's not *local*, is she? Doesn't know one end of the patch from the other. When it comes down to it, there's nothing like knowing the ground. That *has* to be my strongest selling point.' He cuts the air with the edge of his hand – a politician's gesture – then looks up with a flash of humour. 'That, and my grasp of economic affairs, and European Community regulations, and farming subsidies, and opting-out proce-dures. It's like being back at school – three hours' home-work every night.'

'I'm sure you'll pass,' I say. 'I don't suppose you're the right person to ask, but how do you rate Charles's chances?'

'What? Oh . . .' He screws up his face into an expression of open doubt. 'I'm surprised he's got this far, frankly.' He shrugs, rapidly losing interest. 'But far be it for me . . .' He taps his long fingers rhythmically on the table, as if we are in a business meeting and must get back to the agenda. 'What I really need, you know, is a wife.' He laughs, though without visible humour. 'Candidates need wives.'

'I didn't think these things mattered nowadays.'

'Huh, you'd be amazed! The more the family unit becomes an endangered species, the more candidates must conform. The committee like to see the standard set-up. I'm non-standard. That bothers them.'

'Wouldn't it be rather a rush job, finding someone in time?'

'What?' He looks at me blankly for a moment before smiling. 'Ha, ha. Yes, *quite* . . . Which reminds me . . .' He slides his elbows onto the table and, balancing his chin on the thumbs of his clasped hands, fixes me with his most provocative smile, devilish, low-lidded, eyes laden with messages, some self-deprecating, most blatantly appealing. 'I was wondering if you'd come and hold my hand next week. Stand in, so to speak. It's an informal get-together with some of the committee. A sort of preliminary vetting. Next Monday.'

So this is it, I think. This is why you have come. 'Jack, I'm flattered to be asked. But really, I can't, it would be . . .' I trail off, remembering what I am going to ask him in a few short minutes, realising that he is unlikely to take kindly to it if I refuse him this favour. 'Let's go into the garden,' I say, to give myself time. 'Before it rains.'

He isn't overwhelmed by the idea, but follows me through the house into the conservatory where we find we are already too late and the rain is patting heavily onto the glass in slow drops.

We stand at the french windows. 'Can I let you know about Monday?' I say. 'Apart from anything else, I'd have to explain it to Charles and Anne. They'd think I was taking sides. It'd be more than my life was worth.'

He pushes out his handsome mouth. 'I can't see it would make much difference to Charles, quite honestly.'

This is untrue, he must know it's untrue, but I don't say so. Instead I gather my resources and say, 'Jack, you kindly mentioned the possibility of a loan the other day.'

He hardly blinks. 'Of course. I told you . . . I'd be only too glad . . .' He spreads his hands like a street vendor. 'Just tell me what you need.'

'It'd just be until various bits of money come through – the sale of the house, the life insurance, things like that. Though it could be longer. I can't promise – Leonard's a bit vague about the timing.'

'A bridging loan. Of course. How much?'

'That's the thing – I'm not sure yet.'

'But you must have some idea? What does Gillespie say? He must have told you how much is involved?'

'Roughly.'

'Well – shall I talk to him then?'

'No. No . . . I know how much.'

He looks at me expectantly.

I take a wild stab at a number, I leap headlong. 'A hundred and fifty thousand.' It emerges half as a request, half as a plea for mercy.

He pulls back. He gives a forced laugh as if responding to some poor joke, all the time searching my face. Seeing that I am serious, his smile falters, his eyes glint with conflicting emotions. 'Gillespie said it would be twenty at the most!'

So they have already discussed numbers, these two. How stupid of me not to realise.

Reading my confusion, Jack tips me an odd look. 'Unless this is about something else altogether?' He raises his eyebrows, he peers at me. 'Well, is it?'

Quick Jack. Jack who doesn't miss a trick. Jack who can't be fooled on matters of money. I realise that I've misjudged this conversation.

'Something that came up recently,' I admit, looking away.

The rain is beating more steadily, a growing tattoo which blurs the glass and gives our voices a strange resonance.

Jack ducks his head into my sightline. 'It's not this charity business, is it, Ellen?' My silence feeds his suspicions. 'They're not talking you into thinking you owe them something, are they? They're not leaning on you for money, for God's sake?'

It hadn't occurred to me that Jack would know this. I stare at him, wondering why I hadn't realised he would know. Gillespie – or maybe it's Leonard – seems to tell him everything else. I feel exposed and rather foolish.

'No,' I say rapidly, 'it's not that.'

'If they made mistakes, it's *their* business, Ellen,' says Jack, ignoring my remark. 'Nothing to do with you. *Not* your problem. You mustn't even *think* of talking to these people.'

I hear Gillespie's voice in this; I have no further doubts as to who told Jack. 'It's nothing to do with the charity,' I protest more strongly. 'The money's for me.'

He examines my face, he looks doubtful. I feel as though I have the word *liar* tattooed on my forehead.

'What do you want it for then?'

Impressed at my own talent for improvisation, I declare, 'I want to buy a house. I can't bear to stay at Pennygate a second longer than I have to. I'm miserable here. I feel I can't begin to have a life again until I get out.'

'A *house*? Why didn't you say so?' Jack's expression softens a little to compensate for the irritation in his voice.

'I felt you wouldn't understand. It seemed like such an extravagance.'

'I understand,' says Jack, making a visible effort to do so. 'Have you got somewhere in mind?'

'No, but I've got a good idea of what I want.'

'Why can't you rent? It would be more sensible to rent.'

I am so deep into this lie that I am forced deeper still. 'I want a permanent home. For the children's sake. I don't want them to feel unsettled.'

Jack frowns at this, then, labouring his puzzlement, wheels a hand slowly in the air by his head, as if to assist the workings of his brain. 'Well . . .' He stares at me in an unfocused way before turning to look tight-lipped into the garden, 'It's rather more than I . . .' Catching my eye once more, he says defensively, 'The recession . . . Things are a bit tight, even for me. And if Gillespie comes to me for this twenty thousand to cover your general expenses . . .'

Aware that I must shift this moment to my advantage, I suppress what is left of my pride and, using tactics that Jack himself would recognise, I touch his arm, I hold his gaze for much longer than I need to, I put into my expression messages that say: I will be in your debt, I will be suitably appreciative.

The light of calculation and reassessment crosses his face. He says stiffly, 'I can't promise.'

But in saying this, I know he can. Jack isn't short of cash, whatever he may say, but like Harry, like many people who have experienced life without money, it pains him to be parted from it.

As I show him to the door I make my own offering. 'That party. Perhaps if we all arrived together, me and Anne and Charles and you? But I left with you?'

He considers, he sees instantly that he will have the best of this arrangement. We exchange a glance of understanding that, for me at least, owes more to commerce than feeling. He nods slowly. Then in a gesture that shows he is leaving nothing of the old Jack behind, he reaches out to brush my cheek.

The police are late. I use the time to remake my list for the day, pushing some of the calls onto tomorrow so that the afternoon will be clear. I try to picture Dawson as I saw him on his second and last visit, the day before I left for America. I remember the inspector as a dapper man in his mid-forties, on the short side, with a broken nose, slow-moving eyes and the beginnings of a beer belly. He stayed for half an hour or so, sitting in a wing chair, solidly at ease, gazing down the garden towards the river. Like most policemen, he seemed in no particular hurry. We talked about the hazards of sailing the coast, although, like me, he knew almost nothing about tides, currents or small boats. Finally he came to what I took to be the point of his visit, and asked me whether *Minerva* was fully equipped with lifesaving gear. I told him I thought so but suggested he check with the boatyard, who would know exactly what was on board. We hardly talked about Harry.

The coffee has overheated my taut nerves. My mouth is dry, I feel sweat under my shirt, my pulse beats high in my head. I tidy the desk. I crumple the redundant list and drop it into the bin. The scored out 'Simmonds Mitchell' stares back at me from the rumpled paper.

The tension and the heat give me a sort of energy, a false courage. With Margaret busy on the other line, talking to a builder about the broken gutter, I lift the phone and call the City number, and get through to Brian Noakes.

'It's me again.'

'Well, hello, Mrs Richmond.' The jaunty voice betrays only the slightest wariness.

'I've just one question. I want to know . . . is it a Guernsey-based company?'

Out of the stillness behind me, muffled by the heavy study door, comes the soft chime of the front doorbell.

Brian Noakes emits a sound that is half complaint, half chuckle. 'Guernsey?'

Margaret finishes her call with a bang of the telephone and hurries out to answer the door.

'What can I say?' His voice takes on a theatrical ring. 'Let's put it this way, Mrs Richmond, I'm remaining silent . . .' He pauses for dramatic effect. 'And you can take that to mean what you like.'

But I want to hear. 'You mean . . .?'

'That I'm not saying no.'

I catch the murmur of voices in the hall. I picture Margaret on her way down the passage to summon me. 'Would it be called Mountbay?' I ask quickly.

A silence.

'You're not saying no.'

He is delighted with my progress. 'I'm not saying no, Mrs Richmond!'

'Thank you, Mr Noakes.'

'Don't mention it, Mrs Richmond.'

There are two policemen waiting in the hall, both uniformed, one of an age where he must have long since given up ideas of promotion. Sergeant Willis and Constable

Deakin. I make a point of memorising their names.

They have a practised stolidity, though once the formalities are over – the murmured offer of condolence, the apology for bothering me, the recounting of the firearms regulations that demand this inspection – the sergeant slips in a little joke about the bumpiness of the drive, as if to test the conversational temperature. I give a smile which encourages them to settle into a steady well-rehearsed banter – the places they have had to find in their time, the drives they have had to negotiate.

I lead them to the boot room which Harry, in thrall to some grand houses he had visited, tried to persuade us to call the gun room.

Leaving them in front of the gun locker I go to the kitchen to fetch the second key from its hidden place in the dresser. Handing it over to the sergeant with the key from the study, I offer coffee, tea, biscuits. One coffee, one tea; both with sugar.

I go back to the kitchen and put the kettle on. In my mind's eye I see the sergeant turning the keys and swinging open the door of the gun locker. I spoon instant coffee into a mug. I drop a tea-bag into a taller mug emblazoned with Harry's name, then follow it with a second bag; I have the idea that policemen, like repair men, prefer their tea dark and viscous.

The men take longer than I thought. The kettle has boiled and I am pouring water over the tea-bags when a soft rap comes at the door. I hold the kettle steady and lower it carefully onto the counter before turning.

The sergeant stands on the threshold. He asks if I can spare a moment. 'Of course.' I follow his deliberate steps into the boot room where Constable Deakin stands beside the gun locker. No banter now, no eye contact. We take up station in front of the open locker.

194

'The licence, as it stands, Mrs Richmond, is for two shotguns,' declares the sergeant. He holds up the certificate and reads from it. 'As stated here' – he taps the certificate – 'they should both be here in this cabinet. Is that your understanding, Mrs Richmond?'

I look at the open cabinet, at the shape of the long-barrelled gun in its green carrying bag and the empty slot next to it where the second gun should be and the empty carrying bag lying crumpled in the bottom of the cabinet. 'I'm sorry, I really don't know. My husband dealt with the guns. I never knew what the arrangements were . . .' I do not add that I disliked the things so much that I purposely ignored them, that I always thought Harry's cursory training dangerously inadequate for his careless handling of them.

'One gun appears to be missing. Could you tell me where it might be, Mrs Richmond?'

I shake my head in bafflement.

'You haven't seen it about?'

'No.'

'You didn't know that it wasn't in here?'

'I never look.' I add inconsequentially, 'I've been away.'

The sergeant purses up his mouth, a look of gravity. 'It couldn't have got left anywhere, could it by any chance?' he asks ponderously. 'Like in a car boot, for example?'

'I don't think so. I could ask someone to check.'

He doesn't respond, and we stand in silent contemplation of the cabinet with its empty bracket.

'There's been no break-in? While you were away perhaps?'

'No. Well, I don't think so. Someone would have told me.'

He inhales audibly. 'The keys, Mrs Richmond, where were they kept exactly?'

I take him to the kitchen, to the old dresser. Following my directions, he bends down and twists his hand up inside the cupboard to the hook.

'And the other one was kept in the study, in a drawer of the desk.'

'And who would know where the keys were?'

I have to think for a moment. I tell him Margaret, Maurice, Jill, although I'm not sure about Jill.

'And would there be a spare set of keys?'

'Not that I know of.'

He shakes his head. He straightens up. 'And when was the cabinet last opened, Mrs Richmond, do you know?'

'I suppose . . . when my husband last went shooting.'

'Would you remember when that was?'

'In the winter some time.' I take a stab at it. 'February?'

I hear Margaret in the passage. I call to her and explain. I ask her to go and look in Harry's Mercedes, and to see if she can find Maurice and ask him to search the garages, the store rooms and outhouses. The sergeant declines my offer to sit down and stands in the hall by the window, making notes on his pad. The constable wanders in and out of the boot room, looking at doors and windows as if for clues.

I remake the mugs of coffee and tea and take them into the men in the hall.

Margaret reports back, then Maurice. There is no gun. We stand in an uncertain tableau, while the sergeant holds a murmured conversation with Constable Deakin.

Finally the sergeant approaches me and says in a tone that is deliberately low, 'This will have to be reported, Mrs Richmond.'

Sighing, I nod slowly. 'I understand.'

When the policemen have gone, Margaret exclaims in a rare moment of irritation, 'Really! This is all we need!'

Dawson comes at five when I am alone in the house.

He is a little taller than I remember, his belly less prominent, his broken nose more obviously bent. With his calm manner, his double-breasted suit, his highly polished shoes, he might be an insurance salesman, come to renew the house policy. Except that salesmen travel alone, and Dawson has two young officers with him, both plain-clothed. Tall and stiff and watchful, they seem to crowd the hall.

The back-up team sit at either end of the long sofa, while Dawson chooses the same chair as before, by the window, and stares out through the drizzle to the barely visible river. 'What a view!' he says, shaking his head and softly beating his open palm against the chair arm. 'You could look at it all day, couldn't you?' He tuts with disbelief. 'Well, well.'

He turns with the sigh of someone who must attend to business and would prefer not to. 'You realise, Mrs Richmond,' he says, 'that there will have to be an investigation into this missing shotgun? Regulations are very tight nowadays. We have to consider theft, illegal usage, all manner of things. You appreciate?'

'Yes.'

He nods benevolently and with curious intimacy, as if this mutually tedious burden has forced us into some kind of alliance. 'Sergeant Willis told me you had no idea about where the weapon might be.'

'No. I'm sorry.'

'And there was no sign of burglary or theft, I gather?'

'No.'

197

'But the house has been empty at night while you were away?'

'The alarm would have gone off. My neighbours in the cottages would have heard.'

'And there was no break-in before you went away?'

'No.'

'No,' he echoes vaguely, looking abstracted. He stares away through the window again, narrowing his eyes against some imaginary glare. He says almost to himself, 'Do you think your husband might have taken it with him, Mrs Richmond?' He turns with an exaggerated expression of enquiry. 'On the yacht?'

There is a moment of stillness, a moment when I feel the heat pricking my cheeks. 'I don't know. He did take it once.'

'Oh.' Dawson absorbs this, suddenly far less abstracted. 'On the yacht? And when was that?'

'Last autumn. He thought he might have a go at some duck.'

'From the yacht?'

'Yes.'

Dawson's face creases into puzzlement. 'While he was sailing along?'

'Oh no, I don't think so. No, from the mooring. In the afternoon, after he'd been sailing, when he was packing up. It was quiet then. The duck would fly up from the marshes.'

'Ah! I *see*. Of *course*.' He taps his fingertips against his forehead. 'Of course. Shooting's not one of my sports, I'm afraid. I'm a golfer . . .' His mind has already moved on. 'He took the gun just the once, did he, on the yacht?'

'I'm not sure, I'm afraid. He may have taken it several times. But . . .' I shrug.

He smiles attentively, he makes a small gesture of encouragement. 'But—?'

'Well, he probably wouldn't have told me.' I add with a false laugh, 'He knew I wasn't too keen on him shooting, you see.'

'Ahhh.' Dawson gives a slow nod of understanding. 'On the day your husband set off for his trip south, Mrs Richmond – March 26th – you helped him load the boat, if I remember?'

'I helped unload the car,' I correct him. 'My husband loaded the boat. He knew where he wanted everything. I didn't know how to stow things.'

'You didn't notice a shotgun?'

'No, I . . .' I glance away. It is strange how the truth is just as hard to deliver as lies. I look back at him. 'I don't remember seeing it.'

'It's not the sort of thing you'd miss, is it?' Dawson muses, tapping his blunt fingers idly against the chair arm. He chews the inside of his lip and looks beyond me in an unfocused way, like a visitor suddenly inexpressibly bored. Coming to, he leans forward in his chair until his stomach presses hard against his shirt buttons, and says, 'We'll just inspect the gun locker, if we may, Mrs Richmond. And if you would be so kind as to give us the details of the people who had access to the keys. Then . . .' A pause as if he can't quite recollect what he should say next. 'Then I trust we won't have to trouble you any further for the time being.'

We stand up together. Dawson takes a last look out into the rain and shakes his head. 'Amazing, that view. Really amazing.'

I collect the keys to the gun locker and, turning on lights against the gloom, lead the men down the passage to the boot room. Dawson pauses in the entrance and asks with formal courtesy if I wouldn't mind going along with the sergeant and giving him those names and addresses. It occurs to me that this is an effective way of removing me. The sergeant and I return to the drawing-room, where he takes down with slow concentration the names and addresses of Margaret, Maurice and Jill. The task finished, we wait in the silence of two people with nothing to say to each other.

Dawson reappears and takes his leave with a slow dutiful smile, like a guest who has just enjoyed a leisurely tea. 'Thank you for your time, Mrs Richmond. I'm most grateful. Oh, and if you happen to think of anything – my number.' He produces a card from an inner pocket.

I remain at the hall window after their car has gone, staring at the ghostlike trees hovering in the mist, wondering how soon the news will get out. Loyal though Jill and Maurice are, I know with a small stab of resignation that it will be too much to expect them not to talk. And that the news, being touched with drama, is bound to get embroidered in the retelling. I can imagine the story making the rounds of the ornate bar in the Wellington Arms, of the school car-park and weekend drinks parties. People will choose the most colourful interpretation. They will say that Harry must have taken the gun with him on the boat, that he probably used it on himself, that he arranged for the boat to sink in order to conceal his suicide. Needing to appear in the know, they will talk of Harry having money worries, depression, and God-only-knows-what troubles.

This is the epitaph I dread for Harry.

I dread it for the children's sake, because whatever anyone says suicide is still a stigma, something they would have to live with for the rest of their lives. I dread it because these rumours have a way of travelling unbelievable distances and, if the life insurance company gets to hear about them, it may refuse the payout, and then the children's future would be destroyed in a single swoop.

After everything I have worked for.

I stand in the dark hall, fighting down a surge of frustration so violent that I contain it with difficulty.

When I'm calmer, I go to the phone and call Jill.

Josh is just about to have his meal, she reports. Ham and chips and peas and strawberries from the garden. And yes, he seems fine. Happy as Larry.

I ask if some men are arriving to see her.

Lord no, she says, taking time to look out of the window and check. Who would be stopping by to see her? She hasn't had a male visitor under sixty for weeks, not allowing for Alan her husband, who doesn't count. Her laugh fades as I tell her the police will be coming about a routine and rather trivial matter to do with the shotgun licence, how ages ago Harry left one of his guns somewhere, probably at a shooting lodge in Scotland, but that we can't track it down, and that until it turns up the police are duty bound to consider it stolen and will have to make standard 'inquiries'. I load the word with ridicule and weariness, as if I have already had enough of this tedious business.

Jill accepts this story without a murmur. 'All this form filling.' She sighs. 'It never stops, does it?'

Putting the phone down, I allow myself to believe that the absence of the gun might pass unnoticed after all.

I allow myself to hope, but not so much that I won't float the Scottish shooting lodge idea in Margaret and Maurice's direction when I see them tomorrow. And certainly not so much that I won't tell Katie about the missing gun straight away, before there's the slightest risk of her hearing about it from someone else.

Katie is breathless when she comes to the phone; Mrs Anderson caught her on her way to play tennis. I start by telling her about Josh's escapade. She greets this with a dismissive 'Silly boy!' in a camp Hollywood voice that makes me laugh.

'Do you want me to have a word with him?' she adds in yet another of her actory voices, mock stern and schoolmarmish.

'You sound great, darling.'

'Yeah, well,' she drawls. 'They've let me drop history. I mean, they *finally* realised. Like I've been telling them for ever! So . . . Shall I see my stupid brother on Sunday and knock some brains into him?'

'Would you? If you could . . .? We could go for a walk after lunch. I think – well, I know he won't talk to me.' I didn't intend to tell her the rest, but I do: 'He says he wants to go away and board.'

'Oh, *Mum*.'

'Well, maybe he's right,' I say offhandedly. 'Maybe he should go.'

'Oh, Mum,' she echoes more softly. 'But what about *you*?'

'Oh, I'd survive.' I shrug it off with an airy grunt. 'But listen—' I put a lightness into my voice as I tell her that the police came about the gun licence renewal and discovered one of the guns was missing, and that they are going to have to investigate it because they always do when it's guns, and, the neighbourhood being what it is, she may hear about it from someone else.

'Oh,' she says, her voice small and tight. 'Oh. The police, were they all right?'

'Oh yes. You know, it was just a routine thing.'

A pause.

'You're okay, Mummy?'

She calls me Mummy when she is worried about me.

'Me?' I laugh. 'I'm fine, darling.'

So fine that when she rings off, I clutch my head in my hands for a long moment.

The phone forces me back to life. It is Diana. She complains that she is plagued by knocking sounds in her hotwater system and that her stupid plumber is more than useless – a pretext, as are so many of her calls, to talk away her loneliness.

I tell what she wants to hear. 'I was coming over anyway.'

EIGHT

This is just the sort of place I'd like to live in one day. Moreland's rented cottage is typically Suffolk, snug and thick-walled with a low-ceilinged, black-beamed living room, a tiny dining-room, windows that look onto the ancient cottage garden (much in need of attention), a large open fire for the winter, and probably three bedrooms upstairs, the whole thing set among a scattering of cottages on the edge of a village which contains enough life and industry that it doesn't die a death every Monday after the weekenders have gone.

The only thing I wouldn't choose is the river. From where I sit outside the french windows, under a clematis-covered trellis, a stretch of water is visible over the tangle of the adjacent garden, between the creeper-covered corner of the next cottage and the tall side of the Maybush Inn at the river's edge. At this angle the water appears flat and lazy. Dinghies with butterfly-coloured sails dash back and forth, yachts raise their tall white mainsails and slip away towards the sea. Harmless, pretty. But if I listen too hard, I seem to catch the dim beat of wind-flogged canvas. I scent the tang of the salt. I remember, and in remembering I taste my fear again.

Moreland appears with a tray of food and more wine.

'It's rather basic, I'm afraid.' Not so basic: there is ripe Brie and brown bread and fruit.

'It looks fine.'

He puts the tray on the table and plops himself on the other chair. 'I've just been looking at the tides,' he says, raising the bottle in enquiry and refilling my glass, 'and Saturday would be best. It's high water just before eight. I could pick Josh up from the quay and we could kedge in a pool and try for mullet.' He pushes my glass towards me. 'If that's all right.' He gives a characteristic smile, warm but overlaid by seriousness.

The wine is dark and smooth. I take a long sip. From close by comes a burst of vibrant bird-song; a blackbird in the moss-covered branches of an apple tree. 'You will tell me what Josh says, won't you?' I say. 'Even if it isn't what I want to hear?'

I sense Moreland's curiosity, but all he says is, 'I'm sure it won't be anything like that.'

I'd like to agree, but I'm still smarting from one of Diana's more powerful verbal darts. After discussing plumbers and Charles's candidature and running through Diana's usual span of grievances – there is little that doesn't irritate her at some level – we touched on Josh, and I gave her a quick account of his unofficial afternoon off school. From her closed expression I realised she already knew, that Anne must have told her. Lurching forward in her seat, the vodka spilling over the edge of her glass, she fixed me with a narrow pointed look and announced, 'That boy's got out of hand. He needs to get away.' I didn't say anything; for a while I couldn't. Then, shrugging it off, I talked rapidly about other things. But Diana hadn't finished. As I made for the door, she wheezed after me and clutched my arm. Children need to be with other children, she insisted in her most dogmatic tones, not stuck in the wilds with their mother. Believe me, she said.

I drove away in voiceless indignation, wondering why Diana couldn't give me the width of understanding that I have always tried to give her, feeling, rather as Harry must have felt for much of his life, unfairly treated. Arriving at Moreland's, some of my resentment must have been locked into my face because he took a careful glance at me, put a glass of wine into my hand, sat me down in the garden and talked about inconsequential things. Perhaps it was the wine, perhaps it was the calm flow of Moreland's voice, but my anger soon gave way to something much more manageable, a blend of resignation and apathy.

Now, watching Moreland carve the bread, I say reminiscently, 'Strange, but Josh used to tell me everything. I took it for granted. I thought it would always be like that.'

Moreland pauses, his knife in mid-cut, and considers. 'Well, disturbing thoughts are always more difficult to express, aren't they? He's probably feeling lots of things he doesn't understand.'

'Yes,' I sigh, 'I see that. Of course. But he was all right in America, you see.' Abandoning this thought, I take another sip of the rich silky wine, aware that I'm drinking more than I'm used to and it's going straight to my head, but not caring too much.

Moreland puts bread and cheese onto a plate and, leaning across, places it in front of me. He taps the plate and gives the flicker of a smile. I am being ordered to eat. Obediently, I cut some cheese and press it onto the bread.

'I think he blames me for something,' I go on. 'That's the feeling I get anyway. Something I've done. I try to think what, but I just don't know. All I can imagine is that he's been feeling left out. Katie was in such a state after

206

Harry died that I did rather neglect him, I suppose. I don't mean *neglect*, I mean . . .' I stare unseeing into the garden while I grasp the thought. 'Well, I suppose I just assumed that he was all right.'

Moreland has made a sandwich of his cheese and is chewing thoughtfully. 'But children always test their mothers, don't they? It's part of growing away from them. Coming to terms with the fact that their mothers are going to have to be dispensable after all. Everyone gives their mother a hard time. I certainly did. When I wanted my own way. Which, at nine, was nearly all the time.'

I try to imagine Moreland giving his mother grief. 'I don't believe you.'

With a fleeting grin, he ducks the challenge and says, 'Didn't you go through stages? Doesn't everyone?'

'Yes. I was perfectly horrible.' Forced back into these memories, my smile fades. 'But then—' I hesitate, not because I'm reluctant to tell Moreland – I sense a sympathy in him – but because even after all this time my feelings are still extraordinarily confused. 'My mother could be very—' What word to use? 'Difficult,' I suggest finally. 'Not just with me, with my father too. She knew how to . . . twist things round. To build them up, to drag them out, to make us feel that, whatever had gone wrong, it was our fault. Sometimes it was hard to remember what our original crime was meant to be. When it got too much my father used to slip out of the house, usually to the golf club, and not come back till late. And I – well—' My throat swells, old anxieties and resentments block my words, and what I used to do at these times hangs in the air, unshaped, unspoken. 'She wasn't a happy person,' I say at last, frowning into my lap.

'You had no brothers or sisters?'

'No. A pity, really. It might have . . .' I shrug the thought away. 'Anyway, I escaped as soon as I could. Went to art college and got involved with the first interesting man I came across. Well, *unusual* might be a more accurate description. And that was that.'

'He was an art student too?'

'No, music. In his first year at the Royal Academy. But he used to play jazz piano in the student band I was with.'

'You were with . . .?' He gapes incredulously. 'Good God! What did you play?'

'Nothing. I sang.'

'Sang . . . jazz?' He shakes his head and laughs in open amazement.

'I loved it. Singing was . . .' Normally I wouldn't attempt to explain, but the wine has given me a new voice. 'It was the only time I didn't feel socially hopeless. I was rather shy then. To put it mildly. I did my best to fade into things – walls, floors, anything really. Singing did great things for my confidence.'

'I bet it did, I *bet*.' Moreland gives a series of faint nods, as if this at least confirms his picture of me. 'Well . . .' He keeps looking at me with mild astonishment, even admiration. 'And then? What happened then?'

'Then? Oh, Katie came along and I had to give up college. So did Johnnie – Katie's father. Well, he didn't *have* to give up. He chose to. He joined a group as their keyboard player. They were into seventies-style protest numbers. Anti-apartheid, anti-injustice, that sort of thing. The band was on the road most of the time. Katie and I went along too. But it was hard sort of life. No money, no security.' I twist the stem of my glass until the wine dances. 'And too many drugs.'

I leave this hanging in the air to tell its own story of Johnnie's slide into addiction.

We sit in thoughtful silence. The sinking sun dips below the last shreds of the rain cloud and paints the garden with shades of amber. The river, slinking away to the east, reflects only grey.

I turn brightly to Moreland. 'And you? What happened to you?'

A suddenly light in the eyes, a slow smile. 'You mean after I stopped being hard on my mother? Ah ... not a lot, I'm afraid. I didn't have the guts to rebel.' He makes a face of mock regret. 'I thought of getting angry about things but put all my energy into playing sport instead. Then I thought about doing things like going to university but in the end I took the easy way out and went into the Marines. I didn't mean to stay long, just four years or so. It was twelve in the end. But then I did rather take to it.'

'All that self-sufficiency?'

'Well, y-e-s,' he says as if it's rather difficult to explain, 'that's a *part* of it, certainly.' He takes a large bite of his sandwich.

I watch him, I wait. Finally I prompt, 'And the other part?'

He chews slowly, he studies me as if deciding on the type of answer I should have. 'Well, they're really quite different from any other outfit, the Royal Marines. They give you a chance to show what you can do, to operate as an individual, show your initiative within a strong framework – to a degree you don't find anywhere else, not even in the Paras.' Satisfied with this statement, he continues in a lighter tone, 'In my unit we were often working in small teams, just four of us, out on our own. You have to be able to live off your wits in those situations, be totally resourceful, take your own decisions. That was the main attraction. For me anyway. The mixture of routine and not knowing what the hell's coming next. Call it *Boy's Own* adventure if you like.'

209

He gives me a smiling glance that isn't entirely free of defensiveness. 'But while the Cold War was on, the work was important enough. It had a real purpose.' He reaches for his wine. The glass hovering at his lips, he adds, 'And there's also a tremendous sense of family in the Royal Marines.' He knocks back his wine. 'And that includes wives and children. A sense of mutual support.'

I look at him, I am very still. Moreland with a wife. The idea hits me with odd force, I see the inevitability of it, and wonder why I haven't realised it before. A man like this would hardly have reached forty or thereabouts without marrying. The thought disturbs me in some way I cannot immediately identify. A feeling of having been caught out, perhaps. A small resentment at not having guessed.

This does not stop me from being curious to know if I'm right. But by the time I frame the question, Moreland has started to talk about his father, and the moment has passed.

Clasping my wine, I ease my shoes off and curl my feet up into the chair against the evening chill, and watch Moreland's face as he tells me how his father stayed in the Marines for twenty years and started a small wine business in Berkshire on his retirement. He worked hard, held wine tastings and organised promotional weeks. The business was reasonably successful, he thought of expanding.

Moreland looks at me often as he talks, glances that are islands of reassurance in the sea of his story. I sense that he does not tell this story often, that for some reason I have been awarded the privilege of hearing it.

I notice his hands, which are long and expressive. He gestures often, small turnings of the wrist, a spread of the fingers. He smiles ruefully at some turn in his story, and suddenly there is something in his manner, a mixture of solemnity and kindliness, that is intensely attractive.

His gaze becomes preoccupied, he looks past me, he sighs. He tells me how his father's business took a sudden downturn, how his mother died soon after. He pauses. He pulls his mouth down into a grimace. 'Then, just to cap it all, my father was a name at Lloyd's. He was deep into a syndicate that was caught by two of the big disasters, the Alaskan oil spill *and* the 1984 Florida hurricane. He was hit very hard. In the end they called for virtually everything he had.'

'How awful. I'm so sorry.'

He lifts his shoulders. His hands fan out briefly. 'Well, that was the risk he took, I'm afraid.' He adds with a grunt, 'But it almost broke him. Emotionally as well as financially. Knocked the stuffing right out of him. He's never got over it. Never will, I don't think. Having to face retirement without a nest-egg, just when he thought he was all set up. Had to move into a flat and sell the house at a bad price. I did what I could of course, but . . .' After a moment of stillness he casts me a new look, one that is oddly uncertain. Sitting up, he puts his glass carefully to one side and slides his arms onto the table. 'But look – this is part of what I wanted to talk to you about. You see . . . it was Harry who helped us out.'

'Harry?' I make an incredulous sound.

'He let me have a loan. Enough to keep the wine business solvent until it could be sold. That money saved the day, really. Made all the difference between what you might call total disaster and manageable disaster. With the business sold, my father was at least left with something. Not a lot, but enough to keep him going. So you see . . . I owe Harry a great debt.'

I frown, I look away, I feel a mixture of pride and resentment. Harry. Still springing surprises on me at this distance, still living up to all his old contradictions. At

211

least this surprise, if I understand it correctly, is something to be proud of.

Dusk is creeping under the trees. A sharp wind springs intermittently around the garden. I pull my sweater close round my shoulders. 'I'm glad he could help.'

'I'd like you to know,' Moreland says, 'that he offered it quite spontaneously, and without security, and that he never put a time limit on it.'

'Well . . . *good*!' I nod and keep nodding long after I have finished speaking.

'In the absence of any proper arrangement—' With this curiously formal phrase Moreland runs into difficulty, looking down at his hands, pausing, as close to being unsettled as I have seen him. He takes a breath and goes at it in a rush. 'What I did was to repay the money in instalments, every month, whatever I had available. By the time Harry died, roughly half was paid off. Which left a bit over ten thousand. Now, rather than, umm' – he searches for the words with a spiral of his hand – 'worry you directly, I contacted Leonard and asked him to handle the repayment. To say it was a business arrangement.'

'Good Lord!' I stare at him, I lean forward. I shiver and laugh simultaneously. 'It was you! I thought . . .'

'I'm sorry. I didn't mean it to appear in any way – devious.'

'I thought—' But I'm not about to start explaining about Jack.

'That someone was trying to give you a handout?'

'Yes.'

'Sorry. I was simply hoping to avoid any – well, awkwardness. As it was it didn't quite work out that way.' He gives an ironic shrug. 'I was coming to tell you about it when Josh disappeared.'

'Good Lord,' I echo, still absorbing this news, seeing

how someone like Moreland would wish to keep the transaction – and his father's troubles – private.

Moreland sits up. 'You're cold,' he declares. Without discussion, he scoops the food onto the tray and leads the way indoors.

I sit for another moment before following with the wine, feeling pleasantly drugged and astonishingly lucid, wondering why I don't drink more seriously more often.

Moreland is switching on lamps.

'But why pay so much back at once?' I say boldly. 'You don't need to, you know. It isn't necessary.'

He bends down to put a match to the fire and shoots me a backward look that is almost fierce. 'I had the money.'

'And you thought I needed it.'

He stands up. 'I thought you needed it more than I did,' he retorts crisply. '*And* I had the money.'

I have been rebuked. His ability to pay is not really any of my business.

'I—'

But he is already remarking, 'You haven't eaten anything.'

I inspect my bread and cheese. 'No,' I have to agree. Taking the plate, I sit on the floor next to the fire. 'Thank you for the money,' I say earnestly. 'It's very welcome. I certainly won't turn it down.'

Moreland sits in the chair opposite. 'Good!' Any lingering awkwardness evaporates in the breadth and immediacy of his smile.

We talk of other things. Or rather, I prompt him to talk while I listen. It is a relief not to have to think about myself for a change, to forget Dawson and the gun business and all the other lurking worries, to settle back and listen to Moreland's fluid voice as he tells me about his job, how he

213

goes to Saudi Arabia for several days every month, how the itinerant life has its advantages – desert hunting trips with the Saudis, invitations to Longchamps and Ascot – and its disadvantages – the alcohol prohibition – 'not, admittedly, life-threatening, but life-dampening' – laundry always in the wrong place, goats' brains and worse for breakfast – a conspiratorial smile here, as if to admit he is teasing. He touches very briefly on the problem of keeping in contact with friends. He doesn't mention a family.

When the fire becomes too hot, I retreat to a chair, my cheeks burning, though this is probably from the wine, which I continue to consume fearlessly. As the evening drifts pleasantly on, I feel slothful and oddly content and a little euphoric. Moreland, now the subject of the loan is out of the way, speaks with an easy familiarity that assumes common ground, a bank of shared experiences, as if we were old friends for whom everything is half-read; a suggestion that is both restful and beguiling.

I have visions of freedom. I allow myself to look ahead to a time when I will be able to dine out like this with whom I choose, whenever I choose, without thoughts of the past. To a time when my life will be my own again; when, in some yet more distant unformed future, who knows, I might even find someone to share it with.

I'm not so hazy with wine and fantasies of freedom that I don't recognise the danger of looking across at Moreland as I think this. But ideas are harmless and free and almost as intoxicating as wine, and I'm in no state to suppress them anyway. As Moreland chuckles at the memory of a party that he came to in this cottage years ago, the glow of the firelight illuminates one side of his face and accentuates the curve of his mouth and the strong line of his nose, and I let myself wonder how life would be with someone like him.

Before this thought races away with me, I pull myself to an abrupt halt, I bring myself rapidly to earth. A relationship – even the idea of a relationship – is an indulgence I can't afford. Even if by some wild chance Moreland were attracted to me, even if by some wilder chance he were free, it would be madness, and quite unsafe.

My imagination subsides in a rush, though not without a small dart of regret.

Perhaps Moreland catches something in my expression, perhaps it is the suddenness with which I put my glass down, but he stops and says, 'All right?'

'I'd like some coffee. Black, if you have it.'

'*Black* . . . well, I don't know . . .' he teases me gently.

When I fail to respond, he gets up wordlessly and goes to the kitchen.

By the time he comes back with the coffee, I have fought myself some way clear of my wine haze, I have got my mind back on track. Using the courage that only alcohol can bring, I ask something I have wanted to bring up with Moreland ever since I met him. 'Tell me,' I ask, 'what really happened with Harry?'

Moreland is alert. 'I'm sorry . . .?'

'In the Falklands. Harry seemed to have no friends from those days. There was no one at the memorial service apart from the CO and you – apart from you.'

He frowns, he contorts his mouth. 'I couldn't say, Ellen. I hardly knew Harry then. We were in different outfits.'

'But there was *something*.' I sense from his manner that I have struck on the truth.

'Ellen,' he says, looking mildly beleaguered. 'These things . . . Who knows? And after all this time – well, does it matter?'

I consider this. I say reasonably, 'I think it does matter, yes. I suppose it's that I'm bound to hear sooner or later. And that I'd rather hear it from you, now.'

He looks unconvinced.

I laugh oddly, hoarsely. 'Oh, don't think there's anything you could say that's going to surprise me! Nothing about Harry could ever surprise me. I don't have any great and unreal illusions about him, you know. No great *idea* of him that's going to take a dreadful knock.' I play this back to myself while I take a long gulp of coffee, and decide it came out a little more harshly than I intended. I add evenly, 'I just want to understand, that's all. I want to understand everything about Harry. It's my way of dealing with – his death.' And this, I almost tell him, is the absolute truth.

'Maybe there wasn't a reason,' Moreland suggests, fiddling his long fingers. 'Maybe Harry just didn't make any friends.'

I give him a look of disappointment. I shake my head slowly.

Moreland searches my face, he reads my determination. His expression, which has been reluctant, almost obdurate, shifts to one of resignation. He exhales audibly, he shifts in his seat. 'All right,' he begins slowly, 'there *was* something. Just a rumour. The problem with these things, of course, is that you never get to hear the full story. People say things, but you never really know. They might have reasons – old scores to settle, guilt, a need to shift blame, whatever.' He looks away into the fire, his forehead a sudden mass of lines. 'But so far as it's possible to . . . *believe* these things' – he looks back at me – 'it seems Harry's platoon wasn't a very happy one. There could have been all sorts of reasons for that, of course. He could have got landed with more than his fair share of troublemakers. That can happen to anyone – it's happened to me. He could have' – he chooses his words

216

with care – 'lost his grip. One lapse, a time when he didn't make a decision quite quickly enough – something like that. And then if he didn't regain control straight away, the men would have been right on to it. They would resent it. They wouldn't let him forget.' He gives me a quick glance, as if to acknowledge that he hasn't got to the point yet. 'It could be that leadership didn't come naturally to him, that he had to work at it, that he couldn't . . . Anyway, whatever it was . . .' He brings his eyes back to mine, he says in a voice that is suddenly flat, 'The rumour was that Harry's unit didn't advance as fast as it might have, and the men were very unhappy about it.'

The room is very quiet. Only the faint hum of damp wood in the grate.

'I thought one of Harry's men had been injured,' I say, 'that they were delayed by the need to get him to a doctor.'

'Yes. That *was* a problem, so I believe.'

His tone seems to confirm what I already suspect, that an injured man is not a sufficient excuse for lack of action.

'And this rumour,' I ask painfully, 'everyone knew about it, did they?'

'No. Well – in 3 Para, *yes*, I would imagine so. But not outside the regiment. I never heard it outside.'

The famous regimental loyalty, by which they all set such store. 'But *you* heard,' I point out softly.

Moreland's gaze becomes more fixed. 'I had a friend in 3 Para. He told me.'

Not so loyal after all then.

'This . . . failure to advance . . . when was it meant to have happened?'

'During the main push to Port Stanley.'

'About the time you came across Harry's platoon?'

His expression stiffens slightly as if I have touched on

a line of questioning he would rather avoid. 'About then,' he agrees hesitantly.

'So you saw how it was?'

'I'm sorry?'

'With the soldiers. The atmosphere. What it was like.'

'Not really. We came across Harry's platoon in the dark. It was hectic. All anyone wanted to do was flake out for a while. We stayed together just a short time. We swapped intelligence, that sort of thing. Then we went on. That was it.'

I want to say: Long enough to get an idea of how things were, though. Instead I ask: 'And you didn't notice anything?'

'We'd been on the move for three days without much sleep,' he says. 'Quite honestly, we weren't in a state to notice anything.'

I sense that this is all I am going to get.

'Thank you,' I say.

Moreland looks thoughtful, as if he still isn't sure he has done the right thing. 'More coffee?'

'I must go.' This comes out a little more brusquely than I intended.

He catches up with me in the hall. 'Wait. I've got something for Josh.'

He opens a door I hadn't noticed before to reveal a room even smaller than the dining-room, which contains a table and chair and a clutter of papers. He doesn't switch on the light but in the brief moment before he re-emerges I see, spread over the table, large plans of some sort and, on the windowsill behind, a folding leather-framed triptych of photographs. The light is faint but I can just make out indistinct groups of people in two of the frames, and in the right-hand frame a woman on her own, a formal head and shoulders with bare neck and long hair.

'Here,' says Moreland, closing the door behind him. He hands me a book. *Fish of the British Isles*.

He reaches ahead to switch on an outside light and follows me towards the car. The evening is cool. A breeze rattles through the shrubs.

'You don't sing any more?' he asks as we tramp across the gravel.

'What? Oh no!'

'Isn't that a pity?'

We stop by the car.

'You wouldn't think so if you heard me.'

He laughs. 'But you must have been good.'

'That's it – past tense. Out of practice. Anyway, to get the right sound, you have to live the life. Wild. Unhealthy.'

He throws back his head and laughs again, and I am rather surprised and pleased that I have the capacity to amuse him.

'Are you all right to drive?' he asks.

'Fine,' I lie.

He kisses me on the cheek. 'Good night, Ellen.'

The wine makes me sleepy on the way home and it takes all my concentration to arrive safely.

On the kitchen table at Pennygate I find a note from Josh. He must have run over from Jill's soon after I left. The note is propped up against a framed black and white photograph of *Minerva* which normally lives on a shelf in the drawing-room.

The note says: *Mum, Give to Richard. Important.*

The photograph shows the yacht bowling along under full sail with a thin strip of coastline in the background.

I stare at it thoughtfully for a while before standing it on the dresser and starting slowly up the stairs.

*

NINE

Saturday, my second cup of coffee, and I sign the last of the sympathy letters with a small sense of achievement. Something finished, something behind me. *We will miss him very much*. It'll be a relief not to have to write that again. My throat swells each time, my eyes prick with heat.

I have also scribbled cards to all the people, mainly women friends, who left messages earlier in the week, thanking them for their concern, telling them it would be lovely to see them, but not quite yet, not until I have sorted myself out a little more. Perhaps in a few weeks. I send my love.

I wonder what these people are thinking, if any of them have heard about the lost shotgun, if they are talking about it among themselves. I haven't spoken to many people in the last few days – friends have stopped phoning and I don't call back – but the two or three who managed to get past the answering machine didn't mention anything. But then they wouldn't. Or would they? I hover between resignation and a perverse hope. This morning, hope's riding higher, partly because I'm buoyed up by thoughts of seeing Katie for lunch tomorrow, partly because I slept quite well for once; no nightmares until shortly before I woke when, for the first time in weeks, I dreamt about the dory. It was drifting through a fog, somewhere out at sea. It crunched onto a pebble beach, it was too heavy for me to lift. Then the scene shifted subtly and it wasn't me at all but a faceless man who was lifting the boat free of the shingle and pushing it out to sea. Not Harry, though; in the dream Harry was already dead.

I woke troubled but not actually desperate. This is progress.

Carried along by the idea that I am getting somewhere, I take a sheet of paper and start to make a list of things that might raise money. The most obvious is Harry's Mercedes, an expensive model, almost new, which is sitting in the garage. I put this down with a question mark, however. I have the feeling it's owned by Ainswick and not mine to sell. From the transport stable, there is also the dory itself, with sixty horsepower outboard, the jet ski, and the inflatable Zodiac with the small outboard. From the house, the personal computer, the printer; the Jacobean chest in the hall which Harry paid too much for, the mahogany six-leaf dining table with eighteen matching chairs, the massive Victorian bookcase on the top landing: furniture that is too large for any cottage. And while I think of it, the portrait of the prim-faced man in a cavalier hat by an unknown eighteenth-century artist that hangs in the drawing-room, and which I don't think anyone is particularly fond of.

How much will all these luxuries fetch in the middle of a recession? Not, I suppose, a great deal.

Void of further ideas, I look out of the window and watch Maurice working on the vegetable beds, pulling up carrots and beating the earth off them. He follows a ragged rhythm, stooping, forking, straightening with a fearful jerk, knocking the vegetables against his boot and tossing them into a basket; a study, you would think, in how to acquire back trouble. I can never look at Maurice without thinking of the inflatable, and the morning when we brought it up muddy from the quay.

Through the open windows I catch the faint scrunch of wheels on the gravel beyond the garden wall. My imagination adds the click of the letter flap, the drop of envelopes onto the mat. I hurry along the passage to the hall and there, belatedly, is the post. Five letters and two circulars. I flick through the postmarks, but there is nothing from Guernsey. I pour myself another coffee before taking this disappointing harvest back to the study.

I slide my credit card statement to one side unopened; I need time to prepare for that. I pass over a brown envelope from Katie's school – by the look of it, a bill for some extra or another. I stop at an expensive handwritten envelope and extract a letter of condolence from someone I barely remember, an old family friend of Diana's. Optimistic of me to think I had received the last of these letters.

I pick up a flimsy undersized envelope, the sort that is sold cheaply in newsagents and sweet shops. The address is scrappily written in an arbitrary mixture of lettering. My name appears as *Mrs RicHMond*. The envelope contains a slip of folded paper and a newspaper cutting. I recognise the cutting: it's the report of Harry's memorial service from the *Telegraph*. The lower margin has been annotated in the same hand. *So rotten Scum get to be heroEs now!!!*

I stare at this for some moments before slowly unfolding the slim sheet of paper. It says: *What about Joe Congreve! A REAL Hero Betrayed by Scum. Joe's widow got NOTHING. NO fancy service. Britain stinks for Real heroes. But the Right man dead now.*

I flatten the page out, I read it again, I lay it down, I place the cutting next to it, lining the two up symmetrically on the leather. I feel a leadenness, a sense of suspension. I take the words in, but I resent them too, the way they have intruded on me.

I refold the paper and the cutting and slide them back in the envelope. After a time I take them out once more and read the spidery script again. So Harry is scum. And scum betrayed this Joe Congreve. Thus, Harry betrayed Joe Congreve. I suppose this is what I'm meant to understand anyway.

Everyone has enemies, I tell myself. If you have a profile as high as Harry's you are bound to attract envy. This is probably just a disgruntled soldier, venting some long-harboured resentment.

Yet on a harsher level I remember Moreland's words and cannot help being sucked into a grimmer vision of Harry's army days. Unpopularity is one thing, betrayal, as this writer well knows, another.

Did Harry face this sort of talk at the time? Did it, I wonder, stalk him for years afterwards?

If I am completely honest – and this is painful – part of me wants it to be true because then it makes everything more understandable, it gives me a peg on which to hang the destructiveness of those last months. And – come on, Ellen, *come on* – if you're going to be *really* honest it assuages your guilt, it lets you some way off the hook.

With this thought, I abandon the desk and the letter and go through the drawing-room into the garden.

I call to Maurice as I approach. His movements jerk to an uneven halt. He greets me with the faint embarrassment with which he greets everyone, probably including his wife. At fifty, Maurice seems to find plants more rewarding than people. With the garden looking as glorious as it does today, I'm tempted to think he's right.

'Some could've done with leavin' a bit,' he says,

indicating the carrots. 'Might need a magnifier to find 'em in the pot.' Maurice doesn't entirely approve of my preference for baby vegetables.

I tell him they look just fine. We talk about the potatoes and mangetouts, when they might be ready, what is to be planted for the autumn. The autumn: I don't know why I discuss it so earnestly. I may not be here.

At some stage I will have to talk to Maurice about his future. This would be as good a moment as any but I put it off. I tell myself that I can't take any decisions until Gillespie comes back with whatever financial package he scrapes together, but in truth I simply can't face it, not at the moment.

We wander through the larger of the two glass-houses and talk about the plum crop. The air is hot and close with the overblown scent of ripening fruit.

'Oh, by the way, did the police come and see you?' I ask.

He grunts affirmatively. 'Dinner time.'

'And it went all right?'

'Was like you said. Asked about the keys. And the cabinet. Told 'em I never went near the thing. Never touched the guns. Never knew what was in there.'

I spread my palm lightly over a white petunia and press the softness of the petals against my skin. 'I'm sure he must have left it in Scotland, that thing, you know. Margaret and I just can't think where.'

'Sittin' in the boot of someone's car, I shouldn't wonder.'

'Probably.' I smile at him before walking on.

I pause to admire a line of geranium cuttings, set in a row of identical pots. I turn to Maurice with a look of sudden curiosity. 'They didn't come and see you before, did they, the police? While I was away?'

'While—? No.' He thinks about it again. 'No.'

'I just wondered.'

My question has troubled him.

'They had to make inquiries,' I reassure him. 'They always have to, apparently. I just wondered if they'd bothered you, that was all.'

'No.'

'Well . . . good!' I smile again.

We pass through the far door and out into the fresh air.

'Such a magical day,' I gasp, forcing myself to come alive. Maurice looks around with the air of someone who rarely considers days or anything else in these terms. 'Could do with more rain.'

'Maurice!' I laugh. 'Anyway, we've just had some!'

'Not enough.'

I'm still shaking my head when I see Charles's lanky figure strolling across from the house. He raises an arm in a loose-limbed wave. We meet on the lawn.

'You look better!' he exclaims when we have kissed cheeks. 'Gosh, you look better!'

'Do I? Well, yes, I'm all right, I suppose. In fact – yes!'

He blinks at me good-naturedly. 'And Josh?'

'Off on a fishing expedition. So the answer's – fine.'

I tuck my arm into his and we stroll towards the terrace.

'How's it going?' I ask. 'The dreaded candidature and everything?'

'Ah . . . quite *well*.'

His confidence rather surprises me. 'You've got some support then?'

'Can't be sure, naturally. Can't expect rock-solid promises. But I've met quite a lot of the committee now. And I've had a few indications.' He smiles the smile of a schoolboy who's been tipped the wink about a place in the rugby team.

'Oh.'

'You don't sound too pleased,' he says in a tone of mock offence.

'I just—' I stop and face him. 'I never thought this was your sort of thing.' I laugh. 'I thought you were *happy.*'

It's his turn to look surprised. 'I was. I am. But I don't think that's a bar to getting into Parliament.'

'But all that backbiting? All that jockeying for position?'

Ignoring this, he says solemnly, 'I may be wrong, but I like to think I'd do rather a good job. As good as the next man, at any rate. Sorry – *person!* Lord, must get that right, mustn't I!' He chuckles mischievously before rearranging his face into a suitably serious expression. 'I'd certainly work jolly hard at it, I can tell you. Harder than most.'

'I'm sure you would. I know you would. But those ghastly hours,' I remind him. 'All those late sittings. Weekend surgeries. It never stops.' Saying this, it occurs to me that for Charles, living faithfully within a childless marriage, coping with Anne's permanent state of agitated discontent, the long hours may well be a blessing.

'Oh, I wouldn't mind any of that,' he says firmly, and alongside his characteristic twinkle there's a glint of determination that I haven't noticed before.

We walk on. 'Actually, I was wondering if you'd be interested in coming along to a small do,' he says breezily. 'I realise it'll probably be an awful bore for you. Not something you'd normally leap at.' He gives a bark of a laugh. 'But – well, I'd be absolutely thrilled if you could come.'

I dust off a wrought iron chair and sit down quickly. 'You mean, the committee get-together on Monday?'

'Yes! You know about it? You're going? Has Barrow already invited you?'

'Not Barrow – Jack.'

His face goes blank. He shapes his mouth into an 'Oh.'

'I said I'd go. But only if we all went together,' I explain carefully. 'So as not to step on anyone's toes.'

'Together?' He reaches for a chair and lowers himself onto it with care.

'You and me and Jack. And Anne, of course.'

'I see.' Tugging at the knees of his trousers, he sits slowly back in his seat and peers uncertainly at me. 'I see . . .' Then a crooked, rather diffident smile spreads across his face and he shakes his head in admiration. 'You are a clever old thing.'

I make a doubtful face.

'But you're absolutely right!' he declares, brimming with sudden cheer, as if the idea were so brilliant he'd have been proud to think of it himself. 'Best to be non-partisan. Absolutely right.'

It is typical of Charles to take a set-back so graciously. He really isn't suited to politics at all.

'Anne won't mind?' I ask, harbouring the certainty that she will.

'I'll explain it to her.'

I must look less than convinced about this because he reaches across and touches my wrist briefly. 'Dear Ellen. Don't worry.'

He looks away, he acquires a preoccupied expression, he launches himself into his next subject.

'Went to the coastguard again.' He folds his arms, he crosses his legs. 'I did tell you, didn't I?' He unfolds his arms again and links his hands across the front of his ancient jacket. 'Now the upshot is . . . Look, I don't want to give you any false hopes.' He frowns by way of emphasis. 'I wouldn't like you to think that the chances of finding the boat have dramatically *improved* or anything. But well, some new thoughts have come up which do seem worth investigating.'

Beyond the lawn the corn shimmers, the river is freckled with metallic light. 'The Gunfleet Sand thing, you mean? Harry having gone off track a bit?'

'Oh no. That is, we haven't ruled that out. We're still keeping an eye in that direction. Most *definitely*. But no – this is something rather new. Something which could swing the search in a completely different direction. It was Moreland who got onto it, tracked down people who'd seen the boat, worked it all out. I must say, he's absolutely first rate, that chap. Really knows his stuff—'

'*Moreland?*' I say, pushing lightness into my voice.

Charles looks abashed. 'Oh, didn't you—? Didn't I—? I . . . er, meant to say . . . But listen,' he says in the tone of someone who's about to explain everything, 'he's been a tremendous help. Done a tremendous amount of work. Really first class.'

'But why?' I protest.

'You didn't know—? Ah, but Moreland's an expert. He was in the Special Forces, one of their top chaps.' His voice beats with a sentimental pride. 'Knows all about small boats and tides and that sort of thing. These chaps get popped out of submerged submarines off the coast of Norway in midwinter, you know. Have to get ashore and survive. Jolly tough stuff. Not a lot they don't know about these things.'

I look away, suppressing a sense of resentment that contains more than a touch of fear. 'Moreland went with you on Wednesday?' I ask with perfect calm. 'To see the coastguard?'

'Oh yes. That was the whole point, you see. To go over his ideas with them. I must say, the coastguard were pretty impressed. Couldn't argue with it.'

Indignation rubs at me. I have been excluded, I have been, if not lied to, then told less than the truth, like a sheltered child for whom the adults believe they know best. I stand up, I stride to the edge of the terrace, I try to regain some sense of proportion. 'And what is this new idea of Moreland's?' I ask.

'Ah . . .' Charles's voice takes on an eager note. 'Basically, Moreland's discovered that those sightings weren't much good. Those people – the chap on the shore, the crew of the coaster – probably saw quite a different yacht. In fact, almost certainly did. And Moreland has worked out that, allowing for everything – the tides, the weather and so on – the yacht would most likely have ended up somewhere quite *different* from where we thought. Somewhere off to the north. No, what am I saying? The north-east. Yes, north-*east*. Which changes things considerably, of course. It means we could have been concentrating on the wrong area.'

The sun is very high now. Beyond the thin spread of the distant marshes, the sea has crept out of the haze, a soft grey line that makes a border for the long drop of the sky.

'Of course it's just speculation,' Charles says to fill the silence. 'But I must say, it seems to make sense. Worth looking into, anyway.' I hear the slap of his hands on his knees, the scrape of his chair. A bony hand grips my shoulder. 'But don't hold too many hopes, old girl, will you?'

I shake my head slowly. I manage a feeble smile. 'Bless you, no.'

I sit on the quay watching the dinghy snake slowly round the bend and set a steady course upriver. From head-on the craft looks flimsy, like a shell. The effect is accentuated by the smooth arch of water pushed up by the bow which further reduces the hull until the two passengers appear to be sitting in nothing more substantial than a glass bowl.

The smaller figure waves tentatively, then, as I get to my feet and wave back, with more certainty.

The boat, a battered off-white fibreglass dinghy, seems to speed up as it approaches. The gentle throb of the outboard grows to a steady putter then dies back abruptly as Moreland turns the boat towards the shore. The tide is low, the quay high and dry, and he guides the boat in to the crumbling stone ramp of the slipway, whose lower portion has long been buried under a thick layer of silt.

The boat scrunches to a halt and Josh, who has been poised in the bow, leaps out into mud that is ankle deep. I dimly notice that he's wearing his best trainers.

Moreland secures the outboard and calls a cheerful greeting. My muted reply causes him to look up. Catching my expression, he gives me a questioning glance.

Josh is busy hoisting his gear out of the boat in a manner that is affectedly grown-up, all studious nonchalance and self-awareness. I know I shouldn't bring the subject up in front of Josh, I know I should wait, but I can't stop myself saying crisply to Moreland, 'Charles tells me you've been helping out.'

Moreland's eyes register something like regret. He drops his gaze for a moment. 'I didn't think it was worth bothering you.' He makes a movement of his hands, a shrug or something more dismissive.

'Bother? I wouldn't have called it *bother*,' I say, giving a strange half-laugh to offset the tartness of my voice.

'No,' he agrees quickly. 'No.'

We are distracted by Josh, who has squelched clear of the mud and is waiting silently for instructions.

'Ben's mother'll be here in half an hour,' I remind him.

He flops theatrically, he blows out his lips, he gives me a heavy look that says he doesn't want to go out to lunch.

'She's going to take you swimming later.'

He puckers his mouth into an expression of disgust then, glancing at Moreland, rearranges his face into something more reasonable.

I tell him to go up to the house and have a shower, that I'll follow shortly.

He shuffles his mud-caked feet, he casts me a last protesting glance before accepting defeat. He beams a sunny farewell to Moreland, a positive blast of enchantment. He doesn't look at me as he turns to trudge up the path.

Moreland climbs out and, planting his bare feet squarely in the mud, hauls the boat further up the slip. 'I really didn't think it was worth bothering you until something came of it,' he says as soon as Josh is out of earshot.

'But on Wednesday – you could have told me. Why didn't you tell me then? And all this tracking people down, finding the crew of that coaster – I mean, that's not just *anything*! That's . . .' I clamp my arms together, I shake my head.

He climbs up onto the quay and comes towards me. 'No one had talked to these people properly, Ellen. Certainly not the police. No one had been through any of the basics like showing them a picture of the boat. Or asking them which direction the yacht was travelling in.'

I am stubbornly silent.

'Perhaps I should have mentioned it. I'm sorry. But—'

'You didn't want to raise my hopes?' I chant childishly.

He glances away, as if to reduce our mutual embarrassment at this show of peevishness. 'I wanted to wait and see if anything came of it,' he repeats.

'But something *did* come of it!'

'What?' He's filled with quiet alarm. 'Where did you get that idea? Nothing's been found yet. That's the whole point.'

'I meant . . .' But I can't explain. I can't tell him that the news caught me off-balance, that in one lurch it rekindled all my sharpest anxieties. Yet if I'm going to be impatient with anyone, it should, I realise dully, be myself, for having thought that the uncertainty was fading.

Moreland says, 'I never intended to hide anything from you, Ellen.' His gaze is steady and open, the look of an honourable man brought up to behave honourably. How must it be, I wonder momentarily, never to have done anything you were ashamed of?

'Maybe not.' My indignation begins to seem pointless and self-defeating. I say in the tone of a peace offering. 'No . . . But in future I'd appreciate being kept in the picture.'

'In that case, come back to the cottage now. I'll take you through it all.'

'Now . . .?' I glance downriver, already knowing that I'll go.

'It'd be hard to explain without charts. I've got all the charts.'

'I've got to see Josh off to lunch.'

'I'll wait.'

We float out into the stream. I sit on the wooden seat spanning the centre of the boat and trail my feet over the side to wash the mud away. Moreland, sitting in the back, pivots the outboard down into the water and fires the motor with a single pull of the cord. I swing my feet inboard and sit with my back to Moreland, looking ahead.

I had forgotten how much movement there is in the water, how it swirls and ripples, how the wavelets, so insignificant from the shore, slap insistently against the hull. We pass close to *Minerva*'s mooring, an orange plastic buoy with an integral handhold. The current drags at it, pulling it drunkenly over, trailing a small wake behind. The current is strong here, but not so strong as farther downstream. At the river mouth it can draw small craft onto the sand-bars, so they say, and in an easterly wind, when the sea gets rough, a boat can get pounded to death. People hereabouts enjoy telling these stories and Harry used to enjoy listening to them: they added to his craving for excitement. But they made me uncomfortable. My mind would paint the picture too clearly: the deep roar of the surf, the tug of the current, the boat grounding with a heart-stopping crash.

Moreland keeps to the side of the river, out of the stream. Raising his voice above the noise of the engine, he says, 'I talked to Josh.'

I had forgotten about the boarding school discussion. I twist round. 'What did he say?'

'I think he's hankering after the active life. Sport. Other kids. That sort of thing.'

I glance away. Sport. Other kids. The sort of answer a boy would give if he didn't want to admit to what was really bothering him.

'Nothing else?'

It's a moment before he says cautiously, 'I get the feeling he's a bit torn, Ellen. The one thing that really worries him is the thought of leaving home.'

This worries him? I'm not sure I believe it. It seems to me that the one thing which is driving Josh is his determination to leave home – or perhaps, if I can bear to face the thought, it isn't so much home that he wants to leave as me.

With a stab of self-pity, I ask, 'Basically he was keen, though, was he?'

'Well . . . interested, certainly.'

I turn slowly back to face the on-coming river. I let my self-pity roll forward unchecked. I tell myself that I must do what is best for Josh, that I must let him go, that in the long run he will love me the more for it, but these thoughts, necessary and realistic as they are, don't minimise the hurt, or lessen my dread of the loneliness to come.

The boat rocks slightly, and Moreland's hand drops onto my arm and pats it. The sympathy is like a shock.

'I'm all right,' I sing without looking around.

He withdraws his hand.

'I'm all right,' I repeat. I turn my head until he can see from my expression that this is true.

Attempting to lighten the mood, Moreland declares in a tone of mock disapproval, 'They get terribly spoilt, these kids, you know. Hot showers and heated dormitories, for heaven's sake. And videos at the weekends, and out as often as they like.' Still in character, he sighs, 'No hardship at all.'

'You're trying to convert me,' I accuse mildly.

'No,' he says, dropping back into his normal voice. 'I wouldn't do that.'

Approaching the village, the river becomes quite crowded. Boats are clustered around the moorings and pontoons. People sit on yachts with their arms looped over the guardrails, clasping drinks and talking raucously.

Sunbathers lie spread-eagled on the decks or propped awkwardly against open hatches. Children in bright life-jackets row inflatables and sail tub-shaped dinghies with stubby masts to the bellowed instructions of exasperated fathers. Everything is colour and activity. The winter, with its emptiness and echoing secretiveness, seems a world away.

Moreland keeps us out of the main channel, between the outer line of moorings and the loop of marshes and shallows formed by the hook of the river. The first I see of the sailing dinghy is the flash of its rainbow sail as it surges out from behind a moored yacht and heads across our path, on collision course. I look anxiously towards Moreland to see that he's already spotted the boat and is swinging the arm of the outboard across to steer us clear. Looking again I see the face of the dinghy's occupant bob down under the all-concealing sail, the face of a boy no older than Josh. His eyes lock onto us in sudden fear, for a moment he seems immobilised by the sight of us. He vanishes behind the sail again, the bow of his boat starts to turn, as if to pass behind us. But the turn stalls, the dinghy heads straight for us again. Moreland makes an exclamation, the note of the outboard rises to a roar, our boat twists away to the left, we will just pass clear. But the sailing dinghy is in trouble. Already well heeled over, it tips still further, its mast and bulging sail tracing a seemingly inexorable downward arc towards the water. Moreland shouts above the roar and clamour, 'Let the mainsheet go! Let the sheet go!'

The boy, visible now above the sail of the slowly capsizing boat, arches his back, trying to brace himself against the violent tipping of the dinghy. Then, just as it seems that nothing can save him from a dunking, he lets something go – it must be a rope – and the sail shoots out, the mast jerks upright, and with a thunderous flapping and rattling, the dinghy falls unconcernedly back onto an even keel.

'All right?' Moreland calls, but the boy is too dazed to answer. His dinghy, now safely behind us, drifts slowly on, the sails snatching and beating at their spars.

Seeing where he is headed, I cry, 'Mind out! It's shallow there!'

The boy glances back uncertainly, then ahead to where the water, deceptive as ever, looks mild and deep.

'It's very shallow!' I call again.

At last the boy pulls the tiller over and executes a slow disorganised turn, grabbing at a trailing rope and pulling it in as he does so.

While Moreland manœuvres us across the stream towards the landing place I keep an eye on the boy as he navigates his way gingerly through the moorings. When he glances in my direction I wave, but he doesn't wave back.

I become aware of Moreland watching me. 'Well done,' he says.

'But I didn't do anything.'

'You kept him off the mud.'

I look ahead. A sunburst of inflatables and tenders blossoms out from each of the two ladders let into the side of the quay. Like an ice-breaker we have to force a passage through a complaining raft of bumping obstacles to reach the wall. When the dinghy's nose finally touches, I reach for the ladder and, taking the rope – the painter, Harry taught me to call it – I climb the rusting rungs to the top. While Moreland ships the outboard I make the rope fast to a ring.

Clambering up behind me, Moreland follows the painter to the ring and eyes the knot I have used, an unmistakable inspection procedure that I appear to pass.

We start along the road. 'You've done that before,' he says.

'Self-defence.' I add, 'I wanted to be useful at something,' which isn't much of an explanation either.

It was after one of my unhappier experiences on *Minerva* that I got a boatman to teach me the two knots that form my entire repertoire. Harry had lured me out with promises of fine weather and a short trip – 'just to the river mouth'; in the event a journey that took us well out to sea – and a plea to help him entertain his guests, three businessmen who drank a great deal of beer and told schoolboy jokes. Harry, who had a propensity for living out whatever role demanded of him, became the complete skipper to my uncertain crew, all skill and expertise to my ineptitude. He rattled off orders and, when I foundered, slid his guests a pitying glance and took over the task with a small sigh of forbearance.

I did not love Harry at these times.

Then one of my knots jammed into an unsalvageable tangle and Harry flew at me in full hearing of the guests, his eyes bulging with an irritation that he tried to conceal behind a laugh. Our relationship – it still had life in it then – survived the incident because I knew that he was under strain, and that being on the boat often affected him this way. There was something about *Minerva* that brought out the perfectionist in Harry. When things didn't go smoothly, when the smallest item was left out of place, it was almost more than he could bear.

Moreland and I pass the boatyard sheds and come abreast of the boat storage area. At this time of year the area would normally be empty of the long rows of yachts which in winter look like so many beached whales, but this year the long recession has left a sorry tide of vessels for sale or in mothballs, their hulls draped in faded canopies that droop low over grime-streaked paintwork. Amid the keelboats riding high on their splayed skirts of timber props, a small craft crouches squat on the ground, a white work-boat under a blue canvas cover that has retained a pristine brightness. I see the boat, but recognition takes a moment longer.

The dory.

I lose momentum, I come to a slow halt, I take in the fact that the hull is white and polished, that all signs of the boat's last voyage have been expunged, that it looks nothing like it did when I last saw it.

'The yard have fixed it up,' Moreland comments, following my gaze.

We move on. 'Fixed it up?'

'There was a bit of damage.'

I take a moment 'What sort of damage?'

'To one side. A long scrape. And a bash or two.'

'Oh.' My mind races all over the place, I falter again, I look back. I try to work out when and how this might have happened. 'From a collision?' I ask. 'From . . .' From the ship that sunk *Minerva*, I mean to say.

'Possibly,' says Moreland, but his voice is full of doubt. 'Whatever bashed it certainly left some paint behind. But it's just as likely to have come from the trawler that salvaged it, I'm afraid, attempting to come alongside in a sea. I tried to go and see the trawler, to check her paint, but she'd gone round to the West Coast of Scotland. I spoke to her owners though, and they told me her hull is black. Which is the colour they found on the dory.'

Such thoroughness. To pursue things until they can be explained. To follow each fact through to the end and leave nothing unresolved. It is almost . . . *relentless* springs to mind, but that would be the wrong word for Moreland. With him I think it's more a matter of pride, a professional imperative. Also, perhaps, a misguided sense of duty.

'Well done.' Saying this, my heart beats dully at the thought of what discoveries are still to come.

'The dory couldn't be lifted,' says Moreland in the absorbed tone of someone going over well-trodden ground. 'It couldn't be stowed on deck. It had to be towed . . . Now the chap here at Waldringfield' – he taps the large-scale map spread over the desk in front of us – 'the one who says he saw a yacht going downriver at about five that Friday evening, now *he* doesn't remember seeing a dory or any sort of dinghy being towed behind. If it *was Minerva* it seems incredible that he didn't notice it. The dory is fourteen foot long to *Minerva*'s thirty-five – large by any standards.' His voice almost fades away. 'And hard to tow . . .' Suppressing this thought with a lift of his eyebrows and a contortion of his mouth, he slides the map onto the floor, and, almost tipping out of his chair, reaches for another from a large stack at the side of the desk.

I take this moment to glance up at the folding picture frame on the windowsill, to take another look at the woman in the photograph. The contrast of the black and white print is very strong, bleaching out everything except the perfect oval of the face, the large confident eyes, the sweep of the dark hair, the indolent mouth with its half-smile. A vivid passionate face; someone with an appetite for life.

While Moreland unfolds the new map I pass quickly over the other two pictures, one a snap of a family in a

garden – a laughing couple with two wriggling children –
the other a posed studio shot taken many decades ago,
in the forties or early fifties, showing a good-looking man
and a pretty woman in a rakish hat.

Moreland looks up and I bring my attention down to
the map, which is in fact a nautical chart, rather like the
one in the passage at Pennygate, but covering a larger area
and printed with bright colours – the land a rather violent
yellow, the sea partly white and partly blue, with insets of
green, and covered with a scattering of numbers. Most
of these blue and green areas abut the yellow shore, but
many more float out in wide tentacles across the sea: the
shoals. These tongues of colour have titles like Kentish
Knock, North Falls, Gunfleet Sand, Sunk Sank.

'Such names,' I murmur.

But words are insubstantial beings to Moreland and he
murmurs vaguely, 'Colourful.'

He points to the top of the chart, to a river, our river.
'Got your bearings?' he asks.

I nod. From the river the land slopes down and away
to the left until, drawn into the gaping mouth of the
Thames Estuary, it disappears off the edge of the chart.
Directly below is the wide expanse of the estuary itself, a
mass of shoals which ripple out from the river's throat like
blue flames from a cold dragon. And along the bottom,
forming a firm lower jaw, the north Kent coast.

Regaining his impetus, Moreland draws a line with his
finger from the mouth of our river downwards across the
estuary. 'Now the direct course, wind and tide permitting,
takes a boat this way. A small leg round the Cork Sand,
then straight down, leaving the Gunfleet Sand and the
Little Sunk to starboard. Then as you come into the Black
Deep' – he taps a passage that leads between the shoals –

'you have to decide exactly where you're going to cross the Long Sand.' His finger hovers over a long wedge of blue that is overlaid with slivers of green. 'The green bits are the really shallow bits. To be avoided. There are two crossing points you can use in calmish weather, both of which avoid a major detour. The one here is pretty direct.' He draws a path across the blue of the shoal. 'And safe enough, though it looks a bit frightening on the chart, doesn't it? In fact, assuming it was about 21.30, there'd have been a good nine feet at the shallowest point, and the tide still making. You'd have to be very unlucky to hit a bump. *Minerva* drew six feet. She'd have been okay. Plenty of yachts use this route. People with local knowledge. *But* . . .' Engrossed now, locked into his intellectual puzzle, he splays his fingers over the area. 'It was dark and the visibility wasn't that good. You'd have to be pretty sure of your navigation, you'd have to be absolutely confident of your position.' He doesn't say what happens if you get these calculations wrong, but the green patches, which rise out of the blue shoal like bubbles, lurk clearly on either side.

'The other crossing point *here*' – his finger floats a short way along the Black Deep and draws south across the blue shoal again – 'is much deeper, but it also requires a good fix – a confident position – because you don't want to go too near this shallow here.' He prods at a green lozenge close by. 'Now with Decca neither of these routes would be a problem, even at night in poor visibility. The accuracy of the system is such that even if you hadn't bothered to track the tidal flow too accurately, you could soon see how far you were getting pushed off course and compensate accordingly. However . . .' He pushes his lips out, he frowns in thought, he fixes me briefly with his wise eyes.

'It would be a bit nerve-racking singlehanded, and that's putting it mildly. Having to bob down to the chart to fix your position – reading the Decca, plotting it; it's quick but not *that* quick. Having to listen out for ships, having to peer through the murk for buoys and lights, having to lay off your course. Well . . .' He makes a gesture that suggests it wouldn't be something he'd undertake lightly. 'Now if you wanted to be absolutely safe, or the nav aids had broken down and you were left with nothing but guess-work and God, or the fog was really rolling in and you'd lost your nerve for shoal-hopping, *then* . . . Well, you could go outside everything.' His hand follows a loop to the east, across a white sea devoid of blue. 'It's a bit of a detour, of course. But if you were being cautious . . .'

The idea of Harry being cautious hangs improbably in the air. Preoccupied with this or some other thought, Moreland looks across at me in an unfocused way. Then his gaze sharpens, his eyes soften, he smiles briefly before turning back.

'Now this is where the coaster made its sighting.' He lays his finger on a point in the Black Deep. 'At 23.20 hours on the Friday night. As you see, it was just to the west of the second crossing point – not too promising on the face of it. According to the captain – and he seemed fairly reliable – the yacht was heading *east*, which again wouldn't seem too promising. But if the yacht hadn't allowed enough for the south-going tide, which was pretty strong by that time, and was trying to claw her way across-tide to get back into the right position for a dash across the shoal, then it's still perfectly possible, do you see?'

I get the general idea. I give a slow nod.

'But what makes me think it wasn't *Minerva* is something else the captain said.' He sits back in his seat. His long fingers fiddle with a pencil, rotating it slowly back and forth. 'The reason the coaster noticed the yacht was that it nearly collided with her. The captain wopped on his searchlight and shone it straight at her – normal practice. Now in the blur and the confusion the captain didn't notice much – he was probably too busy swearing and cursing – but one thing he was pretty sure about was the absence of any dinghy. Nothing being towed behind. Again, it would have been extraordinary if he'd missed that dory.' He adds quickly, 'Though that doesn't necessarily mean a great deal. It could have broken adrift soon after *Minerva* left the river . . .' He gives me a moment to absorb this, watching me carefully, like a professor taking a student through a long and difficult exercise.

'Now what the captain *did* notice,' he begins again, 'was that both the yacht's sails had numbers on them, and that the sails looked patchy. That's what he called them – patchy. I can only think the sails were racing sails, made of Kevlar, or partly of Kevlar, which is a darkish brown fabric used in ugly great squares on racing sails and looks – well, patchy. Now . . .' His hands are still. 'The lads at the yard here tell me *Minerva* did *not* have numbers on both sails – only the mainsail. And that all the sails were made of standard Terylene, brilliant white. No Kevlar. And no patches.' He rotates his hand; his pencil describes a slow arc. 'Of course, the captain might have been mistaken . . .'

'But you don't think so?'

He shrugs, but I can see he doesn't think so.

A moment of silence passes between us. Warm air wafts in from the window.

Moreland asks with sudden concern, 'Would you like anything? A cold drink? Tea?' He moves as if to get up.

'Thanks, but no.'

'Sure?'

I nod quickly. I look back at the chart. I manage: 'So you think it wasn't *Minerva* they saw?'

He turns his head to catch my words. I realise I have been whispering. 'I'm sorry?' he says.

I repeat it a little louder.

'I think it's unlikely. Also . . . if *Minerva* had been lost in the estuary somewhere, if she'd bumped onto a shoal or been run down by a ship along this route then she'd probably have been found by now. It's mainly shallow water, you see. It's very busy water. Chances are' – he chooses his words – 'something would have trawled into the wreck by this time, or caught a blip on its depth sounder.' He is ticking off the arguments, one by one. 'The only place a wreck might be missed is the Black Deep, I suppose, or the King's Channel, where the water's much deeper. But that's just where the coastguard have been asking people to look, for that very reason.'

I stare unseeing at the chart, trying to picture the Black Deep. I see swirling water and racing tides and ships suddenly bearing down out of the fog.

'And what about here?' I ask, indicating the wide expanse of sea to the east, the route of caution.

'Yes,' he concedes immediately, 'that'd be different. A wreck would be far less likely to be found there.' But from the way he says this, I gather he doesn't think Harry went that way.

'Charles said' – I make an effort to bring my voice up to volume – 'that you'd found something new?' I look up at him.

He pulls in his mouth, he sits forward, he gestures uncertainty, as if to dampen any hopes I might be harbouring. 'Well, I wouldn't say *found* exactly. It was more of an idea really . . . a theory.'

I wait expectantly.

'It seemed to me . . .' Breaking off, he roots around under the chart and pulls out a sheaf of papers and looks at them thoughtfully. 'I took a good look at the weather. I got all the weather reports. Local, national. I asked people who were around the river that Friday. Then I put myself in Harry's place.' He opens one hand, he pauses, finally he says, 'And I decided that unless I was hell-bent on having a miserable time I would never have left that night.'

His words seem to fade out, like a radio that has gone off tune, and it's a moment before I pick them up again.

'. . . There was a gale blowing right through Thursday night into Friday morning.' He leafs through his papers until he finds the one he's after. 'Then all that heavy rain. *Then* drizzle. *Then* mist and fog.' With each point he taps the back of his fingers against the paper. 'And on the Friday night there would still have been a large sea running.' He shakes his head. 'One way and another, I'd have been tempted to stay firmly on the mooring and turn in early with a stiff whisky.' He shuffles the paper to the back and refers to the next sheet. 'Now conditions were *much* better the next morning. Only a thin coastal mist which burnt off as the sun came up. A light northerly breeze, force two to three. Almost perfect. Although if you were being fussy, a bit more wind might have been nice. But . . .' He throws up a hand that says this would have been too much to ask. Reaching down to retrieve the first map from the floor, he spreads it out again. He points to the river mouth. 'Now on Saturday morning, at about six, a yacht was seen going through the narrows here. She was white-hulled. She had a single mast. She was about the right size. *And*' – he says with slow emphasis – 'she was towing a white dinghy. Flattish, like a dory.'

He glances my way, he looks back at the map; he is giving me time. 'It was a rambler who saw it,' he murmurs conversationally. 'He'd parked his car on the north side there. Starting off on a walk. Doesn't know much about boats, but knows what he saw. And it's narrow there, boats pass close to the shore. He'd have seen clearly, even with a mist about.'

Shaping his hands into a cathedral, he rasps the tips of his forefingers over his chin. He waits, but I have nothing to say, no questions to ask, and presently, after a glance in my direction, he picks up the thread again. 'The only thing about the timing of this is the tide. At six it—'

'So early?' My interruption comes from nowhere. I hardly know why I've made it. For a moment I am confused by my own train of thought. 'To get there, he'd have had to start . . .' I shrug. 'At five? Wouldn't it have been dark? I thought it was dark . . .'

He makes a show of consulting his notes, although I sense that he already has the answer. 'Sunrise was a quarter to six. So . . .' He narrows his eyes in calculation. 'It would have been twilight from five or thereabouts. Time to leave the mooring and get down to the river mouth. The journey would've taken an hour, more or less, so . . .'

Nothing unexplained; nothing left out.

Gathering himself again, Moreland goes back to the chart. 'At 06.00, when this yacht was leaving the river, the tide was still running north-east. At up to two knots. If it was *Minerva*, then she would have made slow headway against it, even with the engine running. Now if something disabled her fairly soon – let's say almost immediately – then this tide would have swept her backwards' – he sweeps a hand up the chart – 'and she'd have ended up *north-east* of the river mouth, not to the south at all.'

He pauses, he sucks in his lips. 'You see what I mean?'

Something bothers me, but I can't quite put my finger on it. 'When you say disabled . . .?'

'By whatever it was. Fire. Explosion. Collision.'

The thought comes at last. 'You mean . . . the boat might not have sunk straight away?'

'It's *possible* she went straight down. A collision with a large vessel, something cataclysmic. But if it was something less severe, a fire, a collision with some floating junk – and there's enough of that about – then she could have drifted for quite a distance.'

'But if there was time . . . why didn't Harry call for help?'

Moreland accepts the point with a solemn nod. 'Well, the electrics might have blown, the radio might have been damaged . . . If anything can go wrong at sea, it generally does.'

Through the silence a child's laughter floats in from the lane outside. A car labours up the hill nearby.

'Of course it's just a theory,' Moreland repeats.

I am worlds away, beyond the open window. 'Why didn't he get into the dory then? Why didn't he escape?'

When Moreland doesn't reply, I turn questioningly, but his expression is an answer in itself. Who can know? he is saying. How can any of us know?

'The place where the trawler found the dory on Sunday,' he says, returning slowly to the sea chart, 'seems to fit in with the timing. Matches the flow of the tides, assuming the dory went adrift early that Saturday morning.'

I see the dory floating, empty and aimless.

'The only thing that doesn't *quite* fit—' He pulls away from the chart with a frown, the logician denied the last piece of his puzzle. 'And I was hoping I could check this with you – was the colour of Harry's waterproofs. The rambler said the person in the yacht was wearing a white or mainly white jacket.'

I see the jacket clearly. It's white with a navy band around the bottom and a green collar, made by a popular manufacturer two or three seasons ago.

I take my time. 'He was wearing orange,' I reply. This image is also strong, of Harry motoring away from the quay in the downpour that Friday lunchtime, his bright orange jacket fading slowly into the gloom.

'The rambler could've got it wrong . . .'

'Harry had several other waterproofs,' I say. 'At least three sets. He was always losing them, buying new ones.'

Moreland's interest has sharpened again. 'He kept some on the boat?'

'Yes.'

'White maybe?'

'Maybe. I'm not sure.'

But it's enough for Moreland. His eyes reflect the satisfaction of a loose end that promises to be tied up.

I lean over the desk. I try to translate Moreland's theory onto the chart. I take in the expanse of water to the right of the river mouth. Apart from one or two slivers of blue, it is plain unending white. Deep water. Miles and miles of it.

'Will they try to search it?' I ask.

He gives a slow shake of his head. 'Too large an area. No real reference to start from. No, if anything turns up, it'll be by chance as much as anything else. A fishing boat, something like that.'

I digest this silently, I sit back. 'Then . . .'

His eyes are on me all the time, kind but also suitably detached for the business in hand, an officer's look. 'Not something to count on, I'm afraid. In fact – best not to hope.'

'Actually I—' A small warning bell sounds and I pause, trying to assess how this will sound, how it will be interpreted. 'I *wasn't* hoping,' I say at last, needing to voice at least some of my reservations. 'I've never been hoping. Everyone's assumed . . .' I stare at the chart, I pick at the edge of it. 'You see,' I admit finally, 'I'd be much happier if the boat wasn't found.'

Moreland looks away then back, his face taking on an expression of sudden understanding. 'It'll be painful, I do realise.'

'It's not that so much . . . I just think it'd be better if Harry's body was left where it is. Undisturbed. I think it would be quite – wrong – to go looking for it now. I think he should be left in peace. I'd hate it if . . . Well, I'd just hate it.'

Moreland gropes for a sympathetic approach. 'I appreciate what you're saying. But from a practical point of view, Ellen, if the boat was located, it would make an enormous difference to you. Legally, I mean.'

'But if they find the boat they'll find . . .' I can't say it.

'Ellen . . .' He leans forward, his hand hovers close to mine. 'It's unlikely Harry's body will be there.'

I stare into his face. 'What do you mean?'

'Well,' he says gravely, 'if it wasn't swept away at the time, it probably would have been soon after.'

'Why?' I hear myself asking this as if I were some distance away.

'Because it usually happens that way, Ellen.'

'Why?'

'The currents. The movement of the water.' He is trying to spare me the grim details which my imagination furnishes all too easily – the body bloating, rising, the fish, the processes of the sea.

'I see!' I say tightly. 'I see!' I stand up abruptly.

Moreland rises, looking unhappy. 'I really don't think you need to worry.'

I go to the door. Aware that I'm sounding unreasonable, I half turn and say in a brittle voice, 'Well, I hope you're right!'

Before he can say anything, I gesture back towards the photographs. 'Your family?'

Moreland follows my gaze. 'What? Oh, yes. And friends. And godchildren.'

'Beautiful,' I say, meaning the woman.

He throws me an odd look, laden with messages I cannot read. He glances back. 'My wife,' he says in a flat voice. 'She's in New York at the moment. Her work.'

New York and work fit the face somehow.

Letting the tension go, managing a smile, I ask if he can drive me straight home. 'I've got an awful lot to do.'

'Of course.' Scooping up his car keys, he leads the way out. Meeting the weekend traffic, we talk about the pressures of tourism and the chances of keeping the river unspoilt most of the way home.

Alone in the kitchen, I sit at the table with a full mug of tea, trying to apply some logic to my thoughts. Only when I have drained the last of the tea do I get up and go across the hall to the boot room. The sailing jackets and trousers hang in colourful bundles from the hooks nearest the window. An old jacket of Harry's in a stiff yellow plastic-coated fabric sticks an arm out into the room like an absent traffic policeman. On the next peg the children's matching waterproofs, in brilliant red, hang neatly above their boots.

On the last peg, the white sleeve of my sailing jacket peeks out from under a lightweight anorak which has been draped untidily over the top. Dangling beneath are my sailing trousers in a dark blue which exactly matches the band of blue around the bottom of the jacket.

I extricate the jacket and carry it back to the kitchen and lay it out on the table. I stare at it, the distinctive whiteness, the bright green collar, the blue band around the bottom, and I fold it shop-style, sides in, arms across the back, into half and then half again, until it makes a neat rectangle. I slide it into a plastic rubbish bag and fold the plastic tightly round and seal it with tape. I push the bundle into the kitchen bin, in among the general refuse, then, gathering the top of the liner together, close it with a tier and pull it out of the bin and, carrying it outside, place it in one of the metal bins by the garages, ready for the refuse collector on Wednesday.

TEN

A gale is blustering off the sea. Not an ideal time for a walk on the heath. The wind is so strong that the children and I have to lean into it, plodding heads down, like characters from an illustration in a Dickens story. But I'm glad we came. Sunday walks over the heath were a regular event when we lived at Heath End and I feel it's important to re-establish these rituals, that by reverting to the habits of those happy days we might recapture some of their mood.

We are walking off an indifferent lunch served at an inn outside Woodbridge: overcooked roast beef, pale Yorkshire pudding and dense apple pie. The children ate with uncritical hunger, I with little enthusiasm. Keen to set the right tone for this, the first of what I want to be a string of successful family Sundays, I was too busy guiding the conversation through a series of light-hearted topics. But if I had hopes of a response from Josh, he soon put me right. Since our return he has become skilled at the art of polite inattention, a master of the unfocused gaze, the close examination of his food. Meeting this newly developed indifference, I was struck once again by the feeling that, somehow or other, I have engendered his disapproval.

Troubled by this and other thoughts, I lost momentum.

By instinct or chance, Katie chose this moment to come to life. Emerging from a dreamy mood, fired by a sudden vivacity, she launched into a stream of joky gossip and extravagant tales and scathing skits on the school staff, told with her special blend of theatrical effects and flourishes. When she breaks free from her doubts and sparkles like this, when she uses her extraordinary talent for mimicry, I am overcome by the most enormous pride and admiration. She has such brilliance, such gifts, that I can't help imagining a splendid future for her. Not as an actress – she's far too uncertain for that – but as a writer or journalist, maybe an artist, some occupation which would make full use of her breathtaking flair for observation.

The gossip exhausted, Katie began to tease Josh, reverting to an old banter they both know well, reducing him to grinning affection. Feeding on this, she began to laugh herself, a sound that gladdened my heart, until, in her rapidly escalating euphoria, her laughter took on a fierce, brittle edge. Then I called for the bill and we left.

Now, as Josh spreads his arms wide against the buffeting wind, an aircraft attempting take-off, Katie swoops down on him and, gripping him by the waist, steers him into a series of loops and turns. The two of them gather speed, wheeling in ever wilder arcs, heads down, legs windmilling behind, until they come to a sudden halt and look solemnly out over the heath, catching their breath. Then, draping an arm around Josh's shoulders, Katie leads him on at a slower pace. They walk head to head. I keep back, out of earshot.

They walked like this in Provence last summer, I remember, Katie's arm draped lazily over Josh's shoulders as we strolled through a vineyard one morning, before the heat came up. Harry stayed behind with me, trying to look as though this aimless wandering came naturally to him.

The holiday was unplanned, a sudden whim of Harry's. At two days' notice we flew to Marseilles, hired a car and took a large villa with swimming pool near Gordes. I said nothing about the expense, which must have been considerable, because I sensed that, for almost the first time since he'd lost his seat, Harry was reaching out to us for support, and, in some way I couldn't quite pin down, was reassessing his feelings towards us. Making an obvious effort to rise above his worries, he gave us long bursts of attention, he groaned smilingly at the children's jokes, he watched us with a sort of hungry absorption, as if something had happened to make him see us through new eyes.

Setting a fresh tone, he cut down on his drinking, he swam three times a day, he agreed with only token complaint to come with us on long ambles around the Provençal markets. Best of all, he gave time to Katie. He listened with concentration to her teenage ramblings, he bought her clothes, he encouraged her to try new styles. Once he spent a whole afternoon fine-plaiting strands of her hair.

He experimented with his own appearance too. He bought tight jeans that strained over a stomach that hadn't quite recovered from all those parliamentary lunches, shirts that he wore half unbuttoned to reveal plenty of chest, tie-dyed T-shirts, even – I never thought I'd see the day – a large wallet-cum-handbag of the sort that French and Italian men frequently carry but most heterosexual British men wouldn't be seen dead with for fear of mis-understandings. His hair had grown a little and he let it flop forward over his face, making him look softer and almost boyish.

I watched his efforts with a mixture of delight and, ignoble though it seemed at the time, a creep of doubt. I couldn't help wondering if it wasn't just a phase, if he wasn't simply playing some new role. But as the days went by these questions seemed increasingly irrelevant. It gave me such pleasure to see his absorption in the children, his patience with Katie, who, full of teenage excess, was difficult and charming and exhibitionist by turns. I loved watching the two of them together, talking in the shade of the almond tree or fooling around in the pool or reading side by side on the loungers.

This was the way things should be, I told myself; this was the way I longed for them to stay. If an itch of apprehension remained, I suppressed it.

I can imagine what Molly would say if I told her this story. She would say: Didn't you *see*? The answer is, I suppose I did, but the glimmering was so dark and unimaginable, my wish for our happiness so strong, that it was invisible.

Looking back, it would be easy to say that he was setting things up during that holiday, that there was a sly calculation in everything he did. The model father and husband, chalking up points for good behaviour, putting himself above suspicion. But I can't accept he was that devious. It suggests a sure and overwhelming purpose, and I'm not convinced he had that, not then.

If there was one thing I should have spotted, I suppose it was Harry's lack of spontaneity or joy. Though he laughed and played with the children, though he joined in our games and outings, there was a watchfulness about him, a concentration that was rather too fierce, a darkness that was like a warning. I put it down to business worries.

We had the usual trials that beset all holidays, lost car keys, fits of temper, overtiredness; from me, criticism of the mounting pile of Katie's expensive new clothes which we could have found at half the price in England. We got through these dramas, we made allowances and gave ground, we felt we were happy.

It was Katie who sabotaged the holiday half-way through the second week. For no apparent reason, and with bewildering abruptness, she withdrew into a sulk of mammoth proportions. Everything was foul, everything displeased her, none of us could do anything right. I tried reasoning with her, I tried cajoling her, I even tried being angry, but she put up such a wall of simmering resentment that my words seemed to bounce back at me, loaded with tension.

It was Harry who defused the situation. He showed a degree of tolerance that made my exasperation look unreasonable. Ignoring the worst of Katie's behaviour, he smiled when she least deserved it, he looked understanding at all times, and when her guard was down he slipped an arm round her and gave her a squeeze, as if to sympathise with the tribulations of being almost fifteen. I told him he was being marvellous. Accepting this, he smiled at me inattentively, with only the tiniest glint of shame.

Now, with the children out of sight ahead, I push on across the heath. The wind takes on new resonance. Above the droning and bluster I seem to hear the drag of the sea on the clattering shingle bank that lies somewhere beyond the farthest line of trees. I see the waves pulling at the shore, I hear the thunderous rattle and bounce of the stones, I feel the water sucking at my legs. An echo of panic pulls at my chest, a tug that is like a memory. Then, listening again, the sound seems to fade, and I'm no longer sure it was ever there.

From low-lying bracken and shivering grass, the path winds between tall terraces of gorse which deflect the relentless charge of the wind. Rounding a bend, I find

Katie waiting for me. She grins jauntily and, flipping a strand of hair from her eyes, loops an arm into mine.

'Beastly child,' she remarks carelessly in the general direction of Josh, scurrying ahead. 'Beastly, beastly. Quite the most revolting boy.'

'What's he done?'

'He won't let me have his Walkman.'

'Should he?'

'Definitely. Mine's bust. Only want it till next weekend. Little beast.' She chants a tuneless song, she bounces along at my side, face thrown up against the wind, hair fluttering out behind her. She is still riding high, humming with a nervous high-pitched energy.

'Oh, and he won't talk about school or why he walked out,' she said. 'Silly boy. I told him not to be so stupid. I told him doing things like that is okay so long as you do them for a *reason* and you don't get *caught*. I *mean*.' She rolls her eyes heavenward, she shapes her mouth into an exaggerated look of sisterly scorn.

'Did he say why he wanted to go away?'

'No-o-o,' she drawls dismissively. 'But I'd let him go, Mum. *Honestly*. It'll do him good. He's getting too beastly.' She adds in a bored tone, 'If he goes, I can always come home.' She hums the tune again.

This statement lies between us, burning slowly like a fuse. I say cautiously, 'Well, perhaps when we're settled in a new place. I thought of looking near the school anyway. Somewhere on the other side there, in one of those villages. But you wouldn't want to be home all the time, darling,' I say, forcing balance and reason into my voice. 'Weekends would be plenty. You'd miss your friends.'

She shrugs extravagantly, lifting my arm with hers. 'Oh, I don't know. I wouldn't mind.'

This surprises me. Immediately I begin to worry. 'School not so good?' I ask.

'Oh, it's all *right* . . . But sometimes the guys are so totally *juvenile*.' For guys I read girls. 'They're stuck on the same old things. Rock music, getting married, money – *really*. Obsessed with stupidities. And they pretend to be having these great love affairs!' She makes a face of incredulity. 'They get totally hysterical about these blokes. Calls, letters, you wouldn't believe it – hysterical. I mean, as if it was *important*. Even Jo Mills – of *all* people – she's got this wild crush over some bloke. Slobbers down the phone.' There's a note of injury in her voice which she covers with a defiant, 'I mean – fine, just *fine*, if that's what they want. But I really can't' – searching for the word, she throws a wild arm into the air – '*relate*. I mean, I just feel I'm sort of *beyond* all that.'

Beyond boys. I hope not. But I can see how she needs to persuade herself of the truth of this, how important it is for her to feel she has a high degree of control over her life. And I think for the moment she has her priorities absolutely right. There'll be plenty of time for boys when she's older.

'Otherwise . . .?' I ask.

'Oh, okay.'

'Sleeping all right? No dreams?'

She scoffs, 'Too tired.'

Josh, who has run out of steam, is loitering ahead, stripping bark from a switch of wood.

Ducking her head, Katie says something which is whipped away by the wind.

I lean closer. 'What?'

'One bad night,' she admits crossly, as if I have forced it out of her.

Katie has long had vivid dreams. Since she was twelve – or even sooner, I suppose – she has been prone to waking in the night in a state of panic. Her nightmares revolve around a profound sense of powerlessness – this was how Bob Block summarised it anyway – and the urge-to-flee, inability-to-escape terror that children learn to confront and overcome through the more violent fairy stories has for Katie remained all too real.

We have almost reached Josh. 'Write the dreams down,' I urge her. 'Send them to Bob. He'll be wanting to hear from you anyway.'

She gives a shrug that tells me that she is unlikely to bother. The next moment she unloops her arm from mine and grabs Josh's stick. They tussle, Josh strikes out with his foot, they exchange a barrage of sharp words. We start back in silence. Then, rediscovering her bright amusing persona, Katie wins Josh back with a show of abject affection and teasing flattery. By the time we sight the car, he is laughing again.

It's barely four but Katie wants to get straight back to school. This, I know, is because she wants to avoid the alternative which is to come home. We drive in silence, a silence that is contented and united. I feel that, all things considered, it has been a successful day.

Driving into the school grounds, I try to remember how many family Sundays we managed to achieve while Harry was alive. In the early years, quite a number, probably one in every three. Later, in the political years, it became very few. There was always something going on, lunch parties which drifted on into the late afternoon, more guests for tea and evening drinks, often people the children and I barely knew. Sometimes I didn't manage to give the children any time until they were going to bed.

Katie is reaching for the door handle before the car has even stopped. She prepares to bolt, then, twisting back abruptly, leans over and gives me a breathless hug. 'Mummy . . .'

I squeeze her roughly, I feel a surge of love.

'You're all right, Mummy?' she breathes.

'Me?' I make a face of mock surprise, I grin hard. 'I'm fine.' I am not going to give her the details about the search for *Minerva*, I am not going to tell her anything unless I absolutely have to.

Flinging a last 'Beastly child' at Josh, Katie jumps out and, sweeping her hair off her face with a flip of one hand, swings nonchalantly into the house.

Reversing into a turning place, I come back past the house to find the housemistress Mrs Anderson outside the front door, waiting to catch me.

'I was wondering—' She looks apologetically at Josh in the back seat. 'If you could spare a few minutes.'

Mrs Anderson's sitting-room is dominated by a three-piece suite in one of William Morris's more powerful prints, a swirling whirl of brown and amber that is repeated on the footstool and curtains. I sit in an armchair next to a table piled with exercise books whose covers are almost obliterated by inky doodles.

'I'm sorry to drag you in, but I thought it'd be best.' Mrs Anderson perches on the edge of the sofa, ramrod straight, a wiry fresh-faced woman of fifty or so, with the look of someone whose duty is painful but necessary. 'Are you sure Josh wouldn't like to sit in the kitchen?'

I tell her he'll be fine in the car.

'I'll try not to keep you. It's just that there was an incident on Friday and I wondered if Katie had told you about it.'

I just manage to shake my head.

'Oh.' She raised her eyebrows. 'Well, I thought you should know about it. It was nothing *too* serious. At least not in Mr Pelham's opinion. In fact, he hasn't told anyone but me. He didn't think it was worth bothering the head.' She gives me a little glance, to make sure I have appreciated the delicacy with which the situation has been handled. 'But the thing is, Katie assaulted Mr Pelham. Well, *technically* it was an assault. During a chemistry lesson. It wasn't a blow, really, so much as a – well, Mr Pelham called it a swipe. The back of her hand. It caught him on the cheek. No damage, no marks or anything. But hard enough. There didn't seem to be any reason. At least Mr Pelham couldn't think of any. Katie just seemed to get into a terrible blinding rage suddenly.'

We both ponder this for a moment, I with a small creep of dread.

'No reason at all?'

'Oh, I did ask her,' says Mrs Anderson. 'I spent a long time with her, but she couldn't seem to explain it. She didn't seem to know why she'd done it. She *said* she hardly remembered it.' Clearly Mrs Anderson does not go along with this idea. 'Anyway, we decided to put it down to stress, to all the work she's got to make up, to coming back in the middle of term. But I thought I'd better tell you.'

'Thank you. I'm – grateful.'

'Obviously I'll keep an eye on her. Encourage her to talk. But I have to say that it's rather uphill work at present.'

I look through her and beyond, absorbed by a vision of the chemistry lab. 'Mr Pelham – he, er . . .'

'Yes?'

'Is he at all . . . off-putting?'

'Frightening, you mean? No!' she declares emphatically.

'Very easy-going. All the girls like him. That's what makes it so extraordinary. He's one of the most popular members of staff.'

I would leave it at that, but I sense that some statement is expected of me. 'I can only say that I find it very unlike Katie.' I gesture my bafflement. 'Not her at all.'

I suppose this is what all parents say when their children misbehave. Mrs Anderson's face takes on the look of someone who's been here many times before.

'Well – thank you,' I say again.

'Just as well it was Mr Pelham,' she says as she leads the way to the door.

'Oh?'

'Men don't take these things quite so personally, do they?'

When I look uncomprehending she explains with an impish smile, 'They still forgive temperament in a woman, don't they?'

The recession is unrelenting, so people keep saying, but this street seems to be escaping the worst of it. The cars are only two or three years old, the red-brick semi-detached houses have fresh paint at their doors and windows, and well-tended gardens. In the midst of this tidy uniformity the two properties stand out uneasily, not only because of their size – double-fronted four-storeyed Victorian gothic villas, with carved barge-boards and ornate glass-covered porches, they tower over their neighbours – but because of their evident dilapidation. The threadbare front gardens are littered with bricks and fast-food cartons, the ground-floor windows are boarded over, and the local vandals have ensured that not a pane of the upper windows, not even those of the highest attic, remains unbroken.

The door of the right-hand house stands open. I step into twilight and the scent of damp and decay. Pursuing intermittent rattling sounds, I find Molly in a dim back room, pushing at some shutters which are bulging away from the window.

'God,' she cries, 'I think this place is going to fall apart before we ever get near it. Hold the torch, will you, love?'

She unlatches the metal bar securing the shutters over the window and with the soft tearing sound of rotten wood one of the shutters peels away from its hinges and drops to the floor.

'Damp, damp, damp!' declares Molly, gesturing upwards. 'Probably coming all the way from the roof. Got to the stage where I daren't look.' She dusts herself off and gives me a hug which sends the torch beam arcing round the room. 'How are you? How *are* you?' Without waiting for an answer, she relieves me of the torch and leads me towards the hall.

'Looking better,' she says, inspecting me in the light from the open door.

I raise an eyebrow at her.

Molly shows me over the rest of the ground-floor rooms then we sit on the stairs and spread the conversion plans over our knees. 'Not much wrong,' Molly says airily. 'Nothing that megabucks won't cure. In the last two years these houses have been busy doing what they do best – rotting away.'

'But when it's done, Molly . . .'

'Oh, it'll be great, sure. Only thing, I'll probably be dead by then. Frustration or rage, one'll get to me first.

Either way, I tell you I'll be taking Meacher with me. I'm told by a reliable source' – she lays a forefinger against her nose – 'for which read local reporter, that Meacher takes expensive holidays and has a new BMW. A humble councillor with a new BMW?' She narrows her eyes and scoffs heavily, 'I bet he saved a long time for it.'

I smile at her and shake my head.

'You don't believe me!' Molly declares. 'You think I'm imagining all this, but I tell you, I've got a nose for these things. That planning committee's got a smell about it, and it's not a pleasant one.'

Championing her young offenders against a largely uncaring world, battling the grosser absurdities of officialdom, Molly is apt to see obstruction at every turn.

'What about your tame councillor?' I ask. 'How are you getting on with him?'

'Barry. You mean, *Barry*.' She sings the name, her voice swooping low with amusement. 'Listen, I've drunk so much coffee in the last few days I've got a caffeine-rated heartbeat.' She flutters a hand against her chest. 'He drops in about six every evening. Won't leave.' She gives me a cat-like smile. 'I think he's lonely.'

'And . . .?'

'He's doing what he can. Asking Meacher awkward questions about why the permission can't go through. Trying to get the whole thing onto the agenda for the next council meeting.' She makes a wry face. 'It won't be enough, of course.'

'Why not?'

'Because the local action group's too well geared up. *Someone, somewhere* is feeding them all the right ammunition.' She throws me a significant look. 'Their latest move is to object on the grounds of noise pollution. What really worries them, of course, is that the boys are going to be junkies who'll freak out on the doorsteps.' She slants her eyes. 'Or worse, sneak in and pinch their videos.'

'Perhaps you should have an open day at the Project. Invite the local people.'

She starts to fold the plans. 'What, so they can meet the boys and stare at their long hair and torn jeans and pierced noses and tattoos and have all their prejudices confirmed?'

The sun emerges, throwing a brilliant beam through the doorway and onto the dusty floorboards. Outside, a woman propels a pushchair past the gateway and pauses to stare in at us.

'Have a good look, won't you?' Molly calls but not loudly enough for the woman to hear.

The woman moves on.

'What about Jack?' I say. 'I know you're not keen, but this is just the sort of thing he should be doing to raise his profile. And he respects you, Molly. Really.'

'But he doesn't *like* me. And he knows I don't like him.' She stands up with a rattle of arm bangles. 'I provoke him.'

I get up. I say firmly, 'Molly, he's trying to win the candidature. All you have to do is find an angle in it for him. Just give him the facts, rationally and calmly.'

'I can't argue any way but emotionally, Ellen, my darling. That's the way I am. Anyway,' she says archly, 'he and Meacher are like this' – she presses two fingers together – 'so what's the point?'

This is one of her throwaway lines, the sort of provocative statement that pitches her arguments into the realms of confrontation.

'I should be like you,' she says not too seriously. 'Sensible, reasonable, sweet—'

'*Sweet!*'

'—loved and trusted by men. Someone they feel safe with, someone who brings out the protective in them.'

I roll my eyes.

A softening comes over Molly's face. 'You've never seen it, have you? How men react to you.'

'Because they don't.'

She shakes her head. 'They admire you, they want to take care of you, they want to impress you.'

'Molly . . .' I crease up my face in protest, thinking that, even if there were some truth in this, it didn't work with Harry.

'Harry too,' says Molly, reading my mind effortlessly. 'You brought out the best in him, you know.'

'And then I didn't.' I make a move towards the door.

Molly, realising she has stumbled into sensitive territory, touches my arm, a gesture of regret, then gathers up her voluminous shoulder bag from the stairs.

Shifting to a lighter tone, she remarks, 'I suppose he's going to get selected?'

'Who?'

'Jack.'

'I have no idea. I'm trying to keep out of it.'

'But you're going to this party tonight?'

'I'm afraid so.'

Half-joking but half-serious too, she wags a finger at me. 'Well, don't let Jack use you. Don't let him get the better of you!'

She goes to the door and stares into the sunlit road. Turning back, she leans against the door jamb. 'My councillor told me something yesterday,' she says boldly. 'On our fifth coffee, this was, when he was totally out of control.' She flashed her eyes briefly and suggestively. 'It

266

was about that development by the bypass, the one that Meacher got re-zoned for housing, the one that's going to make Jack his second fortune. Well, Barry told me that before Jack got hold of the land it used to belong to a property company.' She paused, she eyes me meaningfully. 'By the name of Ainswick.'

Ainswick. I realise this must have significance but I can't fit it into the scheme of things, I can't assign it a value.

Molly holds up two parallel fingers, Scout-style. 'Guaranteed reliable information.'

As I try to work out what Molly's getting at, she rushes in ahead of me and brandishes a conclusion. 'Ainswick applied for re-zoning several times and never got it, right? Then Jack buys the land and – bingo!' She casts me a meaningful look, she murmurs sardonically, 'In the circumstances I don't somehow think Jack'll be in the mood to back our unpopular little half-way house project against Meacher, do you? Not when he owes him so much.'

I see Jack leaning against the kitchen counter that night after the memorial service, I see him watching me as I stir Josh's baked beans, I hear him telling me how he fell out with Harry over a piece of land which he'd bought from Ainswick and which had, against all expectations, come good.

'It doesn't necessarily mean . . .' I shrug, reluctant to go into detail. 'Jack's always been lucky.'

Molly's eyebrows shoot up at this. She is longing to chop this remark off at the knees but, with a visible effort, she restrains herself. She says instead, 'There was something else. According to Barry – who doesn't get these things wrong – Ainswick still owns a patch of land on that side of the city, right next to Jack's development.'

I show suitable surprise.

'You didn't know?'

'I never knew anything about Ainswick.'

'Well, it might be worth something!' She delves deep into her bag.

'I don't know . . . The market's meant to be dead.'

'But if the land gets re-zoned! Then it'll be worth a ton. Someone's probably after it already.' She drags some keys out of her bag and gives me a sly glance. 'Maybe even Jack?' The glitter of possibilities burns bright in her eyes. She has no way of knowing, and I am forbidden to tell her, that time is running out for Ainswick.

'Well . . . I'll ask.'

'Do!' she exclaims. 'You never know!'

We step out onto the porch. The worst of yesterday's gale passed in the night, but there is still quite a wind. Small clouds speed busily across the sky and in the neglected garden a plastic bag stirs uneasily against a soft-drink can.

Molly locks the door and, flipping a heavy hasp over an equally sturdy staple, snaps the giant padlock home. 'Ironic, isn't it?' she says, surveying the securely fastened door. 'All this to keep young offenders out, when the whole aim of the project is to get them in.' She drops the keys back into her bag. She peers at me, she hums, she passes a hand laughingly in front of my eyes. 'Ellen?'

I come to.

'I lost you there, gal. No one home.'

Molly wants me to go to a café for lunch, but I tell her I have too much to do.

'Money okay?' she asks for no apparent reason, and I wonder how much she guesses of my troubles.

I kiss her cheek. 'They're sorting it out.'

Driving back to Pennygate, a shadow stirs in the back

of my mind. Sitting at Harry's desk, staring out at the restless trees, I realise that this worry has been circling the edges of my thoughts for some time, that it took one of Molly's remarks to give it definition. When she talked about the patch of land next to Jack's I wondered, as I had wondered so indistinctly before, if everything possible was being done for Ainswick. There was a determined defeatism in Gillespie that seemed out of proportion to Ainswick's situation. I didn't understand then, and I don't understand now, why everything is so unmarketable. I can't help thinking that Gillespie has little incentive to spend much time or effort on Ainswick's affairs.

I also wonder if there are other assets that I haven't heard about. I'm not about to subscribe to conspiracy theories – I will leave those to Molly. I don't think that anyone is failing to tell me these things on purpose. Rather, I imagine they're sparing me these details out of the belief that I won't be interested.

Margaret, having done all she can at Pennygate, is back in the Ipswich office more or less full time. I call her there and ask for the name and number of the City estate agent who is handling the Shoreditch building.

She doesn't ask why I should want the information, though I feel bound to meander through an explanation about someone having asked me to pass it on to them.

I make myself a coffee, I sit in front of the telephone, I plan what I will say, finally I dial. My palms are already damp, my heart fluttering; I don't know why these excursions into the unknown cause me such difficulty.

A female answers in a rapid sing-song. I tell her it's about a commercial property in the Shoreditch area. She clicks me through to a cool-voiced woman who announces herself as Miranda Stephenson.

'Oh yes, we have quite a bit around that area,' says Ms Stephenson, sounding keen for business. 'May I ask who's enquiring?'

It's only a small deception to give my unmarried name and the name of the graphic design company I used to work for.

'And what sort of square footage are you looking for?'

'There was a particular building, in fact. We saw your board up. The Richmond Building?'

'Oh . . . Richmond House?'

'That's it.'

'Let me see . . . I'm pretty sure . . . ' I picture her bringing it up on her screen. 'Yes . . . It's *meant* to be under offer at present.'

'Offer?' I breathe through a mouth that is suddenly dry. 'Oh.' I feel a lunge of relief, a reversal of emotion that leaves me breathless. 'This has just happened then?' I ask, trying to suppress the delight in my voice.

'Well . . .'

'The last few days?'

'No.' Her voice takes on a disgruntled note. 'Actually the property's been off the market for some time but the vendor didn't want the sign taken down.'

My emotions swing back. A moment of stillness before I ask. 'How long has it been under offer?'

'I'm sorry?'

I am speaking too softly. Raising my voice, I repeat the question.

'Well . . . it's been some weeks now.' A hesitation as if she is making up her mind about something. 'If you were interested, you could *try* a counter-offer. There's nothing to stop you. I can't guarantee anything, of course.'

I feel the clarity that weariness and a sense of injury can bring. 'The existing offer, can you tell me—?'

'We know nothing about it,' she interrupts briskly.

It is an instant before I grasp the implication. 'It didn't come through your office, then?'

'No. We were just informed that there'd been a private offer.'

'Some weeks ago?'

'That's right.'

I whisper, 'Thank you, er . . . Ms Stephenson.'

'Would you like details of any other properties?'

'Perhaps . . . next week,' I say, blushing inwardly. 'Can I come back to you?'

Jack fastens his seatbelt and, with a gesture of wonderment, tilts his head at me and says, 'You look absolutely gorgeous.' His voice is low and gravelly, the tone he reserves for comments like this.

I don't know why he says this; I've given him no reason to. Instead of blow-drying my hair I have let it dry naturally into odd waves and kinks. The cream dress I have chosen is plain and unadventurous, I wear no jewellery, not even studs in my ears. I have given my eyelashes only the barest dusting of mascara and have done nothing to lift the colour of my skin, which with the fading of my tan has turned a little sallow. I don't need a psychiatrist to tell me that I am trying to vanish into the background.

I'm already nervous about the time. We're due to meet Charles and Anne outside the local party chairman's house at six-thirty sharp. If we're late the look on Anne's face doesn't bear thinking about.

Making no comment, smiling benignly, Jack starts up

and we move off at a leisurely pace. Manœuvring the car around the pot-holes with an idle swing of one hand, he takes a series of sidelong looks at me. 'It's all in the bones,' he announces with a lazy smile. 'A matter of structure.' His free hand describes the shape of a face, then curves neatly across to drop over my hands which I have carelessly left unattended in my lap. 'Women have either got it or they haven't.' He gives my fingers a squeeze. 'You've got it.'

'Tell me about the party,' I say, making a gesture that requires me to move my hands away. 'Who'll be there?'

'Who *won't*? The committee. All the shortlisted candidates. Even the terrifying Mrs Reeves.' With this thought he brings his hand back to the wheel. 'Hot from some good cause, no doubt. I'm just hoping she'll overdo the credentials. Alarm them with her good works among racially disadvantaged sex offenders or whatever it is she does when she's not being a political powerhouse.' His eyes flash with agitation or annoyance. 'I'm getting quite nervous actually.' He puts on his little-boy-lost look. 'Saturday's only five days away. I'm dreading the grilling. A solid hour in front of the committee, fielding every trick question they can throw at me, and the slightest hesitation a death warrant. And I'm still weak on agricultural policy and Europe. And I think – well, I *know* – someone's going to be gunning for me.'

'Why?'

'Oh, being successful isn't enough to make you politically correct nowadays, even among the Tories; you have to be a community benefactor as well. *Especially* when you're a developer. You're meant to be immorally rich, even in the depths of a recession. To make amends for these filthy great profits that are meant to fall into your lap, you're expected to have donated a good proportion of every development for the last ten years to first-time buyers or old people or some worthy community project. People still have an eighties image of developers – you know, easy money, fat cats in flash cars – that sort of thing.' I think of Jack's immaculate clothes, his air of self-indulgence, the quiet luxuriousness of the car in which we are travelling, and make no comment. 'They don't realise it's bloody hard graft, like any other business,' he says wistfully. 'Nor do they appreciate that the recession's hit us longer and harder than anyone else, and margins have been too tight for all this generosity.'

I almost miss the opportunity, it has come so easily. 'What about the bypass development?'

He frowns distractedly. 'What? Oh, that's *one* project which should pass muster. I've donated the city three prime acres for an out-of-town sports complex. I'm not sure about the timing though ... Announced two weeks ago. They might think I fixed it to coincide with the candidature proceedings. Well, I *did*, of course . . .' He slides me a conspiratorial glance. 'What I don't need is this fellow standing up and suggesting that this charitable work of mine is rather sudden, that I'm doing it just to earn good marks.' We hit a pot-hole and he curses softly. Slowing down, he remarks, 'Harry was much better organised about these things. Regularly made donations – though never *half* as much as people thought – and with a brilliant amount of drum-beating. But then he always had a feel for the old PR, didn't he? We used to argue like hell about Ainswick's philanthropic gestures. I said we weren't running a bloody charity. Harry said it was money well spent.'

We turn out of the drive onto the Woodbridge road and, free of the pot-holes, the Mercedes lunges forward. It's six-ten. Plenty of time; I relax a little.

'The bypass development, it's going well then?' I ask.

He glances at me blankly. 'What?'

'If you can afford to give land away.'

I sense a sharpening of his attention, but then money is a subject that Jack always discusses with concentration. 'So long as the recession lifts in the next two years, it should do all right. Why?'

'Oh, it was only . . .' Without finishing this, I say in a bit of a rush, 'I believe Ainswick still owns some land nearby.' Catching his eye, I raise my eyebrows and turn this into a question.

A beat of silence then Jack says with the air of someone who is not entirely clear, 'Nearby?'

'Close to your bypass development.'

He asks in a voice that is almost liquid, 'Did Gillespie tell you that?'

'I can't remember,' I say, not entirely truthfully.

We come up fast behind another car and Jack peers out to overtake. Thinking better of it, he brakes and tucks in behind.

'Well, I hope he also told you that it's on the wrong side of the bypass and with disputed access.'

'No, I . . . he didn't say that.'

'Well, he should have. That should have been the first thing he told you. He shouldn't have let you think it was in the same sort of class.' He keeps glancing at me as he says this. 'He *didn't*, did he?'

'We hadn't got that far.'

'Ellen, my dear lovely thing' – his hand reaches across to find me again – 'there aren't going to be any miracles, I'm afraid. No immediate restoration of Ainswick's fortunes.' He gives my leg several light pats. 'It's never going to be as simple as that.'

'I hadn't thought it would be,' I say defensively, moving my legs so that his hand slips away.

'Now you're cross with me,' he says in his misunderstood voice.

'Not at all.' Which isn't strictly true. I am upset both by his condescension and my emotional reaction to it. Putting on a businesslike voice, I ask, 'One thing I'm not clear about – perhaps you'd know. The Shoreditch building – is it meant to be on the market?'

'Ummm . . .' He blows elegantly through his teeth. 'I'm not the person to ask about that, Ellen. I wouldn't know.' He reverts to a tone of patient explanation, as if I need things spelled out for me. 'You'd have to ask Gillespie. But . . .' He makes a show of considering the matter, the line of his perfect profile contorted with concentration. 'I would think it *must* be. *Everything* must be for sale.' He asks lightly, 'Why?'

'The agents don't seem to know what's going on.'

'Oh? You've tried them, have you?'

'Yes.'

His eyes dart across. He gives a mirthless chuckle. 'What – chivvying them along?'

'Just – asking.'

'Well done,' he says, repeating it with enthusiasm, as if he is only now beginning to appreciate my resourcefulness. 'Good girl. *Good* girl. They can get bloody lazy, those agents.'

His attention returns to his driving as we pause in the centre of the road to cross the opposite carriageway and pass down a narrow side road which leads to the local party chairman's house. It is only six-sixteen.

'What do you think of Gillespie?' I ask.

'Mmm?' he says with an air of preoccupation. 'Oh, he's

all right.' He spins the car through a tight bend before asking, 'Why?'

'Just wondered.'

'You've seen him since you've been back? He's sorting your finances out?'

'Yes. But . . .'

'Mmm?'

'I do find him – difficult.'

'He *is* rather a cold fish, I suppose. But *solid*. Knows his stuff. Just his manner. Doesn't frighten you, does he?' He gives a fond laugh.

'I wouldn't have said—'

'Ah, here we are!'

It is six-twenty as we turn into the driveway of the chairman's home, a sprawling house in the English hacienda style with a Spanish-tiled roof and balconies with elaborate inward-curving S-shaped wrought-iron railings and heavily rouched curtains at the windows. The lane outside and the drive itself are already lined with parked cars. Undaunted, Jack drives straight up to the house and parks on the garage apron, blocking in two cars. There is no sign of Anne or Charles.

Jack twists the driving mirror round and, squinting into it, runs his hands over his hair.

I don't know why I choose this moment, but I ask, 'Jack?'

He raises an eyebrow at the mirror and sets his jaw more firmly and narrows his eyes, refining some look.

'Mmm?'

'You would tell me, wouldn't you, if there was anything . . .' What am I trying to say? '. . . anything I should know?'

Jack is barely following me. 'What do you mean?'

I don't know how to put it. 'Anything you hadn't told me?'

'What?' Homing in at last, he turns to me in puzzlement. 'Anything I hadn't told you?' he repeats mechanically. 'You mean, to do with Harry?'

'Yes.'

He gives me a strange look, as if he isn't sure how to take this, and declares in mild protest, 'There's nothing, Ellen. Well, nothing I know about. Why? Has something happened?'

'No. It was just . . .'

He glances at his watch. 'Well, whatever it is, I really don't think this is the best moment to discuss it.' Flinging the door open he climbs out and comes round to help me out.

'I suppose I meant – was there anything else worrying him?'

He slams the car door shut. 'Anything *else*?' he says, looking vague again. 'I think he had quite enough to be going on with, Ellen. Don't you?'

Touching his hair once again, he takes my elbow and walks me briskly towards the front door. I look for Anne and Charles among the people straggling up the drive. Sensing that Jack is about to sweep me inside, I hold back, I remind him that we have promised to wait for the others.

'But I saw their car,' exclaims Jack, waving in the direction of the gates, 'out in the road. They're already here.'

'We arranged to meet at the door,' I say. Anne and Charles had suggested meeting at their place, but Jack had pleaded lack of time.

'But they're already here,' Jack insists, unable to conceal a tinge of irritation. He turns aside to greet a couple of approaching guests with robust words and a broad politician's smile. Turning back, his smile pales and he says in the tone of someone who is being unreasonably tried, 'Well, I could go in and check, I suppose.'

'Please.'

Feeling conspicuous, I position myself some distance from the door beside a bed of vermilion begonias which I pretend to inspect with the attention of a keen gardener. It is no kind of cover and I'm soon spotted by some ebullient arrivals who tramp over and tell me how sorry they are about Harry and how much he will be missed. Faced by the prospect of a roomful of equally well-meaning people, I feel a shaft of panic.

Jack's laughter echoes from the porch and he reappears grinning over his shoulder at someone inside the house. Striding quickly over, he announces, 'They're here! I asked Barrow.'

'You're sure?'

'Look, here's Alan!' Putting a firm arm around my shoulders he leads me forward to meet the rotund figure of our host, the local party chairman, who is hurrying out of the house towards us. I don't need to ask how he knew I was here.

'Ellen, my dear,' says the chairman, clutching my hand with visible emotion. 'So delighted you're here. So pleased. But you must come straight in! Can't have you out here. Come in! Come in!'

'Have Charles and Anne arrived?' I ask.

'Er . . . not sure. But Sally will know. Come in, come in.'

I allow myself to be guided as far as the hall where I touch cheeks with Sally, the chairman's wife, a woman with a liking for bright colours and costume jewellery and a deep tan to set them against.

'Ellen!' she cries in a piercing voice. 'But how absolutely

wonderful that you could come! And . . .' Raising her pencilled eyebrows, she looks from Jack to me and back again, a conjectural smile hovering at the corners of her mouth.

The double doors to the main reception room are wide open. Several people turn at the sound of Sally's voice; I see their eyes fasten on me and Jack, I see them pass comment. I realise, with a knot of apprehension, that I can't see either Anne or Charles. From the thick of the room Barrow, the party agent, smiles at me and raises his glass. Catching my signal, he excuses himself and comes over.

He tells me Anne and Charles have not arrived yet.

The anger flows over me like a hot sea. Wordlessly, I turn away, pass quickly behind Jack and make my way to the door.

Too late. Charles and Anne are already stationed by the flower bed, looking expectantly down the drive. As I emerge from the house, Anne glances in my direction and does a double take. Her face darkens, her mouth works rapidly. 'I see!' she hisses as I approach. 'I *see*!' She sucks in a bitter breath, she fights an inner battle. Finally she exclaims, 'So much for a united front!'

Barrow drives me back to Pennygate. Thankfully he doesn't try to talk until we arrive.

'If there's anything I can do, Mrs Richmond?' he says quietly.

'I won't be coming to any more events, I'm afraid.'

'No,' he says, having grasped something of what has been going on. 'I quite understand.'

The house envelops me in silence. Before going to Jill's to collect Josh, I pour myself a glass of wine and go and sit in the conservatory, looking out at the softness of the garden and the metallic sheen of the river, listening to the faint twittering of the birds, drawing my breath slowly from the diaphragm and counting it in and out.

Molly was right; Jack isn't one to miss a trick.

Passing through the kitchen, the red-eyed answering machine blinks lazily at me. I decide to leave it but change my mind and press the playback. A call from Leonard, his voice gruff and remote: a few matters that need discussion. A call from the mother of Josh's schoolfriend Ben.

Then Moreland.

I move closer, I listen to his voice, I picture his face.

Suddenly his words loop out and fill the air. Everything seems to slow down, I have a sense of disassociation and absolute clarity.

It has happened.

They think they have found *Minerva*.

ELEVEN

The fourth day. I wake as the first grey fingers of light touch the room. I wake instantly, with an obscure sense of alarm. I stare at the open window, looking for some movement in the wisteria, listening for a telltale rustle under the eaves.

Nothing. The leaves, black against the lightening sky, hang inert. I get up and go to the window. A mist hangs low and thin over the garden. The silence is very deep, broken only by bird calls that rise sweetly through the stillness.

The wind has gone. After four blustery days when the shipping forecast was peppered with gale warnings and I fancied I could see the whitecaps advancing across the distant horizon, it has finally died. This is the day, then, when the authorities will probably make their first attempt to examine the wreck.

I bathe and dress with care, I take particular trouble with my hair and makeup, then I go down to the study to wait until I can decently call Moreland. In the mornings I try not to call him before quarter past seven. Once – I think it was two days ago – I phoned earlier and, though he insisted he was awake and sounded as pleased as ever to talk to me, I could hear the sleep in his voice.

To pass the time, I spread the chart Moreland has given me across the desk. I know its patterns and colourings by heart, the shapes of the banks, the names of the buoys. Moreland has marked the position of the probable wreck with a pencilled star – we're careful to call it the 'probable' wreck, as if this will protect me from disappointment, though disappointment is not the word I would have chosen.

The pencilled star lies some ten miles off the mouth of our river, in a direction that Moreland calls east-northeast, beyond the northern tip of a sandbank called the Shipwash. I was convinced the water must be deep there – it's coloured white on the chart – but Moreland told me that none of the North Sea is very deep. Indeed, close by the pencilled star, in tiny print, is the figure 22, which is the depth of the water in metres: twenty-two metres, about seventy-five feet. This depth creates no difficulty for the salvage boat, so Moreland explained to me; they simply drop a closed-circuit camera with a light source over the side of their vessel, on the end of a cable. All that is required is a reasonably calm sea.

Like now, like today.

The probable wreck was discovered in just the way they said it would be: snagged on the nets of a trawler.

Moreland gives me these details when I ask for them, which is usually in the early evenings when he and I are sitting in the conservatory having a glass of wine. For some reason I can't bear to hear these snippets of information from anyone else, not even Charles or Leonard. There is something about Moreland that lets me believe against all the odds that he will not bring me bad news.

The trawler was a small one, he told me. It was dragged to a halt when its nets caught on the obstruction. Their echo-sounder had given them no warning; the printed trace showed only the smallest of blips on the sea bed. It took the crew three hours to free the nets. When they finally retrieved them they found gashes and cuts in the mesh, as if the strands had been grinding against jagged metal. No obstruction having been reported anywhere near that position, the skipper followed standard procedure and notified the coastguard.

In the evenings, when Moreland and I are sitting quietly in the conservatory, he frequently tells me that this object on the sea bed could well be a container lost off a container ship, that these containers are always getting swept overboard in bad weather, that they can float for days or weeks before sinking, often ending up many miles from where they were lost. I know he tells me this because he wants to prepare me for whatever is going to happen, and because he is, I sense, increasingly concerned about me, but I don't think either of us is really convinced by the idea.

I'm feeling cold. Folding the chart away, I go up to my bedroom in search of a sweater. Passing the dressing-room door, I open it abruptly, I'm not sure why. I stare at Harry's clothes with something close to resentment. Maybe my mourning has run its course, maybe my compassion has simply run dry, but my memories are hardening. I want his clothes gone, I want his presence removed. Too much is happening; I want my life back again.

I will ask Molly to take the clothes away when she comes over later.

Downstairs again, I make a forbidden cup of coffee – the caffeine has started to give me terrible palpitations – and return to the study. It's only quarter to seven.

I stare at a stack of letters and documents that I should have dealt with days ago, and leaf through them half-heartedly. Succumbing to restlessness, I range through the house, wandering from room to room, standing for a while, looking at objects or pictures or nothing much at all, before moving on again.

I know I'm wearing myself down, I know my nerves are bar-taut and that any weight I might have gained has dropped straight off me again. I realise I should be taking something to slow me down, Librium or one of the other downers they fed me after Harry's death. But what I need more than anything, the only medicine worth having, is an end to this waiting.

Back in the study, threatened by bleak thoughts, I drift into fantasy. This is my new indulgence, my sanity preserver.

I think about the cottage that the children and I will find, the life we will lead there, the simple pleasures we will have. I imagine picking up my career again on a freelance basis, and, to get me out of the house, perhaps doing some volunteer work at Molly's project. An existence that will be remarkable for little but its normality.

I picture all this, but I don't try to match it too closely to reality. Not just at the moment; the gaps frighten me too much.

These fantasies feed pleasantly off each other in an addictive sort of way. I find myself going off in unexpected directions, some of them bizarre, some exciting, some forbidden.

The forbidden ones relate to Moreland. At first I thought of him in the way one thinks of people who are unavailable: I placed both of us in another context, another life. I imagined what might have happened if we'd met years ago.

But in the last day or so my thoughts have shifted and

focused, and I no longer think of the two of us in some hazy hypothetical past, but in the present. These fantasies are, I'm well aware, far from harmless. But whatever the dangers, I don't make much effort to prevent them. I can only live from day to day.

I picture him now, in bed. I see him emerging slowly from sleep. And I think how smooth and firm his skin must be. How I would love to feel his body beside me in the night when I cannot sleep.

I start violently as the phone rings. Before Moreland can say anything, I'm laughing into the phone.

'All right?' he asks.

'Not much sleep,' I admit.

'You didn't take anything?'

'No.'

I said I would take some tablets, I promised in fact, but he doesn't rebuke me. 'Ellen—'

'The wind's gone.'

'Yes. The boat's left. It's on its way out there now.'

My heart is hot against my chest. 'They told you?'

'Just now.'

'It'll be today then?'

'Yes.' Typically he qualifies this, taking me through all the likely snags again. 'Assuming the position they got was accurate, assuming they can locate it. And assuming there's no technical hitch, which is always a possibility with that equipment.'

'Well!' I make a nervous sound. 'Let's hope then!'

Already hungry for his company, I ask him if he can come a bit earlier today, at five or so.

'I'll try. And Ellen—? Try not to think about it too much.'

I do my best. Waking Josh, I chatter incessantly through

breakfast and on the drive to school. He looks baffled by my sudden wave of words, and vaguely wary. He doesn't know about the salvage boat. I have forbidden anyone to tell him. Katie doesn't know either, though strictly speaking this breaks the promise we made to each other in America.

On the way back from the school I meet the postman at the top of the drive and wait while he extracts my mail from the back of his van. I sit in the car and sort quickly through it.

Nothing from Guernsey. It is more than a week since I wrote.

There is, however, a solid packet from London EC1. I open it back at the house, fortified by another cup of coffee. It's from Gillespie and contains a two-page letter, closely typed, and a bound document entitled *Financial Plan*. The plan is twenty pages long. I flick quickly through it, I study a page at random. Under year columns there are ranks of figures, and at the sides, headings covering such things as tax liabilities, mortgages and interest. One category catches my eye. Household expenditure (estimated). It is broken down into things like food, clothing, insurance, domestic staff, equipment. The total is enormous. What is Gillespie thinking of? Does he think I'm wedded to this lifestyle? Does he imagine I can't go back?

Discouraged, I put this to one side, I go through the rest of the mail. There is a handwritten letter from Tim Schwartz. I read it with a sense of inevitability and foreboding.

'. . . *I'm afraid it's becoming impossible for me to hold things off any longer,*' Schwartz says. '*The trustees are asking for an explanation for the delay in finalising the accounts, and I feel duty bound to give them the facts as I know them.*'

Duty bound. Yes, I can see that.

With heavy heart, I start to draft a letter. I say I'm sorry I haven't been in touch but I haven't found anything that might shed light on the matter. Would it be helpful if I came and met the trustees and discussed the problem with them? In the meantime I'll continue to try to find out how the money went astray. Rereading this last sentence, I cross it out and stare at the page, no longer sure of what I'm trying to achieve.

My mind travels out to sea. I picture the salvage vessel. I imagine it as a tug-like craft, squat and functional. I see it wallowing slightly in the swell, I picture a cabin full of electronics, things that blink and flicker and buzz quietly, and in the centre a group of men huddled round a TV monitor which is relaying the picture from the sea bed.

What do they see? *God, what do they see?*

I pick up the pencil again and, crumpling the draft letter into the bin, take a fresh sheet of paper and try again.

The sentences freeze and shift, losing meaning. I reach into the back of the drawer and pull out the Mountbay notepaper, as if the sight of it might yet spring ideas into my head. A company incorporated in Guernsey. A company which is wrapped in secrecy and tax advantages, which is administered by anonymous people, leaving nothing open to public gaze.

But perhaps I'm reading too much into this secrecy. Perhaps secrecy was not the purpose of this company but merely a by-product. Perhaps the little worm of unease that eats at me whenever I think of Harry and Mountbay is misplaced. Even as I think this, the unease curls in my stomach.

I wonder if Harry put something on paper and I just haven't found it. Presumably he would have needed at least one contact number in Guernsey, and some scribbled notes, maybe a bank reference or two.

Damn you, Harry. I could have done without all this.

Damn you . . . I can say that now without any guilt at all.

I look up the dialling code for Guernsey: 0481. I search for the prefix in Harry's diary and old address book. I look through his desk. I don't really expect to find anything, but on this problematic morning the task is suitably mindless and absorbing.

Nothing in the desk, but, driven by a need to leave no corner unsearched, haunted by the thought of finding something in a couple of months' time when it'll be too late, I cannot leave it alone.

Starting on the lowest bookshelves, I remove each volume in turn, glancing at the endpapers and riffling through the text, working my way slowly round the room. The exercise is strangely cathartic; already I feel better for knowing that this one room, at least, will be free of surprises.

The house line rings several times and gets picked up by the answering machine. Jill's voice calls down the passage, announcing her arrival, and presently the low whine of the vacuum cleaner sounds from a far corner of the house.

I reach the second level of shelves and a leather-bound set of Macaulay's essays. Harry acquired these and other old books from a dealer who specialised in ready-assembled libraries of suitably venerable appearance. Harry got round to reading a number of classic political works, but not much else; he said he was too busy keeping abreast of present-day politics.

Above, and probably two hours ahead of me, are modern political biographies – three on Margaret

Thatcher, a cluster of previous prime ministers, the odd chancellor – and works by political analysts. Higher still are travel books and mellow volumes of indeterminate title that have a long-untouched look. On the top shelf are neat stacks of *National Geographic*s and other journals which Harry collected years ago.

After an hour I take a break, still only a quarter of the way along the third shelf. Looking for something to read with my coffee, I take out a large-format book on India which, with several other coffee-table books, is lying end-on in a stack further along the third shelf.

Sliding it back some minutes later, I notice a slim large-format book which has been squeezed into the end of the row by standing it on its front edge.

It is an art book. Of sorts. It contains photographs of firm female bodies with high breasts, dramatically and artfully lit, set against rough stone walls or oddly pro-portioned rooms, the sweeps of flesh taken from unusual perspectives, curving out of deep shadows or illuminated by unexpected shafts of light. The poses are provocative but also, for all their aspirations to high art, rather banal, fingertips hovering on the point of fleshly contact or idly brushing downy thighs.

Harmless, if you like that sort of thing. If it weren't for the girls. They look so young, little more than children, though it is hard to be sure because, disturbingly, their faces are obscured in each shot, either turned away or hidden in darkness or cloaked by falling hair. As if the readers' lusts required a total absence of personality, bodies chopped off at the neck.

Leafing through it, I decide that, for all the artistic gloss, it's really rather tacky stuff. I'm not sure which troubles me more, the headless bodies or my vision of Harry sitting here in the study, looking at them. I don't need to guess what face he put to these lush young bodies. Certainly not mine.

The business line rings.

'I was wondering if you'd received my letter all right, Ellen. And the financial plan?'

Recognising Gillespie's voice, I am transported back to a state of uneasiness. I am thrown, too, by his use of my first name.

I murmur thanks. I explain I haven't had time to look at the plan yet.

'Plenty of time. No hurry.' There is an odd note to his voice which I can't immediately identify. 'I just wanted to say that if it would help at all, I'd be very happy to come up to Suffolk and take you through it.' I realise now: he is attempting to sound friendly. The affability sits uncomfortably on him, like an under-rehearsed performance.

I wonder vaguely what has brought this on. I thank him again. I tell him I'll let him know.

'Of course. Take your time,' he says, as if reasonableness and understanding were his benchmarks.

I prepare to ring off but Gillespie is in a communicative mood. He tells me about the various deals he has done on the mortgage, how he is quite pleased with the terms, how he has tried to cover all contingencies, how he has managed to cover me for at least the next six months.

While he's talking, I prop myself against the desk, I look across the room to where the art book lies open on top of the base cupboards.

'By the way,' Gillespie is saying, 'I'm appointing new agents for the Shoreditch building. I wasn't satisfied that the old ones were performing as well as they might.'

Cautiously I pull out the chair and sit at the desk.

'. . . They've been cutting back on staff, and there's always a price to pay for that. I'm not promising the new people'll find a buyer, of course, but they're highly professional and they should give the thing some new impetus. The market's bottomed out now, so you never know, there might be a bit of interest.'

The suspicion that has been floating through my mind forms and hardens. I see Jack in all this. Jack has been telling tales behind my back.

'Hello? Are you there?'

'I . . . There's never been any sort of offer on the building, has there?' I ask.

'Just the one. But, as I told you, it was derisory.'

'No others?'

'No.' He is wary. 'Why?'

'Someone told me the place was under offer, that it'd been taken off the market.'

'Who told you that?' His voice has taken on all its old smoothness and authority.

If he's been talking to Jack, he'll know the answer to this already. 'I spoke to the agents,' I say.

'Oh, did you?' For a moment I think he's going to comment on this, but he lets it pass. 'Well, I don't know who you spoke to there, but the property's never been off the market.' He adds crossly, 'Why would it be taken off the market?'

I can't offer a reason, and lacing his voice with affability once more he says, 'You'll let me know then, will you, if you want me to go through the plan with you?'

As he rings off I know what he's thinking: he's thinking that he's got off lightly, that I'm a piece of cake.

Returning to the book search, sneezing from the dust –

Jill never seems to reach these shelves – I work my way mechanically along to the end of the row, to the books immediately preceding the gap where the art book had been. It's a moment before I focus on the edge of brown revealed against the exposed back wall of the bookcase. A large manila envelope that has been tucked in behind some *Good Food Guide*s. Jammed into the cleft of the shelf, it resists my tug for an instant before coming away.

Unmarked, quite bulky. I slide my hand inside and pull out photographs. About fifteen of them, though I don't need to look at very many to get the flavour of them.

I feel a small descent into misery, a shrinking. Oh, Harry.

Although these pictures do not stand artistic comparison to the book of erotica, some people might still class them as artistic, I suppose, since there has been some attempt at lighting and what might be considered, by those who study these things, as moderation. The camera has kept its distance, there are no closeups, and in the legal sense, I would imagine the poses fall some way short of obscenity.

But they are explicit enough. The girls have young faces on even younger bodies, small breasts and slim boy-like hips, while the men are older and burly and rough-looking, lorry drivers off the street. But what makes the scenes disturbing is that in all but one of the shots the girls are restrained in some way, with wide straps encrusted with metalwork, or heavy chains, or by men's forearms, thick and dark and muscular. Each picture is like a prelude to rape; or an invitation.

They say even the most balanced of men like an occasional look at these things. I've seen articles where experts say it doesn't do any harm, that it doesn't affect them as lovers or husbands or fathers. I'm not sure about that. I think this stuff is insidious, I think it undermines men's views of women. I think that in the end it diminishes and demeans, and encourages appetites that are best left unexplored.

Did Harry try these things with Caroline Palmer? The thought doesn't bother me in the way it would have done a few months ago. The emotion's gone. My endless compulsion to rationalise has begun to fade. I've learnt to accept that some things are simply unexplainable.

I used to make endless treks over the same lonely ground, wondering if Harry had found me inadequate in bed, deciding that I must have disappointed him in some fundamental way, though I could never think how. But having blamed myself a thousand times I've come round to a more fatalistic view. I've decided that Bob Block was probably right – that nothing I did or didn't do would have made much difference to Harry's underlying state of mind. I've come to realise that Harry's capacity for unhappiness was always there, locked deep in his childhood.

Lovemaking became a strained and unhappy experience for us, almost an act of hostility. One night, as we lay tense and silent after a particularly unsatisfactory attempt, I dared to suggest it might be an idea for us to go and see someone.

What do you mean *see someone*? His voice was ready to pounce.

I don't know, I said, already trying to retreat. A counsellor perhaps. Someone we can talk things through with.

He laughed derisively. A *shrink*, you mean?

Someone who's trained in these things.

And what would we talk about exactly? He was goading me, daring me to dig myself in even deeper.

About our problems, I said weakly.

And what might they be?

I don't know, I said. That's the trouble. I didn't mention Caroline Palmer. I suppose I still wanted to pretend that she didn't exist.

You don't know? he asked scathingly, sitting up and glaring down at me. Well, that's great, he declared, because nor do I!

I was silent. He knew perfectly well what he'd done. But while he refused to face it, while there was no hope of him acknowledging it, I couldn't see any point in saying anything.

For God's sake, he said viciously, what I need is support. And all I get is this shit!

His anger poured off him like a heat, he trembled with barely suppressed rage. For an instant he seemed to hover on the brink of something violent, but then he twisted away and stalked into the bathroom.

A few days later we had a repeat performance. I started it, as always unintentionally. I said something about needing to make the effort to be with the children, and immediately we were back into the lack of understanding I was meant to be showing him, my unreasonable behaviour. This time it was a stand-up argument late at night after too many drinks. And this time the rage rode over him and didn't stop. He grabbed me by the arms, just above the elbows, and gave me a hard shake. I don't think he realised how tightly he was holding me, but the bruises came through the next day.

He was chastened; we both were.

That didn't stop it happening again. This time he gave

me a punch of frustration and resentment. It wasn't a hard blow, more of a tap really, but in many ways it was more hurtful than anything that had gone before.

I knew this wasn't the real Harry, that this rage was quite alien, but that didn't stop me from feeling frightened, as much for the damage it was doing to our relationship as for anything that might happen. I knew it couldn't go on, that there was a risk that we would do irretrievable things to each other. I decided to make a new commitment to our marriage, to give it everything I had, though it would mean forgetting the past and pretending nothing had ever happened.

Looking back – how clear it is, looking back – it was the biggest misjudgement I ever made.

I slide the photographs back inside the manila envelope, place the envelope inside a larger padded envelope and, stapling it shut, take it out to the rubbish bin.

I continue hunting through the shelves until early afternoon when I force myself to go and have something to eat. I take an aspirin for a lurking headache. I go through the motions of walking in the garden and leafing through the mail. I pick Josh up from school. But really I am only counting the hours.

Moreland and I go to the conservatory and sit in our usual seats, adjacent wicker chairs set at an angle to each other, facing the french windows. Moreland opens the wine. After four days this has become something of a ritual.

By common consent we don't refer to the salvage boat. We have already established that there is no news as yet, that we'll be told as soon as there is.

We sip at our wine, we talk unhurriedly. I sense myself slowing down, slipping into a small pool of contentment.

He has this effect on me, Moreland. An illusion of safety.

Josh appears, clutching an assortment of books to his chest, and asks what he should write about for his English essay. He listens attentively to Moreland's opinion, less attentively to mine, and, spinning out the visit for as long as he can, finally pads off.

When he's gone, we talk of inconsequential things. Moreland tells me about a master joiner at the boatyard who got into a brawl. 'Apparently he was a bit upset about his ex-wife getting remarried, and gatecrashed the wedding party.'

I warm to the hot-blooded joiner. 'Perhaps he should have told his ex-wife how upset he was,' I suggest. 'Perhaps she would have changed her mind.'

Moreland looks doubtful. 'Do you think so? I'm not sure people change their minds about things like that. I mean, once they've decided a marriage is over.'

'But who decides when a marriage is over?' I argue mildly. 'If you believe the statistics most people seem to regret getting divorced.'

'Statistics . . .' he says in the tone of someone who treats them with caution. 'But it only takes one person to decide a marriage is over, doesn't it? Then that's that, whether the other person likes it or not.' He says this tightly, with something like disapproval.

'The other person can fight, though.'

'Fight?'

'Try to win the other person back, I mean.'

'Well . . . I suppose. But breaking the new husband's nose could be a bit excessive.'

'I don't know,' I say, only half joking. 'It shows persistence, and persistence can be very attractive.'

'Or very unrealistic.' He adds, with a peculiar little

grimace, 'Better to face the facts, it seems to me.'

A pause. We have come as far as we can on the subject without venturing into more personal territory. Now and again Moreland has mentioned his wife. Very occasionally I have asked about her. Her name is Tricia. She is an expert on medieval tapestries and works for an international dealer. They have no children. She travels a lot. She likes the theatre.

I talk about Harry in similar cocktail-party terms. Places we visited. Parliamentary occasions. Holidays. Saying these things, it occurs to me that in the absence of any other information Moreland must think that Harry and I were happy together.

Moreland starts to tell me about his forthcoming trip to Saudi Arabia, how he has tried unsuccessfully to put it off, how he must leave in two days, but will keep in touch by phone. 'I'll be back on Friday, but I may not be able to come over till Monday,' he announces in an odd voice, 'Tricia's up for the weekend, you see.' He gives me a look as if to say: that's the way it is, I'm afraid.

'Oh.' I put on an over-bright smile. 'How lovely.'

For some moments he seems to hover on the point of saying more, but, changing his mind abruptly, pours more wine instead.

We sit back. Breaking the silence, Moreland asks about my day.

I tell him I have been looking for some information.

'What sort of information?'

'I don't really know, that's half the trouble.'

'Is it important?'

'It could be.'

He waits quietly.

And then I tell him, because it's got to the point where

297

I need to tell someone and Moreland is the only person I can tell. 'It seems some money has been mislaid, money Harry was responsible for.' As I say this, I feel the first dart of shame. 'Money from a charity concert which Harry helped organise. The charity people think' – I glance away down the lawn – 'that Harry knew what happened to it. They think that he diverted the money.' Keeping my eyes on the broken thread of the horizon, I explain about the invoices from Mountbay and, later, the absence of them, the cheques drawn on the charity account that were signed by Harry and countersigned by an elderly trustee, and the lack of paperwork or explanation for the services that Mountbay was meant to have provided. It takes longer to describe the links between Mountbay and Harry and the empty account at Simmonds Mitchell, mainly because I feel bound to paint the fairest possible picture and, wherever possible, to give Harry the benefit of the doubt. 'If Harry did use the money to invest it on the commodities market, then there must have been a good reason,' I finish lamely.

Moreland, who has been listening intently, stares past me, his eyes grave, and moves his head slightly, a gesture of disbelief or disapproval, or both. Finally he asks, 'And what was it you were hoping to find in your search?'

'Anything. An address, a name at Mountbay. Someone who could tell me what happened.'

'But nothing?'

'Not so far.'

'Have you taken legal advice?'

'No. But Gillespie's looked at it. He told me there was no proof, and since there was no proof I should leave it alone. He said the charity would never dare to sue. I'm not sure he's right about that, but even if he is, that's not the point, is it?'

'When did this happen, Ellen? When did the money go missing?'

'Over the last year,' I admit softly. 'The last Mountbay payment was made in January.'

His chair creaks as he leans forward and rests his elbows on his knees. He frowns into the garden. Twice he glances across at me, as if to search for confirmation of a new and disturbing thought, and I realise that he is groping towards a fresh interpretation of events.

'You knew nothing about this Mountbay business before?' he asks at last.

'No. All I knew was that Harry was beside himself with worry. I thought it was just the business. The recession . . .'

'But you think it might have been this?'

'The strain must have been terrible . . . The thought of having lost all that money, the shame . . .'

'You think—' But something holds him back, and I finish it for him.

'I've often thought it might have been suicide, yes.' I look away, I make a gesture somewhere between sorrow and resignation. 'I had a feeling, I don't know why. That's why I took the children away, in case the body turned up and he'd shot himself or something awful and it all came out. That's why I didn't want anyone to go looking for the boat.'

Realisation spread over his face. 'Oh . . .'

'I didn't want the children to have it hanging over them for the rest of their lives. I didn't want them to be saddled with all that.'

'But, Ellen . . .' He's pulling his thoughts back together. 'After all this time, they won't find anything. I mean, no body.'

'Maybe,' I say, my voice heavy with doubt. 'But I'm afraid' – the thought emerges in a whisper – 'that they might find the gun.'

Moreland stares at me.

'I can't be sure . . . I told the police I wasn't sure . . . But I think it went missing that day. At least – I found the locker open the next morning. I know I should have told them that, I *know*. But I couldn't bring myself to. I didn't think it would help the situation. I mean, he sometimes took the gun on the boat anyway. It could have meant nothing. I didn't want to put ideas in their heads. I didn't think it would do any harm . . .'

'God,' Moreland sighs, sinking back in his seat. 'And I thought it would help, to find the boat! I thought it would get you through your legal troubles. I thought . . .' He gestures helplessly, the first time I have seen Moreland at a loss.

'I don't blame you.'

'You should have told me.' He turns to me in vague horror. 'Why didn't you say?'

'I really didn't think there was much chance of anything being found.' I give an empty laugh. 'I didn't realise quite how good you were at tracking these things down.'

'Maybe I'm not. Maybe it isn't *Minerva*.'

But neither of us dares to believe this just at the moment.

'You should have said,' he repeats in mild rebuke.

A slamming door echoes through the house, a voice calls from the hall.

It's Anne. For once Moreland's manners fail him and he turns his mouth down in annoyance. We exchange a look of open disappointment.

I call a hello and take a gulp of wine before getting up to greet them.

Although it is all wrong, although this shouldn't be coming from Anne and Charles, I can see what they are going to tell me. Anne's liquid eyes, her quivering mouth

300

say it all. By the time Charles delivers his sombre statement, I am ready for it.

They have found *Minerva*.

His face creased with feeling, Charles wraps me in a tweedy embrace. Drawing back, holding me at arm's length, he says in his funny brisk way, 'A relief, old thing, eh? Goes part of the way, doesn't it? *Part* of the way.'

Antagonisms forgotten, Anne presses her cheek against mine. 'At least we know now,' she says in a voice that is rocky with emotion. 'We know where he was laid to rest.' She blinks heavily, and focuses on a distant, more heavenly prospect.

For a dreadful moment I think they have found Harry. I turn rapidly to Charles, who shakes his head. 'Just the boat so far, Ellen. Nothing but the boat.'

I look away in case the relief shows too strongly on my face.

Charles and Moreland start to talk. It takes me a while to realise that they are discussing a person called Critchley who is waiting in the hall.

Moreland touches my arm. 'Do you want to come and talk to the coastguard?'

'I'm sure she doesn't want to be bothered,' Charles interjects kindly. 'Do you, Ellen?'

But I do, I do. I want to know everything. 'Yes, please,' I say to Moreland.

Pausing only to suggest that Charles and Anne wait behind, Moreland leads me through into the hall.

It is the fierce-faced coastguard from the memorial service. He stands in uniform, clutching his cap in both hands. He seems discomforted at the sight of me. I think he would prefer to speak to Moreland alone. He greets me with indistinct words of regret. As soon as we're settled in the study, he avoids my eye and addresses his report exclusively to Moreland.

The water was murky, even when the tide was at its slackest, he relates in his soft burr, but they could see it was a yacht. And then, as the salvage vessel swung, they managed to manœuvre the camera over the stern of the yacht and saw enough of the gold-leafed lettering on the transom to identify the name.

'She's lying on 'er port side,' he continues. 'Dug herself down a bit, o' course. The mast looks like it's broken some way up. Bent right over, at any rate. A lot o' rigging about.'

'Any other damage?'

'Not so as could be seen. But then she was on 'er side, like I said.'

'Nothing else?'

He shakes his head. 'No, but . . .' A pause. He flicks a glance in my direction but fails to meet my eye. He says tightly to Moreland, 'Likely they'll be sending a diver down.'

A moment of stillness. Moreland says, 'A diver? Why?'

I notice the hatching of deep lines that fan out from the coastguard's hard eyes, the broken veins that cover his cheeks. 'Have to cut things away,' he states, 'so no more nets get caught. Mast and rigging and maybe a stanchion or two.'

'But they'll leave the hull?' Moreland asks.

'That'll dig itself right down,' the coastguard replies ponderously. 'That size o' vessel, won't take long. It's all sand.'

They talk on. Moreland goes back over several questions, asking for detail, querying things. He asks again about signs of damage, but the coastguard can offer no more information.

Hardly listening any more, I begin to consider how I will break the news to the children.

Only when the two men stand up do I realise they have finished. We walk back to the hall.

Moreland whispers to me, 'I'll just see him out.'

I find Josh in the sitting-room, planted in front of the television. Anne's round form is perched uncomfortably on the floor next to him, her plump arms gripping his shoulders, her head tilted protectively to within an inch of his, her corseted bosom pressed against his chest. Josh flashes me a fierce look, as if he blames me for this intolerable act of affection.

'Just catching up with the news from school,' Anne says briskly, sending me eye signals to show she has said nothing about the boat, signals that I can see Josh picking up rapidly. Leaning on a chair arm, panting hard, Anne pulls herself slowly to her feet. 'Well,' she exclaims with heavy tact, 'I'll go and see how Charles is getting on.'

Josh fastens his attention back on his programme, something about wildlife in Siberia. Now that he has been so thoroughly alerted to the atmosphere, I realise I will have to tell him what is going on, although this is not the moment I would have chosen.

I crouch beside him. I say simply, 'Something's happened. I'd like to have told you later, after everyone's gone, but . . .'

He says nothing. I reach for the remote control and press the mute button. In the silence I say, 'I expect you'd like to know straight away.'

Staring furiously at the flickering screen, he gives a violent shrug.

Kneeling, I put an arm round his shoulders. I begin gently, 'They've found the boat – *Minerva*. Not far away.

303

Well – out to sea a bit. The coastguard found it today. They just came and told us.' I add, as if further explanation were needed, 'It's there on the bottom. On the sand.'

Beneath my arm, Josh's body feels stiff. He doesn't say anything.

Then I say with an enormous effort: 'They don't know yet if they'll find Daddy as well.'

Eventually I pull away a little and take a look at him. He is glaring at the carpet, his face taut with suppressed emotions.

Casting about for a point of contact, I say, 'Moreland – Richard – might be able to tell you more. I . . . didn't get all the details. He's got them all. Shall I ask him to come and tell you about it—'

Josh makes a noise half-way between a snort and a gulp, an exclamation of frustration or anger, and, twisting away from me, rolls onto his feet and stalks head down from the room.

I call after him, '*Josh*—' But I don't pursue him. I wouldn't know what to say. Sinking down onto the floor again, I am filled with a dull sense of inadequacy.

Moreland finds me there a few minutes later. Taking my hand, he helps me to my feet and onto the sofa. We sit beside each other on the edge of the seat, hunched forward, our knees touching.

'The diver, Ellen. It's not about the rigging or cutting things away . . .' His hand hovers over mine, then grasps it firmly. 'It's the police. They want to have a look inside.'

I feel a pull in my stomach, a terrible lurch. 'But I thought . . . He said . . .'

'For some reason he didn't want to mention it in front of you.'

'The police?' I echo in a dying voice.

He nods.

'But why?'

'They want to check. They more or less have to, apparently.'

A pool of coldness forms in my stomach. 'Have to?'

He sighs unhappily. 'According to Critchley, they have no choice. They're duty bound to try and find out what happened. And since the boat's fairly accessible . . .' He hesitates, locked in some internal debate. 'Also . . . because all the hatches were closed.'

I feel a sharper descent, like the beginnings of death. 'Oh?' It takes me a while to ask: 'Is that – something?'

'It's – not what one would expect.'

For an instant I free fall towards despair. Then somehow I breathe, I breathe steadily, forcing myself to respond to the slow inner count that comes back to me from the past. I take a painful step towards acceptance. I force myself to realise that nothing I can do now will prevent what is to happen. Agonising though it is, I have to accept that I have done my best, and I have failed.

They are going to find Harry's body.

I give Moreland the faintest nod, to show that I have understood.

'I'm sorry,' he says.

He sandwiches my hand between both of his and raises my hand against his cheek. This gesture unlocks something in me, a rush of self-pity, a hunger for reassurance. I drop my head against his shoulder, I feel his arm come around me and pull me against him, I reach an arm round his neck. In the few moments before we hear Anne's steps coming along the passage, I cling to him wordlessly.

A brief moment of comfort before I too begin to sink.

TWELVE

'Actual bodily harm? Oh, that's just a black eye or three!' declares Molly in answer to Katie's question. 'A tap on the chin. No more than your standard dust-up, really.' Reducing her eyes to slits, she floats a fist across the table in Josh's direction. 'Your *grievous* bodily harm, that's a bit more serious. Blood and gore. Ambulances and hospitals. Short of intent to murder, but not much.'

Katie digests this. 'And after that?'

'What? Next worst?' Molly responds brightly. 'Well . . . wounding, I suppose. Knives. I've got one lad at the moment, slashed someone in a gang fight, took off the other guy's *lip*.' She acquires an astounded expression. 'I mean, how do you take off a *lip*?'

The children ponder this with suitable gravity. Conversations with Molly are seldom less than educational. I spoon the last scrapings of sauce over Josh's spaghetti and take the dish to the sink.

'And after wounding?' Katie asks, pursuing some solemn logic of her own.

'Thanks, darling,' says Molly, blowing me an airy kiss as I put the carrot and celery salad on the table, salad which she herself has brought, along with the bottle of powerful Bordeaux we have just opened and some runny

Brie and the rich chocolate pudding waiting on the counter.

'After wounding . . .' Molly muses. 'It's robbery, armed robbery, things like that . . . But my lads haven't usually got to that stage. They don't usually learn about shotguns until they're banged up on remand. Notice I said *until*.' She sighs and shoots Josh a companionable look, as if he were of an age and understanding to share her pessimism. 'Mind you, given a gun tomorrow, most of them would probably manage to shoot themselves in the leg. They generally manage to cock things up. Part of their charm.'

Josh chews his spaghetti distractedly.

Katie sips her wine-and-water and replaces the glass on the table with concentration, shifting it about until she has fixed it in some predetermined position. 'What happens to them?'

'What, when they do armed robbery? Well, depending on how many other convictions a kid's chalked up – and we're likely to be talking long lists here – then it could be I.T. – intermediate treatment. But more likely, it'd be straight to a young offenders' institution. And' – the declaration is fatalistic – 'a guaranteed life of crime.'

'After robbery?' Katie asks without looking up.

'What – *even* worse, you mean?' Rolling her eyes, Molly refills my glass in a great surge that pushes the wine to the very rim. 'Then you're into rape, attempted murder, murder . . . Spying. Treason. Have you been to the Tower, Josh? Seen what they did to traitors in the old days? *Gory.*'

Josh nods vigorously, half afraid that she will go into detail.

'But we don't get the serious offenders,' Molly resumes. 'Normally it's just theft and more theft. That's all they think about, my boys – money, money and more money. The way they see it, there's absolutely nothing wrong with acquiring it from other people. In fact they're usually surprised when we want to lock them up for it.' She takes a gulp of Bordeaux. 'Even, in some cases, honoured.'

Not for the first time since we sat down, my eyes are drawn to the trees outside, my infallible wind indicators. The copper beeches stand tall and still in the evening light, the oak too; only the fingers of the ash tremble occasionally. Calmish, then, out at sea. Did the diver get down today? Nobody has called to tell me, and I have not called to find out. Once, in my impressionable youth, I used to imagine I possessed a degree of intuition, the result of a couple of prophetic statements I made that happened to come true, undoubtedly by chance. But now, though I stretch my mind out into the distance, though I wait for some dormant instinct to flicker into life, no whisper comes back to me.

'Why don't you get them?' Katie is asking Molly.

'The serious offenders? Well – in this part of the world, though you may find it hard to believe, there aren't that many. Not *yet*. And then' – she shrugs – 'by the time they get out they don't usually count as young offenders any more.'

Katie seems satisfied, and loses interest.

'Not hungry?' I ask Josh, who's stirring wreaths of spaghetti round his plate.

He shakes his head and puckers his mouth. A hush descends. The business line rings distantly in the study – I have unplugged all the other extensions. Today is candidate selection day, and it will almost certainly be Anne or Charles or Diana, wanting to give me the news. I will be more than happy to hear about Charles' interview, how he feels it went, but not while Katie is here, not when I am anxious to make her trip home an experience she will want to repeat.

Molly, glancing round, says with a cheerfulness that is almost pitched too high, 'Well, enough of *that*! I want to know *all* about the worst excesses of the school staff. Caught any of them smoking behind the lavs, Josh? Swearing in the corridor? Mmm? Spitting in the flowerbeds?'

Josh giggles.

'And you, Katie? What're your lot up to? Does the head sneak off to raves wearing shiny black leathers, mmm?'

Katie looks up and frowns.

'They're always up to something,' Molly declares with her rich laugh.

'She's a crabby bitch,' Katie says with unexpected vehemence.

There's a sharp silence. Molly, who's used to this sort of language, doesn't blink an eyelid.

'Katie,' I say quietly. 'That's enough.'

She turns and glares at me. 'Well, she *is*!' Then, dropping her eyes, flushing angrily, she scrapes her chair back and parades out of the room.

I leave it a while before going in search of her. I find her in her room, sitting at her desk with her back to me, hunched over a magazine. 'Could you drive me straight back?' she announces without looking round.

'If you like.' I sit on the bed. I pick up one of her teddy bears and fluff up its ears. Finally I ask, 'What was all that about?'

Without looking round, she raises her shoulders almost to her ears and says nothing. I give the bear a hug and wait, in case she should change her mind.

Yesterday, when I drove to the school to tell her about the discovery of *Minerva*, she took it with extraordinary calm, as if she had prepared herself for it. I was impressed by her control, by her touching concern for me and how I was coping, but now I wonder how deep this self-possession really went. I know that visions of the boat form the stuff of her nightmares. I know that her imagination, like mine, is far too graphic for these things.

She stands up abruptly and slides me a quick look from behind a curtain of hair. 'Sorry,' she declares, exhaling sharply. 'Sorry.' She scoops her hair back. 'It's just – the bloody staff get up my nose sometimes. They're so sodding pathetic.'

I hate this language she has taken to using; it's not like her at all. But I don't say anything. I recognise that this offhand manner is part of her defence mechanism, that, among her schoolmates, it probably gives her street credibility and therefore distance. I just wish she wouldn't use it on me.

On the journey back to school, Katie puts a hand on my arm and makes a wry face. A peace offering. But not, it seems, a prelude to explanation. As soon as we draw up at the door, she plants a quick kiss and is gone.

When I get back, Molly and Josh are playing a furious card game, slapping cards loudly on the table, shouting challenges, grabbing at each other's stacks. I leave them to it.

The searching of the bookshelves has become like an old obsession; I'm no longer sure why I'm doing it but I can't rid myself of the compulsion. As I work my way along successively higher shelves, the volumes become increasingly unlikely. Victorian books on fishing and hunting, old editions of *Who's Who*, text books from Harry's university days. I search without real hope of success, continuing only because I've so nearly reached the end.

Breaking off briefly to put Josh to bed, I climb the library ladder to the topmost shelf and tackle a collection of classic French novels in the original which I never knew we had, and which will certainly never have been read, since Harry didn't speak more than ten words of French.

'Treasure hunt?' Molly asks from below with a laugh that doesn't entirely hide her curiosity.

'Sort of.'

I flip open the final volume, and, with blatant disregard for the well-being of the spine, hold the book upside down by the covers and shake it vigorously.

'Give me a clue,' she says as I climb down the ladder.

'I'm looking for something – I don't know really – a paper, a letter . . .'

'What – from Harry?' she says nervously.

'Yes.'

'Not a *note* or something? God, you don't think . . .?' She gives me a horrified look.

'I don't think anything.'

Molly laughs with relief. 'I was going to say . . . Whatever happened, my love, I don't think Harry killed himself. He was far too tough. A born survivor.'

I don't get to sleep until late, three or so. And then it is only to wake in the first light of dawn, roused by a thought that has arrived from nowhere, mysterious yet fully formed. It won't leave me alone until I have crept out of bed and padded downstairs. I collect the first key from the desk in the study, and go into the kitchen. Reaching into the dresser, I lift the hidden key off its hook and, passing quickly across the cold hall in my thin-soled slippers, I go into the boot room and turn the separate keys in their locks and swing open the door of the gun locker.

The lone shotgun stands in its carrying bag, the second bag crumpled and empty at its side. Crouching, I search through the clutter of cartridge boxes and belts and bags lying in the bottom of the locker, then, working my way up the inside, look along the single upper shelf. There are several dusty manila envelopes, an empty cartridge carton, four loose cartridges standing on their metal rims, a box of fishing flies with a transparent lid, and one glove. The first envelope contains an instruction booklet on shotgun maintenance. The next envelope, which has been ripped almost in two, its corners curled and dusty, holds a much-folded guarantee. The last envelope, a heavy-duty full-size A4, unlabelled and unsealed, lies beneath the empty cartridge box, and looks newer. It contains four or five sheets of paper. Drawing them out, the first thing that meets my eye is the letterhead, *Mountbay (Guernsey) Ltd*.

I stare at it for a long moment before sliding the papers back inside. The house is very quiet. Closing the locker again, I take the envelope to the kitchen and lay the papers out on the table. Diverting to put on the kettle, I sit down in front of them and space them out.

Five sheets in all. The sheet with the Mountbay heading is the first of a two-page document entitled 'Heads of Agreement'. A letter from a bank in St Peter Port, Guernsey. An unheaded page of jottings – mainly figures – in Harry's handwriting. A bill from a hotel in Palma, Majorca.

The hotel bill, made out to a Mr J. Meacher, I relegate to one side and examine the page of jottings. But though there are dates and figures and, on the right-hand side, what appears to be a running balance, it's all very cryptic. Each entry is identified by initials and what might be dates – only days and months, no years – and the figures themselves are denoted by single or double digits with decimal points. These numbers may well represent larger amounts – hundreds or thousands or more – but there's no way to know.

Pulling my wrap closer around me against the early chill, I turn to the letter from the Guernsey bank. Marked strictly private, addressed to Harry here at the house, it is dated just over four years ago and is signed by the manager. Under the subject reference *Mountbay (Guernsey) Ltd*, the manager writes to confirm that he is in receipt of the bank draft for fifty thousand pounds and has with effect from the above date opened a thirty-day deposit account in the name of Mountbay (Guernsey) Ltd. He quotes the account number and emphasises the need to quote the authorisation code for telegraphic transfers. Overdraft facilities will only be possible by prior arrangement.

I read this oddly tantalising letter once more before turning to the last offering, the two-page 'Heads of Agreement' on the Mountbay headed paper. The document has been word-processed, the right-hand margin neatly justified. The agreement, so the text begins, is made between Mountbay (Guernsey) Ltd and J. H. Hoch of Liechtenstein (Nominees). After three paragraphs of dense legalese, the terms of agreement are itemised, one to three on this page, four to six on the next. The text is stiff with holdings and options and rights, and the second sheet doesn't look much better, though I hardly have time to read it before my eye is caught by the signatures at the bottom.

For the Liechtenstein company there is a foreign name, precisely and legibly reproduced. For Mountbay, Harry's squiggle and flourish. And beneath it a second signature, the long loose scrawl that is unmistakably Jack's.

'Well, what a treat,' Jack declares expansively, leading me towards a deep chair in the conference area of his light-filled office. I have been here once before, about two years ago when I came to touch Jack for funds for Molly's project. The room looks different, though I couldn't say how. New decor perhaps. Or maybe it's the magnificent desk, an immaculate art-deco style piece in pale cross-grain veneers, with, at one corner, a large leather-framed photograph of the prime minister, facing outwards across the room. The Sunday quiet seems unnatural. When I was here before, there were voices and telephones and the sound of heavy traffic outside.

Jack, in weekend garb of dark blue slacks and smoky-green open-necked shirt, both immaculately pressed, stands by the chair. 'To what do I owe this pleasure?' Before I can reply, he states as if in answer to some question of mine, 'Not long now. Tomorrow. Well, the *official* announcement anyway.' He slides me a jittery grin: the candidate in an agony of suspense. 'Someone's going to slip me the wink before then, of course. Should be about seven tonight.' He waits until I'm properly settled before crossing to the opposite chair. 'I really don't think anyone could fault my interview. Didn't put a foot wrong. Even the sods who were gunning for me couldn't catch me out. Managed the two trick questions just like that.' He snaps his fingers. 'I knew it went well, of course. You sense these things.' He sits back, he beams confidently at me, though his gaze is oddly unfocused, as though fixed on some more attractive prospect. 'But who can tell?' he says with uncharacteristic equanimity. 'If I don't get selected, well—' He gives a careless shrug to suggest that losing would be no more than a minor inconvenience.

You'll be mortified, I think to myself. You'll bay about injustice. You'll probably move to another town.

Rubbing his hands together, he peers at me with fresh

concentration. 'So!' He turns his palms outwards in a gesture that says: here I am, gleaming with success, no time to spare, but still at your service.

I reach into my bag for the envelope of documents.

'By the way,' Jack says, 'I did try to call you when I heard about the boat. Couldn't get through. Then what with one thing and another . . .' He screws up his handsome face in plea for understanding.

'It's all right.'

'I'm so sorry. Poor you. What a shame.'

I blink at this.

'Well, you must be fed up with the whole thing,' he says. 'It must be a bloody nuisance, having everything dragged out like this.'

Odd that Jack should be the one person to appreciate this, though nuisance isn't perhaps the word I would have chosen. 'It'll hurry the formalities up, so Leonard says.'

But he isn't really listening. He's looking expectantly at the papers I have pulled out of the envelope.

I pass the heads of agreement across. Sitting forward, Jack brings the document into his lap with a deft twist and I watch his eyes fix on the Mountbay letterhead. His expression is unreadable. Quickly he skims the first page and flips over to the next. When he finally looks up, it is to raise his brows ironically. He waits for me to speak.

'What's it about?' I ask.

Casting the paper onto the low table between us, he sits slowly back and, making a cradle of his hands, watches me over the tips of his fingers. 'Mountbay was Harry's baby. I haven't had anything to do with it for years.'

'But . . . at one time?'

'I was involved, yes. But in a purely nominal capacity.'

Not sure where to take this, aware of how very still Jack is and how sharp his eyes are, I progress yet more slowly. 'When was this?'

'Oh, it must be five years ago. And then for no longer than a year – if that.'

I absorb this through the sluggishness that comes from lack of sleep. 'But what did it do exactly – Mountbay?'

'Do? It didn't do anything. It was set up as a convenience, a vehicle for moving money around.'

Again I wait for him to help me along, again I wait in vain. Finally I ask: 'What money?'

'Money,' he repeats unhelpfully.

I am struggling now. 'You mean – business money?'

He blinks lazily, though his eyes have lost none of their keenness. 'I imagine so, yes.'

The minimal response again. As if he wants to absolve himself from responsibility for this conversation.

'Jack—' Out comes my nervous laugh, sounding strident. 'I'm very tired, there's a lot going on, it would be nice if you could be a little more forthcoming.'

He gives a show of incomprehension. 'I'm answering your questions, aren't I? What else do you want to know?'

I shake my head. 'Everything.'

'Well – ask away.'

'You're not making things easy.'

'I'm telling you what I know,' he says reasonably. 'Ask away.'

Seeing that he is not to be shifted, I move wearily on. 'So – Mountbay was part of the business?'

He purses his lips. 'Oh no. It was quite separate.'

'I don't understand.'

Jack taps his forefingers against each other in what could be irritation or reflection. 'Harry needed to keep it

316

separate because he took to using it for purposes that were – how shall I put it – that took him slightly near the mark.'

This time I wait him out.

His eyelids droop in forbearance as he explains, 'There were certain advantages to channelling payments through Mountbay. Financial advantages. But, well – it was a grey area. Open to interpretation, you might say. The purposes of the payments would have had to be argued with the Revenue. It was easier, in the end, not to let them know.'

I am careful to show nothing, and certainly not surprise. Outside in the street, an ambulance siren whoops past. The afternoon sun glows hotly against the slatted blinds.

'Where did the money go? What was it used for?' I ask.

Jack's hands fly open briefly. 'I don't think that matters.' His tone is final. Proceed no further, he is saying, I have judged it best that you don't know. But I can't help wondering if he is sparing me this knowledge for my benefit or his own.

'I'm sorry,' I say, determined not to put off for once, 'but are you saying you don't know? Or that you can't say?'

He lifts his shoulders. 'It's irrelevant, that's all.'

It seems I'm not to have all my questions answered after all.

Sweat is damp against my blouse. I find my thread again. 'I've discovered Harry had an account with a commodities broker called Simmonds Mitchell. Was that—'

'After my time. Harry started all that after he and I parted company.'

All that. He makes it sound ominous. 'You knew about it?'

Jack gives me a look which suggests that I have managed to strike out in another unsuitable direction. 'I knew *of* it,' he replies testily. 'Indirectly, anyway.' He tucks in his fine jaw, he tightens his lips, he says disapprovingly, 'Harry had been dabbling in commodities for some time. *Investing.*' He instils the word with scorn. 'The chances of making money in the commodities market are about on a par with winning at roulette, and probably a great deal worse. Harry made the classic error of thinking that he could cover his liabilities by doubling his risk. He thought a quick flutter on the market would fill a few yawning chasms in his cash flow. Well ... I imagine that's how it was,' he adds ingenuously. 'Harry wasn't exactly forthcoming about these things.'

I think: but you knew all the same. Just as you knew all about the charity money the other day. I glimpse Gillespie's shifting figure in the background again.

'Did Harry say anything to you?' I ask. 'About his losses?'

'He didn't have to. If he'd have won he'd have been laughing, wouldn't he?'

'He didn't say ...' I can hardly bring myself to ask, '. . . where the money might have come from?'

Jack gives me a look that says this is not wise to ask.

This is it then, as close to an explanation as I'm ever likely to get. But, having got this far, I'm not sure what I have really gained. A little more certainty perhaps. The knowledge that there's absolutely no hope of the missing money turning up.

'Thanks.'

Jack flutters his fingers graciously. Then, fixing me with a thin smile, he adds, 'I'm sure you'll appreciate that it wouldn't be a good idea to mention this to anyone. It doesn't bother me – I cut the ties long ago – but for the sake of Harry's reputation.'

I give an unhappy nod.

'And, Ellen – no more enquiries about Mountbay. It would only draw attention. You appreciate?'

I let his words reverberate a moment longer before asking with a laugh, 'What do you mean, more enquiries?' I'm thinking of my letter to the Guernsey bank; I'm thinking that he knows about it.

He shoots me a look in which realisation and annoyance are keenly merged and for an instant I have the wild impression that I have caught him out. 'Enquiries,' he repeats solidly, taking his time. 'As in questions to Gillespie.'

'Ah.'

He starts to get up.

'Jack—'

'Mmm?' He perches restlessly on the edge of his seat.

'There was something else. I wondered . . .' I draw out the photocopy of the hotel bill I made this morning. '. . . if this meant anything to you?'

Jack takes the copy from my hand and examines it. He pushes out his lip, his expression shifts to one of puzzlement, though not before I fancy I see a flash of something like displeasure dart over his features. Languidly he lifts his low-lidded eyes to mine and gestures ignorance.

'The guest's name . . .' I direct him back to the bill.

'What . . .?' He frowns at the paper. 'Meacher?' He glances back at me, as if he's trying to get the drift of my reasoning.

'The chairman of the planning committee. Isn't that his name?'

Jack makes a show of taking another look. 'Could be.' He regards me with sudden amusement. 'What a mind you have, Ellen!' He waves a hand loosely in the air. 'Okay. Well, if it *was* Meacher, what can I say? These things have been known to happen. It would be unrealistic to say they didn't. But it's all pretty harmless. A cheap holiday, the odd weekend, things like that. These people get paid next to nothing. They expect this sort of perk. Part of the job.' He regards me coolly. 'Harry wouldn't be the first developer to have promoted his interests in this way, Ellen.'

Molly's dark suspicions about Jack and his relationship with the planning authorities flicker through my mind and I wonder fleetingly if Meacher has taken any holidays at Jack's expense.

I start to gather up the Mountbay papers.

'I'd be careful of those,' Jack murmurs, drooping a lazy finger in their direction.

Doomed to be slow on the uptake, I look up questioningly.

'Best to get them shredded. I can do it for you, if you like.'

I hold them closer to me. 'But I thought I might write to the bank . . .' I put on an obdurate face.

'As you wish. But it's very unwise.'

I hesitate.

'I'm just telling you what's best for you.' When I don't reply he stands up and says irritably, 'Well, don't say I didn't warn you.'

I get slowly to my feet. We walk towards the door.

Pausing at the threshold, Jack reverts to his father-figure tone. 'Gillespie looking after you? Talked you out of this house-buying idea yet?'

I busy myself with the fastening of my bag, I look noncommittal.

Jack stands close in front of me and shakes his head. 'There is no house, is there, Ellen? *Is* there?'

'I want to move,' I declare. 'I'm longing to move.'

He regards my protest with open scepticism. 'I talked to Gillespie. We worked out that a loan of thirty thousand should see you through for the time being. I'll be glad to top it up if necessary. But no more than that, Ellen. Sorry.'

I feel a childish resentment. 'I see,' I say stiffly. 'May I ask why?'

'We think you'll only give it to this stupid charity.'

'That's my business, I would have thought.'

'Well – *hardly*. Anyway, it's not just a matter of the money. You don't seem to understand that any talk of money or restitution—'

'I wasn't going to—'

'*Any* talk of money or restitution,' he continues firmly, '*any* discussion at all, would be as good as announcing that Harry was guilty of something. You do realise that?'

I must look unconvinced, because he steps closer and takes me lightly by the forearms and says in a tone of patience wearing thin, 'Do I have to spell it out for you? Nothing can be proved about this missing money, Ellen, because so long as there aren't any papers lying around there's no way they can trace Mountbay back to Harry. That was the whole point of Mountbay, you see, the reason it was set up the way it was – so there'd be no possibility of any comeback.' He pauses to let this sink in. 'The only way they might pin anything on him is with *those*.' He points towards my bag and the papers. 'What Harry was thinking of, I don't know, leaving that sort of stuff around.' He swivels his eyes heavenward, then, fixing his considerable gaze on me again, insists, 'Without proof all they can accuse Harry of is incompetence – something these charity people seem to be pretty good at themselves. And incompetence is a very different thing from fraud, Ellen. Putting it mildly. Now you see why you mustn't admit to anything at all. Why it would be dangerous to keep those papers . . .'

Against my will I see the wisdom of this. With bad grace I reach into my bag and pull them out. Jack plucks them from my hand and, leading the way into the outer office, switches on a large shredding machine. He leafs quickly through the sheets. 'The hotel bill – is there an original?'

I hesitate for only an instant. 'No.' This of course is untrue; the original is at home. But it isn't a Mountbay document, it can't be dangerous, and a stubborn perversity makes me reluctant to give up quite everything to Jack.

He feeds the papers into the jaws. 'You're worrying too much anyway,' he says dismissively. 'If anything does come out, there'd be a bit of whispering – well, a bit of a fuss, maybe – but in the end the whole thing would die a death.'

A bit of talk, some fuss. He makes it sound harmless, but it seems to me that a whisper, far from dying a death, is the one thing that lives for ever.

The rest of Sunday passes slowly, with unreality. I feel both connected and detached, like an actor stepping in and out of a half-learnt role. My family come and go, as if responding to a set of stage directions that I haven't had the chance to see.

By the evening I am good for little but supper in front of the television. Molly insists on staying another night, and I don't try to argue her out of it. We watch a comedy. I find myself laughing, though the programme isn't that funny.

I drive Josh off to bed at nine. We don't say much. I think he's as exhausted as I am. Downstairs, a phone rings and I hear Molly answer it. A moment later she calls for me to pick it up.

As I make my way to the bedroom extension something inside me beats a warning.

Mrs Anderson's tone is buttoned down tight, but not so tight that I can't pick up the tone of indignation beneath. 'I'm going to have to ask you to collect Katie and take her home, Mrs Richmond.'

'What's happened?'

'What's happened,' she says coldly, 'is that Katie's behaviour is totally unacceptable. Under *any* circumstances, *whatever* difficulties she may be having.'

Oh, Katie.

I say, 'But what—'

'I'd prefer not to go into detail.' Her voice rises abruptly then steadies again. 'I think all future discussion should be carried out by the head.'

I start to apologise, something of a reflex action with me, then, remembering that Katie is someone I don't need to apologise for, I halt and inform her that I should be there in twenty minutes.

First there are certain rituals: the bath, the bar of old-fashioned soap, the fresh towel, the crisp white night-dress, the hair-brushing, the childhood cup of cocoa. Then we lie in my bed, side by side, my arm round her shoulder, her sweet-smelling hair against my cheek. Like old times. I have left a night light on, but Katie still shifts slightly against me as if to check that I am really here.

Finally I murmur, 'Well . . .?'

A flutter of tension that eases again. 'St-u-pid,' she sighs at last, in a sing-song. 'Bit of a disaster. *Sorry.*'

'What happened?'

She moves her shoulders in what may be a shrug. 'I said something, that's all . . .' The bravado slips, she exhales unhappily. 'I called Mrs Anderson a stupid cow. Well, she kept on at me, kept using this awful voice, like *sickly*, trying to get me to talk about what she calls my *problems*. Putting her arm around me – I *mean*!' She shudders. 'Sick! I *told* her – I don' wanna talk about it. I told her!'

Waiting for the rest, I look out at the soft windless night and the scattering of stars.

Finally she says in a defeated voice, 'And then – well, I sort of bashed her. I didn't *mean* to, I just . . .'

I give it a moment before I ask, 'When you say bash . . .?'

'I dunno . . . a sort of punch, I suppose. I didn't *hurt* her or anything. I just,' she breathes deep draughts of self-disgust, 'lost my cool.'

I say gently, 'Like with the science teacher?'

I sense her surprise. 'Sort of.'

'And what happened with him?' I ask in a neutral tone.

'He's just a creep!' she exclaims as if I should know this. 'Pure *grease*. That smarmy smile, hand on your shoulder, coming close to look at your work all the time – I mean, his face *this* close.' She closes her thumb and forefinger to within a millimetre of each other. 'Thinks he's so *wonderful*! And oh-so innocent, oh-so incredibly amazed when I told him to lay off. A total creep! And all the staff think he's so *totally perfect*!' She twitches with indignation. 'But he's *yukky*. Complete *yuk*!'

I have two pictures, one of a schoolmasterish hand patting Katie's shoulder, an innocent gesture of encouragement or congratulation that this man has probably been using for years; the other, of him looking at Katie in open admiration, as many men have been doing since she was twelve or so, and failing to take his eye away in time, leaving his hand a moment too long, overstepping the mark a fraction.

It doesn't really matter which of these pictures is closest to the truth; it's the way Katie sees it. It's the way she interprets even Mrs Anderson's fumbling attempts at kindness as an unacceptable invasion of her space. If Katie has made any progress in the last weeks, it's not in the direction of trust.

Mrs Anderson probably thinks Katie is a neurotic, ruined by a doting mother. She cannot appreciate, and certainly I can never tell her, what Katie has been through.

I lie awake for a long time after Katie has gone to sleep. Finally I creep downstairs to make myself a hot drink. I find Molly in the sitting-room, watching a late movie, puffing on a forbidden cigarette, a habit she was meant to have given up six months ago.

'Is she all right?' she asks anxiously.

I nod.

'What happened?'

'Nothing. She's just upset.'

'What about?'

'Everything, I suppose.'

'She hasn't said?'

'No.'

Molly, who can spot an evasion a mile off, shoots me an admonitory frown.

I admit wearily, 'She had a row with her housemistress. Then something unfortunate happened. Apparently Katie lashed out at her.'

'Oh.' Molly manages to give the sound a wealth of meaning.

Ignoring this, I go through into the kitchen.

'Look, sweetie,' says Molly, coming in behind me and

settling on the opposite stool, 'don't get me wrong, *please* don't get me wrong, but you don't need this, you really don't. Not at the moment. I really think you should consider getting some help. Counselling or something.'

'I'll be all right.'

'I meant for *Katie*.'

I knew she meant for Katie. 'She'll be all right, too.'

Molly fights an internal battle that rages across her face. Finally she says, 'I just don't think you should have to deal with this on your own. Not with everything else that's going on. No one should.'

'Funny,' I say, 'the head seems to agree with you. She thinks Katie needs a psychiatrist.'

Missing the irony in my voice, Molly says quickly, 'Well, I'm not so sure about psychiatrists. They just bugger people up, if you ask me. But counselling. I've seen plenty of kids that a bit of counselling did wonders for. *Wonders.* You know – someone from *outside*. Someone who isn't involved.'

'Katie'll be all right,' I say again.

Molly stays silent with difficulty. Finally she feels bound to say, 'Sweetheart, don't rule it out. Sometimes family aren't the *best* people to deal with these things.'

I make a performance of the tea, pulling out pot, cup, saucer.

Molly sighs. 'I hate to see you getting so upset. She always makes you upset.'

'I don't think that's quite fair.'

'I'm sorry, but she does. She knows exactly how to wind you up.'

'Don't, Molly.'

'But it's true, sweetheart. Got to say it. She *does*. Somehow she always manages to get to centre stage. If there

326

isn't a drama, then she manages to make one happen around her.' Molly looks pained. 'I'm only saying this because I love you and I worry about you and I don't think *anybody* should have to cope with this alone. I'm not saying Katie isn't feeling all this intensely, I'm sure she is, I know she loved Harry, but really . . .' She is going to say more in the same vein, but thinking better of it, she murmurs, 'Well, it isn't fair on you.'

So Molly also believes that Katie is a case for treatment, that I have been too indulgent.

Something heaves up inside me, an explosion of internal fury. I have the urge to shout her down, to crush these ideas of hers, to make her realise how deeply unjust they are. I want to cry, Yes, she's difficult! Yes, she's demanding! But what do you expect? How could she be any other way when she's so dreadfully and irretrievably damaged? When she was so completely deceived?

But I cannot say it, I must never say it. To do so would be to admit that Katie is the real victim in all this, and I will never add to her pain or risk her precarious balance in this way.

To rid myself of my anger, I direct it back to Harry.

There were times long before that day in March when I felt I could have killed him for what he had done to Katie.

If he were here now, I could kill him still.

Later, in the stillness, a sound. The scrunch of car wheels on gravel, growing closer. I avoid Molly's questioning glance. I take a mouthful of coffee and wait. When the doorbell rings, I get up calmly, as if I've been expecting someone. Crossing the hall I have the sensation of looking backwards at this moment from a point far in the future.

Two cars are visible through the side window. I swing the door open to a solemn triumvirate. Charles, Leonard and, in a linen suit that looks as though it's had a long day, Inspector Dawson. Or perhaps it's Chief Inspector Dawson, I've never been quite sure.

'Ellen – I would have phoned but . . .' Charles waves a hand, looking oddly stricken.

Leonard, gaunt-faced, severe, stands slightly apart, looking at a point just to one side of my head.

'May we come in, Mrs Richmond?' says Dawson in his easy, salesman's voice.

'Please.'

I put on some lights in the drawing-room. Dawson positions himself by his usual chair facing the bay and the garden. We sit down, I in the armchair opposite Dawson, Charles and Leonard deeper in the room in seats that circle the fireplace, as if we are two groups of people having separate conversations. Dawson fastens his deliberate gaze on me, he puts his stubby fingers together and says without preamble, 'Mrs Richmond, I have to inform you that earlier today we retrieved a body from the sea and that it has been formally identified as that of your husband.'

I take a long moment, I unfasten my gaze from Dawson's, I look down at my hands.

'Where?' I manage at last.

'From the boat. Inside the boat.'

'Inside,' I echo, hearing my voice die away. I feel a surge of sadness. Or relief. It's hard to tell.

In the well of silence that follows I half turn to Charles, who meets my eye in unhappy confirmation.

Dawson's unmoving gaze waits on mine. 'With regret,' he continues in a drab voice, 'I must also inform you that a shotgun was found beside the body' – a pause, a moment of deathly stillness – 'and that from a preliminary examination it would appear that Mr Richmond suffered wounds commensurate with having turned the shotgun on himself.'

I stare, I can only stare.

'I'm sorry.'

I close my eyes, I have a sense of disconnection.

I dimly hear someone moving across the room, then Leonard is at my side, pressing a glass into my hands. I bring the water to my lips and drink.

Leonard's dry bony hand finds its way into mine. I hear the rasp of his breath beside my ear, and he murmurs, 'Not to blame yourself, Ellen. Not to blame yourself.'

Old resentments rise, freshly charged, into my chest. I blink back sharp tears. Through this sea of feeling I'm aware of Dawson watching me with a blend of detachment and discomfort, someone who hasn't found the breaking of bad news any pleasanter with the passage of time.

He waits for my attention.

'There are certain formalities,' he begins when I look up at him again. 'Routine investigations which will take some time, I'm afraid. We are hoping, circumstances permitting, to raise the yacht. Hopefully in the next few days. Obviously we'll try to minimise the distress to yourself and your family. Keep things as low-key as possible. And I hope you'll bear with us during what I realise will be a difficult time.'

Uncertain of what he means by this, I nod vaguely. Leonard, still hovering, draws up a chair and sits close beside me.

Dawson leans forward a little, as if to exclude Leonard from our conversation. 'I realise this has come as a great shock to you, Mrs Richmond. I've no wish to keep you from your family at this time. But it would be most helpful if you could tell me what reasons you think your husband might have had for taking his own life.'

'There were money troubles . . .' I start tentatively, looking to Leonard, inviting him to take up the story.

But before Leonard can speak, Dawson raises an excluding hand and says, 'Go on, Mrs Richmond.'

I rest my fingers briefly on my eyelids. 'There were debts,' I say unsteadily. 'Business debts. Personal debts. I didn't realise quite how bad they were, not until recently. He never told me these things . . .' I think of the children, I force myself to go on. 'Then there was his political career. When he lost his seat in the last election it was completely unexpected. He—'

'Yes?'

It's a moment before I can say, 'It was an enormous shock. He took it very badly . . .'

'Did he seem particularly depressed in the period just before he disappeared?' Dawson pressed on. 'In the last few days or so?'

'I don't know. I've thought about it a lot. But with my husband it was hard to tell. He wasn't a great talker, not about this sort of thing anyway.'

'But you've been thinking about it, you say? So it had entered your mind – that he might have taken his own life?'

'No. No. It was just those last few days I kept thinking about, that's all.'

'Any particular reason?'

My throat seizes, blocking my words. Finally, I manage, 'All the things I didn't say. All the things I wish I'd said.'

'Nothing happened around then?' he asks. 'No events that upset him in any way? Nothing that might have had a bearing?'

I go back through my memory, which has become fragmented and oddly jumbled, so that I'm no longer absolutely sure of what is real and imaginary. 'The only thing . . .'

'Yes?'

'There were some business calls that seemed to upset him. I felt – it was no more than a feeling – that there was some crisis.'

'News of some sort?'

'I can't be sure, but I think so.'

'And this news, whatever it was, he took it badly?'

I almost say, *he took everything badly*. 'He was very worried, yes.'

'But he never talked about taking his life?'

'No.' I shake my head slowly. 'No.'

Dawson takes a long breath and says almost as an afterthought, 'Would you say he was capable of taking his own life?'

I wrestle with this. When my answer emerges, it is as much an admission of my own failure as Harry's. I whisper, 'Yes.'

Thus do I condemn you, Harry.

Dawson's mouth lifts at the corners, his puffy cheeks swell. He has the answer he wanted.

THIRTEEN

We were sitting on the shady balcony of the apartment in
La Jolla, staving off jet lag, when Katie began to tell me
about the bad times. Josh was playing computers with
some kids next door, the drone of the traffic on the boule-
vard two blocks away had sunk to a lazy hum, and a
welcome breeze was drifting in from the ocean. We were
talking in a desultory way about clothes when, grasping
the opportunity such as it was, I asked her in unemotional
tones about her shopping expeditions with Harry. How
were they? Were they – it was always hard to find the right
words – difficult?

Screwing up her eyes against the bleached light, looking
out over the palm-lined street towards a vivid Astroturfed
lawn opposite, Katie said just as casually, They were okay.
Then, with a grudging sigh, Well, not too bad.

How do you mean? You mean – caution, caution –
there were some things that weren't so good?

It was just, like, this *feeling*, she said in her flat child-
voice. I dunno. She shrugged hard. I tried not to think
about it. Like if I didn't think about it, it would go away.
I thought that maybe if I was dead nice, if I did the trips
and wore the clothes, then he'd be pleased with me and
everything would be okay.

Pausing, she attacked some well-picked skin on her forefinger.

It wasn't that anything happened, she added, knowing how paranoid I was on this point, how I felt driven to ask about this even at the cost of making her retreat.

He didn't touch you? I couldn't help asking, my heart cold against my ribs.

He held my hand, things like that, she said briskly. That's all.

I knew she was telling the truth; it was just that I couldn't hear it too often. I had developed this retrospective distrust of Harry's every action, and, excruciating though it was, I had to rake through each event.

Another day, as we walked along the broad glaring sand, past the whooping volley-ball players and the strutting girls, Katie talked about the French holiday. As so often in the conversations that followed, her mood was at first remote and unpromising. It was as though she needed to withdraw into herself, to create some distance from me before she could talk about these things.

She'd been dead worried about the holiday, she said. She'd been worried in case she spoilt things . . .

Spoilt things. It was all I could do to let this pass.

Everything was okay for a while, she said. He seemed to . . . She groped for the words. Well, it was like he didn't *crowd* me. Like he was making an effort to be . . . okay.

With what in mind? I wondered bitterly.

Then, she went on dully, then . . . Responding to the memory, she lengthened her stride, she glared down at the sand. It was like it was before, she said. Just . . . suddenly. She didn't know why it changed so quickly. She couldn't think what she'd done. She didn't think she'd done anything.

And what did he do? I asked in my most detached voice.

For a time I thought she wouldn't answer. Sort of hugs, she said finally. Just hugs . . .

I had, I thought, become a master of impassivity, of the carefully arranged expression, but Katie, taking a glance at my face, reached for my hand and gave it a solemn pat. This role reversal that she practised then, her dutiful concern, produced terrible upwellings of emotion in me, and I had to turn away and talk of something else.

After the beach, Katie was silent for several days. Her sessions with Bob Block were, I think, absorbing her completely. Then, when we were unpacking groceries one afternoon, stealing curls of toffee crisp ice cream from a giant tub and sucking them off the spoon, the subject of Christmas came up. It was Christmases in general, but, glancing into her face, I knew we were both thinking about the last one.

This was the time when I should have realised, the moment when the situation was first written out for me, if only I hadn't been so determined not to see. It was three days before Christmas. I came in late after ferrying Diana back from a party and, finding the study deserted, the TV off and the rest of the floor in darkness, I went upstairs in search of bed, Harry, and the children, in no particular order. Our bedroom was empty; I registered vaguely that Harry must be downstairs after all. Out of long habit I went along the corridor to check on Josh, who, as always in sleep, was completely dead to the world, lying flat on his back, making soft purring noises in the back of his throat, looking beautiful and new and miraculous, as only a child can look.

Coming to Katie's room, seeing her light was still on, I knocked briefly and reached for the knob. I remember my sense of anticipation; the holidays had just begun, I was thrilled to have her home again. I remember, too, the instant of surprise as the door was flung open and Harry stood before me, his skin flushed, his mouth slightly open, his shirt skewed at the neck, and beyond, Katie's white face stared out from the bed. As we stood in a silent tableau, the signals came at me thick and fast. A tension hummed through the space between us, and the air contained something I couldn't pin down, something ugly and disturbing. I saw in Harry's face irritation and resentment, and a strange shadow, like guilt. And in Katie, in the long moment before she turned away and buried her head in the pillows, an expression of injury.

Looking back, I realise the atmosphere positively reeked of Harry's craving. But though my instincts insisted something was wrong, though I couldn't rid myself of this unease for several days, I finally shut it out. I have always tended to push uncomfortable thoughts to the back of my mind, to hope in some vague unchannelled way for the best. And when Harry told me that Katie had been difficult, that she had trounced off in a temper, that he had gone to her bedroom to make peace only to be goaded into a row, I believed him.

I believed him, I overrode my instincts, and that was my great failure, the whip with which I now beat my back.

The thought of Harry having sexual feelings for Katie, let alone putting them into practice, was to me so unthinkable that it didn't begin to enter into the realm of possibility. Such things simply didn't happen to people like us. I still thought of us as ordinary people then – though, by almost any standards, Harry was far from ordinary. Deep down – I see this now, perhaps I always knew – he was irretrievably damaged in some way.

Anyway, my limited capacity for suspicion was already filled by his infidelity with Caroline Palmer. If Harry was engineering scenes with Katie, if he was using her against me in some way – and this was how I came to interpret what had happened – then I decided it must be part of some emotional game plan, some way of driving a wedge between us. I didn't imagine for one moment that Caroline Palmer was the heroin-substitute, the methadone, to his real addiction.

But then I saw everything in terms of our relationship, and how it had failed. It was soon after the French holiday, which for a time seemed to offer such hopes, that a deep ache of anxiety lodged itself in my stomach and wouldn't go away. At first I blamed business problems, political failure; all the worries we were sharing. It was some time before it dawned on me that our relationship itself was slipping away. I began to feel Harry exercising his considerable determination against the very idea of us, as though he had weighed things up and decided our marriage simply wasn't worth the effort any more.

Agonising over this, I failed to see that there was another side to this coin of unhappiness, that Harry's fascination with Katie had grown into something altogether darker and more obsessive.

With the brilliance of hindsight, I see how it began; how, as Katie began to grow up, Harry used to watch her with a speculative expression that was midway between admiration and puzzlement, as if he couldn't quite believe how sweet and lovely she was. Since I felt the same sort of wonderment when I looked at her, since I thought it both natural and not a little miraculous that Harry should feel the same affection for Katie as he did for his own son, I was thrilled at the attention he gave her. I was pleased when he used to break off from whatever he was doing to talk to her. I was touched when he stroked her hair at bedtime, or ran a knuckle softly down her cheek. It was more than I had dared hope for. I couldn't believe my good fortune.

Katie, using more instinctive touchstones, knew better, though she could never rationalise her feelings. Even when she talked it through with Bob Block she couldn't put it into words; she just knew she had to get away.

The boarding school. Why didn't I guess? Not the real nature of the problem – I could never have guessed that, not then – but why didn't I see that she didn't really want to go? That she felt driven to leave home because she felt so uncomfortable there?

As we packed the ice cream away at La Jolla and talked of Christmas, the memory of the bedroom scene hung between us. Katie wouldn't give me details then. All she would say was: it wasn't bad-bad. Later, when we had established a means of communicating the more emotional information through the neutrality of Bob Block, I learned that, if not bad, the Christmas incident had certainly been worse than anything that had happened before.

There was a certain amount of touching, Bob relayed.

Touching, I echoed, dying quietly inside. You mean assault.

After Christmas, Katie kept telling me, things were better. The rest of the school holidays and the first half of the spring term there were no shopping expeditions, no unexpected visits to school.

This, of course, was because I was watching him. Tracking his movements. Looking for evidence of Caroline Palmer. Ironic. The hunter on the false trail.

Wretched Katie, wretched me. Both deceived.

I've thought a lot about the nature of blame and forgiveness. I don't blame Harry for being the way he was. I loved him as much for his faults as his more obvious strengths.

But this isn't to say I can ever forgive him; I can't. Understanding is quite separate from forgiveness. You can only forgive acts that people commit unthinkingly, in a rush of weakness, in the heat of the moment; things that you yourself might have done under the same circumstances.

But Harry didn't do what he did unthinkingly. He planned it. It was this realisation, more than anything, that suspended all feeling, that gave me the strength to do what I did. It was this realisation that eats away at me still.

I find the office of The Rumanian Orphans Relief Fund tucked away above a print shop in a run-down terrace of late-night grocery stores and kebab houses and launderettes between Queensway and the Russian Orthodox church. The lino on the stairs has seen better days and there's a smell of stale spices and disinfectant. The door at the top sports the charity's logo and, tacked on beneath, a stencilled sign inviting entry. Inside, two work-weary women sit tapping at computers amid stacks of mail. The walls are papered with press cuttings and photographs of volunteers grouped around relief lorries at what I presume to be Rumanian orphanages.

Tim Schwartz's office, which leads off the outer office, is a more spacious but no less overstretched room. The surfaces of the metal and melamine desk and conference table and the tops of the battered grey filing cabinets are stacked with documents and box files.

Schwartz looks mildly disconcerted at seeing me, as if I have come unannounced and he is having to tear himself away from something important.

He is wearing a voluminous shirt tucked unevenly into his jeans. His narrow face is made more severe by a pair of metal-framed Einstein spectacles. He clears a seat for me then wheels his own chair round the desk and leans back in it, his arms crossed in the attitude of someone who is not likely to be impressed by what he is about to hear.

I unfold my prepared piece, written in the late hours of last night. Mindful of Jack's warning, I am anxious that there should be no misunderstandings.

'While in no way accepting . . .' My voice cracks. I clear my throat and start again. 'While in no way accepting that my husband had any responsibility for any funds . . .' I pause over the awkward phraseology. '. . . that might have been due to your charity, and on the understanding that what I am about to offer should in no way be seen as connected to any other matter, such as these funds, I would nevertheless like to offer, as a gesture of good faith, a contribution to your charity. In view of my present finances, this contribution will be smaller than I would like, in the region of twenty thousand pounds for this year.' I glance up and find Schwartz's eyes glinting with what looks like a hostile light. 'In future years,' I continue uncertainly, 'I would expect to make further donations. These donations will continue for as long as I am able to make them, and for as much as I can afford.'

Schwartz's mouth twitches downward. 'That's it?'

'I'm sorry?'

'These future donations,' he says tautly, 'you can't specify . . . ?'

'No, I . . . Not at the moment. Though I should have a better idea in a couple of months.'

He screws up his mouth. 'Mrs Richmond, frankly your

offer amazes me. *Amazes* me . . .' He lifts an unbelieving hand. 'I mean, this money never belonged to your husband. It wasn't some kind of *loan* to be repaid at his – or your – convenience. It belonged to *this charity* . . .'

I see slippery slopes before me, just as Jack prophesied. 'It's the best offer—'

He cuts in aggressively, 'I mean, we *are* in agreement as to who the money belonged to, aren't we?'

'I don't think . . . I don't really feel I can . . .' I hear my voice ebbing away. '. . . discuss it.'

'We're going to pretend your offer is unconnected, is that it?'

Reluctant to be cornered, I waver, only to realise that hesitation is an answer in itself.

'We're going to say you're making these donations out of the blue, are we?' he continues derisively. 'And the charity's meant to show extreme gratitude, I suppose?' He gives a faint snort. 'The fact is, Mrs Richmond, that we need this money *now*. We have major capital projects that have got to be carried out before we can even begin to think about the children's emotional and educational needs. We've got to get the orphanages functioning. I don't think you realise – these children are still having to live in the most basic conditions. The staff spend all their time wrestling with prehistoric laundry and kitchen equipment. The plumbing doesn't work, the heating fails—'

'I've no doubt you need the money,' I interrupt unhappily. 'And if it was in my power to wave a magic wand and send enormous quantities your way, believe me, I would, I *would*.'

Partially mollified, he falls into a grudging silence.

'And if I personally had anything else to give,' I say, 'then I would give it. But my husband's estate isn't going to be worth very much. I have the house, but there's a big mortgage, and by the time it's sold . . . There should have been some shares, I thought there were some shares, but it seems they're not mine after all.'

'I'm sure you're doing your best, Mrs Richmond. I don't doubt your goodwill. That's not the point.'

We eye each other uneasily as we both ponder the point, which, I don't need reminding, is that the charity is without its money.

I refold the paper. 'My offer . . .' I venture at last. 'It's not a lot . . . I realise . . . But hopefully it would go some way . . .?'

'Forgive me,' Schwartz retorts, 'but it's really pointless to discuss this. A large sum of money has gone missing. And the simple fact is that it belongs to us.' His hands fly out in indignation. 'We want it back.'

'I don't think . . . that'll be possible.'

He slowly refolds his arms. 'Oh? Why?'

'Because it isn't there.'

'You know this?'

'Well . . . I'm pretty sure,' I murmur.

His eyebrows rise. 'You're pretty sure? I'm sorry,' he says with elaborate sarcasm, 'but what does that mean?'

Not at all certain I'm doing the right thing, ignoring all sorts of warning signals, I hear myself say, 'We've looked. Everywhere. We can't find any money.'

'You can't find any money. I'm sorry, but that's hardly our problem. Why shouldn't it be in some bank somewhere?'

He has me there, of course. He also has me deep in admissions that would appal Jack. 'We did find a hidden account. But it was empty.'

He puts on a knowing expression, as if to say: well, you would say that, wouldn't you?

'We tracked the money some of the way,' I tell him,

'but I'm afraid it seems to have been lost. All of it.'

Now he is taking me more seriously. '*Lost?*'

'It seems so.'

'You're telling me you *know* it's all gone?'

Deeper still. I tell him we're as sure as we can be.

He searches my face, as if to gauge the truth of this. 'Great!' he hisses bitterly. 'Bloody great!' His mouth twists into a childish grimace, which, perversely, serves to make him appear more human and less frightening.

'I'm very sorry . . .'

He glares at me, not trusting himself to speak. Finally he manages: 'So what are we meant to do exactly? Forget it ever happened?' He twists his head to stare furiously out of the window before coming back with, 'There's no way we can do that! We can't just write it off like some bad debt! I have to tell you that the trustees intend to instruct lawyers,' he presses on. 'Not to mention the police.' He is angling for some greater reaction from me. 'And they're absolutely right!' he cries in a final outburst. 'It's theft! And of the most craven and disgusting sort!'

In the pause that follows, he pulls back a little, he says almost contritely, 'I'm sorry. I didn't mean to . . .' He makes a gesture as if to claw some of his remarks back.

But we both know he meant every word.

Leaving, Jack's warnings reverberate through my mind and I wonder if I haven't given too much away.

'He didn't get enough support, that was the trouble!' Anne declares emotionally. 'He just didn't get enough support!'

She looks to Charles and, briefly, Diana, but I am aware that her comment is aimed at me. It's a theme she has hinted at several times in the last hour but not openly voiced until now. We are sitting in Anne and Charles's drawing-room indulging in desultory speculation about why Harry should have taken his own life.

Charles mumbles tensely, 'I don't think that's quite right, dear. I really don't. I think there were all kinds of pressures . . .'

Anne's voice rises again. 'But if he'd been able to *talk* to someone. *That's* what's so dreadful . . .' Unable to bring herself to look at me, she directs her resentment at Charles. 'Someone should have realised. *Someone.*'

I suppose I should defend myself – I think Anne is hoping I will – but I don't want to be drawn into an argument that will distress us both.

Diana drawls some inaudible comment. Forced to repeat herself, she rasps crossly, 'Never a talker, Harry. Never. Not to anyone.' She blows a dismissive breath through drooping lips and reaches, fumbling, for a cigarette. She has shown little emotion apart from irritation, as though she would like to get hold of Harry and give him a piece of her mind.

The room is hot and close. The curtains are partially closed, though whether against the sun or as some mark of respect for Harry I'm not sure. In the reduced light the densely patterned fabrics seem heavy and overblown, the gilt-framed landscapes dark and stormy, and, on the ancient Persian rugs, the sleeping dogs are like lumpen black shadows.

Charles says, 'I think we just have to accept that he was good at hiding his worries. After all, he hid them well enough from us.'

'What are you talking about?' Anne retorts tearfully. '*I* knew something was wrong! *I* knew! It was just that I didn't want to interfere. I thought I'd be getting in the way. I thought I wouldn't be *welcome*. But I knew all right!' Her tremulous voice rises into an accusing silence.

'Whatever any of us did or didn't do personally,' Charles says, 'is rather by the way now. I really don't think there's any point in going over it time and again. He was obviously determined to do what he did—'

'How can you say that?' Anne returns sharply. 'Harry wasn't the sort of person to give up. When did he ever give up?' She glares at us emotionally, daring us to answer. 'He must have felt so *lonely* to even *think* of doing such an awful thing,' she cries in a tone of high reproach. 'That's the worst of all. Not having anyone to turn to!'

'Anne, *please*.' Charles purses up his face in rare exasperation, and Anne closes her mouth abruptly, looking wounded.

I get up and Anne's liquid eyes follow me as I position an ashtray under Diana's toppling ash. Before I can retreat, Diana's long claw-like fingers close on my arm. 'You were hard on him, you know. You shouldn't have been so hard on him.'

I stare at her, too astonished and hurt to speak.

'Couldn't live up to it all,' she declares.

I don't try to ask her what she means by this, I just pick up my bag and with a tense goodbye leave the room. Charles catches me at the door.

'Ellen dear – don't take any notice. Please. They're just upset.'

I breathe hard and nod. I let him walk me to my car.

'It's the sense of having been so useless,' he goes on. 'That's what's makes us all so *cross* with ourselves.'

'Yes.'

'They didn't mean it.'

'No.'

344

He squeezes my hand.

'I'm sorry about the candidacy,' I say, remembering that condolences are in order.

'Oh, there we are,' he says phlegmatically. 'I didn't really fit the bill, did I? I mean, I'm a bit of an anachronism. Small-time landed gentry dabbling in politics – outmoded. Jack's much more the image – thrusting and successful and all that. I think they've made a wise choice.'

'Yes,' I say, 'I think they probably have.'

When I get home the children are watching their favourite soap and Molly is scraping burnt debris out of a pan.

'Bloody press,' she declares, abandoning the pan. 'Kept phoning. So I put a message on the answering machine saying we were unavailable and not taking messages. Is that all right?'

I tell her that's fine.

'Oh, and your father called earlier. He didn't seem to know what was going on. I wasn't sure what to do, so I sort of told him. Sorry, I just thought maybe . . .'

I tell her that she did the right thing, that I'm glad it was someone else who told him. My father will be finding the idea of suicide embarrassing, even threatening, and I'm sure he would have had great difficulty in finding something to say to me.

Molly pours coffee and cranes at the jotter pad by the phone. 'Oh, and Margaret got a fax at the office from Richard Moreland – in Saudi Arabia, is it? – saying he couldn't get through, and could you fax him back.'

'Could you ask Margaret . . . No—' I pick up my coffee, I start for the study. 'Thanks, I'll call her myself.'

Margaret is not at home but I leave a message on her machine asking her to fax Moreland in the morning and tell him what has happened. Though I miss my daily talks with Moreland, I'm not sorry to be communicating with him at one remove. I can't entirely forget that it was he who led the police to Harry's body, that I have him to thank for this sword of doom that hangs over my head, and just at the moment I feel rather confused about that.

While I'm speaking into Margaret's tape, I remember something I was going to ask her yesterday. I thought of it on my way back from Jack's, while I was still smarting from the sense of inadequacy he always seems to produce in me. Reaching into a drawer, I take out the Majorca hotel bill with Meacher's name on it and check the date – it was some five years ago – and ask Margaret if she could look it up for me in the office diary and tell me what was happening around that time.

When I return to the kitchen Molly is getting ready to leave.

'Sure you'll be all right?'

'Sure,' I say.

'You know, I keep thinking . . .' She hesitates, she puts on a expression of studied puzzlement. 'This suicide thing – don't take this wrong – but I just never thought he had it in him.'

In the end it is easier to shut ourselves away for a few days. I inform Josh's headmistress that he won't be attending school until further notice; I ask Molly and Jill if they would be kind enough to shop for us; I have the answering machine refer calls to Margaret, who phones in twice a day with the messages; and Jill's husband frees the hinges of the ancient gates at the end of the drive with a hammer and chisel and swings them shut for the first time in living memory, although, strictly speaking, we are acting illegally by barring public access to the ancient bridle paths which criss-cross the estate.

I'm glad of our isolation. I enjoy walking with the children and doing things we used to do when they were younger and I seemed to have more time, like setting nature projects and reading aloud. I rally them to these pursuits in a relentless way, all heartiness and positive thinking like some scout-mistress. It's not that I'm insensitive to their moods, I'm just anxious to show them that life goes on, that, while we need to come to terms with these new events, it's also important to draw strength from each other.

I tell neither of them about the post-mortem, which Charles informs me is being carried out on Wednesday morning. Nor do I tell them that the operation to lift the yacht is under way until, after a failed attempt on Wednesday afternoon, it is finally accomplished late on Thursday. Not understanding the possible significance of this – and I do not explain it to them – they listen to this news with curiosity but no alarm.

Later we discuss the funeral, which I'm hoping to arrange for early next week: how it should be, the sort of hymns Harry would have liked. Twice I give Josh the option of staying away, but this causes him to glare at me accusingly, as if I am trying to deny him his rights from some deep and dishonourable motives of my own. I am careful not to suggest it again.

We talk about suicide too, or rather I talk about it and the children listen. I tell them how people with lots of problems can get so worried about them that their bodies get worn down and stop working properly and send all the wrong chemicals round the brain and then the brain stops working properly and these people become very ill, though neither they nor anyone else may realise it, and that this illness is as real as if they had broken a leg or needed an operation. I try to explain how, even though Daddy loved us all just as much as he ever did, the illness was so bad that it blotted out his memory and his feelings and, though he never wanted to leave us, he felt he had no choice. I consider telling them about the insurance money and how, if everything had gone to plan, it would have been his legacy to us, but on balance I decide against this.

With difficulty, because it's something that disturbs me too, I also tell them about attitudes to suicide, how people who don't understand about illnesses of the brain think that it's simply a lack of will, that only weak people kill themselves, when in fact you have to be very strong to do it. How some people like to suggest it's the dead person's fault, when it's no one's fault at all. How families can feel very guilty, as though they might have been able to prevent it, when it can be quite impossible to foretell. I say that none of us could have guessed what Daddy was going to do, that he gave no clue.

Such a painful discussion was never going to be easy, and both children are upset by it, albeit in different ways – Katie looks cross, as though she would rather not hear about it at all, while Josh seems overwhelmed by the unfathomable mysteries of the adult world. But I know I'm right to force them through it, that before they face other people they must understand how unfairly the outside world may judge our tragedy.

Friday is the kind of day when the world seems to have rolled to a gentle halt. The heat hangs over the wheat fields, a single whisp of cloud floats in the haze of the sky, and the river is dull as an old mirror. In the late afternoon, as the haze thickens into a sulphurous band that blurs the horizon, I think about Moreland. I wonder whether he's back at his cottage yet, and if so, whether he's waiting for his wife there, or has brought her down with him from London. I wonder if she's as striking as her photograph; I wonder if, for all her attractiveness, she is good to him.

We decide to eat supper on the terrace. As the children carry out the last of the dishes and bicker amiably over who should go back for some forgotten cutlery, the doorbell sounds.

'I hope this isn't inconvenient, Mrs Richmond,' says Dawson, standing in the porch, 'but I was just passing. A few words?' He is looking hot and uncomfortable, his skin glistening, his hair damp at the temples. Sitting heavily at the kitchen table, he cranes his neck and runs a finger inside his collar.

I put a glass of iced water in front of him and invite him to take his jacket off.

He meets the suggestion with slight disapproval, as if I am encouraging him to break some rule, and briefly shakes his head. Clasping his hands together, he settles his elbows on the table.

'Perhaps you could tell me, Mrs Richmond,' he asks in a monotone, 'would you have described your husband as a meticulous man? Something of a planner?'

For some reason, this wasn't the sort of question I was expecting. 'Well . . . in business things, yes. He had to be. Otherwise . . .' I shrug. 'Not especially. It depended . . .'

'He had made a will?'

'Oh yes.'

'And he had insurance policies?'

'Yes.'

Dawson sips at his water and brings his slow eyes back to mine. 'And there was no note, Mrs Richmond?' he says quietly. 'You would have told me if there was a note, wouldn't you?'

'There was no note.'

'No,' he agrees as though the question was hardly worth asking in the first place. 'No . . .' He contemplates the table for a moment. 'A thorough man, though?'

'Well, I . . . On things that mattered.'

'And what sort of things mattered?'

'Well . . .' I face multiple images of Harry. 'Oh, the usual things, I suppose. Work, money, career – his political career, I mean.'

'And his family, I imagine.'

I tilt my head questioningly.

'He would have been concerned about you and the children.'

'Well, yes.'

'Did he talk about that? About your future?'

'From time to time—'

'In the period just before he died?'

'Not really. No. Not then.'

'But he must have had some worries about you. Respecting your financial situation.'

I see where this is leading. 'He didn't talk about it. Not particularly.'

Dawson rests his thumbs against the flattened bridge of his nose and squints briefly at me before saying, 'Your husband was very thorough when it came to his death, Mrs Richmond.'

A beat of alarm. 'Oh?'

'Perhaps you could suggest a reason?'

'When you say thorough?'

'He didn't talk about insurance policies at all?' Dawson says, ignoring my question. 'In the period just before his death?'

'No.'

'But the life policy was substantial?'

'Well – yes. So I'm told. I never knew much about it . . . It wasn't something we discussed.'

'Ah.'

The unknown pulses high in my chest. I ask again, 'You said he was thorough?'

Dawson's eyes lock on mine. 'He sawed through two plastic pipes, wide pipes that would let the water in rapidly. He then' – a pause – 'shut himself inside . . .'

I absorb this carefully. 'You mean . . .?' I wait until he spells it out for me.

'So as to be sure he wouldn't be found.'

Ah. We are back to the unthinkable things that unrestrained bodies do, the way they rise, the way the currents pick them up and carry them off to more public places.

'And you think he did all this for a reason?'

'Most people leave notes, Mrs Richmond. They like the world to be in no doubt as to what they have done, and why. It gives them an easier mind.'

'But not if . . .?' I want the thought finished for me.

'Well, the circumstances would be different if a man was thinking of his wife's financial welfare, wouldn't they, Mrs Richmond?' Catching my remaining uncertainty, he explains gently, 'For his wife to claim on the insurance, he would need to go out of his way to hide the true nature of his death. Go somewhere he wasn't likely to be found. Leave no note.'

I nod sharply, humbly. I lower my head.

Dawson drains his water and lumbers to his feet. 'Thank

you for your time, Mrs Richmond. I very much appreciate it.'

On the way to the front door, I slow down. 'The post-mortem,' I ask, 'that's all . . . *over*, is it?'

'It will be shortly.'

'And . . . there's no doubt, I suppose . . .' I wait but he gives me no help. '. . . about what happened?'

He gives me a sorrowful look. 'Mrs Richmond, it wasn't an accident.'

I press a hand to my head as if to restore my brain. 'No. No, of course not . . .'

I watch him climb into his car beside one of the blank-faced young officers who came before. Without thinking, conditioned to a thousand leave-takings, I give them a hearty wave as they drive away.

Returning to the children, I find myself tipping Katie a soft wink.

It is only later, when I am alone, that I give a shape to the small glimmer I am feeling, and realise that I am allowing myself to believe that the worst is over.

FOURTEEN

'I'm afraid it won't be possible to fix a date *quite* yet, old thing,' says Charles, coming to a halt near the edge of the ditch and casting me one of his more oblique looks.

We are talking of the funeral.

'Why not?' I ask.

He clasps his arms, he blinks rapidly, his mouth turns down. I notice how very overheated he looks, and how very worn, his eyes drooping, his skin scored with an old man's lines, and I wonder what sort of a time he's having at home with Anne. 'Apparently these things always take time,' he says. 'No way round it. The police have to finish all their inquiries before they can, you know . . . actually sign things off.'

I suppose he means, before they can release the body. I look out over the ripening wheat which stands motionless in long furry waves. For some reason I had made up my mind that we would be able to get the funeral behind us. I wish someone had told me sooner.

'I thought the police *were* finished,' I say.

'Oh, I'm sure they *are*!' Charles insists, as if he can reassure me by force of will. 'I think it's just a matter of paperwork. Red tape.'

Red tape. I can only think of the post-mortem. What

else could it be? I can only imagine it isn't over and done with after all, a thought that has me draining the last of the wine from the warm glass I'm clutching stickily in my hand. I have already had one more glass than is good for my thinking, and probably my judgement as well.

'And the inquest?' I ask.

'Likely to be adjourned again.' He screws up his face apologetically. 'The coroner's office can't give a date for the hearing proper. All depends on the police again. How long it takes them to wrap things up. Got the impression the police aren't too speedy in these matters. Could be weeks. Even months.'

Momentarily confused, I have a grim thought. 'The funeral, that won't take—?'

'Oh no! Oh no! That'll be much sooner. Much sooner. Different lot of paperwork.'

'Paperwork . . . But what paperwork, Charles?'

He seems surprised at my persistence. 'They just talked about *formalities*. I rather assumed . . . They didn't give any details.'

But it has to be the post-mortem. What else could it be? I have a sense of powerlessness.

I look back to the terrace, to where Molly and Margaret sit under an umbrella with their coffee, to where Katie lies face down on the sunbed, plugged into her Walkman, and Josh stands by the barbecue poking at it with some sort of stick. As I watch he throws something onto the embers which makes them flame up and causes him to step back smartly and look around to see if anyone has noticed.

'I was going to put the house on the market,' I murmur.

'But . . . you can, can't you? I thought things were clear now.'

Now that there's a death certificate, he means. Now that, legally speaking, I'm a widow.

'I was going to wait until after the funeral,' I explain. 'I didn't want people all over the house.'

'Of course you don't. But surely, a bit of a delay won't hurt—'

'Things have changed,' I explain. 'I was relying on the life insurance, you see. That was virtually the only money I had. But suicide doesn't pay.' The irony was completely unintentional, and I give a bleak chuckle.

Charles blink rate shoots up. Beads of sweat dance on his eyebrows. 'No. Well, in that case . . .' I can't tell whether it's my attitude that embarrasses him, or the talk of money.

We start to walk again, following the edge of the lawn towards the rose garden and the heavy mantle of blooms, which hang vivid in the sluggish air. Now and again Charles pushes out his lower lip and funnels a draught of air upwards over his glowing nose. He is wearing his customary weekend outfit which, irrespective of the season, consists of baggy trousers and a long-sleeved, heavy cotton check shirt designed for altogether sharper weather.

'I've been wanting to say Anne's really sorry for what she said the other day,' he says, growing awkward. 'She was upset, you know.'

I tell him what he wants to hear. I tell him I didn't take it too seriously. 'But she may have had a point, you know. Maybe I wasn't supportive enough.'

His head comes up sharply. 'No, not at all! No, I thought you were superb with Harry. A great support!'

'I was hard on him towards the end.' Why I tell him this I'm not sure. Perhaps I need to know what Charles thinks of me in the light of Harry's suicide. Perhaps I want to prepare him in some small way for the truth.

'They were difficult times, Ellen. You mustn't blame yourself. I really don't think Harry could have asked for

355

more.' He moves his hand as if to touch mine, then swings it back diffidently. 'You were always so *loyal*.'

Loyal. Still this immaculate picture of me. Even if I suddenly announced that I drove Harry to it, I doubt he'd believe me.

We pause in front of a bed of crimson floribunda roses, their heads hanging low in the heat. At last I broach the question I have been wanting to ask Charles for some time, and for which I have engineered this stroll.

'I wanted to know—' My stomach floats upwards. 'How did they identify Harry's body?'

His damp face contorts with dismay. He makes a nervous sound. 'Ellen . . . Dear girl, what can it matter now?'

'I'd like to know, that's all.'

'But . . .' He gestures helplessly.

I try to explain that not knowing is far worse than anything else. Far, far worse.

His shoulders hunch forward, he fights some inner battle. Reaching a decision, he says with a sigh, 'Well . . .'

I wait.

'Dental records,' he offers at last, his voice gathering strength. 'Partly. And partly direct identification.'

I digest this slowly. 'Direct? But who by?' But even as I ask this, his expression gives me my answer. I touch his arm. 'Why didn't you say? You should have said.' I add, 'How awful for you.'

He brushes my pity aside with a shy gesture, a man who likes to think that in circumstances such as this feelings are something of an irrelevance.

I have a vision of the mortuary, of Charles staring down. I feel sympathy for him, but also, it has to be said, relief for myself, because he was there and now he will be able to tell me what I want to know.

'Was it . . . bad?' I ask very quietly.

He gives a brisk shake of the head.

'You could tell . . . that it was him?'

Enlightenment passes over his shaggy features; he thinks he understands why I am putting us through all this. 'Oh yes. There was no doubt it was him, Ellen. No doubt.'

'I mean, he wasn't . . .?' I wait for help. Getting none, I murmur, '. . . damaged?'

Another wave of comprehension. 'Oh no! No . . .' he says gently, 'the *damage* was in the chest, Ellen.'

He still hasn't grasped what I'm after. I know perfectly well where Harry was shot. It's the rest that worries me.

'I meant, after all that time in the sea, wasn't he . . .?' But I can't say it.

Charles is there at last. 'Oh no. He was remarkably . . .' It takes him a moment to find the word. '. . . *untouched*.'

'But I thought . . .'

He looks as though he might try to spare me the details but, catching my expression, he pushes his shoulders back, he says in oddly formal tones, 'Apparently the water's the critical factor – the water temperature, that is. And it was pretty cold. Also . . .' He describes a circle in the air. 'Being enclosed . . .' He waves the hand again, but feebly.

'Enclosed?'

'Being inside the cabin.'

'That made a difference?'

He fastens his mouth down and nods.

Finally I have it; the closed hatches, the sealed cabin, the lack of creatures that might swim in and – I use this careful word of ours – *damage* him.

No wonder the post-mortem isn't finished yet.

'Thanks for telling me.'

Charles's eyelids flutter. His tired face folds itself into a smile. 'Dear thing,' he says gruffly.

We head back across the lawn, which, after a brief revival during the rains, is growing large yellow patches again. The tableau on the terrace has shifted, I notice. The children are sitting together on the sunbed, Margaret has vanished and Molly is standing with her arms folded, glass cradled in one hand, waiting for us.

'I thought I'd take this lot for a swim,' she calls as we approach, tilting her head in the children's direction. Only when I am much closer does she tell me in a low voice which Charles cannot hear, 'The police have just arrived. Margaret's got them in the study.'

I glance quickly towards the children.

Following my gaze, Molly says matter-of-factly, 'I haven't mentioned it to them.'

I ask half to myself, 'But what do they want?'

Molly peers at me. 'You all right?'

I pull myself together. 'It's the way they come unannounced.'

I go to the children and try to sell them the swimming idea. I remind them that we have been offered the use of a pool by friends while they're away on holiday. But one glance at Katie's face and I can see that, though Molly may not have told her about the police, she has picked up the fact that something is going on.

'I've got to go and talk to the police for a while,' I explain immediately.

Katie gives me a hard stare, as if to ask whether I'm keeping anything from her. Even after all this time, she still has these moments of doubt. I touch her shoulder soothingly. 'It's just a routine thing. It won't take long. But why don't you go and swim?'

I can see the effort it takes her to summon her optimism. 'Okay,' she announces suddenly, getting to her feet.

Josh clambers up after her. I would speak to him, I would reassure him too, but he has gone before I have the chance.

Entering the study, I am met by the gaze of one of Dawson's blank-faced young officers. Dawson himself is standing at a bookcase, squinting at titles. He is wearing a suit in an eye-catching shade of mid-blue with a slight sheen to it.

He turns unhurriedly. 'Mrs Richmond,' he says with a small gesture of greeting, 'sorry to bother you again.' We meet in the middle of the room. 'But I was wondering if you could spare me some of your time? A few formalities. I would hope to have you back within a couple of hours or so.'

'Back?'

'We'll need to go to the station.'

'Oh,' I say, giving myself a second or two. I glance at Margaret, who is looking cross on my behalf, then back to Dawson. 'It can't wait?'

He makes a regretful face. 'No.' It seems to me that there is a doggedness in his gaze which wasn't there before.

'And we can't do it here?' I ask.

'Not really. I'm going to need a statement, you see. And that can't really be done elsewhere.'

'A statement,' I echo.

'A standard requirement.' He makes a reassuring movement, a spreading motion of his hand. 'We have to put things on record.'

But why now? I wonder.

I say, 'Then . . . of course.'

'Oh, and . . .' Dawson says in the casual tone of an

afterthought, 'you might like to speak to your solicitor. See if you would like to have him with you. Many relatives do in these circumstances.'

In the pause that follows, the young officer shifts his weight slightly, and I find myself looking into a face that seems to have borrowed its studiously stony expression from a dozen bad films.

'But if you'd prefer not . . .' Dawson lifts his mouth into a meagre smile.

'I think perhaps . . .'

Dawson tilts his head.

'. . . that I will call him. If you don't mind.'

'Of course not, Mrs Richmond. That's your privilege.'

The room is box-like, with a narrow window set high in the wall. It is painted cream with a black floor and stained wood skirting, and has the sickly smell of industrial cleaner and room deodoriser. The furniture consists of a rectangular table, with one end pressed up against the wall, and, around it, the four chairs on which we sit, and, by the door, a fifth chair on its own. A battered tin ashtray, emblazoned with the name of a popular lager, empty of butts but caked with stubborn ash, lies on the table before me, alongside the heavy circular stand which supports the thin shaft of the microphone. The recorder itself sits on the edge of the table, against the wall. The formica surface of the table, shiny and otherwise unmarked, is scored by a single groove as if something very sharp has been dragged across it.

A uniformed policewoman has brought me tea in a plastic cup. Leonard, at my side, has accepted some water which he doesn't touch. The young officer opposite him stares out at me over the rim of his drink, while Dawson, facing me on the other side of the microphone, stirs sugar into his coffee.

'Not the most comfortable of surroundings,' Dawson says with a grunt of apology. 'But the recorder saves us having to stop every few minutes to get things down on paper. Saves a lot of time.'

I nod my understanding, though I am finding this more unsettling than I imagined.

The overhead light drains Dawson's skin of colour and accentuates the fractured ridge of his nose and the pouches beneath his eyes, so that when he offers me a quick smile the warmth, if it is there, is lost.

'Just have to get the recorder going,' he says. He presses a button or two, and, in a lumbering monotone, gives the date, the time, the place, his and the other officer's name, and my name and the fact that I am giving my statement in the presence of my solicitor, Mr Leonard Braithwaite.

'Have to go through all that, I fear,' Dawson says, instilling his voice with sudden intimacy, 'otherwise we can't transcribe from tape to paper. Can't use it for the record.' He clears his throat, he sips his coffee. 'Now . . . I'll have to ask you to go over one or two matters that we've already covered, so you may have to bear with me.' The washed-out smile again. He settles his forearms on the table, he clasps his hands loosely together. 'Perhaps we could start with Mr Richmond's general state of mind in the weeks before 26th March. How would you describe it?'

I tell him what I told him before, about the pressures on Harry, the disappointments he suffered, the debts that he kept to himself and which I only found out about later. Going through it again, I hear myself honing the story, embellishing it in small but significant ways, painting

Harry a little closer to despair. I don't like myself for doing this, but that doesn't seem to stop me.

Dawson leads me onwards with an interest that is methodical, often kindly, but never less than attentive.

'And the day of his disappearance, he gave no sign of being particularly depressed?'

'No more than usual, no.'

'There was no indication that he had any desire to take his own life?'

'No.'

'And he had never talked about taking his own life at any point in the past?'

'Never. It never entered my mind. I suppose it should have. I suppose if I'd thought—'

'Perhaps we could just go through the events of that last day, Friday, 26 March.' His low voice, steady and smooth, coaxes me forward. 'How did the day start?'

I have to think for a moment. 'We got up at about eight. Maybe just beforehand. We had breakfast. I went to the supermarket to get some food—'

'What time was that?'

'Nine. About then. I must have got back – I don't know – about quarter past ten? Harry was loading the car with gear for the boat. I sorted the food out, put it in boxes, took it out to the car. Then we drove down to the quay.'

'And when was that?'

This preoccupation with time. I try to think. 'At about . . . it must have been eleven-thirty.'

'There was a lot of this gear to load then, was there?' he asks in a tone of puzzlement.

'Not that much. Clothes, charts, food. It was only a weekend trip. Two, three days at the most.'

'But it took until eleven-thirty to load?'

'Well, yes. Harry kept getting sidetracked.'

'Oh. In what way?'

'Phone calls, that sort of thing.'

'Ah.' He nods, he drains his coffee. 'Business calls?'

'I think so. I just heard him on the phone.'

He cants his head slightly to one side. 'You never saw a shotgun in the car that day?'

I take this slowly. 'No.'

'Not something you'd miss really, not something that size,' Dawson remarks more to himself than anyone else. 'Would you think?' he asks, coming back to me.

I lift my shoulders. 'Harry'd already loaded a whole pile of waterproofs and boots and things like that. It could have been hidden underneath something, I suppose.'

Dawson gets a distant look as if seeing the possibility of this for the first time. Fixing his gaze on me again, he says gently, 'The firearms licence was for two shotguns, to be kept in a locker at the house. When did you first realise that one was missing?'

I work backwards. 'Three weeks ago? Whenever it was that the police officers came for the inspection.'

'No one had looked in the locker since your husband left on his final trip, since 26 March?'

'No. Harry was the only one who ever opened it.'

Seeming to lose his concentration for a moment, Dawson twists his cup slowly in his fingers.

I turn to catch Leonard's eye, wondering if he is happy with the way this seems to be developing into a question-and-answer session, but if he is concerned he gives no sign, and merely raises his eyebrows as if to say, not long now.

Dawson is asking, 'Did Mr Richmond ever leave a gun on the boat at all?'

'I'm not sure. It wasn't something I ever asked about.'

'And Mr Richmond didn't mention it?'

'No.'

It must be air-conditioned in here. I am beginning to feel chilled.

'So you loaded the car – could you take the story on from there?' Dawson's tone has softened again, as if he has just reminded himself of my situation and the need for a sympathetic approach.

'We drove down to the quay. I waited in the car while Harry went to fetch *Minerva* from her mooring and bring her in to the quay—'

'Forgive me—' Dawson asks with exaggerated politeness. 'But that took how long?'

'I suppose half an hour. No, a bit more. Forty minutes perhaps. Then we loaded everything onto the boat.'

'And you didn't notice a gun at this stage?'

'No.'

'And you would have, do you think, if it had been there?'

'Well . . . I honestly can't say. Harry carried some of the heavier loads. It could have been in there. I wasn't really looking. The weather was appalling. It was bucketing down. We were trying to get the job finished as quickly as possible.'

'Of course. Please . . .' He bobs his head. 'Go on.'

'When everything was in the boat I sat in the car while Harry stowed things away inside. Then I helped him get away. Untied the ropes.' I anticipate the next query with: 'It must have been about a quarter past one.'

'And he was heading where at this point?'

We have covered this twice before in the past, but I

364

suppose that counts for nothing now that we are setting down the definitive version, and I am doubly aware of the need to get it right. I explain how *Minerva* could not stay at the quay on a falling tide, how Harry had to take her out to the mooring until the time was right to go downstream, how he was aiming to get to the mouth of the river at about six that evening and make a night passage round to the South Coast.

'And that was the last time you saw your husband, was it, Mrs Richmond, when he took the yacht away from the quay?'

The question throws me. I'm not sure what lies behind it. For an instant I read suspicion in his expression, I seem to detect an undertone to his words; then, forcing myself to recognise the improbability of this, seeing instead Dawson's lumbering adherence to step by step procedure, I confirm that it was indeed the last time I saw him.

'And did you see him stop at the mooring?'

I shake my head. 'It was raining so hard. I couldn't see that far.' I reach for my cup and slide it closer.

'So you never saw the yacht stopped at the mooring?'

This sounds like the same question. 'No.'

Dawson lifts a blunt finger and scratches at the chipped surface of his cheek. 'So what did you do then, Mrs Richmond, after he'd gone?'

'I went home.'

He waits for me to elaborate, then prompts: 'And what did you do there?'

We have never covered this before. 'I gave my son his lunch, I helped him with his project, I did some chores. Not very much really.'

He gives a series of slow professional nods, like a doctor listening to a long-winded patient. 'And later?'

'I dropped my son at Jill Hooper's and went to have supper with Molly.'

We establish Molly's identity as Miss Molly Sinclair, and her address.

'You spent the evening there?'

I nod. This being insufficient for the demands of the tape, he raises his eyebrows patiently and waits until I have given voice to a yes.

'And you left Miss Sinclair at what time?'

I sip at the tea which is tepid and bitter. I make a show of searching my memory. 'It must have been about ten,' I say finally. 'I thought it was later, I think I may have told you it was later, but it just seemed that way because we started the evening so early. I'm sure it can't have been later than ten.'

Dawson leans slowly back in his seat, and flexes his shoulders like someone easing a troublesome back. He gives a sudden smile, as if to apologise for the distraction. 'You went straight home?' he asks, finding his coaxing voice again.

'Yes.'

'Arriving when?'

'Well, it must have been ten-thirty or so, I suppose. If I left at ten.'

'Once at home, you stayed in the house?'

This, too, is new territory. 'Well – yes.'

'You didn't go out again for any reason?'

My heart gives a solitary tap against my ribs. 'No.'

'You didn't go down to the river?'

'No, I . . .' Then, as understanding comes: 'I never thought Harry might still be there. It never occurred to me.'

'And now – do you think Mr Richmond *was* there?'

Does he expect a guess? An opinion? 'I don't know. He

366

hadn't said anything about staying. He seemed set on going that night.'

A pause. I cradle my cup with both hands, though the tea offers little warmth. I see Leonard glance at his watch and wonder if he will try to limit the length of the interview. I hope so. I'm not sure I can go on much longer without making mistakes.

Dawson dips into the silence. 'After you'd returned home that night, did you hear anything at all? Anything unusual?'

'Unusual?'

'Any sound. Anything you particularly noticed?'

But I sense he has a particular sound in mind.

'Outside, you mean?'

He nods.

'Not that I remember.' I look at Leonard and back to Dawson. I make a gesture which suggests it would be helpful to know what sort of sound I am meant to be remembering.

Ignoring this, Dawson continues on some predetermined course. 'The day of the twenty-sixth, did Mr Richmond injure himself in any way?'

'Injure?'

'Incur any knocks, bruises, that sort of thing? That you know of?'

So this is what they have found at the post-mortem. This is the worst they have found. A bubble of relief ripples up inside me.

I shake my head. 'But he was always bumping himself on the boat. Coming back with bruises.'

'But there was nothing you noticed that day of the twenty-sixth? Nothing he remarked on?'

'No.' I look to Leonard, wishing he would follow up

with the obvious question. Finally I ask it myself. 'Why? Was there something . . .?'

Dawson looks doubtful about answering this, though whether from a desire to spare my feelings or ingrained caution it's hard to tell. 'A bruise was found,' he states with magisterial solemnity. 'On the side of the head.'

For an instant, imagination and memory mix, become indistinguishable. I see Harry in the boat's saloon. I see him falling sideways, his head meeting the corner of the folded table. The next moment the picture shifts and my imagination casts it quite differently, and I wonder how I could have conjured up so sharp an image.

Perhaps Dawson reads something of the strain in my face because he glances up at the wall clock, then at his watch, and says, 'We can leave it there, if you like, Mrs Richmond. Finish off another day.'

I nod mutely.

Dawson scrapes his chair back and makes to rise. Then, straightening his fingers in a gesture of recollection, he leans forward again. 'Did, er, Mr Richmond have any particular enemies that you know of?'

I almost laugh. I thought they only asked questions like this in films. 'Not that I'm aware of.' Even my answer sounds like something from a script.

'Nobody who wished him harm in any way?'

I blink incredulously. Can he be suggesting that Harry's death might have been suspicious? That a cutout villain – some business rival – felt so aggrieved that he somehow plotted against Harry? The idea is so fantastical that I don't know what to say.

Dawson takes his answer from my face. 'No?'

'No.' I emphasise this with a firm shake of the head.

Dawson leans into the microphone and signs off.

Leonard helps me stiffly to my feet. As Dawson comes round the table, I find the courage to ask, 'That sound you thought I might have heard – you didn't say what it was meant to be?'

Coming slowly to a halt, Dawson lifts his heavy head and frowns at me, as if weighing me up afresh. Finally he says impassively, 'A person has stated that he heard a sound on the river late last night. He thought it was a gunshot.'

There is a deep pause. It is left to Leonard to break it.

'But that can't have anything to do with this matter, surely? If it was on the river.'

'Quite so,' says Dawson evenly. 'But as I'm sure you'll appreciate, we still have to make the appropriate inquiries.' He inclines his head towards me. 'Sorry to have kept you so long, Mrs Richmond.'

'Not at all.' Producing what I hope is a suitable response, I give a brave little smile.

I had forgotten about the anonymous letter with its newspaper clipping. Or perhaps I hadn't forgotten, but had pushed it to the back of my mind. After supper, gripping a second glass of wine that Molly had pressed into my hand, I leave her and the children watching TV and take myself to the study. I locate the letter half hidden by an opera brochure at the back of the drawer.

I read it in the context of Dawson's questions. An enemy? The writer of this cowardly little note certainly qualifies. But venom is a long way from wishing someone harm, and further still from doing something about it. This pitiable person would probably run a mile from any thoughts of violence. But if Dawson is set on the idea of enemies, if the gunshot and the bruise are lodged in his mind, then this, at least, would give him something to focus on.

There are dangers. It could complicate everything irredeemably. It could harden Dawson's thinking, move him permanently away from the idea of suicide, make him determined to search out new evidence. Perhaps I'm crazy, perhaps without this, Dawson would simply drop the whole idea of enemies.

Yet even as I think this, I feel he will not. It is the gunshot. People don't fire shotguns around here late at night. The occasional poacher maybe, once in a blue moon. But it's sufficiently rare for Dawson to be thinking, not surprisingly, that the gunshot could have been the same one that killed Harry. That something happened to Harry while the boat was still in the river.

... *Betrayed by Scum. Britain stinks for Real heroes ... the Right man dEad now.*

I fold the letter and place it on top of the desk. The more I wonder whether it would be wise to show it to Dawson, the more undecided I become. I sit staring out into the garden, and wonder why things are moving so rapidly in the wrong direction. Though is it the wrong direction? Maybe not. This is the worst of it: I can't make up my mind.

I am roused by voices coming down the passage. Molly's burble, the low murmur of a male voice.

I realise: it is Moreland. I jump up, I check the drawers are closed. My own instincts fluster me; sometimes I forget what I am trying to hide and what I can safely reveal.

Molly, chattering brightly, leads him in. He is looking handsome in jeans and a pale-blue shirt. He seems both unexpected and familiar, a new friend that I have known

370

for ever. I feel a fast-beating pleasure, but also a sense of distance which I know it would be wise to maintain.

He grips my arm briefly, his only concession to sympathy, though for some reason this affects me more than any extravagant gesture.

'They've lifted the yacht?' It's a question but also an expression of concern.

I explain roughly what has happened and what the police have told me so far, how until today they saw it as a carefully planned suicide, set up to be undetectable, so that I could claim the insurance money.

'Until today?' Moreland prompts.

'Now they seem to want to know if Harry had any enemies.'

I am aware of Molly's eyes on us, picking up signals, trying to work out what if anything is in this relationship which I have told her so little about.

'The trouble with the police,' she declares, claiming Moreland's attention, 'is that they're not very bright. Once you've grasped that, you've grasped everything.'

While we discuss the IQ of the police she continues to examine Moreland with open interest until, with a show of tact, she takes herself off to catch a favourite programme.

'How are the children?' Moreland asks as soon as she has gone. I had forgotten this way he has of making me feel that I am being cared for, of making me feel, moreover, that I want to be.

I tell him that it's hard to be sure how they are coping. Katie seems to have accepted the fact of Harry's suicide, but Josh has gone quiet and won't speak much. Not, at any rate, to me.

'And *you*?' He makes a concerned creased-up face.

'Oh, I'm all right. Well . . .' I make a wild gesture, I give

371

a wry laugh. Why pretend? 'I wish the police didn't have these odd ideas. They seem to be looking for something *unusual* about Harry's death.' Unusual. I don't know why I say this. Everything about Harry's death was unusual.

I start to recount Dawson's questions, partly because it seems natural to tell Moreland, partly because I'm curious to hear his reaction. I settle in Harry's seat while Moreland wheels the typing chair over and, sitting at the side of the desk, slides an elbow across the leather and props his head against his hand. I had forgotten how beautiful his hands are, how he looks at me with an expression that seems to understand everything I am feeling.

'Perhaps Harry did have enemies,' I say. 'But ordinary enemies. Business enemies. With all the deals he did it would be funny if he hadn't fallen out with a few people along the way. He could be' – a stab of disloyalty – 'abrasive. But for someone to actually want to *do* something about it? A contract killing or something? I assume that must be what's in Dawson's mind. It's mad!'

'He didn't say why he was asking? What had given him the idea?'

'Not really. Except . . .' I make light of it. 'Oh, there was a gunshot. Someone is meant to have heard it late that Friday night. But it could have been poachers,' I declare, testing the argument, gauging the sound of it. 'There are plenty of poachers around. Or it could have been a farmer taking pot-shots at rabbits in his head-lights. Anything.'

But a spark of interest glitters in Moreland's eye. 'This person, did he hear where the shots came from?'

'He thought, the river.'

'What time was this?'

'Dawson didn't say.'

'What about the kind of sound? Was it loud, a bang, or more of a crack?'

But I don't know this either.

Moreland absorbs my limited information with an oddly speculative look, as if he were matching it to some previous knowledge. 'Did Dawson say anything else?'

'No.' As an afterthought I add, 'Well . . . there was this . . . *bruise* apparently. He asked me if Harry'd bumped his head that day. I told him Harry was always bashing himself on the boat, that he wasn't very good at holding on when the boat lurched, that sort of thing. At the end of a weekend he was always covered in bruises.'

Moreland listens with concentration before losing himself in some distant thought.

'What worries me about this talk of shots and enemies is that it'll get back to the children,' I sigh. 'You know how these things travel. I wish Dawson would leave it alone.' I wait for Moreland to agree with me.

'I realise it's difficult for you, Ellen. But I think he has no choice. I think he has to follow everything up.'

So here I have my independent appraisal: Dawson isn't likely to let go.

I look down at the cheap envelope lying in front of me. Realising that I may yet regret this, with some sense of going against my better judgement, I slide it slowly across the desk towards Moreland.

I don't say anything. I wait for him to take out the letter and the tattered press cutting and read them.

'When did this come?' His voice has darkened.

I tell him it was shortly after the memorial service.

'You haven't shown it to Dawson?'

'I didn't think it was important. You think . . .' I lift this into a question.

He gives me a reflective look before returning to the letter and reading it again. 'I think perhaps he should see it.'

'But this is just some pathetic little man, surely? Someone with a chip on his shoulder?'

He makes a who-can-tell face.

'Who's Joe Congreve?' I ask, though I have already guessed the answer.

He tucks the cutting inside the letter. 'He was the soldier from Harry's unit who got killed.'

So you know his name, I think. You know more than you let on. 'Tell me,' I say.

Moreland considers, he eyes me as if he is weighing up what I can take. 'Some of Harry's unit felt very aggrieved about Congreve's death,' he begins gravely. 'They felt that he was exposed to enemy fire unnecessarily. That the order to send him out on his own was' – he chooses the word with care – '*flawed*.'

'And they blamed Harry?'

'Feelings run high at times like that.'

'But ten years later?' I protest.

'I'm sure you're right,' he agrees suddenly, 'there's probably nothing in it. But I think the police should see it all the same. I could take it along, if you like. Fill in the background for them.'

I sigh, an agreement of sorts.

Moreland slips a hand over mine, and his grip is warm and firm. I glance down at his hand. When I look up again it's to find him frowning and smiling at the same time, a mixed message if there ever was one.

FIFTEEN

Katie has never talked to me about the 'bad-bad' time, the day four weeks before Harry's death when he finally got to her. She has never told me, and I realise now she never will. She told Bob Block, of course, but under the terms of the confessional. Before then she used to encourage Bob to tell me selected elements of her story, to act as impartial broker of the more difficult emotions. But not for this. She knew, I think, that it would hurt me too much.

But then I had already worked out when it must have happened. There was a weekend when Katie came out from school and I was away most of Saturday evening at one of Molly's fund-raising events. A friend of Katie's called Lucinda was meant to be staying the evening. I don't know why Lucinda left early, or when precisely Harry drove her home, but she wasn't there when I got back. Perhaps Harry engineered her departure, perhaps he planned it in advance. Perhaps, seeing the opportunity, he was simply incapable of resisting it. Who knows? Even now I'm not sure that his actions can be judged by any normal standards. I think that by this time he had sunk so deep into his own nightmare that his actions were inexplicable, even to himself.

But whatever led to it, at some point after he had driven

Lucinda home and Josh had gone to bed, he must have got Katie on her own.

When I came back at midnight and put my head round the study door – a move I undertook with caution at the best of times – he cast me a dismissive half-glare and declared impatiently that Lucinda was long gone and both Josh and Katie were in bed asleep. I was too tired to question this, too preoccupied to wonder why Katie wasn't up, watching her favourite late-night programme. All I wanted, I remember, was to sink into bed.

The next day we all drifted, barely connecting. I hardly saw Harry at all. Josh disappeared into the garden. Katie failed to appear for lunch. When I knocked on her door she announced she had stomach ache and wouldn't be getting up. Her voice was thick, her face puffy. I thought she must be coming down with something, I offered to call the doctor, but she wouldn't have it. All she'd agree to was to take some paracetamol washed down by a fizzy vitamin C drink. When I drove her back to school that evening, there was a blankness in her face.

Yes: that was when it happened.

I worked it out for the first time during that endless night on the boat, waiting for the dawn. It wasn't a great feat of deduction, not then, not after the events of the evening. I remembered how, soon after that Sunday when Katie had stayed in bed, she had failed a maths test and dropped out of the house play, how she had become monosyllabic on the phone. How, when Mrs Anderson noticed her sudden weight loss and sounded the alarm, I pronounced on the subject of anaemia and vitamin deficiencies – anything to avoid more painful truths – and took Katie to our doctor who, finding nothing physically wrong, suggested a touch of anorexia or school phobia or a mixture of both, and prescribed antidepressants. I didn't argue. Even if school phobia was wide of the mark, I was forced to face the larger truth of what he was saying, that Katie was disturbed in some inexpressible way. As I saw it then, there was only one thing that could be disturbing her, and that was our troubles at home – Harry's depression, my clumsy attempts to keep things running smoothly, and overlaying it all, our silent warfare, which, in my simplicity, I thought I had managed to conceal from both Katie and Josh. I should have known that children pick up on these things, that someone as intuitive as Katie was bound to absorb this tension and take it into her vulnerable heart.

Katie swallowed the antidepressants for a day or so, but when she next came home from school the tablets weren't in evidence and I think she must have thrown them away.

I believed love and communication offered the best medicine anyway. Having told Katie too little, I overcompensated and proceeded to tell her what I later realised, with some agony, was far too much. I spelt out Harry's troubles as far as I knew or guessed them, I emphasised the terrible pressures he was under, I explained how the situation was taking its toll on me as well and, if I wasn't my usual self, it was because I tended to worry too much. I implied that our problems were at a critical stage. I spoke to her as an adult, I didn't try to hide anything – except the affair with Caroline Palmer – and in so doing I can't rid myself of the suspicion – some days it's a certainty – that I helped bring about our disaster. I think I laid such a burden of responsibility on Katie, I painted the picture so dark that she felt she couldn't add to my problems by even hinting at what had happened, that if she said anything it would only make life unendurable for all of us.

She was right. It would have made life very difficult. But, though she had no way of realising it at the time, staying silent was going to make things far, far worse. Poor Katie: trapped.

I remember sitting with Katie in her bedroom as I catalogued Harry's woes, and the way she kept her eyes firmly on her lap, the way she wouldn't look at me. When I asked her if she understood what I was saying, her only response was a faint nod. At the time I felt she was being less than sympathetic. When she wouldn't answer my hug, I thought she was being unnecessarily difficult. Though, loving her as I did, not wanting to aggravate the anorexia, I didn't say this. I took care to let her know that she had our unconditional support. I told her that we'd always be there for her, that all she ever had to do was call, that in difficult times that was what families were for. Ironic, really.

And then – more ironic still – I looked around her bedroom which had been newly decorated in her favourite colours, lemon yellow and pale blue, with Osborne & Little chintz cushions and frilly curtains, and, sitting there on the bed, I thought how pretty it all looked and how, here at least, she must feel safe and secure.

In America, during those first weeks, this scene kept coming back to me, part of my regular programme of self-torture, in which I became Katie, I became fifteen and hurt and bleeding, I was there in the bathroom wiping the blood from my legs, I was hand-washing the sheet and hiding it in among the other laundry. I was degraded, diminished for ever. And then I put myself through the final betrayal, sitting in the lemon-yellow and blue bedroom, listening to my mother tell me about my stepfather's problems, how they were so great that he deserved all my understanding and support. And with this, both I and the person that was Katie died a little more inside.

The need to punish myself was very deep. For a while it became an obsession. I flooded Bob Block with self-reproach, I bombarded him with tears and mortification. But in time even guilt wears itself down into something more manageable. And, as our return to England grew nearer, so my instincts for self-preservation reasserted themselves. If I was to have any hope of protecting the children, I knew I had to get some sort of grip on the future.

Katie brought it home to me once when we were in Yosemite Park, in a designated viewing area where we were permitted to get out of the car and admire the scenery.

Reading her mood, I asked: Okay?

Fine, she said without much enthusiasm.

Tell me if you want to.

Her head was down, her arms were clasped tightly around her waist. She took a long time to answer.

Sometimes I feel bad about . . . how I feel. Sometimes I don't feel the way I should . . .

She was talking about Harry's death.

I can understand that, I said.

But it's *awful*. It's awful to think like that.

It's natural, though. I often feel the same.

You do?

Yes. Sometimes I'm glad he's dead.

She wasn't quite ready to believe this. She shook her head.

No, I said. *Really*. He was so ill, darling, he was so *unhappy* that I actually think he's better off. Happier.

Harry's illness featured heavily in our discussions then.

Bob Block had encouraged us to fasten on to it, both as an explanation for his behaviour, and as a means of coming to terms with our feelings about his death.

But Katie was not to be moved from her mood of self-condemnation. She said, I still feel . . . it was all my fault.

Your *fault*, baby? How could it possibly be your fault? It was never your fault.

But, Mum, I—

You did *nothing*, Katie. *Nothing*.

But I did! she cried in frustration. I *did*!

This was old ground, though not yet sufficiently well travelled for Katie's needs.

Listen, I said sternly, there are some things that it's right to blame yourself for, and others that it's just plain wrong to even think about blaming yourself for. You *know* which is which.

Bob Block had taken her through this many times. But that didn't stop her from giving me a look that was pure child, and asking miserably: You really think so?

I really think so.

She took what reassurance she could from this, which wasn't perhaps a lot just then, and looked away to where Josh was hanging over the rail that corralled tourists away from the edge of the gorge.

But I keep thinking, Mum. If something happened to you . . . she said, voicing the dread that never leaves her.

To me? I laughed.

Yes.

Nothing's going to happen to me.

I couldn't bear it.

Oh yes, you could, I said firmly.

But in my heart I knew she was right. She would fall apart.

This reminder came just in time. It concentrated my mind during those last days before we came home. It forced me to go through everything that had happened, to work out where we were vulnerable, and how I could best protect us; it made me realise how vital it was to get my story right.

Now Katie seems overcome by the same lethargy that gripped her before Harry died. I noticed it creeping over her at the weekend. She has lost the wish to do anything. She certainly shows no desire to get back to school. Her headmistress, having fired off a stiff note of disapproval, following it quickly with lavish expressions of sympathy at what she described as the nature of Harry's death – this arriving only two days after the discovery of Harry's body, a gauge of the efficiency of the local grape-vine – finally, two days ago, made an offer to have Katie back.

But Katie doesn't want to go. She can't say why. She doesn't seem unhappy exactly, but she has distanced herself from me. For the last two nights she has stopped coming into my bed for our nightly chat, she has stopped searching me out, and though she accepts my expressions of love, she does so passively, without focus.

I can't seem to lift her out of this mood; perhaps I'm the wrong person to try. But with the weekend over, Molly is back at work, and Margaret, who only comes in on Mondays now, isn't close enough to her. Josh has gone back to school, grumbling loudly but, I think, secretly relieved to be away from the house.

So we are alone together, Katie and I, but subtly apart. I would like to share my worries with her – how often have I sworn to her that I would? – but, having laid that kind of burden on her once before, I'm not about to do it again. Besides, how can I tell her that my reassurances might be meaningless? That I'm not so sure I'm going to be around for her after all? That, despite everything I have tried to do for us, luck might to be turning against me after all, and that I live in hourly expectation of being found out.

Maurice pulls at the handle and the door follows a slow backward arc into the underside of the roof. Sunlight floods the lower shelves along the rear wall of the garage, with their cargo of dusty boxes and old awnings and spare oars, and slants down over the rolls of carpet and unwanted furniture along one side.

Dawson steps in and looks at me questioningly.

I indicate the right-hand corner, which is in deep shadow, and follow him across the floor. We stand in front of the green tubular bag with its overflowing bulges of grey rubber.

'This is it?'

'This is it,' I confirm.

'It's what you'd call an inflatable?' Dawson asks with the air of someone who is keen to learn.

'Yes. Well – we used to call it the Zodiac. That's the make. A Zodiac.'

'And this is what Mr Richmond used?'

'Sometimes.'

'Not all the time then?'

'No. He used the dory a lot.'

'To get out to the yacht?'

'As a tender, yes.'

Dawson draws his heavy brows down and rubs his chin

in a gesture of incomprehension that is almost theatrical. 'Forgive me, Mrs Richmond, but you'll have to explain these terms to me. I am a nautical moron, you see.'

'Sorry. For getting out to the mooring and back again.'

'That's a tender, is it? Something for getting backwards and forwards?'

'Well, I think so. But don't rely on me. I'm not so brilliant on these things myself.'

'Aha.' We share our moment of nautical inadequacy. 'What about, er – voyages?' Dawson continues, using the word self-consciously. 'Did Mr Richmond take the inflatable along with him then?'

'He didn't go on many long trips,' I explain. 'Two at the most. And they weren't even that long. Round to the next river. Down to Burnham.'

'But he took the inflatable on those occasions?'

'I don't know, I'm afraid. But I suppose so.'

'You didn't go with him?' he asks benevolently.

'Oh no. I used to get nervous and very seasick.' My half-chuckle emerges as a choking sound, as though I were feeling sick again now.

'And when the inflatable wasn't on the yacht, where was it kept?' Dawson picks at each word, feeling his way through what is still unfamiliar territory.

I think for a moment. 'Down at the quay. Sometimes. Or here. It varied.'

'So on occasion, when it wasn't in either place, it would be safe to assume it was on the yacht?'

I shrug.

'You don't think so?' His mouth shapes itself into a smile of professional inquiry.

'I just don't know. It was Harry's department. He never told me what he was doing with the boats.' Reaching some

383

threshold, I say in exasperation. 'Forgive me, but I can't see what this has to do with anything. I find it – upsetting.'

'I'm sorry to put you to the bother, Mrs Richmond.' His expression is opaque and intractable; he doesn't intend to answer my question, nor does he intend to stop asking his own.

He directs his interest to the shelves, casting a look along the back wall, before turning to face the light, peering out into the drive with creased eyes, to where Maurice is standing beside Dawson's acolytes, the flat-faced police officer from before who, I have finally grasped, is called Fisher, and a chubby constable who looks about sixteen. Beside a van are two more officers, wearing paper overalls.

'The morning of Saturday, 27th March, you went down to the quay and you found the inflatable there?' he says. 'Is that right?'

'Yes.'

He looks back at me. 'You expected to find it there?'

'Well – yes. Harry had asked me to pack it up and put it away.'

'I'm sorry—' Dawson inclines his head towards me as if he has got hard of hearing. 'He asked you to—?'

'He asked me to take care of it.'

'Though that was usually his department?'

'Yes.'

'What did you think about that?'

I frown my lack of understanding.

'About him asking you?'

I wonder what he expects me to say to this – that I thought it was unusual? Or is he after a more personal reaction, like annoyance? 'I knew he was short of time. It was no problem. And Maurice helped.'

'Ah yes.' Dawson regards Maurice solemnly. 'You carried it up from the quay, did you? You and Mr – er, Crick?'

'We drove it up in the Volvo, yes.'

He takes this in with a slow nod, and turns to take another look at the swollen folds of grey rubber discharging from the mouth of the taut green bag. 'Looked normal, did it, when you found it?'

'I'm sorry?'

'The inflatable. Nothing to notice about it?'

'No. A bit muddy, that's all.'

'Muddy? Was that usual, for it to be muddy?'

'It's a very muddy river,' I explain. 'So – yes. Most things get muddy.'

He puts his face close to the dinghy with its largely mud-free skin.

'I gave it a bit of a clean,' I say, anticipating his question.

He looks at me with something like disappointment. 'Water? Soap? That sort of thing?'

'Water and a sponge. Then Maurice gave it a proper clean up here, before he packed it away.'

Dawson contemplates the dinghy one last time before offering me a formal smile and starting back towards the light. 'Oh,' he says matter-of-factly, 'you wouldn't mind, would you, if we took it away for a short while?'

I raise my shoulders powerlessly.

In the garage entrance Dawson stops suddenly and splays out a hand, as if remembering something. 'Oh, and would it have had a motor, the inflatable?'

'There's a small outboard somewhere, I think. But it was hardly used.'

'Ah. It wasn't with the inflatable then, when you collected it from the river?'

'No.'

'So without a motor people would have—?'

385

'Rowed.'

'There'd be oars then?'

'Yes.'

He looks back into the interior expectantly. 'And where would they be?'

I had forgotten the oars. I call across to Maurice and ask him where they are. Immediately he lopes past us and is only restrained from pulling the oars out from where they stand in a dark corner behind the shelf ends by Dawson's hasty intervention.

Dawson gives instructions to the officers in overalls and goes to talk to Maurice while the men wrap first the Zodiac then the oars in copious plastic and carry them to the van. They wear rubber semi-transparent gloves, like medics.

'Oh, one last question,' Dawson says, tramping back across the gravel towards me. 'The – er, *dory*. Where was it exactly when you saw your husband off that day? On that Friday, 26 March?'

'Inspector . . .' I sigh, I don't try to hide the fact that I am finding this a trial. 'I don't know. I really don't know.'

'But you would have noticed if he had attached it to the back of the yacht?'

'Probably. Possibly. It was raining. I wasn't really looking.'

'It would help if you could remember, Mrs Richmond.'

Before I can stop myself I sing out testily, 'It would help if I knew why.'

Dawson glances down at his feet. When he looks up again, he regards me with altogether cooler eyes. 'The point is, Mrs Richmond, we have to consider all aspects. We have to consider the full range of possibilities.'

'I do see that,' I say with a sigh. 'But when you say possibilities . . . it worries me.'

He says solemnly, 'We have to eliminate the possibility of another person or persons being involved, Mrs Richmond.'

Out comes my incredulous laugh, a small explosion of sound that pierces the silence. 'But that's ridiculous.'

Dawson makes a regretful gesture, as if he would like to be able to agree with me. 'That letter was not very pleasant, Mrs Richmond.'

'But it was nothing very serious, Inspector.'

'You say that, Mrs Richmond, but we don't know that for sure, do we?'

I don't feel strong enough to argue this again – we have already been through it once in the house. And I don't want him ticking me off a second time for not having told him about it before.

I clasp a hand to my head, I rake my fingers back through my hair.

'Please don't upset yourself, Mrs Richmond. It's purely a matter of following up on available information,' he explains, reverting to police-speak. 'There's a person we need to trace and eliminate from our inquiries.'

This is new. I am confused. 'A person? Who?'

I have to press him before he says grudgingly, 'The person we believe most likely to have written the letter. I can't tell you more at present, Mrs Richmond, though I will, of course, keep you informed.'

'But why do you need the inflatable?' I indicate the Zodiac wrapped in its plastic sheath inside the open van.

'It's just a question of checking everything out, Mrs Richmond. Tell me again, Mrs Richmond, where you found it exactly, that Saturday after Mr Richmond's departure?'

'By the quay.'

387

'In the place you would expect to find it?'

I realise I am getting myself into a corner that I might regret. I say vaguely, 'There wasn't really a normal place for it.'

'But you found it easily enough? By the quay?'

Mistake, Ellen. Mistake. But I am committed now. 'Yes.'

'And the dory? You didn't notice it attached to the yacht when your husband left?'

'Well, I . . . Maybe.'

'You're saying that you did, Mrs Richmond?'

'No, what I'm saying is that I'm not sure. Does it really make any difference?'

'A great deal, Mrs Richmond. If he didn't have the, er, *dory*, with him at that time, then that would certainly be significant.' Even in my jumpy befuddled mood I can see that the dory could not have found its way to *Minerva* by itself, that if Harry left it at the quay, then someone else must have taken it out to the mooring.

Dawson pulls a finger and thumb down the edge of his lapel, he takes on a studious look. 'It is anyway an *odd* choice of vessel to take to sea, the dory, so I believe. Being of a large and more solid construction. Something you would not choose to take behind a yacht under normal circumstances. I gather this, er, style of vessel is extremely difficult to, er, *tow* along behind . . .'

Moreland. I hear your voice here. I can see you painstakingly leading Dawson through it.

'. . . and that it would slow progress a great deal. And that in violent weather it would be something of a liability. That it could even sink. Or . . .' He searches for the expression. '. . . turn turtle.'

'But if you're intending to kill yourself the circumstances are hardly normal,' I point out.

Dawson considers this. 'No,' he agrees finally. 'Which is why' – he lifts his chin, he squints down the bumps and curves of his nose at me – 'it would help if you could place the, er, *dory* on that Friday in March.'

A slam. One of the overalled officers is fastening the rear doors of the van. Beside him Fisher laughs, his face disjointed by a scornful smile.

'I'm sorry,' I say to Dawson.

'It was of course quite a large vessel as, er – *tenders* – go. You don't think you would have noticed if it was attached to the back of the yacht?'

'I suppose so, but . . . No, I can't be sure.' I turn my eyes heavenward, showing suitable despair at my own inadequacies. 'Sorry.'

The salesman's smile, in which all disappointments are carefully concealed, returns to Dawson's face. He nods slowly. 'If anything comes back to you, perhaps you would . . .?'

'Of course.'

He walks me to the front door, inclines his head in thanks and starts towards his car. I hear him stop, the scrunch of his feet on the gravel. 'Oh, one thing I meant to ask,' he calls, strolling back a short way. 'There was a ship-to-shore radio on the yacht, I believe. But would Mr Richmond have had any other means of communicating? A mobile phone, for instance?'

My breath is tight. 'He owned one, certainly.'

'And he had it with him that day?'

I lift my hands. I give a weary laugh. 'Inspector, you keep asking me these things. And I simply don't know.'

A three-line letter from Gillespie, who wants to know if I

have had a chance to study the financial plan, and, if so, if I'm ready to give him a decision.

I place the document with its impressively printed title on Harry's desk in front of me, I study the introductory remarks, I turn to the ranks of figures with a growing sense of hopelessness, I am lost by page three.

I push the document away, a child who doesn't want to face the unpleasant. I lower my forehead to the desk and rest it on the cushion of my fingers. Thoughts of Dawson and the dinghies crowd my brain. It occurs to me that he will probably have removed the dory from the boatyard and taken it away as well, though I'm not sure what he thinks he will find when the dory has been overhauled and repaired and burnished, when the gouges have been filled and the alien black paint rubbed away.

And the inflatable, what is he hoping for there? I am back at the quay, sluicing and sponging at the stubborn mud. I am standing on the garage apron, watching Maurice apply the hot water and detergent, standing over him as he starts his systematic circular scrubbing.

Tired, I slip momentarily into a nightmare where I am slithering about in blood and mud, unable to extricate myself from the dinghy, and in the far-off house Katie is sobbing.

'Under the circumstances, which the trustees have agreed are somewhat exceptional, they are prepared to accept an offer along the lines we discussed.'

It is Tim Schwartz's turn to sound as though he is using notes.

'Hello?' he says when I don't reply. 'Hello?'

'Yes, I'm here.'

'But they have asked if it would be possible to make a

390

higher initial payment.' He sounds crisp, the reluctant messenger.

The call has caught me in the kitchen. I work my way round the end of the counter and slide a stool under myself. 'I'm not sure I can manage that.'

'Well, perhaps you could suggest a timetable of payments? A formula for discussion.'

'Well . . .'

'Some idea. Very rough.'

'I'll have to come back to you. Could I?'

A pause. 'Is there a problem?'

Hearing a sound, I twist round. It is Katie, who drifts past and heads for the fridge.

'I am rather tied up at the moment.'

'Ah. Yes.' A thin sort of sympathy. 'When you have a moment, then.'

'Yes, I'll try . . .'

'Mrs Richmond, forgive me but I seem to hear a note of doubt. You haven't changed your mind?'

Katie stands at the open fridge, head on one side, hand on hip and takes something from a lower shelf.

'No, not at all,' I say. 'No, it's just a question of finding the time.'

'I don't mean to press you, but when do you think that might be?'

'Umm . . . Next week?'

Katie pulls bottles out of the door and, emerging with her arms full of fruit, Coke and mineral water, swings the door shut with a deft movement of her foot. As she turns and starts back across the room, I notice she has a small tart covered with whipped cream jammed into her mouth.

'Shall I call you on Monday then?' says Schwartz. 'Oh, and . . .'

A muffled exclamation. Katie has ground to halt and

is standing stock still, gaping at the section of tart that is sliding down the slope of her bosom in a trail of whipped cream, gliding past the tightly clutched bottles, until, dodging the fingers she struggles to put in its path, it drops stickily to the floor.

'The trustees asked me to convey their formal regrets,' Schwartz is saying, 'about your husband.'

I watch Katie, wondering which way this is going to go. Her shoulders droop a little, she glares at the long smear down her T-shirt and then, with perfect timing, unable to resist the comic opportunity, her face comes alive and she turns to me with eyes popping, brows raised high, lower lip thrust out, a caricature of injured innocence.

'I'm sorry?' I manage.

'The trustees. They send their regrets.'

Katie holds her pose, playing it for all she is worth. She has a cream moustache on her upper lip. The laughter rises irresistibly in my throat and I have a job to say, 'Oh, thank you. I mean – thank them.'

I sense Schwartz's confusion. Deciding, apparently, that I am near to tears, he says grudgingly that there is really no pressure on the timing, he could make it Wednesday if that would be easier.

Ringing off, I give Katie her laughter and applause. Not a performer to have her head turned by such easily won acclaim, she takes this with cool grace, but I fancy her eyes glint with satisfaction.

Still laughing, I hug her, bottles, cream and all.

She guffaws into my neck.

Mercurial Katie. Still my girl.

I pull back. Seeing the emotion in my face, she drops her eyes, she begins to turn away.

'Don't, Katie. Don't, sweetheart.'

She pauses, she makes a face, she wages some internal debate. 'When the police come . . . I get frightened.'

I'm silent for a moment. 'Yes,' I murmur with feeling. 'Yes, so do I.'

And she comes back to me then, and we lean against each other, two battle-weary warriors resting between skirmishes.

Jack calls, 'Come up! Come up!'

The idea of visiting Jack's bedroom is not something that fills me with enthusiasm, but since he warned me that this was the only time he had to spare I don't seem to have much choice. Climbing the stairs, I think of all the females who must have trodden this path over the years. Did they go in hope? I wonder. In love or lust? Did they imagine they would be the ones finally to catch him?

The bedroom is sparse: a large bed, and on the wall above it a large and intricate Eastern print which looks vaguely erotic, though I don't examine it closely enough to find out; a side table, a trouser press and a wall of built-in cupboards.

'Here.'

I find him through the far door, in a bathroom tiled in a startling blend of red and navy. He blows me a kiss through a beard of shaving foam. He is wearing a striped robe which gapes at the chest.

'Congratulations again,' I say.

He beams and waves me towards a seat on the lavatory, whose lid he closes with a flourish. 'Hasn't quite sunk in yet,' he says, grinning quietly. 'And I've still got to win the damned seat for us, haven't I?' He turns back to the mirror and, raising his chin, pulls the razor up his neck, removing a neat strip of white.

'So . . .?' Half turning, he peers down at me.

'So . . .' I take a long breath; I tell myself that this will only be hard if I make it so. 'I still need that money.'

He rinses the razor under the tap, and, squinting into the mirror, removes another band of foam. 'Just tell me,' he says with an edge to his voice, 'are we going to have a rerun of our last conversation?'

'No,' I say tightly. 'No . . . I don't think so.'

'Good,' he drawls. 'Good. So what's it for this time?'

'It's for me.'

He slides me a look in the mirror. 'What does Gillespie say? Has he said you need it?'

I am so nervous my stomach is pushed high against my ribs. 'I haven't discussed it with him.'

'So we *are* going to have a rerun,' he says with undisguised irritation.

'I'm asking you as a friend, Jack.'

'And I'm turning you down as a friend, Ellen!'

I feel a pull in my chest, a lurch that is close to anger, and it carries me forward. 'Jack . . . I feel that we have a collective responsibility about this charity. A duty to try and put the matter right.'

'Duty!' The razor jolts to a halt, his eyes bulge at me from the glass. 'You have to be joking!'

I know that if I'm to get through this, I'm going to have to avoid his eyes. Fixing my gaze on the dark glazed tiles to Jack's right, I say cautiously, 'You see, it seems to me that Harry's troubles started with Ainswick, that if Ainswick had been doing all right he would never have been tempted to – take short cuts.'

Jack gives a harsh contemptuous sigh. 'It was his own fault! I told you, the Shoreditch idea was a disaster.'

'Yes, I realise . . . But there were so many other things that seemed to go wrong. Not getting permission for the bypass land—'

'I explained about that.' And his voice carries a warning.

I plough on, I tell myself I'm not going to be frightened of Jack any more. 'Yes, I know what you told me. I know. But you left a few things out, didn't you? When you got the bypass land, it was Meacher who promoted the development for you, wasn't it? You know him well. But when I showed you that hotel bill, you pretended you didn't recognise his name. And then it occurred to me . . . That Majorcan holiday. You said Harry had arranged it, you suggested it was Harry who dealt with Meacher. But the date on the hotel bill . . . it was five years ago, almost exactly, and I checked with Harry's diary. He was here then. He wasn't away. He didn't go to Majorca with Meacher.'

'No, well, he didn't have to, did he?' Jack said tautly. 'He just paid for it.'

Forgetting to avoid his eyes, I look into the mirror and say, 'But *you* went, Jack. You went to Majorca with Meacher.'

He turns and reaches slowly for a towel. 'Now what gives you that idea?' And there is a ring to his voice, part threat, part caution. He rubs the towel slowly over his chin, and above it his gaze is very hard.

'Well . . . Margaret looked it up in the office diary.'

He drops the towel over the edge of the sink, he folds his arms, he says in a voice of exaggerated wonder, 'Now, why would Margaret want to do that?'

'I . . . asked her to.'

'You asked her to!' He drops his arms, he advances until he is standing over me. Faced by his gaping wrap, I get slowly to my feet. 'And why did you ask her, Ellen?' he demands caustically. 'What was the purpose of this little bit of detective work?'

'I wondered why Harry had kept the bill, I suppose.'

'You wondered. And have you decided on the reason?'

I look away, I take my time. 'I think maybe he knew it was significant.'

'Ah. You think *maybe* he knew it was significant,' he repeats with relish, like a vindictive teacher leading a pupil towards ritual humiliation. 'And what do *you* think, Ellen? Do you think it's significant?'

I make an ambivalent face.

'Why would it be *significant*, Ellen?'

'Perhaps he thought' – I throw up a tentative hand – 'that Meacher was more of a friend of yours than he was of his.'

Jack regards me unblinkingly, his mouth spreads into an imitation smile. 'Tell me, did you keep that bill?'

I don't reply, which is an answer in itself.

'I thought so.' He takes a pace back as if to get a better look at me, then thrusts his face close again. 'There's a word for people like you, you know.'

I brace myself.

'Well, this *is* a threat, isn't it? It sounds very much like one.'

'Jack, it's not a threat.'

'Oh, isn't it? Then why didn't you destroy the bill?'

I think about this. 'I felt I couldn't.'

'That's right,' he says, proving his case, 'you felt you couldn't.'

I sigh, 'It's not like that.'

But Jack is nodding tightly, as though he has got my measure at last. 'So what's the arrangement, Ellen?' he says, with an elaborate air of enquiry. 'I pay off Harry's debts and you take good care of the bill, is that it?'

'You make it sound . . .'

'How do I make it sound?' He spreads his hands in

mock innocence. 'How, Ellen? Like you are doing a deal on me, like you are twisting my arm?'

'I just feel that we share responsibility.'

'Responsibility? Now there's that big word again!'

Suddenly I am tired of his bullying. 'Okay,' I say in exasperation. 'If you like – I *am* twisting your arm. All right. Yes. *Yes*.'

He nods with the satisfaction of the inquisitor who has finally got the admission he wanted.

I take a moment, I calm myself. 'But I would never do anything with the damned bill, Jack. I'm not interested in creating more problems. I was only trying to point out that maybe Ainswick had more than its fair share of bad luck, that if things had gone better then Harry probably wouldn't have done what he did. I was just trying to point out that he didn't get the breaks he might have done. That maybe you could have done a little more to help.'

Jack doesn't try to argue with that. His aggression subsides a little. 'So . . .' he says crisply. 'I'm meant to do this out of the goodness of my heart, am I?'

I don't answer that one.

He gives a mirthless laugh. 'A bloody philanthropist! Well, let me tell you, I've got more than enough good causes already.' He returns to the basin and picks up the towel and presses it hard against his face.

He is still smarting because I have put him at a disadvantage.

'Jack, it's more than that,' I argue sombrely. 'It's for me and the children too. I can't bear the thought of it coming out. I really don't think I could stand it.'

'But I told you—'

'Not even the slightest whisper. I couldn't bear it.'

'Aahh,' he says, as if this made sense at last and he never

believed my altruistic motives in the first place. 'So the image is not to be tarnished. The pristine Ellen is not to be shamed.' He gives a sardonic little laugh. He crosses the space between us and, pausing to enjoy my unease, grasps my neck and kisses me full on the lips.

He pulls back. 'So I'm to be kind to you, am I?' There is acceptance in his face, but also the harsh glint of calculation.

It's very dark outside Moreland's cottage. The drive is empty, no lights show. I park a short way up the lane and wait. I angle the car seat back and close my eyes. The air is alive with hidden sounds. When the wind breathes in through the window I seem to hear above the faint rattle of the laurel leaves the ripple and swash of the tide against the river bank at the bottom of the hill, to catch the distant rasp and pull of the surf at the river mouth, and to feel once again the fear that came with the mist and wrapped itself around me, cold as death.

His car wakes me. Trying not to look too furtive, I walk to the gate and, keeping well back, peer into the drive.

A light springs on, the front door swings open, throwing a wide beam into the darkness.

He is alone. I feel relief, but something else too, a sort of satisfaction.

He twists round at my call, he gives an exclamation of surprise. He comes to meet me and leans forward to kiss my cheek. Maybe I turn my head a little, maybe he does, but our lips almost touch and I catch, mingled with the male scent of him, a breath of wine.

'What's happened?' he demands. 'Has something happened?'

I make a stab at humour. 'Just about everything.'

Unsure of my mood, he leads me into the hall and inspects me under the light.

'No – nothing really,' I admit. 'Just . . . Dawson came and took the Zodiac away and asked endless questions about the dinghies.' Then, unreasonably: 'You might have warned me.'

'I didn't realise. I thought . . .' But he leaves it unsaid. He is looking striking in a dark suit and a cream shirt with the top button unfastened and the knot of his tie slackened, as though he had wrenched at them on the way back from wherever he has been, in sheer frustration at having to dress up.

'He seems to have got the idea there was something odd in Harry taking the dory,' I say with only the faintest note of irony.

'I did tell him I thought it was a bit unusual,' Moreland confesses.

'I thought you might have,' I say in mild rebuke. 'He also seems to have acquired a prime suspect for the anonymous letter. Someone' – I find myself mimicking Dawson's tone – 'he wishes to eliminate from his inquiries.'

Moreland has the grace to look a little uncomfortable. 'Yes,' he says, 'I told him about that too.'

'You had someone in mind then?'

'As soon as you showed me the letter I knew who might have written it.'

'I see,' I say stiffly. 'Someone you already knew about?'

'Ellen, I'd have told you before. But I thought it'd be unnecessarily . . .' He has trouble finding a word that won't offend me.

'Upsetting?' I offer.

He makes a face of apology, he concedes my right to feel injured.

'Perhaps I could have made up my own mind about

that,' I say in a small voice. 'Perhaps I can now.'

'Yes.' He drags at his tie until it gives way altogether, he slips off his jacket and throws them onto a chair, as if to announce that this is going to take time in the telling. 'I'll make some coffee.' Inviting me to follow, he goes into the kitchen and fills the kettle.

'I told you,' he begins, 'that we stumbled on Harry's platoon that night?' Forgoing a spoon, he shakes instant coffee direct from the jar into the mugs. 'And his men didn't seem too happy and they felt bitter about Congreve's death?' He leans back against the counter, he folds his arms and beneath the fluorescent light his face takes on deep lines and harsh shadows. 'They were in a bit of a mess,' he says in a reminiscent tone. 'The first thing they did was to shoot at us. That can happen any time, of course. But this wasn't exactly the heat of battle. We were up near Teal Inlet, with no Argies for at least fifteen miles. We had the advantage of knowing that, of course – we'd been recceing the southern shore of Teal Inlet, three of us. But even allowing for the fact that the Paras' intelligence wasn't up to ours, they were pretty jumpy.' He shakes his head at some distant memory. 'Anyway . . . We were on to them before they were on to us – they were making enough noise, God only knows – clattering, yakking. We gave them a shout, and the first thing the buggers did was to fire at us. Luckily, having suspicious minds and cautious natures, we'd kept our heads down. They realised their mistake soon enough, or someone did, and they called out for the password. When we'd finished cursing them, we called back and established contact. But even then, we didn't move until they'd made a firm promise not to blow our heads off.' The kettle boils and clicks off. He looks distractedly at the steam as it curls around his shoulder.

'We were glad to see them. We'd been on our own for three days, we were tired. We'd missed two RVs – rendezvous – we were facing a hard slog to get to our emergency RV. We were glad to meet up with our own side. Swap intelligence, get some kip.' He pours the water. 'But it was hard to sleep. For me anyway. I kept hearing things that made my hair stand on end. I mean, open insubordination from three or four men, and the rest not saying a word, not telling the discontents to shut up as they would in any normal troop. And everything angled in our direction, so we'd have no doubt about how unhappy they were. As if they didn't care what sort of trouble they got into so long as they could tell someone how browned off they felt. And there was Harry, failing to control the situation. He made the odd attempt, but it was crystal clear that he'd totally lost it. I couldn't identify the troublemakers in the dark of course. But Harry must have known who they were all right. But he didn't try and bring them to book, didn't knock the situation on the head. I suppose us being there made things worse for him, but by the time I realised how bad it was, my mates were kipping, I didn't want to kick 'em awake and tell 'em we had to get going again. So in the end I made myself switch off and go to sleep as well.'

He pulls a carton of milk from the fridge and sniffs at it before raising it in offering. I keep to black.

Moreland scrabbles in a drawer for a spoon and scoops sugar into his mug. He takes a long time stirring it and when he looks up his expression is grave. 'I told you, too, that they felt let down. That, rightly or wrongly, they felt their mate's death might have been avoided.' He watches me to see if I need reminding of the implication of this.

'They thought it was Harry's fault?'

'It was just a few of them – but yes, they did.'

401

'And was it?'

He gives a single shake of his head. 'Who knows? My men got the story – or a story of sorts – which I heard later. But who can tell? When someone buys it in what seem like unfair circumstances, it's all too easy to shove the blame around.'

He takes my coffee from my hand and, tipping his head towards the door, leads the way through into the sitting room. We settle on either side of the cold hearth. I notice a couple of cigarette-ends in the grate, and on a side table a glossy fashion magazine, and on the mantel a vase of shop-bought flowers that are past their best.

'What we didn't realise was there'd been the most almighty scuffle before we arrived. A man called Atkins had gone all out for Harry. There was another incident of sorts while we were there, just before dawn as we were getting ready to leave. It didn't get so far as a scuffle, but it was pretty close. I heard retching, I thought someone was puking. But it was Atkins choking. His mates were sitting on him to stop him from having another go. He kept thrashing about. In the end I asked Harry what was going on. He said the man had gone mental. But my men told me another story later, that this man Atkins was Congreve's mate, and had tried to throttle Harry.' He pauses. 'I never told anyone about this,' he murmurs. 'I felt it was Harry's business. Nothing to do with me.'

I try relating this distant tale to my present situation, I try fitting Atkins into the scenario that Dawson is painting, but the whole thing seems to belong to another Harry, to a world that I have never quite grasped.

'So . . .' Moreland puts his coffee aside and leans forward, his elbows on his knees, his hands loosely clasped. 'Atkins seemed the obvious place to start.'

402

I never imagined a name would be put to the poison-pen letter. I never thought there would be a person to pursue.

'I don't see it,' I say firmly. 'Harry killed himself. Anything else is just ridiculous.'

'I know it may seem that way but . . .'

'Everyone keeps going on about the dory. Harry always loved the dory because it had a big engine and went like stink. Rowing irritated him. It was just like him to take the dory along when he shouldn't. Anyway' – I seize on the point – 'if he was going out there to kill himself, he wouldn't have cared which boat he took. It wouldn't have made any difference.'

'Why take a dinghy at all, then?' Moreland argues softly. Before I have time to feel outmanœuvred, he continues in his most gentle tone, 'And – I'm not sure if you know, perhaps Dawson hasn't told you' – he pauses questioningly – 'but there was something else that was odd. The inflatable – it was seen early that Saturday morning, stranded on the mudflats above the quay.'

And I told Dawson I found it at the quay. I say this aloud: 'I told Dawson I found it at the quay.'

'You must have a good neighbour, then. Someone who fished it off the mud and brought it back for you. But Wally Smith saw it there in the morning, first thing.'

Wally is the gamekeeper on the next-door estate. Stupid of me not to realise that someone would see it. Stupid. And such an unnecessary lie to tell Dawson. I am starting to make mistakes. I wonder if Dawson realises I have lied, or whether I can still extricate myself. I wonder how many other mistakes I have made.

'Dawson saw Wally?' I ask in bemusement. The idea of Dawson talking to my neighbours fills me with fresh insecurities.

'I think so. But Wally had told several people anyway.'

People? Or was it you, I wonder, who just happened to have heard about it and then passed it on to Dawson?

'So . . .' Moreland takes a slow breath. 'What with one thing and another – the letter . . . the bruise . . . the gunshot' – he gives each a quiet emphasis – 'you can see how it looks to Dawson.'

'Tell me,' I ask quietly, 'how it looks to him.'

He gives me an odd frown as if he can't quite make out the spirit in which I am asking this. 'Well . . .' He splays out both hands, palms down, he begins tentatively, 'Well . . . I suppose it could be that this person – Atkins or whoever – took whichever dinghy was still at the quay and used it to get out to the mooring. The attack took place, and then he decided to take the yacht out to sea—'

'Why would he bother to do that?'

Moreland concedes the point immediately. 'I'm not sure. Maybe there was a struggle and there was a lot of blood or whatever' – he doesn't flinch from this – 'some sort of evidence that couldn't be got rid of anyway. So he decides to make the whole yacht disappear. He casts off the inflatable, which drifts onto the mud bank, he keeps the dory, takes the yacht out to sea, starts it sinking, heads back to shore in the dory, lands on the beach, pushes the dory off again, it's found drifting the next day. And then . . .' He trails off. He makes a doubtful gesture, as if to admit that it doesn't really hang together.

I give a loud exclamation which takes Moreland by surprise. 'You mean that this soldier knew the river and all the sandbanks, knew how to start *Minerva*'s engine, knew how to start the dory's outboard?' I laugh again. 'I hardly think so.'

404

Moreland smiles with me for an instant before saying, 'Well, the engines wouldn't have been a problem for Atkins. He comes from a family of offshore fishermen. But the river . . . yes, that does seem a bit much.'

I stare at him. 'You've been checking up on him?'

'I made a call today, yes.'

'And Dawson – he's been checking too?'

'I would think so.'

I have a vision of this man Atkins under arrest for a crime he didn't commit. 'But you don't think there's anything in it?' Then, almost pleadingly: 'Do you?'

'I think . . .' He shoots me a considered look. '. . . that it's pretty unlikely.'

I feel relief. 'And you've told Dawson?'

'I pointed out a couple of things, yes. I told him a Para would never choose a shotgun. Not his thing at all. More like a knife. And then why wasn't he seen? Someone must have seen him, if only when he made his way back from the shore.'

'From the shore?' I echo.

'If he landed the dory on the beach, he'd have had to get away, get back to his transport. I don't think Dawson had thought of that.'

'No,' I murmur, miles away.

'And as you say, why bother to go to all the trouble of sinking the yacht?'

I look away, disentangling my thoughts with difficulty. 'So does Dawson understand that? Does he see . . .?'

'The problem is, it wasn't the first time that Atkins had put pen to paper. Margaret told me – has told Dawson – there'd been malicious letters before.'

'*Before?*' I am still the actor, but I have stepped sideways into a strange play where I have been given a part without lines and the other players seem to be making up the story as they go along. 'Why didn't Margaret . . .?' I lift a knowing hand. 'No, don't tell me – she didn't want to upset me.'

Moreland keeps a diplomatic silence.

'These letters,' I ask, 'how many have there been then?'

'At least three, she says.'

And she told you about it, I can't help thinking. In view of the writer's military connections, I suppose she would, though this doesn't entirely quash my sense of aggrievement. 'And they were from this person?'

'They weren't signed exactly. But they were from the same person.'

The coffee has sent me into a sweat, I feel the heat spreading down my back, dampening my shirt. The room seems oppressive. I hear myself exclaim, 'God! God!' I sink back in the chair and cover my eyes and rub them viciously.

I hear Moreland get up. He squats in front of my chair. 'Ellen, don't . . .'

'But this is all so ridiculous,' I cry. 'I thought we knew where we were. I thought we knew Harry had killed himself.'

'I know. I'm sorry. I feel partly responsible—'

'Well, yes, you are!'

He flinches slightly. He takes a long breath. 'But I never intended to do anything – to uncover anything – that would hurt you in any way. I promise that was the very last thing I intended.'

'No, well, I'm sure.' I hear the peevishness in my voice, and gesture it away. 'Tell me something . . .'

He shifts his position, resting an elbow on the chair arm and propping his chin on his knuckle. He has this expression, this way of looking at me, that is so full of reassurance and goodwill and something like affection that there are times when I feel I could tell him literally anything, that, whatever I chose to confide in him, however much I was asking him to overlook, he would make the necessary leap of faith.

And then there are the other times when I glimpse the unbending integrity that runs through him like a rod, and it's like a warning, and I pull back, heart beating, from the brink.

'Tell me . . .' I search his face. 'Why have you bothered with all this? Why have you gone to so much trouble?'

He looks wary. Or reticent.

'I mean, it's not that I'm not grateful. Well, perhaps grateful isn't quite the right word,' I say drily. 'Appreciative. But Harry wasn't a particular friend of yours. In fact . . .' I almost say: I can't believe you liked each other at all. ' . . . you weren't close. And the debt – well, that wasn't really such a big thing, was it? So . . .' I shrug. 'Why?'

He considers this for a long moment. He looks down, and when he looks up again there is something new in his eyes, something I have never seen before, a brighter, more uncertain light. 'It was partly the debt,' he says slowly. 'In the beginning anyway. Partly, the professional challenge. Proving that I could locate the yacht. Thinking, in my arrogant way, that it was bound to help your financial situation.' He glances down again, and I sense a nervousness in him, and suddenly I know what's coming, and I feel a nervousness too.

'But then . . . it was concern for you and the children.' His eyes stay on me, and I read in them all manner of things that I am half frightened, half hungry to read; and I have this sense of rushing forward into something that I don't want to prevent.

I can only think of repeating, 'Concern?'

The language of this new dialogue doesn't come easily to him either. Finally he says, 'I wanted you to be all right.'

Sensing that the moment might slip away, not wanting it to, unable to think of what to say, I reach up to touch his hand where it rests against his face, and it seems to take for ever for my hand to reach his, I watch it moving with infinite slowness and all the time I am aware of him watching me and my heart beats so high in my chest that I think he must hear it. Reaching his hand, I touch it lightly with my fingertips.

He twists his hand around mine and grips it against his cheek.

'I meant well, Ellen.'

'I know.'

'I just wanted you to be free of it all.'

'I know.'

He kisses my hand. And his eyes, with their strange light, are still on me, and the space between us is so full of feeling that it's like a heat.

My head roars with a sense of freedom and certainty. In the past, love has always been a considered thing for me, a blend of emotion and judgement and desire. But this is much simpler. This is disconnected from the future, and I have no doubts.

Suddenly I want him desperately. I want him to fill the lonely spaces around me, to smooth my pain.

I move first, but he is only an instant behind me. We come together, and I put all the signals he needs, if any more be needed, in the way I open my mouth to his. I shift closer and slip an arm round him and grasp him hard, like someone who has no intention of letting him go, which, just now, I don't.

We don't so much kiss as consume. Our mouths stretch wide, our tongues search and reach past each other. I slide

408

down off the chair until we are kneeling against each other.

After a moment I feel him pull away; I try to follow him with my mouth.

'Ellen, Ellen . . .' He cups my chin in his hand. 'We should talk about this.'

I narrow my eyes at him. 'I don't think so.'

'My situation is . . . complicated.'

I shake my head. I go for his lips again.

'Tricia and I have talked of separating. In some ways, we have already, but—'

'It doesn't matter.' I smile to show him that I really mean this. I put my fingers against his lips.

'But I don't want you to—'

'I won't.'

He laughs close to my mouth. 'But you don't know—'

'Oh yes, I do.'

He would try to say more but I don't let him. I cover his mouth with mine, I lick the edge of his cheek, I drop my hands and grip the perfect roundness of his behind. Then, in a gesture that might have surprised me a short time ago, I make the move that will take us past any last opportunity for retreat. I get slowly to my feet, he rises with me. I pull his arms around my back, I lean my body against his, I signal that I am ready to be taken by the hand and led upstairs.

So brazen have I become. So open.

We undress with the lights on. His body is beautiful, lean and smooth. In the moment before he reaches for me, he takes my face almost roughly in his hands and says, 'I never meant you any harm, Ellen.'

Later, as we lie hot and damp in the darkness, still half entwined, he tries to talk of the future again, but I deflect him, I speak of other things.

It's only later still, when he has walked me out to my car

and we are standing in the pre-dawn chill, postponing the moment of separation with soft kisses, that he succeeds in silencing me.

'I'll try and talk to Dawson,' he says, 'but I think it may be too late. I think he's rather hooked on the idea of finding a villain for the plot.'

SIXTEEN

'They want to see us at one-thirty,' Leonard complains at the other end of the line. 'Very short notice. I said it was rather *inconvenient*. An objectionable young police officer – *Fisher*. Most impolite. So unnecessary. Shall I put them off? I feel like putting them off,' he adds, showing rare pique.

I suspect that they aren't to be put off so easily and I tell him not to bother to try, that I'd rather get it over with anyway. I ask him if he wouldn't mind picking me up, although it will put an extra forty minutes on his journey. I know – though I don't explain this to Leonard – that driving will be beyond me.

I make a joke of it to Katie, I tell her that they're hauling me in for a grilling. I say to come and bail me out if I'm not back by midnight. She isn't fooled, of course; she can see that this front of mine is paper-thin. Oddly – but perhaps not so oddly – she rises to the occasion. She relishes the opportunity to take charge of me; it is almost as if she has been looking forward to it. She helps me choose something to wear; a loose-fitting jacket, cool slacks. She brushes my hair and thrusts lipstick and eye pencil into my hand and stands over me while I put them on. She marches me downstairs and forces me to consume orange juice and toast.

Katie my protector, bossy and capable. Through the haze of tension that presses in on me, it occurs to me that I have been denying her any role but that of victim, that in trying to shield her I have been reinforcing her sense of powerlessness, and this is something she would like to be free of.

On the doorstep she gives me a brisk kiss, she wags a finger in front of my nose. 'Don't let them bully you,' she says.

I hear little of what Leonard says on the drive to Ipswich. Something about proving the will, the price the house is likely to fetch, documents he is preparing for me to sign.

Inside the police station the desk is busy. While Leonard tries to attract the attention of one of the three officers who are helping people find their way through forms or listening dead-eyed to involved tales of woe, I take a seat between a sprawled unshaven man with stained trousers and a plump black woman with a sad smile whose look seems to say we are all going to be here a long time. When Leonard finally manages to get his message across and someone has spoken into a phone, we are asked to wait. If there is air-conditioning in this part of the building it isn't working too well and the heat contains odours of fried food from long ago and too many unwashed bodies in too small a space. Leonard paces back and forth, stopping regularly at the desk to ask how long we will be kept waiting. Coming back to me, he stoops and mutters, 'Outrageous for you to be treated like this. In your circumstances.'

My circumstances. That's just it; I have the feeling they have changed.

It is shortly before two when Fisher finally appears and leads us down the soundless corridors to the same chill interview room as before. Dawson rises heavily to his feet and comes round the table to shake my hand. His face looks pouchy and tired. His smile is brisk and impersonal.

While tea is being fetched no one speaks much and when Dawson trumpets into a handkerchief the sound fills the room.

This time, as soon as the uniformed policewoman has brought the tray of plastic cups, she occupies the chair by the door, and I notice that, in addition to Fisher at the table, there is another young officer who takes a seat against the wall.

When everyone is settled, Dawson faces me and we go through the usual business with the tape recorder. Dawson's voice is muffled and nasal from a congested nose. A pause while he arranges his hands neatly on the table, then he lifts his chin and, offering me an unreadable expression, says, 'Mrs Richmond, I have to inform you that as from this morning we are treating the death of your husband as a suspicious event.' He gives this a moment to settle before adding, in case I haven't got it: 'In effect, we have begun a murder inquiry.'

I see Leonard's hands jerk, his head come forward. His mouth moves soundlessly before he manages to gasp, 'There must be some mistake—'

This is not perhaps a remark to endear itself to Dawson and I wonder if Leonard, fine drafter of wills and conveyor of house titles though he is, isn't going to find this situation beyond him.

Without offering a reply, Dawson brings his grey eyes back to me. 'I realise this has come as something of a shock, Mrs Richmond. I'm very sorry indeed.' Then, as if remembering the correct procedure for such circumstances: 'Would you care to take a moment or two before we continue?'

413

I realise some reaction is expected of me, though the dryness in my throat, the troop of butterflies cavorting in my stomach are real enough. I whisper increduously, 'I don't see . . . I can't . . .' I drop my head, I squeeze my eyes shut. Coming up again for air, I ask unsteadily, 'But *who*? Why?'

'These are matters we are seeking to establish.'

'But – you have some idea?'

'Our inquiries are only at a preliminary stage. We can't say as yet.'

'But . . . you're sure it was . . .?' I ask emotionally. 'That someone . . .?'

'We have reason to believe so, yes,' he says solemnly.

I say, '*God!*' several times.

'Would you like a moment?' Dawson offers again, creasing his eyes against some nasal tickle.

Realising I'm unlikely to get much comfort or advice from Leonard, at least for the time being, I shake my head. Dawson's face contorts suddenly and he twists away to sneeze into a hastily opened handkerchief. Unexpectedly, without any warning at all, a tear rolls out of my eye and plops onto my hand. I look down in surprise and brush the dampness from my eyes with the back of my hand.

Dawson, having missed this, crumples his handkerchief into a ball and says, 'As I'm sure you'll appreciate, Mrs Richmond, under the, er, circumstances we will be needing to make very rigorous inquiries. And that will necessitate going through everything with you again in greater detail. Obviously we would appreciate it if you could give us the fullest possible information.'

I nod mutely.

'If we could start with a couple of points?' This is more of a statement than a question. The avuncular civility has faded, and I catch the cool draught of his professionalism. 'The day you helped your husband prepare for his yachting trip, that is, Friday, 26th March of this year, did you at any time during the course of that day see a shotgun that might or might not have belonged to your husband?'

The question swells to fill my mind. Why is he asking me this all over again? I teeter on the brink of all the things I am about to say that can never be unsaid.

Dawson tilts his head. 'Would you like me to repeat the question?'

'No. No – I didn't see a gun.'

'Not in the car, not in the yacht?'

'I didn't go in the yacht,' I point out softly.

He acknowledges this with a small movement of his fingers. 'Around the yacht, then?'

'No.'

He dabs at his nose and makes a loose phlegmy sound in the back of his throat. 'You didn't see a gun anywhere then?'

The repetition takes an effort. 'No.'

He unfolds and refolds his handkerchief, a rumpled off-white cotton square that looks as though it has done long duty, and searches out a section to receive the next blow.

'Your husband owned two, er, *tenders*, I believe – a dory and an inflatable, the latter also referred to by yourselves as the Zodiac. Could you tell me which vessel, if any, was at the, er, quay that day?'

I shake my head. 'I don't remember, I'm afraid.'

Dawson looks down at the table and it may be my imagination, but I think I see annoyance tug at the corners of his mouth.

'Did you see either of these, er, *tenders*, anywhere else that day?'

'Not that I remember.'

Another pause, a cooling in the air between us. Fisher shifts in his seat but I am careful not to meet his eyes.

'Moving on,' Dawson says ponderously. 'Regarding the inflatable dinghy, also referred to as the Zodiac – could you tell me where you found it on Saturday, 27th March, the day after you helped your husband prepare for his yachting trip?'

This has come much sooner than I thought. I feel light-headed and it is an instant before I realise I am holding my breath. 'I'm glad you asked that,' I say in a forced tone. 'Because, um . . . very foolishly' – I feel my mouth twitch into the semblance of a smile which I swiftly extinguish – 'I didn't quite get that right before. In fact . . . I didn't tell you the truth.'

There is a silence like cold or darkness. Fisher glances at Dawson with a knowing flicker. Dawson, whether from anticipation or long practice, shows no reaction. His heavy lids blink once. 'Now why did you do that, Mrs Richmond?' he asks in a lugubrious tone.

'I thought . . .' I shake my head at my own stupidity. ' . . . it would only muddle everything. That . . . you'd start to take this Atkins idea seriously.'

In the corner of my eye, I'm aware of Leonard frowning at me in dismay.

'Ah,' says Dawson drily. 'You didn't think we should do that then?'

'I thought the whole Atkins idea was quite mad, frankly. Nothing to do with Harry and what happened. I thought if I told you about the dinghy—'

'The inflatable?'

'—the inflatable, then you'd think there was something in it, and everything would get stirred up again. Just when

416

it was all beginning to quieten down. Just when I was getting the children settled again. I thought it would only confuse things . . .' I trail off, gesturing my penitence. 'I didn't realise.' I add humbly, 'I'm sorry.'

Dawson takes a long troubled breath, the schoolmaster faced by the errant pupil. 'Mrs Richmond, you must have realised the *seriousness* of failing to mention this.'

I give a remorseful nod. 'Well, *now* . . .'

'At the time?'

'No, I . . . really didn't.'

Dawson snorts, clearing some obstruction from the back of his nose. 'So where did you find the inflatable?'

'It was sitting on the mud.'

'Where on the mud?'

'Upriver from the quay a way.'

'How far exactly?'

'I'm not very good at distances. Umm – fifty yards? A bit more?'

'You could see it from the quay?'

'Yes.'

'And what did you do?'

'When I saw it? Well, I thought it had just drifted there, hadn't been tied up properly. And I went and fetched it.'

Dawson unfurls the dismal hanky again. When the blast of his hooting has died away, I can hear above the faint hum of the recorder the sound of someone shouting in the corridor outside.

'May I ask how you fetched the inflatable back exactly?' He affects the look of someone in need of enlightenment.

'Well, I waded out through the mud and I paddled it back to the quay.'

'Paddled? Forgive me, I want to be clear. Is that the same as rowing?'

417

I answer dutifully, 'No. What I did was to sit in the front of the dinghy and use one oar as a paddle, first on one side then the other. I've never been very good at rowing.'

'It was hard, paddling?'

'No. The current was with me.'

'The current was with you?'

'The tide.'

'Ah. It changes, does it?'

I wonder if he is having me on. 'The current moves downriver when the tide's going out, and upriver when the tide's coming in. I had to learn that,' I say with a short laugh, sounding too eager.

'When you were doing this paddling, and later, at the quay, did you notice anything unusual about the inflatable?'

'I'm sorry?' We both know that I heard, we both know that I am putting the moment off.

His eyes are watering. He blinks rapidly to clear them. 'Was there anything in or on the inflatable that caused you to take notice of it?'

'You mean—?' But he doesn't help me. 'Well, there was mud,' I say. 'I'd brought a lot of mud in . . .' I lift my shoulders. 'Nothing else. What else should there have been . . .?' I look to Fisher, to the officer by the wall, as if they might give me the answer. 'What sort of thing?' I am sounding anxious again.

No one answers me.

'You gave the inflatable a clean up?' Dawson continues.

'I got the worst of the mud off, yes.'

'And the oars? They were there in the inflatable when you found it on the mud, were they?'

I think carefully. 'Yes.'

'And you used them to paddle back?'

'Well, just the one, yes.'

'And were they muddy as well, the oars?'

'I didn't notice. I don't think so.'

'And there was nothing else about them? That you noticed, I mean?'

It comes to me then. The oars. It is the oars. I didn't clean the oars well enough and they have found Harry's blood on them.

'Did you wash the oars as well, Mrs Richmond?'

My nervous inappropriate smile springs up before I can suppress it. 'They may have got a splash of water. But no. I mean, I didn't sponge them or anything like that.'

It is definitely the oars. And realising this, I try to grasp where this might lead, I'm swayed by new uncertainties.

Reaching some juncture in his own thoughts, taking his time, Dawson inserts a handkerchief-clad finger up each nostril and submits his nose to a thorough clear-out. He gives a heavy sigh. 'Pity you didn't tell us about this before, Mrs Richmond,' and when he looks up his expression has hardened, and my confidence falters and I am not at all sure he has believed a word I have said.

There's a cry a child makes that kicks at your deepest instincts, that has you sprinting, sick with nameless terror, towards the source, ready to defend, fight, tear, rip, kill. Once when Katie was five she got lost in a crowd and when her scream rang out it turned my heart to ice. Another time, when she was about seven, her cry took me pounding across a friend's garden and into battle with a terrier that had her by the sleeve of her dress. I dragged the dog's jaws apart with a strength I never knew I had, and which came, I think, from sheer necessity.

When Katie got through to me at Molly's that Friday evening, the sound she made down the phone wasn't a cry exactly, more of a wail, but, with her frantic sobs and the realisation that for some reason she wasn't at school but at home, I was soon racing out to the car and fumbling with the ignition and pushing my foot flat against the floor in mindless reaction. During the journey to Pennygate I talked myself out of the more excessive scenes of doom and disaster, I told myself that Katie often got things out of proportion, but as soon as I got into the house and called out and heard Katie's answering cry from upstairs, the terror came thudding back.

She was sitting in my half-filled bath, fully clothed, the water dark and murky.

I kept asking what the matter was, I kept asking until my voice became like a chant in my ears. For a while she was completely incoherent, shivering hard, rolling her head, sobbing in juddering spasms through a mouth that was pulled back in a long grimace. When she finally managed something intelligible, it was just a few garbled words. But if I had been slow in the past, if I had managed to close my mind to everything I didn't want to see, I quickened up then, I got there in a single wrench of understanding, and it was like stepping off a ledge into nothingness.

For a while the anguish was so great that I clung to Katie, and together we rocked back and forth, sending waves across the murky water.

Then she shivered more violently, and I helped her out of her clothes and drained the cold dirty water and poured hot clear water and helped her bathe herself. I wrapped her in a large towel and put her in my bed and held her tight against me and stroked her hair and told her over and over again that I loved her. And all the time I was shrivelling inside.

I gave her sleeping pills, two strong ones, and as soon as she began to quieten down, I asked the questions that I half dreaded to ask. I kept my voice low, low and calm; I began with what I hoped were the less disturbing things. What made you come home from school? How did you get here? For a while it seemed she wouldn't answer, and when she finally did the words came spasmodically, in blurred moans and gulps. At last I made out: 'Said you were there . . . promised . . . *promised*. Said . . . you were . . . fetching things. Promised . . .'

The rest came in equally uneven snatches, but finally I understood that Harry had phoned her at school, had promised her that I was there with him, that the two of us wanted her to come over for supper, that she was to get a taxi.

I absorbed this in agonising lurches. He had said I was there. He had lied to her. But it was more than that; he had done it, I realised, to deceive her into thinking she was safe. In understanding this, I also understood, with the shock of the obvious, that Katie had known she was at risk, that she had been living in fear.

And then there was only one question to ask. It was all I could do to keep my voice under control as I whispered, has this happened before?

When she didn't reply I asked her again. But she turned her head deeper into the pillow and blocked me out, and her action was an answer in itself.

I felt emotionally sick, I wanted to vomit all the love I had ever felt for Harry clear of my body. I wanted to void all my feelings and be rid of them for ever. And fuelling my despair and revulsion was my own sense of failure. I could only think that I had let this happen, that I should have seen.

And then I thought of the way Harry had lured Katie away from school, I thought of the planning he had put into it and something shifted inside me and I felt this peculiar coldness, a gathering of altogether fiercer emotions.

I had reached the age where I thought I knew everything there was to know about myself, I thought my boundaries had been marked out for me, that I had experienced every kind of happiness of which I was capable, every kind of anger. But when I thought of Harry and what he had done, my emotions sped out into entirely new territory, and I felt this rage. It was nothing like the occasional flashes of childhood heat I'd felt when provoked by my mother, it was nothing like the weary anger I'd felt at the more testing times in my marriage. This was a worm of resentment and fury that uncurled inside me, feeding on itself until it filled me up, I was bursting with it, and it drove every other thought from my head.

Leaving Katie to sleep, I pulled on a coat and slipped out of the side door and through the gate onto the track. As I strode rapidly down to the quay, stumbling now and again, jarring my legs in the darkness, fresh realisations came to me, I saw new layers of deceit and betrayal. Muttering aloud, my voice like a second presence, I pushed on, unstoppable.

At the quay there was only the dory, its heavy engine shipped, and no key for the ignition. But then I saw the way the tide was running and remembered the paddles that were always kept under the back seat, and, buoyed by determination, I cast off and struck out into the stream and let the current carry me away. It was dark, there was still a heavy mist, but I never doubted I would find *Minerva*. My rage would carry me there.

Dawson is called away and, returning briefly, suggests a half-hour break. Leonard and I go for a walk in the heat of the street and look unsuccessfully for somewhere quiet to sit down.

'This is so terrible,' Leonard keeps murmuring in hushed tones as we trudge towards some tea shop that is meant to be a couple of streets away. 'So *terrible*. But in some ways perhaps it's a *consolation* to know it wasn't suicide.' He looks anxiously for my response. Getting none, he says in his practical voice, 'Do you want me to tell the family?'

The thought of anyone else knowing is painful. 'Not yet.'

'The newspapers – I'm afraid they'll find out.'

The tea shop has gone, another victim of the recession, and we turn back.

I agree: 'The family then,' and the enormity of what is happening comes home to me.

When we reassemble in the interview room it is with a sense of familiarity, everyone in the same seats, the tea and tape recorder ceremonies unfolding with the smoothness of ritual.

Dawson's cold seems to have worsened. His eyes have acquired a glassy look, the skin around his nostrils has become red and inflamed, from time to time his voice croaks or seizes altogether. The weary cotton handkerchief has gone, replaced by a box of tissues which he dips into with faint reluctance.

Leonard, determined perhaps to make up for his earlier

423

confusions and inadequacies, makes a statement about the unacceptability of keeping me too long, considering it is already late in the afternoon. It is, in fact, five.

'No one will be kept longer than necessary,' Dawson says thickly, tidying some papers on the table in front of him and turning his attention to me. 'Mrs Richmond, could we just go over a few things concerning that evening of Friday, 26th March?' His manner has hardened, and I have the feeling that it isn't just his cold which is aggravating him. 'You went to Miss Sinclair's for a meal at about six p.m.?'

I agree.

'What time did you leave Miss Sinclair's?'

'I think I said – it must have been about ten.'

'Are you sure about that?'

'Well . . . it could have been earlier. I don't remember.'

He gives me an odd look, as though he knows this to be untrue. 'You went straight home?'

'Yes.'

He coughs uncomfortably, as if his chest is causing him pain. 'And then?'

'I did a few chores and I went to bed.'

'What time would you have got to bed exactly?'

'About twelve, I suppose. Something like that.'

'Did you receive any phone calls that evening after you got back?' And suddenly he is staring at me intently. And I too am very still, because while I have been dreading this, I have also been preparing for it. I know my lines, there is no problem about that, but I am short on rehearsal and I'm not sure my delivery will be up to scratch.

I make a show of searching an imperfect memory. 'I don't remember any, no.'

424

'Nothing at about eleven-fifty?'

'I don't think so. But I could well have been in the bath, and then I might not have heard the phone. In fact, I often don't hear it. I usually have the radio on, you see. When I'm in the bath.'

'So if there'd been a call at eleven-fifty, it would have gone unanswered?'

'The machine would have picked it up eventually.'

'I see.' This emerges as a croak. 'And then you would have played the message back at some point?'

'Yes. In the morning, probably.'

He clears his throat with a loud hawking sound. 'And was there a message the next morning?'

I shake my head. I blow out my lips. 'It's hard to remember after all this time.'

His eyelids droop. 'Would you have remembered if it had been a call from your husband, Mrs Richmond?'

I stare at him. I whisper, 'Of course.'

'There was no message the next morning from your husband?'

I am still staring at him. Coming to with difficulty, I shake my head.

'You're quite sure about this?'

'Yes. But I don't understand . . . you're saying my husband called that night?'

Dawson pulls in his lips and says in a significant tone, 'A call was made from your husband's mobile phone to your home at eleven-fifty that night.'

I am openly bemused.

'And you're saying there was no message?' Dawson asks.

'No.'

'Would anyone else have played the message tape back?'

425

I shake my head uncertainly. 'They shouldn't have.'

'So what could have happened to his message, do you suppose?'

I hunch in my chair. I raise a baffled hand. 'Perhaps he didn't leave one.'

'The call was logged at six minutes, Mrs Richmond.'

A clammy sensation creeps over me. It is all I can do not to freeze entirely. I had no idea it had been so long. I look away, I feel a trickle of sweat inside my shirt, and the longer I founder, the more I sense I am giving myself away and the greater the swell of panic. For an instant I have an urge to admit to everything, to get it over and done with, but somehow I manage to drag my eyes back to Dawson's and slowly shake my head.

'You have no explanation?'

'No.'

'There was no one else in the house who may have taken the call?'

Another rush of anxiety: he knows about Katie. He must know! Everyone knows! Then, slowing down, play-ing his voice back in my mind, I hear his note of pedantic enquiry, and I tell him calmly that there was no one else in the house.

He doesn't argue; he doesn't repeat the question.

In my relief I have a momentary vision of Katie lying half-comatose in my bed, of the phone ringing, of her reaching groggily to answer it. I see myself back on *Minerva*, clutching the mobile to my ear, repeating myself time and again, getting nothing but wild incoherent mum-blings until at long last she seemed to understand what I was saying. Back in a while, back in a while. Just sleep, darling, just sleep. It's going to be all right, I promise it's going to be all right. Not such an important message perhaps, but vital to me. I couldn't have left her without a word; I had to know the drugs were working and she was going to sleep.

We go over the foibles of the answering machine, the frequency with which it has lost messages in the past. I tell Dawson it has jammed occasionally, that it is impossible to tell when it has lost messages.

We return to the bath I took that night, how long I stayed in it, how loud I was playing the radio.

Then it's back to the answering machine. And again. The same questions in slightly different form. How it could have lost a message. Whether I think it lost Harry's message that night.

And every time he repeats a question, I feel it's a small step closer to the end, because I sense he doesn't believe me. It is his determination against mine, and I'm not sure that mine is the stronger.

Dawson picks up one of the papers in front of him. 'Your husband also called your daughter's school at' – he brings the sheet a little closer – 'six-thirty.' Lowering the paper, he regards me with raised brows. 'Were you aware of that?'

'No. But then he can't have spoken to her.'

'Why not?'

'Well, she would have told me,' I say unsteadily. 'In fact, the last time she spoke to him was on the Tuesday. She said so.'

'So who would your husband have spoken to then, on the Friday?'

I shrug lightly. 'Oh, one of the seniors, I expect. You phone the house and leave a message with one of the senior girls on duty, asking your daughter to call back.'

He screws up his face and presses his fingertips to the

427

side of his head in a practised show of puzzlement. 'So she would have got a message?'

I am falling, falling. And in danger of taking Katie with me.

'No . . .' I grab at something, anything. 'Often they can't find her. She's somewhere else in the school. The message gets lost. So you call back and . . .'

He leans forward and cocks his head to hear me better.

'. . . you just try again.'

'Just try again,' he echoes ruminatively. 'That's how it works, is it?'

I nod breathlessly.

I must look odd or ill because Leonard glances at me anxiously and Dawson asks me if I want more tea and raises an empty cup to the policewoman. Suddenly everyone is in motion, stretching, standing up, collecting cups, and I have gained recovery time. Dawson retires into a corner with a bunch of tissues to hoot and trumpet in private. Leonard gives me a bleak look and pats my arm.

When the fresh cups stand in front of us and the door is closed once more, Dawson sinks solidly back in his seat. Beating a fist against his chest, he says, 'Apologies. Hope I'm not blowing germs your way.'

'You should take something for it.'

He looks at me blankly.

'My grandfather always used to say, take a candle and a bottle of brandy to bed. Light the candle and when you see two flames, blow them both out and sleep through till morning.'

He regards me with slight puzzlement until, getting the humour, such as it is, he gives an awkward mirthless smile.

'Now . . .' He pulls his face down into an expression of gravity, as though I needed reminding of why we are here.

'Perhaps we could move on to the period leading up to Friday, 26th March? The few weeks prior?'

Debts. Anonymous letters. After the phone call ordeal, I greet these subjects with something approaching relief.

'May I ask' – and his tone is contrite, as if he wished he didn't have to mention it at all – 'how things were between you and your husband?'

I grip my cup more tightly. 'Well—' I say eventually, 'we were under a lot of strain. All his business worries, the debts, not being able to talk about them ... Our relationship certainly suffered, yes.'

'There were no other problems between you?'

Ah, I have the drift now. I see where this is leading. I make a non-committal shrug. 'Well, every marriage has its ups and downs.'

Dawson draws in his lips, he takes his time. 'Were you aware that your husband was having a relationship with a woman named Caroline Palmer?'

Now who has been talking? I wonder. Margaret? Or Jack?

I say it straight out. 'Yes.'

'How long had you known about it?'

'Since October.'

'And how did you feel about it?'

'I was upset. When I found out. But then I realised it wasn't serious, I realised it was something that would pass. I learnt to live with it.'

'You, er, tackled your husband about it?'

'No.'

He contemplates the table. 'Not once?'

'No.'

'Why not?'

'I didn't think it would do any good.'

429

Dawson frowns before rubbing a tissue mercilessly across the end of his nose. 'But you were unhappy enough to, er, keep tabs on your husband, to keep an eye on him?'

Jack: it is Jack who has told them.

I can't decide whether I should try to deny this. I hear myself say, 'For a while, yes.'

'You were jealous, in fact?'

Where is this leading? But even as I wonder, a part of me already suspects. 'Upset,' I correct him. 'I was upset.'

Dawson's look suggests that I am trying to split hairs. He says heavily, 'Didn't you take to trying to find out where Mr Richmond was? To phoning your husband's flat in London? To calling friends to ask them where he was?'

Yes: definitely Jack. He was the only person I ever called to ask where Harry was. He was the only one who knew how I felt about Caroline Palmer. I wonder if this is Jack's way of getting back at me over the charity money.

'There was a time,' I admit, 'when I needed to know where he was. A time when I was particularly upset.'

'When you were jealous?'

I give in. 'If you like.'

Dawson pulls his shoulders back, a gesture of satisfaction. 'And, er, the reason your husband was trying to get the yacht round to the South Coast, that was connected, wasn't it?'

'He was going cruising.'

'Wasn't he in fact taking it there to act as a weekend meeting place for himself and Miss Palmer?'

'He may have been.'

'And this was a fact that you were well aware of?'

'Well – I guessed.'

'You knew?'

'As good as,' I concede.

'And you wanted to prevent it if you possibly could?'

There is a pause, a collective holding of breath, as the implications of this question fill the room.

I am being accused.

Leonard finally feels moved to say, 'Inspector, is this really necessary?'

Dawson leans closer across the desk and says in a low voice, 'I'd be grateful, Mrs Richmond, if you would answer – did you try to prevent your husband from leaving?'

I blink tearfully. 'No.'

'Why didn't you tell me the truth about the inflatable dinghy straight away, Mrs Richmond?'

'I told you . . .'

'But the real reason?'

I shake my head, I make a gesture as if to say, why are you asking me this?

Dawson sighs. 'Mrs Richmond, that phone call from your husband' – and his voice is heavy with regret – 'you did in fact answer it, didn't you?'

Leonard moves as if to intervene again and is cut short by a rapid twist of Dawson's hand. I feel the ground slipping away from under my feet and there's nothing to hold on to.

'No,' I breathe.

He turns an ear to hear me better. 'I'm sorry?'

I repeat my denial in a stronger voice.

Dawson leans back in his chair, coughing roughly. Recovering, he gives me a mournful stare. 'Perhaps you'd care to think things over, Mrs Richmond?'

'There's nothing to think over,' I say, with a bravado I do not feel.

'Shall we say ten o'clock tomorrow?'

'Josh?' I try putting a hand on his shoulder, but he

shakes me off with such force and resentment that I pull back to the edge of the bed and look helplessly towards Katie.

I make one more attempt. 'I really do think they've made a mistake, honey,' I say, with a sincerity that rings falsely even in my own ears. 'I just don't believe that anyone would want to hurt Daddy. I just don't believe it. I think the police had it right before, that there was no one else involved, there was just ... *him* ...' I trail off, aware that I have lost the will to fight even on this front, which is almost the most important one of all. We have been here for half an hour, the three of us, going over the same ground – or rather Katie and I have been picking the police's ideas apart while Josh has lain rigid, resistant to all offers of love or comfort.

Katie says, 'I think they watch too many films, the police. I think they fancy themselves zooming around finding clues and arresting people and looking cool and all that stuff.' She paces to the head of the bed and looks down at Josh, inert on the duvet with its bright red and green racing car pattern. 'Hey?' She nudges him gently. 'Hey?' She ducks her head down to get a look at his face. Getting no response, she pulls a face as if to say she'd do better on her own, and, feeling defeated, needing no second prompting, I retreat.

The thing is, I don't blame Josh for giving up on us. He would have to be blind and deaf not to realise that Katie and I had a separate agenda in America, he would have had to be totally insensitive not to feel excluded. Perhaps, with this final shock, he's run out of faith. What can I say to him? Believe me, Josh? Why should he believe me when I don't believe myself any more?

Moreland is late. Like a child I go to the window in the

hall and look out, as if this will be enough to bring his car into sight. Waiting there, I lean my head against the glass and feel the blend of clarity and confusion that exhaustion brings.

Clatterings take me to the kitchen, where I find Molly bent over a saucepan, stirring briskly.

'I'm not sure anyone's going to be hungry,' I tell her.

Her head comes up, she stops. 'No,' she agrees immediately and switches the gas off and chucks the spoon down as if the idea were so obvious she should have thought of it herself. 'No,' she sighs. Wiping her hands on her apron, she reaches for the cigarette smouldering in the adjacent ashtray and inhales long and hard. 'Drink?'

I wouldn't mind something but decide against it. I need to clear my mind, not muddle it. I have this notion, based on nothing but the shallowest of hope, that if I think hard enough some ideas might yet come to me, that against all probability I might yet persuade Dawson that I have nothing to tell him.

'What is it, honey?' Molly cocks her head at me, blowing a plume of smoke expertly past her nose.

I have been staring. 'I want to ask you something,' I say after a moment's thought. 'A sort of favour.'

Molly stubs out her cigarette. She makes one of her more extravagant gestures, all wide arm movement and chinking jewellery. 'Anything.'

I draw her to the table and we pull out chairs and sit hunched knee to knee. 'The thing is, the police will probably come and talk to you again. If they do . . . would you . . . well, I'd be grateful if you didn't tell them about the call from Katie. That night?'

She knows the call I mean. She's already shaking her head. 'Haven't mentioned it before. No reason to mention it now.'

433

'Also . . .'

She urges me on. 'What?'

'You must say no if you have any doubts. If you feel unhappy about it . . .'

She brushes this thought aside.

'It's just . . . they might understand things better if you told them that I was worried about Harry.'

'Well, you were!'

'Yes. But I mean particularly worried that evening.'

'Of course.' She shrugs as if to say, is that all? 'Anything particular you were worried about? Was he ill? In a bad mood?' She's enjoying the challenge, but I think she's also relieved that I haven't asked for more.

'A bad mood, I think. Depressed. And that's why I left early.'

'Did you leave early?'

'It might have been before ten.'

'Oh. But you went to see if he was all right?'

'Yes.'

She presses her cheek to mine. 'No problem.'

'It's just that I don't want—'

Pulling away sharply, she holds up a hand. 'No, don't tell me,' she says. 'No need.' And she looks pleased with herself for this display of discretion, as if we were involved in some harmless game and she is proud of having grasped the rules.

The phone rings and, taking on her self-appointed role as guardian of the peace, she gets up to answer it.

'Charles – *hello*,' she says into the phone, rolling her eyes in my direction. Receiving my not-at-home signal, she proceeds to tell him I have taken a sleeping pill and gone to bed.

Ears towards the drive, I'm finally rewarded by the

434

sound of a car. Slipping out through the kitchen door, seeing the scruffy black Golf, my worries are momentarily pushed aside and I feel all the half-forgotten emotions of a new lover, the blend of excitement and apprehension, the foolish hopefulness. Watching Moreland climb out of the car, I measure him against my image of him, and he hasn't changed. If anything he seems more familiar, like someone I have known a long long time, and I feel a surge of affection that at any other time I might easily take for love.

When he looks up, he doesn't have to tell me that something is terribly wrong, it's written all over his face.

'Have you got a while?' he says. He doesn't kiss me, he doesn't even touch me, he just stands there looking grave and stern, and my throat is suddenly dry.

I nod wordlessly and go back to tell Molly I'll be away for a time. I return to find him holding the passenger door open for me.

When we're bumping down the drive I ask, 'What is it? What's happened?'

He frowns ahead, he answers with difficulty, 'I'd rather tell you when we get there.' He glances briefly towards me. 'If that's all right.' And his politeness is almost worse than anything else.

At the main road we don't turn left towards Wood-bridge and Moreland's cottage, we go the other way, towards the sea. If I think of speaking again, I am silenced by the grimness of Moreland's profile, the tightness of his lips. We pass through one village and another, we turn onto a smaller road, and then into a lane that is barely wide enough for two vehicles, and suddenly I know exactly where we're going.

The sun is almost set, the land is darkening, and only

the tops of the taller trees are brushed with gold. The fields fall behind us, then the last of the trees, and we descend onto a verdant table of reclaimed marshland, and then there is nothing ahead of us but the mass of the shingle bank that rises in a giant rampart against the sea.

The single-track concrete road dissects the flatland, wriggling briefly over two dykes, before slanting up the back of the shingle bank, with its bedding of sand and tussock grass. Half-way up the slope the road forks, one branch carrying on towards a group of coastguard cottages which stand in incongruous isolation on the top of the bank, the other turning left, up and over the top of the shingle. Taking the left turn, negotiating a barrier that says NO VEHICLES BEYOND THIS POINT, we rise over the brow of the bank, and the sea spreads out before us, filling the horizon, vast and broad and dark as pewter.

The top of the bank is wide. Before the sand and meagre vegetation give way to the mass of grey pebble, there are large brackish pools and, running parallel to the sea, a ribbon of pitted and crumbling concrete, a remnant of some World War II defence system. Moreland negotiates the concrete for a distance then, choosing his spot, points the car towards the sea and parks. When he turns the engine off, the silence is filled by the rumble and rasp of the waves dragging at the stones below. Hearing this, I am scrabbling to find my footing on the stones again, the salt is sharp in my eyes, the waves are pulling at my legs.

Moreland places his hands high on the steering wheel and leans his forehead against them as if he were deeply tired. Straightening up slowly, staring out to sea, he starts to speak in a voice that seems for all its control to be close to despair. 'A couple of days ago, when I was taking the Atkins idea seriously, when it seemed to fit everything, the dinghies and so on, before I'd thought it through properly, before *you* helped me to see that it was a non-starter . . .' He pauses and almost glances at me before fixing his eyes on the sea once more. '. . . I tried to work out how Atkins could have done it. The sheer logistics.' He makes a derisive sound and murmurs bitterly, 'Ever the detective!' Pushing himself onwards with an effort, he continues, 'I reckoned that Atkins would have had to come ashore somewhere along this stretch of beach before pushing the dory out to sea and making his way back to his transport. But where was he most likely to have landed? And how did he get back to his transport, assuming he had some? I couldn't see him taking the dory all the way back up the river. Too visible, too obvious. So where did he land? Much further north than here and he'd have had to swim the Ore or walk miles and miles to Aldeburgh or beg a lift on a military ferry, and still be a long way from his transport, assuming he left it somewhere near Pennygate. No, the way I saw it, if he had any sense at all he'd have come in somewhere near here and taken the path back over the marshes.'

He stops for no apparent reason and, turning away slightly, narrows his eyes as though examining something on the horizon. Concentrating again with reluctance, he resumes in a slightly brisker tone, 'So I asked around. The local lads, the fishermen, a bloke I'd met who has one of the coastguard cottages here as a weekend place. Anyone who might have seen anything. I even went back to the rambler, the one who saw *Minerva* motoring out of the river. But . . . nothing.' He looks down at his hands, he squeezes his lips, and still he finds it easier not to meet my eye. 'Then the chap in the coastguard cottages called me today. He said there was someone in one of the other cottages, an old guy who lives there all the time, and I should speak to him. So . . . I went there this evening.'

Beyond him in the middle distance, the cottages stand in ghostly silhouette, small Gothic follies against the fading sky.

Moreland turns at last, he looks at me, and his expression is at once appalled and sad, and I have a rush of feeling for him, for both of us, because I know what he's about to say.

'He saw a boat drifting early one morning, he wasn't sure of the date exactly, but it was about the right time. In March anyway. A weekend. A white boat, open, like a dory, though he couldn't be sure about that either. He didn't think there was anyone in it. He watched it for a bit. It drifted steadily north and then he lost it in the mist. While he was watching he noticed someone coming up over the shingle about where we are now, someone wearing a white waterproof jacket with some colour on it – green, he thought. He particularly noticed because the person staggered and fell and lay down for a while. He thought of going out to see if the person was all right but when he looked out again the person was getting up. He went down to the kitchen shortly after and saw the person passing the back of the cottages, and taking the path down onto the marshes.' Moreland's frown deepens, his voice trembles slightly as he says, 'He said it was a woman. He was quite sure it was a woman.'

The silence stretches out between us.

'Tell me he was wrong, Ellen.'

But I can't tell him that. It would be useless to try.

SEVENTEEN

'It was me.' I say it quickly as though this might lessen the impact.

Moreland twitches slightly as though an unseen insect has flown against his skin, he stares at me with faint horror and open bewilderment.

I look away. There are moments you fear and try to plan for, moments you think about so much that you can't focus on them any more, and then when they finally arrive they aren't as you imagined. I feel a sense of loss, but mainly I feel a bleak relief.

I make a gesture of appeal or apology. I say again, 'It was me.'

'You were on *Minerva*?' Moreland asks thickly.

But I can't answer this without answering everything. Needing more time, I wind the window down and let the breeze bowl in, cool and damp from the sea, filling the car with the low clamour of the pebbles clinking and rattling on the beach below.

'*How?*' Moreland demands. '*Why?*'

I sigh, I begin emotionally, 'It was Harry. You may not have realised, but he was in a terrible...' But this is wrong. If I am going to get through this story with some self-respect, if indeed I'm to have any hope of being believed after the untruths I've told, then I must do it without the more unedifying dramatic trimmings.

'Can I go back a bit?' I ask rather formally.

He indicates: anything.

But the beginning still eludes me. I could start with Harry losing his parliamentary seat, with Ainswick's troubles, I could even start with the affair with Caroline Palmer, but I'm not sure that these tales would add much to the story, which is straightforward enough. If only I can get it right. But I must get it right, for Katie's sake as much as my own. Lies are not so hard to tell, but they're extremely hard to fix in the memory accurately, so that they emerge unaltered every time.

'Harry . . . was . . . unhappy.' I begin haltingly. 'Things had been going wrong for a long time. He had been under terrible strain. He was very depressed. He felt things were never going to work out for him. He felt he was sinking deeper and deeper . . .' I am losing momentum. Gathering myself again, I continue, 'I couldn't seem to offer him any support. I couldn't reach him. He cut himself off from me. From everyone, I think . . .' I pause as though to consider this afresh. 'I think he was clinically depressed. I mean, from being something mental it had become physical as well. You know – the wrong chemicals in the brain. An illness. Needless to say, he wouldn't go and get help. That wasn't his way. He couldn't admit to anything that he couldn't deal with himself.'

I hate these half-truths, I hate my veneer of plausibility. Beneath it I feel transparent, I feel that Moreland must see straight through me, so that when I glance up I'm rather surprised to find him watching me with sympathy.

'That Friday,' I hurry on, 'I had the feeling that something was terribly wrong. I mean, worse than usual. He

440

was in such a strange mood when we were loading the boat. Not there at all. Doing things mechanically. Half dead. I can't put my finger on it quite. A feeling of doom and despair. Hopelessness. And going singlehanded in that weather! I was sick with worry. I went down to the quay in the afternoon to see if he needed anything but of course I couldn't make contact. I mean, the boat was there on the mooring and I shouted and waved, but he never heard me. The mooring's quite a way out, it's hard to hear on the best of days. I tried calling the mobile phone but he must have switched it off or something. When I got to Molly's that evening I couldn't stop worrying. I kept think-ing – well, that was it, I wasn't sure what it was, exactly. A feeling. A sort of foreboding, I suppose.'

Such a performance. The details, the embellishments. It seems I have an instinct for these things.

'So I came home early. I went down to the quay. It was very dark. I couldn't see *Minerva*, I couldn't see a light. I thought he must have gone. In a way I hoped he had – sailing always cheered him up, made him forget his troubles. And it was such a big challenge, taking the boat so far on his own; I thought it would give his confidence a lift, get him going again. But the weather still looked so horrible – wind and rain – that I rather hoped he hadn't gone after all. I thought it would be too much for him, sailing at night in that wind.'

Pausing, I stare out through the windscreen and More-land follows my gaze. The sky is fading fast, the sea is dark as slate.

'I kept an eye on the weather for the rest of the eve-ning,' I resume and he watches me again. 'Kept the win-dows open, listened for the wind. It dropped right away. I was relieved. I thought of Harry somewhere in the middle

441

of the estuary with all those ships around, I thought he'd be much safer with the wind gone. I went to bed, feeling a bit easier about things. Then . . . oh, about eleven-ten' – I have caught Dawson's obsession with precision – 'well, some time just after eleven, I heard the . . .' I lift my head as if to hear the sound again. '. . . the *shot*. It was a long way off, muffled, but I knew what it was. A shotgun. I mean I've heard enough of them. There's quite a bit of shooting around Pennygate in the winter.' I make an indeterminate gesture. 'I also knew . . . somehow . . . that it was Harry. I just . . .' I lift a hand. '. . . *felt* it.'

The breeze stiffens, I turn my face to meet it. Moreland shifts forward slightly as if to keep sight of my face.

'I drove down to the quay and there was a light. It could only be *Minerva*. It was in the right place, the right distance away. I knew then . . . somehow . . .' I shake my head, I look down at my hands. 'So I went out. To look.' I sense Moreland's unvoiced question. 'It was the dory, I took the dory,' I tell him. 'It was the only thing there. But I didn't know how to lower the engine into the water. I got the torch from the car, but I still couldn't work it out. And even if I had managed to get the engine down, I wasn't sure how to start it, whether you just turned the key or what. So I paddled. I saw the way the current was going, and I realised I could go with it. I almost missed *Minerva*, though . . .' I wince at the memory. 'Almost got swept past. Had to paddle like mad. Just managed to grab the Zodiac and pull myself up to *Minerva*.'

I brace myself. The vision is very strong and, though I have been back to the yacht many times in my mind, now that I try to put the picture into words the scene has become doubly vivid, like an etching that has sprung into full and awesome colour.

'He was . . . dead.'

Moreland nods in the manner of someone hearing what he has expected to hear.

'There was no doubt,' I whisper. 'I mean – that he was dead. I checked, I felt for . . . you know, pulse and things. And . . .' The memories crowd closer still, my voice constricts in my chest, it's all I can do to say, 'His eyes . . . were wrong. You know – open.'

Moreland nods again.

'The gun was beside him,' I murmur. We contemplate this in our separate ways before I continue in a new voice, 'I sat there for a long time. I don't know – an hour or so. Oh, I covered him up,' I add swiftly, as if this were an important point. 'I covered him with a chart; it was all I could find. It was wide . . .' But this is too painful and I abandon it with a shake of the head. I see the blood still. The astonishing redness of it as I bent over him. The way it glistened in the light. The awful gape of his mouth which seemed to yawn up in front of me even when I had turned away.

'Then I just sat there.'

Just sat there and wept, though I don't say so. Wept and railed and sobbed until my throat was hoarse, until, catching the sound of my own voice, I recognised the futility of it all and shuddered to a halt.

'I felt so frustrated and angry,' I relate calmly. 'I kept going over it all in my mind. I couldn't understand why he'd been so . . . Why he couldn't have *told* me . . .'

Moreland's hand arrives on my arm and grips it dutifully.

'That's what's so hard. That he never talked about it.' Saying this, I allow old emotions to rush in. I remember what enraged me so profoundly as I tied the dory to the

443

rail and pulled myself onto *Minerva*'s deck, as I prepared to go into the cabin and confront Harry; it wasn't his failure to tell me about his troubles – I never really expected anything else – but the realisation that he had deceived both Katie and me with such dedication and skill, that he had never faltered in his determination to deceive.

Moreland's hand is strong and warm on my arm.

'I realised why he'd done it,' I announce with a sigh. 'The only thing that could have made him do such a thing . . .'

Moreland withdraws his hand and waits attentively, his face shadowy against the last streaks of light.

'The Rumanian orphans money – I think he was about to be found out. I think they were on to him, and he couldn't bear the shame.' I watch a ship far out at sea, its lights like pinpricks in the growing cushion of darkness. 'There were the debts as well, of course. And the pressures on his business. And . . .' I hesitate, 'other things. But it was the thought of scandal, I'm sure of it.'

After a time Moreland murmurs, 'What happened then?'

'Then?'

'On *Minerva*,' he prompts gently. 'What happened then?'

'Oh . . .' I pull myself back into the story. 'Oh, I thought and thought. *God*, I couldn't stop thinking. About what had gone wrong, about the terrible waste of it all, about the absolute sheer *uselessness* of what he'd done. And then . . . Then I started thinking about the children . . .' I glance at the childless Moreland, in sudden doubt of his understanding. 'About what this would do to them. How they would be saddled with having a suicide for a father. How people would always whisper about it behind their backs. How it would become a label, stuck there for ever. How they'd never be free of it. And I was angry.' I turn blindly to Moreland. 'I was angry with Harry for having been so selfish. I know it seems – *bad*. I know it was *wrong*, but – I just couldn't help it. I just felt – angry.'

'That's natural,' Moreland says flatly. 'I'm sure that's natural.'

'Then I realised, of course – the suicide was nothing. *Nothing*.'

This is the difficult part. If I am going to lose Moreland anywhere, it's going to be here.

'I realised that the shame of having had a father who'd killed himself was nothing compared to the shame of having had a father who was a fraud – someone who stole from orphans! Whose only decent action in the whole of his life was to kill himself – well, that's the way people would see it, wouldn't they?' I grimace involuntarily at the thought. 'I just couldn't bear it. The thought of the shame being visited on the two people who least deserved it. Who were least able to deal with it. I felt – and I know this wasn't fair, I know Harry was very ill at the end – but I felt he should have thought of that. He should have thought of the children. And since he hadn't, I realised I would have to instead.'

I sense in Moreland a sharp curiosity as to what's coming next, and, though it may be a product of my shaky confidence, the first stirrings of incredulity too.

'I kept thinking about the children,' I hurry on. 'How I'd do absolutely anything to spare them the shame of it. How they had their whole lives ahead of them. With Harry dead, it seemed to me that they were all that mattered, that my first – my only – responsibility was to them.'

Searching the shadows that mask Moreland's eyes, I

seem to glimpse scepticism. But then his cheeks crease into a brief smile of encouragement, and I realise that he is still with me.

The breeze is fierce and cold on my neck, I wind up the window almost to the top and the swish and claw of the dancing stones fades into the sound of our silence.

'Then I realised there might be a way of protecting them after all,' I say. 'I'm not sure how it came to me. Thinking about the charity, I suppose. Imagining how the trustees might be persuaded to forget the whole thing. I thought that if I could pay them back then they might agree not to say anything, that the fraud would never get out. Harry didn't have any money of course. I knew that. But I thought perhaps I could borrow some. Or sell things. Or . . . and then I realised.' I give a bitter laugh. 'Harry had a life insurance policy. I wasn't sure how much exactly, but a couple of hundred thousand at least – enough to repay the charity – well, that's what I thought at the time. And then I realised – the final irony! – it would never pay out! Not for suicide. They never do, do they?' I attempt a sardonic laugh that rings unpleasantly in my ears. '*God!* I couldn't believe it. I sat there – *sick*. I felt this unbelievable hopelessness. This sense of complete defeat. Even the insurance – no good! I just felt it was the end of all of us, not just Harry. And I think perhaps I was still in shock. I don't know. But I must have been because otherwise I could never have done what I did. I couldn't even have begun to think of it.' I press my head back against the seat. 'Well . . .' I say meekly. 'You can guess the rest.'

Moreland's voice is low, close to wonder or disbelief. 'You took *Minerva* out to sea?'

'Yes.'

'You . . .' He hardly knows how to put it. '. . . sank her?'

I nod faintly.

While Moreland absorbs this with a long dazed intake of breath I replay what I have just told him in my mind, and the more I go over it, the less convincing it sounds. I see nothing but holes, I see the sheer unlikeliness of the great thinking session I'm meant to have had in the cabin in the presence of my husband's body, and I have this urge to go back and embroider over the thinner patches, to make a more convincing job of it. But some cautionary instinct holds me back, something tells me that this will only smack of uncertainty and desperation.

'Tell me,' Moreland says with some awe, '*how*? How did you manage it?'

'The boat?'

'The whole thing.'

I rub a hand over my face. 'You may well ask. By guess and by God as much as anything else. And by frightening myself to death.' My voice shakes at the memory.

'But you'd never been out of the river.'

'No.' I gave a rocky laugh.

'Tell me then. Tell me how.'

Here is the other Moreland, ex-Royal Marine, master seaman and survival expert: the compulsive matcher of facts to evidence.

This part of the story isn't hard to tell; it can be lifted complete from my memory, a series of desperate moments linked by intervals of more absolute terror. Though, wary as ever, I check the journey for pitfalls before starting out. 'Well . . .' I say at last, 'I had all night, you see. To prepare. *Minerva* was ready to go. Harry had done it all. The electrics were on – something he always talked about, getting the electrics on, but something I wouldn't have had a clue how to do on my own. And the key was in the ignition. I tried it and the engine started first time. I went back to the house first, though. I took the Zodiac and rowed back to the quay and went up and got some things. Warm clothes, waterproofs . . . And a saw, I took the saw from the garage.'

'You knew how you were going to do it? With a saw?'

'Oh no. I mean, I wouldn't have known. But ages ago Harry got me to help him with some repairs. Well, *help* . . . I just stood there giving moral support really. This was back when he first had the boat and was still keen on doing these things himself. He was taking a pipe off some of those things that brings water into the boat – a sort of nozzle thing—?'

'An inlet.'

'An inlet. Anyway when he eventually got the hose off, the water gushed in. Just gushed in. He hadn't turned the wheel thing off properly—'

'The stopcock.'

'The *stopcock*. It was jammed. And while he was trying to get it to work the water kept gushing in. He managed to shut it off eventually, but it gushed in for quite a time. I mean, so fast. I'd seen how long it had taken him to get the hose off. He had to put heat on it and things, it was a terrible job – and Harry was quite strong – so I knew I'd never be able to do it that way, that I'd have to find another way. I thought a saw would be easiest. The pipe was made of that soft bendy plastic. I didn't think I'd take very long to cut through it.' Hearing this, I'm struck by the calculation in my voice. I say, 'But I didn't plan it, not like that. I mean, the whole thing just sort of *happened*. It was . . .' But it's hard to explain my thought processes, and in the end I don't try.

'When I got back to *Minerva* the dory was the most

448

difficult thing. I had to make sure I could get it to work when I needed it. It took me for ever to get the outboard down into the water. I tried everything. I thought it was just a matter of pressing some lever. I didn't realise you had to lift the outboard and operate the lever at the same time. And it was so heavy, the engine. I got there finally, but it took a long time. And then *starting* it. I'd never had much to do with the dory. I'd ridden in it but never driven it. I wasn't sure what you had to do. There was meant to be a key hidden under the back seat – I'd seen Harry put one there anyway – but when I looked it wasn't there, and I thought I'd have to go all the way back to the house to find a spare. I almost gave up then. But . . . I couldn't.' I rub my fingers savagely over my forehead. 'I was in a state. Frantic. Not thinking straight. All I knew was that I had to do *something*. I wanted to make things *right*, you see.' I glanced at Moreland as though for reassurance. 'Impossible, of course. Nothing could be right, but I still felt I had to try. I felt it was the only way any good could come out of what was otherwise an absolute disaster.'

In the pause that follows Moreland glances away, his profile unreadable. Beyond him, a car's lights sweep over the coastguard cottages and, coming to rest behind them, die abruptly.

'In the end I found the key for the dory on *Minerva*. In the chart-table drawer, right there with all the other keys. I tried it, but nothing. I mean the key turned, but nothing happened. The thing seemed dead. I'd seen the way Harry pushed the handle forward when he started it, the handle by the steering wheel – what is it?'

'The throttle. Well, throttle and gear combined, probably.'

'The throttle. I tried it every which way, and finally got

449

the engine to turn. But it still wouldn't start. Eventually I found that knob – you have to push it in, don't you?'

Moreland nods. 'To put it out of gear, yes. It wouldn't start in gear.'

I tap a finger against my temple in a gesture of dull-wittedness. 'Well, I got there, finally. It took long enough. But I finally got it started.'

I am deafened again by the howling outboard, which seemed to fill the river, an invitation to everyone to come and investigate, or so it seemed. I'm back in a state of indecision about whether to let it run for a while – it sounded so sick and spluttery – or to turn it off again and have the cover of silence. I held out for a minute or so. The silence, when it returned, roared in my ears, almost as loud as the engine.

'I waited then. Under the hood in Minerva's cockpit. Until there was enough light. I may have slept for a while – but I don't think so. When the time came I started the engine. I was shaking with fright. It was so bad that I was sick in the end. Had to go to the rail and heave. I felt a bit better then. I went and undid the mooring, and raced back to the cockpit and pushed the lever forward. I was so relieved when she started to move. I hadn't been sure she would, you see. I thought . . . I don't know.' My doubts seemed unexplainable at this distance. 'She seemed to go more or less where I wanted. I'd worried about that too, about whether I could steer her. It probably sounds silly to you, but I'd never done it before, not really. Only when Harry told me to hold the tiller for a minute while he did something important. I'd got as far as the fact that you moved the tiller the opposite way, but that was about it. Anyway, I got the hang of it – well enough anyway. Then I was busy looking out for the buoys. I couldn't remember

450

where they all were, I was frightened of missing one, but I knew about the colours, red to the right. I kept saying it: red to the right. There were posts, too. I wasn't sure about them, I just guessed, but the moorings weren't a problem. I knew you went between them at Waldringfield. I knew where the mud was just there.'

'I remember,' Moreland comments softly.

I had forgotten our trip downriver to Waldringfield. Something in his tone makes me realise that the incident with the sailing dinghy, the way I warned the boy away from the mud, had stayed sharp in Moreland's mind, that he had stored it carefully away, along with my unsuspected talent with knots.

'I wasn't so good with the Zodiac,' I murmur as if we were discussing knots now. 'I can't have tied it on very well. It drifted away in the night some time. From the mooring. It wasn't there in the morning, anyway. I found it later, when I got back.'

'On the mud where Wally Smith saw it?'

I responded vaguely; I had already moved on. I'm back on *Minerva*, coming to the narrow river mouth. I'm seeing nothing ahead of me but the empty sea. I'm feeling the first swaying movements under my feet. The shoals are ahead and the fear is tight around my stomach and I'm feeling sick again.

'Coming out of the river I had no idea where to go,' I resume. 'I just headed out. It was misty, I couldn't see very far. I knew there were shallows somewhere, everyone was always on about them. The *shoals*. But I couldn't see any markers. I thought there was meant to be a buoy somewhere, but I couldn't see it. So I just hoped and prayed. The waves got bigger – well, they seemed big to me. They made the boat roll and lurch. I fell over once.

And then . . . And then the water ahead was . . . different. Flatter. Covered in ripples and small pointed waves.' I flutter my hand in the darkness. 'I knew immediately. I just – knew. I turned the boat away and tried going another way. And then I realised I'd turned too far, that the line ahead was the shore, that I was heading back again.' I frown. 'So I turned again. I probably went in a complete circle. And then I thought of looking at the compass. But I wasn't even sure how *that* worked. I had to think for ages about which direction I wanted. I couldn't work it out. I mean, I knew I should go east, roughly, but what was that on the compass?'

Moreland, thinking perhaps that I don't require an answer, takes a moment to spring to life. 'Ninety degrees.'

'Ninety . . . Ah.' I remember the dancing dial, the way it moved in the opposite direction to the one you thought it would, the way it kept moving in one direction even after the boat had started turning in the other. 'Ninety. Yes, I thought it must be something like that. But it was too late by then' – the memory snatches at my voice – 'because I was in the shoals again.' I suffer the horrors of perfect recall, I see the peaking frothing water. 'They seemed to be everywhere, the waves. All around. In the end I pressed on because there was nothing else to do. I sort of *froze*. I can't explain. I was so frightened I just stopped thinking. Cut everything out. Went into a complete daze. Then—' I take a second to breathe. 'There was this awful crash. The boat stopped dead. I fell forward. I felt as though we'd hit a wall.' Reliving it, I pull back slightly against the seat. 'I thought we'd had it. I thought that was it, that the boat was going to sink under me there and then. I thought . . .' I sigh, I shake this off. 'Then she sort of skidded round and leant over a bit and I felt her

452

bumping. I realised there was still a hope. I put the engine on faster – Harry used to do that when he got stuck in the river at low tide. It made an awful noise. I thought it was going to stop altogether. Or blow up.' I laugh grimly. '*Minerva* was shuddering and shaking. It was hard to tell what was happening, the water was swirling round so much. Then, I don't know, I had the feeling we were moving again, slowly, slowly. She leant over again. And then . . .' I exhale suddenly. 'We were free.'

I don't tell him about my diatribe, my screams to all the powers that be and ever were, to every god that might exist to hear my prayers and deliver me from my nightmare. I don't mention that I collapsed onto a seat afterwards, and sat there limply, muttering over and over to myself like some madwoman, moaning with relief and fright.

'I kept going,' I say, recovering with an effort. 'It was very misty. All around. I never saw another thing. I took a point on the compass – I can't remember what it was now. I couldn't stick to it anyway. I was all over the place. But I tried to come back to it now and again – roughly, anyway. And I just kept going. I don't know how long for.' This period is still a blur, a time when I lost the measure of many things. 'The boat lurched all over the place. The waves seemed enormous, though I don't suppose they were. One of the sails got itself unravelled and started flapping about. But I left it. I could hear things crashing around in the cabin, but I couldn't face going down . . . I couldn't bear to . . .' I drop my face into my hands, I see Harry's body again, the chart that didn't quite hide the hideous wound. Raising my hand, I catch the breeze through the top of the window. 'I just kept going.'

A faint luminosity comes off the sea, a suggestion of a

watery presence amid the greater darkness, but inside the car all I can see of Moreland is the shape of his head, the line of his nose.

I plunge on before I have the chance to think about what comes next. 'Finally I realised how far I must be getting from the shore. I stopped. I . . . got everything ready. I pulled the dory in and tied it alongside. I got the outboard going, to be sure it would work . . .' I break off, eyes burning, confused again by the lucidity of my actions then, which seemed to have a momentum of their own, quite independent of my chaotic thoughts. 'I thought of giving up again. To do such a thing. I realised there'd be no going back, that it was quite – irrevocable. I realised that in some ways . . . it was a terrible, *terrible* thing . . .' I draw in long breaths, I drop my head on my chest. 'Because Harry would never be buried properly and . . . his body would be . . .'

I must be whispering, because Moreland leans closer. 'I'm sorry?'

I lift my head, I say more distinctly, 'I thought of . . . him there. Of the things that would happen to him . . . And I couldn't bear it. That's why I closed the hatches when I left. Closed them tight. To shut him in. I couldn't bear . . .' This thought drifts into the ensuing silence. I try to push the image of Harry's body from my mind, just as I tried to escape it on *Minerva*.

I force myself on. 'The pipes, they didn't take long. I cut through two in the end. The water poured in. It wasn't long before it started coming over the floorboards.' But again I have difficulty in going on. Tears are dripping slowly onto my hand. 'Then I said prayers for him – every prayer I could remember. And I said goodbye. From everyone.' I wipe a drip from the end of my nose with the

454

back of my hand. 'And then ... I went. I left *Minerva* pointing east – well, what I hoped was east – and put the engine lever forward so she'd keep moving.'

'And you put the auto-pilot on?'

It seems there's nothing that Moreland doesn't know or guess.

'I pressed a button and hoped, yes. I didn't know if it was going to work.'

'The boat wouldn't have kept straight otherwise.'

'Ah?' I say, only half listening.

Moreland lifts a hip and, pulling something from his pocket, presses a handkerchief into my hand. I blow my nose hard. I mop up generally.

'You found your way back?' Moreland's tone is reverential, though whether for me or Harry I can't tell.

'Back? Yes.' I make a sound of disbelief. 'By sheer luck. I was in such a state, I didn't think, I just set off. The mist was bad and when I looked back *Minerva* was fading fast, and then of course I realised I had no way of finding the shore, that I was going to get totally lost.' I groaned at my idiocy. 'I turned back straight away. But even then I couldn't see her – *Minerva*. She'd disappeared – in those few seconds while I was turning. I panicked, I thought I'd be going in circles for ever. I thought ... well. ...' I laugh shakily at the memory of everything that went through my head. 'But then I glimpsed her through the mist. Just. *Just*. It was a job getting back on board. I tripped over the rail. I fell on my shoulder and bashed my head. And then I nearly lost the dory! Nearly let go of the rope!' I hear Harry correcting me: the *painter*, Ellen, it's called a bloody *painter*. 'It was awful going back on board. *Awful. Minerva* was getting lower in the water. And ...' I close my eyes involuntarily, I see the water lapping around Harry's body and this is almost the most terrible memory of all. 'I searched,' I say through a throat that is seized tight. 'I searched and found a compass. And then I left again.'

The waves popple and hiss and whisper below. Listening, I remember my first sight of the beach, the long line of the shingle as it emerged shadowlike from the soft wall of mist. I wasn't sure what I was seeing, I didn't care, I headed straight for the deepening line. The shingle was steep, it was hard to land. The pull of the water was very strong, the way it surged up the stones, and dragged and sucked back. I had to go in up to my armpits to turn the dory round and push it out to sea. A wave took my legs from under me, I fell, the water went over my head, and I imagined what it was like to drown.

'Well,' Moreland murmurs, sounding dazed. 'Well . . .' Then: 'You're going to have to tell them, Ellen.'

These things are so easy for Moreland; you simply establish the honourable path, and follow it.

'They'll think I did it for the money,' I tell him.

'What?'

'Well, I did partly. Remember.'

'But if you explain about the charity—'

'No. Never. I can never do that.'

'But surely—'

'No.' I say with sudden vehemence. 'They'd dig it all out. The fraud, the debts – it would become public property. There'd be a terrible scandal. Then everything I did would have been for nothing. For *nothing*.' I add more calmly, 'And then they'd be bound to charge me with something, wouldn't they? They'd have to, I'm sure they would. Failure to report a death, perjury – something like that. It'd get dragged through the newspapers with the rest of the scandal, and the children would have two parents to be ashamed of.'

He tilts his head in understanding or mystification. 'All right,' he says, sounding troubled. 'Tell them you did it for the children then. To spare them the fact that it was suicide.'

I ask seriously, 'Do you think they'll believe that? Do you think so?' I'd like to think it was possible, but voicing it, the chances seem increasingly remote. 'I think they'll find it hard to believe I went to all that trouble just for the happiness of my children. I think money will figure much larger in their thinking. The fact that I was trying to claim the insurance. That's fraud, isn't it? I think they'll find it hard to believe it wasn't the main reason I wanted to hide Harry's body.'

'You underestimate yourself, Ellen. I think you're the one person who can talk of protecting her children and be thoroughly believed.'

'You think so!' I almost laugh aloud. 'I'm afraid I don't quite have your faith. You're forgetting, I've told them an awful lot of lies. Why shouldn't I still be lying? In fact . . .' I give a strange excited laugh. '. . . since they're convinced it was murder, why shouldn't it have been me?'

'Come on, Ellen. Don't be silly.'

'It's not so silly,' I say, feeling frightened. 'Think about it.'

'Come on.'

My voice wobbles. 'I'm perfectly serious.'

'But why would you have wanted to kill Harry?'

'Ah. Well, we were going through a bad patch, you see. He was having an affair.'

'Oh.' Moreland digests this slowly. 'Oh,' he says again. 'But that's hardly a reason to kill someone.'

'Isn't it? I thought that was precisely why lots of people killed each other.'

Not judging this worthy of a reply, Moreland blows dismissively through his lips.

With a leaden feeling, I tell him, 'The money's not all, I'm afraid.'

I feel him scrutinising me through the darkness. 'What do you mean?'

This is the difficult part; this will involve a leap of trust which I'm not entirely sure I'm ready to make. I put the decision off a little longer by telling him about the Zodiac's oars, how the police have found Harry's blood on them, how they interpret this as a sure sign of foul play.

'Well, that's explainable,' Moreland states. 'You used the Zodiac, you obviously must have had some blood on your hands.'

Blood on my hands. What a ring it has.

'Yes,' I agree. 'But then . . . there was a phone call. From the mobile phone on the boat. To the house. Late that night. The call was answered, they know that. They thought it was Harry calling me. I persuaded them that the answering machine picked the call up and lost the message. Or rather, I failed to persuade them. I don't think they believed me for a moment. If I tell them what really happened, that it was me on the boat, that I made the call, they'll want to know who I was calling.'

'And? Who was it?'

'That's the trouble. I can't tell them.'

Moreland makes an uncertain movement. 'I don't understand.'

My senses reach out through the darkness towards him. To trust or not to trust? I hover on the brink. Suppressing the last quiver of doubt, I make the leap. 'It was Katie. She'd come home from school unexpectedly.'

'*Katie*. But why can't you tell them that?'

'Because she's on the point of a nervous breakdown

458

already. And if they question her, she'll almost certainly have the real thing.'

Moreland's confusion is almost tangible. 'Katie? But why?'

'She was complete devastated by Harry's death. You may not have realised. She almost flipped. I had to take her to a psychiatrist. She's still very shaky.'

I leave him with this for a moment. Then I murmur, 'I can't risk Katie. I can't risk Josh either. Whatever I've done wrong, the truth would crucify them.'

'But Ellen. *Ellen.*'

'I know, *I know.* Don't tell me – it's a mess! I know . . . But trying to explain it will only make things worse! And what's to stop them making something really bad of it? The blood on the oars. Why shouldn't they think I did something much, much worse?' I leave the worse thing – that is, murder – to float unspoken before us.

Moreland leans forward and, gripping the wheel high on the rim, stares out through the windscreen, shoulders hunched, like a demon driver in full flight. Then, some internal debate resolved, his shoulders fall and he sinks back.

'Then you mustn't tell them,' he says tightly. 'You mustn't tell them anything.'

Reprieved. I allow myself a moment of thanksgiving, an inner smile of relief.

'You must hold on . . .' He's thinking aloud. 'If you just hold on they'll lose interest. They're bound to, sooner or later.' He turns to me. 'Stick to what you've already told them. Don't budge an inch. Don't show the slightest doubt. I mean – don't overdo the confidence, but don't let them rattle you either.'

'They frighten me,' I tell him truthfully.

Moreland's hand finds mine. 'Just stick to your guns.'

'I get so scared.'

'I'll be here for you.'

I am suddenly breathless. 'You will?'

He takes my head in his hands, he kisses my forehead solemnly. 'Oh yes, dear Ellen. Yes.'

EIGHTEEN

Christmas approaches, and life unwinds gently before me.

Sometimes when I'm out shopping, I pause and give up silent thanks. Or when I'm cooking, or at the Project, or at my drawing-board. I close my eyes, I feel this surge of gratitude, I savour my sheer good fortune. I tell myself that I'll never take anything for granted again, not the obvious things, not the simpler things, and certainly not the fact that I'm free to lead the uneventful life I have wanted for so long. I stop and ask myself what I have done to deserve so much, and I'm not sure. But if gratitude in any way contributes to luck, then I feed it regularly, with reverence.

Even greater rushes of feeling come to me when I'm lying close to Moreland in the night. This is partly the euphoria of love, of course, which has been an undreamed of bonus of these last few months, partly my belief that nothing bad can happen to me while Moreland and I are together. And indeed, nothing has. Richard manages to give me a disproportionate belief in myself, to fill me with much of his very considerable confidence. During the long summer, when Dawson was still pressing hard, Richard talked me steadily through my worries, rehearsed me carefully before each interview, persuaded me that I was capable of holding out against Dawson. Having committed himself to the idea of protecting me, he has applied himself to the job with single-minded devotion. Counsellor, supporter, lover, friend; always there for me, just as he promised.

When I stop to consider my luck, I also ask myself what I've done to deserve Richard, and I don't know the answer to that either.

I've heard nothing from Dawson since October. Officially, the investigation is still open, still a murder inquiry. But since Atkins was found to have an unshakeable alibi and no other suspects have come to light, since in effect nothing is happening or is likely to happen, the team has been wound down from what I believe was once thirty officers, to twelve, then five, and though no one will confirm it, I'm told that no officers are actively working on the case at present. That isn't to say Dawson has given up. I know he hasn't. He told me as much at our last meeting. It had been the usual question and answer session, we had gone through our lines like performers in a long-running play, our voices flat, almost bored, we had trailed off into an inconclusive silence, when Dawson brought his palm down on the table, a gesture of finality, and announced that he would walk me out to my car.

'There's a tradition,' he said as he held the car door open for me, 'that a case stays open until it's closed.' He eyed me speculatively. 'You can rest assured, Mrs Richmond, that as far as I'm concerned this case will remain open for as long as is necessary.'

'I appreciate that very much,' I said without a trace of irony. 'Though you know how I feel about the murder idea.'

He inclined his head in acknowledgement. 'Just as *you*

must appreciate, Mrs Richmond, that I really can't be satisfied with suicide.'

'Perhaps we'll just have to accept that we'll never know for sure.'

'That doesn't bother you, Mrs Richmond?'

'No,' I announced after some thought. 'Not any more. All I want now is a quiet life.'

'Ah. But we don't always get what we want, do we?'

But I have got exactly what I want, that's the amazing thing. The niggling fear never quite leaves me, of course, but then I never expected it would. It is anyway a pale shadow of what it was in the summer. While the murder inquiry was in full swing I couldn't rid myself of the dread that some new evidence would come to light, something ugly and irrefutable; that Dawson would discover Katie was at home that night, that the old man in the coastguard cottages would realise the significance of what he'd seen and go to the police, or that it would occur to Dawson to question him and the other people who have a view of the shingle bank. None of this ever happened, but the accumulated tensions of this and my other worries erupted in a long bout of flu which left me weak and depressed. It was several weeks before I got over it, and some of that time I was in such a shaky state – mind as well as body – that if it hadn't been for Richard I'm not sure I wouldn't have stayed in bed and turned my face to the wall.

Now, my energy has come back, I can sleep for as long as six hours at a stretch, and without nightmares, and more often than not I reach the morning with a sense of hope and optimism. The only time I can't sleep is when Richard is away. In October when he was in Saudi for a week, I went out and bought a dog from the nearest dogs' home. Jiff is a mutt of unknown parentage and all the things I said I wouldn't have, large and long-haired and an indefatigable transporter of mud onto furniture, but he's affectionate to the point of idiocy and when I'm alone lies warm and woolly on my bed.

I finally moved out of Pennygate in September, a week after the sale was agreed and two months before completion. I went to a cottage ten miles inland, in a small village where people leave you pretty much to yourself. The place is only rented, it could do with some paint, the windows are draughty – Richard has had to attack them with putty and tape – but it has a cosy feel to it, a certain well-worn charm, and the fires draw well. When Richard and I lie in our bedroom under the eaves we hear scufflings in the thatch. Richard mutters darkly about vermin, but I find it rather companionable to share a roof with the local mice. The cottage stands alone on the fringes of the village, half-way up a narrow dead-end lane, so that few people have reason to come past the gate. This suits me fine, since I still have something of a phobia about the press and treat anyone looking over the fence with suspicion.

The press had a field day with the murder story, so Molly told me later. Every national newspaper and the evening bulletins on both main channels. There were reporters camped at the end of the drive, and photographers who used the ancient rights-of-way to walk within a few hundred feet of Pennygate and zoom in on the cars parked in the drive. First the house phone, then the business line, had to be left off the hook, and someone at the police station must have tipped them off about my next visit to Dawson because when I drove up with Leonard there were four or five photographers waiting.

Such interest couldn't last, thank God, but if I'd hoped for a rapid return to peace and quiet I was soon put right by a persistent piece of unpleasantness, a journalist from one of the tabloids – I later discovered he wasn't fully accredited – who pounced on me one day in the village and kept reappearing at regular intervals like a bad smell that won't go away. He had a leering grin, a greasy collar and a battered trilby. We called him The Bookie. Once he tried to talk to me when I was shopping with Richard and got more than he bargained for – Richard's language was startlingly succinct – but the episode left me nervous for a time. The last thing I needed was a story of the widow-quick-to-take-lover type. But maybe Moreland frightened him more thoroughly than I realised, because nothing appeared. Not then.

Once I had moved into the cottage, I slipped into a quiet almost hypnotic routine, which I have been following with enthusiasm ever since. I do two afternoons a week at the Project as a volunteer. I have no particular skills to offer young offenders, except perhaps to listen. I think I must listen quite well, or maybe the boys recognise some fellow feeling in me because, now they've got to know me, most of them seem happy to talk. I don't say a lot, I ask the occasional question, but I take them seriously and, when provoked, give as good as I get, which they seem to appreciate, albeit guardedly. They are, as they say themselves, full of shit. Boasters, liars, smirking gloating vandals, kids who would steal – have stolen – from their own grandmothers, even supposing they know who they are. They have only a distant curiosity about the notion of right and wrong, like package-tourists who view foreign customs as quaint and nonsensical. But, as in all the best hard-luck stories, the boys have their redeeming features. Most have never had anything that resembles a proper home, some have been abused, all have been neglected.

Without exception they can barely read and write. It seems to me that they went wrong because there wasn't any other way to go, and I of all people can sympathise with that.

Molly is so busy with builders and plumbers that I hardly get to see her at the moment, except to share her frustrations and woes at the delays in opening the new half-way house. But at least it is going ahead; the planning permission came through in July. Molly is convinced that her coffee-and-charm sessions with her tame councillor won the day, and she may well be right. I certainly wouldn't suggest otherwise.

I spend four mornings a week at the drawing-board. I've had quite a few commissions now; well, three – a logo for a woman's boutique in Ipswich, the design for an estate agent's news sheet, and – a major job – a corporate image for an expanding transport business. It was hard getting back to work, harder still to feel confident. I had to give myself imaginary briefs and work through dozens of ideas before I felt I could accept a paid commission. I still haven't got to the stage where I feel I can go out and market myself – the jobs so far have come through friends – but I'm getting there. I'm beginning to recapture a sureness of touch, a certain satisfaction.

On Wednesday mornings I write the children between two and three sheets of A4 each. I try to get the letters into the post by one-thirty so they'll arrive on Thursday and break up the week for them. Most parents don't bother to write, they just get their children to phone, but I like to put things on paper. Not only does it make me cover a much wider range of thoughts and ideas than I ever would chatting aimlessly on the phone, but it makes for an altogether more powerful statement. Devotion, commitment, a readiness to take pains; all the things I want the children to know and feel when they open those thickly packed envelopes.

Katie has done better at school this autumn, her marks have climbed from rock bottom to borderline acceptable. She may even scrape some results next summer, though I'm not banking on that. More importantly, she has been much calmer and outward looking, as though she has decided to put the past behind her and get on with life, a development that fills me with tentative relief.

I'm not so happy about Josh. In fact, I feel very confused about him. He has gone to a boarding school in Norfolk, some forty miles away. Friends tell me I have been wise and farsighted to let him go, sometimes I even manage to persuade myself that it was a sensible decision, but most of the time I'm cross with myself for giving in. I feel it can only force us apart, and that frightens me.

He seems to have settled in well enough – the staff haven't mentioned any problems anyway – but when he comes home a dark tension settles over him, and unvoiced indignation. Much of this resentment gets pushed my way, he gets quite difficult on occasion, but, as I try to remind myself, parents always get the brunt of these things. I try to give him the benefit of the doubt, I think of it as a stage he is going through, some lingering reaction to all the dramas of the summer; a cry for attention perhaps. But I can't pretend I don't miss the easy, loving boy I used to know.

The rest of the time? I walk, I shop, I cook, I wait for Richard to come home. Recently his work has taken him to London and often he doesn't get back until late. I wait like a bride, table laid, supper in the oven, heart lifting at the sound of every distant car, breath tight at the thought of the moment when supper will be over and we climb the stairs to our cosy bed under the eaves.

I don't think about the future too much; I feel it's unlucky somehow. It is enough that Richard loves me, that he has finally separated from his wife, that he has promised he will never leave me.

I have something approaching peace of mind. I am far luckier than I deserve.

A couple of weeks ago Charles came to see me. He sat stiffly by the fire and sipped at his whisky with the uneasy manner of a UN official undertaking difficult negotiations.

'It would be nice if we could all get together again,' he said wistfully.

I reminded him that it wasn't me who was holding things back, it was Anne, and he nodded sadly at that. He could hardly disagree.

Anne doesn't actually come out and say so – not to me anyway – but I know she thinks I haven't told the truth about Harry's death. She doesn't go so far as to point the finger of blame at me – even she, with her overblown imagination, doesn't believe I'm a murderer – but she thinks I'm covering up in some way. *Obstructing the course of justice*, she has been heard to say. What motives I'm meant to have for this I don't know. A secret lover, perhaps, whom I was entertaining at Pennygate that night when the call from Harry came through. Or a lover whom I'd sent to kill Harry and who was phoning from the boat to tell me he'd completed the job. The fact that this lover has never appeared, that I'm seeing Richard, doesn't seem to figure in Anne's thinking, but then she doesn't approve of my relationship with Richard anyway. She thinks I've been indecently quick off the mark. But then as a faithless wife, presumably one more lover is neither here nor there. Who knows? Anne's mind is unfathomable.

'Perhaps you and the children could come over for Boxing Day?' Charles suggested. 'Tea, or something?'

I told him I didn't think it'd be a very good idea.

'The children then. Anne would love to see them. And so would their grandmother. They've bought them all sorts of presents.'

But I didn't like the idea of the children going to Anne and Charles's on their own. I didn't want them picking up disturbing messages about me.

'I'm sorry,' I said. 'Perhaps when Anne's feeling better about things.'

Charles accepted this with a small sigh. 'I'll do what I can.'

At the door he asked me how I was managing generally.

'Just fine,' I said.

'Money all right? All sorted out?'

'All sorted out,' I said.

This wasn't strictly true, but it's not something I discuss with anyone but Richard and my new accountant, a discreet and hard-working young man from Woodbridge. Now that the largest assets are sold, it's clear that I'm going to be left with very little. Pennygate got a poor price, barely enough to cover the various mortgages, the furniture and pictures achieved disappointing prices at auction, and the yacht insurers have refused to pay out because the yacht was 'scuttled'. Leonard has fought this, just as he has pressed the life insurance company, citing the police's decision to treat the death as murder, but the company insist that while there's any doubt about the manner of Harry's death it's against policy to pay out. Leonard remains determined, but

I have written all the insurance money off. Things are going to be tight, but I'll manage.

The Rumanian orphans got their first cheque in July. For a time I worried about raising anything like enough money for the next instalment, but, having thought it through, I have decided to go back to Jack and ask him if he can find something in his charity budget for next year. I don't feel too bad about this. His various companies have gone from strength to strength, he has acquired another prime site on the outskirts of Ipswich and I read in the local paper that he has sold an office block in the middle of town, presumably at a profit.

He has also managed to pick up a couple of bargains. In October, two months after Ainswick went into liquidation, I asked my new accountant to find out what had happened to Ainswick's assets. He discovered that within a month of liquidation the receiver had sold the Shoreditch building to a company called Redfern, who sold it on almost immediately to a Hong Kong investment company. Redfern, it turned out, is a wholly owned subsidiary of Conquerall Properties – a telling name – which is registered at Companies House as a private company ninety per cent owned by Jack Crawley.

Ainswick's parcel of land near the bypass was also acquired by Jack at a knock-down price. Although, as chance would have it, it now seems that the land might not be quite so useless after all. According to an obscure notice in the local gazette – brought to my attention by Molly's councillor – Jack's company has successfully applied for a change of use for this plot, along with the granting of the all-important access across the intervening council-owned land.

Jack with the golden touch.

I know I should feel bitter; sometimes I do. Whichever way you look at it, the children and I have been cheated.

But what am I going to do about it? Looking at it bluntly, my options are extremely limited. I could take legal action, I suppose, but I suspect that, being Jack, he will have covered himself very carefully and it will be extremely hard to prove anything. These cases can take thousands in legal fees and drag on for years, without any guarantee of success. And I mustn't forget that when it comes to fraud I live in the largest glass-house of all, and that it might be extremely unwise to start throwing stones.

No, taking everything into account, I prefer to think that things will get balanced out in other ways, that when the children and I need anything, Jack will help us out. Indeed, he's already agreed to pay Josh's school fees, and, if I have trouble in finding Katie's fees next term, which is very probable, then I have no doubt he will help us again. Ever since I found out about the bypass land, I haven't felt too bad about going back for more. Jack has no children, he is very rich; I like to think that contributing to our welfare makes him happy.

One thing about the murder inquiry – the only advantage, one might say – is that Jack has been keen to keep his distance. As a suicide's widow I merited a certain pity, but murder has a taint to it, a suggestion of dark deeds and scandal, and I think Jack worries about his image. Our dealings have become brisk and businesslike, which is only appropriate when you consider the nature of our arrangement, about which neither of us has any illusions.

I decided some time ago; this was going to be the most complete Christmas ever.

Richard says I have missed my vocation and should

have been a military logistician, the way I have planned it. Lists, highly targeted shopping expeditions, secret present-wrapping sessions. With the children due home in two days, I have done the decorations to death. Every mantel and picture is draped with holly and red ribbons, there are garish lights round the porch -- Richard suggested I should go the whole hog and have them flashing on and off -- while the tree fills an entire corner of the small living-room, its branches laden with lights and glass balls and silver circles and glitter that I brought from Pennygate. Beneath, I have laid out the presents so they look bulky and tantalising. Mistletoe hangs in the hall, and waiting on the children's beds are enormous green felt stockings embroidered with festive robins and pieces of fake holly.

On the food front, I intend to reach new heights. For Christmas lunch, I plan turkey with mushroom and olive stuffing, accompanied by roast potatoes, carrots and sprouts and bread sauce and gravy: the full trimmings. And afterwards, mince pies and brandy butter and plum pudding with lucky twenty-pence pieces. Though no baker, I have managed to make a traditional cake with frosted icing, decorated with (shop-bought) chocolate yule log, scarlet-sugared Father Christmas, and a 'Merry Christmas' in red plastic and *diamanté* that looks as though it too should flash on and off.

In the ten-day lead-up to the big day itself, I have planned all sorts of outings for the children: cinema trips, shopping expeditions, visits to friends, video showings at home.

Apart from persuading Moreland to dress up as that great chimney escape artist Father Christmas -- a role he has firmly declined -- I think I have covered absolutely everything.

*

472

Waking early, I watch the first glimmers of light creep in under the thatch and apply my mind to composing clues for a treasure hunt that I'm planning for an evening in four days' time, when some friends are bringing their children over to supper.

As soon as Moreland shows signs of life I try him with, 'I'm old and venerable, I hurry for no one, but young people regularly look up to me.'

Moreland mumbles, 'Grandfather clock.'

'Oh! Too easy then.'

'Too easy because I got it?'

'Well, I like to think I can fool you sometimes.'

'No chance.'

And he rolls over and pulls me close against him and kisses me just how I like to be kissed.

'The problem with you,' I say, hooking a leg over his waist, 'is that you're too bright.'

His mouth travels onto my neck. 'Just as long as you think so.'

We are well down the road to making love when the phone rings.

'Leave it,' Moreland breathes.

But even as he says this he gives up the idea and rolls onto his back to let me reach over and pick it up.

'Sorry, darlings,' says Molly's voice, 'but there's something in the paper. I think you might want to see it.'

'What sort of thing?'

'A story.'

'Bad?' I ask.

'Well – not too good. Listen . . . I'll bring it over.'

We're up and dressed by the time she arrives. The story is splashed across two pages of a popular tabloid. I don't need to read the byline to realise that The Bookie has

473

finally sold his story. It doesn't take long to get the gist of it. Under the headline *SO WHO DID KILL YACHTING MP?*, the story, based on 'exclusive information', states that the police have finally ruled out an SAS-style revenge killing and now believe that the murderer was someone well-known to Harry Richmond. Evidence from 'exclusive sources' points to a well-planned attempt to conceal the crime.

There is a lot of background detail, a rerun of the story so far, then the revelation of the 'exclusive' evidence. The blood on the oars. The inflatable left high and dry. The shotgun blast. The late-night call to the house.

If Harry Richmond was killed by a shot heard at 11.30 p.m., as police believe, then who made the late-night call from the boat to the house? The Bookie demands. *And who took the yacht out to sea and sank it?*

I feature quite heavily. I was up at the house through the latter part of the evening but 'claim' that I didn't hear the phone call. I rescued the inflatable from the mud the next morning but 'claim' that I didn't think it was worth reporting.

Then, as if that wasn't damning enough: *Ellen Richmond has been interviewed eight times by Ipswich police.*

We all know what that means in tabloid-speak. It means that the police are convinced I'm guilty but can't find enough proof.

'I don't think anyone takes any notice of this sort of thing,' says Molly, protesting too much.

But they do, they do. And Richard knows it too, because he is grim-faced as he puts an arm round my shoulder. The paper, for all its gossip and slick journalism, has an enormous circulation and is read by politicians, the media, most of my friends and probably half the village.

And I thought the risk had passed. I sink into a chair.

I accept a black coffee. I half listen to Richard as he tells me that these stories blow over in time, that thinking people take them with a pinch of salt.

I say abruptly, 'The children.'

I catch Katie on her way out of her first class. Luckily she had seen and heard nothing. The newspaper is one that the girls in her house take regularly, but with the end of term disruptions no one has read it yet.

When I give her a rough outline of the story she groans and sighs and says angry things about newspapers and journalists. Then, more plaintively, 'How *could* they? Why don't they leave us alone?'

I ask her if she wants me to come and collect her a day early.

'No, I don't think so,' she says uncertainly. 'No. That would mean we minded, or something.'

'You're sure? The girls are bound to see it. They might say things.'

'No, I'll be fine,' she says in an altogether tougher voice. 'No problem. We always knew, didn't we? I mean, there was always a chance of this sort of stuff. But are you okay?'

No problem, I declare, adopting the jargon. I tell her that it's like water off a duck's back, that friends are the only people I care about and they're not going to take this sort of thing seriously, that it'll blow over in time.

'You're not on your own?' she asks.

I tell her I have Molly as well as Moreland. Positively surrounded, I joke weakly.

I don't feel such urgency about reaching Josh. I'm pretty sure he doesn't get to see newspapers at his age – not gossipy rags like this anyway – though I leave a message for his housemaster anyway.

Both Moreland and Molly offer to stay with me, but I

send them off to work and sit at my drawing-board, tinkering fruitlessly with ideas for a bathroom fittings brochure.

The phone rings solidly. I monitor the answering machine – a couple of reporters, friends I'm not ready to talk to – and pick up the handset only when I hear the voice of Josh's housemaster.

'I guessed it'd be about that,' he says when I explain. 'I'm afraid one of the day-boys must have said something already. We have no control over what day-boys read.'

'Josh—?'

'He's rather upset.'

My heart lurches. 'What did the boy tell him?'

'I don't know. It didn't seem the time to try and find out.'

'Is he very upset?'

'Well, he is in a bit of a state, yes.'

I ask if he could arrange to get Josh packed, as I'll be picking him up and bringing him straight home.

When I arrive Josh is sitting in the dormitory next to his trunk, which one of the matrons is packing for him. He is like a small statue, pale and immobile. His eyes are puffy from crying. He gives me a strange glance as I go to hug him, as though he can't believe I'm here.

Driving back, I hold his hand as often as I can, I tell him everything I told Katie. I say it's a lot of nonsense, the stuff they put in the papers, that as far as these editors are concerned it's anything for a good story, that we have to be strong, the three of us, and rise above hurtful things.

I ask what the day-boy said, but the question so obviously disturbs him that I don't press it. Back at the cottage, he picks at his lunch without interest. His movements are minimal, as if he will attract less attention that way. I go

476

through everything I told him in the car for a second time, but it's like pushing against glass, I don't feel I'm getting through. I try a couple of other approaches, but I realise with a sense of failure that I don't really know what to say to him. In the end I light a fire and leave him curled up on the sofa with Jiff, watching an old film.

I manage to track Moreland down at the boatbuilders in Ipswich. He says he'll come straight away and I move restlessly around the house until he arrives. Typically he has stopped on the way to buy me flowers and a card on which he has written a supportive message.

I give him a punishing hug. I say humbly, 'You're the best present I ever had.'

'Just remember – the press don't matter. Nobody can possibly matter except the people we care about.'

'Keep telling me.'

'I'll keep telling you.'

'Thanks. For being here, I mean.'

'Oh, it's no great hardship really,' he smiles.

He kisses me, and I cling to the sense of safety that only Richard can bring me.

Just as typically, Richard has brought something for Josh as well, an adventure magazine and some favourite chocolate-coated nuts. With conspicuous tact I leave the two of them alone in the living-room and lose myself in the kitchen.

They emerge after fifteen minutes and Moreland announces, 'We thought we'd change and go into town for a burger. If that's all right?'

'Save me cooking!' I say with nervy joviality.

Watching them leave, it seems to me that Josh has brightened up already.

I spend the time sewing and watching TV and monitoring the answering machine. After eight, I start to listen for the sound of Moreland's car.

Jiff leaps up at one point and barks frantically, but it's only the rain pattering against the windows. Later I go out to replenish the wood-basket. Somewhere at the edge of the garden branches creak and rub complainingly. And beyond everything, way off in the dim distance, I seem to hear the sea on the shingle once again.

I pause, I listen, and I shake a mental fist at the trickery of the wind. The shingle is all of fifteen miles away. I laugh. I think: You won't get me that easily again! Nothing will! I'm free of all that. Newspaper stories won't harm me, nor Dawson's little campaigns. I feel too strong to be frightened any more, and the realisation is like a small revelation.

I return to the warmth and light, a crab scuttling happily into its shell.

At nine I decide Richard must have taken Josh to the cinema. Or they have met up with friends. No, the cinema; otherwise they would have phoned. By ten, my apprehensive nature has pushed its way to the surface and I'm beginning to remember how treacherous and narrow the roads are, how it only takes one crazy driver to cause an accident.

Thirty minutes later I hear the slamming of a car door, and, all fears forgotten, I hurry to let them in.

Moreland carries a sleepy, blinking Josh over the threshold and, forestalling questions with a shake of his head, takes him straight upstairs. Wordlessly he helps undress him, and I don't interfere.

'Good night, my darling.' I lean over the bed to kiss Josh.

'Night, Mummy,' and he puts his arms around my neck

and turns his cheek to meet my lips and there is a relax-
ation in him, a warmth to his embrace which thrills me.

'What did you say to him?' I whisper to Moreland in
the passage.

'Oh, nothing in particular. Listen . . .' He glances away.
'I have to go and write something. Could we talk about
it later?'

I look at him. I have this feeling. 'Later?'

'It'll only take half an hour. But I've just got to get it
done.' He smiles briefly, but his eyes don't smile with him.

'Is there something wrong?'

'I want to tell you what Josh said. But it'll take a
while to explain properly. And I've really got to write this
thing first.'

'Something's wrong,' I repeat.

He makes a gesture of impossibilities, and my heart
sinks at this small evasion.

'What is it?' I press.

'I promise – just half an hour.'

I look into his face and I see all kinds of messages that
frighten me to death.

'But I want to know now.'

'Half an hour,' and I can see he is not going to be moved.

Giving in, I say with a small smile, 'No longer?'

'No longer.'

He turns away and I let him go. I have a bath, I lie on
the bed with a book in front of me and cover the same
passage time and again. I can't rid myself of a sense of
foreboding.

When Richard has been gone twenty-five minutes I hear
a sound, a door closing. When he still doesn't come, I start
to get off the bed. As I swing my legs down I hear a car.
I sit there and I hear it drive away from the house. I

leap off the bed and race downstairs and throw open the front door.

His car has gone.

I stand there until I begin to shiver. Retreating, I look in the living-room, I look in the dining-room where Richard does his paperwork. I turn back into the hall.

Then I see it. On the table by the door, an envelope, with my name written in Richard's clear script.

There is no 'Dear Ellen'.

I have to tell you what Josh told me this evening. You were right to be concerned about him. He's in a bad way, mainly because he's terrified that you're going to be arrested and taken away, and he feels very confused about that. He has good reason to think this might happen, because he saw you on the night his father died. I will try to put it down exactly as he told me. He said that his supper at Jill's made him ill and he got up to be sick. He saw lights at Pennygate. Thinking you must be home and wanting to see you, he pulled some clothes on and sneaked out of Jill's and came across to find you. Inside the house, he heard crying. He was frightened and hid in the kitchen. When you came into the kitchen and took a key from the dresser he hid behind the door. He didn't say anything because he thought you'd be cross with him. He saw you go into the boot room and come out with a shotgun in your hand and leave the house. He called to you then, but you didn't hear. He followed you as far as the edge of the garden and saw you go on down to the river. He waited for a while then went back into the house. He waited at his bedroom window for a while, to see if he could spot you coming back. Then he heard the sound of a shot.

This is what he told me.

I'm afraid I told him something I shouldn't – I told him

I was sure there was an explanation. It was wrong of me to abuse his trust in this way, to raise his hopes artificially, but I couldn't bear to let him see how utterly shocked I was, or for him to think bad things about his mother because of me. Poor little blighter will find out all about betrayal soon enough.

Unless your concern for your children is entirely pretence, I suggest you think of a story to tell Josh. It'll have to be something pretty convincing. Otherwise he's going to spend the rest of his life wondering what happened that night, believing you killed his father, and that will screw him up for ever.

I don't think I'm in the market for more lies myself.

I'm sorry I couldn't tell you this to your face. I didn't think there'd ever be a situation I would run from, but I was wrong.

I'll get my stuff collected, if you'd be good enough to pack it.

There is no signature.

NINETEEN

The best that can be said for moving house is that it weighs your mind down with so many trivialities that you don't have time to think of other things. I got the timing wrong though. I should have left the move until late September, when the children will be gone and another dreary winter will be looming ahead and I'll be only too glad of something to keep me busy. As it is, we moved two weeks ago, towards the end of August, just when I had intended to spend what they call quality time with the children, and to help Katie get herself organised for America. I don't know who drove each other madder during the move, the children or me. They couldn't believe how disorganised I was, and I suppose I did rather leave things to the last minute, but their ideas of packing were pretty bizarre too, with whole drawers left unemptied and miscellaneous debris left under beds. In the end they took charge, which was no bad thing. I needed a bit of leadership.

Now we're beginning to settle in, I tell myself it's good to be in our own place, bought and paid for, thanks to a little help from my friends and a building society. I give myself all the arguments about laying the foundations of a solid future, about the importance of providing the children with a firm base. I ignore my own restlessness, which scratches at me like rough cloth. But constant travelling wouldn't be the answer. It's not a change of scene I'm after, but a quieter mind, and that's not so easy to find.

It was Molly who goaded me into moving. I think she got fed up with seeing me in that dank cottage during the long winter. She pushed me into looking at houses in March, I made a fruitless bid for a half-timbered cottage south of Woodbridge at the beginning of May, and found this in June. It's tiny, the kitchen's a cheap add-on, far too many things needed doing to it – the builders were in for five weeks – but the living-room is south-facing, the garden sunny, and Jack thought it was a good buy, and you can't get a much higher recommendation than that.

We're still camping. Boxes remain unopened, and I can't muster a great deal of enthusiasm for finding fabrics or getting coat hooks screwed into walls, so the interior is spartan and likely to remain so for some time. But the kitchen and bathroom function, I have a place to put my drawing-board; we can live.

The summer holidays are almost over. In three days Josh goes back to his boarding school where he has developed an unsuspected talent for art, aided and abetted by an inspirational teacher called Mrs Daly, who keeps telling him he could be really good, which is very pleasing.

The day before that, Katie leaves on an exchange visit to a college near San Francisco. It's only for a term, she'll be back by Christmas, but you'd think she was setting off on an uncertain voyage to an unknown continent. Cards and messages arrive daily, her friends send her such weight savers as jars of marmalade and framed photos of themselves, she has stocked up with packets of her favourite muesli. When she isn't spending hours on the phone, squawking with excitement, she is railing at the inadequacies of her new clothes, about which she was ecstatic just three weeks ago.

I hold a farewell lunch for her. The day is warm enough to have it outside, which is just as well since we're too many to fit comfortably inside the cottage. We sit at two trestle tables put end to end and covered with white cloths, like a French wedding party. In the best tradition of such feasts, the family have assembled for the occasion. Charles sits on my right, Diana on my left, and Anne on the far side of Jack. I didn't really expect Jack to come – he's always telling me how busy he is – but I think he has a sneaking liking for family gatherings and, now that he's had time to get used to the idea, a pride in his role as uncle-figure and benevolent provider. Not that anyone is meant to know about that, though some seem to have guessed, a fact for which Jack himself is probably responsible. Molly tells me that he has been dropping hints in various quarters, and I can just imagine him murmuring with a suitable show of modesty, *well, I do what I can, you know.*

Having guessed about my financial arrangements, some people have drawn quite the wrong conclusions. Only the other day, when I mentioned a lingering debt, Anne said, 'Can't Jack look after that?' I gave her a questioning glance and she raised her eyebrow slightly and gave me a knowing look as if to say, you can't think I'm a total fool. And I have heard there are whispers in other quarters.

Jack doesn't help this kind of rumour by dropping in on me at odd times, rather in the manner of a wise investor inspecting an asset. He is still wary of being seen with me in public – I remain something of a talking point, I gather, and the talk isn't entirely free of speculation – although this prudence only serves to lend his furtive visits, in which he is careful to park his highly conspicuous car down a side lane, a somewhat suggestive air.

But I don't care what people think. I'm content that Jack and I have reached an understanding that has become almost amicable, and so long as the faintest whiff of scandal attaches to me, I know that his interest in me will never step beyond the proprietorial, which suits me very well.

This doesn't prevent him catching my eye and throwing me his most charming low-lidded smile.

Anne and I have also reached an understanding, though it's an altogether more uncomfortable and less well-defined arrangement. We go to pains not to offend, we address each other courteously, we try to smile, and as I look at her now, she raises her glass and calls, 'What a wonderful day!' But I have no illusions about what this show of family unity costs her. She still thinks I am guilty of something. I catch it in her face sometimes, and I get the impression that she shrinks when I come near.

'What's she talking about?' croaks Diana, who's getting increasingly frail and confused. 'It's cold. *Cold.*' And for an instant it could be Harry, there is such a similarity in the intonation of the voice, in the profile of the nose they shared. I lift her cardigan from the chair back and drape it round her shoulders, and wonder briefly what Harry would have been like in old age.

Molly, in a flowing cotton number, sits on the far side of Charles, next to one of Katie's three school friends, pretty fresh-faced girls wearing the mandatory sloppy T-shirts and torn jeans and long hair which they constantly scoop back from their foreheads with a nonchalant rake of the fingers. Their languid movements and flashing eyes are directed towards a young man called Biff, whom Katie invited as a 'sort of friend'. Biff has startling blue eyes and

485

a quick smile and seems to be saying fascinating things. Josh is delighted by Biff too, not because of anything he's saying, but because his name rhymes with Jiff, and every time someone mentions Biff's name the dog, who's confused enough about moving house, jumps up and barks, which sends Josh into paroxysms of laughter.

At the far end of the table sits Katie, the loveliest of them all, with her gleaming hair and smiling eyes, all ethereal composure broken by eruptions of exhilaration. Watching her, I think of the wonderful time she's going to have in America, of the life that stretches before her, and I tell myself that everything I did was worthwhile, every last awful deed, and that I don't regret a thing.

I tell myself this, though it isn't strictly true. I do have regrets, and the greatest is Moreland. It's at moments like this, when I'm surrounded by family and friends, or at night when I'm alone in the emptiness of my bed, that I feel his loss the most. I tell myself that there was always going to be a price to pay, that I should count myself lucky that it's not a great deal worse, that I could have been caught and sent to prison for an unimaginable number of years, that indeed I'm fortunate that Moreland's sense of honour will not permit him to go to the police. I tell myself that I will get over him in time, but the pain lingers, an old wound that I pick at in my dreams and reopen constantly.

After Moreland left I learnt that time is a lumpy commodity, that it passes with plodding slowness or in bursts of distraction that are all too brief. I learnt that there are ways to reduce your awareness of being alone, that having the TV on all the time provides a permanent backdrop like auditory wallpaper, that you can believe a dog is almost human if you talk to it often enough and with sufficient feeling, that if you make yourself cosy and comfortable and warm your bed with an electric blanket and plant a TV at the end of it, you can fool yourself into believing life's treating you well.

'Ellen?'

They're all laughing at me.

'Miles away!' Charles says affectionately.

'Sorry,' I say, sitting up and smiling back.

Jack is on his feet, wine glass in hand. He raises an eyebrow at me as if to check that I'm finally paying attention before announcing in his best parliamentary voice, 'A toast. To Katie. May she have every success at her new school.' Needing no lessons in timing, he leaves it a second before adding, 'And not get into too much trouble.' Amid laughter, he raises his glass.

'Katie!' everyone cries, and she glows with pleasure.

Her glance slips my way. I lift my glass and silently mouth her name. We exchange a look in which nothing is left out.

Packing has never been one of Katie's stronger points, and we spend most of the next morning trying to fit an impossible quantity of gear into her case.

'Can Biff come with us to the airport?' she asks casually.

'Well, I suppose so. Does he really want to come all that way?'

She flashes her eyes at me as if I'm crazy to ask. 'Course.'

'You like him?'

'Oh, *Mum*.' She puts her hands on her hips with an expression that says: you of all people!

I retreat hastily, I throw up my hands. 'I didn't mean . . . I meant – he's nice? He's going to be a real friend?'

She gives me the benefit of the doubt. 'Yeah. I mean, he's *okay*. And he wants to come, so . . . Damn! My Walkman's packed up.' She pushes the buttons repeatedly. 'Batteries flat!'

'We can buy some at the airport.'

She doesn't answer but marches next door into Josh's room, and I make a mental note to replace whichever batteries she is pinching from her brother. I hear her pulling open drawers and rooting around, then a long silence. After a time I put my head round the door. She is standing by a half-unpacked box reading what looks like a letter. She turns and holds it out to me. 'Here.'

I'm about to admonish her for trespassing, but something in her expression gives me a beat of alarm, and I reach out and take it.

I stare at Moreland's handwriting. The letter is addressed to Josh, and dated June, towards the end of the summer term. I don't mean to read more than a line or two, but it's impossible to break off, and I go through to the end. It's a newsy letter peppered with anecdotes and enquiries in the tone of someone who's written many times before, and had replies too.

'Did you know?' demands Katie.

I shake my head.

'How dare he! The ratfink! What a cheek!'

I read the beginning again. *Dear Josh, Cricket was never my game either! All that standing around for hours waiting for the ball to come your way and then when it does, and you have to make a catch, you have two dozen kittens because you're so terrified of missing it.*

'You should tell him to get lost.'

I fold the letter and slowly shake my head.

'After the way he left! You should tell him to mind his own business!' She studies me for a moment, she reads my expression and sighs. '*Mum* – he was a rat!'

'No.'

'He just walked out!' And there is still hurt in her voice, because, despite giving him a hard time, she liked Moreland too.

'He didn't walk out. I told you, I asked him to go.'

She doesn't want to contradict me, but she doesn't believe me either.

'There were good reasons. Really.'

'Sure,' she says dismissively.

And suddenly I don't want Katie to think that Moreland is just another man who lets people down.

'He had a conflict of interest,' I explain, pushing the letter back into the chaos of the box.

'Oh yes?' she says archly.

And, facing her again, seeing how grown up she has become, I tell her what I have never told her before. 'He thought I helped Harry to kill himself. Or worse, that maybe I pointed the gun.'

She digests this. 'Why?'

'He found out I'd been lying to him. He found out' – and I say it in a tone of total acceptance – 'that I took the shotgun down to the river that night. Before the shot was heard.'

Understanding comes to Katie's face. 'Josh told him?'

'But you mustn't blame Josh.'

'Oh, Mum,' she sighs, 'why didn't you tell me?'

Because I didn't want to upset her. But I don't say this, I just shrug.

She studies me again, and all kinds of conflicting emotions pass over her face. Then, moaning slightly, she comes and puts her arms around me. 'Oh, Mum.' After a time she pulls back and takes another reading of my face. 'You mind,' she accuses me.

'No. It wouldn't have worked anyway. Really. If it hadn't been that, it would have been something else. *Really.* We just weren't suited.'

She shakes her head with high drama. She is at an age where she puts love on a pretty high plane, and you either love someone with burning passion or not at all.

I am beginning to wonder if I have made a mistake in telling her the truth.

'You could still tell him. Why don't you . . .' She wrestles with a decision, she contorts her mouth, finally she says, 'You could explain a bit about . . . you know, *me*. I mean, I wouldn't mind. If it was just him.'

But she would mind, I know that she would. 'That's a very sweet offer, darling, but I honestly don't think it would make any difference now.'

'Why not?'

'Oh, all sorts of reasons. Too late. Too much water under the bridge.'

And because he wouldn't be so ready to believe me, because he would see the holes in whatever story I tried to give him and shoot it down in flames, though I don't say this.

'I wouldn't mind. If it made a difference.' She is mildly offended at having her gesture turned down.

'Sweetheart . . . No. Really.' And I'm careful to remove all trace of regret from my voice.

This doesn't stop her from acquiring the troubled look she always gets when the past comes back to haunt her and she doesn't quite know how to cope with it, and I say quickly, 'Come on, let's go and finish the packing before it drives me completely crazy.'

There's something about going away that brings out the chaotic in Katie. Having stayed up late – I don't know what time she finally turned out her light – she is almost unrousable in the morning. When she finally gets up she drifts around unproductively for at least an hour before managing to get dressed. Then, just to drive me to distraction, she announces fifteen minutes after we're meant to have left for the airport that she's lost her air ticket. By the time we finally get the show on the road – Josh, Biff, Katie, plus air ticket – we're half an hour late and I'm driving with white knuckles.

But we make up time and the tension drops away and I start to chuckle at the children's convoluted jokes. At the customs gate I am the model parent. I don't say too many embarrassingly motherly things, I am practical and briskly loving. It's Biff I feel sorry for. Katie, having sent him across the terminal to post a letter, then rewards him with the most perfunctory of farewells, a brief, 'See you!' and the sort of distant gaze that stars bestow on fans when they're finding adulation a bit of a bore. Josh and I get hugs and grins.

Waving her off, I feel happy for her, but at the same time I'm not in the mood to talk, and I'm relieved when the two boys discuss dogs and sport most of the way home.

With only a day to get Josh organised and packed for the new school year, I'm thrown straight back into name tapes and missing sports gear and shoes that suddenly don't fit any more. As we sit beside the trunk ticking items off against the list, Josh tells me what shoes will double, which sports shirts are unnecessary, and I'm struck by how much his confidence has grown since the winter.

I still tremble at the thought of what Josh witnessed, it still wrenches my heart to think of the burden he was carrying for all those weeks. Until his father's body was found I like to think he'd largely blocked the memory out,

491

that he didn't in any way interpret what he'd seen or match it to events. But later, when the gun was found beside his father, I hate to think what went through his mind. I have never pressed him on the subject so I can only guess, though this, of course, is almost worse.

It was hard holding out against Dawson, but the most challenging story of all was the one I had to construct for Josh. Not only did I have to explain my actions, but I had to do it without destroying Josh's belief in me and in the memory of his father. This was a tall order. Abuse was never on the agenda – no ten-year-old could cope with that – and I could hardly pretend I'd taken the gun down to the boat and let Harry commit suicide in front of me, so in the end I hatched an entirely different scenario that relied on Harry's death being purely accidental. When Josh gets older he may see the gaping holes in this version of events and if he ever questions me I'm going to have to think of something better, but in the meantime he seems more than satisfied. I think he was desperate to grasp any explanation, however unlikely, so long as it relieved him of the guilt of seeing what he saw and the anxiety of my possible arrest.

Now, like any other boy who's coming up to eleven, he's preoccupied with school and friends and seeing the latest videos, and if the past still bothers him at all, he doesn't seem to dwell on it.

On the drive to school, I hover on the point of asking him about Richard. I am curious to know how long the correspondence has been going on and whether Richard ever says anything about me. But in the end I never quite say anything. I would hate to put him on the defensive, to make him feel that I've been prying, or to put him in a situation where he feels he has to lie to me.

I come home to a house that is empty save for a prancing

Jiff, and immediately plunge into gloom. Molly, who knows my moods all too well, has arranged to come over later, armed with wine. But this does little to forestall my sense of loss and isolation. It still baffles me as to how I have managed to find myself in a strange new village without either of my two wonderful children. No doubt I'll pull myself together in a couple of days, I'll get back into the routine, I'll put some theatre dates into my diary and persuade myself I have a social life, but the truth is I'm useless at being alone and always have been.

Allowing my self-pity a short unimpeded burst, I sit disconsolately in the bare living-room eyeing the new paint where it's run and the floorboards where they're still hopelessly uneven, before dragging myself upstairs to do something useful like stripping the children's beds.

I have not been into Katie's room since she left. An envelope sits prominently on the pillow. I feel a leap of affection and gratitude at her thoughtfulness. It is just like her to leave a farewell message when I need it most.

Then I read what she has scrawled on the front of the envelope.

Mum. Don't be cross with me. But this is like a present from me to you. I thought about it very carefully, and it's definitely what I want to do. I love you, Mum. You've been the best.

Fumbling, I tear open the envelope and pull out four sheets: photocopies of a letter in her own handwriting. My heart lurches as I skim through it. I double back a couple of times, but there's no mistake. I feel dizzy. It's all here, she has left nothing out. I am breathless with astonishment.

Then all emotions are swept aside by an eruption of fear as I realise the enormity of the risk she has exposed us to.

'*Oh, Katie,*' I cry.

Trying to contain my anxiety, I reach for my address book, I start for the telephone, I stare at my watch, I go back to the letter, I return to the telephone and dial Moreland's number.

Before it can ring, I drop the receiver back into the cradle.

The phone will not do: I will have no peace until I find the letter and watch it burn.

The street where Moreland lives lies in a maze of similar streets to the south of Clapham Common, in an area of road-bumps and chicanes and other deterrents to through traffic. The terraced houses are grey-bricked and bow-fronted and packed close together behind tiny front gardens with no trees. Nearly all have been gentrified, with white-painted windows and bright glossy doors and flower tubs, prudently chained to walls.

There are so many cars that I have to park in the next street and walk back. Moreland's house has a blue front door and a smart brass knocker which needs a polish. There's no one at home. Through the uncurtained bay window I see a sofa covered in a modern pattern, a simple standard lamp, a large pastel print on a white wall. I can't see through the letter box which has a flap over the back of it.

I go and sit in the car for a while, then, as lights start to blink on, I cruise back and find a parking place just two doors away on the opposite side.

At nine, people are still coming home from work, smart professional girls, young men in pinstripes, nobody over forty. TVs go on, curtains are drawn, people stand with drinks in their hands. And still I'm filled with irrepressible

494

fears. My thoughts skid between the efficiency of the postal service and the arrangements Moreland is likely to have made for his mail if he has gone away. Perhaps his wife is back. Perhaps she deals with the mail, perhaps she will eventually open the door to me.

By ten I am badly in need of a loo and relinquish my parking space to drive to the nearest half-respectable pub to use the facilities, squalid as they are.

When I return there are lights burning in Moreland's house.

I park in the first available slot and walk back and knock firmly.

I hear an internal door and firm footsteps approaching. I feel myself being scrutinised through the spyhole, then there's the sound of a heavy lock turning and the front door swings open and a startled Moreland stands under the light.

Before he has a chance to say anything, I blurt out, 'I need to know if you've got a letter from Katie.'

I notice how tanned he is, how clear his eyes are, as though he has just come back from holiday.

He stares at me, his mouth moves a couple of times as though he would answer if he could remember the question. Then, taking in what I have said, at last, he glances over his shoulder, he throws out a hand. 'I've only just got back. I don't know.'

He gives an uncertain smile which is poised some way between warmth and doubt. Then, reading the urgency in my face, he says, 'Hang on a minute,' and steps back into the hall and picks up a pile of letters from a side table. He comes back, shuffling quickly through them.

He holds up an envelope and I see Katie's writing and feel a great surge of relief. I nod rapidly.

'Why don't you come in?'

'No,' I say hastily. 'No, I . . . I just wanted to know that it hadn't gone astray. And that you'll promise to destroy it.'

'Should I?'

'She wants you to.'

'Oh. Am I allowed to read it first?' He says this lightly, not expecting a refusal.

'I'd rather you didn't.'

He frowns at this. 'What about Katie – does she not want me to read it either?'

I hesitate before shaking my head.

He says not unkindly, 'Is that a no, she doesn't want me to read it, or a no, she's not against me reading it?'

When I don't reply, he says with a touch of his old sternness, 'You'd better come in.'

'No.' And I'm already retreating down the path. 'I'll come back in a minute,' I call, 'when you've decided.' And I walk quickly away before he has the chance to say any more.

I sit in the car, recovering slowly. My nerves are so taut, my emotions so extreme, that it is some moments before I stop trembling. Through this haze of feeling, I imagine Moreland switching on the standard lamp and settling back on the patterned sofa and unfolding the letter. I see him starting to read.

I reach into my bag and draw out the copy that Katie made late that night on my desktop copier, and, as Moreland reads, I read with him by the sulphurous light of the street-lamp.

Dear Richard, I was upset when you left us that time. Mum tried not to show it but she was very upset too. It's hard when your Mum has a boyfriend. You have funny feelings about it. You don't like to think of sharing your Mum with anyone, which is sort of selfish, I know, but you can't help it. And after everything we'd been through I didn't want anyone around _ever_. *But I have to say you were okay, always dead straight with us and great with Josh and if I gave you a hard time sometimes, I'm sorry. I never really meant to. I just felt very protective about Mum. She's been so great to me. Not just my Mum, but my best friend too. The reason I'm writing to you is –* there's a line crossed out – *because I think what happened at Christmas was unfair on her. It's not right for you to think bad things about her because it just isn't true. It probably won't make any difference now, but I want you to know what happened and I'm trusting you not to tell anyone, for Mum's sake and mine. In fact, can you promise right now to burn this the second you've read it?*

Such trust, my Katie. Even after everything.

What you have to know is that my stepfather had been abusing me. Mum didn't know and I couldn't tell her. I felt so ashamed and confused. I thought it was my fault somehow, that if I pretended it wasn't happening it would go away. I've had therapy since then and I can talk about it now, but then I felt so miserable I wanted to crawl away and die. I know now that Dad wasn't well, that he was sick, and that helps, to understand that. I also know that what he did was very wrong, but I didn't understand that either, not then. I know that may seem crazy, but victims often feel that way, they feel it's all their fault. When it started I just prayed for everything to be all right again. I thought perhaps if I just kept out of the way, then Dad would forget about it.

That night, he phoned me at school from the boat and said to come and join him and Mum for dinner. He said

497

Mum was just getting some food from the house and that I was to get a taxi over and if Mum wasn't at the house, then to come down to the quay and he'd pick me up in the dinghy. He promised me faithfully that Mum was there. I didn't think he was telling me lies because she'd said she'd be down there most of the day, helping him to get the boat ready and everything. And he kept promising, he kept saying she was there.

Yes, he was a brilliant liar, Katie, he could fool anyone.

Harry spoke to my housemistress and got permission and I took a taxi over. There was no one in the house when I got there and I never thought of checking the calendar to see where Mum was. I just went straight down to the quay and Harry was waiting for me. Half-way to the boat I suddenly thought, what if Mum isn't there? But it was too late then. And Harry seemed okay. Like he didn't say anything to make me realise.

Then I got on the boat and saw Mum wasn't there. I asked Harry to take me straight back. I begged and begged him. He said to calm down, not to be hysterical, that he wasn't going to hurt me, but then he did bad things to me. I mean, he raped me. I'd never fought him before, not when it happened the other times, but I fought him that time. He kept saying he loved me and cared about me, but he wouldn't stop. I got something, a lamp, and hit him on the head but he still wouldn't stop and when he did stop he said terrible things which weren't true, awful things about me, and I went crazy. I must have gone a bit mad because I don't remember much, but I got a knife. I didn't mean to hurt him so much, I just wanted to hurt him a bit, and to make him stop and not do it again. But the knife went right in. I hardly pushed at all but it went right in and Harry fell down and went white. It's hard to write this because you're probably thinking what a terrible person I am. I can only say that I didn't mean to kill him and that it's the worst thing that ever happened to me in my whole life and that if I could bring him back right now, I would.

You didn't have to do all this, Katie, you could have left some of it out. And thinking this, I am filled with strange pride.

I couldn't believe it but he died just like that. I couldn't believe it, but he did. He wasn't breathing. I tried things, but it was no good. And then I totally panicked. I could only think of getting Mum. I got the rubber dinghy and rowed to the quay and ran up to the house and saw that she was at Molly's and called her. She came straight over and gave me sleeping pills and put me to bed. Then she rushed down to the boat. When she came back she didn't say anything to me about what she was going to do, but everything she did after that was to try and protect me. Everything. She took the shotgun and went back to the boat to make it look like suicide. She said it wasn't a hard thing to do, to use the gun, because he was already dead. She says that, but I think it must have been very hard really.

My eyes fog up, my throat seizes. 'Yes, it was hard,' I say aloud. 'Very hard.'

Poor Mum, she thought that would be enough. She didn't realise.

'No, I didn't, I didn't,' I sigh, gripped by helplessness again.

I don't know what went wrong, she wouldn't really talk about it, but for some reason it was no good. She realised they'd guess straight away what she'd done. Then she had the idea to take the yacht out to sea.

You make it sound so easy, Katie. But it took hours and hours to work out.

And she took the boat out to sea and sank it. It was an

awfully hard thing for her to do when she hates the water and doesn't like boats. She didn't tell me everything that happened, but I think she nearly got lost and thought she was going to die too. It was so brave of her and I think she was crazy to do it, but I'm glad she did. I couldn't have got through this without her, I just couldn't.

I should say that Mum couldn't have told you all this even if she'd wanted to because she promised me a long time ago that she would never tell a living soul for as long as she lived. She told me so I'd feel safe, and it helped a lot, though I was always frightened that the police would find out. But she said that at the very worst they'd accuse her of trying to conceal a suicide. She said she might go to prison for a few months at the most, but it would be a small price to pay and whatever happened I was never to own up because she'd never ever forgive me if I did. I was terrified of her going to prison and it's just great that it hasn't happened because I couldn't have taken it.

I can never forgive myself for what I did. I know it was wrong. But then what Harry did was very wrong too.

'Yes – wrong,' I echo, as if she could hear me now and needed support.

While I'm in America I'm going to have more therapy. I know this won't make things right either, but at least maybe I can work my way through everything a bit better then.

It's been hard for Josh too. He saw Mum take the gun, though we never realised until Christmas. It must have been awful for him thinking Mum had done something bad. As soon as we realised what he'd been thinking we told him a bit of what happened, as close as we could anyway without making him feel too bad about Dad. I told him that it was all my fault. I didn't say about the *abuse. Mum felt it'd be too much for him. I made it sound like an accident instead. I told him that Dad had been drinking, which was true, and was maybe on pills as well, and had been in a foul mood. And that I'd been no better, that I'd said a lot of stupid things that had made him even madder, that he grabbed me to tell me off, but the boat rocked and he stumbled and we both fell and I had a knife in my hand because I'd been chopping things for supper. I made it sound like a complete accident, <u>so you must never tell him the truth</u>. Poor Josh. It's been hard for him, not just thinking those things about Mum but feeling left out. He thinks we should have told him the truth at the beginning and perhaps we should.*

I've told you everything because I don't want you to think badly of Mum. She's too good for that. But writing this letter is scary. It's a big thing for me to tell someone. You always seemed like someone I could trust, so I hope you won't let me down, and will burn this straight away.

I got your address from Mum's desk. And then I called you two nights ago and didn't say it was me (if you were wondering who the call was from). I wanted to check you were there.

It will probably drive Mum crazy, me having written, but I wanted to.

Katie.

PS. Could you write to me in America (P.T.O for address) and let me know you got this all right and everything?

I fold the sheets carefully and put them back in the envelope. I sit in the long silence, I start slightly as a sports car engine roars into life close by. I watch a long-haired blond woman walk past with a long-haired blond dog. I give it another five minutes before I make my way back.

This time Moreland opens the door almost immediately. Without a word, he takes me gently by the arm and leads me inside and closes the door. He grasps my hands and, lifting them to his mouth, kisses them in a gesture that would be flamboyant if it weren't so full of feeling, then, with another courteous old-fashioned movement, he signals me to follow him down the passage and into the kitchen.

The letter lies open on the table. Still without saying anything, he takes a metal wastepaper basket which he must have brought from another room and, placing it in the middle of the floor, he suspends the first page above it and puts a lighted match to it.

'I should have guessed,' he says solemnly.

'But why?'

'The call you made to Katie from the boat. Her nervous breakdown.' He gestures hopelessly with the burnt match. 'The way you were so desperate to protect her.' He sets the next sheet alight.

'But no one was meant to guess.'

He won't be mollified. He says in a tone of disbelief, 'I should have realised.'

I hand him my copy. 'You'd better burn this too.'

He holds the papers in his hand. He starts to speak only to halt abruptly and throw me an unhappy glance, before winding himself up to try again. 'All this time – ever since Christmas – I was tortured by the thought of how wrong I'd been about you. I couldn't believe I'd been so badly taken in. So thoroughly deceived.' And his face tightens at the thought. 'But you know, the worst thing – the *worst* thing – was thinking how carefully you must have worked everything out, how you must have planned it all!'

'Planned it . . .' I smile faintly. 'No, Harry was the planner.'

'Taking the yacht out to sea,' he continues urgently, as if he must explain himself with all possible speed. 'It was *that* more than anything, Ellen. The more I thought about it, how tough you must have been to do it, the more I persuaded myself you were capable of anything.'

'But I had to take it, you see. I had to take the yacht.' I gather myself for one last excursion into the past. 'The suicide; when I decided to try it, I realised I had to make it look right, that if I was going to do it at all I mustn't make a mistake. I knew it would only take one thing, just one thing, and I'd be found out. I'd read somewhere about traces of gunpowder or whatever it is people get on their hands when they kill themselves. I knew you had to get that right. So . . . I put his hand on the barrel of the gun.' I stare at the wastepaper basket, at the last wisps of smoke. 'I wrapped his other hand round the trigger. I wiped my fingerprints away. I thought I'd managed it.' I pause, seeing again the terrible sight in the cabin. 'Then I realised' – I press my fingertips against my temple, I give a bitter laugh – 'I realised it was all for nothing. I'd missed the most obvious thing of all. You see, there was no bleeding. I shot him and there was no bleeding. I realised they'd know straight away. They'd know he was already dead when he was shot.' I look away to a draining-board that is cluttered with upturned saucepans and draped with a dish-cloth that is none too clean. 'And that wasn't all,' I say, and the visions crowd in on me. 'When I pulled the trigger, I wasn't holding the gun tightly enough or something, because it jerked a bit to one side and' – I grimace – 'it didn't cover the knife wound. Well, I *thought* it didn't. They never found it, in fact, the knife wound, so I must have . . . *managed* it after all. But I thought they'd find it. I thought everything would be an even worse disaster than before. And then . . .' I gesture inevitably. 'I was faced with having to do something. With having to hide the whole terrible mess.'

Moreland is very still, I feel him watching me. And then his hand is squeezing mine hard and he is saying my name in a ragged voice before he turns slowly back to his task and, taking the copy letter, sets light to each page in turn.

We watch the last page fall flaming into the bin.

He says, 'You knew I wouldn't hesitate, didn't you? To burn this?'

'I knew. But I had to be sure. I couldn't help it. You may have noticed, I have a tendency to worry about these things.'

His eyes flash with affection. 'I had noticed.' He throws the burnt match into the bin. 'I'll write to Katie,' he says, 'I've kept the address.'

'I know you'll say the right things.'

'What worries me' – and he fixes me with that uneven look again – 'is what I can say to you.'

I think about this for all of a second. 'I think that you could tell me that you'll come and see us sometimes. I know Josh would love it. And Katie, too.'

'And you?'

'Me probably most of all.'

BETRAYAL

For Andrew,
with love and gratitude

One

I WOKE WITH a terrible start, my heart crashing against my ribs, and fumbled for the burbling alarm. Sinking back on the pillow, I waited for my heart to quieten down and my brain to stop racketing. Dream fragments jostled disturbingly in my mind. Most were nightmarish, riddled with scenes where I was caught red-handed in some misdemeanour. Only one held any comfort, and for a moment I clung to the warm echo of a time long ago, a faded image of a remote bay and firelight, and, at the water's edge, the slim elusive figure of Sylvie.

Then, in the harsh dawn light, this, too, plunged into nightmare as it came to me with a fresh lurch of disbelief that Sylvie was dead, and that I would have to wake to this stark knowledge for the rest of my life.

My violent awakening hadn't disturbed Ginny. She lay on the far side of the bed, her thin arm reaching out across the pillows towards me, the eye-mask reducing her face to a ghostly triangle of mouth and chin. At some point in the night she had turned on the light and taken a pill. She had glanced towards me but I had feigned sleep. In the dark of the night I had felt too raw for conversation, too unsure of where

1

it might lead. Ginny hadn't been fooled, she'd known I was awake, but we'd both kept up the pretence.

I slid out of bed, sending a shower of papers to the floor: the amended buyout terms I had tried to read at one-thirty or whenever it was I had got to bed. Soundlessly, I put the pages into some sort of order and noticed that my hands were trembling. I showered and shaved, nicking the scar on my upper lip as I always did when I was tense or more than usually overtired. Some beads of watery blood dropped into the basin and I wiped them away with a tissue. I didn't have to look too closely into the mirror to know that the worries of the last few months were stamped all over my face.

I reached for a cord jacket, the sort of thing I generally wore for a day at Hartford, but, remembering the message I would be delivering to the people there, I changed it for a suit of sober grey worsted. I must have lost some weight because the waistband was slack and I had to search out a pair of braces.

I went down to make some three-spoon coffee to keep me awake on the journey. It was barely six-thirty but someone had already been into the house. The girl we contracted to do the flowers must have been to market early because through the open door to the laundry room I could see several large buckets crammed with fresh blooms standing amid spatterings of water. That meant we were having a party tonight. It also meant that, not for the first time, it had slipped my mind. The prospect of a houseful of chattering people filled me with dismay. I dimly

2

hoped it wasn't going to be a charity event, then at least I might know a few of them.

A soft conspiratorial knock sounded from the hall. I unbolted the door to find Julia, my assistant, poised tensely on the step.

In my jittery state I assumed bad news. 'What's happened?'

'Nothing's happened,' she said hastily.

'Then what are you doing here?' I asked, more in curiosity than annoyance.

She handed me a file. 'I thought you might want this.' She made a doubtful face that admitted to the thinness of the excuse.

I waved her in. 'A bit early for you, isn't it?'

She gave a short laugh, glad that I could still tease her. 'I *have* been up at dawn before, you know. Well – once.'

The file was one we both knew I didn't really need. I raised a questioning eyebrow.

'Today's *Times*,' she announced. Pulling the business section out of her bag, she found the page for me.

It was in the snippets column, the place where they put the news that isn't going to influence share prices. The source, whoever it was, had been meticulous with the facts. 'Buoyant' china and lighting manufacturer A. L. Cumberland, fresh from its takeover of – and it stung me to read it – 'debt-ridden' HartWell Glass, the family-owned crystal and tableware company, was putting HartWell's loss-making Hartford Crystal division up for grabs. Cumberland's chairman was quoted as saying that slow-moving crystal did not

3

mesh well with Cumberland's dynamic mass-market product profile.

But it was the final paragraph that really needled. *After years of lacklustre sales and low investment, Hartford Crystal would seem ripe for absorption by brand leaders in the highly competitive export-dependent crystal market. An attempted management buyout led by HartWell's erstwhile joint managing director and major shareholder, Hugh Wellesley, is thought to be facing an uphill struggle.*

Julia remarked, 'A bitch, eh?'

'Yup,' I said bitterly.

'I thought you'd better see it.' Julia fought a losing battle against her indignation. 'You can't help noticing the timing!' she hissed. 'I had an idea something like this was coming, that's why I went and got the papers on the way over.'

If she meant to surprise me, she succeeded. 'You knew?'

'Well, I guessed. Don't ask how. You wouldn't approve.'

Not yet thirty, Julia was the best assistant I'd ever had, exceptionally shrewd and efficient, yet when she'd first arrived her attitude, openly cynical and opportunistic, had rather disturbed me. Now I took a more ambivalent view.

'You think it came from inside Cumberland?'

She gave me a heavy look. 'I *know* it did.'

She meant it had come from Howard who, until the takeover, had shared the managing directorship of HartWell with me. In the process of courting Cumberland and negotiating the takeover, Howard had managed to secure himself a seat on the Cumberland

4

board and a lucrative share option deal. For Howard there was no such thing as an old loyalty, and the moment he'd stepped over the Cumberland threshold six weeks ago he'd belonged to them, heart and soul.

'It could have come from a City guru,' I suggested.

'Sometimes, Hugh, I think you're too trusting for this world.'

I shook suddenly, the tensions welled up, I heard myself snap, 'And sometimes I think you're too damn sure of yourself!'

Her eyes rounded, she stared at me, eventually she stammered, 'Sorry. You're right. That was out of order.'

'It's just . . .' I pressed a hand to my head, I couldn't explain.

Julia was still looking astonished. I think she had been under the illusion that I never lost my temper.

Regaining some control, I gestured apology. 'It's just that I don't want to think about who might have done it. Not when it's too late to do anything about it.'

'No, of course . . .'

There was a short silence while we both recovered from our second angry words in the two years we had worked together. The first, I realised with dismay, had been only yesterday.

Finally Julia said in a muted voice, 'I know you said you wanted to drive yourself down to Hartford, but I've got a driver on standby just in case. I thought you'd be exhausted.'

'I'll drive myself.'

She gave it one more try. 'It's such a long way and he's just outside.'

But I wouldn't have been comfortable arriving at Hartford in a chauffeur-driven car, not when there was an axe hanging over the factory's future.

'No, but thanks anyway.' I took *The Times* and *Telegraph* from her and opened the door.

'Sorry I was out of line,' she repeated unhappily. 'I think you're right, it's altogether too early for me.'

'For all of us,' I smiled.

She hesitated. 'You're looking terribly tired.'

'I'll catch up on the weekend.'

'If there's any more I can do. To take some of the load . . .'

'I don't think so, but thanks anyway.'

She paused on the point of saying more, then, thinking better of it, declared, 'Good luck for today. I hope it goes well. You really deserve it!' In a gesture that was uncharacteristically demonstrative she reached out and grasped my hand in both of hers before striding off down the street.

In the kitchen I quickly leafed through the papers. I turned each page with an odd mixture of dread and hope, but there was nothing more about Sylvie. The initial report two days ago had been sparse: a woman's body had been recovered from the River Dart; it had been identified as that of Sylvie Mathieson. I wasn't sure what I expected now. Some details of how she had died perhaps; some idea of what the police were doing. But maybe there was simply nothing to report. Maybe the police had imposed a news blackout. The uncertainty did nothing for the anxiety that coiled and twisted in my belly.

I gulped the rest of my coffee and thrust the *Times*

article into my briefcase. Crossing the kitchen, I glimpsed the flowers again. I picked out a white fluffy bloom – it might have been a dahlia – and, not really sure what I meant by the gesture, carried it upstairs and propped it on the pillow next to Ginny. I took a sheet from the pad and scribbled 'Sorry'. I didn't know what I meant by that either. All I knew was that flowers and notes were thin substitutes for all the time we never had together.

Looking down at Ginny, I felt the familiar blend of bewilderment and guilt, mainly guilt. Things hadn't been right between us for such a long time, and I didn't really know why. But then my whole life seemed to have gone adrift, and I wasn't absolutely sure why that had happened either.

I changed my mind about the flower – too crass – and thrust it into the bin.

I was halfway down the stairs when Ginny's voice cried out, 'Hugh. *Hugh?*'

She was sitting up in bed, her mask pushed back over her head. 'What's the time?'

She looked so fragile that I felt a pull in my chest somewhere, a tug of emotion and regret.

'Sorry, I didn't mean to wake you—'

She focused on me. 'Where are you going?'

'Hartford.'

'Must you?'

'I've got a meeting.'

She seemed momentarily confused by this and I guessed she was still groggy from the sleeping pill or whatever it was she had taken in the night.

'You won't be late back?' she asked.

'I'll do my best.'

'You haven't forgotten tonight?'

'No.' But I couldn't maintain the pretence. 'What's the party for exactly?'

Usually Ginny would cast me a flicker of resentment at such lapses, as though I made a point of forgetting these things simply to belittle the importance of her work, but nothing showed on her face. Instead she said dully, 'It's for the premature baby unit, the fund-raising committee. I promised ages ago.'

'Am I essential?' Seeing her eyes widen in reproach, I added hurriedly, 'I'll try not to be too late. I'll do my best.' For all her shoulder-rubbing with the great and the good, for all her grace and poise, Ginny had never found it easy to face the world on her own. Even as I made my promise I knew with sinking heart that I'd be unlikely to keep it, and that by letting her down I would yet again be fulfilling her gloomy expectations of me.

Aware of the time, I moved towards the door.

'It's the last party,' Ginny said abruptly. 'No more after this.'

I turned back. I wasn't sure what to make of this statement, except that it was meant to be momentous in some way. 'No more?'

She gave a slow shake of the head and pressed her fingertips to the corners of her eyes. I tried to read the signs. Was I expected to question her, to listen to whatever social disappointments or imagined slights had led to this decision? If so, Ginny's timing was as unerring as ever; she always managed to choose a moment when I was rushing off to some meeting or so tired that I could barely think. Yet she could never understand how this, more than anything, doomed our conversations to failure before they had even started.

'I'm desperately late,' I ventured. 'Otherwise—'

I waited for the soft glance of injury she produced on these occasions, but her face was bare of emotion. She gave the faintest of nods, and my heart lifted as it always did when we avoided a tiff.

'I'll see you later,' she said, reaching up to pull the mask back over her eyes. 'Oh, and Hugh?'

Trying not to show the slightest impatience, I put my head back round the door.

'Take care, won't you?'

She said it with strange solemnity, and it struck me again how very thin she looked.

'Of course.'

'You're overdoing it at the moment.'

'Just until the buyout's over . . .'

Her eyes were unfocused, she was hardly listening. 'Well, take care anyway.'

Winding my way through the Chelsea streets, driving out through the suburbs, I did take care. The coffee and lack of sleep had made me light-headed and I didn't entirely trust my reactions. But as the well-worn road to Totnes unwound before me and my mind skittered over the myriad problems that lay ahead, my concentration began to waver. To keep alert, I turned on the radio and aimed the air vents at my face.

The *Times* article kept returning to haunt me. The

more I tried to persuade myself that it wouldn't diminish our chances of funding the buyout, the more damaging it seemed to become. And, when I really wanted to torture myself, which was quite often, I imagined Zircon, the venture capitalists who were backing our bid, having second thoughts and pulling out altogether.

Needing to take some action, however unproductive, I called Julia on the car phone and asked her to find a corporate PR adviser for us. Then I spent a fruitless twenty minutes trying to locate Pollinger, our contact at Zircon, but, despite mobiles, pagers and home numbers, he seemed to lead an elusive life.

In search of distraction, I switched on the radio again and, finding a discussion programme, raised the volume until the voices filled the car.

I was on the M5, somewhere past Taunton, when a blaring horn brought me to my senses with a jolt of adrenalin. A car was looming up in front of me. In the instant that I realised it was stationary I also knew that I couldn't possibly stop in time. I jerked the wheel to the left and braked hard and felt the car kick round as the rear wheels lost their grip. I must have twisted the wheel the other way because the car performed a snake-like manoeuvre and skidded again as it shot across the middle lane, narrowly missing the front of a large coach. The inside lane came at me in slow motion, any approaching traffic hidden by the bulk of the coach, but the lane must have been empty because the next moment the car was shuddering sideways across the hard shoulder and hitting the kerb with an almighty bang that almost lifted me off my seat.

The car rocked to a standstill, the engine stalled. All I could hear was the radio newscaster droning on. I sat motionless with my hands clutched to the wheel, the sweat cold against my ribs, until someone opened the door and asked me if I was all right.

I heard myself say I was okay. I must have sounded convincing because, after the man told me several times to stop driving like a bloody maniac, he slammed the door and walked back to the coach, which was parked some way ahead on the hard shoulder.

It was a long time before I could think about setting off again. I kept reliving the near-miss and the seconds preceding it, when the newscaster had spoken Sylvie's name. His cool detached voice kept running through my mind, like a tape being played over and over again, yet only two words really registered, and both felt like something driven against my heart. *Stabbed and bound.*

I got shakily out of the car and heaved the sparse contents of my stomach onto the grass verge. When I felt a bit better I walked round the car to look for signs of damage, but the wheels seemed all right, the tyres still had air. Not knowing what else I should check, I got back into the driver's seat and, after a last five minutes with my head back and my eyes closed, I started the engine.

I drove gingerly, half expecting knocking sounds or wobbles from the steering, but after a time I forgot to worry about the car and slowly accelerated to mid-lane speed, my mind miles away again, in a dark and distant place.

I arrived at Hartford half an hour late. Driving in through the gates, I tried to picture the factory through the eyes of potential investors. With its twenties architecture, drab brickwork and mean windows, the place had the air of old glories long faded, while its clusters of ventilation pipes and aluminium chimneys suggested spasmodic and piece-meal modernisation. Only the recently completed warehouse, a spare metal structure in cobalt blue, emitted anything approaching an up-to-date image. *Lacklustre sales . . . Low investment . . .* The newspaper's comments were ill-founded but they still pricked at me.

George Banes came out to meet me. The production director was a burly man, his large belly testing the fastenings on his shirt, with a thick head of hair that had been silvery grey for as long as I had known him, which was almost twenty years.

'Thought the traffic might delay you,' he commented, as we shook hands and made for the entrance, 'so I told the staff we'd meet at ten minutes to noon.'

'You explained that it was just an update?'

'I did. I said you wanted to keep them abreast of developments but that there was nothing definite at the moment.'

Even now, in my state of preoccupation, I couldn't walk through the doors of the factory without feeling a proprietorial thrill. I was too much my father's son, too deeply instilled with his old-style paternalistic pride not to feel an attachment to the place that was decidedly emotional.

George took me into the office that had been my father's and would have been mine if Howard hadn't pressed for what he liked to call an integrated management structure, and insisted we put the management and sales of all three divisions under one roof at Slough.

The room was virtually unchanged since my father's retirement ten years ago. His wide oak desk stood in the same spot by the window, the ancient wooden in- and out-trays squatting on a worn leather surface that still bore the pattern of a hundred ink marks. When I was a small boy this room had seemed cavernous, and my father, behind the mass of his desk, an oddly distant figure. It was only when he finished his business and took me down to the factory floor and chatted in his easy soft-voiced manner that I had felt I knew him again.

George brought coffee and we sat down at the conference table.

'So it's all signed up with Zircon?' he demanded eagerly.

'It's signed.'

'No quibbles with the business plan?'

George and I had worked so hard on the business plan that we knew every word and financial projection by heart. 'No quibbles with the business plan,' I reassured him, and saw his eyes spark with satisfaction. 'But I tell you, George, whatever happened to them on the playing fields of Eton, it turned their hearts to stone.' I was thinking of the additional leverage the venture capitalists had demanded, and the personal guarantees covering the fifty per cent of my personal worth that was not already committed to the buyout. 'They've made financial pain into an art form.' I managed an ironic laugh.

'But they're behind us now, that's the important thing.'

'They still have their doubts about me, I think. Or rather the idea of me.'

'What? *Why?*'

'According to the City, family firms are breeding grounds for inefficiency and nepotism. And a family buyout – well!' I rolled my eyes. 'That's even more unhealthy. Incest.'

'But that's ridiculous! It's not like that here. Don't they realise that? We've always been a team, for God's sake! And, this buyout – well, we're all in it together, aren't we?'

We certainly were. George was putting fifty thousand cash into the buyout, and another fifty thousand against his house. So were Alan and John, the other Hartford directors. But that was how the venture capitalists liked it, to have the whole lot of us over a financial barrel.

I passed George the page from *The Times*. 'This may not help.'

George read the article and spluttered, 'What's this? Years of low investment? What are they damn well talking about! We've upgraded the batching plant, for God's sake. We've installed the stem-pulling machines—'

'It's nonsense, of course—'

14

'And lacklustre sales! They've stood up bloody well, considering. Apart from Packenhams.'

This was one of our worst blows, being de-listed by London's second largest department store.

George thrashed a hand against the paper. 'Who gives them this rubbish?'

But I didn't try to answer that.

George hadn't cooled down yet. 'It makes Hartford sound like some cottage industry filled with Luddites! As if we'd fought change tooth and nail!'

The irony wasn't lost on either of us. While Howard and I had been running the company it had hardly stopped changing. That was the whole trouble. We had moved too far, too fast, expanding rapidly into mass-market glass and chinaware just as trading conditions began to worsen. While my father was alive he hadn't liked much of what we had been doing but had never tried to interfere. I was glad he had died in February. It had saved him the anguish of seeing quite what a mess I had made of everything.

'At the end of the day it's only a newspaper story,' I said.

George, forcing himself back to his natural state of optimism, declared, 'Right! Right!' He laughed loudly and abruptly. 'We never thought it was going to be easy, did we?'

I laughed too, awkwardly. This deal was the hardest thing I had ever attempted. In the six weeks since the Cumberland takeover, I had been cut loose from the new parent company to run Hartford Crystal on a nil-salary basis, while simultaneously planning to buy it out. Raising the three million pounds of leverage from the banks, keeping all the financial and legal balls in the air, pulling together all the strands of what was an amazingly complex deal, was a Herculean task which, even on an eighteen-hour day, was stretching me to my limits. Much of the time I was suffused with a wild conviction that we would pull it off, and then I flew on adrenalin. At other times, faced by endless setbacks, I settled into something more mechanical, a mindless persistence fuelled by the determination to save what I had so foolishly jeopardised.

There was no mystery about my motives. For me this buyout was about restitution. My father had worked hard for twenty years to build up the company and pass it on to me in good shape, while I had worked hard for ten to achieve nothing more, it seemed, than to let it slip away and threaten the livelihoods of all the people who worked for us. I wanted it back, I wanted to show what I could do with it now that I was free of Howard and his remorseless drive for diversification. I wanted to make a success of it for my own sake, certainly, but more than that I wanted to feel I could look the employees in the eye again.

George and I talked our way through the monthly sales figures and were just starting on the cash flow analysis when a woman's voice sounded in the outer office. There was something about it, the suggestion of a lazy laugh, of dark overtones, that caught at my memory and chilled my heart.

'You all right?' George asked.

'Fine.' Reaching for my coffee, I promptly knocked

16

it over. Trying to retrieve the cup, I got that wrong too and sent it flying across the table.

I muttered 'Jesus!' Then as I picked the cup off the floor: 'What an idiot!' I gave a disbelieving laugh. But as soon as George had gone in search of a cloth I sat in silence, wondering what on earth was happening to me and whether this was just frayed nerves or a form of delayed shock. Whatever, the loss of control frightened me, and I was unnerved by the thought that it might happen again.

By the time George returned with a roll of kitchen paper, I was staring bleakly at the pool of coffee, trying to suppress visions of dark water and Sylvie's flesh, mutilated and cold.

'Do you want something to eat?' George asked when he had finished clearing up. 'A sandwich? Biscuits?'

'Thanks, no.'

He peered at me. 'You look as though you need something. If you don't mind my saying so.'

I shook my head and jumped to my feet. 'We'd better go.'

As we made our way towards the factory floor George's secretary hailed me from her office. 'Mr Hugh, a message from Dr Wellesley. He'll be free from twelve-thirty.'

'Hugh or Mr Wellesley,' I corrected her half-heartedly, having largely abandoned the hope that the long-serving staff would drop their archaic terms of address. 'My brother will be at home, will he?'

'Yes. And there was an enquiry from a Detective

Inspector Henderson. No details. Just could you call him?'

She gave me a slip of paper with a number. The area code was Exeter. 'Thank you.'

I glanced at the number again, then, stuffing it into my pocket, walked quickly away. George caught up and started singing the praises of some training scheme, but I was hardly listening. I was wondering what questions the police would ask me. I had no doubt it was Sylvie they wanted to talk to me about, it could hardly be anything else. We must have been seen together, on the pontoon perhaps, or the boat. Such things did not go unnoticed in a small community like Dittisham. Ever since Sylvie's death I had been telling myself that this summons would come, yet now it had materialised I felt oddly shaken.

We reached the batching plant and I managed to ask the warehousemen some sensible questions about the new forklift and the revised storage bay layout. The route George and I took through the factory had been laid down since the beginning of time. After a circuit of the storage bay which took us past pallets of silica, lead oxide, litharge and potassium, we inspected the computerised batch mixer, then, after a few minutes with the batch quality control staff, we went through to the heat of the blowing room.

The dull roar of the furnaces still stirred me in some atavistic way. The transmutation of the dry amalgam into clear lava still seemed like some mysterious alchemy. The groups of schoolchildren and visitors who toured the factory on the overhead walkways lingered longest over the blowers as they ballooned and moulded the cooling lava into shape, or beside the cutters as they chased the designs into the glass, waiting in nervous delight for them to make an error and abandon the goblet, tumbler or bowl to the reprocessing bin with a crash of splintering glass. But for me the fascination had always lain here, in the unimaginable heat, in the impenetrable trembling magma that seemed incapable of any transformation, let alone the miraculous metamorphosis into a material both dense and transparent, both complex and flawless.

Bill, our senior master blower, raised his eyebrows in greeting. Many years ago when I had worked here in my university vacations, sweeping floors and wheeling bins, Bill had tried to teach me to blow the simplest shape. My best effort sat at home somewhere, a far-from-round object of uneven thickness with a trail of bubbles up one side.

The factory buzzer cut our tour short at the grinding and polishing area. Following George towards the canteen, the ideas for my speech, such as they were, seemed to scatter, and I wished I'd made more time to prepare.

As the staff gathered I greeted as many as I could by name. A few had been at Hartford for thirty years or more; some twenty; a good number for more than ten. There were two entire families – father, sons, daughters-in-law. We even had a grandmother and granddaughter on the payroll. A hundred and fifty employees in all, people whose lives were dependent on this factory, and – never had I needed less reminding – on my ability to restore its fortunes.

The moment came. George called for silence and I stepped forward, beset by strange emotions.

'As soon as the takeover was agreed I promised to keep you in touch with developments,' I began. 'I also promised you that we were going to do everything in our power to get this management buyout off the ground.' Voicing it, I felt a new weight of responsibility. 'Well, the good news is that we've reached agreement with some venture capital people called Zircon. They're going to put up about a quarter of the money. That still leaves a full half to be raised from the banks, and I won't pretend that it's proving to be easy, because it isn't. We're in the second round of talks with two banks, the Chartered and the West Country Mutual. We haven't been turned down yet. That's all I can tell you so far.'

I caught the eye of Madge, grader and glass washer, sitting solidly on a chair directly in front of me. She was glaring at me: a combative expression, an anxious one, or a combination of both.

'Now, when Cumberland took us over I warned you that sentiment would play no part in their calculations. And though they've given us first call on buying Hartford, we still have to match the best price on offer. I have to tell you that according to our latest information they're talking to Donington and maybe some other companies too.'

The feeling of disconnection hit me again. Without warning my brain did an abrupt shift, a sort of sideways jump, and I completely lost track. When I finally managed to speak, I stumbled, not sure if I was making sense. I heard myself say, 'Now we're very attractive . . .' A lone titter rose up, and, glancing uncertainly towards the sound, I grappled for the thread of my argument. 'Our name and reputation are the attractions,' I said at last. 'And of course our designs. But valuing a name and reputation is not the same as valuing a workforce.'

That had sounded all right, but my brain was functioning with agonising slowness. 'People like Donington have the capacity to produce the Hartford range at their own plants so, if they outbid us, well – you can imagine. This factory will almost certainly close.'

I was back on track at last, my mind free of whatever had constrained it. I thrust some optimism back into my voice. 'But we can make damned sure that doesn't happen! We can make sure that our bid is bigger and better than anyone else's!' I paused, trying unsuccessfully to gauge their mood, before plunging on. 'Now, we've already asked a lot from you, I know that. And you've responded one hundred per cent and that's the entire reason we've managed to keep going as long as we have. But the venture capital people want one more undertaking, and that's what I've come to ask you today. They want a formal undertaking that you'll agree to a two-year period of wage restraint.'

I explained how this would work, how their share options and profit-sharing schemes would remain unaffected. I told them that if it had been left to me I wouldn't have asked them for anything in writing, but venture capitalists were altogether more cautious animals.

I said a lot more of what I hoped were the right

things before halting with a sense of relief. My brain was clear, but my momentary disorientation had shaken me and I didn't want to risk it happening again. I had no intention of going on, I certainly didn't mean to get onto emotional ground, but my judgement was all over the place and, without any idea of where it might lead, I found myself saying forcibly, 'You know, some people believe tradition's a bad thing, that it's the enemy of change – the great modern god Change. But I believe that the traditions we've built up here really matter, that they actually *help* us to change in a productive way. We've been together so long that we think like a family, we take each other into account, we're not just out for ourselves and to hell with the next man . . .' I broke off, aware of how pretentious this must sound to people who, at the end of the day, just wanted a regular job like everyone else. 'What I mean is – I believe that this company is worth fighting for. And not just for what comes off the end of the production line. But for the way we do things here.'

A voice piped up, 'We certainly do it our way!' and there was a ripple of laughter followed by a call of 'You can say that again!' and a smattering of applause.

Buoyed up by their irreverence, I laughed with them before delivering a few last words.

When I stepped down my shirt was damp with sweat and I pulled at my collar to loosen it. Madge brought me a glass of water. 'No need to worry about us, Hugh.' After twenty-five years at Hartford she

22

used my name with a disarming familiarity. 'We're the least of your troubles.'

'Madge . . . That's good to know.'

'We don't mind the wages, we don't mind being asked to do the overtime, what we *don't* like is being second best to cheap glass and tableware.'

'I never meant Hartford to be second best.'

'Got your head turned, didn't you?' Madge prided herself on her blunt speaking. 'Big ideas.'

I couldn't deny it and I didn't try.

Madge, who was a grandmother ten times over, gave me the sort of admonitory nod she probably reserved for her own middle-aged sons.

George and I lingered for a few minutes answering questions before walking back to the office.

'Good speech,' he exclaimed delightedly. 'Just what we needed.' He caught my expression. 'You weren't happy with it?'

I gestured inarticulately. 'Take no notice of me. Too much on my mind.'

'You really don't look well. I noticed the moment you arrived. Are you sure you won't have something to eat?'

'I'm all right.' I made a feeble attempt at humour. 'Just a nervous breakdown. Well – if I could ever find the time.' I looked at my watch and made for the door.

Before leaving, I found an empty office and phoned the Exeter number. Detective Inspector Henderson wasn't available but I spoke to a Detective Sergeant Jones who asked if I could call in during the afternoon.

'Will it take long?'

'Can't say, sir.'

'I have to be back in London by seven. I could give you half an hour at two-thirty. If you wanted longer we'd have to make it another day.'

'Very well, sir. We'll see you at two-thirty then.'

'Who should I ask for?'

'Anyone on Detective Inspector Henderson's team.'

I thought I knew where the police station was, but asked for directions just in case. It was only after I'd put the phone down that I realised that Sergeant Jones hadn't offered to tell me what the matter was about and I hadn't asked him.

George walked me to the car. 'They're right behind the buyout, you know,' he said. 'Everyone here, they'll back us all the way.'

Behind my smile, I was beset by doubts. Having worked so single-mindedly towards the buyout, having pursued it to the point of obsession, it had suddenly lost focus and significance, like some all-consuming passion that inexplicably falls flat. I told myself that my loss of momentum was due to exhaustion, to the punishing pace I had forced on myself in recent weeks. I kept telling myself this because I didn't want to think about my other problems and how they were eating into my confidence.

The road was clogged with the last of the summer caravans, there were roadworks in the town, and I didn't turn onto the Dartmouth road until almost a quarter to one. I drove as fast as I dared and probably faster than I should have. I had the idea that if I was forced to concentrate on my driving then I wouldn't have time to think.

It didn't work, of course. My thoughts simply became less controllable, popping up like muggers in the night. I kept thinking of the last time I had travelled this road, heading not for my brother's place, but for Dittisham and my old family home, standing empty on the dark river. It seemed incredible that I had driven along this road just five days ago, that I had travelled with longing still dragging at my heart, and that when I had arrived at the house and opened it up and drawn back the curtains and put on all the lights I had still half hoped that Sylvie would see my childish signal and come.

I turned off the road into David's drive with relief. I couldn't have faced Dittisham today.

Furze Lodge was an early-nineteenth-century rectory in the grand style, with eight bedrooms, a staff flat and stable block in grounds of five acres. Seeing the immaculate garden, the freshly painted doors and windows, I wondered how much the place cost David and Mary to run. It couldn't be less than fifty thousand a year, not with a live-in couple and at least two horses. When you added the school fees – they had a boy and a girl, both teenagers, both at expensive boarding schools – the charity events Mary hosted and the rest of their community commitments, their expenditure must have exceeded David's income as a GP by a very wide margin indeed. Like me, he had relied heavily on his HartWell dividends. Like me, I imagined he had been feeling the pinch.

I found David in the rather gloomy study which

doubled as a consulting room for his private patients. He sat behind his ancient kneehole desk in a charcoal pinstripe suit complete with waistcoat and watch chain, and when he looked up he eyed me over gold-rimmed half-moon spectacles, so completely the doctor that he had taken the image almost to the point of parody.

'You look terrible,' he remarked immediately.

'Thanks,' I said. 'I'm glad I'm not one of your patients or I might get depressed.'

'Have you seen anyone?'

'What? No. I'm fine.'

He was shuffling paper as he talked. 'You should see someone.'

'I'll be all right once this business is over. It's just frantic at the moment, that's all.'

'Are you sleeping?'

'Don't find the time.'

'What about those tablets I gave you? Have you been taking them?'

I vaguely remembered the tablets he was talking about, but couldn't think where I'd put them. 'Probably not.'

'They don't work unless you take them regularly.'

'What are they meant to do anyway?'

David pulled open a drawer, took out a bottle of pills and chucked them across to me. 'Don't forget this time.'

It was easier to put them into my pocket than to argue. Until this summer David had rarely showed much interest in my health, and I had never expected him to. David was two years older than me, we had been close as children, but since growing up we had never been too involved in each other's lives. If I'd ever stopped to consider our relationship, I suppose I would have described it as practical.

'How are things with you?' I asked automatically.

'Me?' he said in a tone of self-mockery. I noticed that his hair, once so dark, was greying rapidly at the temples and that his cheeks were criss-crossed with deepening lines, though these signs of age did little to detract from his patrician looks, which women found impressive enough to remark on. Like me, he seemed to have gone against the trend and kept his waistline. Unlike me, he had lost none of his hair. 'Oh, I survive,' he said with irony.

'The old loves playing up?' South Devon was retirement country, with a population that David had once described as ninety and skyrocketing.

'They get ill and fed up,' he said heavily. 'They want magic potions.'

Watching him tidy his desk it occurred to me that he, too, was a tired man, and that he was tired because he didn't enjoy his work. With his sharp brain and wide skills, he would have made a good consultant, but though he'd completed two years as a senior houseman he had failed the big surgical exams and never given them another shot. This had caused my father much grief, not because of the failure itself, but because David hadn't had the backbone to persevere. For my father, lack of effort was almost the greatest sin of all, and doubly so when you were blessed with inherited money. He believed that financial security gave you a duty not to depend on it, that it was almost immoral to rely on the sweat and tears of previous generations. It seemed to Pa that David had succumbed to the easy option, and he never quite got over it.

I looked nervously at my watch.

David stood up. 'I'll fetch Mary.'

But he made no move towards the door. Instead he glanced back at me and said in his cool professional voice, 'You heard about Sylvie Mathieson?'

'I did, yes. Awful.'

'She was stabbed apparently.'

'God,' I breathed.

'Dumped in the river.'

'They have no idea who—?'

'No.'

I wasn't sure I wanted more details, but I couldn't stop myself asking, 'Where did they find her?'

'On the first bend there, near the Anchor Stone. The body was caught against a rock. Dead less than a day, they think. Wrapped in plastic, tied up with rope.'

'God.'

David picked up a pen and examined the nib, then put it down again as if it had been guilty of distracting him. When he spoke again his tone was hedged with reservations, as though he were still debating the wisdom of mentioning the subject. 'She was all over the place, you know.'

I stared at him, my mouth suddenly dry. 'What do you mean?'

'Oh, the full bit,' he said airily. 'Lovers. Drugs.'

My stomach tightened. I felt an unreasonable anger. 'How do you know?'

'Oh . . .' His shrug implied contacts in the right places. 'One hears.'

I wanted to ask him why he was so quick to believe such rumours, but I pushed myself to my feet instead so that he couldn't read my face. 'She was always a free spirit,' I proclaimed. 'She always went her own way.'

I didn't have to look at him to know he was wearing a sceptical expression.

'Thought you'd better know, that's all.'

I turned. 'Me? Why?'

'Well, you were in love with her once, weren't you? ' He spoke in the curt voice he used to distance himself from anything that bordered on the emotional.

'Yes . . .' Why had I thought he meant anything else? 'Yes, I was. Yes.' And saying it, I had a fleeting memory of those distant feelings, so intense and innocent and full of hope. 'A long time ago.'

'Look—' David began irritably. But he broke off at the sound of footsteps in the hall.

Mary came in and her face lit up. 'Hugh!' she sang.

I went to kiss her cheek but, with the reproving tut of a mother hen, she pulled me into a generous hug. Standing back to inspect me, she cried, 'How *are* you?'

'I'm fine.'

She shook her head and rolled her eyes in mock exasperation. 'I don't know . . . Is it worth it? Just look at you!'

29

'Don't *you* start,' I protested. 'David's bad enough, giving me pills.'

'It's not pills you want, it's a rest! Isn't it, darling?' she flung at David. Turning back to me. 'You'll stay for lunch at least?'

'I've got to leave at two.'

'Hopeless!' she declared. 'Hopeless!' And her eyes flashed with their habitual amusement.

I said, 'I can always come back again if we don't get through it—'

'I meant, you have to eat! I'll go and fetch something now.' She threw a questioning look at David. 'Shall I?'

'Well, perhaps we can just get started . . .'

'Fine!' she said immediately. 'In a minute then!' She perched on the chair David had pulled up for her and fixed me with a bright stare. I had always liked Mary. She was a determined extrovert who believed that the secret of life was to laugh at whatever came your way. If her high spirits were sometimes a little relentless they hid a compassionate and generous personality, quick to leap to the aid of those in trouble. A solicitor who had given up her practice on marrying David, she did good works on the boards of hospices and children's homes, and was a prison visitor at Dartmoor.

She had a sturdy body with an angular face, ruddy cheeks, and eyebrows that seemed too dark and bold for her colouring, and her appearance wasn't enhanced by her practical tweed skirt, shapeless jumper and cropped hair. But if her looks were plain,

30

they were thoroughly redeemed by her unwavering good nature.

She could not have been more different from Howard, either in appearance or personality, and sometimes I had to remind myself that they were brother and sister. Mary was so much a part of our family, both in spirit and fact, that I tended to forget she might sometimes have divided loyalties. When our two families had jointly and harmoniously controlled HartWell this had not been an issue. But if Mary had felt torn over the acrimonious falling out between Howard and me, she had been very discreet about it.

'We've looked through this buyout proposal thing,' David began, leaning back in his chair and pulling his spectacles off his nose in a practised gesture. 'I can't say we're a hundred per cent clear on *everything* . . .'

So I took them through it, item by item. The investment opportunity, the risks, the potential for significant capital gains. I told them what the new team had already achieved, what was left to get right. When I talked about the future, how we believed we could turn the company round in a few months, some of my old fire returned, I began to sound evangelical again.

Mary listened with partial attention, her sharp eyes on mine, a smile hovering at the corners of her mouth. When I had finished she looked meaningfully at David, and I guessed she was prompting him to ask some pre-arranged question.

'Yes . . .' murmured David, catching her eye.

'Suppose we put in, say, fifty thousand now, could we put in more later?'

I tried not to show my disappointment. Only last week David had been talking about a minimum of a hundred and fifty thousand. 'It would be difficult,' I said carefully. 'You see, there's only going to be so much equity and once the buyout's gone through, that's it, there won't be any more for sale.' I glanced from one to the other and wondered if they had actually decided on this reduced figure but didn't like to tell me.

Mary recognised my anxiety and gave me a sympathetic little grin.

David roused himself to murmur, 'After the last two years, the losses . . .'

'I know. And that's why I want you to come in with us, David. To make good your losses. The potential is there, we believe that very strongly.'

Engrossed in some inner deliberations, David narrowed his eyes and tapped his fingertips together.

Mary tried to catch his attention again but, failing, shrugged at me and said in a theatrical whisper, 'We wanted to ask – what about income? What income could we expect?'

'There would be no dividends until we got into profit.'

David picked up on that. 'And that could be years?'

'Hopefully a lot less.'

'*Hopefully*,' he repeated with a censorious look, as though he had succeeded in catching me out.

I started on our strategy then, how we intended to go out and sell ourselves hard on the Hartford name and quality. But catching the expression of boredom on David's face, an expression I knew so well – lids hooded, his dark winged eyebrows lifted outwards in a satanic arch – I cut it short.

'Listen—' I said forcefully, 'I'm putting everything I have into this. I wouldn't be doing it unless I believed *absolutely* that we could pull it off.'

Mary exclaimed in mock horror, 'Everything?'

'Certainly all the cash I have. And' – I gave a weak chuckle – 'quite a lot I don't. I'm borrowing as much as I can.' And far more than was safe or wise, though I didn't say that.

I tried not to think of how much I stood to lose if the buyout failed, and how much I had at risk if it succeeded. I tried to forget how very overextended I already was. Ginny and I had a lifestyle that didn't come cheap. We had second homes in Provence and Wiltshire, we had staff and cars, until last year we had bought good modern pictures, and we entertained on what could only be described as a grand scale. Even allowing for all this, the outpouring of cash was so relentless that I could never quite grasp where it went. Since last year when the HartWell dividends had plummeted and I had taken a voluntary reduction in salary, we had tried to cut back. Ginny had been in charge of the economies, but for some reason I could never understand her cuts seemed to make little impact on our bank balance, and whenever I thought of the future I felt an upsurge of panic.

Mary screwed up her face in an extravagant imitation of alarm. 'I hope you're not expecting us to do the same!'

'Of course not. I wouldn't want you to. You must only invest what you can afford.'

David drawled, 'And if the company goes down the plughole?'

'It won't.'

'But if it does?' he insisted with a tinge of impatience.

'Then the banks would get first call.'

'And we'd get—?'

'Nothing.'

He grimaced, '*Exactly!*'

I was aware of Mary watching me closely again. She gave a sudden chuckle. 'A bit of a gamble then!' She made it sound like a flutter on the horses.

David sat forward. 'We'll need time to think about it.'

'Of course.' I looked from one to the other. 'Though it would help enormously if you could give me some idea of how long you'll need.'

David pursed his lips. 'I don't know—' He shot a look at Mary. 'The weekend? Say, Tuesday?'

She shrugged her agreement.

'Tuesday then.'

It could have been worse. Suppressing the urge to press my case further, I mustered a grin.

In the short silence that followed, Mary jumped to her feet. 'I'll go and do that lunch!'

'I'm not sure I've got time, Mary.'

She wagged her finger at me. 'It's only a sandwich. Won't take a moment.' There was something brittle, almost peremptory, in her tone. She paused at the door. 'Have you told Hugh about Dittisham, David?'

34

'Ah . . . no.'

Mary caught my eye and, reverting to her more familiar role, made a face of jokey forbearance as she disappeared into the hall.

'The thing is, we might have a buyer,' David told me when she had gone. 'Someone who wants it pretty quick. We heard this morning. Prepared to pay the asking price.'

I felt a pinch of loss. Dittisham had been the home of our childhood, the place in which I had spent many untroubled years, the house in which our parents had lived all their married lives. Until our mother's death twenty years ago, it had stood at the very core of the family. Yet while the child in me hated to think of other people living there, the realist knew that, with Pa dead too, it had to go.

'When do these people want it?' I asked.

'In a month.'

'You'll let me know, will you? I'll need to clear some stuff out.'

'You can't clear it out now?'

'No chance.' Reminded as always of the time, I reached for my briefcase and jumped to my feet.

'Hugh—'

There was something about his tone, a warning note, which made me pause. He came round the desk and, half sitting on it, folded his arms. 'The thing is . . .' he said with a sigh of annoyance, 'the police have been asking about Sylvie.'

A small pull in my chest somewhere. 'Asking?'

'They came to see me yesterday.'

'You? Why you?'

David frowned as if I were being particularly dense. 'Because she was my patient.'

I must have let some of the surprise show in my face because he said, 'Didn't you realise?'

I gave a shrug. 'No . . . Well, I simply never thought about it. You didn't say . . .'

'Anyway, the point is' – and he hesitated as if he would rather have avoided the whole subject – 'they seem to think that Sylvie was on the boat a few weeks ago.'

I didn't need to ask which boat he meant. During the summer David and I had been keeping an eye on Pa's cruiser *Ellie Miller* while we decided what to do with her.

I made a show of puzzlement. I asked evenly, 'Why do they think that?'

'They didn't say. Listen, it's none of my business, but . . . Well, be careful of those cretins, won't you?'

'Careful?' But we both knew what he meant.

'If Sylvie was seen on the boat with you, they might make too much out of it. Assume you were, you know –' he flapped an impatient hand – 'together.'

'Did they say that?' I blurted.

'No, *no*. But you know how their minds work. One-track. In *my* experience, anyway.'

I had been so desperate to talk to someone about Sylvie for such a long time that I almost told him then. I wanted to explain the extraordinary hold she had always exercised over my imagination, and in telling him perhaps to explain it better to myself. I think I wanted to hear him say that he understood,

36

that it could have been the same for him. Yet something held me back: an instinct for secrecy, a fear of being misunderstood, a doubt as to how he would receive such confidences. David had never been one for letting his feelings get the better of him; as far as I knew he had never lost his head over anything, far less a woman.

I said abruptly, 'They've already been in touch, actually.'

'The police? You've seen them?'

'Soon. In half an hour, in fact.'

'Oh!' He looked at his watch, reached back over his desk for his diary and flicked a page over. 'If you want me to come along, I *might* be able to swing it.'

'I don't think that'll be necessary.' But the fact that he'd suggested it planted a small seed of anxiety in my heart.

'Sure?'

'Sure.'

'All right,' he conceded immediately. 'But don't forget, Hugh – they have small brains. Strictly one-track.'

Two

THE DETECTIVE settled himself in his seat. 'Sorry to have kept you, sir.'

'I am rather pressed for time,' I remarked. 'Is this likely to take long?'

His look suggested that police business did not hurry for anyone, especially people who liked to think they had more important things to do.

Taking the cap off his pen, he began to write laboriously on a pro forma pad.

'E . . . S . . .' I said, reading my name upside down. 'After *Well*, it's E . . . S . . .'

'Ah . . .' He amended it to *Wellesley*. 'And your address?'

I gave it to him, complete with post code.

'That's central London, is it, sir?'

'Yes. Chelsea.'

'Now . . .' He fixed me with a bland stare. 'You were acquainted with Sylvie Mathieson, were you, Mr Wellesley?'

'Yes.'

'And did you know Sylvie well?' His use of her first name threw me a little, it made our conversation sound like some casual discussion about an old friend. But then the whole interview had an unexpectedly informal air, with the comfortable chairs, the open door, the chatter floating in from the passage and the way the interview had been allocated to neither Henderson nor Jones, but to this Detective Constable Reith, who, with his smooth unshadowed chin and clear complexion, looked far too young to be doing this or any other job.

'At one time I knew her well,' I said. 'We met – oh, fifteen or sixteen years ago. But I didn't see her for a long time after that, not until this summer in fact.'

'This summer. And did you see her often?'

I inhaled abruptly. 'No. She came to the boat once. No – twice.'

'The boat?'

'My father's cruising yacht. My father died recently. I was keeping an eye on the boat. Pumping it out, that sort of thing. She swam by one day.'

He blinked. 'Swam by?'

'Yes, swam up to the boat. We started talking. She came aboard for tea.' Tea: how quaint that sounded, redolent of afternoon and sunlight and respectability.

'Where did this happen?'

'At Dittisham. The boat's moored in front of my father's house.'

'And when was this?'

'It must have been—' I frowned with the effort of memory. 'June? Some time then.'

'And the other time Sylvie came to the boat, did she swim over on that occasion as well?' He was intrigued by the swimming, as if this marked Sylvie out as some kind of oddity.

'No, she was rowing a small dinghy. She was on her way to another boat.'

'And which boat was that?'

'Oh, I don't know its name. But it's an old-fashioned boat, thirty-five feet or so, a white cutter with a bowsprit. Moored a little further down river, past the ferry.'

'You saw her go to it, did you?'

'Well – I knew she was on her way to a boat. I assumed it was that one. I'd seen her on it before.'

'You'd seen Sylvie on it before?' he repeated stolidly.

'Yes.'

'And when was that?'

'She was with a group of people, they were going off somewhere. It must have been around . . . the beginning of July? Yes – the beginning of July.'

'Did you recognise the people she was with?'

'No.'

'You could point the boat out to us, though?'

'I *could* . . .' I made no effort to conceal my reluctance. 'But I'd rather not. I don't come down here very often. I'm just on my way back to London now. It would be rather inconvenient. I'm extremely busy at the moment.'

'I mean – if necessary.'

'If necessary,' I conceded, trying not to sound openly uncooperative. 'But I'm sure the harbour master will be able to tell you straight away. There can't be many cutters with bowsprits moored the other side of the ferry.'

Reith nodded in an unfocused way. 'So, er . . . apart

40

from these two visits, did you see Sylvie on any other occasions?'

'I saw her by the river once. We chatted for a minute.'

'And that was all? You saw her just the three times?'

'To talk to, yes.' And saying this I felt a sudden heat, a prickle of sweat against my shirt, and thought what a poor liar I would make if I had to do it on a grand scale.

'Did you know who she mixed with? Who her friends were?'

'No,' I said a little too hastily. Then, more matter-of-factly: 'The only time I saw her with anyone was when she was on the boat with that group. And once I saw her walking with someone. Well, I *think* it was Sylvie. She was a long way off.' How these tiny untruths seemed to slip effortlessly off my tongue. Yet I could hardly admit that I had watched her covertly through binoculars, like some pathetic Peeping Tom.

'It was a man she was with?'

'It looked like it, yes. Though he had long hair. Noticeably long, onto his shoulders or even longer.'

'And she didn't mention the names of any friends when she was in conversation with you?'

'No.'

Reith shuffled a piece of paper. 'Now, Mr Wellesley, where were you between noon on Saturday last, the thirtieth of September, and noon on Sunday, the following day?'

I thought I had maintained my expression but

41

perhaps he caught a hint of alarm in my eyes because he added coolly, 'A standard question, Mr Wellesley.'

As I met his unwavering gaze he suddenly didn't seem so young any more. 'Of course . . .' I cleared my throat. 'On Saturday I worked in my office in Hammersmith until mid-afternoon. I left at . . . it must have been about three. Then I drove straight down to Dittisham. I arrived at dusk – so, about seven-thirty, I suppose. I opened up the house—'

'What house are we talking about, sir?' He was making detailed notes now.

'My late father's house – Dittisham House. And then . . . I drove into Dartmouth to buy some food—'

A pause while he got it down. 'So, what time would that have been?'

I really had to get this right. 'Oh . . . eight-fifteen? Maybe a little after. Yes, about eight-thirty.'

'And where did you shop, sir?'

'Well, I went to the Co-op first, but it was closed, so I went to the Spar shop by the church. It was the only place I could find. That was open, I mean.'

'Which church is that, sir?'

'Which church?' I repeated, momentarily confounded by the pedantry of the question. 'I've no idea what it's called, if that's what you mean. But the one right down in the town, near the quay.'

I wondered if he was writing so slowly out of an overdeveloped sense of clerical diligence, or a perverse wish to delay me even longer. 'Then?' he asked at last.

'I went back to the house. My wife arrived shortly afterwards.'

'Your wife? And her name is—?'

'Virginia Wellesley.'

'Mrs Virginia Wellesley.' I watched him record it in block capitals. 'And she is of the same address?'

'I'm sorry?'

'London. She lives with you at—' He peered at his notes. 'Glebe Place?'

'Yes.'

The conversation had taken on a fantastic quality, both predictable and bizarre. The leisurely nature of the proceedings, the meandering questions, seemed grotesquely inappropriate to the terrible event that had brought us here.

'So at what time did you get back to the house and see your wife?'

I went through the motions of dredging my memory again. 'Well – nine or so.'

'And then?'

'We had some supper and went to bed.'

'And the next day?'

'Oh, wait a minute, I forgot . . . That evening my brother called in briefly, at about ten.'

'Your brother being?'

'David Wellesley. Dr Wellesley. He practises in Dartmouth.'

Reith held his pen awkwardly, knuckles bent like a child, and the nib laboured ever more slowly across the page. 'And the next day?'

'Help . . .' I rubbed my forehead. 'We must have got up at about eight and then we worked on the house and the boat. Clearing out cupboards and attics, that sort of thing.' Yet again I waited for his pen

43

to catch up. 'Then in the evening we went back to London.'

'What time would that be, sir?'

'When we left? Oh – nine. Just after.'

He read laboriously through what he had written, then looked up and smiled his bleak professional smile. 'Thank you, sir.'

Even then I wasn't sure he had finished until he closed his notebook and got to his feet. I rose and shook his hand. 'I hope you find whoever did it,' I said. 'She was . . .' What was I trying to say? Why had I even started? '. . . a lovely person.'

'Was she, sir?' And his eyes slid away knowingly.

I drove fast again, often touching a hundred, sometimes exceeding it, stopping only to buy petrol and a mineral water. Julia called me on the car phone and gave me the messages in her cool staccato. The Chartered Bank had brought forward our next meeting to the following day at eleven-thirty, which I took as a wholly encouraging sign, but my satisfaction evaporated with the next message. Graham Moncrieff, the leader of our legal team, had called to say that he'd hit a problem with the Cumberland lawyers. It seemed Cumberland were backing out of their agreement to lease us the Hartford properties, and were suddenly insisting we buy the factory and warehousing outright.

For the second time that day I almost had an accident, straying out of my lane to earn a prolonged blast from a Range Rover.

Containing my anger and disbelief only with difficulty, slowing down to a sedate sixty, I told Julia to fix a meeting with Howard for some time the next day.

'You don't have any slots left.'

'Breakfast. Evening. Midnight, if necessary. But some time tomorrow, Julia.'

I asked her to save the rest of the messages and rang off. I needed time to calm down; I needed time to absorb the full implications of Cumberland's about-turn. If they forced this issue, if they made us purchase the factory, we would have to raise more money, another million at the very least. Just when we'd presented our final figures to the banks; just when we had the last of the money almost within our grasp. Cumberland weren't just moving the goalposts, they were taking them away altogether. Finding another million would be hard: we had tapped every source, we had called in every debt, we had milked every contact.

If this manoeuvre was designed to defeat us then it registered high on the scale of dirty tricks. But was it a manoeuvre? Did Cumberland want us to lose, or did they simply want to squeeze more cash out of us? Howard would know. Though whether he would be prepared to tell me was another matter.

This was the aspect of business I had always disliked and tried my best to avoid, the backbiting and chicanery, the breaking of trust, the pressing of every last advantage until your opponent bled. Howard regarded my scruples as a quaint but fatal flaw. He thought I was soft, and he was probably right. But I quite liked the idea of leaving the dignity of my opponents intact; if it was a flaw to dislike making enemies, then I possessed it in good measure.

I was going to be late. I almost called Julia to ask her to let Ginny know, but in recent weeks such second-hand messages had resulted in ruffled feelings. Ginny had accused me of finding excuses to avoid calling her. Realising that there was a small but undeniable grain of truth in this, feeling ashamed of it, I determined to call her myself.

'I've been held up,' I said as soon as she answered. I could hear voices in the background.

'Will you be very late?'

'Seven, I hope. Seven-thirty at the latest. If you don't mind me unwashed.'

'I don't mind if you don't.'

She sounded so subdued that I asked, 'Are you all right?'

'Feeling a bit rough. A touch of flu, I think.'

One of the voices in the background was male, a caterer or maintenance man. In the old days we would have joked about Ginny having a secret lover, but we didn't joke about that sort of thing any more.

I said, 'I'm sorry not to be there to help.'

'I'll manage.'

'You're sure you don't need a doctor?'

'No, no. I'll just go to bed as soon as everyone's gone.'

It was a quarter to eight by the time I finally turned into Glebe Place. The party was larger than I'd imagined. After a long hunt for a parking place – the garage was blocked, the adjacent streets tightly packed – I followed some guests into the house to find a wall of backs in every doorway and people spilling out of the drawing room into the conservatory.

A woman loomed up. 'Hello, Hugh! What a super party! You always give such super parties!'

Mouthing greetings, wearing my best smile, I moved through the room in search of Ginny. I finally spotted her by the fireplace, her back to me. She had done her hair a new way, or perhaps it was an old way that I'd forgotten, pulled severely back and held at her neck in a thick band, though this did nothing to diminish the brilliance of her hair, which was auburn and exceptionally glossy. She was wearing a plain black dress and when she turned I noticed that, apart from pearl earrings, she wore no jewellery. This didn't prevent her from looking exquisite; nothing could ever do that. She had a heart-shaped face with high cheekbones, a fine nose, and winged eyebrows that gave her an elfin quality.

She was smiling at someone. It was a smile I recognised, brittle and nervous.

'I'm here,' I announced unnecessarily. 'Everything okay?'

'The caterers got the food wrong.'

'Is it serious?'

'It's all doughy stuff. And spiced chicken. They forgot the smoked salmon parcels and the roulades!' She exhaled with a tiny shudder. 'Well, it's too late now, I suppose.' Her eyes, bright with illness or anxiety or both, darted constantly around the room. For a moment we stood silently amid the cacophonous swell, two castaways in a storm of our own

47

making, then Ginny drifted away and I found myself talking to a City man about interest rates.

Slowly I succumbed to the rhythm of the party: enquiring after health and business, deflecting questions, spinning thin jokes, talking but not listening too well. The champagne made me tired and slow-witted, and I soon abandoned it for mineral water. Later someone made a speech about the premature baby unit and the need for funds and we all applauded.

A voice sighed at my elbow. 'Hello, you.' It was Caroline Adam, a friend of Ginny's and something high-powered in PR. She had wide red lips and tousled silvery blonde hair and was tall enough to look me straight in the eye. 'The man of the moment,' she declared.

'I am?'

'I call you two the golden couple. So beautiful, so clever, so – *everything*.'

I couldn't begin to respond to that, and didn't try.

'How are you in fact?' There was a slyness in her manner.

'Fine,' I said.

'And Ginny? She's looking a bit pale. I noticed straight away.'

'She thinks she might have flu.'

'Ah,' Caroline breathed, her heavy-lashed eyes fixed on mine. 'But you guys are okay?' Her smile did nothing to take the edge off the question.

A sickening thought struck me: that Ginny had confided in this woman, had spilled out the most painful details of our unhappiness. And fast on this thought came the idea that Ginny had talked about my visits to Dittisham, had even – a sinking thought – read something suspicious into them.

'Couldn't be better,' I said with terrible joviality.

Caroline searched my face, and I had the feeling that little escaped her voracious eyes. 'Glad to hear it,' she said at last. 'So many people falling by the wayside. Owing their last bootlace to Lloyd's. Jobless at fifty. Reduced to selling herbal remedies from their dining rooms. No wonder marriages creak under the strain. And we're all meant to be more caring!'

Had Ginny suspected something all this time? Had she thought I was having an affair? As the idea took hold, my spirits shrank at the prospect of the confrontations ahead.

'Though when it comes to caring,' Caroline was saying with a provocative smile, 'I think you poor beleaguered men have had a raw deal. I think us beastly women have pushed you too far, and you all need spoiling and cosseting again, just like in the bad old days.' She gave me a look that wasn't entirely frivolous.

The noise seemed to rise up around me, the drink sang in my brain, I had reached some limit that I barely recognised. With an indeterminate salute, I moved rapidly away and escaped into the garden. I knew I shouldn't let the Carolines of this world get to me. Mischief-making was a compulsion with her and if it hadn't been such a very long day I would have remembered that sooner. I would also have remembered that, whatever else Ginny had reproached me for, she had never hinted at infidelity.

Besides, our unhappiness had set in long before the summer, at some point in the long years since love had given way to bewilderment.

Standing there in the sulphurous darkness of the London night, the party a distant murmur, I tried to picture a time when things might be different, when the business would be back on its feet, when Ginny and I would be happy again, when in some miraculous way I would be free of worry and guilt. But the idea wouldn't form, it seemed too remote, and, taking a last breath of damp leafy air, I trudged back towards the house.

A few guests lingered remorselessly until nine-thirty, and we didn't close the door on the caterers until after ten.

'You go to bed,' I told Ginny. 'I'll finish down here.'

'I'm all right.' She sat on the edge of a chair by the fireplace. 'I don't think it's flu after all.'

'Are you sure?'

She gave a faint nod, her eyes doggedly on mine, and I realised she wanted to talk.

I poured myself a brandy, almost certainly the last thing I needed, and sat in the chair opposite. 'Well, that seemed to go all right, didn't it?' I said with forced brightness. 'I don't think anyone noticed the food.'

She sat like a governess, her arms held into her sides, her shoulders braced, austere and unyielding. 'How was your day?' she asked.

'Oh, you know . . .'

'No, I don't. Tell me.' And she fixed me with a look of strange intensity.

'Well . . . I told the Hartford staff what was happening. I saw David and Mary for lunch.'

'And what was it you told the staff?' she persisted solemnly.

'Oh, I gave them the latest news in all its glory!'

'Please, Hugh – I'd like to know.'

If I looked surprised it was because Ginny had never shown much interest in the details of the business. 'Sorry,' I said penitently. 'What did I tell them? Well . . . I made Cumberland sound pretty ogre-ish. I said they'd sell Hartford to the highest bidder, and, if it didn't happen to be us, then the staff faced almost certain redundancy. I said the future under a buyout would be pretty tough. But I think I made the bad times with us sound marginally more attractive than being out of work.'

She was listening intently, a small frown on her forehead, so I went on, explaining some of the risks involved in making our bid, and the hard work that lay ahead.

'But you believe in the buyout?' she said. 'It's what you want?'

'What I want?' I gave a shaky laugh. 'I think so! When I last did any rational thinking anyway.'

'There you go again,' she said, her voice rising.

'Where again?'

'Not answering me properly.'

'I'm sorry.' I heard the note of injury in my voice and suppressed it. 'Yes, it's what I want.' Articulating this gave my feelings new force. 'Yes. *Yes*. I can't just let it be written off. Not when it's got so much going for it. Oh, I know what you all think,' I said as if she represented the rest of my family. 'You think it's just the *tradition* or something, that I'm incapable of letting go. But it's not just that. It's the people at Hartford, and the place . . . I love it! I love everything to do with it!'

Ginny said gravely, 'So long as it's what you want.'

'Okay, and I want to be the person running it!' I conceded, as if this had been in dispute. 'I want to run it because I think I can do a better job than anyone else. With the right team beside me – and without crazy delusions of grandeur!' Just thinking about Howard stirred me to anger once more, and it was a moment before I took in what Ginny was saying.

' . . . I phoned the estate agent, threatened to take the house elsewhere unless they drummed up more interest in Melton. The man suggested some ads in the glossy magazines – which *we* pay for, of course. I agreed, but I told him he was on trial, that we'd give him six weeks at the most. Then . . .' Some thought distracted her, she blinked rapidly. 'Then . . . I asked the Murrays which agent they used for their place in France. Those local people are sharks, you know.'

Her calm acceptance caused me a flutter of remorse. 'I'm sorry it's come to this.'

She dismissed this with a slight lift of her shoulders. 'Too many houses anyway.'

'But you loved Melton.' And she had loved the house in Provence too. Her great passion was for decorating, her great talent for putting furniture and objects and colours together in fabulous combinations. She had made the houses into showcases, and their loss would be far more painful for her than for me. But at least we were talking about it. There had been a time when Ginny seemed to think that I wanted to sell the houses for some capricious reason of my own, out of perversity, or even, in her blacker moments, because I wanted to undermine her in some way. For a while I had hardly dared to ask how the agents were getting on.

I ventured another risky subject, the matter of the costly couple who ran Melton. 'The Kemps, have we managed to . . .?'

'Yes, yes. They left a week ago. I told you.'

'You did? Sorry.' Another apology, another small descent.

'Mrs Hoskins has agreed to go in three times a week.'

'Well done.'

'Will we have to sell this place as well?' she asked in a voice that was deliberately calm.

'No, of course not!' I made a poor stab at humour. 'No, I thought we'd go mad and keep at least one roof over our heads! The doorways along the Strand are a bit draughty. And you don't meet the same class of dosser, so they tell me . . . Old Etonians, Lloyd's bankrupts—'

'Please don't!' she exclaimed suddenly, and the tension stretched out between us. 'I do wish you'd just – *tell* me things! Sometimes you treat me like an idiot!'

'I *am* telling you,' I responded mildly. 'And I've never treated you like—'

'But if you're going to be at Hartford all the time, we can't live up here, can we?'

'In time we could certainly think about moving nearer, yes.'

She exhaled sharply with exasperation. 'Of course we'll have to. It's the only thing to do.'

I wasn't sure what to make of this Ginny, vibrating with the usual tensions, yet unexpectedly and miraculously focused.

'But we don't have to live at Dittisham, do we?' she demanded.

'No.'

'But you *were* thinking about it.'

It had been the briefest of suggestions, made soon after my father died, when I was still in a state of disbelief. The thought of losing both my father and the house where I had grown up had seemed too much to bear, and for a few weeks I'd nursed emotional ideas of restoring the place and using it for summer weekends. My imagination had cast a golden wash of nostalgia over the prospect; I had seen children in the garden again, and barbecues on the terrace, and Easter treasure hunts, and expeditions on the river. 'It was just a thought. But no, it's being sold. There was an offer today.'

'Ah.' And the relief showed in her face.

We both looked away into the unlit fire. The fake logs were so cleverly finished with ash and scorch marks that they were indistinguishable from the real thing; Ginny had seen them in America and ordered them specially. I felt her glance back at me, gathering herself to speak again.

'That girl – the one they found in the river – did you hear anything?'

I kept myself steady, I showed nothing in my face. I brought my eyes back to hers. 'Oh, David mentioned something. She was stabbed, apparently. Then dumped in the water.'

'They haven't got any idea who did it?'

'I don't think so.'

A pause. 'You might have told me, you know.'

'Told you what?'

'That it was *her*.' And Ginny's voice was charged with an emotion I couldn't read.

I didn't say anything.

'That she was the one you were in love with.'

I took a slow breath. 'It was a long time ago, Ginny.'

'But it *was* her?' And her voice trembled slightly.

'Yes.'

'The one you wanted to marry, but couldn't.'

'Who said that?'

She dropped her eyes briefly, as if caught in some subterfuge. 'Mary.'

'Well, I wouldn't believe everything Mary tells you,' I retorted, wondering what else Mary had said. Then, to soften my words: 'Honestly, darling . . .'

'I don't mind, it's not that,' she said, her voice high. 'I just wish you'd told me.'

'Really, it wasn't anything . . .'

'You did want to marry her though?'

There was a relentlessness in Ginny, an inability to let go, that reverberated through our arguments like the beat of a discordant drum. Hearing it now in her voice, knowing what was to come, I said hotly, 'It never got to that stage. There was never any

55

question . . .' She was waiting for me to elaborate. 'Sylvie was very young,' I explained unhappily. 'Only sixteen.'

Something in the way Ginny took this, the suggestion of a nod, made me think that she already knew, that Mary must have told her, and, fired by the drink and the endless day, I felt a surge of resentment against this exchange of notes.

Ginny took a moment to frame her next question. 'You saw her this summer?' And the coolness of her voice did nothing to disguise its tautness.

'Once or twice.'

'And she was' – the hesitation again, the careful choice of words – 'living in Dittisham?'

'I don't know. I didn't ask.'

'Mary said she was running a shop. Pottery or handicrafts . . .'

'Well, Mary would be the one to know.' I threw the last of the brandy down my throat and got up.

'Mary thought—'

I twisted away to hide my exasperation and despair. I was so exhausted, I had survived so much today, that I longed to shout out, to beg her to leave it alone and give me some peace.

'She thought the police would want to question everyone who was near the river on the weekend.'

Constrained by habit, or possibly futility, I made myself turn back and say, 'Yes, I expect she's right.'

'So they might want to question us?'

I gestured the possibility.

'And you? Because you used to know her?'

'Yes. Well, in fact—' I would have given anything

not to talk about it just then, but one bad moment was probably as good as another. 'They already have. Today.' And I thought: now we start the argument in earnest. Because I have failed to tell her immediately. Because she'll think I have something to hide.

But she was very still, her eyes fastened on my face. 'And?'

'Oh, it was just what you'd expect. They asked if I knew Sylvie. If I'd seen her this summer. It didn't take long. Mainly because I didn't have much to tell them.'

A progression of thoughts flickered over Ginny's face like shadows across a screen. 'There we are, then,' she exhaled finally.

It was a moment before I realised that there was to be no row after all, that she was going to leave the subject alone. With the relief came an extraordinary fatigue, like a coat of lead.

'I must get to bed.'

'Yes,' she declared. 'You've had it! So've I!' She swung away and walked towards the stairs without looking back.

Yet I didn't sleep immediately. And nor did Ginny. We lay on either side of the bed, facing away from each other, and I thought that this must be the lone-liest feeling in the world, to lie beside each other yet find ourselves unable to reach out, to have things to say yet find it impossible to speak. Also – and the thought travelled painfully out of the past – to remember how different it had been at the beginning, the closeness – and yes, the love – that we had once felt for each other, and to realise that, for some reason that neither of us understood, those times seemed to have slipped for ever beyond our grasp.

Later something made me wake. The wind, the distant pattering of rain. And close by, the sound of Ginny's breathing, coming in uneven jerks. A tiny gasp, then another. I rolled over and put my hand on her shoulder. She stiffened and held her breath. I moved to touch her cheek beneath the mask, to feel the tears I knew I would find there, but she pushed my hand away and said in a harsh voice, 'What is it? What's the matter?'

I had no answer, and in the end it was easier to say 'Nothing' and turn away.

It was just before seven-thirty as I pressed the security code into the keypad at the entrance of the HartWell offices in Slough. The panel shrieked at me and for a moment I thought Cumberland must have had the code changed, but I must have had the code wrong first time because at my second attempt the door buzzed its acceptance. I noticed that the heavy inner doors of solid glass emblazoned with the HartWell logo had not yet been replaced. That logo. Howard and I had argued about every detail of it – the style, the size, the colour, you name it. In those days we had thrived on argument, it had been the lifeblood of our partnership, a stimulus for problem solving and fresh ideas, a constant source of hilarity, and the only way we knew to keep our minds sharp in the face of our terrifying success. Well, success that had been terrifying for me anyway; Howard took it as his due.

In the early days of our expansion into mass-market glass and china we had measured success in terms of turnover and profit margins. But profit margins don't protect you from recession or cut-throat tactics by your competitors. And for Hartford, heavily dependent on exports, margins don't defend you against the dollar taking a nosedive from which it never recovers.

I looked into my old office. The large Hartford crystal vase dating from the fifties stood in its usual place on the side table, now bereft of flowers. The aerial photograph of the Hartford factory still hung on the wall next to the dusty outlines of the two pictures I had removed to my temporary office in Hammersmith: a photograph of my father greeting a young Prince of Wales at Hartford during a visit in the seventies; and a picture of me as a self-conscious eighteen-year-old, trying to blow crystal.

No amount of framed pictures or crystal vases could ever have made me feel comfortable in this hermetically sealed glasshouse. Slough may have been equidistant from Hartford and our factories to the north, and convenient for Heathrow, but for me, imbued with the hands-on philosophy of my father, the place was a bureaucratic no-man's land that had left me feeling dangerously out of touch.

I waited in Howard's outer office. One thing I had learnt to rely on in my years with Howard was that he would always be late for our meetings, and, knowing full well that today would be no exception, I determined to remain calm.

It was ten to eight when Howard made one of the

silent entrances at which he was so proficient. I looked up and there he was, filling the doorway. He was wearing a dark suit, expensively cut to disguise the weight which had settled evenly, and, despite his much-vaunted gym expeditions, it seemed permanently, over his broad frame. Crossing the room, he slid a hand elegantly down one lapel and unbuttoned his jacket with a flick of his thumb.

'Is it just us?' he asked in feigned surprise.

'Who else was there meant to be?'

'I thought – lawyers, accountants. No?' He affected this ironic air when he wanted to intimidate me.

'Don't talk rubbish.'

He attempted an ingenuous look, something he had never quite managed to master, and I noticed that his grey eyes were looking puffy, and his hair, normally immaculate, was unkempt around the collar, while his cheeks were beginning to develop an unhealthy mottled look. But then if my social life was full, Howard's was frenetic. Since his divorce four years before, he frequently featured in the glossy magazines that Ginny liked to read, pictured with a string of society women. When I had last chosen to listen, someone had told me that he was keen to marry the twice-divorced daughter of a landed duke.

He unlocked his office and led the way to his desk.

'This isn't to do with the buyout then?' he drawled, sinking into his high-backed leather chair.

'Of course it is!' I said tightly, avoiding the strategically low-seated guest chair opposite his desk and fetching a higher one from the conference area.

'And you really don't feel you want anyone else here?'

Recognising this as a no-win question, I ignored it and demanded, 'What's this problem about the leasing agreement for the Hartford properties?'

But he was still playing games. 'I need coffee,' he announced languidly, casting around as if this might cause a cup to appear out of nowhere.

I growled, 'Forget the coffee. I've only got fifteen minutes.'

Suddenly he laughed, a rich chuckle that rumbled on after he had stopped smiling. 'Hugh,' he scolded. 'Always in such a rush.'

'Too damned right!'

He regarded me with something approaching affection, though it could just as easily have been pity, and then, this show of indulgence having served its purpose, which was to wind me up, he got down to business.

'Is there a problem?' he murmured.

'You know damn well there is. It was agreed that we could *lease* all the properties from Cumberland. There was never any talk of buying!'

'Oh?' He affected puzzlement. 'Wasn't there? Are you sure you aren't thinking of the earlier discussions? At the first merger talks perhaps?'

I was never sure why Howard liked to call the takeover a merger. Because he had instigated the deal perhaps. Or because it boosted his view of his own standing on the main board. 'You know perfectly well which discussions I'm talking about, Howard,' I said, determined not to give him the satisfaction of seeing me lose my temper. 'When the outline buyout terms were agreed. In August.'

Howard grimaced elegantly. 'I don't think anything was actually *decided*, Hugh.' He made a show of testing this recollection against his memory. 'No,' he murmured, 'I'm sure I'm right in saying Cumberland didn't commit itself to a leasing arrangement.'

'It was agreed in principle, Howard!'

'It was just one *option*, Hugh.'

'More than an option, Howard! A commitment!'

His face took on an expression of forbearance wearing thin. 'Whatever your recollection, Hugh, the situation is that Cumberland cannot possibly agree to a leasing agreement. In a buyout you expect the customer to *buy*. Cumberland doesn't want the Hartford properties left on its books. It wants to dispose of them. *Not* unreasonable in the circumstances.'

'Unreasonable if you've made a commitment.'

'Hugh – a commitment is something in writing, something agreed by one's lawyers.'

'For Cumberland, maybe.'

'Come – for anyone, surely.'

'So do I take it the matter's no longer open to negotiation?' I said stiffly.

'On the price?' he asked, deliberately choosing to misunderstand.

'On the option to lease!'

He sighed with a sort of paternal irritation. 'I thought I'd made it clear, Hugh. Didn't I make it clear?' He spread his hands questioningly. 'Leasing is not an option.'

Despite my intention to remain calm, I heard my

resentment break through. 'Cumberland are reneging, then? I just want to be quite clear.'

'Hugh, I strongly object to that. There's no question of reneging. How can there be when we never agreed anything?'

'You realise this could sabotage the entire buyout?'

'Oh?' He was suddenly a picture of imitation concern. 'Well, I'm very sorry to hear that, I really am. I know how hard you've been working on it.'

'Come on, don't tell me you didn't realise!' I said bitterly.

'Realise?' The shrug was hopelessly exaggerated. Such a bloody bad actor. But then overplaying the scene was all part of the satisfaction for him. 'How could I realise, Hugh?'

I shook my head, not trusting myself to speak.

'Surely the additional cash won't be that hard to find?'

He was fishing, he wanted to know just how far we had got with the banks, but I was damned if I was going to give him that sort of information. 'It's not the money, Howard, it's the timing, as you well know! The Cumberland board have had the outline agreement for six weeks – *six weeks* – and they suddenly decide on this *now*. That's as close to sabotage as you can get!'

'Well, I'm sorry but Cumberland can hardly be blamed if you've rushed things at *your* end, Hugh. The proposal had to be evaluated very carefully. You couldn't expect us to do it overnight. I'm sorry if you're going to have to go back and renegotiate with the banks, but that's hardly our problem, is it?'

Looking at him, a suspicion formed in my mind. It came to me that Howard himself had engineered this whole situation, that, for some reasons of his own, he wanted my bid to fail.

I stood up. I fully intended to leave with my pride intact, but my anger got the better of me. 'Sleeping all right, are you, Howard?'

'Oh, come on, Hugh,' he said with the injured air of someone fending off an unprovoked attack. 'That's always been your trouble, you know – taking things personally.'

'With you, I don't know any other way to take them.'

'Business is business, Hugh. You've never been able to grasp that, have you?'

The morning tailback began just beyond Heathrow. As I joined the haze of shuffling traffic, I thought back over the years of my partnership with Howard. Though I'd never harboured too many illusions about him, while I'd seen him instigate some pretty ruthless manoeuvres in his time, I'd always liked to think there were certain limits beyond which he wouldn't go, that the sixty years during which our two families had jointly owned and run HartWell counted for something – a remnant of loyalty, perhaps, a fragment of sympathy – and that he would draw the line at actively plotting against me.

I liked to think such fine noble thoughts because if I didn't I began to contemplate walking away from the whole miserable business and going to live a hermit's life in France. I'd had such thoughts before, in early summer when the full extent of the crisis at HartWell was becoming clear, when I realised that Howard had engineered the takeover behind my back, when I began to appreciate just how completely I had let the real control slip from my grasp. Then I was dogged by a sense of worthlessness and futility: my mid-life crisis. An absurdly frivolous term for the doubt that had taken to descending on me without warning, turning my thinking inside out, making me question things that at my age did not bear questioning. Despairing of the present, clutching at the past, harbouring visions of what might have been. Hungry for escape and solace; ripe for the idea of Sylvie.

Fumbling with the radio, I turned on the eight-thirty headlines, knowing that there would be nothing about Sylvie, yet needing to hear it for myself. An exercise in reassurance. Or paranoia.

The traffic did not ease and I reached the three-room office suite in Hammersmith five minutes before Julia and I were due to leave for the meeting with the Chartered Bank. I had rented this place as a temporary London base while we negotiated the buyout. It wasn't so much an office as a space from which I made calls and sent letters. All the meetings – and there were up to three a day – took place at the City offices of the various bankers, lawyers and accountants acting for us or for Cumberland. Very occasionally meetings were held at Hartford itself, four hours' drive to the south-west.

Before Julia could collar me, I phoned Moncrieff to check what I already knew, that we had no legal remedy against Cumberland for reneging on the leasing agreement. I followed this with a swift call to Pollinger at Zircon to alert him to the fact that we would be asking for more money. He warned me that unless I was prepared to give Zircon a bigger slice of the equity then the most I could expect from them would be a quarter of the extra million.

Julia put her head round the door. 'I know I shouldn't, but I couldn't help overhearing. That bastard!' I didn't need to ask who she was referring to. So far as Julia was concerned, Howard had rat status.

'It would have been a board decision, Julia.'

'Yes, but who proposed the idea?'

'No point in worrying about that now.'

'That's what you always say.' Instantly she made a disclaiming wave of the hand. 'Sorry. *Sorry.* What I meant was, *I* wouldn't be half as forgiving. You're too nice, that's your trouble.'

'It's nothing to do with being *nice*,' I grimaced, smarting at the compliment. 'It's a question of being realistic.'

Julia conceded this with a dubious face, and looked at her watch. 'We've got to go.'

'One more call,' I bargained.

My bank manager was a bland insubstantial character named Elliott. With the various personal loans I had been forced to negotiate, I had got to see quite a lot of him over the last two years. He did not sound surprised that I was asking for money again.

'This mortgage would be additional to your existing building society mortgage?'

'That's right.'

'Five hundred thousand is rather a large sum for a mortgage, Mr Wellesley. That sort of sum would usually come into the range of a business loan, subject to business rates.'

'But you'll consider it?'

'This would be in addition to the loan on the country property?'

'That's right.'

A pause. 'So on the Chelsea house, the new mortgage would take the loan up to ninety per cent of its value?'

'That would be on a conservative valuation. But – yes.'

'Well – I'll look into it,' he said cautiously. 'But, Mr Wellesley, are you quite sure you want to put your home at stake?'

'Yes.'

'You have considered what would happen if your business were to fail?'

'Yes,' I said testily.

'And your wife – she's happy with the arrangement?'

'I realise she'll have to agree to it,' I said. 'I'm aware of the law.'

'Very well. I'll come back to you as soon as I can.'

Julia appeared in the doorway wearing her we-really-have-to-leave face, but I held up a delaying hand and, when she had frowned her disapproval and disappeared, I called Ginny, only to get the answering machine. I told the tape I should be home by eight. It was only after I'd rung off that it occurred to me that Ginny might have flu after all and be lying ill in bed. She was prone to catch all the nastier bugs and to suffer them badly. Convalescence, with its inactivity, always depressed her, and it was then that I became acutely aware of how isolated she was without children. During the five or so years when we had actively discussed our childlessness and gone through various fertility investigations I had once or twice mentioned adoption, but she had brimmed with dark resentment at the idea, as though it were an admission of defeat or an allotment of blame, and I hadn't brought up the subject again. Now we never talked about children at all.

Julia came in briskly. 'We really have to go.' She tipped her head to one side and cast me a sharp glance. 'Are you okay?'

'Don't you start.'

'You look awful again.'

'What do you mean *again*?' I grabbed my briefcase and sprang to my feet. 'You're as bad as my old nanny. I'm fine.'

But I can't have sounded too convincing because as we headed for the door she demanded, 'When did you last eat?' Interpreting my silence correctly, she announced that she would get some sandwiches on the way.

Hurrying down the stairs I tried to concentrate on the crucial meeting ahead. I dreaded pitching to bankers, it was like reasoning with wet dough. They were malleable enough, you felt things were shaping up, but at the end of the day you were never quite sure what you had ended up with.

We emerged fast into the lobby. Through the doors

I could see Tony, the driver Julia regularly hired to take us into the City, standing at the bottom of the steps beside his Rover. Two men crossed in front of the Rover and came up the steps towards the entrance. I swung the door back for Julia just as the first of the visitors pushed through the opposite door. I registered a crumpled raincoat, sparse greying hair, a thin mouth in a fleshy face. The second man was younger, taller and fitter. I wasn't sure what it was about them – the white shirts, the well-worn clothes, their air of purpose – but, coloured by the events of the previous day, my imagination moment-arily cast them as policemen.

I hurried on towards the car.

Tony had the rear door open and I was just about to duck in when a voice called, 'Mr Wellesley?'

I straightened up and looked round. Julia said sharply, 'Can I help you?' and turned to intercept the approaching men.

The one with grey hair ignored her and continued towards me with the rolling gait of someone with a hip problem. Digging into his breast pocket, he pro-duced a card mounted in a leather case and, holding it up at eye level so there was no possibility of my missing it, announced himself as Detective Inspector Henderson.

'You are Mr Hugh William Wellesley?'

'Yes.'

'I'd like to ask you to accompany me to Exeter, sir, to help us with our inquiries into the death of Sylvie Mathieson.'

I felt a draining in my stomach. 'But yesterday – I saw your man Reith. I told him everything.'

'We'd be grateful for more details, sir,' he said in a flat voice. 'And a statement, if you don't mind.'

I spread my hands helplessly, I opened my mouth a couple of times to speak, I felt a sudden heat. 'I'll be glad to help in any way I can – of course,' I said at last. 'But I'm on my way to a vital meeting and I'm already late.' I glanced towards Julia as if for support and met her startled gaze.

'The matter is rather important, sir.'

Disbelief and mounting alarm made me exclaim, 'So is *this*! You don't understand, Inspector – I *have* to get to this meeting!'

Henderson pondered this with the air of someone who has heard a lot of excuses in his time, but my incredulity and panic must have made some sort of impression because after a show of consideration, he agreed to wait. I told him my meeting would take one and a half hours. We settled on two.

In accepting this, I realised with dismay that I had agreed to go all the way back to Exeter.

Three

WE ARRIVED in darkness and monsoon rain. The approaches to the police station were blocked by manoeuvring cars, and we were forced to scurry head down through the deluge to the shimmering entrance. Inside, Henderson shook the water from his collar and pressed his thin hair down to his scalp. Wiping my forehead, I glanced up and saw David.

I grinned weakly. I'd guessed he might be here, I knew Julia had called ahead, but the sight of his sardonic face still gave my spirits a lift. The long journey from London had done nothing for my peace of mind.

David had someone with him, a young thin-faced man with floppy blond hair and a cast in one eye. 'This is Charles Tingwall of Ruthven & Forbes,' David announced. 'He's here to look after your interests.'

I wasn't sure how I felt about this. To my impressionable mind, programmed by a hundred television dramas, hiring yourself a solicitor suggested you had something to hide. But in the next more considered moment, I realised that, irrespective of appearances, it was a sensible precaution that I would be foolish not to take.

Tingwall gave me a dry handshake and turned to Henderson.

'On what basis is Mr Wellesley here, Inspector?' The two men moved to one side, as if for negotiations. I could just hear the policeman recite, 'We are hoping Mr Wellesley can help us with our inquiries into the death of Sylvie Mathieson.'

Tingwall then asked: 'Is Mr Wellesley here as a witness, then, or a suspect?'

'As a witness.'

'In which case—'

I didn't hear any more as David said to me in a robust voice that seemed to carry across the reception area to the duty officer at the enquiry window, 'What did I tell you? Small brains.'

I frowned a protest at him.

Deliberately misreading my look, he added, 'Don't worry, Tingwall will get it sorted. He came highly recommended.' He added in a tone that was almost offhand, 'Have they said why you're here?'

'No.'

'Well . . . it has to be the lover scenario, doesn't it?'

'Oh thanks. *Thanks*.'

'What else could it be?' he said with a flicker of impatience. 'I told you – they've got one-track minds. Just remember, they're guessing. Don't let them rattle you. Just tell them where to get off.'

I wasn't so sure it would be that easy. I wasn't so sure I would feel quite so confident on this alien territory.

Tingwall and Henderson turned back.

'I'd like some time with Mr Wellesley,' Tingwall announced.

Henderson offered, 'Five minutes?'

'I'm sure Mr Wellesley could do with a sandwich and a wash and brush up.'

'Fifteen, then.'

'Twenty?' Tingwall raised an eyebrow at me. 'Mr Wellesley's come a very long way.'

Henderson yielded with a cursory nod before limping away.

For some reason this well-practised professional exchange did nothing to reassure me.

I said I wasn't hungry but Tingwall sent David off to buy sandwiches anyway and led me to a bench in a corner of the reception area, away from the lugubrious gaze of the duty officer.

'Now, Mr Wellesley,' Tingwall began in a hushed tone, 'I just want to be sure – they didn't arrest you?'

'Arrest me? *No.*'

'They didn't caution you?'

'No.'

'There was no mention of anything you may say being given in evidence?'

'No.'

'Fine.' He gave me a brief smile which was undermined by the cast in his left eye. 'And you haven't said anything to them already?'

'I gave them a statement yesterday.'

This was obviously the first he'd heard of it. 'And what did you tell them exactly?'

I gave him a rough summary, and found myself

wondering for the hundredth time where I might have slipped up.

'And you didn't say anything in the car on the way down?'

'What? No.' Apart from a couple of offers to stop at service areas, Henderson and his cohort Phipps had maintained a steadfast silence during the entire journey. If their intention had been to unnerve me, then they had partially succeeded.

'Have you anything to add to yesterday's statement?'

'No.'

'They haven't given you any idea of why they've asked you back?' Tingwall enquired cautiously.

I shrugged, 'No.'

'And you yourself can't think of any reason?'

'No.'

Tingwall tapped his fingers together pensively. 'Well, if they've got their wires crossed, I mean if they're completely on the wrong track, then you must say so.' He waited for a sign that I had understood this. Getting nothing back, he spelled it out again. 'If they have some notion that's completely wrong, then you must put them right.'

The thought of what they could have got wrong made me feel ill, but I managed a faint nod.

'Now, you should be aware of your rights—'

'My rights?' I protested. 'God – you make it sound as though I'm about to be charged or something.'

'I apologise. I didn't make myself clear. I meant your rights at interview.'

'I'm not sure that makes me feel a whole lot better.

The way everyone's going on I'm beginning to feel like a suspect.'

'The police do that to everyone, I'm afraid. It's their way.' He gave the unconvincing smile again. 'Now, you are here in an entirely voluntary capacity, to help them with their inquiries. As a result, nothing you say can be held against you. If, however, they suddenly decide to caution you, mid-interview or whatever, then I must warn you that everything will change.'

Far from bolstering my confidence, this conversation was eroding it fast. 'So you think I *am* a suspect?'

'Er – no, Mr Wellesley.' Tingwall chose his words with the care of someone picking his way over barbed wire. 'Not at all. At the same time . . .' He was struggling to get it right. '. . . they don't usually bring someone all this way unless they think, rightly or wrongly, that he or she has information of some kind.'

Even in my more optimistic moments I'd realised that the police wouldn't have sent their big guns to bring me all the way down here unless they believed I had something to tell them. But it was one thing to think it, and quite another to hear it from a professional.

'In that case,' I said, 'you'd better spell it out for me.'

Now that he was on firmer ground, Tingwall moved confidently into his stride. 'The important thing to remember is that you don't have to answer any questions you don't want to.'

My anxieties shot back to the surface. 'Won't that look bad?'

'It doesn't matter how it looks. If there are any areas that you feel are best left unanswered – for whatever reason – then you shouldn't answer them.'

'But it's not like that,' I murmured. 'I told them everything yesterday.'

'Fine. But bear it in mind, all the same,' Tingwall said.

I felt bound to ask, 'And if I don't want to answer? What do I say?'

'I leave that up to you,' he said with curious emphasis, as if there was an obvious conclusion to be drawn from this.

I didn't understand and said so.

'Well, let's put it this way . . .' His disconcerting squinty eyes seemed to focus somewhere on my left cheek. 'It's better to say you can't remember than to be vague or to change your mind. And if you're simply not sure of something, again, don't just take a stab at it, don't give a vague answer. Just say you can't remember. Keep it simple.'

I took a long breath. 'Okay.'

David came back with the sandwiches, but I still wasn't hungry and, leaving David with Tingwall, I asked the duty officer the way to the gents. The basins were smeared with dirt, one was missing its plug, and the taps were the type that switch themselves off after yielding a niggardly trickle. I splashed some water over my face and washed my hands. Drying my face with a paper towel, I told myself I felt refreshed.

When I got back to the reception area David was

pulling on his coat. 'I'm going over to the hospital. I'll come back later.'

'Don't feel you have to.'

'Well, it's hardly out of my way, is it?' he replied in the brusque tone he used to discourage further discussion.

I followed him outside and we stood under the dripping porch. 'I was thinking,' I said, 'if this gets out, if the press get hold of it . . . *Christ.*' The idea was enough to shake me.

'I've talked to Tingwall about that. He's dealing with it.'

'He is?'

'No guarantees, though. The press are always sniffing around. He can only try.'

I clamped my eyes shut in an attempt to close out images of the newspaper headlines. 'What a time to choose!'

David couldn't think what I was talking about.

'The buyout!'

'Oh.'

'The Chartered Bank is on the brink of committing itself. The thing's practically off the ground.'

'Well, that's good.' But his tone conveyed a lack of interest.

'Off the ground, subject to raising the rest of the money, I mean.'

I said this so that he wouldn't think I was taking his support for granted, but he interpreted it as an untimely attempt to push my case.

'Yes, well,' he said with visible irritation, 'Give us time, eh?'

'I didn't mean that.' But it was too complicated to put the matter right and reluctantly I let it pass.

David looked at his watch. He frequently gave this impression of needing to be somewhere else; it was one of his stratagems for keeping people, particularly difficult patients, at arm's length.

'Listen,' I said, 'Ginny doesn't know where I am. I thought it best, in case she worried – you know. But now . . . well, I'm not so sure. I'd hate her to hear about this from someone else.'

'Ah, she knows, in fact. I called and told her.'

'You did?' I should have been annoyed at such peremptory action, and part of me was, yet Ginny would have had to know sooner or later, and I was quite relieved that David had been the one to tell her. He could always be relied on to down-play a crisis, and his uncompromising brand of logic would have checked Ginny's tendency to overreaction.

As if to confirm this, he said, 'I told her not to come down. I said there was absolutely no point, that it was just a routine thing and she was best at home.'

'And she was happy about that?'

'Oh yes,' he said emphatically.

I said with a tremor of emotion, 'Thanks.'

With an offhand wave and a sharp twitch of the mouth in what might have been intended as a smile, he went out into the rain.

Tingwall announced our readiness and a uniformed officer let us through a security door and along a passage to a door marked Interview Room 2. This was a different room from the one where I'd talked to Reith. The floor was uncarpeted, the chairs hard and upright, and there was a tape recorder at one end of the table. The fluorescent lighting gave off a ghostly flicker, and there was a stale tang of cigarettes and heavily scented floor polish.

Tingwall and I sat on one side of the table, Henderson on the other, with Reith to his left. Phipps stood against the wall, by the door.

Henderson intoned some preliminaries in an expressionless voice, thanking me for my willingness to help them with their inquiries – as if he had offered me much option – explaining that he simply wished to establish one or two facts. His thin, lipless mouth was like a slit set at random amid the broad heavy features. He had the skin of a heavy smoker, porous and etched with webs of deep lines, and his eyes were hooded and droopy as a spaniel's. It was a spent and punished face, but not, I felt, a stupid one.

He repeated most of the questions that Reith had asked me the day before. How did I know Sylvie, when and where had I seen her in the last few months, what had happened when we met.

I took my answers slowly, matching them to the ones I had given Reith the day before, conscious of Henderson's washed-out eyes and his air of quiet watchfulness. As we progressed, part of me stood outside myself wondering what sort of an impression I was making, yet the more self-aware I became the more unnatural I sounded to my own ears and the more I felt I was exhibiting the body language of someone with something to hide.

'To summarise then,' Henderson said, 'the first time you saw Sylvie Mathieson this summer was when she swam to the boat and you had tea together for perhaps forty-five minutes?'

'Yes.'

'The second time she also came to the boat and you—'

'She didn't come on board,' I corrected him mildly. 'She just tapped on the hull.'

'So she remained in this other boat she came in, and you talked for ten minutes?'

'Yes.'

'And the third time you met on the quay?'

'We bumped into each other, yes.'

'And you talked for—?'

'Oh . . . two, three minutes. At the most.'

'So, it was just the three times then?'

I hated the way that repetition etched these details deeper and deeper into the stone of fact. 'I think so, yes.'

'You *think* so?'

'Well, as far as I remember.'

His eyes flickered to life. 'Your memory could be faulty then? Might it have been four times that you met, or five, or even more?'

'No. *No*. If it was more than three, then it wasn't much more. Four at the outside.' This was sounding terrible. I was beginning to appreciate Tingwall's warning about vague answers.

'Well, if it was four, on what other occasion did you meet her?'

'Look, I'm not sure I did meet her again.. But if I did it was probably on the water. But really, I can't remember.'

I felt sure Henderson would pursue this, but for some reason he took on a distant look, and asked, 'You spent a lot of time on the water this summer, did you?'

'A few weekends, that's all.'

'Out sailing?'

'Only once. Mainly I was just doing the maintenance.'

Appearing distracted, Henderson dropped his eyes and gave a slight nod. When he looked up again his gaze had regained its watchfulness. 'How would you describe your relationship with Sylvie Mathieson?' he asked, and suddenly there was a charge in the air.

'Well – old friends, I suppose. Though we hadn't seen each other for many years.'

'Nothing more than that?'

So David was right: I was to be cast as Sylvie's secret lover. 'No,' I said.

'You weren't involved in a sexual relationship?'

I took a moment to answer. I wanted to strike the right note, somewhere between indignation and candour. 'No.'

'Just . . . er, *friends*?'

'That's right.'

His old man's eyes appraised me coldly. 'You had known each other in the past?'

I had already told him this. 'Yes.'

'When was it that you met exactly?'

'It must be . . .' I frowned with the effort of the mental arithmetic. 'Sixteen years ago.'

'And what was your relationship then?'

I didn't want to answer that, not with anything

that approached the truth anyway. The very thought of telling this leery grey-faced man with his pasteddown hair and tight collar what I had once felt for Sylvie made me bristle. Eventually I said, 'We used to go out together.'

'She was your girlfriend?'

'For a time, yes.'

'Was it a sexual relationship?'

My resentment rose in a hot wave. I threw a glance at Tingwall, who was already protesting, 'That can hardly be relevant to your present inquiries, Inspector.'

'We're talking about sixteen years ago,' Henderson said reasonably. 'Surely that's not a problem, Mr Wellesley?'

Before Tingwall could interject again, I said hotly, 'Well, it is, actually, because it's really none of your business.'

'You prefer not to answer the question then, Mr Wellesley?'

'That's right,' I said shakily.

There was a shift in the atmosphere then, a palpable hardening in their attitude towards me. I felt as though I had the word *suspect* tattooed across my forehead.

'May I ask how long this non-specific relationship lasted?' Henderson asked drily.

I thought about not answering that as well, but murmured grudgingly, 'A year and a half.'

'You were how old at the time, Mr Wellesley?'

I had no doubt he knew the answer to that, he just wanted to hear me say it. 'I was twenty-six.'

'And when you met Sylvie Mathieson she was fifteen years old?'

'Sixteen.'

'Er . . . Not if it was sixteen years ago, Mr Wellesley.'

'I remembered her as sixteen – but you may be right.'

'I ask because I'm wondering if that's why there appears to be a difficulty over the question.' When I made no response he explained, 'If she was fifteen, a sexual relationship would of course have been illegal. If it would help, I can ask about your relationship after Miss Mathieson had turned sixteen. What was the nature of it then?'

Tingwall broke in angrily, 'I think we've established that this question can have no relevance to the present inquiry, and that my client is perfectly entitled not to answer it. He is here to help with your inquiries, Inspector, not to be grilled on his personal life.'

Henderson accepted this with a splaying of his thick fingers, a slight shrug of the shoulders, as if the approach, though doomed to failure, had been worth one last try.

'Well, let's move on then,' he said, sticking out his fleshy chin with something like relish. 'Perhaps we could go over your movements last weekend? In some detail.'

He wanted everything. What time I had left for work on the Saturday morning, what I had done in the office, who could vouch for the fact that I had left Hammersmith at about three.

'There was no one else there,' I explained. 'I was alone in the office.'

'No security staff?'

'At the main door, yes. But I don't know the weekend staff, and they don't know me. There are dozens of companies in the building. I just rent rooms there.'

'So no one saw you leave?'

'No.'

'And nothing to confirm the time you started your journey?'

I thought for a moment. 'No.'

'And you say it took you four and a half hours to reach Dittisham?'

'Well – a little less. I arrived between seven-fifteen and seven-thirty. But longer than usual, certainly. The traffic was terrible. There was a crash on the M4 near Swindon, a big tailback.'

'No one saw you arrive at Dittisham?'

'Not that I'm aware of, no. Someone in the village, maybe.'

'You came through the village?'

'It's the only way to the house.'

'What car were you driving?'

'My BMW.' A memory stirred. 'But I did stop for petrol.'

'Where was this?'

'I can never remember the name of the place. It's on the motorway somewhere this side of Bristol. But I'll have the receipt somewhere.'

A glimmer of something like disappointment showed in Henderson's face. 'So what time would this have been?'

'I don't know. About five-thirty, I suppose. Maybe even later. Six, possibly. The jam was terrible.'

Henderson leant back in his chair and eyed me thoughtfully before saying to Tingwall, 'Perhaps this receipt could be found?'

Tingwall played hard to get. 'I'll look into it,' he said.

Henderson brought his attention back to me. 'So you didn't see anyone when you arrived at Dittisham?'

I was finding this a strain and made no effort to hide it. 'No,' I sighed heavily.

'You went straight to your late father's house?'

'Yes.'

We established that on arriving I had done some fairly normal things like putting on lights, having a drink, taking a look around.

'And then?'

'I went into Dartmouth to buy some food.' Anticipating the next question, I added, 'It must have been about eight-thirty when I got to the Co-op and found it shut.'

'If I may interrupt,' Tingwall cut in smoothly. 'It couldn't have been any later than eight when Mr Wellesley arrived in town.'

There was a silence while we stared expectantly at Tingwall.

'My client's brother, Dr David Wellesley, left a meeting in the town just before eight and saw Mr Wellesley driving along Duke Street shortly afterwards.'

'Dr Wellesley is sure about that?' Henderson asked.

'Quite certain.'

'Was he alone?'

'Was who alone?' Tingwall asked, deliberately choosing to be obtuse.

'Doctor Wellesley.'

Tingwall pulled an expression of exaggerated surprise, as if he couldn't imagine the relevance of the question. 'I *believe* so, yes. I could check, of course. But, er, there's no doubt about the time and place.'

'And he can make a statement to that effect?'

'If *necessary*, of course.'

Henderson turned back to me with a fusion of disappointment and irritation written on his face. He had thought I was his man, and he didn't like the idea of getting it wrong.

'And your wife arrived at about nine?' he asked mechanically.

'Yes.'

'And you were together for the rest of the weekend?'

'Yes.'

'Very well, Mr Wellesley, that'll be all for the moment,' he said crisply, pushing his chair back. 'But I'd be grateful if this petrol receipt could be found,' he said to Tingwall. 'And I'd like Mr Wellesley to return in the morning to make a formal statement, if he would be agreeable. And I'd be grateful if Mrs Wellesley could make a short statement too.'

Catching my glance, Tingwall launched into negotiations over Ginny, asking if a statement was really necessary, and if so, whether she couldn't make it in London. Then they moved on to David's statement and whether that was really necessary either, but by that time I was hardly listening. I was adjusting to the idea that I seemed to be off the hook.

David slowed as we approached the entrance to Furze Lodge. 'Sure you won't change your mind?'

'No,' I said. 'Thanks anyway.'

'The children'll be doing their own thing. They won't bother you. I'm lucky if they talk to *me*.'

'It's not that. Really.'

David shrugged as he accelerated past the gates. 'There mightn't be any bedding at Dittisham, you know. Mary's been clearing things out.'

'I'll find something. Don't worry. I just need to crash out . . .' I explained lamely.

'Fine.'

For several minutes we continued in silence towards Dittisham, with only the hiss of the wipers and the swish of the wet tyres and the blurred beams of the headlights on the shining road ahead.

Since picking me up from the police station David had talked almost continuously, a dry monologue about tying up the last details of Pa's estate, about the children's progress at school; about anything except what had just happened. I was grateful not to have to talk, I needed time to regain my equilibrium, but now there was something I had to say. 'I'm not sure you did the right thing, you know – telling Tingwall that – but thanks anyway.'

He knew perfectly well what I was referring to but affected a lack of interest and understanding.

I said it for both of us: 'Telling Tingwall you saw me in town.' I had already broached this at the beginning of the journey, but he hadn't responded then either. 'But look, David, I don't want you to get yourself into a corner.'

'Don't be ridiculous!'

'You say that, but what happens if they find out? Who knows, I might have been seen somewhere else at eight, driving through Dittisham, something like that.'

'But you *did* go into town about then, didn't you?' And he threw me a look of complete innocence.

'David – it was more like eight-thirty.'

He tossed a hand in the air. 'A few minutes. So what?'

'Half an hour,' I argued unhappily.

He slowed to take the steep hill down through the village. 'I wouldn't worry about it.'

'Wouldn't it be best not to tie yourself to a definite time, though, just in case?'

'Really, Hugh.' He shook his head as if I were a total mystery to him.

A whorl of leaves spun across our path as we turned through the gates of Dittisham House. The security lights blinked on, the shrubs glinted darkly, we rounded the slight bend and the house rose up before us, its tall windows gaping blackly like empty eyes. This was the moment I had been dreading, the moment when the memories would pounce. And for an instant the images did rear up, of Sylvie leaning lazily against the french windows, the sunlight making a halo of her hair, and then, like turning the page of an album, a darker picture took its place, of Sylvie on the boat, shivering in my sweater, hair dripping wet, mouth poised provocatively in that laughing way of hers.

Then we parked, the wind shivered against the car and the images faded. I thought that if this was the worst it would get then I would survive it.

Something was different about the house but in the shadowy beams of the outside lights it took me a moment to work out what it was. The ceanothus that covered much of the stonework, forming a ledge for the upstairs windows and an arch for the porch, had come away from the wall and fallen, broken and shrivelled, onto the gravel in a forlorn heap of rotting leaves. Pa had only been dead a few months, yet already the place seemed to have acquired a long-abandoned air. For a moment I felt so woebegone that I considered going to stay at David's after all.

'Lucky to be getting the price for this place, you know,' David remarked. 'Not many houses fetching the full whack nowadays.'

'It's the water,' I suggested. 'People love the idea of water.'

David, having chosen to live inland, wasn't ready to admit to the drawing power of the river. 'Mmm,' he grunted dubiously. 'It's a good-sized house, remember. Not so many of those around.'

And not so many that were quite so pretty either. An early-nineteenth-century villa with an Edwardian extension, it had floor-length windows and on the river side two bays with a verandah supported by iron trellises. The garden fell in a succession of two terraces and a lawn to the river below.

'Drink?' I asked brightly.

David hesitated, and I realised how much I wanted him to accept.

'But if you can't . . .' I offered immediately. 'If you have to get back . . .'

'Well . . . Unless you're desperate?'

I was desperate to talk, but this wouldn't be what David had in mind. For him a couple of stiff drinks were a palliative against the trials of the day, not an excuse for unburdening the soul, an exercise he had always regarded with the greatest suspicion.

'No, I'm fine,' I said.

'You've got a key?'

'I left one in the porch, thanks.' I pushed open the door and the wind swooped into the car. I couldn't leave without saying, 'You were dead right, by the way.'

'Oh?'

The wind shook the door, threatening to slam it, and I pulled it shut again.

'About what the police had in mind. I was meant to be the jealous lover.'

David gave a derisive grunt. 'I told you, they're cretins.'

He restarted the engine and, still shaking his head, waited for me to get out.

'Look, when you said she had lovers—'

He made a face. 'Did I?'

'Yesterday. You said she was all over the place, that she had several lovers,' I persisted.

He shrugged dismissively. 'It was just gossip.'

'But this gossip – did it mention me?' I was still brooding over what had brought the police to my door.

'No, *no.*'

'Nobody even hinted . . .?'

'No! There was no mention of any names. It was nothing like that.'

'What about the chap with long hair, the one she went around with? Presumably the police are on to him?'

'God only knows. Really, I have no idea.'

'You'd think the police would be on to him.'

'Perhaps they are,' he said briskly.

But still I couldn't leave it alone. After the events of the last week I had to talk to someone. 'The thing is . . . well, I didn't quite tell them everything. You see, I did see something of Sylvie this summer. More than I said I did, anyway. She . . . I—'

'Look, I'd forget it, if I were you,' he cut in, his eyes alight with impatience or anger. 'I wouldn't discuss it with anyone.'

I felt like saying: Since when were you anyone? With an effort I stayed silent, but the reproach must have shown in my face because he made a grudging gesture of appeasement. 'Best to let things lie.'

'I wasn't actually planning on talking to a whole lot of people about it,' I protested.

'Not with anyone,' he repeated in the tone of a stern parent.

It's amazing how your family can undermine you, how in the space of a few words they can catch you unawares and demolish your confidence. What did David imagine I might be about to admit to? What did he think I knew? When we were young he had had a talent for putting me down, for ridiculing my efforts, and for an instant I felt echoes of old humiliations and childish resentments, the younger brother once more.

We said a stiff goodnight. Watching him drive off, I felt relieved to be alone.

The house was cold but once I had turned on some lights and put a match to the gas fire in Pa's study the gloom soon lifted. The good furniture had gone to the salerooms some weeks ago, but the heavy damask curtains still hung at the windows, the carpets and older rugs remained, Pa's battered kneehole desk still straddled one corner, and there was a comfortable chair to pull up to the fire.

The Scotch wasn't on the mantelpiece where I had last seen it and for an anxious moment I thought Mary or Mrs Perry, the cleaner, had removed it, but after a quick hunt I found it standing in solitary state in the cupboard where the family photo albums had always lived. There were no albums there now, and I assumed the family mementoes were accumulating at Furze Lodge with David and Mary.

I poured myself a hefty measure and took several large gulps before topping the glass up again. Until this summer I'd never been a great drinker – I'd never particularly liked the sensation of losing my wits – but tonight like a few other nights recently I wanted a small measure of oblivion.

The wind was racketing in the chimneys, the windows were humming and rattling to a frenetic rhythm and, outside, the rushing trees sounded as though they were about to storm the house.

The phone made me start. Imbued with the day's paranoia, I considered not answering it.

'There you are,' gasped Ginny when I finally picked up the receiver. 'How did it go?'

'Not an experience I'd like to repeat.'

'But it's over?'

I gave a pale laugh. 'I sincerely hope so.'

'They've finished with you?'

'It looks like it.'

She made a slight sound, an exhalation or a sigh. 'Well, thank God for that.' A pause, then: 'You're staying there?'

'I'll get a train back tomorrow.'

'When will you arrive?'

'In the afternoon some time. Not sure when.' I didn't say I had to go to Exeter first to make the statement.

A hesitation, then she said in a rush, 'Why did they want you back? What was it all about?'

'I've no idea.'

'But there must have been a reason,' she said, and there was an edge to her voice.

'They didn't say, Ginny. But they want you to make a statement, I'm afraid.'

'What do you mean?'

'It's a routine thing,' I said, playing it down. 'Establishing where everyone was. They just want to confirm that we met up at nine that night and left for London on Saturday evening.'

She didn't reply.

'Ginny?'

'When? When do I have to make this statement?'

'There's no hurry, I don't think. There's this lawyer Charles Tingwall who's arranging it for us. He's fixing it so you can do yours in London. It won't be very complicated.'

'And it's a routine thing, you say? They're asking everyone?'

'Well – people who were around,' I lied.

I could hear her breathing, always a sign that she was getting tense. 'I see.'

'I'll tell you more tomorrow. All right?'

Another pause, and I knew she was working up to something. 'But why did they want to see you? Please tell me. They must have given you a reason.'

'They didn't.'

'What did they ask you, then? What sort of questions?'

'Look, I'll tell you all about it tomorrow.'

'Will you?' I caught a note of accusation in her voice.

'Of course.'

'Of course,' she echoed in a tone of open scepticism.

'Sorry?'

'Nothing.'

'Ginny – they had it all wrong.'

'Did they?'

Suddenly I felt beleaguered. Where was the unconditional family support? First David, now Ginny.

Suppressing a dart of self-pity, I said, 'Tomorrow, Ginny. Let's talk about it tomorrow.'

Her voice broke slightly as she said a curt 'Fine', and I could picture the uncertainty and reproach in her face. I nearly called her back, I fully intended to, but, unable to face more questions, I poured myself another Scotch instead.

I took my drink to the window and stared out into the darkness. A light on the far side of the river blinked through the flickering branches, the wind whistled in the eaves. Draining my glass, I pulled at the bolts of the french windows and walked out into the blustering gale. Crossing the stone terrace to the steps, I felt my way down to the next level where sodden grass pulled at my shoes. A last flight of steps and I was descending the sloping lawn towards the water. The arches of the pergola rose dimly to one side, the bare branches of the fruit trees swished angrily near by, the deeper blackness of the summer-house loomed somewhere to the right. Misjudging the distance, I almost walked into the low wall that marked the river boundary.

The wind was barrelling down the deep cut of the river, pulling at my jacket, buffeting my ears, and it was much colder. The darkness was so thick that I couldn't make out the state of the tide, whether the water was high or there was a sea of mud, though I fancied I could hear the rip of the ebb close by. A sprinkling of lights gave height and form to the ridges and creeks of the opposite banks, while away to my right the lights of Dittisham and the ferry landing gave shape to the curve of the river. But the water itself was hidden, a secretive ribbon of ink coursing towards the sea.

Somewhere in front of me was *Ellie Miller*, lying to her mooring, her squat shape lost against the greater blackness of the night. No cabin lights showing now, no laughter echoing across the water, no lazy rippling of the tide in the warm summer air. Maybe it was the drink, maybe it was the tensions of the day, but I felt such a jumble of emotions that my eyelids pricked with fierce heat and I gasped for breath. Visions came: of water pressing into Sylvie's mouth and eyes, of her body bumping against the rocks, of unspeakable wounds in her flesh. The images were vivid yet curiously opaque, like my images of Sylvie as she had been in life. I saw her clearly: I saw her dimly. She was featureless and exhilarating and proud; she was distant and elusive and cold. She was open and devious; she was sensuous and cruel and base. I realised then that she would baffle me just as thoroughly in death as she had confused me in life.

I turned away and stumbled up the slope. Above the thrashing of the trees I heard a baleful cry. I stopped. It rose again, a chilling sound carried high on the wind. It seemed to come from the river, and in a moment of disorientation and fear my nightmare roared back to life and everything stalled inside me, my heart and breathing seized, and I was overcome by a sensation of imminent disaster.

The next whoop brought me bumping back to reality. It was a very human sound, very much in the present. Looking up the slope I saw a figure outlined against the french windows.

'There you are!' sang Mary as I climbed the last of the steps and entered the pool of light. Drawing me inside the house, she gave a theatrical shiver. 'Wow, it's wild out there!' Railing against the climate, she pulled the windows shut and drew the curtains. 'I've brought some sheets for you!' she declared heartily. 'And some breakfast. Can't have you camping! But how are you? I want to know how you are!'

I couldn't hide my feelings, perhaps I didn't try, because when she took a better look at me her face creased into a picture of concern. 'Oh, Hugh!' she sighed. 'That bad?'

'Just a bit tired and emotional.' I laughed to make it sound like a joke. I went in search of another glass. 'I'm awfully glad to see you.'

'You should have come and stayed with us, you twit. But I know – ' she added with a laugh and a flip of the wrist ' – the kids are home for the weekend! You're not the only one. They get too much for me sometimes. All those teenage moods. All that ghastly music – rock or rap or whatever it is.'

I fetched a chair from Pa's desk and offered her a whisky which she accepted with a show of conspiratorial glee, as though drinking was always a bit of a lark.

We sat on either side of the fire.

'So,' she grimaced sympathetically. 'What a beastly day for you.'

'Yes, as days go . . .' I sank back into my chair. 'Cumberland put another million quid on the price of the buyout. Just when we'd raised most of the money.'

'I hope that wasn't Howard's doing.'

'Oh . . . I wouldn't have thought so.'

Perhaps it was my hesitation, perhaps it was something in my tone, but Mary rolled her eyes and sighed, 'Oh, you don't have to hide it from me. Nothing surprises me about my brother. You know, I'll be glad when the buyout's over and our two families never work together again.' She tutted, 'But this extra money – will you be able to raise it?'

'I don't honestly know.'

'It's too bad, after all your efforts . . .' She watched me for a moment. 'Now what about the police? Were they horrible?' Her tone was feisty, like a warrior who at the slightest provocation would take up cudgels in my defence.

'It may seem crazy,' I said, 'but for a while back there I really thought they were going to lock me up.'

She wasn't sure how seriously she was meant to take this and her mouth jerked into an uncertain smile. 'Poor Hugh! How awful!'

'They seemed so *fixed* on me. That's what was so bloody terrifying.'

She looked fierce again. 'They gave you a bad time?'

'It felt like it, but then I haven't exactly got a lot of experience to measure it against. But you know the worst thing? It was not knowing why they'd called me in. Was my crime to have been seen with Sylvie? Christ, if that's a crime! Or did they think they had something else on me – you know, something they didn't tell me about? I suppose that's how they get people,' I laughed grimly. 'By making them think they know something damning about them.'

'Skunks!' Mary declared. 'It's just bullying, isn't it?' Taking a gulp of her drink, she eyed me over the rim of her glass. 'They didn't give you any idea then? What it was?'

I shook my head. 'With all these lovers she was meant to have, you'd have thought they'd have had plenty of other candidates to interview.'

Mary looked at me with open interest. 'She had lots of lovers?'

'According to David.'

'Really?' Her eyes flashed, she gave a sudden snort. 'Well, well! We all knew about the youth with the long hair – at least, we *assumed* he was the lover – but as for the rest . . . Mmm!' She widened her eyes in anticipation of disclosures to come. 'I must get David to tell me more.'

'He says he doesn't know any more. It was just a rumour.'

'A rumour. Ahh.' She looked away into the fire, then, trying to lift my mood: 'But they're satisfied now, the police?'

I considered this. 'You know something? I'm really not sure. I have this feeling that they'll come back.'

'Come back . . . But, Hugh, that's ridiculous – why should they?' Yet the question wasn't entirely rhetorical, there was curiosity behind it, and I realised that Mary, like the rest of my family, didn't seem to have ruled out the possibility that I had something to hide.

'I was going to ask *you* actually,' I said. 'Was I meant to be having an affair with Sylvie? Was the neighbourhood buzzing with it? If so I'd really like someone to tell me because I seem to be the last to know.'

'I've never heard anything.' But her tone was so hedged with reservations, her manner so strained, that I looked up sharply. Taking the opportunity with obvious relief, she said, 'Look, Hugh, I'd better tell you – it's just possible Mrs Perry may have told the police something.'

'Mrs *Perry*? But what?'

'That she saw your car outside Sylvie Mathieson's cottage. In fact . . . well' – she made a regretful face – 'we both did. I was driving her, you see. Her car had broken down, she hadn't been here for weeks, and the place was getting so dirty that I drove her here one day and picked her up again when she'd finished. And on the way back we saw your car . . .'

Something folded in me then, my defences evaporated, and all the accumulated tensions spilled out in a rush of dread. 'Oh God . . .'

Mary asked tentatively, 'You, er . . . didn't tell the police you'd been there?'

'No.' I clasped a hand over my eyes.

I heard her scramble to her feet. Crouching beside my chair, she gave me a rough comradely hug. 'Hugh, they can't make too much out of that.'

'No?' I exclaimed bitterly. 'They'll assume I've lied about everything, won't they?'

She sat back on her sturdy haunches. 'But an assumption? That's nothing, *nothing*.'

I looked into her strong irrepressible face, I saw the concern there, and the fierce loyalty, and I said,

'Mary . . . It wasn't the only thing I didn't tell them about.'

She said in a small voice, 'Oh dear.'

Neither of us spoke for a long moment, then she said almost gruffly, 'Do you want to tell me about it?'

Aware that I was taking a step whose consequences I hadn't begun to consider but not caring too much, I said weakly, 'It's a complete mess, Mary.'

'Hugh . . . don't be silly!' She grasped my shoulder and shook it, as if to imbue me with optimism. 'Wait . . .' Getting up, she replenished our glasses from the bottle on the mantel before pulling her chair closer and sitting down with a look of anxious concentration.

'I don't know where to start . . .'

But I did know. I knew exactly where I should start if I was going to make any sense of it. 'There was this dreadful week,' I began slowly. 'A nightmare week at the end of the most appalling month.' I paused. 'I think I cracked up a bit . . .' I thought about this. 'Yes – that was it, really. At the end of the day, Mary, I think I went off my head.'

Four

'DAVID CALLED it depression. He even pre-scribed me anti-depressants. Typical David! If only it'd been that simple. Pop the pills and lose your troubles! But it wasn't depression, you see. Not in the way he meant it anyway. It was sheer disbelief. Everything was going wrong and I couldn't seem to do anything to stop it. The business was in trouble and still sliding, the banks were moving in for their pound of flesh, and it suddenly hit me – I mean, quite suddenly, in the period of a day or so – that we were in real danger of losing the company. And then . . .' It was still mortifying to say it. 'Howard was going behind my back, setting up the takeover. It took me for ever to realise it. God, I was so slow! Good old Hugh – blind to the obvious!' My laugh sounded bitter to my ears.

'And then . . . things were difficult at home. Ginny thought – well, I don't know what she thought, that was half the trouble – but we started to disagree over nothing, everything. There was this awful *wall* between us. We couldn't seem to make contact. We seemed to wear each other down the whole time. And the money . . . She couldn't see how desperately we needed to cut down, she had this blind spot. She just . . .' But my words were stifled by the peculiar mixture of exasperation and guilt that Ginny always seemed to engender in me, and I returned to less confusing ground. 'You know the worst thing, though, about the company? The worst thing was knowing that it was my own stupidity, my own pig-headed bloody idiocy that had got us into trouble.'

'Come on – what about Howard?' Mary protested. 'It must have been his fault too.'

'Oh, Howard didn't know any better,' I exclaimed sweepingly. 'Howard was the ideas man, always had been, while my talent, such as it was, was for keeping us on the tracks financially. That was the theory anyway. But then I completely lost it! I let myself get seduced by ideas of easy money and limitless expansion. Pure conceit. I thought I knew best, you see! Prudence, restraint, all the things Pa had preached – well, they were just quaint and outdated, weren't they? Leverage was the name of the game. You borrowed up to the hilt, you traded right up to your limits.'

'But the board, the accountants,' Mary argued, 'they should have realised, surely?'

'They were under Howard's spell, just like the rest of us. And everything seemed to go so well at first, you see. Profits booming. Sales rocketing. Except for poor old Hartford, of course, which was left in the dumps.'

'So it all seemed hopeless?' she said, drawing me back to the story.

'Not immediately, no. For a long time I believed the situation could be salvaged. I worked like mad on the restructuring plan, I took a pay cut – half my salary. I really thought I could get it all together.'

'Then?'

'Then . . .' The memory caught me with fresh force. 'Then I realised what Howard was up to.'

I found out purely by chance. One day my driver was off sick and it was Howard's driver, Brian, who chauffeured me to our bankers for yet another fraught meeting on restructuring – a City euphemism for raising more money at heavy cost. I made some remark about the traffic and Brian launched into a stream of good-natured complaint about contraflows and road-works, and how it was getting increasingly difficult to outmanoeuvre them. Stafford last week had been a particular challenge; he told me, because an accident on the M6 had caused a ten-mile tailback.

I thought of reasons for Howard to go to Stafford, I came up with a few, all perfectly plausible, yet, even as I tried to talk myself into believing them, a single thought chimed insistently in my mind: that Cumberland had its headquarters in Stafford, along with three of its four factories.

Watching Brian in the rear-view mirror, I went through a show of searching my memory. 'Ah yes . . . that was Howard's meeting with – who was it?'

Brian was about to reply when his eyes jumped guiltily and there was an awkward pause before he mumbled something unconvincing about some lunch engagement Howard had had at a hotel whose name he couldn't recall. When he dropped me off he was still looking uneasy, and then I knew all I needed to know.

Over the years I had discovered that there were only two ways of approaching Howard on subjects he wasn't ready to discuss. One was to lift his mood with a joke; the other was to tackle him head-on, with something approaching aggression.

The next morning as soon as he was free I strode into his office and planted myself in front of his desk. I hadn't slept much the night before, my nerves were humming, and I could feel a pulse beating high in my head. Howard glanced up from some report and raised a lazy eyebrow.

'Tell me about Cumberland,' I said.

He sank back in his chair. He took his time. I could almost see his mind working. 'Cumberland?'

'You've had a meeting with them?'

'There's no need to get upset, Hugh,' he said smoothly. 'I was just opening out our options. The beginning of a contingency plan, if you like. Something to consider if the banks get threatening.'

A wild inarticulate anger rose over me, I had to clamp my lips together to stop them trembling. 'How could you?' I knew it was the wrong thing to say to Howard, for whom a moral stance was always a source of irritation, but I was beyond discretion.

'Look, it's no good taking an emotional line on this,' he intoned in his most infuriating way. 'That's been half our trouble, Hugh. No objectivity.'

I couldn't begin to work out what objectivity had to do with betrayal. I said unsteadily, 'Behind my *back*, Howard.'

'Don't be ridiculous!' he declared. 'It was just a preliminary chat to see how the ground lay. Nothing to get excited about. I was going to talk to you about it today. I mean, just *think* about it, Hugh,' he argued archly, 'I could hardly progress anything without you, could I?'

'And how *does* the ground lie, Howard?'

Reverting to old mannerisms, he gave a cat-like smile and dropped a half-wink in an expression that wouldn't have looked amiss on a used-car dealer. 'I tell you – they're rather hot for us! Oh, they're not letting on, of course, but they'd be mad not to progress the idea and they know it.'

'And what exactly is the idea, Howard? A takeover?'

He looked offended. 'God, no! A merger. A *merger*,' he repeated, as if I were incapable of taking it in first time. 'Integration of administration, distribution and sales. Big savings to be made, Hugh, big savings.'

'And where would Hartford fit into this?'

He tightened his lips and slowly shook his head as though I had conjured up this remark just to try him. 'Hartford is a great asset, Hugh. Nobody's going to throw it away, now are they?'

Staring at him, then, I wondered which of us had gone mad, whether he had always been like this or I was the one who had changed. It seemed incredible that we had ever worked happily together, or that I had ever trusted him.

But even then I hadn't really grasped the situation. 'No more clandestine meetings,' I warned him. 'No more going behind my back, Howard. No more going behind the board's back!'

The way his eyes slid away, the knowing look that drifted across his face told me the rest of the story.

'I *see*. How silly of me,' I said bitterly. 'You've been setting the scene for the board, have you?'

'Hugh, all this anger really doesn't help, you know. I do wish we could discuss this rationally.' He gave a small sigh and waited, as though a little sensible reflection would cause me to see the childishness of my ways.

'And your family?' I asked as levelly as possible.

'My family are all in favour of finding a happy conclusion.'

A suspicion leapt into my mind. 'And *my* family? Where do they stand?'

He spread his hands, the picture of baffled innocence. 'I wouldn't know. But presumably they're aware of how precarious the situation is? Presumably they've read the financial reports? I mean – I *presume*.'

He wanted me to see through him. He wanted me to think he'd already persuaded my family to vote for a takeover. He wanted me to think it, and, hating myself for being so easily manipulated, I did.

'Thanks for letting me know,' I said tightly.

Howard shook his head again and pulled himself indolently to his feet. He paused, running his hand down his tie as if to test its smoothness. 'Sometimes it's important to remember that there's no disgrace in making money, Hugh. No disgrace in cashing in one's hard-earned assets and reaping the rewards of success.'

'*Success?*' Sometimes Howard simply robbed me of speech.

'Success.' He lifted his head to the sound of it. 'You seem to have a problem with that, Hugh.'

'No, Howard, no. I don't have a problem with that.'

I stopped sleeping then. I spent hours staring into the darkness, burning with disbelief. The shock wasn't so much that Howard was prepared to sell the business out – he had absolutely no sentimentality where money was concerned – but that after all our years together he was prepared to treat me with such contempt.

In the next couple of days I embarked on a frantic damage limitation exercise. I phoned each of the board in turn, I threw together a paper listing the reasons a merger would be a bad idea, but of course Howard had been there ahead of me. He'd laid his ground very carefully. He'd already won them over.

'It was then I began to lose heart, Mary. Or to lose faith in myself, which probably amounted to the same thing. I began to question things I hadn't questioned in a long time. Wondering why on earth I'd been slaving away for most of my working life if it was to get stabbed in the back by my partner.'

Mary nodded ruefully at this. She never took exception to criticism of Howard; sometimes she actively endorsed it.

'I thought of all the years that had just vanished – just *gone*. I thought of the hours I'd worked, all the evenings and weekends I'd never got home, all the time I'd never found for Ginny . . .'

'She never seemed to mind too much.'

'Oh, she never complained. But it mattered. It mattered a lot. We were always in such a rush that in the end I think we simply forgot how to talk.' I grasped at a new realisation and floated it tentatively. 'Or we were frightened to talk. I think there may have been something of that too. We were frightened in case we had to face up to how . . . *wrong* things were. How very differently things had turned out from the way we'd expected.'

Mary leant forward and turned the fire down.

'And then . . . oh, it was everything, really. I began to think a lot about Pa. How much I missed the old devil – you know? And how little time I'd found for him towards the end.'

'Not your fault.'

'Oh, but I should have *made* time, Mary. You can always make time if you really try. I didn't try hard enough. I think I was ashamed. I didn't want to have to tell him how badly the business was doing. I didn't want to admit how everything he'd worked for was slipping away.' Halted by force of memory, I felt a fresh pull of affection and loss. The old man had maddened me sometimes, especially when I was a young man; he had been forceful and opinionated, he had been shamelessly paternalistic, particularly towards women, my mother included, but he had also been a spectacularly successful human being, full of warmth and feeling, and ingrained with a strong sense of duty and loyalty.

'So you were feeling pretty low?'

'Low? Yes – *low*. But you know something?'

Mary shook her head, and her sharp eyes did not leave my face.

'The idea of losing the business was terrible, of course it was, but I would have bounced back all right. I was stunned – yes, and angry, too – but it was more of a *reaction* than a state of mind. I hadn't really given up. I was just exhausted, utterly wiped out. All I needed, really, was some sleep and the chance to work things out. A bit of time, that was all.'

Mary read my expression and raised an eyebrow. 'But you didn't get it?'

'It wasn't Ginny's fault,' I insisted, betraying my guilts. 'People, fund-raising, parties . . . It was her whole life. I'd left her alone so much, what else did she have?'

Mary's face was still, deliberately so.

I continued to argue unhappily, 'What else did she have? No, whatever went wrong, Mary, it wasn't Ginny's fault.'

It was on the Friday at breakfast – the first breakfast we'd managed to have together in some time – that I realised what sort of a weekend lay ahead.

Ginny peered at me and exclaimed, 'Oh, such woe!'

I arranged my face into something more cheerful and mumbled about bankers giving us a hard time, and how life would be a lot easier without them.

When I picked up the newspaper she turned away to make the orange juice. The whir of the electric

110

squeezer rose to a sudden shriek. 'This thing's playing up,' she tutted. 'I might buy us one of those shiny steel things. You know, the smart Italian jobs that look like cappuccino machines.'

She poured the juice into a glass and wiped her slender fingers on a cloth. She stood in profile, the glossy fall of her hair tucked behind one ear, her features unreadable, and for an instant she seemed like a stranger, someone I had always known yet hardly knew at all. I looked away abruptly because the idea frightened me so much.

She put the juice on the counter and, sliding onto the stool opposite, flicked her hair back from her forehead with a characteristic sweep of her hand. 'I thought I'd leave about ten, as soon as the fish man delivers,' she announced in the light rapid tones she used to discuss arrangements. 'You did order enough wine, didn't you, darling? It's soup then fish then duck, remember.'

It came back to me then that we were having one of our social weekends in Wiltshire. Ginny always went down to Melton early to make sure everything was ready. 'How many people?' I asked, trying not to think of the expense.

'Twelve. And Cook thinks the pudding could do with some dessert wine. Is that all right, darling? I mean, I would organise it, but . . .' She gave a tiny shrug. She took a strange pride in boasting that she knew absolutely nothing about wine, except whether it was any good or not, which she could establish at the first sip.

Weekends at Melton followed a pattern. We gave

a dinner party on the Friday or Saturday with never less than four courses produced by a hired cook we referred to as Cook, and served by the male half of our housekeeping couple masquerading as a butler. On the Saturday we went to some sporting event with our house guests – usually racing or polo – and on whichever evening we were not entertaining we dined at another large house. On Sunday nights, if no guests were staying on, I caught up with some of my paperwork before getting up at five-thirty to drive to London.

'You'll be sitting next to Lady Werner,' Ginny informed me. 'She's on lots of boards and welfare organisations. Limps a bit, injured herself hunting years ago, still very horsy. They've got lots in training, Derby-winners and things . . .'

I tried to speak, but Ginny was at full gallop.

'. . . But she's a trustee of the family charitable trust, you see, along with Sir Frank – they run it together – and they give big donations . . . well, the trust does. We might get as much as fifty thousand for three years running. And they're awfully nice really—'

'Ginny—!' It came out more harshly than I meant it to.

Her eyes widened, her mouth twitched. 'What?'

I was going to bring up the subject of our expenses, but I faltered. I wasn't sure I could face the inevitable upset. I could never work out if Ginny believed against all the evidence that she was cutting back, or whether she was simply incapable of doing so, but whenever I mentioned the subject she grew so prickly and defensive that reasonable discussion became virtually impossible.

'Nothing,' I said hastily. 'Anything else I need to do for the weekend?'

'Absolutely not,' she declared with the touchy pride of a born organiser. Then, eyeing me: 'What on earth's the matter?'

'Just desperately tired, that's all.'

'I can never understand why you have to do it all. Why can't some of these people take the work off your hands?'

But I didn't have the energy to explain. 'They just can't.'

When she realised I wasn't going to elaborate she tightened her mouth and went to fetch fresh coffee. Returning, she rested her small chin on her hands and blinked rapidly, a sure sign that she was nervous of whatever she was about to say. 'By the way,' she began with studied casualness, 'Eddie Maynard's going off to that shooting school for a weekend course. He wanted to know if you were interested in going with him, but I said you were far too busy—'

'Ginny,' I said with more patience than I was feeling, 'it's not a matter of being too busy. I'm simply not interested in shooting, and that's all there is to it.'

'But you used to be.'

'No, Ginny. I may have said once—'

'More than once.'

'Only as a sort of joke,' I protested.

'I see,' she said in a small voice, as if I had altered my story simply to make her look foolish.

She had clung to this ridiculous hope that I would

113

take up shooting for some time; why, I could never fathom. I loathed guns and it saddened me to see wild ducks hanging in people's game larders.

'Having a place in the country doesn't mean we have to do what country people do.' I realised too late how critical this sounded.

'It's not that!' she protested, breathing fast. 'You seem to think I want you to take it up for some . . . some . . .' She agitated her hand. 'For some *snobbish* reason! I just thought how lovely it'd be for you to have an interest down there, something that'd give you a bit of exercise and fresh air. And you make it sound . . .' She was gasping for air now, wheezing from low in her chest. I fetched her inhaler from the basket in the corner of the kitchen. Grabbing it, she pulled two squirts into her lungs.

I dropped an arm lightly round her shoulders. 'Darling, I didn't mean it like that.'

'Oh, yes you did,' she cried between gulps.

'I just like to relax at Melton, that's all.'

She fought to speak. Eventually, after an agonising pull on her lungs, she managed to gasp, 'You really think other people's opinions are important to me! It's so insulting!'

I dropped wearily onto the stool next to her.

'That's what you think, isn't it?' she demanded.

What I really thought came to me with the clarity that only unhappiness can bring: that it was in Ginny's nature to strive for perfection, that she couldn't bear any area of our lives to fall short of some far-reaching ideal, and that, by setting herself such high standards, she doomed both of us to constant struggle. With this insight came another, equally clear: that I was deeply weary of this self-imposed burden, that I would gladly leave it all behind.

'I think it'd be nice to slow down a bit,' I said.

She cast me a guarded look. 'Slow down . . .? In what way?'

'Try not to do quite so much.'

'You mean – my charity work?'

'Of course not, no! I meant, see friends less often. Have more evenings to ourselves.'

She was fighting for breath again. 'But we don't see people *that* often! And you've always said you loved seeing them! And now suddenly . . .! You're being very confusing, Hugh. And very unfair!'

'It's partly the expense,' I said, grasping the nettle. 'We have to cut back.'

She cast me a look of quiet injury, as if I had broken all the rules of fair argument. 'I know that,' she said stiffly.

'Any joy with the accounts?' I tried to hit a light note, absolutely free of reproach.

She gave a long rasping cough and reached for her inhaler again. 'I've had a look through the bills, if that's what you mean.'

'You can see, then, that we're way over budget.'

'But we never had a budget, darling! You talk about this budget as if it was something passed at a board meeting.' Her eyes were exceptionally bright, close to anger or tears. 'I never knew anything about this budget until you invented it! You seem to think I've been spending money like water! D'you think I don't check the bills? D'you think I don't get the best prices?

And I can't just cancel dinners arranged *months* ago. It's taken me a *year* to get the Werners to dinner, a whole year!'

'All I'm saying is that we really must cut back.'

'You make it sound as though it's my fault—'

'No, no,' I said hastily. 'Of course it's not your fault . . .'

'Provence was your idea!'

This was old ground. 'Yes.'

'And Melton.'

I let that one pass; it simply wasn't worth arguing about. 'Melton *has* to go as quickly as possible,' I said.

'D'you think I don't know that?' she cried. 'I've been on to the estate agent every day! *Every* day!'

I remembered other things, the redecorating of the drawing room here at Glebe Place that appeared to be going ahead though I thought we'd agreed to cancel it, and the housekeeper in Provence who was meant to have left last month but still seemed to be in place, and I got that sick clammy feeling I always got when I realised that our spending was still way out of control.

'I'm doing all I can!' Ginny declared, sparking with reproach. 'You make it sound as though I'm trying to make things worse or something!'

'Of course I don't think that. I just—' But a futility blocked my words.

Ginny's mouth was buttoned down in that expression of hurt and abandonment I knew so well, and, with a swoop of defeat, I reached for her hand. 'Sorry, sorry . . .' I wondered how many times we said sorry to each other in the course of an average tiff, and

116

how little this immense weight of apology seemed to achieve.

'It's all right,' she said, with a glint of the uncertain humour she used to signal the end of our arguments. 'I'll cut down on the cat food and serve up leftovers and fire Consuela. And if all else fails I can always go on the streets.' She gave a brave little smile. 'Not past it yet.'

I took my cue. 'You can say that again. You'd make a fortune.'

As I put my arms round her I had the sensation of falling off the edge of my life and not being able to stop.

'Do you shoot?' asked Lady Werner.

'No, I'm afraid not.'

'Ride?'

'The last horse spotted my beginner's label at fifty yards and rubbed me off against a tree.'

Lady Werner had the generosity to laugh before turning to respond to the man on her right. It was a relief not to talk for a moment. I was finding conversation hard, partly because I'd drunk too much wine – I was making the most of the last of the good claret I'd laid down ten years ago – partly because my troubles kept blundering into the forefront of my mind, obstructing my words.

I stared dimly at the brilliant scene before me, at the banks of candles and flowers extending down the table, at the rich ruby glow of the wall hangings, at the blood-red and gold of the wine reflected off the

117

crystal; I saw Ginny at the far end of the table, her marble complexion and fine-etched beauty perfectly framed by the vibrant colours around her. I watched her tilt her head towards Werner and listen with rapt attention, and I felt disconnected from the scene, like an imposter in some exotic spectacle.

When the party moved to the drawing room for coffee, I slipped away upstairs and sat in the quiet of the bathroom, gripping my head in my hands, staring unseeing at the carpet. When a return could be avoided no longer, I splashed cold water over my face and made my way back downstairs.

Fortunately Werner wasn't a demanding conversationalist. I only had to slip in the occasional nod or comment to keep him going for half an hour on the subject of art sponsorship. Harder to stomach was a lawyer called Hodgworth-Hill, whose smooth overbearing manner and open contempt for what he called the common herd began to grate on my overstretched nerves. I wondered why Ginny had asked him; I couldn't imagine he was involved in charity work. Listening to his gabble I felt a sudden upsurge of resentment. I had the suspicion he would be the last of the dinner guests to leave and I was right.

'But he's staying,' Ginny declared when I caught her in the hall. 'I told you! Come and play backgammon!' she urged with feverish gaiety. 'Come on! We'll set up two boards!'

She pulled at my hand but I mumbled an excuse about needing to go upstairs for a minute.

Her return to the drawing room was greeted with a cheer. I heard the bombastic tones of the lawyer, followed by shouts of raucous laughter and the clink of glasses, and something overturned inside me. I stood there in the hall, trying to make sense of my raging thoughts, aware that I had reached some terrifying crisis but not absolutely sure what it was about, let alone how to contain it. I only knew that I couldn't face another moment among these people, that I had to get away.

Once the urge to flee overtook me, it became a desperate compulsion. I didn't stop to think where I would go or how long I would stay away, I didn't pause to consider Ginny, I only knew I had to escape. I raced upstairs and, throwing my evening clothes on the floor, pulled on some old jeans and a sweater. Pausing only to scribble a note to Ginny, I blundered out to my car and careered off.

It was madness to drive. I was way over the drink-driving limit, but the stupidity of what I was doing was lost in my greater panic and the need to feel that I was, in some muddled way, regaining a degree of control over my life.

I set out blindly, yet there was never any question of where I would go. Dittisham was the one place I could be alone, the one place where I would have a chance to think.

There was little traffic, the motorway was like a wide black tunnel, I had the sensation of flying. Somehow I stayed awake, miraculously I didn't kill anyone. Arriving at Dittisham in the dead of night, I wandered from room to room. I couldn't get over how quiet it was. The hush was miraculous, an all-enveloping cocoon of calm. It seemed to me that I had never really noticed it before, that my mind had been closed to such things for a long time.

Exhaustion made me maudlin. I felt a sudden longing for the past, for the simplicity and focus of my early life. I thought of my father and how much he had meant to me. I grasped at the more elusive memories of my mother, dead for more than twenty years, and thought how little I had really known her.

Eventually I climbed the stairs and, hesitating outside the guest room Ginny and I had always used when we came to stay, passed on down the passage to the small room that had been mine as a boy. It was a storage room now, stacked with trunks and tea chests, but an old metal bed still stood in one corner, and, perched on a rickety table next to it, a lamp from my Indian travels, crowned by a parchment shade. Beneath the bed were my watercolours, hundreds of them, bundled into cardboard folders, relics of the years when I'd had the ambition to paint. It was many years since I had attempted any sort of picture.

Opening the window, I lay down on the hard mattress under an ancient blanket. There was hardly any wind, just a faint movement in the air, but it must have been wafting from the river because I could hear the faint lapping of water. Stupefied by the memories of a thousand untroubled nights, I slept like a child.

'Nothing gentle about the way David woke me, of course. Rattled the bed head. He wasn't too pleased with me.'

'Well, we hadn't had the best of nights,' Mary commented drily. 'Ginny called at something like two, then again half an hour later, not to mention the calls the next morning. We told her you probably weren't answering the phone, but she wanted David to go and find you there and then, in the middle of the night.'

'I didn't hear the phone, I'm afraid.'

'Why should you?' For the first time it struck me that Mary actively disapproved of Ginny's permanent state of edgy anxiety.

'I didn't mean to worry Ginny.'

'David flatly refused, of course. To go out and look for you. Until the morning anyway.'

'I wasn't leaving her – it was nothing like that,' I said, seeking to justify myself further. 'I never stopped loving her . . .' But in saying this I was no longer sure what I meant by love, and whether it must always contain so much effort and pain. 'She worked so hard at everything, at making our lives . . . *full*.'

Mary studied her drink. 'But you had to get away,' she reminded me.

Defending Ginny was something of a reflex with me, but for once I let it pass. 'Yes, I had to get away.'

'We all need space from time to time.'

'Yes.'

But my response was too half-hearted for Mary. 'Nothing wrong in that,' she argued.

'No. You're right.'

She nodded firmly.

'So . . . There was poor David,' I said, finding my way back into the story. 'He made the mistake of asking me what the matter was – and got the lot. All my angst, yards of it. The business, Howard, Pa's death. And of course, me and Ginny . . . It just poured out, I'm afraid.'

'I hope he was sympathetic.'

'Well, you know how he is. Not his strongest suit. But on the whole – yes. Apart from the one subject that he really should have learnt to leave well alone by now. He kept on about fertility treatment and whether Ginny'd tried the latest method, whatever its name is. He'd sent us some information about it. He was convinced that not having children was at the root of our problems, and however much I told him that it wasn't an issue he just listened with that maddening all-knowing expression on his face. Sometimes I think he sees absolutely everything in medical terms, even relationships.'

Mary raised her eyebrows slightly at this, but made no comment. She never voiced any grumbles about her marriage, although among the family it had long been acknowledged that my brother wasn't the easiest of people to live with.

'Anyway, at the end of it all he declared that I was just depressed, and gave me some tablets. Typical David! Nothing that can't be fixed by getting dosed up! Oh, don't get me wrong – I didn't really expect any more. I mean, David has quite enough on his plate, doesn't he? People's troubles all day long. No, it was enough to have someone to talk to – that was all I needed really.'

I looked into the fire. 'But then, Mary, the strangest thing, the strangest thing . . .' I hunched forward as the memory gripped me. 'We went down to the river

– David wanted to look at the river wall or whatever it was that needed repairing – and I was rambling on about the past, about the summers we used to have, the golden times – I was still in a bit of a state, I can tell you – and, talking about those years, the best years, I thought of Sylvie. Nothing too surprising about that – we'd spent that long summer together, do you remember? The one when it was really scorching?'

'I remember.'

'But the thing was – just as she came into my mind, at the very instant I thought of her, I looked across the river and there she was! I thought I was dreaming. Well, I thought I was seeing things, actually. Then I thought it must be someone else who looked just like her. She was in a dinghy with a whole lot of other people, going up river. But that hair, the way she sat, her profile . . . David couldn't see the likeness, but for me it was blinding. I felt a great bolt of recognition and – well, I'm not sure what. Hope? Something like that. I couldn't get her out of my mind. I was overwhelmed . . . bewitched. I had the strangest feeling – this sounds mad – that everything would be all right if I could get to see her again, that she would be able to *save* me in some way. Crazy! *Crazy!* But you have to remember I wasn't thinking straight. I still hadn't had much sleep – what time did David come over that morning? Seven? Eight? So, four hours at the most. I wasn't sure what was real any more. I told myself my mind was playing tricks. But somewhere deep down there was this tiny irrational ray of hope that it *was* her. Part of me was desperate for some sort of escape, I suppose, and Sylvie represented something precious and beautiful. She was my Avalon; or the *idea* of her . . . I'd been so happy with her, you see. I'd felt so full of – *possibilities*. It was the only time in my life that I'd felt free.' The wind roared outside, the house creaked like an old ship. I looked up. 'I don't know – is this making any sense?'

She gave a slight nod, though her eyes seemed to have taken on a harsher, more judgmental light.

'By the time I went out to *Ellie Miller* that afternoon, I'd persuaded myself it was a hallucination. I'd slept a bit by then, I'd come down to earth with a bang, I was feeling bloody awful, in fact—'

'What were you doing on *Ellie*?'

'Oh, checking her over, pumping the bilges. David asked me to go out, to save him a trip. I was glad, actually. It gave me a reason to stay down. I couldn't have gone back to Melton. I couldn't have faced anybody just then.'

'No.'

'But Mary, I'd forgotten how utterly glorious the river could be. It was a perfect day, quiet, warm, no one about. It was so peaceful! So I stayed on board for a while, sitting there on the mooring, drinking Pa's whisky, thinking things through. Mentally, it was rather a toss-up between shooting myself and dying of sheer love of life. I was a bit emotional, to say the least.'

Sitting there on the boat I had remembered all the good times I'd had when I was young, the trips with

Pa on *Ellie Miller*, the passages up the coast, the expeditions ashore; the excitement of the night watches, the running jokes we'd enjoyed, the long companionable silences.

It was on one of these trips in my late teens that my father had confided in me about his early life, about his strained relationship with his own father, the lack of communication and affection, and how he had strived to succeed because he'd felt it was the only way to win his father's approval. He wanted it to be different for me. He wanted me to succeed for my own sake, and because I loved the business.

There had been a time when I'd resented his blithe assumption that I would follow him into the business. At seventeen I'd made up my mind to become a designer, which was the closest I could get to being an artist and still get paid. My father hadn't tried to talk me out of it exactly, but he'd got various family friends and godparents to point out some of the disadvantages. I hadn't improved my chances by failing to get in to the first two art colleges I'd tried. And when I was offered a place at Oxford to read languages, I began to recognise the inevitability of what lay ahead. My father was characteristically generous, sending me round the world in my gap year, funding all my travel in the vacations. After that I felt it would have been ungrateful not to give the business a try.

I hadn't regretted my choice, only my failure to make a success of it.

I missed my father. No one tells you how to grieve properly, how much pain to expect, how much guilt and anger, and whether it's normal to have long periods when you feel nothing at all. In the months since his death, my grief had seemed both inadequate and incomplete.

Going to the chart table, I lifted the lid and found his job list lying on the top of the charts where he had always kept it. I picked it up with gentle hands and laid it on the table. Seeing the elegant hand-writing made shaky by age, the neat columns of jobs with all but three systematically crossed off, I wept for him at last.

'And then . . .' The picture burned brightly in my mind. 'Sylvie appeared. I heard this knocking on the hull and I went up on deck but I couldn't see any-thing. No boat, nothing. Then the knocking came again and I went to the stern and there she was in the water. Well, I couldn't believe my eyes. I just stared at her. Then she laughed at me, and, Mary, it was like a dream only *more* so. You see, she hadn't changed. She was just the same. It was as though . . . as though *nothing* had changed.'

My throat was dry, I coughed, and Mary passed me the last of her whisky.

Gulping it, I echoed, 'She was just the same.' I saw her standing in the cabin, with that dramatic colour-ing she had inherited from her French mother, the long black hair sticking wetly to her shoulders, and the white translucent skin touched with faint freckles; and I could only wonder again at the smoothness of her skin, the way it was completely untouched by time, as if she'd skipped all the intervening years and lived no other life.

'I pulled her out of the water and she scolded me for letting her stand there and shiver. I just laughed because she was talking to me as if we'd last seen each other a few hours ago. That was her gift . . .' I reached for a thought I had never fully identified before. 'Her gift was for *intimacy*. She could make you feel you were the only person in the world, or at least the only person she really cared about. She made you feel that being with her was everything, that there couldn't be anything more important or more exciting. That suddenly everything was possible. And I needed that, Mary! I needed to feel . . . well, that I could have some sort of life away from all the pressure, the endless succession of disasters. That I could forget – for a while anyway – and be . . .' I gave an ironic gasp. 'Be *free*.'

I heard Sylvie's voice again, that extraordinary rich voice of hers that could communicate so many different, often contradictory, messages. She was sitting in the saloon, wrapped in the only towel I could find and an old waterproof jacket of Pa's, a whisky in her hand, with her head tilted to one side, chin tucked in or suddenly thrown up in that French way of hers. Only her gaze was unwavering, her almond eyes fixed on mine with a glittering absorption, as if no time had intervened and we had never stopped being soul-mates. She told me about her new life, the pottery shop in Dartmouth where she was working, the cottage she was renting just outside Dittisham. She loved it here, she told me. Her return was a spiritual thing, she needed to be in touch with elemental things, with water and wind and creativity. She was going to start sculpting. Near water she felt empowered, she could draw on wells of creativity, she felt supremely in touch with her body and her spiritual energies.

No one I knew talked in this way. Among my contemporaries this would have been dismissed as New Age psycho-babble, yet Sylvie imbued it with a sort of grandeur, and an earthiness too. There was an undercurrent of self-indulgence there, a strong hint of physicality and hedonism. But then even at fifteen Sylvie had exuded a powerful animal sensuality, a breathtaking sexual assurance, which, with her flamboyant defiance for convention, had produced an overwhelming effect on the rather staid young man I had been when we'd met.

The effect she had on me as we sat in the boat drinking whisky sixteen years later wasn't terribly different. I laughed too much and too quickly, I heard myself trying to impress and amuse her, I felt a ridiculous effervescent pleasure. With a sense of the miraculous, I felt myself come alive again.

When she got up to leave she rested the back of her hand against my face, and gave that little cat-grin of hers, all enchantment and promise.

Mary clasped her hands under her chin. 'Then?' She was urging me forward, and I realised how late it must be.

'Then?' I sighed. 'Well, I had to see her again. In

fact, I couldn't think of much else. It was a desperate thing – a sort of compulsion. I couldn't get her out of my mind. It was . . .' But the memory caught at me, and stalled my thoughts.

After a while Mary said softly, 'You had an affair?'

Distracted, I stared into the fire, I shook my head in lingering disbelief. 'For a long time nothing happened. I thought she was just wary of involvement, I thought it was her conscience. That she was bothered by me being married. Quite funny, really, in retrospect.' My smile emerged as a bleak grimace. 'By the time I realised she had no conscience whatsoever, it was too late. I was completely hooked. I'd completely lost my judgment. And she used that, she used *me*.' Saying it, I felt a fresh plunge of humiliation. 'She led me a complete dance. That's exactly what it was – a dance!'

Mary said something which I missed, and she had to repeat it. 'Did you see her last weekend?' Her voice had a sudden tension to it.

'No.' Then, as I absorbed the implications of what she had said, I stared at her. '*No*, Mary, I did not.'

Mary said rapidly, as if to get it over and done with, 'You weren't on the boat with her?'

'No.'

She cast me an odd look, as though something about this disturbed her.

'*Mary.*'

'I only meant that it wouldn't have looked too good if you had been,' she explained in a rush. 'That was all.'

'I did not see her last weekend,' I repeated forcefully.

She nodded but her eyes still held a spark of doubt.

'I hadn't seen her for two weeks!'

She held up a defensive hand. 'Hugh, I believe you. Really. *Really*.'

The ringing of the phone cut into the unhappy pause that followed.

It was Tingwall. 'Look,' he said, 'I didn't want to bother you so late, but I thought you'd better know that I've had a call from the press.'

'Christ. What did they want?'

'I think I've quashed any ideas they might have had. Told them you and your wife were just possible witnesses because you lived on the river. That sort of thing.'

'Did they buy it?'

'One can but hope.'

Five

GINNY APPEARED on the landing above, a wraith against the sunlit window. 'You're back,' she declared, sounding agitated. She touched an anxious hand to her uncombed hair, then to the fastening of her wrap. 'What's the time? I fell asleep.'

'It's about four. Are you all right?' And asking this, I wasn't sure what sort of response to expect. Even at the best of times I found it difficult to gauge Ginny's mood.

'It was flu after all,' she said matter-of-factly, 'but I think I'm over the worst of it now. And you? No more from the police?'

'No.'

'Well,' she breathed, 'that's something. And me? Do I still have to . . .?'

'Tingwall's arranged for you to go to Chelsea police station on Monday, if that's all right. They'll only need a brief statement.'

She nodded solemnly.

Turning towards the bedroom, she paused for long enough to catch my eye and issue a silent but unequivocal plea. The moment of account was not to be delayed, I realised, and climbing the stairs I attempted to prepare myself for whatever was to come, wrath or recrimination.

She was smoothing the bed. 'I'm sorry about what I said on the phone,' she announced immediately, and there was a note of rehearsal in her voice. 'I didn't mean to be unhelpful.'

'No . . . I wasn't too helpful myself.'

'I just wanted to know what the police thought they were up to, that was all. I was worried.' She was on the point of saying more but, ducking her eyes, sat down abruptly at her dressing table and began to brush her hair with sharp strokes that made it crackle.

I asked, 'Do you want to talk about it now?'

She twisted round and said, 'Please,' as though we had plucked this subject out of the air.

I sat on the edge of the bed. 'Well . . . They knew Sylvie had dropped in to see me on the boat a couple of times. This was ages ago, June some time. I'd already told them that. And I'd told them I'd bumped into her by the ferry once. But for some reason – and I've no idea what – they came down on me like a ton of bricks. The full treatment.' I gave a shuddering laugh. 'They have this way of making you feel they're not going to believe a word you say. Scary. *Terrifying*. Anyway, they were extremely keen to know where I was when Sylvie was killed. Luckily, I could account for most of that Saturday – David saw me in Dartmouth hunting for food and then you arrived and then David popped in later . . . So, one way and another, there wasn't time for me to have been anywhere else.'

She absorbed this with stern concentration. 'And

you've no idea what it was that made them pick on you?'

I shook my head.

'But there was *something*?'

'Possibly – presumably . . .'

'And they didn't tell you what?'

'No.'

She gave an anxious laugh which hid none of her curiosity. 'But what reason could they have had for dragging you all the way down there again?'

'Ginny, I don't know.'

She searched my face for the lie, and I met her gaze as best I could.

She looked away. 'What else did they want to know?'

'Oh, you can imagine. How well I knew Sylvie, that sort of thing.'

'And they were happy with . . . what you said?'

I shrugged. 'They had to be, didn't they?'

She drew a ragged breath. 'How could they do it anyway – drag you off like that? Did they have the right?'

'I'm not sure, darling. But it would have looked strange if I'd refused, wouldn't it?'

She considered this. 'Yes, I suppose it would.' She twisted the hairbrush in her lap, her delicate features etched with unease. 'And you don't know what it was that made them want to see you again?'

'No.'

She made an attempt to smile. 'But you must have some idea.'

Here it was again, the inability to let go, the

133

constant chafing. 'I really don't know, Ginny. But they must have thought I was having an affair with Sylvie, mustn't they? If I was meant to have killed her I would hardly have done it without a reason, and that's the obvious one, isn't it?'

I could hear the sound of her breathing, the rasping that preceded an attack, and I wondered how long it would be before she reached for the inhaler.

'And you've no idea what made them think . . .?'

It wasn't a challenge this time, more a craving for reassurance. So I denied it again, because it was far too late to do anything else.

Conflicting emotions passed across Ginny's face, then with a jerky movement she put the hairbrush back in its place on the dressing table. 'Well, at least they've got it straight at last!' she said, striking a bright nervy note. 'We can begin to forget the whole wretched business.'

She was waiting for me to agree; she wanted to hear me say that I was putting everything to do with Sylvie behind me.

'Let's hope so.'

She shot me a sharp look.

'It's the press,' I explained. 'They seem to have heard about my visit to the police. And we all know what they're like. Given half a chance, they'll blow it up out of all proportion. That'd be all I need, with the buyout coming together.'

She was blinking rapidly, pulling hard on her lungs. 'But how did the press hear about it?'

'Who knows? These things get out, don't they?' And for no apparent reason I thought of Howard.

Her forehead wrinkled into a rare frown, and I noticed how strained she was looking, and how dark were the shadows around her eyes. 'What happened? Did they phone?'

'They called Tingwall. He seems to think he's palmed them off all right.'

She shook her head. 'It's not so easy to palm them off! They have a way of coming back. We should make a plan.'

Ginny's mother had been a famous beauty who'd led what in charitable terms might be described as an eventful life, with three husbands, numerous lovers, and an unwavering talent for attracting scandal. After a childhood in the spotlight, Ginny had good reason to consider herself something of an expert on the press.

'The thing is . . .' she murmured, thinking her way through it. 'You must be sure to speak to them if they call. Be completely open. Utterly polite and terribly nice. Even jokey. Mummy always said that you could get away with murder if you made the press laugh.' She looked at me with her great fluid eyes, the irony of what she had said completely lost on her, or calmly unacknowledged.

'I'm not sure I'm quite up to cracking jokes, Ginny.'

'Be jolly, then. Carefree. If they catch the slightest hint of panic around you, they'll be back for more, like jackals.'

This was what I always forgot, her astuteness, her talent for reading situations.

'It's terribly important to appear friendly,' she

stressed. 'You can be rather cool, you know. I've heard you with journalists. You can sound rather offhand.'

'Can I? I hadn't realised. Well, I'll do my best.' I picked up her inhaler from the bedside table and took it across to her.

'Tone makes all the difference . . .' But she could hardly say it, she was so short of breath.

She took the inhaler from my hand, drew on it greedily and gave two or three harsh coughs. From the gardens below came the sound of children playing and the wail of an electric lawn mower. I kept forgetting it was Saturday.

After a while I asked, 'All right?'

She nodded impatiently. She never liked to talk about her asthma. 'Oh, Julia came by with a stack of papers for you. I put them in the study.'

'Thanks.'

She twisted round on the stool and examined her face in the mirror. 'Will you have time for dinner?' Above the breathlessness her voice was still taut.

'Of course. I'll make time.'

'I thought we'd have something silly, like eggs and baked beans.' She reached for her face cream and I saw that her hand was trembling.

I felt a surge of remorse. 'Ginny—'

'It's all right!@' she declared, smearing the cream fiercely over her cheeks, 'I'm not going to ask if you had an affair! I assure you – I don't want to know!' Abandoning her face abruptly, she clamped her hands together on the surface of the table and stared down at them. She whispered, 'But I would like to know if you loved her.'

I stared at her dumbly in the glass.

'And don't lie, please,' she added, her voice rising sharply. 'I couldn't bear it.'

'I didn't love her,' I said.

She looked up and our eyes met in the mirror. I saw hope in her face, and wretchedness.

'I didn't love her,' I repeated.

She searched my expression, then, gasping, looked down and nodded rapidly.

'It was—'

'No! Don't say any more!' She fumbled for the cream again. 'Don't!'

I felt a familiar gust of helplessness and uncertainty. Did she mean it? Sometimes her most effusive denials turned out to be cries for reassurance which, despite the absence of firm clues, I was meant to decipher and assuage. I was still searching for the right thing to say when she glanced up and said briskly, 'I'll see you later then. You really don't mind eggs and baked beans?'

Relief made me smile stupidly. 'Can't think of anything better.'

She nodded again, and returned to her makeup.

I leant down and kissed the top of her head. When I looked up again she had averted her eyes.

With the paperwork was a note from Julia. 'I can't find that petrol receipt,' she wrote. 'I don't think you ever gave it to me. It's no great problem. I can get the details from MasterCard and/or the service station, but I just thought I'd mention it, in case you had it lying around.'

I looked in the compartment of my wallet where I usually put receipts and credit card counterfoils before handing them over to Julia at the end of each week. The petrol receipt wasn't there, nor the credit card voucher. I remembered handing my card to the cashier at the service station, I remembered signing the slip, but the rest of the exchange, like the drive itself, was a blur. I had spent the journey trying not to think about Sylvie but thinking, in the end, of little else. All sorts of fantasies had crowded my brain: I imagined her waiting for me at Dittisham, I heard the phone ringing as I walked in, or if these were too much to hope for, I saw myself finding a note, telling me where to find her. They were desperate impossible fantasies, born of obsession. I knew full well that there would be no sign of her, that as usual she would be doing her best to avoid me, and that if I was to have any chance of seeing her I would have to go and search for her myself.

Nearing Dittisham I persuaded myself that I would be able to exercise some self-control, that I would have the strength of will to maintain some dignity and stay away from her, yet I knew perfectly well that I would go and look for her. I was incapable of stopping myself. The urge to see her was like a craving. I was consumed by the need to know what had gone wrong, why she had so brutally cut me out of her life. I was desperate to retrieve what she had so tantalisingly proffered and so abruptly snatched away; I wanted the euphoria again, the surge of long-forgotten emotions, the sensation of being completely and spectacularly alive. I knew our affair was over, yet I couldn't accept it. I needed to know if she'd intended to humiliate me, if she'd meant to set me up quite so effortlessly: I needed to know just how thoroughly I'd been deceived.

Approaching Dittisham, I went through a pantomime of normality. I avoided Sylvie's cottage and drove straight to the house. I forced myself to go inside and turn on the water heater, to pour myself a drink and sit by the window as if I intended to have a quiet evening. I even convinced myself that I would be satisfied by going upstairs to David's old bedroom and focusing my specially purchased binoculars on the stretch of river just beyond the ferry where the white yacht with the bowsprit lay at her mooring. But the stillness of the scene, the complete absence of life on board were both a torment and a challenge. It was then that I gave up all pretence of self-possession and drove off in search of her.

I had spent an hour on some amended cash flow projections when Ginny buzzed through to say that David was on the line.

'We're just on our way out,' he declared, ever swift to establish that his time was limited. 'Wanted to let you know what we've decided for the buyout. It'll be fifty thousand. Can't do more, I'm afraid.'

Overcoming my disappointment, I said, 'David – thank you.'

'The thing is, we've tied up quite a bit in this trust

for the children. And the terms of the trust – you know, we're simply not allowed to invest in anything risky.'

'I understand.'

'Well, there we are.'

'You won't regret it.'

'I should hope not!' And his tone wasn't entirely facetious.

'Thanks again for yesterday.'

'Mmm?' he murmured distractedly, and I could hear the sound of turning pages as his attention wandered.

'For coming to the police station.'

'Oh, that reminds me,' he drawled. 'Mary heard something on the lawyers' scandal-vine this morning – you know how she is for having her ear to the ground. She was going to call you. She didn't get a name,' he said, meandering towards the point, 'but she heard that someone got hauled in for questioning late last night.'

'But who? Does she know?'

'I told you, she didn't get the details,' he said in his busy voice, the one he used to presage the end of his conversations. 'But I told you it would be all right, didn't I?' David's confidence had a certain steamroller quality to it, a momentum that did not allow for dissent.

'Yes, I suppose—'

'Got to rush.'

'David, I can't thank you enough for putting your faith in the buyout—'

'Not a bit,' he cut in and, with a grunt that might have been a goodbye, he rang off.

I brooded for a long time, wondering who Henderson might have hauled in for questioning. The unprepossessing long-haired youth perhaps? The owner of the white cutter? Or another of this tribe of lovers that Sylvie was meant to have had?

She was all over the place. David's words still reverberated in my mind. I had always known that Sylvie lived by her own rules, that her addiction to the sensual took her beyond normal limits, but I had pushed the obvious consequences of this thought from my mind. During our affair I had not dared to face the idea that I was sharing her with someone else. I had been too frightened of the emotions that such a suspicion might unleash in me.

The wail of a siren sounded from the direction of the King's Road. Gazing out into the dark gardens, beyond the tracery of branches to the lights of the neighbouring houses, I felt immensely glad that it was all over, that I had recovered most of my sanity and equilibrium. I had not liked myself very much while I was in thrall to Sylvie, I had not enjoyed being in a state of misery and abject longing; most of all, I had disliked being at the mercy of emotions that were so intense, obsessive and ultimately demeaning.

The siren echoed in the distance. Returning to the present with a sense of relief, I pulled out a sheet of paper and set down the figures that were already written large in my head. A shortfall of a hundred thousand from David; one million more to be found on the total price tag of the company. Against this I might be able to raise five hundred thousand on this house and Zircon might come up with two hundred and fifty thousand. I didn't need to be an Einstein to see I was still short by three hundred and fifty thousand.

I didn't blame David for reducing his investment. The takeover had brought him some shares in Cumberland and a little cash, but the total was less than a third of what he could have expected a few years back if we'd sold HartWell at the height of its fortunes. And for all I knew he and Mary might need cash for other things: they might be planning early retirement, they could even be up to their ears in debt. David might have been my brother, but so far as his financial affairs went I hardly knew him at all.

Given enough sweat and tears, I could probably raise the extra money from the Chartered Bank, but I was loathe to go back to them cap in hand unless absolutely necessary. At best it would look as though George and I had failed to do our homework properly, at worst we would simply appear incompetent. Then there was the time element. Renegotiations could take weeks and I suspected that Cumberland would use the time to solicit a better offer from elsewhere and announce a tight cut-off date for final bids. When I really wanted to frighten myself I imagined that the juicy offer was already on the table and that Howard had planted his million-pound bombshell to raise the stakes, and, accidentally or otherwise, jeopardise our chances of success.

Three hundred and fifty thousand. It shouldn't be too hard to find, so long as nothing happened to rock

142

the boat. I tried not to think of the press and the positive storm they could raise without uttering a single word of libel.

I scribbled a line through my calculations and threw them into the bin. I heard Ginny approaching to summon me to supper, and an absurd bubble of contentment rose up in me at the thought of baked beans at the kitchen table with my wife.

'Everything went into the wash.' Already Ginny's expression was taking on the defensive look she acquired whenever she thought she might have done the wrong thing. We were in the dressing room, standing in front of the open wardrobe.

'What about the beige cords?'

'They went to the cleaners.'

'And you didn't happen to notice anything in the pockets?'

'No.' She said it a little too quickly, and I guessed she hadn't looked. 'Was it something vital?' she asked.

I shrugged, 'Not really,' and began to get undressed.

'What was it?'

'Just a receipt.'

'What for?'

'Oh – petrol, that's all.'

'But you have to find it?'

She had sensed something. It was ridiculous not to tell her. 'The police want to have a look at it. To establish what time I was on the motorway last Saturday.'

This seemed to confuse her. 'On Saturday?' She half turned towards the wardrobe as though to start undressing, only to turn back with a frown. '*Saturday*? And it's important, the time you got the petrol?'

'The police think so.' I threw my socks into the basket and reached for a robe. 'I told them I arrived at Dittisham shortly after seven, but they weren't inclined to believe me, not without some backup anyway. Not the most trusting of souls.'

'And it's *lost*, this receipt!'

'Oh, it doesn't matter. It's not essential.' I explained how the information could be tracked down through the credit card company.

But something was still disturbing her. 'What will it tell them, the receipt?'

'Tell them? That I was somewhere near Bristol at five-thirty that afternoon. Well, I *think* it was five-thirty, but I'm not so sure now. I wish I hadn't said five-thirty, in fact, in case I was wrong.'

'Could you be wrong?'

'Who knows? It wouldn't be the end of the world anyway.'

'You say that! But supposing it was earlier? Could it have been earlier?'

'Well, maybe half an hour or so – not a lot.'

She was looking appalled.

'Ginny!' I laughed, putting an arm around her shoulders. 'It's all right, really.'

But she wasn't so easily pacified. 'You *say* that . . .'

'I *know* it.'

She cried, 'You can't *know*.'

'You worry too much.' I drew her into an embrace

and rested my cheek against the richness of her hair. Her stiff body seemed to tremble in my arms, like a frail storm-tossed bird.

I began to rock her slightly and to murmur soft reassurances, as I had always done in times of stress or reconciliation. Her body did not yield.

I whispered, 'It's so good to be home, Ginny. You can't imagine.' I meant, good to be home with just the two of us and no hordes to be wined and dined, though I didn't say that.

Eventually I pulled back a little and, cupping a hand under her chin, leant down to kiss her.

She didn't retreat, but she didn't kiss me back either.

I didn't blame her, I didn't expect instant absolution, but I did need to know that forgiveness wasn't a total impossibility either.

'Ginny,' I whispered awkwardly. 'Darling . . . if I caused you any grief then I'm—'

She gave a small cry and wrenched herself free. For a moment she agitated a hand at me, unable to speak. 'Not now,' she gulped, her eyes brimming. 'I can't deal with that *now*!' She turned and hurried into the bedroom.

'Ginny!'

But something prevented me from pursuing her, futility or weariness. Retreating to a hot bath, I stayed in it for a long time. I comforted myself with thoughts of a not-too-distant time when life would be more settled, when memories of this summer would have faded and Ginny and I would be established not too far from Hartford, in a country house that might look something like David's, with land and gardens and an interior with enough potential to stimulate Ginny's designer instincts, a time when we would have adjusted our lives to an altogether gentler pace and in some as yet unidentifiable way moved our relationship forward, into calmer waters.

It was after midnight when I finally went into the bedroom. The lights were off but I knew Ginny wasn't asleep. Going softly round to her side of the bed, I leant down and kissed her head.

Her eyes glittered up at me.

I said, 'Do you want me to sleep in the other room?'

'I'd prefer it if you didn't.'

My heart lifted. 'Then I'll stay.'

'I don't want to be alone.' It was a statement delivered without emotion.

I thought of all the weekends when I had left her to go down to Dittisham. 'No.'

'I don't think I could bear to be alone again.'

Was this the bargain then? A commitment to curtail my freedom?

I steeled myself to say, 'I'll never leave you alone again, I promise.'

'That would mean so much. If you could manage it.' There was no irony in her voice.

A little later, as I was beginning to doze off, she propped herself up on one elbow, and without switching on the light, shook a tablet from a bottle and washed it down with water. When she settled down again her foot touched my leg and she did not move it away.

*

It was a good twenty years since, as a fresh-faced graduate with more confidence than sense, I had undertaken my sales training under Ronald Simms and got my first inkling of what it was like at the sharp end of the business. Ronald Simms was a representative of the old school. He worked his patch to a hallowed schedule, he knew the names of the buyers' children and the ailments of their wives, he wore white shirts with starched collars which did permanent battle with his Adam's apple, and he called me Mr Hugh, just as he called my father Mr Richard.

Sitting in the lounge of the Churchill Hotel with the Packenhams buyer I was reminded of the time Ronald and I had been preparing to pitch a difficult sale. 'You remember what I told you?' he'd remarked. 'That with the Hartford name there's no such thing as a cold sale? Well, that doesn't stop some sales from being a bit chillier than others.'

This sale was definitely on the chilly side. Miss Stevens, who with her doll face and timid posture appeared a disconcerting twenty though she must have been a good eight to ten years older, had been the Packenhams china and glass buyer for two years, and was showing no chinks in her considerable armour. She had de-listed Hartford Crystal five months ago because we had given Harrods a better price, and since walking into the lounge and offering me her limp handshake she had made it plain that she wasn't about to relent.

'Miss Stevens, I can only say I'm horrified by what happened. I can assure you quite categorically that it's never been our policy to discriminate. I can only imagine it was an appalling error on the part of the sales people. The only thing I can do is to offer you my sincere apologies. And my personal guarantee that it will never happen again.'

Her unyielding look said: It's a little too late for that now.

'All I can tell you is that things are going to be different at Hartford once the buyout goes through. We're putting everything we have into it – financially, I mean, as well as blood, sweat and tears – and we wouldn't be doing that unless we believed one hundred per cent in the product. You see, we feel we have something really special in Hartford crystal. We feel—' I broke off as another of Ronald's maxims came back to rap me over the knuckles: Don't tell them what to think, tell them what's new. 'What's new,' I said, 'is that Hartford will be run by the people on the spot, the people who know the business backwards. And I can honestly say that we're going to make a damned sight better job of it.'

Behind Miss Stevens' spectacles something stirred, though it was hard to tell what sort of emotion it might be. 'It wouldn't be hard to make a better job of it,' she commented in her wispy voice.

'But, Miss Stevens, however successful we are – and we *are* going to be successful – none of it'll be any good if Hartford crystal isn't on sale in Packenhams—'

My mobile phone sent up a warble from my briefcase. 'I'm so sorry,' I said rapidly. 'Only my secretary has this number and she wouldn't call me unless it was extremely urgent.'

Miss Stevens looked at her watch as she reached for her coffee.

I snatched up the phone and growled, 'Yes?'

'*Sorry*,' Julia hissed, 'but there's a photographer snooping around outside the office and your wife just called to say there're a couple at Glebe Place too. Thought you ought to be warned.'

'Hell.'

Above the coffee cup Miss Stevens' eyes, enlarged by her lenses, watched me speculatively.

'Have they phoned, the press?'

'No.'

'Well, let me know if they do. And don't say a word to anyone about this, will you?'

'Of course not,' she said indignantly. 'Oh, and George called to say he thinks he can raise another forty-five thousand.'

I dropped the phone into my case. 'I'm so sorry about that. It was, umm . . . urgent.' For an instant I imagined that the photographers had followed me here, that they were waiting for me to leave the hotel. 'So . . . I was saying that . . .' I groped for my thread. 'Our plans . . . Yes, we're going to advertise in the colour supplements over the three weeks leading up to Christmas, and what we'd really like to do is mount a special spring promotion with Packenhams.' I brought out a folder and passed it across to her. 'It's all in here.'

Miss Stevens slid her cup onto the table and sat forward, preparing to leave.

'Look,' I said hastily, 'I very much want you to change your mind about us, Miss Stevens. I'm not sure how I can achieve that, but – well, I'm going to keep trying!'

'Mr Wellesley, I'll consider your proposals. That's all I can say.' Her little-girl voice reminded me more than ever of a shop girl fresh out of school. Standing up, she smoothed the skirt of her bad suit. She hesitated before announcing, 'My father risked our home for his business.'

I didn't say anything.

'He lost both the house and the business.'

'I'm sorry.'

'So were we.'

'Miss Stevens – we're not going to fail.'

She eyed me appraisingly. 'No,' she said, 'I don't suppose you are.' And in the moment before she turned away she gave me a look that wasn't entirely unsympathetic.

'They're standing right outside the door,' Ginny told me. Her voice faded and crackled in the earpiece as my cab swung along the Bayswater Road. '. . . Photographers and a reporter.'

'How many?'

'Three of them. I have to go out in a minute. But I know what I'm going to say to them.'

'Ginny . . .' I didn't want her to realise how appalled I was. 'Wouldn't it be better to say nothing?'

'Don't worry – it won't be much.'

I felt powerless. 'Well, be careful, for God's sake.'

'I will.' She sounded listless, or depressed; it was hard to tell with such a bad connection.

'How are you feeling?'

'Me? Umm . . .' She took her time. 'Oh, all right.'

'What about the doctor?'

'That's where I'm going, to see him.'

'Let me know what he says, won't you?'

'Yes.'

'Don't let him give you any old thing.'

'No.'

She had slept most of the day before. When she'd finally got up we had spent the time like two battle-weary warriors home from the fray. After the tensions of the previous night we'd kept a respectful distance, speaking little and with caution. Over an early supper we had discussed the sale of Melton and its contents, and I had drawn some comfort from the prosaicness of our conversation. Later we'd watched television in bed and as we'd fallen asleep Ginny had made no objection when I'd slid an arm loosely round her waist.

I said, 'You haven't been to the police station then?'

'I didn't feel well enough.'

'No, of course not. I left a message for Tingwall, to warn him you might not be up to it. He'll square it with the people at Exeter.'

'While you're on,' she said. 'The petrol receipt, have you . . .?'

'Julia's still chasing it. But it'll be fine, really.' A roaring came over the ether as though we were entering a tunnel. 'Take care,' I shouted. 'And do watch out for those people.' I had a vision of the photographers pushing their lenses into Ginny's face.

151

'Don't worry.' Her voice was breaking up badly, but I thought she said, 'I'm used to them, remember.'

Nearing the office I peered over the cabbie's shoulder, but there were no photographers outside the building and no one loitering in the entrance. I strode inside with an itchy feeling between my shoulder blades and a powerful urge to look behind me.

Julia told me the photographer had abandoned his vigil twenty minutes before.

'And it was definitely me he was looking for?' I asked, knowing the answer.

She put the messages in front of me and nodded. 'He tried to get information from the security man. Wanted to know if you'd been in today.'

I tried to shrug if off, I tried to tell myself that they would lose interest quickly enough, but all the time a small doom-laden voice wondered why they should come now, when the police had finished with me.

Julia waited for me to read the messages. 'Oh, that petrol receipt?' she said. 'I got the MasterCard details. It was the Gordano service station on the M5. Just past Bristol. And the time – you've no idea what I had to go through to get this, I had to bribe the station manager to sort through all his till rolls! Anyway, it was four-fifteen.'

I felt a pull of apprehension. 'Are you sure?'

'Yes.' But giving me the benefit of the doubt she hurried into her office and came back with her notebook. 'Here we are.' She showed me the entry. 'Four-fifteen.'

I'd been miles out then. I had told Henderson five-thirty to six. What on earth had made me say that? I realised that, far from leaving the office at three, I must have left long before, maybe as early as two. I had been in such a state of confusion that afternoon that anything was possible.

I could see now that it had been a mistake to commit myself to such a firm guess. Being half an hour out might have looked understandable, but a whole hour was going to seem careless. Yet it was the easiest thing in the world to make a mistake about the time. Well, I hoped that was how the police would view it anyway. Suddenly I needed reassurance. I was about to call Tingwall when Julia buzzed through to tell me Mary was on the line.

'Hang on,' called Mary the moment I greeted her. In the background I could hear the squawky voices of cartoon characters on the television, then, rising above the sound, Mary yelling good-naturedly to someone to turn the thing down.

'Henry's home with flu,' she complained cheerfully. 'If it's not one thing it's another. Listen, did you speak to David? Did he call you?'

'Yes. Look, I'm really very grateful for your support.'

'But it's only fifty thousand.'

'Whatever you feel comfortable with is fine with me.'

'Well, it's not fine with me,' she declared in the crisp authoritative tones she'd retained from her legal days. 'I'd like to put in some of my own money.'

'Mary, that's sweet of you, but I couldn't accept it.'

'Why not?'

'Because . . . I wouldn't feel happy.'

'Why wouldn't you feel happy? It's my money. Nothing to do with David. Oh, I'll tell him, if that's what you're worried about – though I very much hope it isn't!'

I knew Mary had money of her own; quite apart from the HartWell shares which she and Howard had inherited from their father, they had also been left antiques and silver and cash, though I'd never been clear on how much was involved, nor the extent to which Mary's capital had been merged with David's or tied up in the children's trusts.

She asked, 'How much do you need?'

I laughed, 'Mary, you don't want to ask!'

'I am asking!'

I laughed again. 'Okay . . . As of today we're still short by three hundred and five thousand. Assuming Cumberland agrees the valuation.'

'Can't manage all of that, but you can count me in for a hundred thousand.'

'*Mary.*'

'Actually on second thoughts I might not tell David. What do you think? No, no . . . I'll have to, won't I?' She sighed, an overblown sound made for effect. 'He won't like it, will he? You know how he is – caution, caution. Never backed a horse in his life.'

'Mary, I don't know what to say.'

'Don't say anything, then. Oh!' She gasped. 'One person who must never find out – Howard!'

'There's no risk of that, Mary. We're not exactly speaking.'

'You'll keep it totally anonymous? Just you, me and David?'

'Of course.'

'Well, there we are then!'

'Mary, you're amazing.'

'Since you mention it . . .' And she gave a gravelly laugh.

'You don't want time to think about it?'

'I've done my thinking. And my thinking says you're going to make me rich.'

'Mary, I'll certainly do my best.'

She gave a hum of amusement and we said goodbye.

I sat in a state of barely controlled elation, knowing that there was still some way to go, that I mustn't on any account think of celebrating, but feeling too optimistic and too starved of good fortune not to do so.

Julia came in and, catching my mood, demanded, 'The good news?'

'Only two hundred and five thousand to go!'

Julia thrust a fist into the air, and performed a curious shimmy with her hips.

Pushing thoughts of the press to the back of my mind, I rang Hartford to tell George, then spent the rest of the afternoon calculating the revised figures for Zircon, which Julia typed and sent off by special messenger, and arranging the necessary meetings for the rest of the week. There were three sets of documents to be finalised urgently: the company articles for the new firm, Hartford Crystal Ltd; the Shareholders' Agreement with Zircon; and the agreement for the new company to purchase the assets, trading names and working capital of the old Hartford Division. I wanted everything ready for signature before the end of the week, in case Howard pulled a fast one. It was an ambitious schedule, but not an impossible one.

At five, lifted by the satisfactions of the day, I said to Julia, 'You know something? I'm beginning to think we're making some progress.' I was too superstitious to talk about success.

'I keep telling you – the light at the end of the tunnel isn't always an approaching train.'

I had been trying Ginny all afternoon and getting the answering machine. Now the line was engaged. I hoped the doctor had given her some vitamins. It was a long time since I had seen her so low, though I hardly needed reminding that much of the responsibility for that lay at my door. I hated the idea of having made her unhappy, yet it seemed to me that unhappiness had been creeping up on us for a long time, and that without it I would almost certainly have resisted the final slide into betrayal.

There are a dozen ways to block out unhappiness. Ginny and I had chosen work, as much as we could fit into a single day, so that we never had time to question the purpose of it all.

I knew the structure of Ginny's days, where she went, who she saw; I knew about the committee meetings, the working lunches, the hours on the phone, the shopping; but I had never known if these activities were a real source of contentment to her. She had always taken her duties seriously, the duties of keeping house – the food on the table, the flowers and decorations, the supervision of the diary – and the duties of her charity work, which she undertook with immense conscientiousness; but did she feel a sense of achievement at the end of it all? She never expressed any views one way or the other. She seemed to distrust discussions of happiness, as though such scrutiny would tempt fate and undermine whatever joys she did possess.

I was packing my briefcase when Julia buzzed through to say that Tingwall was on the line.

'I was going to call you,' I said immediately, and started to tell him about the petrol receipt.

'Perhaps we can leave that for another time,' he interrupted. 'I have bad news, I'm afraid. The police want you to come in again, and this time it'll be as a suspect. They've served a number of search warrants on us.'

My heart thumped once against my chest. 'What do you mean?'

'They've obtained warrants to search Dittisham House, and the *Ellie Miller*, and to remove your car.'

The room seemed to sway, I felt the blood drain from my head. 'You're joking!' I could hardly get the words out. 'You're bloody joking!'

'They'll arrest you on suspicion as a formality. But please remember it's not the same as being charged.'

'Christ . . . *Christ* . . .' I found my way onto my chair. 'Why? *Why?*'

'They don't have to tell us, I'm afraid. And we have no way of finding out.'

'But there must be some reason!'

'In so far as the police have to show the magistrate good cause before he'll sign the warrants – yes, there must be. Magistrates do vary, of course, some let things through on a nod, but on the whole . . .'

My disbelief was overtaken by the painful realisation that, like it or not, I had to deal with this nightmare which had so suddenly and firmly attached itself to me. 'The boat, you say? And the car?'

'I've arranged for your brother to hand over the keys to Dittisham House and the boat. They've got your car.'

It took me a moment to grasp what he was saying. 'They've got it?'

'They're at your house. I said you'd surrender to them there. I thought you might find it more convenient.'

'They're there *now*?'

'Yes. And Mr Wellesley? I need hardly tell you not to say anything until you get to Exeter. I'll see you there.'

'Charles?'

'Yes?'

It hit me suddenly, the enormity of what lay ahead, and my throat swelled, I felt a surge of panic and self-pity. 'This whole thing is ridiculous!'

'I'm sure.'

'They're quite wrong.'

A slight pause. 'We'll sort it out.'

'They're wrong.' I heard the entreaty in my voice, and the desperation.

'Just remember not to say anything on the way down. All right?'

I blurted something to an astonished Julia before walking blindly down to the street and hailing a cab. The driver set off at a fair lick and as we sped towards Chelsea I had the sensation that everything in my life was moving too fast, like a film run at double speed. I tried to prepare myself for what was to come but my mind was all over the place, caught between despair, reason and a growing panic. Sporadically I tried to reach Ginny on the mobile but the line was always engaged.

I'd forgotten the photographers. As we entered Glebe Place I saw them clustered around the gate. Thrusting money at the cabbie, I walked through their clicking lenses, not looking at them but not hiding my head either.

Ginny must have been watching for me because she opened the door as I approached.

Phipps and Reith were standing behind her in the hall.

Ginny whispered, 'They have a warrant.'

Reith stepped forward and delivered in a dull monotone, 'Hugh William Wellesley, I am arresting you on suspicion of the murder of Sylvie Anne Mathieson—'

I began to shake my head.

'—You do not have to say anything. But it may harm your defence if you do not mention when questioned something which you later rely on in court. Anything you do say may be given in evidence. Do you understand?'

My brain responded, but it took a little longer for my lips to obey. 'I understand.'

Ginny said, 'I would like to accompany my husband to Devon. I hope that'll be acceptable.'

Reith exchanged a look with Phipps. 'If you wish, ma'am.'

'And my husband will need a few minutes to wash and collect a change of clothes.'

Reith looked uncertain, but he must have decided I wasn't suicide material because he nodded abruptly and stood back to let me pass.

Ginny followed me upstairs to the bedroom and closed the door rapidly. 'What have they found out?' she breathed.

'Do you think I know? Do you think they called and told me?' Hearing the childishness in my voice, I groaned, 'Sorry. *Sorry.*'

'Hugh – we've got to think this through.'

'There's nothing to think through! There's nothing we can do!' I was choking with frustration. 'This time it'll be all over the papers – you realise that? Over everything. Christ!'

Ginny gripped my forearm. 'Hugh – we must think!' she gasped. 'We must think!' And her voice was trembling. 'Listen – what did you tell the police? No, no,' she corrected herself with an impatient wave of both hands. 'No – what I mean is, was Sylvie ever in the car with you?'

I didn't understand what she was getting at. 'I think . . . once.' I went through the exercise of sifting my memory, though I knew perfectly well I wasn't mistaken. 'Yes. Once.'

'Did you tell the police that?'

I looked at Ginny and suddenly I began to understand. 'Oh God.'

'And the house? Did you say she'd been there?'

I shook my head miserably.

'Tell me what you did say, tell me!' And she was alive with a furious energy.

'It's not so much what I did say, it's what I didn't say. When they asked me when and where I'd seen her, I just didn't mention the house. Or the car.'

Ginny closed her eyes for a moment as if to absorb the full impact of what I was saying. 'And she *touched* things at the house?'

'What?'

'Doors. Glasses – I don't know, I don't know. *Things.*'

I saw Sylvie watching me over the rim of her glass, I saw her holding a cup of coffee. 'Yes, she touched things.'

There was a silence like darkness. Ginny took a sudden breath and seemed to speak by sheer force of will. 'They'll know then.'

I sat on the bed and leant forward with my head in my hands. 'Oh, Ginny . . . I'm so sorry. I'm so sorry.'

'No, no!' she cried. 'Listen!' She sat beside me and pulled my hands away from my face and shook my shoulder until I looked at her. 'I'll say that *I* invited her to the house.'

'What?'

She nodded sharply. 'I'll say you introduced us, and I saw her in the village and invited her for coffee. I'll say it was just at the end of August. I'll say you

were out on the boat, getting it ready for the weekend—'

'Ginny, *Ginny* . . .' My heart squeezed with gratitude, she meant so well. 'But darling, they'll want
exact dates, times. It simply wouldn't work. If – no,
when they found out you weren't there – it would
only make things worse.'

She clamped her lips together, she intertwined her
long nervous fingers, she gave a small ironic laugh.
'But I *was* there that weekend, you see.' She took a
breath halfway between a rasp and a sob. 'And I did
see her. I saw her at the house.'

I could only stare at her.

'I didn't go to Provence,' she explained. 'I drove
down to find you.'

I looked into her face, I saw the slight shame there,
and the hurt, and knew it was true. 'Oh, Ginny.'

She was straining to breathe but when I tried to
fetch her inhaler she grasped my arm and held me
back. 'I saw you go to the boat too. I saw you sailing
off. But Hugh, I wasn't the only one. Someone else
saw you go – someone at the inn – and they told
David, and David asked me if it had been me on
board, and I told him it was. I said it was me!' As if
to impress this on me, she shook my arm again. 'And
then Mary asked me as well, and I told her. I told her
it was me. So that's what we've got to stick to, Hugh,'
she urged through the labouring of her lungs, 'that's
what we must swear to! We must say that it was *me*.'

I felt an inner crumbling, a sudden loss of will.
The idea of committing myself to more lies was bad
enough, but to try and carry off such fragile deceits

seemed utterly futile. 'It's no good, Ginny. It's no good.'

'What do you mean?' And her grasp was very tight.

'They'll find out. Honestly, Ginny, it'll only make things worse.'

'No!' Her vehemence took me by surprise. '*No! What are you thinking of! What are you thinking of!*' She was trembling again.

'It'll be better to tell the truth. They'll find out anyway!' And the thought sent me into a new chasm of despair.

'You can't! You can't!' She knelt in front of me and clasped my face in her hands so that I was forced to look into the fierceness of her eyes. 'Think of *me*, Hugh! Think of *me!*'

The tears sparkled angrily in her eyes, she cried for breath. Hurriedly I fetched her inhaler. As she pulled the drug into her lungs her gaze didn't leave my face.

'Ginny, I'm sorry,' I said wearily. 'I'm so very sorry.'

'Don't be sorry,' she gasped angrily, 'be brave! Be *brave!* For me, Hugh. *Please.* Do it for *me!*'

Six

I'VE FORGOTTEN what excuse I found for going back to Dittisham that first time. To sort out attics, to do some work on the boat. It didn't matter, really, because Ginny soon got the message that I wanted to be on my own. Coming on top of my late-night flight from the house party, this did little to ease the tension between us. Ginny wanted explanations and reassurances which I could not give her, while I dreamed of solitude and peace of mind, longings which I dared not voice for fear of making things worse.

We were meant to be having dinner with some friends from New York on the Friday, and Sunday lunch with neighbours, but I said I couldn't face people, which was true, and suggested Ginny go without me, which I knew full well she would never do.

I had a conscience about that, but it got lost in the desperation to get away. That week I had been on a two-day whistle-stop to some of our major customers in France and Belgium, I had been fighting the banks tooth and claw on a daily basis to extend our loan arrangements, and at an acrimonious meeting the HartWell board had outvoted me and passed Howard's motion to open formal merger discussions

164

with Cumberland. By Friday I was drained of small talk, I was incapable of putting on a front for other people and pretending that things were just fine. Things were far from fine, and I knew that the greatest crisis of all was in myself.

Sylvie had been drifting through my mind ever since the swimming incident two weeks before, yet I told myself I wasn't going back to Dittisham to see her. I told myself I was going back to Dittisham to sort myself out, which contained more than enough truth to placate my conscience.

I reached the house after midnight on Friday and slept through until six, which in those insomniac times was something of a record. Then, seized with the fierce energy that exhaustion brings, I drove into town and took the ferry to Kingswear and, parking up on the cliffs, walked the coastal path until my legs ached. On the way back I took a detour into Brixham and, finding a dingy cafe near the harbour, devoured a plate of limp bacon and crusty eggs, washed down with bitter tea.

On returning to the house I made a half-hearted attempt to sort through Pa's books, but restlessness soon had me wandering aimlessly from window to window and back again. Eventually I put the books to one side and walked down the garden to the edge of the water. Down river, beyond the ferry, I could see the old-fashioned cutter with the bowsprit that Sylvie'd told me she and her friends took out most weekends. This Saturday the boat floated at its moorings, devoid of life.

I sat on the bank, watching the tide creeping in

and the gulls squabbling in the sky above *Ellie Miller* and the scurrying ferry as it carried the hikers and holiday-makers across to Greenway. I stayed for almost an hour, finally trudging back up the hill when heavy clouds covered the sun. Approaching the house I heard the phone ringing, but something prevented me from hurrying to answer it and by the time I got inside it had stopped.

Still unable to settle, I went into town again and drove the streets until I found the pottery shop where Sylvie worked. It was a small place squeezed into a row of handicraft shops in a narrow street near the harbour. Brightly coloured pots and bowls lined the shelves that straddled the window. Through the open door I could make out a fiftyish woman in an ethnic dress sitting by the till, reading a newspaper. She seemed to be alone. I drove on to the supermarket, roaming desultorily among the shelves, buying whisky, milk and breakfast cereal, before ending up in a pub and passing an unsatisfactory twenty minutes with a beer and a solid meat pie.

As soon as I got back to the house I went upstairs to David's old room and looked down river.

The cutter had gone.

I felt a ridiculous sense of aggrievement, as if I had been unfairly excluded. I searched the house for binoculars and, finding none, strode down to the water's edge to take another look. There was no doubt: the cutter had gone, leaving a squat wooden dinghy at her mooring.

My resentment burned on childishly. When I made sense of this absurd emotion, I realised it was based on envy, a naive and sentimental longing to be part of Sylvie's adventure, to sail off to God knows where, as we had done in the languorous days of that endless summer long ago, to some quiet cove maybe, or France, or nowhere very much at all. I yearned for the simplicity of those days, when we were faced by nothing more challenging than a trick at the tiller or a change of sail. Most of all perhaps, I yearned for the love and laughter we had shared, and which seemed to have faded inexorably from my life.

I had told Ginny I would be back by the following evening but I found reasons to put off my departure. Sorting Pa's books took a lot longer than I'd thought – or I made sure it did – then I persuaded myself that I needed to get out to *Ellie Miller* and pump her bilges. In the soft summer afternoon I collected oars and rowlocks from the garage and walked through the village to the quay.

I found the dinghy underneath two others in a stack of tenders jostling for space on the end of the ferry pontoon. Setting out, I didn't take my usual route to *Ellie*, which was to run parallel to the mud flats until the river widened a little and I could cross where the current was weakest, but rowed straight into the ebbing tide which would carry me close by the cutter's mooring. When I reached the mooring, there was nothing to see, of course, just the buoy and a battered plywood dinghy with badly chipped gunwales and a gash down one side.

Ellie had quite a bit of water in her, so I guessed David hadn't been aboard for a while. Once I had pumped her dry I looked around for other jobs to do:

anything to delay my return. I pottered about for an hour or so, running the engine, doing odd bits of maintenance; and all the time I was keeping an eye out for the cutter's return.

Closing the engine compartment, on the point of packing up and going home, I looked out through the main hatch and saw the top of a mast in movement. I climbed up the companionway for a better view, and there was the white cutter, coming up to her mooring. I counted four people on board. Even at that distance Sylvie's slim figure was unmistakable.

It was then that I should have understood the nature of my secret hopes for Sylvie. My agitation should have warned me, and the unwarranted hostility I felt at the sight of the two men in the group, one of whom I immediately cast as Sylvie's lover.

The four were in a hurry to get ashore. If they had a mainsail cover they didn't put it on, and they forgot to tighten the halyards, let alone tie them off to the shrouds. As they pulled the dinghy alongside and started to load it, Sylvie stood in the cockpit, hands on hips, and I had the idea she was arguing with one of the men, a tall figure with bushy fair hair. The second man, a wiry figure with dark shoulder-length hair, got into the dinghy and took the bags handed down by the other woman.

I reached into the companionway for the binoculars. By the time I had focused on Sylvie, she had moved to the side deck. If she wasn't arguing with the fair-haired man then she was putting her message over pretty forcefully, weaving expansive gestures in the air, and I almost laughed to watch her, her body was so expressive. The fair-haired man seemed to make a point of turning his back on her before climbing down into the dinghy. Finally, after another exchange of words, Sylvie chucked a dismissive hand in the air and, with apparent bad grace, joined her companions in the dinghy.

Up until that moment I might still have held back, I might have persuaded myself to keep my distance, but as the fair-haired man rowed the dinghy towards the quay Sylvie twisted in her seat and, in a pose that would have looked utterly affected if it hadn't been so typical of her, thrust a hand into the water and, turning her head as if to watch the ripples, let her cheek fall against her shoulder.

Quite suddenly I felt sure she was looking at me. It was as though she had known from the beginning that I was there and had expressly engineered this scene for our benefit.

I lifted my hand and waved to her, and though I couldn't be absolutely sure it seemed to me that she returned my smile before turning back to her companions. This small inconsequential smile rapidly took on a mammoth significance in my mind. My pulse quickened, I felt a foolish excitement. It was then that I knew I must see her again.

By the time I reached the quay she and her friends had disappeared. I hurried back to the house and, sitting at Pa's desk, spent half an hour composing a note. I would love to see her again, I wrote; our meeting on the boat had been all too brief, I would be down the next weekend, would she be interested in going for a sail . . .

In my new mood of calculation I realised it would be better to meet on the boat where there was no danger of David or Mary walking in on us, where the exigencies of finding crew members often threw the unlikeliest of people together. Even then I recognised that any relationship I might have with Sylvie, however innocent, would need to be discreet. Sylvie carried her sexuality too blatantly for anyone to believe she was capable of anything so casual as friendship. Even at fifteen, her style, her indifference to opinion, had attracted misunderstanding and gossip.

I found an envelope and, sealing the note, drove into town and posted it through the pottery shop's door before heading back to London.

The week brought a succession of crisis meetings. Galvanised by inflammatory talk of imminent financial disaster from Howard the board voted to rush the takeover proposal straight to the shareholders, which was little more than a formality when half the shareholders sat on the board, and the rest were married or related to them.

Facing almost certain defeat, I functioned in a schizophrenic state of acceptance and despair. I threw myself at problems, as if by sheer force of effort I might find some miraculous solution to HartWell's difficulties. I rarely got home before ten and then it was only to work until late in the night. Conversations with Ginny seemed to be confined to the subjects of meals, transport and laundry.

I tried not to think about the weekend, yet the idea

of seeing Sylvie glittered quietly in the back of my mind like a distant beacon across a dark sea.

By Friday what I had discounted as unshakeable tiredness had turned into the first flutterings of fever. That didn't stop me from driving down to Dittisham, of course. I told Ginny I needed to work away from the telephone.

There was no message from Sylvie at the house, no answering note on the mat.

I had a bad night, sweating heavily and periodically kicking the covers off, only to wake cold and shivering a short time later. I came to at nine the next morning, my mouth parched and my forehead burning. I found some aspirin in a medicine cabinet and took a couple. Then I dragged a duvet and pillow down to Pa's study, and, pulling the sofa in front of the open windows, lay propped up against the arm so that I could see down the length of the garden to the river. Armed with a jug of water and a book, I dozed sporadically.

I woke to see a figure standing in the window. It was Sylvie.

You're ill, she said with a small sniff.

You don't sound very sympathetic, I smiled.

No, I'm not, she declared, because it means we won't be able to go sailing and the weather's perfect.

You would have come? It was the foolish question of an anxious lover.

She gave that laughing shrug of hers. Yes, why not?

I offered: I might be well enough by tomorrow.

But that prospect didn't seem to interest her.

I couldn't stop looking at her. I had forgotten the way her hair clouded out from her head and fell softly to her shoulders. I had forgotten the fullness of her lips and the way she pushed them forward whenever she finished speaking, so that every statement, however mundane, seemed to contain an invitation.

Next weekend, I said. Let's make it next weekend.

She lit a cigarette and sniffed again. Leaning back against the window frame, she gave me a sideways look, her almond eyes slanted like a cat's. Can we go to France? she said.

France? I repeated stupidly.

She was serious. She was waiting for my answer.

Well, I said hurriedly, it would be great, of course it would, but the boat's not really in commission. And I'm not sure I am, either. I mean, I haven't been sailing for a long time.

Her fluid lips had taken on a brooding look. It would be so nice, she said. And she gave the 'nice' an enticing quality.

My heart pulled with long-forgotten excitement. I knew I would agree. The thought of leaving my muddled life behind for a couple of days was irresistible.

I don't know, I said, putting up a last pretence of reluctance. I could ask the yard to look at the boat, I suppose. They could probably get her ready in time.

Her smile seemed to say: You see how easy it could be.

I hope you can navigate, I said, only half joking.

Sylvie frowned. Don't you have GPS?

It's installed, yes.

She flashed her eyes at me. Well, then.

I don't know how to work it, I admitted.

But *I* do, she said.

I shook my head and laughed. Can you organise the food? I asked.

She repeated with mock horror: Food? as though she never deigned to touch the stuff.

I laughed again because her ploy was so outrageously transparent and because I was soaring with a feverish elation.

Where would we go? I asked.

She drew on her cigarette and blew out a long plume of smoke. Cherbourg.

Cherbourg? I said. But it's always so crowded.

She looked away. Oh, there's a good restaurant there. And I want to buy some shoes.

Shoes!

She gave another sniff. Yes, shoes. And now it was her turn to laugh.

I tried not to remember how easy it was to get to Cherbourg but how very hard it was to sail back against the prevailing winds.

We could leave on Friday? she asked.

We'd have to, I said, to be sure of getting back on Sunday.

That's good, she said.

We wouldn't have very long in Cherbourg.

Who cares? It'll be wonderful! And she gave a low chuckle, a mischievous smile.

I looked at that smile and suddenly my desire for her expanded into something so intense that it seemed to grip my heart, to rob me of breath. But if in that moment my longing sharpened into something

173

more passionate, it also darkened into something more possessive. Even then, before our affair had begun, I was haunted by the thought that she would leave me.

Tell me what you've been doing all these years, I asked her.

She waved her cigarette dismissively in the air.

I pressed her: No, really – where have you been? What have you been doing?

The past, she shrugged. It's over. There's nothing to tell.

Come on, Sylvie, I remonstrated lightly.

But she wouldn't tell me, not much anyway. All she would say was that there had been good times and bad times. She had travelled a bit – she tilted an upturned hand towards what might have been far-off places – then she had lived in Paris, then the Midi. Then . . . She shrugged. Really, she said, the past is past. The important thing is that I'm here and I'm going to do my sculpture and I feel so happy and free. She repeated: So happy and free! And languidly, in a gesture that contained an element of self-parody, she laughingly raised her arms as if to embrace the sun.

I had no reason to think that this lazy extravagant rapture was anything but an expression of genuine pleasure. I did not glimpse the determination in her eyes, nor the singlemindedness.

She turned back to me. You look bad, she said.

Thanks for your encouragement, I laughed.

Isn't anyone looking after you? she asked in mock surprise.

No one knows I'm here.

She came closer and peered at me. Have you taken anything? she said. I have this herbal stuff that cleanses the bloodstream.

Anything that does things for my bloodstream must be good, I said.

Shall I bring some food, too?

I thought you refused to have anything to do with food.

Ha, ha, she said. But you're sick, aren't you?

And that's different?

That means I'll take pity on you. She poured me a glass of water as if to prove it. Coughing suddenly, she pulled out a handkerchief and blew her nose.

You don't sound so good yourself, I said.

She brushed this thought aside with a flip of one hand.

Will you eat with me? I asked.

Her lips formed an arch of uncertainty, her shoulders rose slightly, not so much a shrug as a granting of possibilities. What would you like to eat? she asked.

I'm not too hungry at the moment.

But you will be later. She was already moving towards the windows.

Will I?

Oh, I think so, she said, and there was a subtle but deliberate duality in her voice that made me laugh again.

Grinning back, she fluttered her fingers in farewell and was gone.

When will you be back? I called after her, suspecting, quite rightly, that I would get no reply.

I dozed again, but fitfully. My sleep was disturbed by a recurring dream in which I was waiting endlessly for Sylvie aboard *Ellie Miller*, only to look up and see her on the white cutter, sailing away with her friends. In the way of such dreams I opened my mouth to yell to her but no sound came.

The telephone woke me and took me unsteadily across to the desk. It was Ginny, wanting to know if I was all right. I told her I had flu and would be heading back at around noon the next day. If I hadn't been feeling so rough I would have remembered that mention of flu was bound to be a mistake. Ginny would fret, she would urge me to hire a driver to take me home, and, though she wouldn't mean to, she would be unable to leave the subject alone and then, despite my best intentions, I would become brusque and impatient until, finally, we both retreated, bruised and hurt.

But you can't drive with flu, she said.

I'll be all right by tomorrow.

But have you still got a temperature?

No, it's gone. I'm sure it's gone.

But Hugh, you mustn't even *think* of driving while you've got a fever.

I really do think it's gone.

But you must be very weak.

Honestly, darling—

A movement caught my eye and I looked round to see Sylvie moving silently into the room with a bag of shopping under one arm.

176

She put a finger against her lips, making conspirators of us both, and I felt a lurch of guilty excitement.

Really, I'll be fine, I said to Ginny as I watched Sylvie disappear in the direction of the kitchen. If not, I'll catch a train.

Promise?

Feeling a twinge of remorse, I said: I promise. And it didn't make me feel any better to know that remorse alone wouldn't stop me from going to France with Sylvie the next weekend.

Ashamed of my capacity for duplicity but unable, it seemed, to suppress it, I did not interrupt Ginny's repeated expressions of concern, I took time to reassure her. Yet the moment I had put the phone down I pushed thoughts of loyalty and conscience to the back of my mind and hurried towards the kitchen, my heart beating absurdly.

Sylvie was standing by the kettle, waiting for it to boil.

It tastes disgusting, she said.

What does?

What I'm going to give you.

I creased my nose. I'm not very brave, I said.

I think you talk nonsense. And she used that tone of intimacy again, the one that suggested we might still be lovers.

Do I have to? I said.

Things that are good for you are always hard to swallow.

Always? I said, assuming a roguish expression. Oh, I do hope not!

I thought I was so witty, I thought I was so dazzling. But that was the effect she had on me; she made me feel attractive and clever again, and in restoring my self-esteem gave me a new sense of my own possibilities.

I inspected the meal she had brought. A tin of soup, a tin of sardines, a few tomatoes, a couple of bread rolls, two apples.

A banquet, I said facetiously.

She lit a cigarette and held it between thumb and forefinger, like a screen gangster. I didn't have any money, she said.

You should have told me!

She smiled her cat-smile. Why? Would you have given me some?

I cast my eyes heavenwards in mock despair.

Are you nice and rich? she asked, and, being Sylvie, it was a direct question.

Rich is a relative word, I said. But I've got enough to take us to France at any rate, and give us a good meal when we get there.

She considered this with the pretence of gravity, and gave a characteristic sniff. Well, it's a start, she said. And she tilted me an expression of mock disdain.

A start? I said, thrilling to this game of words. A start of what? A start to where?

But she turned away as the kettle boiled and, pouring some hot water into a mug, stirred in some grey powder. She lifted the potion to her nose and pulled down her mouth in a show of disgust before handing it to me.

That bad? I said.

Let's see just how brave you are, she said, and her eyes issued all sorts of challenges.

The liquid was far too hot and, putting the mug to one side, I held her gaze for a long moment before stepping into the space that separated us and, reaching slowly up, rested the back of my hand against the softness of her cheek. Her eyes, which seemed at a distance to be almost black, glittered with a fierce amber light, and when I began to move the back of my fingers against her skin her lids drooped in bliss, like a basking cat.

I ran my palm down her hair and onto her neck and she let her head fall back as if to open herself up to me.

It was she who heard the sound first. She straightened her head and her eyes flashed a warning. Then I heard it too, the crunch of a car on the gravel.

I made a face and, leaving Sylvie where she was, crossed to the hall window to see David getting out of his car. I went back to alert Sylvie, but there was no sign of her in the kitchen and it wasn't until I had looked into the study and the garden that I realised she had vanished.

David wasn't too thrilled to see me, especially when I told him I'd been ill, because then he felt duty-bound to do doctorly things like taking my temperature and pulse. If he thought it strange that I should have come down on my own without telling him or Mary, then he didn't comment on it. He had come to check the house and didn't stay long. As soon as he had gone I went out into the garden and called Sylvie's name but, though I waited hopefully, she did not return.

I called the boat yard first thing on Monday morning and they promised to go and inspect *Ellie Miller* within the hour. I should have remembered that for boat yards time is an elastic concept. When I chased them up on Wednesday they'd only just decided that *Ellie*'s fastenings looked a bit dodgy around the stem and she'd need to come out of the water for a week while they fixed them. I questioned the need for such drastic work, but I was only making noises to vent my disappointment. I had learnt enough from my father to know that fastenings were serious, and that you didn't put to sea if they weren't in good shape.

I sat through two interminable meetings that afternoon. Whenever the discussion flagged, my mind strayed to ways of salvaging the weekend. It would be difficult to stay at Dittisham – David dropped in at odd times to check the house and Mary was still clearing the attics – and I had the feeling that Sylvie's cottage wouldn't be suitable either, though I didn't care to think too closely about why that should be. A hotel then? A weekend abroad? There would be a risk of discovery but, overruling my last shreds of judgment, I persuaded myself that it would be too small to worry about.

As soon as I had the chance I found a private phone and, my stomach tight, my palms damp, I called the pottery shop. A strange female answered and, overtaken by some guilty reflex, I put the phone down without speaking. Calming myself, I called again and asked for Sylvie, to be told that she wasn't in and might not be in again until Friday. The woman wouldn't give me Sylvie's number but offered to take mine and pass it on. I didn't leave my name, I just said it was about the weekend and gave the number of my direct line at the office.

But I couldn't leave it there, it was all too indefinite, so I sent a letter by express delivery to the pottery shop with a note asking the shop to forward it urgently. In the letter I explained to Sylvie about the problems with the boat and suggested, with all the subtlety of a determined man, that a quiet weekend at a guide-recommended hotel on the northern edge of Dartmoor might be quite fun. Or else – trying to pre-empt Sylvie's disdain for the mundane and predictable – a couple of days in Nice or Madrid. I asked her to ring me at the office as soon as possible, or, if all else failed, I would meet her at Dittisham on Friday at six.

She didn't ring. I tried calling the pottery shop but it was always the same woman and I kept putting the phone down. On Friday I skipped a midday meeting and drove down early in a state of jittery anxiety.

I went past the pottery shop but it was closed. I opened up the house and waited until past six but she did not come. I poured myself a whisky and forced myself to wait for another half hour before climbing the stairs to David's old room and going to the window.

I had to brace myself to look down river because part of me dreaded what I might see. The cutter was not at her mooring.

I topped up my whisky and forced myself to wait for another two hours. At ten, despite the evidence of the absent cutter, I went looking for her. I knew the pottery shop would be just as empty as before, but that didn't stop me from driving past and peering into the darkened interior.

On the way back I examined every cottage I passed, as if their lights might provide some clue as to which was Sylvie's. Several had cars outside, but I didn't know if she had a car, let alone what make it might be.

I parked near the bottom of the village and went into the pub overlooking the ferry. As I made my way through the crowd to the bar I recognised some men from the boat yard, and with them an assistant harbour master named Horrocks who had known my father well. They were a jovial loquacious bunch, flushed with beer, and, after I'd bought them a drink, it didn't take long to bring the conversation round to the white cutter. Oh, that lot! they cackled derisively. The hippies and weirdos! The boat was called *Samphire*, they informed me, and her owner was a dropout by the name of Hayden who had once been a professional skipper on a massive private yacht in the Med and now lived up Totnes way with no apparent means of support.

She's a pretty boat, I said to explain my interest.

Pretty on board too! cracked one of the lads. All the boys got long hair!

I asked if they cruised far. The same wag reckoned they went just as far as they needed to go out of sight of the shore and start one of their sex and drugs parties. With drunken relish he told me that earlier in the summer they'd been spotted in a quiet bay prancing around the deck naked or as near as dammit.

They went to Alderney a lot, Horrocks the assistant harbour master told me more soberly, but this weekend he happened to know they were headed for Barfleur. That was the destination they'd filed with the customs anyway, though he doubted they'd make it back in a hurry with a westerly gale forecast.

I slept badly, waking regularly through the night. At first light I went to the window in David's room and looked down the river. Driving rain blotted out the dawn and it was another half an hour before I could be certain that the cutter hadn't yet returned to her mooring.

I closed up the house and drove back to London. I don't remember what reason I gave Ginny for coming home sooner than I'd planned, something about the weather being so dreadful that I couldn't work on the boat. Having received my decision to spend yet another weekend at Dittisham with a burst of exasperation, she greeted my unexpected return in stony silence.

Haunted though I was by Sylvie, I wasn't yet so obsessed that I could abandon Ginny for a third weekend running, and we spent a quiet two days at Melton, with only a drinks party and a casual supper with neighbours to be survived. I don't know whether Ginny had decided tenderness was her best tactic or had recognised that beneath my moods and preoccupations lay a bedrock of despair, but she treated me with cautious affection and sudden eruptions of bleak humour. When we made love I thought of Sylvie and had the decency to feel ashamed.

I might have kept away from Dittisham for another weekend, maybe a lot longer, if Sylvie hadn't called. She came through on my direct line and, in typical Sylvie fashion, did not give her name or even say hello, but announced herself with a question.

Is the boat ready? she asked.

It was a moment before I could speak. What happened to you? I said at last.

What do you mean? she said with breezy innocence.

You know what I mean, I said sternly. When we were meant to be going to France.

But the boat wasn't ready. You said it wasn't ready.

Yes, but I'd made other plans for us, if you remember. I was expecting you. You could at least have let me know. I heard the peevishness in my voice and tried to suppress it.

Oh, but it wouldn't have been any fun going somewhere else, she said. It's so lovely to sail. I love to sail.

You seem to get plenty of sailing on *Samphire*.

She gave a dreamy murmuring laugh, and I couldn't tell if she had missed the reproof in my remark or had merely chosen to ignore it.

She asked: So is the boat ready? Can we go?

It's not that easy, I said. And saying this I remembered how true this was, how Ginny had arranged something for the weekend and I would have to lie to her if I was to get away.

Ahh, Sylvie said. It was a long lingering sound, a sigh but also a signal of dwindling interest.

I have other plans, I explained. But it was a feeble attempt at resistance; I had been prepared to forgive her the moment I heard her voice.

So we can't go?

I made more doubtful noises to bolster the remnants of my pride, then caved in. It might be possible, I said.

Possible?

Possible.

You don't sound very keen.

It's not that. I *am* keen. But after last time how can I be sure you'll turn up?

Oh, I'll be there, Munchkin.

The nickname caught me unawares and bowled me back to the past, to a time when her promises had contained untold possibilities and our greatest intimacy had sprung from the exchange of our most secret thoughts.

We'd have to leave by six, I said.

Sure, she said. And I had the idea she was wearing her cat-smile.

Give me your address and number, I said, in case there're any problems.

Will there be problems?

No, but I must be able to get hold of you, just in case.

She hummed a little, as though considering the merits of my request, then informed me lazily that she lived at Blackwell Cottage up Farrars Lane. She could never remember the phone number, she said –

a statement I tried not to greet with scepticism – and took three shots at it before deciding that she probably had it right.

Where shall we meet? I asked.

I don't know. The end of the pontoon, by the dinghies?

No, I said quickly, thinking of who might see us.

Oh, Hugh, she sang teasingly, you haven't changed, have you? All right, pick me up from *Samphire* then.

Is that all right?

Sure, she said.

I said: If you don't turn up, I'll kill you.

She laughed, as though I had made a really witty joke.

Don't forget the food, I said, but she had already rung off.

A doggedness overtook my thinking then, a sort of tunnel vision that left out the more uncomfortable truths. My life was in danger of going off the rails; I knew in my heart that an affair was the very last thing likely to put it back on track, yet I couldn't let go. I clung to the idea of Sylvie as a drowning man clings to a lifeline. I found justifications. I told myself that Sylvie had been the great unrealised love of my life, that she had belonged to a golden future which had been unfairly denied me, and therefore, by some circuitous logic, that I had the right to reclaim her. I persuaded myself that, after stoically enduring the strains of my marriage, I deserved something more exhilarating and undemanding. And the final time-worn excuse: Sylvie's world in no way impinged on mine, Ginny would never find out, no harm would be done. I told myself all this, and sometimes I even managed to believe it.

I didn't like myself very much when I lied to Ginny again, but that didn't stop me from carrying it off effectively. I managed to look her in the eye when I told her I wanted to go sailing at the weekend. Only when she offered to join me did I feel a touch of conscience. Knowing how much she disliked boats, I realised that this suggestion had cost her some effort. But guilt made me unkind, I told her bluntly that I preferred to go on my own.

Ginny flinched slightly. But why alone? she asked.

I need time to think, I said.

But can't I help?

You help a lot, I said. You really do. I just need time away from everything.

It was that Melton weekend, she declared. Something happened then, didn't it? Why can't you tell me what it was?

It wasn't anything in particular.

But you ran out of the house without a word! You just disappeared!

All those people, I said in a fit of honesty. I had nothing to say to them.

So I shouldn't have invited them?

I'm not saying that, I said wearily. It was probably me.

But you didn't like them?

To lie or risk the truth? I said at last: Not all of them, no.

She began to breathe hard, her face took on a cornered look. She said: So it was my fault, then.

I closed my eyes briefly before saying: Ginny, it's not a question of fault. The how and why isn't important, don't you see?

But she didn't see. She gave me a long wounded gaze before tightening her mouth and leaving the room. I found her crying in the kitchen and, like two actors doomed to repeat our lines in a long-running drama, we began our habitual progression through apprehension and reassurance, doubt and comfort. While Ginny demanded to know where she had gone wrong, I repeated the well-used phrases that would eventually restore us to a rocky equilibrium. It seemed to me that we succeeded in reaching an uneasy reconciliation not because either of us was ever truly consoled by what the other had said, but because the prospect of the alternative was too terrible for either of us to contemplate.

I promised to make more of an effort with her friends, I promised us more time together, but I would not give way on the matter of the weekend, and the next day Ginny announced stiffly that she would go and stay at Melton on her own. I felt remorse, but mainly I felt relief.

I ordered a hamper from Fortnum's and supplemented it with some basics from the Dittisham village shop when I got down on Friday afternoon. I tried not to look at the weather, but it was impossible to miss the flailing of the trees and the angry cat's paws on the water. I persuaded myself that the gusts couldn't be stronger than force five, but when I went to pick up an almanac from the chandlery they told me there was a gale warning out.

The first spatterings of rain freckled the water as I rowed out to *Ellie* and by the time I had unloaded the stores and got the boat ready for sea it was hammering down. When I set out for *Samphire* at ten to six the outlines of the cutter were barely visible through the murk.

I waited in *Samphire's* cockpit, getting increasingly damp and anxious. Sylvie finally appeared at six-thirty, a crouched figure in yellow waterproofs emerging from curtains of rain. I called a bright greeting but she did not reply. Leaving her dinghy tied to the cutter, we went on in mine.

Fabulous weather! I exclaimed wryly. Would you believe it?

But she did not speak until we stood dripping in *Ellie's* saloon.

I suppose this means we won't be going, she said.

It doesn't look like it, I said and told her about the gale warning.

Her eyes narrowed, she gave a very French display of displeasure, a hiss, a flash of her eyes, and a clamping of her hands to her upper arms, as though to contain her annoyance.

Think about it this way, I said in my most cheering and, I hoped, beguiling manner, the view here is better than Cherbourg and the chef's willing if not able. We have wine. We have food. Even – I made a triumphant gesture – candles!

She did not begin to relent until we were on our second glass of wine. In my mood of insecurity I tried too hard to amuse her, I spoke too loudly, I rattled around the galley like some television chef, stirring extravagantly, making bad jokes, dispensing wine with wild sweeps of the arm. Against logic I felt I was responsible for her discontent and must lift her out of it. But then I was still running blind; I wouldn't have recognised reality if it had come and knocked me on the head. It was a long time before I understood that it was not me who was the main attraction, but France.

We ate, we opened a second bottle of wine. Sylvie emerged slowly from her preoccupations. For a time she sat motionless in her seat, barely listening to what I was saying, then, thrusting an elbow onto the table, she rested her cheek on her hand and watched me with amused detachment. She went to the loo and when she came back she seemed to have made up her mind to enchant me again.

She began to talk lazily, tantalisingly, leading the conversation off in great meandering loops or changing direction abruptly, delighting in her ability to catch me out in small inconsistencies, scolding me now and again in that teasing manner of hers; and once again I had this exhilarating idea that I was the only person in the world for her, that, deep down, there had never been anyone else.

She sneezed, I thought she had a cold, but when I fussed over her she laughed at me fondly and reached across the table to touch my face.

The energy left her as rapidly as it had come. She fell into a dreamy silence, her glass tilted in her hand. I moved onto the seat beside her, my heart racing high in my chest, my nerves taut with hope. Removing her glass to the safety of the table, I touched her hair and kissed her gently on the lips before pulling back, constrained by uncertainty.

She smiled her animal-smile, her eyes narrowed and she came towards me with her head arched back and her lips open.

I rushed at her then, all finesse cast aside. I pushed my mouth onto hers, I grabbed for her breast, it was all I could do not to rip at her clothes.

She flicked her tongue against mine, she gave a low sensuous moan, and it seemed to me that I had never wanted anyone or anything so much in my life.

At first the change was almost imperceptible. Her mouth slackened a little, she became heavier in my arms. Then, quite suddenly, her responses died away altogether and she sank limply against the back of the seat. I stared at her in disbelief. I called her name. She stirred once and laughed softly, then fell into an impenetrable sleep. I shook her, I shouted, but there was no rousing her.

I railed at her, at the wind, at the whole damn world, at myself; by turns I became philosophical and angry and maudlin. Eventually I grew tired. I stretched her out on the bunk and covered her with a sleeping bag, and lay down on the opposite side of the saloon.

I must have slept that night but it didn't seem like it. The gale racketed until dawn. I lay listening to the whine of the halyards and the thrumming of the mast and the fierce slap of the water against the hull, and I felt the night would never end.

The sun was high when I woke. I saw the empty wine bottles, and beyond them, the empty bunk.

She had taken the dinghy.

It was half an hour before I managed to hitch a lift from a passing boat and get ashore. I drove directly to Farrars Lane. Blackwell Cottage was set back from the road behind an overgrown garden. It was a tiny run-down place with mean windows, peeling grey paint and a rusting transit van standing inside the gates on a patch of weedy gravel.

I beat on the door. The silence reached out derisively, and I hammered again, my fist keeping time with the pounding of my heart.

A sound; a door opening or closing. Unhurried steps approached across an uncarpeted floor, the latch clicked and the door opened an inch or two to reveal a man's eye and dark uncombed hair falling across an unshaven chin. The face pulled back. I pushed the door open and stepped into a tiny hall with dark paint, cramped stairs and the smell of damp.

I shouted at the receding back of the long-haired man: Where's Sylvie?

He kept going up the narrow passageway, and I shouted again.

I'm here, Sylvie said. She appeared from the dark front room. I was just coming to find you, she said.

I didn't trust myself to speak.

She lifted a shoulder, she spread a palm. She said again: I was just coming to find you.

Who the hell's he? I jerked my head up the passage.

Joe? He's an old friend. That's all, she said, reading my mind only too well.

Oh yes? I heard the infantile sarcasm in my voice.

Yes, she insisted laughingly. I've known him for ever. She reached up and passed a comforting hand down my cheek, and I shuddered under her touch.

She seemed completely unaffected by the night's alcohol. Her eyes were clear and bright, her skin had a translucent sheen. Her loveliness stood out in stark contrast to the dinginess of the cottage.

Shall we go? she said, and she led the way down the path.

We got into the car and still I couldn't speak.

I had to come and collect something, she explained. I thought I'd get back to the boat before you woke.

Well, you didn't, I said. And there was a choke in my voice.

She put a hand on my knee. Poor Munchkin, she said. Her lips formed the shape of a kiss, her hand moved on my leg, and there was nothing in either gesture that was not completely deliberate. She said: Let's go to the house.

She could have suggested an alleyway and I would have agreed. From that moment on my anger and my lust became inextricably entangled and I never managed to separate them again.

We drove to the house in silence. Once inside we stood slightly apart, weighing each other up as though for combat, then Sylvie took my hand and pulled me upstairs and into David's old room.

I stood before her, not moving, not speaking. Perhaps she liked that, perhaps that made it into a game for her, because she smiled to herself before reaching forward and sliding her hand under my shirt.

Her eyes were very black as her hands travelled over my chest and up my back and then down, down over my bum to curl inwards around the back of my thighs.

I didn't respond immediately, I didn't want her to see how deeply engulfed I was. When I finally touched her it was to grasp her shoulders, but in my attempt to keep some control I must have gripped her more tightly than I realised because she flinched slightly and shivered.

I held my grip. Her lips opened, she gave a harsh sigh, a challenge or a capitulation. I realised with a blend of fascination and exultation that there were no barriers for her, that in her greed for experiences she set no bounds, and the realisation was an incitement to a more terrifying desire. In that moment I was finally lost.

We just made it to the bed. It was over in minutes. Later we made love in the study on the sofa with the lights on.

During the night she disappeared, leaving no word. Her telephone didn't answer. This was the pattern of things to come, the pattern of uncertainty and torment that Sylvie practised on me so effortlessly.

It was not long after this, in late July, that Cumberland agreed in principle to the buyout. Leaving Howard and the lawyers to negotiate the finer points of the takeover, I spent much of the next two weeks at Hartford, drawing up a business plan. George offered to put me up, but I always found excuses to stay at Dittisham.

Sometimes Sylvie would announce that she couldn't see me; she never felt she had to give a reason and she laughed at me when I demanded one. And when she did agree to meet me she would often be late or, worst of all, simply fail to turn up. Then, sick at heart, dismayed at my own weakness, I would look for her at the cottage or the shop, I would train my newly purchased binoculars on *Samphire*, I would walk through the village to the quay. Many times I would swear to finish with her, yet I continued to search for her with the same ghastly masochistic craving.

When I finally tracked her down I would question her pathetically, my humiliation mingled with undiminished longing. Finding me in this mood she would regard me with pity, and when I reached for her would pull away impatiently and leave without explanation. In those moments I began to understand how people could kill each other.

When she did let me make love to her – just twice in those two weeks – it was on the promise of making the long-delayed trip to France. I still didn't get it, of course; I was still too dazzled to understand the significance of France.

I couldn't get away over the following two weekends – a family wedding, then a batch of buyout meetings – but I slipped down midweek a couple of times. By then I had lost all restraint, and all caution too. I took risks, I left cryptic phone messages with long-haired Joe – calling myself M, my token to discretion – and once I took Sylvie out to dinner at a restaurant in the country where we could easily have bumped into people I knew. She laid down her terms at that dinner, she said she didn't want to carry on unless we could get away to France. In my blindness I was flattered, I thought she wanted to relive our old adventures, to escape the madding crowd and be alone with me, and, desperate for my moment of happiness, I heard myself promise faithfully to take her to France the next weekend.

By tradition Ginny and I always left for a ten-day break in Provence on the Friday of the August bank holiday weekend, but at two days' notice I told Ginny I couldn't go. I said I had too much work at Hartford, that she should go on her own for a day or so to prod the estate agents into action and inspect the house. If she had put up a fierce argument, if she had challenged me about an affair, my conscience might have got the better of me, but she didn't, and with an adulterer's logic I took her acceptance as some kind of permission.

I couldn't get down to Dittisham until midnight on the Friday. Sylvie was waiting for me at the house. It was too late to go out to the boat that night, so we picnicked in the study by the french windows. The anticipation was like a drug. My head was light, my pulse racing. We made love on the sofa with the curtains undrawn.

As Sylvie moved over my body I thought I heard a sound outside but, lost to the sensations of the moment, I quickly pushed the idea from my mind.

Seven

HENDERSON PREPARED unhurriedly, arranging his papers, checking the recorder, ignoring me.

Tingwall poured me a cup of water and murmured, 'Okay?'

I nodded, trying to suppress my nerves. 'We'll get a break at some point?'

'Oh yes, I'll make sure we do.'

'I don't want my wife sitting there for hours.'

'Don't worry, we won't go on all night.'

It was the same interview room as before. Reith was sitting a foot or so back from the table, to Henderson's left. Phipps was propping up the wall by the door. The air was hot and stale as though the room had just been vacated by another team in pursuit of a sweating quarry. For an instant I wondered what the air was like in prison, whether it was like this or worse, whether it stank of sweat and urine and drugs, and fear whispered in my stomach.

The tape recorder was switched on. Henderson intoned some preliminaries, informing me the interview was being recorded and that I could take a copy of the tape away with me if I so wished. He then logged the time, the place, and identified each person in the room.

He slid his heavy forearms onto the table and raised his gloomy eyes to mine. 'Mr Wellesley, could you please take us through your movements on Saturday, the thirtieth of September?'

'I got the time of the petrol wrong,' I announced straight away. 'It was earlier than I thought. Four-fifteen.'

'And where did you buy this petrol?'

'At the Gordano service station.'

'And that's on the M5?'

'Yes, just this side of Bristol.'

'Four-fifteen . . . So what time did you leave London?'

'It must have been nearer two-thirty. Maybe even two.'

'In your previous statement you stated that it was three o'clock.'

'I was working hard that day. I was under a lot of pressure. I didn't notice the time.'

'And what time did you arrive in Dittisham?'

'At about quarter past seven.'

'So it took you three hours to get from just past Bristol to Dittisham?'

'Yes.'

'Though the traffic jam you mentioned in your previous statement was *before* Bristol, *before* you stopped for petrol?'

'The traffic was heavy everywhere. It was a Saturday.'

'But three hours, Mr Wellesley?' He tilted his ponderous head. 'Even if the traffic was heavy it would be extremely unusual to take that long, surely?'

I shrugged. 'Well, that's how long it took.'

'These timings seem rather uncertain in your mind, Mr Wellesley.'

'No. I've got them right now.'

'How can you be sure when you arrived in Dittisham?'

'I noticed the time because I needed to buy some food and I realised the village shop would be closed.'

'Yet you can't account for this unusually long journey time?'

'No. Yes. I mean – I can only tell you what happened.'

'Indeed,' he said, and the scepticism showed in his voice.

He looked down briefly. 'What time did you arrange to meet Sylvie Mathieson that day?'

My mouth dried slightly. 'I had no arrangement to meet her.'

'Come now. You had an arrangement to meet her early that evening, didn't you?'

'No, I did not.'

'You had an arrangement to meet her on your father's boat, the *Ellie Miller*?'

'I had no arrangement to meet her that day.'

'Not that day?' He affected a look of curiosity. 'Another day then?'

'No.'

'You met Sylvie on the boat regularly, didn't you, Mr Wellesley?'

I glared at him. I didn't reply.

'I repeat, you met her on the boat regularly?'

'I told you – I met her there twice.'

'You also went to her home, didn't you? To Blackwell Cottage?'

I realised, then, that his information could only have come from Joe. Long-haired, spaced-out Joe.

'You went to her home more than once?'

I shook my head.

'Could you speak out, please, Mr Wellesley?'

'I've told you how often I saw her.' I was fighting for time. I was trying to work out if Joe would be able to identify me after a brief glimpse through a crack in a door and a slightly longer look in darkness when he was stoned out of his mind. I was also trying to decide whether drug addicts were likely to be regarded as reliable witnesses.

'The question I'm putting to you, Mr Wellesley, is whether you met her regularly?'

'I had no arrangement to meet her that day,' I repeated doggedly, not answering the question.

'But what about all the other times?' Henderson said, still asking it.

'I told you how often I met her.'

'Three or four times?'

'Yes.'

'But that was all lies, wasn't it, Mr Wellesley? You saw her much more often than that, didn't you?'

'I did not meet her on that Saturday.' It was the only tactic I could think of, to repeat the point like a liturgy.

'You're not answering my question, Mr Wellesley. You met Sylvie Mathieson on a regular basis, didn't you?'

'I did not meet her on a regular basis.'

200

'You're denying it then?'

I thought of Ginny, of what she had asked of me, and he got his direct answer at last. 'Yes.'

Henderson turned down his rat-trap mouth and moved on. 'You went on a trip to France on the boat, didn't you? At the end of August?'

'Yes.'

'You went with Sylvie Mathieson?'

'No. I went with my wife.'

Henderson raised his brows slightly at that. 'You went with your wife?'

'Yes.'

'Are you sure about that?'

'It's hardly something I'd be mistaken about.'

His mouth compressed into a sharp line, he fixed me with his droopy eyes. 'Presumably not.' He addressed himself to Tingwall. 'Would Mrs Wellesley be prepared to make a statement to this effect?'

Tingwall gave me the briefest glance. 'Er, I would have to confer, obviously, but I imagine there will be no difficulty.'

Returning to me, Henderson murmured, 'But you did go on a trip with Sylvie Mathieson at some point, didn't you, Mr Wellesley?'

'No.'

'What – no trip at all?'

'No.'

'Never mind France. Anywhere . . . Up the river?'

I exhaled harshly. 'No.'

Henderson tapped his stubby fingers twice on the table. 'What about there in the harbour then? You spent time with Sylvie Mathieson on the boat there, didn't you?'

'Just the once, as I told you. And the time she rowed over and talked to me from a boat.'

'Perhaps you'd care to reconsider your answer, Mr Wellesley. You see, there are witnesses who will say they saw Sylvie Mathieson on the' – he referred to his notes – '*Ellie Miller* more than once or twice. They'll say they saw her there several times.'

'I've already told you she came to the boat just twice.'

'And you don't want to add to that statement?'

'No.'

'But there *were* other times, weren't there, Mr Wellesley?'

'I've told you.'

'And what about these witnesses, the ones who saw Sylvie visiting you on the boat?'

'I have no idea.'

'Come now, Mr Wellesley, we know you saw her regularly. Why not tell us about it?'

This was his method then, a kind of verbal bullying. The technique was transparent enough, yet I could see how it might wear people down, how they might tell him what he wanted to hear just to win some respite. I wondered if he realised that in most respects I was already won over, that I hardly needed any wearing down, that if it hadn't been for my solemn promise to Ginny and the dire interpretation I felt sure he would put on any admissions I might make, I would have told him the truth about the affair half an hour ago. An affair was nothing, after all, compared to murder. This thing had gone on too long and become too frightening for considerations of pride.

'There's nothing more to tell.'

Henderson appraised me with open interest, trying to gauge whether I was mad or simply stupid.

'What about Saturday, the thirtieth of September? You met Sylvie Mathieson there on the boat, didn't you?'

'I've told you – no.'

'You met her because you were having an affair with her, didn't you?'

I made no answer.

'You met her in the same way that you'd met her many times before, but this time you had an argument which got out of hand and you killed her.'

Everything had been leading up to this statement, yet the baldness of it still took me aback.

'That's not true.'

'Perhaps you didn't mean to kill her. Perhaps it was just a moment of anger.'

'Listen—' I tried to maintain a reasonable tone. 'I did not see her that day. I did not arrange to meet her. And I certainly did not kill her. And no matter how many times you ask these questions, no matter how often you suggest these – *things* – nothing's ever going to change that.' I added emotionally: 'Because it simply isn't true.'

Reith exchanged a knowing glance with Phipps. Only Henderson's expression did not alter.

'It isn't true,' I repeated, lifting my hands helplessly.

My words fell unheeded into the silence.

Henderson sighed, 'Let's go back to Saturday, the thirtieth of September, shall we?'

I looked at Tingwall but his absorbed expression gave me no guidance.

We went over it again in minute detail, the unusually long journey, the period that Henderson referred to as unaccounted time, the rest of the weekend. We went back over how well I had known Sylvie, the two visits to the boat, the conversations. We continued in this way for an hour or more. I made no slips, I had learnt my story too well by then, yet the air seemed to grow steadily closer, the lights harsher, and I was glad when Tingwall asked for a break.

Henderson agreed calmly, 'Very well.' He went through the signing off procedure for the benefit of the tape, then switched off the machine. 'Oh, and Mr Tingwall? We would like Mr Wellesley's fingerprints, if that's acceptable.'

Tingwall's squint intensified. 'This would be for elimination purposes, would it?'

Henderson conceded with a faint shrug. 'If you like.'

Tingwall asked for a moment to confer and took me into the corridor. 'Listen,' he whispered, 'if we refuse I have the feeling they'll just slap a charge on you, and then the prints'll be compulsory anyway. So it might be best to agree. It seems to me that the longer we put off a charge, the better.'

I nodded meekly and we went back into the room.

'Mr Wellesley will be happy to comply,' Tingwall announced.

'I believe Mrs Wellesley's downstairs, is that correct?'

Tingwall confirmed it.

'I trust she'll also be agreeable to providing prints?'

'Is this necessary?' I demanded.

Studiously ignoring me, Henderson looked to Tingwall for a reply.

Henderson's attitude suddenly infuriated me. 'I'm asking,' I said, 'if this is really necessary.'

Tingwall began to speak but I hushed him with a splayed hand.

When Henderson finally addressed me it was grudgingly, as though he was granting me an unnecessary indulgence. 'To conduct an elimination process,' he intoned, 'we have to have the prints of everyone who had access.'

'That's an awful lot of people,' I retorted, though I didn't know what access he was talking about. 'My whole family for a start!'

Tingwall cut in smoothly, 'Will an hour be all right, Inspector? Mr Wellesley will need something to eat before everything closes for the night. And I will need time to confer.'

Henderson looked at his watch. 'Fingerprints in fifteen minutes? And we'll continue the interview in the morning at nine.'

Tingwall nodded, and drew me aside. 'It'll be a night in the cells, I'm afraid. But I'll bring in a sandwich, otherwise you'll get nothing till breakfast.'

'How long do I have to stay here?'

'They can hold you twenty-four hours without charge. Thirty-six with the superintendent's say-so.'

'I didn't mean to get angry,' I said.

He raised an eyebrow.

'Will it count against me?'

Tingwall caught my bleak attempt at humour. 'Listen – compared to most of his customers you're a saint.'

I waited in the stuffy interview room with a yawning Phipps until Tingwall reappeared.

'Mrs Wellesley has agreed to the fingerprinting,' he said when Phipps had left. 'She asked for you to be present. And I said I thought that could be arranged.' There was admiration in his voice, and deference; it seemed that Tingwall had been rather taken by Ginny.

'Listen,' I said, 'am I going mad or . . . If there were drugs in Sylvie's body then why aren't the police looking into that side of things? Why aren't they chasing those connections?'

Tingwall's eyes took on a wary light. 'Drugs? Were there drugs?'

'That's what my brother said. He'd heard from somewhere – the hospital, some doctors. And if she was into drugs there must have been dealers, drug addicts . . . Perhaps she was in debt to them. Perhaps . . . I don't know – but something.'

Tingwall mulled on this. 'It would certainly seem like an area worth investigating,' he said cautiously.

'So why are they ignoring it?'

'We don't know they are. They could well be looking into it.'

'Oh yes?' I said heavily. 'Well, it doesn't seem that way to me. It seems to me that they've made up their minds.'

'It's not easy to tell the police what to do, Hugh. They don't always like it. But I'll try.' He didn't look too hopeful.

Phipps came to lead us to the fingerprinting room. Ginny was already there, sitting apart from the waiting officers. When she saw me she rose hurriedly and kissed me. Standing in that dreary room with her classy Joseph suit and her long slender legs and her curtain of shining hair, she looked like a vision visited on a wasteland.

'All right?' she whispered, and there was no mistaking the question in her eyes.

'All right,' I said, and my look told her what she wanted to know, that I had kept my promise and stuck to our story.

She clutched my arm in a gesture of encouragement and complicity.

We stood at the desk side by side like a couple in a register office. When Ginny offered up her hand to the sergeant I saw that she was trembling. As the sergeant rolled the first of her fingers across the paper she gave a shudder that travelled the length of her body. When the last print was taken she exhaled suddenly and, wiping the ink from her fingers, turned and gave me an anxious lopsided smile. Looking at her then I couldn't imagine why I had ever thought I didn't love her.

In the morning they let me out of the cell to wash and shave. I turned down the large fried breakfast and settled for dark tea and dry toast. Tingwall appeared at nine, looking very young with his smooth scrubbed skin and bright expression.

He told me the interview had been postponed and no new time fixed.

'Is that good or bad?'

'Impossible to say.'

'So I could be here all day?'

'Yes.'

I didn't ask about the press, because I knew that if there wasn't anything in the papers today, there would be tomorrow, and I wasn't ready to face up to the consequences of that quite yet.

'They've asked for your wife to make her statement this morning so I've arranged it for eleven. Your sister-in-law is driving her in.'

'Will I be able to see her?'

He made an apologetic face. 'Probably not.'

Ginny had stayed the night at Furze Lodge. David and Mary would have been kind and attentive, but probably rather overwhelming too, and I suspected that she would be feeling the strain.

After Tingwall left I asked for pen and paper, which the duty officers let me have, and, in an attempt at normality, I balanced the paper on my knee and tried to work on some marketing plans. But the gesture was hopeless, I simply couldn't concentrate, and after a while I lay on the bunk staring at the ceiling, wondering how people could survive this for days on end. At noon a plate of fish and chips arrived with a gluey pudding and more strong tea. At one Tingwall came to tell me that Ginny had made her statement without a hitch and the whole thing had been completed in just over an hour.

'She did very well,' Tingwall remarked with an odd embarrassed smile, as though he were especially proud of her. 'They haven't said anything about you,' he added. 'No interview time set.'

'Is that good or bad?'

'Can't say. They may be waiting for something.'

The afternoon was endless. By three I was pacing the cell, by five I was asking for Tingwall. It came to me then that, unnerving though imprisonment may be, it is not the lack of freedom which most undermines you, it is the sudden powerlessness, the sheer inability to communicate.

They finally called me at nine. We took our places in the interview room like seasoned players. At first Henderson did not diverge from his routine. He retrod the same ground, I carefully repeated my answers. The new question was an hour coming. We were going through the weekend of Sylvie's death when Henderson said: 'On the Sunday you were away from your wife for some of the time, is that right?'

I wondered exactly what Ginny had told them. 'There were lots of chores to be done that weekend,' I said. 'We split the tasks between us. Mostly I was in the house, and yes – for some of the time my wife was doing other jobs.'

'She was away on the boat for two hours?'

'I can't remember how long she was there, but yes, she went to the boat.'

'You asked her to go there?'

'No. No, it was . . . There were certain jobs that only I could do – sorting through trunks, papers, that sort of thing. It was simply the way it worked out, that she should go to the boat.'

'What was she doing on the boat exactly?'

'Oh . . . Cleaning it out, taking things off. Preparing the boat to be laid up.'

'Laid up?'

'Hauled out of the water and put ashore for the winter.'

'She always did that job, did she?'

'No, it was my father who did that sort of thing. It was his boat. He always looked after it.'

'So why should your wife go and do the job? How would she know what to do?'

I understood now. I had sent Ginny to the boat as a ploy to get her out of the house and win time to cover up my crime of the previous night. Or perhaps they weren't absolutely sure when Sylvie had been killed. Perhaps they thought I had done it on the Sunday morning and calmly proceeded to carry her body down to the river in full view of the walkers and rowers and weekend sailors, and dumped her in the river.

'My wife knew the boat well. She used to sail on it when we were first married. She knew what had to be done – clearing out the galley, taking off the bedding – that kind of thing.'

'That was what you asked her to do, was it? The galley and the bedding?'

'I told you – we didn't go into detail. I left it up to her. She's very good at all that.'

Henderson pondered this. 'And while she was away you . . .?'

'I went through a trunkful of old letters.'

'You didn't see anyone?'

'Well – no. I was up in the attic.'

'No one came to the house?'

'Not that I know of. I probably wouldn't have heard the doorbell.'

Henderson watched me tensely. 'And what time did your wife return?'

'About one? No – twelve-thirty.'

'And then what happened?'

'We had lunch. As my wife will have told you.'

He was still for a moment, then in a display of disappointment or resignation he fanned out his fleshy fingers and flexed his shoulders before moving back to old ground.

And that was the turning point, though I didn't realise it immediately. Henderson went through the motions for another half hour or so, but his voice took on a weary tone, he looked at his watch from time to time, and Tingwall, reading the signs, began to push for an end to the proceedings. Like barrow boys, they began to negotiate. Taking me aside, Tingwall asked me if as a concession I might be willing to stay in the area for a couple of days.

'Do I have to?'

'No. But it might persuade them not to apply for a custody extension.'

And so I agreed because by that time I would have done almost anything to get out of there.

It wasn't until I walked into the reception area and

saw Ginny that I allowed myself anything approaching relief.

She gasped when she saw me. 'Thank God,' she kept saying. 'Thank God.' And she began to cry, half laughing as she did so.

'It may not be over,' I said.

She searched my face, she absorbed this slowly. 'Well, let's cross that bridge when we come to it.'

It was almost midnight when the taxi dropped us at Furze Lodge. David opened the door.

'You shouldn't have waited up,' I said.

'What the hell,' he said airily, and kissed Ginny on both cheeks.

'I'm rather tired,' Ginny announced in a subdued voice. 'I think I'll go straight to bed.'

I offered to bring her up a hot drink. At first she said not to bother, but perhaps she understood that in my inept inarticulate way I was trying to show my gratitude to her, because she changed her mind and said if there was a camomile tea she'd love one, otherwise anything would do.

I followed David into the kitchen and watched him hunt vaguely through a couple of cupboards. 'We're not really into herbal stuff,' he declared apologetically. Eventually he found a lone sachet of peppermint tea.

'Well?' he demanded as he filled the kettle and plumped it on the Aga.

'Well . . . they've let me out, but they think I did it.'

'Think or know?'

'Actually,' I protested stiffly, 'there's nothing to know.'

'I meant,' he retorted with a flash of impatience, 'what evidence do they have?'

'They're not saying.'

Shaking his head, he disappeared and came back almost immediately with a bottle of Scotch and two glasses.

'David, you said that Sylvie was into drugs—'

He slung the glasses onto the counter between us. 'Did I?'

'Yes. You said so the other day. You said she was into all sorts of stuff.'

He slopped some whisky into the glasses and pulled his mouth down into an expression of denial. 'I don't think so.'

'For Christ's sake, David!' He had done this when we were younger, made some bold statement only to disclaim it later and somehow shift the blame for the misunderstanding onto me.

Under my furious gaze he made a grudging concession with a lift of one shoulder, and waved an ambiguous hand. 'It was a rumour, that was all. Hospital gossip. You know – the police pathologist drops a hint. Or it might have been a forensic technician. But it's not too reliable that sort of thing. Believe me.'

'But she was your patient.'

'Ha!' My naivety brought a hint of bitter amusement to his face. 'You think patients tell their doctors everything? You think they tell them about their secret drinking and their forty fags a day and their extracurricular pills?' He lifted his eyes expressively.

'Sylvie only came to see me a couple of times and the subject of whether she was on drugs didn't *exactly* come up.'

'What about the people she mixed with?'

He took a swig of his drink. 'Haven't a clue.'

'There was that deadbeat with the long hair.'

'Which one?' he exclaimed sardonically, as if his surgery was beset by long-haired deadbeats.

'Joe something.'

'Doesn't ring a bell.'

'And someone called Hayden.'

He shook his head. 'Not one of mine. Well – so far as I know.'

'She used to go sailing on Hayden's boat. That's what they said at the boat yard, anyway.'

'And he's a druggy, is that it?'

'Someone must have been.' I dragged my hands wearily down my face. 'Oh, I don't know, I don't bloody know, David. It's all such a bloody nightmare.'

'Well,' he said laconically, 'it's not worth panicking about, is it? They can't get you for something you didn't do, can they?'

'I hope not,' I said fervently. 'But sometimes . . .'

'For what it's worth,' he continued in the same brisk tone, 'we'll do what we can. You know – support and all that.'

After such a day my emotions were running close to the surface and when I thanked him my eyes misted over, the words caught in my throat.

Looking alarmed at this display, David said sharply, 'I gather they want our fingerprints.'

'Yes,' I said, pulling myself together. 'For elimination purposes – that's what they call it. Tingwall can explain it better than me. Apparently you don't have to agree, but if you don't they could insist.'

David gave a shrug suggesting that it was no skin off his nose, then turned away to deal with the boiling kettle.

'The family contacted me,' he said over his shoulder.

'Family?'

'Sylvie's brother. Jean-something. Jean-Paul.'

A memory flickered, an image of a self-absorbed guitar-playing youth who had appeared once or twice during that distant summer. 'God . . . I'd forgotten.'

'An *academic* of some sort. Bristol.'

'What did he want?'

David poured hot water into a mug. 'Oh, where to go for the burial arrangements, that kind of thing.'

I hadn't thought about her family. I hadn't thought about the funeral. 'When will all that be?'

David dunked the bag of mint tea uncertainly into the mug, then lifted it out and, creasing his brows in faint annoyance, dropped it in again. 'Oh, not for quite a time, I wouldn't think.' He added casually: 'He wanted to know how to get in touch with you.'

'*Me?*' The thought disturbed me profoundly. 'Why?'

'Not sure. Old time's sake maybe.' And I couldn't tell if he meant this ironically. 'Anyway I talked him out of it.'

'He didn't realise that I was the prime suspect, then?' I said with a lurch of self-pity.

'Probably not, no.'

This was the way of the future, I realised. In my new state of social unacceptability I would have to rely on my family to shield me from unsuitable encounters, and my lawyers to protect me from the worst intrusions of the press.

David yawned and rubbed his eyes savagely with his forefingers.

'Sorry,' I said immediately. 'I'm keeping you up.'

'No, if you want to talk . . .' He stood there doing his best to look approachable, but it was not something that came easily to him, and it showed in the restlessness of his eyes and the wariness of his manner. As boys we had told each other everything, we had been accomplices in many a misdemeanour and covered for each other steadfastly, yet in our early teens David had abruptly distanced himself from me and the world in general, and in the muddle of adolescence I had never been sure why.

'Thanks for the offer,' I said, 'but I'm exhausted.'

He nodded with what might have been relief and, turning off the lights, led the way upstairs.

I carried the tea in to Ginny as she lay reading a magazine in bed and, placing it on the table beside her, kissed her on the forehead. She smiled a loyal smile, and it came to me that, if I was to be locked away, this would be the worst deprivation of all, the loss of such moments of quiet domesticity.

After a restless night I woke early to a clear sky and scents of autumn. I lay in bed and remembered waking to a morning like this not so long ago and thinking how lucky I was to be alive. That must have been before the cash flow crisis, before David told me that Pa had cancer.

Ginny had taken some pills and was still asleep. I got up quietly and, making myself some coffee, carried it out into the freshness of the garden. My shoes darkened as I wandered across the dew-laden grass. Above me the leaves of the oaks were saffron, lemon and gold, and on the far side of the croquet lawn a maple blazed. Somewhere a lone bird was calling. It was best not to consider the beauty of it all; that way lay depression and despair.

A sound made me turn and there, in a reprise of our meeting at Dittisham House, was Mary, waving hard. She closed the door behind her and came striding towards me in her Barbour jacket, knee-length skirt and gumboots, her round face cracked into a smile.

'I meant to stay awake last night,' she declared indignantly as soon as she had kissed me. 'I told David to give me a shout the moment you arrived! Honestly!' With a flick of the hand, she gestured the futility of such expectations. 'But listen – how are you?'

'How am I?' I considered this with a mournful laugh. 'Oh, for public consumption, I'm fine. You know – full of righteous indignation and protesting my innocence from the rooftops. But in reality . . . Quite frankly, Mary, when I'm not feeling choked I'm scared stiff.'

'They've found out, have they, about you and Sylvie?'

I lifted my shoulders. 'God only knows. They're not saying.'

'And what have *you* told *them?*'

'Nothing.'

'Nothing,' she repeated thoughtfully, as though she wasn't entirely convinced of the wisdom of this but didn't like to mention it.

'Well, what am I going to tell them, Mary?' I argued with sudden heat. 'That as it happens they're dead on track, that I've lied through my teeth, that I had a wild affair with Sylvie, that I had every reason to kill her—'

'*Every* reason?' she interrupted with a small embarrassed laugh.

In telling her, I realised that I was testing the story against a time when I might have to deliver it on a larger stage. 'Well, she'd dropped me, hadn't she? Finished the whole thing. Just – without warning. For no reason at all. She wouldn't say why. In fact, she wouldn't communicate at all. She deliberately avoided me. Just . . . cut me out! She was brilliant at that,' I added wryly, 'at shutting people out.'

'*Oh,*' Mary murmured, her face puckered with concern. 'Oh. I hadn't realised.'

'Oh, I knew it was no good!' I declared. 'I knew the whole thing was hopeless! I realised she wasn't the same person. I realised she'd changed out of all recognition. In many ways she was utterly *un*likeable. But still, but *still* . . . I couldn't *stop* myself, you see. I just couldn't.'

Mary absorbed this with the faraway look of someone attempting to imagine a passion completely outside her own experience. 'Poor old thing,' she said at last. 'How awful for you!'

We strolled towards the croquet lawn.

'When was this?' Mary asked.

'Oh—' I muttered vaguely. 'At the end of August.'

A pause. 'You mean – when you sailed to France?'

'Thereabouts.'

'Aha.' And she drew the sound out until it took on a wealth of meaning. 'I realised it must have been Sylvie on the boat with you.'

I halted.

'Ginny's always hated sailing so much.'

'God. Does anyone else . . . David . . .?'

'I don't think so.'

'The thing is . . . we're saying it was Ginny. We're telling the police we went to France together. Ginny's absolutely determined. She's making a statement about it. You won't . . .' I gestured feebly. 'I mean . . . not to anyone?'

Mary fixed me with her most fiery look. 'If you weren't in such a state, I'd take that as a bloomin' insult!'

'Sorry. *Sorry,* Mary. Sometimes I get paranoid.'

She shook her head fondly and we continued our walk.

'Hate to mention it and all that,' she said after a while, 'but Ginny wasn't anywhere else when she was meant to be sailing with you, was she? I mean, nowhere *obvious.*'

'No.'

Whether she was simply being tactful or had

deduced that Ginny had come secretly to Dittisham, she didn't ask me to elaborate on this curious answer.

I hesitated, knowing I was about to test Mary's patience yet further. 'I'm going to be paranoid again,' I announced. 'But I've got to ask – you haven't told David anything at all, have you? About me and Sylvie?'

'Don't be ridiculous!' She threw her head back and gave a sharp laugh, half amusement, half scorn. 'He wouldn't listen anyway!'

We had reached a bench set on a small rise overlooking the croquet lawn. Pulling a scarf out of her pocket, Mary began to sweep the dew from the seat with broad strokes.

'Oh, it's not that he isn't *concerned*', she assured me. 'It's just that he doesn't like to hear about anything even faintly disturbing. Never has done. He's the original ostrich when it comes to problems and crises. Just blanks them all out. That's why he should never have been a GP – can't deal with the patients. And that's why I've brought up the children almost single-handed. Oh, don't think I'm bleating!' she added breezily, beating the last drops from the wood with whip-like flicks of the scarf end. 'Because I'm not. It's just the way he is. I don't *mind*. Having stuck with his foibles for all these years, I'm certainly not about to give up on him now!' She gave another bray-like laugh and, sitting down and crossing her muscular legs, patted the seat next to her.

'What happens now?' she asked in the bracing tones of a pragmatist.

'Oh, more questioning, I suppose.' I sank disconsolately onto the seat. 'But I want Tingwall to press them on what *else* they're doing. On why they haven't bothered to look into the rest of Sylvie's life. Like her drug connections for a start.'

Mary threw me a glance. 'She was involved with drugs?'

'One way and another.'

'Blimey!' she exhaled noisily with a kind of baffled admiration, as though other people's lives never failed to amaze her. 'She told you, did she?'

'Me?' I gave an ironic laugh. 'Hardly. But then if I'd been in my right mind she wouldn't have had to. It was staring me in the face. She had a runny nose half the time. And she'd be morose one minute and go off to the loo and, hey presto, when she came back she'd be full of life again.'

'And you're saying the police haven't realised this?'

'No,' I conceded. 'I suppose they must have done. I mean, if David knew . . .'

'David knew?'

'Some rumour on the medical grapevine.'

'Ah.'

'But the police don't seem interested in following it up – finding out about her pals, where she got the stuff from, that sort of thing.'

Mary, picking her way cautiously through alien territory, ventured, 'You mean she might have been mixing with dealers and other dubious specimens?'

I chucked the dregs of my coffee onto the grass. 'That's exactly what I mean.'

221

In the silence a light aircraft droned overhead and we both looked up at it.

I said in a rush, 'She worked for them.' I got it out quickly before I had second thoughts.

Still following the plane, Mary took her time. 'She worked for the dealers?'

'The trips she took on *Samphire*. They were all about drugs.'

Mary turned to examine my face. 'They had them on board?'

'They picked them up in France. I don't know exactly what sort of stuff it was, but it was hard stuff. Powder of some sort.'

Mary waited silently while I found the words to tell the rest of the miserable tale.

'Sylvie fell out with her chums,' I began. 'Well, I guess she did because suddenly *Samphire* went to sea without her or didn't go to sea at all. *So . . .*' I spread my hands derisively. 'Alternative plan. Set up in business on your own. Find a mug with a boat, preferably someone who's pretty naive and malleable—'

'Oh, Hugh.'

'—Use him to get you to France.'

'Oh no.'

'—Collect your package, allow your dewy-eyed lover to stand you an expensive meal before getting him to sail you back. Then leave him to carry the can.'

Mary looked alarmed. 'You mean you got *caught?*'

The memory gripped me and I shuddered. 'So nearly, Mary. So nearly.

*

222

As *Ellie Miller* crept out from under the lee of the land and caught the first uncertain gusts of wind, I felt the elation of someone who had forgotten the extraordinary illusion of freedom you get at sea, the sense of leaving the world behind.

I went about the boat, trimming sheets, tightening halyards, entering the log, and relived the exhilaration of my boyhood trips, when my father had expected no crew member to stop until all the tasks were done, when no sail was considered trimmed until it had passed his beneficent scrutiny, when, at twenty, I was first entrusted with the job of navigator. The pride I had felt, and the fear of failure, and the satisfaction when the destination was made.

The wind was westerly and fresh. It was *Ellie*'s weather, a steady force five on the quarter, downhill all the way. As the old girl gathered pace she groaned and creaked in grumpy contentment, like a grandmother exercising her stiffened joints. Water hissed and surged along the hull, the crockery rattled in the galley, somewhere wood moved complainingly against wood. Hearing such long-forgotten sounds, feeling the movement of the boat under my feet, it seemed to me that, in abandoning sailing for all these years, I had left something important behind, a part of my past, a part of myself.

Sylvie sat in the cockpit for an hour or so, chatting desultorily, before going below to sleep. After lunch, I dozed for a couple of hours while she kept watch. When I came back on deck she was in one of her more ebullient moods. She told me a little more about her life in France, though not so much that I could piece many facts together. There had been a house in the Midi, with, it seemed, several people in residence, though she wouldn't be drawn on their relationship to each other. Lovers, husbands, wives; it was all very vague. Had it been a happy time? I asked. Oh, happy enough, she said. Then she turned her almond eyes on mine and said in that low sonorous voice of hers: But not happy like we were happy, Munchkin.

That was all it took, one small remark, and my heart squeezed with foolish joy, and, for a short time at least, the doubts that constantly lurked at the edges of my feelings for Sylvie faded away. In a moment of euphoria all my romantic notions of undying love came rushing back, I thought in ludicrously grandiose terms of the great wheels of fate that had brought Sylvie and me together again. For a short while, until the unease returned, I was besotted again.

As dusk fell and we sighted the beams of the Casquets and Cap de la Hague, the breeze stiffened and *Ellie* picked up her skirts and rushed headlong for land at a galloping six and a half knots. We tied up in the marina at half past midnight. The strange thing was that, though I had nurtured visions of sleeping beside Sylvie in some quiet harbour ever since our affair had begun, something made me retreat. I still wanted her terribly, but it was an ugly craving that drove me to make love to her that night, an urge to possess her at all costs, almost an act of retribution for the helplessness she engendered in me, and once I had left her body, once she had curved against me ready for sleep, something about the intimacy of the position and its implications of domesticity unsettled me and after a few minutes I crept away to a bunk in the saloon.

I woke to find Sylvie on her way out to buy croissants and bread. There was a tautness about her that morning, a barely concealed impatience, and no sooner had she returned than she announced she wanted to go out again.

The shoe shops open? I grinned.

She shrugged: And other things.

I asked if it could wait half an hour while we had our coffee.

You don't have to come, she said, and behind the empty smile there was a dark cold look in her eye.

But I want to, I said lightly, trying to dispel the tension.

She sat still for a minute or two, then climbed up the companionway. I thought she was waiting for me in the cockpit, I didn't hear her step onto the pontoon, but, light-footed as she was, she must have gone immediately, because by the time I had taken a last gulp of scorching coffee and gone up to find her she had vanished. Suppressing a fury, I locked the boat up and walked briskly towards the town.

Approaching the shopping area I saw her distinctive figure a long way ahead, turning a corner into a side street. I accelerated to a jog then a steady run but on reaching the corner she had disappeared. It was a street of small family shops: a brilliantly lit *boucherie*, a musty *librairie*, a *boulangerie* with a queue snaking out onto the pavement, then – I congratulated myself – a shoe shop. The window was plastered with sale signs so it wasn't until I went inside that I realised she wasn't there.

My resentment flared again, I felt a surge of anticipation. For the first time I imagined hurting her, taking her arm and squeezing it until she yelped.

At the end of the street was an open market set in a small square. The place was crowded, the stalls tightly packed, but I saw her almost immediately. At first I thought she was eyeing the baubles on a trinket stall, but then she turned to the young man beside her and spoke to him, and I realised with a jolt that they seemed to know each other.

Stupefied, I watched as they walked purposefully towards a narrow lane radiating off the square to the south. Following at a distance I saw them pause halfway down and turn into a doorway. For ten minutes I waited a few yards away, my imagination ballooning uncontrollably, my temper simmering. I was on the point of beating on the door when she calmly reappeared, alone.

I stepped forward so that she could not fail to see me.

She showed no surprise. Rather she gave a vague sign of recognition, as if she'd half expected to find me there, like someone who, having been kind to a stray dog, can't shake the animal off. She walked past me without breaking her stride so that I was forced to catch up with her. This small act was typical of her insensitivity, one of the many small humiliations that she perpetrated quite thoughtlessly and indiscriminately in pursuit of her own interests.

I grabbed her arm and spun her round. How dare you waltz off like that, I hissed.

I thought you'd be bored. I had this errand to do.

Errand? I crowed sarcastically. What, meeting someone?

She shook her head in exasperation or dismissal, and then I did something I had never done in my life before – I hurt a woman. Living out my violent imagining, I gripped her arm until she went white and winced with pain.

Don't ever treat me like that again! I shouted before walking blindly away.

I had lunch alone, going over and over the affair in my mind, wondering how one person could push me to such terrifying extremes of emotion. I had always considered myself a mild man, someone who kept his reason under pressure, yet when I had gripped her arm I had been shaking with rage. It frightened me to have lost control so completely; it terrified me to think it might happen again.

When I returned to the boat Sylvie was sitting on the foredeck reading a book. Ignoring her I went below. She followed and, coming up behind me, circled her arms round my waist and laid her head against my back.

Don't be cross, she sighed. We were having such a good time.

But you just walked off!

I wasn't going to be long. Please, Munchkin, life is too short.

How do I know you won't do it again?

I won't, I promise.

I cross-examined her about the man at the stall, I demanded to know what they'd been doing together in the flat or whatever the place was. He was just a friend of a friend, she said, someone who worked in the market; she'd simply been collecting something from him, a favour for the mutual friend.

I gave up then, because no answer would ever satisfy me nor quell my darker suspicions.

And I forgave her. I forgave her because I wanted the pain and humiliation to end. And because the dreadful sick longing was still dragging at my heart.

Just don't do it again, I said weakly.

Later we went to an expensive restaurant and had a mediocre seafood dinner which took over an hour to arrive. We had agreed to start the return trip immediately after the meal, though that didn't stop me from drinking far too much, and it was more by luck than judgment that we bumped only one boat as we manoeuvred out of the berth.

The wind was dead on the nose, force four or five. After half an hour bucketing about in a nasty chop I returned my dinner to the ocean and, leaving much of the helming to Sylvie, spent a miserable night between the cockpit and the guardrails, retching on an empty stomach.

Dawn brought little improvement. The wind rose to a stiff six or seven and showed no signs of backing. In her day *Ellie* had been a tough old girl, but with all the talk of fastenings and planking I didn't dare drive her too hard. By midday we had made good a paltry thirty-five miles and I was beginning to despair of ever getting home. Seeing my exhaustion, ignoring my half-hearted resistance, Sylvie took a long watch in the morning and again in the afternoon, leaving me to curl up on a sodden bunk and, oblivious to the drip of a persistent deck leak, catch some sleep. I loved Sylvie then, I loved her toughness and her resilience and the fearless face she turned to the wind, a wild child in a wild sea.

At six the wind finally backed, and we began to make up some time, but it was still four in the morning before we turned up the path of the Kingswear light. Motoring past the Blackstone, Sylvie handed me a brandy and I drank it in one.

Any lingering anger I might have felt about the Cherbourg episode was lost in the euphoric camaraderie one always feels at the end of a hard trip and my gratitude to Sylvie for being such a game crew. We had another brandy and she blew an alcoholic kiss against my mouth, and I felt ridiculously happy again.

We rounded the Kingswear bend in that strange time before the true dawn, when the shadows seem to play tricks, when shapes form and instantly dissolve again. Glancing towards the fishermen's quay beside the station, I saw a large motor launch against the piles, and in my imagination it seemed to me that men were standing on the deck.

As we continued up river, Sylvie kept looking astern and when I asked her if she would go below and find the searchlight she didn't respond. Instead she made a hiss of intense irritation. *Shit! Merde!* she cried angrily. They're coming! Hurry! Hurry!

I looked behind and saw nothing. What the hell do you mean? I demanded.

But she would only growl: Hurry! And when I didn't react she grabbed for the throttle and pushed it as far forward as it would go.

For Christ's sake! I argued, trying not to succumb to the atmosphere of panic. As we charged through the lines of moorings, I kept glancing over my shoulder and finally I saw what Sylvie had seen: some way astern, against the myriad illuminations of the town, the steaming lights of a motor vessel were moving, coming our way and gaining steadily. When I looked ahead again Sylvie had gone below. Controlling my fury with difficulty, I kept shouting at her, asking what the hell was going on.

When she finally reappeared she was almost naked. In the ruby glow of the compass light I saw brief underclothes and a dark band around her waist. Touching the band I felt the smoothness of heavy parcel tape which she appeared to have wound around herself several times. I couldn't work out what the tape was for until she turned to clamber onto the side deck and I saw the bulging packet held to the small of her back. I reached out and prodded the packet: under the plastic it was soft, like flour or sugar.

I kept shouting: What the hell, Sylvie? But it was more of a cry of disbelief than anything else. Even I could no longer ignore an interpretation of events which sickened my stomach and deadened my heart.

I went on yelling at her above the engine noise but she didn't answer. She was too busy working out where we were along the river, how far from Ditti-sham and where she might be able to climb ashore if she swam for it now, and balancing these factors against the speed of the approaching customs launch.

Above the throb of the engine Sylvie shouted: I wasn't on board, you understand? Not on any of the trip! You went alone! Stick to it or we'll both be in trouble!

Then she clambered over the rails and lunged headfirst into the darkness. Her dive made hardly a ripple. I kept looking back but I didn't see her surface. It was part of her luck, or possibly her judgment, but just a few seconds later the customs boat's powerful searchlight sprang on and bathed *Ellie* in a blaze of blinding light.

I slowed down, I let the launch catch up and come alongside. I answered their challenge. Name of vessel? Where from? Home port? I hesitated over 'How many aboard?' before replying with an uneasy heart: One.

The launch towed *Ellie* to a mooring and two officers came aboard. They went through the ship's papers and my passport. They did not seem surprised that I was alone. They asked me if I had notified them of the boat's departure for France. When I admitted that I had failed to do so they asked me if I realised I had broken the law. I did now, I said. I explained that I had not sailed for some years, that I was out of touch, but all the time I was waiting wretchedly for the moment when they would search the boat and find Sylvie's handbag and passport and all the other signs that there had been someone else on board.

In the end their search was pretty cursory, just a rummage through the lockers and bilges, a hand thrust into the sail bags. They took no notice of the fact that some of the clothes were female. Wherever Sylvie had hidden her handbag she had made a good job of it.

Maybe it was the reference to having lived on the river for many years or the mention of a doctor brother having charge of the boat, but they let me off with no more than a stern caution.

I took *Ellie* up river to her mooring in a state of blank exhaustion. I found Sylvie's handbag in a side pocket of her holdall. It contained hairbrush, lip salve and moisturiser. No passport, no money, no identification. I realised she must have put them in the bundle so artfully strapped to her back. Clever Sylvie. Sly Sylvie. Not missing a trick. Never missing a trick, even with me.

Once ashore I drove straight to the cottage. I told myself that I needed to be sure that Sylvie had survived her swim, but the truth was far uglier and less altruistic. My anger was cold and bleak, I wanted to have it out with her, I wanted to know if my deepest suspicions were correct and she had been using me all along. I wanted to hear it from her mouth.

I walked into the cottage without knocking. There was no one in the lower rooms. Taking the dingy stairs two at a time, I peered into a back bedroom so strewn with clothes and junk that the floor was virtually invisible. Approaching the front room, I heard a slight sound from inside and, heart hammering, hesitated for a second before thrusting it open.

Some dense material must have been fixed over the window because the small room was very dark except for two candles burning either side of a large bed which filled virtually half the available space. Sylvié lay propped up on the pillows, entirely naked and uncovered, like something from a Botticelli. Beside her was the dark hairy figure of Joe, equally naked, like something from a horror film. Sylvie turned her head towards me with immense slowness as though it were very heavy, and creased up her eyes with the effort of focusing. Joe was on another planet altogether, blowing out his lips and chuckling wildly to himself like a bin case.

Sylvie, focusing at last, gave a warm smile and a low laugh. Come and join us, she said.

Joe's manic giggles followed me down to the car and fed my nightmares for weeks to come. In one dream I watched Sylvie dive into the water with a lead weight tied to her back. When I realised she was drowning I did nothing to save her.

Eight

I WOKE beside Ginny in the airy yellow guest room at Furze Lodge and wondered, as I had wondered on each of the previous two mornings, if this would be the day when I would be summoned again. Sometimes I saw the delay as a sign that, despite their investigation of houses, boats and cars, the police had found nothing against me and would soon be forced to admit their mistake. At other less confident moments I saw the delay in more sinister terms. I imagined that somehow or another they had assembled a few miserable scraps of evidence against me and were simply waiting for the right moment to return.

The uncertainty lurked in my gut, I couldn't eat, I slept badly, yet on this morning, as each morning before it, I got into a company car and drove to Hartford as if life were perfectly normal.

I had told George and the others about my arrest, I had made no bones about being under suspicion. I had even managed to make a thin joke about the possibility of being arrested again. They may have noticed how shaken I was, they may even have suspected that so far as my relationship with Sylvie was concerned there was unlikely to be smoke without fire, but on the face of it they refused to take the idea seriously and studiously avoided the subject, as if the outcome of the investigations was so much a foregone conclusion that it required no comment. And so, in the midst of my personal emergency, we continued to work flat out towards the buyout, due for completion in two weeks' time. George was pursuing another fifty thousand, Alan thought he'd identified an investor good for a hundred thousand, we were near agreement with the staff on the wage and productivity agreement, and later in the day the Chartered Bank people were arriving for their crucial tour of the factory.

There was no need to make any sort of announcement about my arrest to the Hartford staff. With forensic people all over Dittisham House and *Ellie* beneath plastic sheeting at the boat yard under a twenty-four-hour police guard, with divers searching the river bed around *Ellie*'s mooring, the news might as well have been broadcast in ten languages on all four channels. The local rag could also have saved itself its rather coy report about an unnamed man being arrested and released on police bail, and printed my name two inches high.

The staff did not mean to make life uncomfortable for me. They smiled to my face and did not stare at me until my back was turned, but their curiosity was so palpable that whenever I went down to the factory floor I felt like an exhibit in a zoo, and it wasn't long before I found excuses to stay away.

Evenings at Furze Lodge had developed their own tensions. While David retreated into his habitual mood of preoccupation, Mary compensated with a bracing show of family solidarity. Her constant flow of chatter gave conversations a certain momentum, it was impossible to distrust her good intentions, yet after a couple of days the verbal onslaught began to wear family affections thin. There was a brittleness in Mary's manner, a determination in her cheerfulness that didn't allow for weakness or doubt, and for me, in my questionable state of confidence, this approach left out too much.

I don't know what I'd expected from Ginny – not a great deal in the way of understanding perhaps – but I had misjudged her. By sheer force of will she managed to impose a rigid dignity on herself, a kind of all-encompassing calm, and, knowing what this must have cost her, knowing how alien it was to her anxious jittery nature, I was doubly grateful. It was as though she had taken a decision to rule herself out of the equation, to suppress her own feelings and concentrate all her efforts on me. When under this new guise she offered small gestures of support, when her thin fingers reached for my hand and grasped it, I was terribly moved.

On the Wednesday evening as we sat in the kitchen after David and Mary had gone to bed I said, 'I wouldn't be able to survive this without you.'

She shot me a look which contained a flash of uncertainty. 'We'll get through it,' she said.

'Once this is over everything'll be different. I promise.'

Her eyelids began to beat. 'Will it?'

'I'll cut down on work, we'll spend more time together.'

'Oh Hugh.' Shaking her head, she said without rancour, 'You'll always work too hard. You won't change.'

'But I want to change. I don't want to go on in the same way. What's it achieved, all this work?'

'It's made you happy.'

'Has it? Once, maybe. But I keep thinking of what it's done to us. It hasn't made *us* happy, has it?' I really wanted to know. 'Has it?'

She said in a wary voice, 'I thought we *were* happy. At least I always felt happy when you were happy.' She stood up abruptly and took the coffee cups to the sink. 'And when you weren't happy any more . . .' She hesitated before saying with sudden anguish, 'Then I didn't know what to do.'

'You should have said something.'

'Should I? But, darling, what would I have said? It seemed to me that everything I did was wrong, that you were determined to . . . move away from me.' She shook her head to deter me from denying it. 'No, it's true, you know it's true.'

'I never blamed you for anything. I just felt – *besieged.*'

She came back to the table. 'I would have done anything to help. Anything. I felt so useless. Worthless. I felt you didn't need me any more.'

'Ginny – it was never a question of not needing you any more. I just . . . lost my way.' But my avowals were beginning to sound contrived even to my own ears, and I fell back on a more certain truth. 'Well, I need you now, that's for sure.'

She smiled ruefully at that, and when we went to bed we held each other for a long time.

Ginny's mood of containment held until Thursday when Tingwall told us that the police wanted her back in Exeter for a further statement. Then, despite her attempts at calm, she showed some of her old nerves.

'It must be the trip to France,' she gasped.

'Why?'

'They didn't ask me very much about it before. Only dates, things like that. They must want more detail.'

We were sitting side by side on the bed in our room at Furze Lodge, the only place where we could be certain of being alone.

'It'll be all right, won't it?' she asked. 'So long as we stick to what we said. That's the important thing, isn't it?'

The desperation of her plea did little to reassure me, not only because it reminded me of how thin our story about France was and how easily the police would see through it, but because it made me suspect that, however much she denied it, Ginny believed I had a lot more than France to hide.

'That's the thing, isn't it?' she repeated, seeking some reassurance of her own. 'To stick to it?'

'I suppose so.'

'You don't sound very sure.'

'Ginny – I'm *not* sure,' I admitted straight away. 'Oh, I know saying we were together seemed like the best thing to do at the time,' I argued cautiously. 'I'm not blaming you, darling, but I can't help thinking how bad it'll look if the truth comes out.'

'How would it come out?'

'I don't know. But it has to be a possibility, doesn't it?'

'You were seen in France?'

'No. Well – not that I'm aware of anyway. Though we had dinner at that restaurant in Cherbourg, the one all the British go to, and you know how it is, there's always someone, isn't there? And then when we set out we rowed out from the pontoon in full view of the village—' I halted, remembering that Ginny herself had seen us, that Ginny had been on the shore somewhere, watching secretly, and an avalanche of unhappy thoughts followed as I wondered how long she had been there and what else she had seen that weekend. I closed my eyes involuntarily at the memory of Sylvie and me on the sofa at Dittisham House, in full view of the uncurtained windows.

'Even if no one saw Sylvie, there's still . . .' I hesitated, weighing up the wisdom of delivering such a belated and unwelcome truth. 'The thing is . . . on the way back from France, coming up the river that night, the customs came and boarded us. Well, not *us*. Sylvie wasn't there. She'd disappeared, swum for it. There was just me. But the point is, I told them I was alone. They could *see* I was alone. And now we've told the police you were on board. If they compare notes with the customs how do we explain you not being there? Why would I have wanted to hide *you*?'

Ginny looked down at her hands and I could hear

her breath catching in her lungs. She didn't speak for some time. Finally she raised her eyes towards the window and announced in a tight voice, 'We have to stick to what we said.'

'Yes,' I murmured, though it was more to convince myself than anything else.

Ginny had started to overbreathe and, in an effort to regain control, she tightened her mouth to slow her intake of air before blowing out with a slight hiss, like a smoker exhaling a long plume of smoke.

'Could you take me through it?' she said between breaths. 'What you told them? I want to be sure of getting it right.'

I thought back to the interview room and Henderson and the long stream of questions. 'All I said was that it was you who'd come to France with me, not Sylvie. I didn't give them any details, though. They didn't ask for any.'

'But I must have them, mustn't I?' she pointed out. 'In case they ask.'

So I told her what time we had left the river, and how perfect the weather had been on the way over and how quickly we had reached Cherbourg. I described the market place and the restaurant and the dinner, and the long hard slog back across the Channel. If the police challenged her about the customs raid, I suggested she tell them that she had been in a hurry to get ashore and had asked me to drop her at a jetty in the town where she could find a cab. As an explanation it didn't make a lot of sense, but it was all I could think of.

Ginny absorbed this with a fierce concentration,

chewing on her lip, nodding from time to time like an earnest student.

'And the last weekend, when she died, can we go over that again, just in case?' Her voice faltered and she disowned this display of weakness with a brief grimace.

'I simply told them what happened. How I got down to Dittisham at about seven-fifteen—'

'I meant—' She wheeled a hand. 'What did *we* do? What did you tell them about *us*?'

Here was the focused Ginny, the one who always caught me off-balance. 'Of course . . .' I made another effort of memory. 'I just told them what we did. I said you arrived at about nine, that we had a basic supper.'

'Was I expected?'

'They didn't ask me that. But . . . I certainly didn't say you weren't.' I remembered the sound of the front door opening and the sight of Ginny appearing in the doorway, and how I had stood there in blank surprise.

'Why had we travelled down separately?'

'They didn't ask that either.'

She ventured, 'I could have been held up in London, doing some homework for a committee meeting, couldn't I? What do you think?' she asked anxiously. 'Will that do?'

I laid my hand on hers. 'I'm sure that'll be fine.'

She didn't withdraw her hand exactly, but she didn't welcome the distraction either, and I took my hand away again. I said, 'They didn't ask any of this before?'

'No, it was just times and events, nothing else. Did I say I was arriving at nine or . . .?' She was thinking

241

the thing through as she went along. 'Or hadn't we said a time?'

'We needn't have said a time.'

'The evening then . . . I'd told you I'd be getting down some time in the evening,' she recited before leading herself resolutely on. 'And after that?'

'Oh, I said we had supper. I didn't give them many details – nothing about what we ate or anything like that – then I said David popped in at about ten and stayed a few minutes. Then we went to bed at about eleven-thirty. It *was* about then, wasn't it? Then they asked about Sunday. I was vague about when we had breakfast – I thought about nine – then I said we spent the rest of the day going through the house and the boat.'

'Going through them, that's what you said?'

'Yes . . . Clearing everything out of the house before it was sold. Sorting through the attics, that kind of thing.'

'And the boat?'

'I said we were getting *Ellie* ready to be laid up. They weren't sure what laid up meant,' I added, recalling Henderson's pedantic query. 'I had to explain. They seemed interested in the fact that it was you who'd gone to the boat while I'd stayed in the house.'

'Yes?' she urged.

'I explained that I was busy with Pa's papers, that it was left to you to do the other jobs. I said I didn't tell you to go to the boat, that it just sort of worked out that way.'

'And? What else?'

'That was all.'

'Those were your exact words?'

'I think so. But darling,' I said gently, 'I don't think we have to match our stories word for word. In fact, it'll sound really odd if we do.'

She gave me the look she reserved for my less intelligent statements. 'I do realise that,' she said with a show of patience. 'But I still needed to know.'

'Sorry,' I said, wondering how she put up with me. '*Sorry.*'

'What about the rest of the weekend?'

'I told them we had lunch at about one. That we worked on through the afternoon and left for London at about nine.'

She was waiting expectantly again.

'That was it,' I said.

She looked thoughtful, then, reasserting her new-found composure, said, 'I just wanted to be clear.' Some doubt must have remained on my face because she added, 'I'm frightened of saying the wrong thing, that's all.'

She didn't speak during the drive to Exeter. She looked intently at the road ahead, and I had the feeling that she was going over the story again in her mind.

To avoid any chance encounters with the press we'd arranged to meet Tingwall at a hotel on the outskirts of town before he took Ginny on to the police station.

As Tingwall came across the lobby I searched his face for a hint of developments, but he was too busy giving Ginny a mushy dumbstruck stare to be sending out those sorts of signals.

'What's the news?' I asked, bidding for his attention.

He dragged his gaze towards me. 'News?' he echoed. 'Oh, nothing, I'm afraid. And nothing on the car or the house, either. No saying when they'll be finished with them.'

'What about getting back to London?' I sighed. 'I've had to miss a couple of important meetings.'

'If you can hang on a bit longer. Say, till the weekend.'

'And if something comes up and I have to leave?'

'Let me know. *Please*. Just let me know.'

Before I could say more, Ginny touched my arm, as if to remind me of why we were here.

'All right?' I murmured to her profile as we walked out to the car park but, keyed up for the ordeal ahead, she didn't reply. Tingwall sped ahead and opened the door of his car for her and waited solicitously while she got in. He closed the door like a chauffeur, softly, with only the faintest click. I saw him smile to her as he got in beside her.

I stood and watched them drive off but she didn't look back.

Beginning a potentially long wait, I sat in the car and prepared to make some calls. I hadn't shouted my troubles from the rooftops, I certainly hadn't mentioned them to the people at Zircon or the banks, and Julia had been careful to put the postponed meetings down to general scheduling problems. A small paragraph announcing 'an arrest' had appeared in two of the national dailies that morning, but either the police had been laudably reticent or some legal principle prevented the press from saying too much because neither report had mentioned my name. I had been hoping my anonymity would last but the moment I got through to Pollinger at Zircon I knew my period of grace was over.

The tone of his greeting warned me before he said crisply: 'Hear you've had a spot of bother.'

'This police inquiry, you mean?' I said casually. 'I was interviewed, yes – the victim was someone I'd known years ago – but that was it.'

'I heard, *arrested*.'

I didn't try to deny it. 'The police overreacted a bit, to put it mildly. But they let me go straight away without charge.'

'All sorted then, is it?'

'Yes,' I lied.

'Not good for the buyout.'

'I'm aware of that.'

'This sort of rumour needs to be knocked firmly on the head, Wellesley, otherwise it could keep doing the rounds. Get fixed in people's minds.'

I wasn't sure I knew how to go about killing any sort of rumour, let alone one this salacious. 'How did you hear?'

'Me?' Pollinger had gone into the City straight from Winchester; he wasn't used to being asked to reveal his sources. 'Look, all I can tell you is that if the story isn't all over the place by now, it soon will be.'

'What do you think, then? A press release?'

'A bit of a sledgehammer, old chap. A letter to your backers might be a bit more politic.'

Pollinger was right about the news travelling fast. Julia confirmed it as soon as I spoke to her. Most of Cumberland knew, she told me, and at least two of their lawyers, and possibly the Chartered Bank, though she couldn't be absolutely sure about the bank, short of asking them outright. Oh, she added caustically, Howard had called, asking if it was true that I had been charged with murder. She had taken the liberty of telling him that, if his spies couldn't do any better than that, he should think about taking them off his payroll. She hoped that was all right.

It was a strange feeling sitting there in a car park on the outskirts of Exeter, knowing that my life was being picked over in a dozen offices up and down the country. I could imagine how thrilled the banks were at the prospect of loaning their money to someone who looked as though he might be charged with murder at any moment. And I could see Howard hastily diving into his damage limitation mode, rapidly distancing himself from me and the buyout, and casting it about that, in all the years we had worked together, he'd always had his doubts about my stability.

I asked Julia to draft a fax to Zircon and the banks, explaining the situation and setting their minds at rest. I didn't have the heart, or the nerve, to make any more calls after that. I sat listlessly in the car, watching the traffic go by and thinking of Ginny. I pictured her in the stuffy interview room, sitting straight-backed on the worn chair, meeting

Henderson's cool gaze as she told him about the cup of coffee she was meant to have had with Sylvie at Dittisham House. I saw Henderson searching her face as she described bumping into Sylvie in the village and inviting her over. I heard him ask her what she and Sylvie had talked about. Then – the tactic was so obvious that I winced at not having thought of it and warned her – I heard him trying to catch her out, asking her what Sylvie was wearing, whether she'd been driving a car, and if so what sort of car it had been. I pictured Ginny pale and tense in the face of this crisis, yet, oddly, I didn't hear her falter. Though I replayed the scene several times, though I built up Henderson into some kind of super-sleuth, Ginny's aura of composure remained unassailable in my mind.

My confidence wavered only when I thought of the places where the police might have found Sylvie's fingerprints – in David's old room, on the bed post – and how hard it would be to explain their presence after a single coffee session. But you could go mad thinking things like that. You could go mad wishing for the hundredth time that you hadn't lied about something so mundane as an extra-marital affair.

I closed my eyes. I must have dozed for quite a time because it was dark when the sound of the passenger door woke me.

'How was it?' I asked Ginny as she climbed in.

She sank into the seat and shook her head. 'I'm so tired,' she sighed. 'I'm so tired. Can we just go back, please?'

As I drove I kept glancing across at her. She had

her head pressed against the headrest and her eyes closed. After a minute or two she said, 'I'm not sure. How it went.' And there was something in her voice that sounded a small warning in my mind.

'The weekend in France?'

'He didn't ask about that.' Each word seemed an enormous effort for her.

'Nothing at all?'

'No.' Her voice was so faint I could barely pick it up.

'And having Sylvie in for coffee?'

'No.'

'What – *nothing*?'

'Oh, I told him,' she murmured. 'I told him, but he didn't want that.'

'What did he want then?'

She didn't speak for so long that I began to think she hadn't heard. 'He wanted to know how often I'd been at Dittisham.'

I tried to read her profile in the reflection of the lights. 'What did you say?'

'I said . . . I said I hadn't been down very often. Just three times. He . . .' Another pause. 'He wanted dates. I told him I'd need my diary, that I'd have to let him know. But it wasn't that he really wanted . . .'

'What was it then?'

She dropped her head forward and her hair fell across her cheek. 'That last weekend,' she whispered. 'He wanted to know all about that last weekend.'

'What, the times or . . .?'

With great weariness she lifted her head again and looked ahead. 'Sunday. Mainly the Sunday.'

'What about the Sunday?' I had to force my attention back to the road.

'Everything.' She echoed bitterly: 'Everything.'

'But what about it?' I repeated doggedly.

She didn't reply.

'*Ginny* . . .'

'The boat. It was the boat.'

I had a bad feeling then, a sick foreboding. When I next glanced across, Ginny had half turned her face towards me, her expression hidden in the darkness.

'They know she was killed on the boat.'

My stomach lurched, I had a strong sense of unreality. I looked for a place to stop and there was nowhere. Finally I saw a farm gateway and lurched to a halt across it. '*They said that?* They said she was killed on *Ellie*?'

'They didn't have to say. It was obvious.'

'What do you mean?' I cried.

'Everything they asked . . . Everything.' Her voice was harsh, close to desperation or tears. 'Wanted to know who'd been on board . . . Why I'd gone out there on the Sunday . . . Whose idea it was . . . Why I'd scrubbed the floor . . . Had I noticed any marks or' – she could hardly say it – 'stains. *Stains.* They didn't have to say, did they? They *know*. They know she was killed on the boat.'

'That's ridiculous!' I argued. 'You must have got it wrong! You must have!'

She shook her head, and kept shaking it.

'But Ginny, that's crazy! How can they . . . How can they . . . Christ! It's ridiculous! You *must* have got it wrong!' I babbled on like this for a moment or two until I drifted to a forlorn halt and, leaning my forehead against the wheel, closed my eyes. 'Christ.' And this time it was an expression of dread.

I heard the squirt of Ginny's inhaler. She gave a couple of deep coughs before whispering in a raw voice, 'Let's get home.'

The two men from the Chartered Bank were in their mid-forties, wearing almost identical grey suits, and with the untroubled faintly jocular air of employees of large organisations who have never known what it's like to risk their own money or have their careers seriously on the line.

They liked the glass blowers best. They stood back and shook their heads in self-conscious admiration before venturing forward for a closer look. They asked the standard questions. How did the team of blowers manage to produce the correct shape and thickness each and every time, how did they prevent bubbles from getting into the walls of the glass, and how long did they work before taking a break.

They peered dutifully at the cutters manipulating the blanks against the cutting wheels, they inspected the packing room, and then George and I led them back to the front hall to present each of them with a gift set of six wine goblets and a decanter, which they could safely take home without having to mention it on their tax returns.

We smiled as we escorted them out to their car and shook hands. They smiled back. None of this smiling fooled anyone. No final commitment had been made, no date had been fixed for signing the loan agreement. The two executives would only say that they were returning to the bank for 'final consultations' and would let us know within three days. It was inconceivable that these final consultations would not involve discussion of my fax, transmitted the previous day to all our backers. Julia had written the text. While avoiding blatant untruths, she had managed to suggest that rumours of my arrest were little more than pernicious gossip, put about by those with a vested interest in seeing the buyout fail. When she first read it out to me I'd told her that this was incendiary talk, that allegations of conspiracy could easily backfire, but with so many distractions I was no match for Julia at her most persuasive, and the fax went out more or less as she had drafted it.

George and I waved the car off and strolled back. It was a lovely autumn day, bright and clear with a slight bite to the air. The factory looked almost handsome in the afternoon sunlight, its dingy bricks tinged with a rosy hue, the ventilation pipes gleaming like the funnels of a steamship. The main doors had been given a hasty coat of blue paint for the bankers' visit while the flower troughs on either side were newly planted in scarlet and white. The old place looked like a middle-aged girl tarted up for a new lover.

'I'm sorry if I lose it for us,' I said.

'What do you mean?' But he knew exactly what I meant.

'This trouble of mine – it could be more of a liability than we realised.'

251

'Nonsense.' He gave me a glare that was both a denial and an acknowledgment.

'Look at it from their point of view.' I tipped my head in the direction of our recently departed guests. 'Would you commit two million plus to someone who might be locked away for life?'

'But you're not going to be locked away.'

'They don't know that though, do they?'

'You're beginning to sound like Howard, for God's sake!'

Realising his gaffe, he gave an exaggerated grimace.

'What's Howard been saying?'

'Hugh . . .' He made a gesture as if to suggest we forget the whole thing, then almost as quickly lifted a resigned hand to concede the uselessness of trying. 'Oh, he's been bleating on.'

'Saying?'

'Talking some tripe about assurances. Saying Cumberland requires assurances.'

'Oh, yes?' I laughed grimly. 'What kind of assurances?'

'That we're in a position to continue with the buyout. That sort of stuff.'

'Or else? What was the "or else"?'

'Hugh, he was just making noises. You know him.'

'What was it, George?'

'Oh, he talked some stuff about having to consider the best interests of the shareholders.'

'He wants to break our agreement?'

'He didn't say that.'

'But that was what he meant.'

'You know the way Howard is – it was just talk.'

I didn't believe for a moment that it was just talk. Howard would have seized any excuse to block our bid and prevent me from making a success of Hartford. He couldn't bear the thought of my showing what could be done with the company when he wasn't around to interfere in it.

The era of extended lunches and early weekends might have died with the eighties, but at four on a Friday afternoon it was still hard to find a lawyer at his desk. Moncrieff's assistant told me that he was at a meeting out of town, while the rest of the legal team were tied up elsewhere and weren't due back in the office until Monday. I called Julia and asked her to reach Moncrieff at home that evening and set up a meeting for the next day.

'And if he can't do Saturday?'

'Sunday, then. And I want a meeting with Howard and the Cumberland people on Monday.'

'Something's happened?' Julia asked.

'Not if I can help it.'

With the decision to leave for London hot in my mind, I stuffed my papers into my briefcase and, amid memories of happier departures, unhooked my coat from the ancient coat stand that had stood sentry since my father's day, and hurried out into the passage.

The traffic was slow. I tried to call ahead to Furze Lodge to warn Ginny to start packing, but the line was engaged. I also tried to contact Tingwall, but I wasn't too sorry when the receptionist said he wouldn't be back that day. It gave me the excuse not to tell him what I was doing until later, when it would be too late for him to try and talk me out of it.

Mary appeared at the door as I drew up.

'How were the bankers?' she called brightly.

'Oh, grey suits. Vapid. Banker-ish.'

'What did they come up with?'

We went into the house. 'Not a lot. Nothing so risky as a commitment anyway. Mary – we'll be leaving tonight. I want to thank you for everything. For putting up with us all this time.'

Surprise passed over her face, then doubt, and finally a sudden effusive delight. 'They've said you can go?'

'No, but I'm going anyway.'

Her expression fell away. 'But do you have to go tonight? You couldn't leave it till morning?' She was trying to tell me something. 'It's Ginny,' she admitted at last.

Instinctively I glanced towards the stairs. 'What's the matter with her?'

'Nothing serious. David's given her something.'

'She's ill?'

Mary raised an eyebrow and gave me a look that contained a trace of disapproval. 'She hasn't been eating. She's been spending most of the day in bed. David thinks it's stress.'

Bemused, I cast back over the last few days. I hadn't noticed Ginny failing to eat, not when we'd been together in the evenings anyway. And days in bed – nobody had mentioned anything about that to me, certainly not Ginny. None of this prevented me

254

from feeling an immediate responsibility; where Ginny was concerned my guilt had no end.

'If that's the case, all the more reason to get home,' I told Mary as I made for the stairs.

Ginny was lying propped up in bed, her eyes closed, a magazine open on her lap. As I came in she twisted her head on the pillow and, murmuring a hasty greeting, sat up on one elbow.

I came round the bed and said, 'I thought we'd go back to London.'

She asked no questions. She simply said, 'Are we leaving now?'

'If you're up to it.'

She nodded and rubbed her eyes before throwing back the covers and getting up.

'Mary says you haven't been eating.'

She made a dismissive gesture. 'Mary doesn't know everything.' She went into the bathroom and began running some water.

'You are happy to go back tonight?' I called. 'You would tell me if you weren't?'

She reappeared. 'Whatever you want.' But she spoke carelessly, and I wondered what sort of tablets David had given her, whether they were addling her brain.

'We'll have a holiday once this is over,' I said lightly. 'Somewhere wonderful, like Barbados.'

She lifted her head and considered this. 'That would be nice,' she said and went back into the bathroom.

Following uncertainly, I found her in front of the mirror, smoothing the skin beneath her eyes. Still staring at her reflection, she dropped her hands and asked contemplatively, 'Do you love me? I mean, just a little?'

I made a sound that came out all wrong, an exclamation that was almost a snort. 'Of course I do. More than a little, Ginny. A *lot*!'

'I couldn't bear it if you didn't love me at all. If you hated me.'

I came up behind her and put my arms around her. 'Ginny, I love you very much. I couldn't have managed anything without you.'

'I've got things wrong a lot of the time, haven't I?'

'Nonsense!'

'Oh, I have. I know I have. Things haven't worked out the way you'd hoped, have they? Our life has been – *different*. But if I've tried too hard – oh, you don't have to say anything, I know I've tried too hard – it was only because I loved you.'

'Ginny!' The snort again, as though I couldn't think of what to say. 'You mustn't blame yourself for anything! You've been wonderful. Everything I could have asked for.'

'Not everything,' she corrected me gravely, frowning at her hands. 'Not everything . . .' Her eyes found mine again. 'But it hasn't been so terrible either, has it? Not so bad?'

I turned her towards me and hugged her. When I drew back I gave a shaky smile. 'I do love you.'

'I'm just sorry,' she breathed. 'Sorry . . .' And she might have been apologising for the entire world.

'Let's go home,' I said.

We packed steadily. Ginny finished before me and

went and stood at the window, looking out into the dusk.

From the front of the house came the distant crunch of wheels on gravel. Something about the sound made me glance up. Ginny had heard it too. She stared at me, her face blanched of colour. For an instant neither of us moved, then I strode out onto the landing and across to a front window that looked down onto the drive.

Two cars, several uniforms, Henderson getting out.

The scene lurched, my stomach jolted, and I had the sensation of losing my balance. I made my way blindly back to the bedroom.

'It's them! It's the police, for Christ's sake!' Fury had me charging rapidly towards the stairs, ready for blood or battle.

'Hugh!'

But I didn't stop and I didn't look back. The doorbell rang through the house. At the bottom of the stairs I met Mary coming from the kitchen.

'Shall I call the solicitors?' she offered in a worried voice.

I shook my head as I went to the front door and wrenched it open.

Henderson stood before me with Phipps and Reith, and in the rearguard four uniformed officers, two of them women.

Henderson gave me a lugubrious nod. 'Mr Wellesley. Perhaps we could come in?'

'Just get on with it, Inspector,' I said, my throat tight with indignation. 'Just say what you've got to say! But I warn you, you'd better be exceedingly sure of your ground.' I could feel myself trembling, and there was a heat in my face.

Henderson hesitated and looked past me into the hall.

'Just get on with it!'

His gaze fastened itself on a point over my left shoulder.

With a half-glance I saw Ginny moving up beside me.

'Mrs Wellesley,' Henderson said, and it sounded more like a statement than a greeting. His eyes still fixed on her, he turned to face her more fully and for some wild unaccountable reason I suddenly realised what was coming, and even as he opened his mouth, I cried, 'No—'

'Mrs Virginia Wellesley, I'm arresting you on suspicion of the murder of Sylvie Mathieson—'

'*No!*'

'You do not have to say anything. But it may harm your defence—'

'Don't be bloody ridiculous!' I protested. 'This is absolutely crazy!' Phipps moved forward and placed his body halfway between mine and Henderson's, forcing me to step back.

'. . . something which you later rely on in court . . .'

I stared at Ginny. She was very still, her eyes lowered.

'. . . Anything you do say may be given in evidence.'

'This is mad! *Mad!*'

But Henderson's voice was grinding on. Then, reaching the end of his chant, he was asking Ginny

258

if she understood and she was giving the shadow of a nod. Then everyone was in motion. The policewomen were coming forward and beginning to usher Ginny outside, the detectives were moving out toward the cars. Only Henderson remained.

'For Christ's sake!' I cried furiously.

Henderson said to me, 'Perhaps you'd like to pack up a few things for your wife, Mr Wellesley. Or . . .' he glanced towards Mary '. . . whoever.'

But I could only repeat, 'You're mad! She knows nothing! She wasn't anywhere near the river!'

'Mr Wellesley, we'll be leaving shortly. I do recommend you pack a few things for your wife.'

But my brain was bursting, I couldn't hear.

Mary's voice said, 'I'll go.'

Henderson began to turn away but I grabbed his arm. 'Just tell me,' I pleaded. 'Just *tell* me – *why*? What has she done? What could she possibly have done?'

Henderson made a doubtful face, then, taking a quick glance over his shoulder as if to make sure no one was within earshot, said in a low murmur, 'There is a substantial case to answer, Mr Wellesley.'

'Like what?' I gasped.

He spread his hands, gesturing impossibilities. 'I'm sorry.'

'Like *what*?'

But he had turned away. Unable to grasp the full enormity of what was happening, or unwilling to, I followed him numbly to the car where Ginny was already sitting between the two female officers. I was about to call to her when Mary's voice came from behind: 'Which one, Hugh? Which case? *Hugh?*'

Turning, it took me a moment to understand that she was referring to our suitcases which she had brought down from our room. I fetched Ginny's case and handed it to a constable.

Engines were being started. I remembered Ginny's inhaler. I just had time to race up and fetch her handbag and hand it in through the car window before the final door slammed and the cars sped away.

Watching the last car disappear into the lane I felt Mary's arm around me, and realised that the angry gasps I could hear were the sounds of my own despair.

Nine

'WHAT REALLY worries me,' I said, hearing the emotion that was never far from my voice, 'is that she won't survive in that place. It'll make her ill. I mean, worse than she is already. The dirt, the conditions, the filthy sanitary arrangements. No *lavatories*, for God's sake. It'll kill her. Just kill her.'

'I appreciate your concerns, Hugh,' Tingwall ventured gently. 'But I did make full representations. I sent in the doctor's letter. I checked with the medical staff and they're fully aware of her condition. She's under permanent supervision.' He added in a transparent attempt at cheerfulness, 'And she seemed okay when I last saw her. She said her room was all right. She said they were looking after her.'

The fact that Ginny had talked to Tingwall when, on both of my visits, she had hardly spoken a word to me shouldn't have bothered me quite as much as it did, yet I couldn't shake off the feeling that she was excluding me on purpose. 'We have to get her out of there,' I insisted unreasonably.

'We'll do our best, Hugh.'

We had only just begun our meeting yet already I was facing the wall of helplessness that seemed to dominate all my recent discussions with Tingwall.

'I'm sure you'll try your best but, if you don't mind my saying so, it seems to me that precious little progress is actually being made.'

Tingwall frowned at the surface of his desk. 'Hugh, I realise that the whole thing must be very difficult for you. I realise how anxious you are. However, we're faced with these procedures, and we have to follow them, with no guarantee of the outcome.'

I held up a hand. 'Hang on. What are you saying exactly? Are you saying' – and my voice hit a warning note – 'that we might not get bail?'

'I'm not saying that, Hugh, not at all. But bail is very much the exception in a case like this. We'll have to show good cause, we'll have to argue it carefully.'

'So?' I made a gesture of bafflement. 'If anyone has good cause it must be Ginny, surely.'

'We can certainly set out a case—'

'What about getting a QC? Surely we should have a QC on this?'

'We can certainly approach Counsel—'

'Charles – let's just hire the best man there is. Tomorrow. The *best*.' I was steamrollering him, I knew I was, but the law, with its nonchalance and mind-bending complexities, was testing my patience.

We were sitting in Tingwall's office, a tall room at the front of a converted Georgian house on a noisy road near the centre of Exeter. This was my third visit in a week; my third visit since Ginny had been formally charged late on Saturday night; a week in which I had seen her brought to court and remanded in custody, in which I had twice made desperate ineffectual attempts at conversation in the bleak visiting

262

room at the prison near Bristol; a week in which I had gone through every shade of disbelief and despair, during which I had attempted to apply logic and reason and emotion to what had happened and found nothing but incomprehension and dread. My thoughts went round and round and came out nowhere. My nights were riddled with nightmares and sudden panics. Confusion and doubt had wrenched my anchors away; I drifted back and forth on the tide of my uncertainties, ready to believe anything and nothing, to fight on and give in, to challenge everything and question nothing.

'I'm not saying we won't get bail,' Tingwall was saying. 'Not by any means. But I don't want to raise your hopes too far either.'

'But what could be the problem?' I asked, trying to hit a conciliatory note. 'What reason could they have for refusing?'

Tingwall interlaced his bony fingers. 'Obviously there's no suggestion that Ginny—' He caught my glance. 'You don't mind? She asked me to call her that.'

'No. Of course.'

'There's no suggestion that she's about to abscond or reoffend – that's hardly an issue. But with a murder charge the magistrates are bound to consider other factors, like the medical report.'

'Well, that'll be devastating, surely. She's already had two bad attacks. What more do they want? Her asthma's triggered by stress and dirt and damp.'

Tingwall gave a slow nod, like a bow. 'We'll certainly cite that, yes. I've already written to Ginny's specialist asking for a letter. But the court will also have the psychiatric assessment to consider—'

'Psychiatric assessment?' I was instantly defensive. Every time I thought I was getting to grips with the procedures something like this turned up, another bolt from the blue.

'I did mention it,' Tingwall pointed out delicately. He waited for some sign from me before continuing, 'In serious cases they always ask for a psychiatric assessment, partly to establish whether the accused is mentally capable of facing charges—'

'Sane, you mean?'

'Yes.'

I couldn't bear the euphemisms that crept in, the fine obfuscating language. 'If you could keep it simple . . .?'

Tingwall took this reprimand on the chin, with a quick frown of contrition. 'Also,' he continued, 'to assess whether the accused is likely to be a danger to him or herself.'

'Suicide?' I laughed dismissively. 'Ginny wouldn't do that. Not unless she's forced to stay in that place at any rate.'

'Maybe not.' Tingwall felt his way carefully forward. 'But, Hugh, I have to tell you that our man Robertson—' He peered at me. 'You remember, I said it was important to get our own assessment?'

'He's a psychiatrist?' In my shock I could remember none of this.

'Yes. He saw Ginny on Wednesday, and' – he made a regretful face – 'I'm afraid his findings aren't as unequivocal as I would have wished.'

264

Suddenly I was full of pain. 'He's saying she's unbalanced?'

'What he says is, he feels he cannot vouch entirely for Ginny's state of mind. Not at the moment, anyway.'

'But who is this Robertson?' I demanded, looking for an escape. 'Is he the best person? Do we want a second opinion?'

'He was recommended. But we could consider getting someone else in, yes. But before making a final decision I think we should be guided by Counsel.'

We had completed another circle. 'What are we waiting for then?' I asked. 'Why haven't we got a QC?'

'The best QCs are very busy, Hugh. I'm making enquiries, I'm trying to find out which of the top names are available. It's not always easy to get the person you want.'

I pushed myself to my feet and took my frustration to the window. 'Okay,' I said, descending into sudden weariness. 'So how long is all this going to take?'

'The bail application? I think we should hold it for another week. It'll give us time to prepare really thoroughly, to get this second medical opinion, if that's what we decide.'

Outside, the good burghers of Exeter meandered along the pavements, going about their errands, wearing their own troubles on their faces. I wondered how many had read about Ginny's appearance in court and what they had made of it, whether they had skimmed the item or picked over it with avid curiosity. Whether they, too, had decided she must be slightly off her head. Picturing Ginny's life being raked over in this way was almost more than I could bear. Yet I knew full well that the news coverage so far was as nothing to what would come if the case went to trial.

I turned back. 'This psychiatric assessment – it's standard, is it?'

Tingwall gave me an odd indecipherable look. 'We *could* have refused it.'

I was incredulous. 'Then why the hell didn't we? Why didn't we—' A notion lodged in my head; it seemed so obvious that I couldn't think why it hadn't come to me before. 'How many murder cases have you handled before this, Charles?'

Tingwall inclined his head to acknowledge the fairness of the question. 'Perhaps I could answer that by mentioning that, contrary to what many people think, murder's a fairly rare crime, and this region must have one of the lowest murder rates in the country. And most of the murders that do occur are domestic or fairly straightforward or both, by which I mean there's usually very little doubt as to who was responsible. It's more a question of why, and whether it was self-defence, and so on. There are very few – extremely few – cases in which the facts are . . .' he chose his words '. . . rather more open to interpretation. So, to answer your question, this firm has handled three murders in the last eighteen months, which is a lot by local standards, in fact two more than any other firm in Exeter. Now if Ginny feels she would like to go to people with more expertise, then I would understand completely, and I would do my best to hand the case on to another firm in good order, if that was what she so wished. As for the psychiatric assessment . . . I can only say that I thought it was for the best.'

I dropped back into my chair and regarded Tingwall's thin intense face. 'What's your opinion?' I asked drily. 'Do you think Ginny would do better elsewhere?'

Tingwall pondered this with his habitual diligence. 'Some of the big London firms would certainly have greater experience in this type of case. Against that, a local firm has the advantage of local knowledge, and of being on the spot, with experience of the local courts. A big city firm might have more immediate access to the right experts, to specialist knowledge, but a small country firm, if it does its homework properly, wouldn't let that be a problem. If at first you can't find the right expert,' he recited with a forefinger in the air, 'then you keep looking until you track him down.' He grew solemn again before cocking me a half-smile. 'Being a small outfit, we might also try harder.'

Despite his youth and relative inexperience, despite the gaffe over the psychiatric assessment, my first instinct was to stay with Tingwall. Yet this was Ginny's future we were talking about. Getting this decision right was probably the most important thing I could ever do for her. Before putting the matter to Ginny I decided to check it out with some lawyer friends in London. I said, 'I'll have to speak to my wife.'

'Of course. It's for her to decide.' He gave a

diffident smile. 'Perhaps I should say ... if she decided to entrust me with the case I would give it my very best shot. Everything I had.'

'I'll tell her that.'

A slight softening had come over Tingwall's face, a shadow of his fascination for Ginny, grown distant now, and sadder.

'You're visiting her tomorrow morning?' he asked, resuming a suitable briskness. 'Give her my best regards, would you? And tell her I'll see her before court on Monday.' Behind him the calf-bound legal tomes marched brashly along the shelves, at his elbow a stack of files teetered precariously, and I wondered how many other cases he had on the go.

'What'll happen on Monday exactly?'

'Not a lot. The Crown Prosecution Service will ask for a further remand, and I will ask that it be set for a week, and the magistrates will agree. And that's it.'

'We don't question anything?'

'The evidence, you mean? Not at this stage, no.'

'When, then?'

Tingwall's narrow eyes flicked away briefly, he pursed his lips. 'It's highly unlikely we would want to challenge anything before the trial. Though that can't be decided, finally, until we see the prosecution's evidence.'

I said with disgust, 'And the trial's eight months away.'

'It could be six.'

'And there's no chance of getting the case stopped before then?'

Tingwall was looking uneasy, as he always did

when I talked in this way. 'I think we have to face the fact that it's very unlikely.'

My frustration resurfaced. 'It all sounds so *negative.*'

Tingwall considered this with detachment. 'I would hope – realistic.'

I pulled my hands down my face and let my anger go. I knew I shouldn't take my disappointment out on Tingwall, yet a part of me needed to challenge the frightening mood of inevitability which seemed to have attached itself to Ginny's case.

'You think the evidence is that strong?' I hadn't meant to ask this; I wasn't sure that I was ready to hear the answer.

'As laid out by the police,' Tingwall stated cautiously, 'as specified by them, the evidence would seem sufficient to take the case to trial.'

So far I had avoided discussion of the evidence. There are things that aren't that easy to face. But now, finally, I braced myself to confront the facts, partly to test Tingwall's knowledge against my own, but also – there was no denying it – to feed my own hunger for understanding, to embellish the reel of film that kept running through my head with images and colour.

'Tell me what they have,' I asked calmly. 'As you understand it. The evidence so far.'

Tingwall shot me a questioning glance, then stood up. 'Of course. Coffee?' He went to a side table and, pouring two cups from a Thermos jug, brought them over. He pulled up a chair and, setting it at an angle to mine, sat on the edge of the seat, hunched forward with his arms resting on his knees, and began to speak in the gentle measured tones of a storyteller.

'I asked the police for a summary of their main evidence immediately after Ginny was charged. And it was the same as the evidence listed in court on Monday. Now it's possible they may be holding something back on the principle that you don't give away any more than you have to at this stage of the proceedings, but I doubt it. In a case like this I think they'd produce everything they had, just to be sure. So . . .' He clasped his hands together. 'The first thing they stated was that several traces of the victim's blood had been found on the floor of the *Ellie Miller*, thus establishing the boat as the scene of the crime. Now this was a categorical statement, based on forensic evidence, so we can assume that they have run DNA tests and so on. Then . . .' He paused to take a sip of coffee and gather his thoughts. 'Then they said that Ginny's fingerprint had been found in a bloodstain on the boat, and that this blood was also the victim's.'

I had meant to keep quiet, but I said, 'This forensic stuff, it's cut and dried, is it?'

'Usually, yes. In the case of DNA, particularly so.' He was like a cat on a precarious ledge, choosing the safest place to step. 'With other forensic evidence, it can sometimes be . . . open to interpretation. Often it's a matter of the individual expert's opinion – and opinions can differ. Very occasionally they differ considerably. What we can do, of course, is hire our own expert to examine whatever evidence it is and run his own tests. If his findings give us a chance of challenging the prosecution's expert, then – well, obviously we'd pursue that avenue rigorously, get a third opinion and so on. The first step – and I think I mentioned this to you the other day – is to get a pathologist to carry out a post-mortem for us. I've made enquiries and Dr James Bagnall could do it next week. He's the best man, quite famous now. If the police pathologist has missed anything, he'll find it. And his opinion would count for a great deal. He's done a lot of murders – all the ones you read about.'

And now this one: another to be read about.

'I'll go ahead then, shall I?' Tingwall asked. 'With Dr Bagnall?'

'Yes,' I said, trying not to think of Sylvie's body and what would happen to it under Bagnall's knife. 'I interrupted you. On the evidence.'

Tingwall's disconcerting gaze flicked up to me, before fixing itself on the floor some five or six feet in front of him. 'Next . . . The police are saying that they have a witness who saw Ginny rowing out to the boat on the *Saturday* afternoon, when she says she was only just starting out from London. Now identification evidence is always soft evidence, and if this was the only thing the prosecution had to go on we'd certainly consider challenging it at an early stage.'

But it was not the only evidence, and he moved quickly on. 'Finally, they cited Ginny's own statement, that she went to *Ellie Miller* the next day, the Sunday, and scrubbed the boat clean. The inference being that she was removing blood and so on.'

In the silence that followed I replayed that Sunday

morning in my mind, as I had replayed it so many times in the last week. I saw Ginny in jeans and a loose top, packing a plastic bucket with cleaning materials to take out to the boat. I held her face close to my mind's eye and searched her expression for signs of trauma and despair, I recalled snippets of our dialogue and scanned the casually uttered words for intimations of disaster, yet I found nothing, no hint at all. Casting Ginny in an innocent role, I saw someone keen to participate in the boat-orientated life at Dittisham from which I had excluded her for so long that summer, eager to muck in and show me what she could contribute, and, in so doing, make a go of our marriage again: Ginny the peacemaker, fraught with nothing more sinister than anxiety. Then I cast her as someone frighteningly different, a person I scarcely recognised, someone calculating and vindictive, cold and methodical, someone who was capable not only of committing such a terrible act, but of behaving as if it had never happened, and in this incarnation her mild agitation that morning finally took on a guilty significance.

Tingwall murmured, 'Of course we must wait for the prosecution to serve their statements on us before we can be absolutely sure of what we're up against, and that won't be for some weeks yet.'

'But at the moment it looks pretty bad?' I said, staring straight into his crooked eyes.

'I wouldn't use a word like bad, Hugh. But there's certainly a serious case to answer.'

This judgment, though I had been expecting it, was like a band tightening around my heart.

I braced myself to ask, 'What's the worst that can happen?'

'The worst?' He jerked his head back slightly, as though recoiling from an unpleasant task. 'I really . . . That's something for the QC to advise.'

I persevered, 'If she was found guilty?'

He said with great reluctance, 'For murder, it's a mandatory life sentence. But Hugh, there are bound to be mitigating circumstances, the chance of a lesser charge—'

'Bound to be?'

'Of course! Ginny's case is never going to fall into the same category as a cold-blooded gang murderer. There are so many ways to play this, Hugh. She could plead guilty to manslaughter on the grounds of diminished responsibility, for example. She could say she was under such intolerable strain that she lost her head. She could say she was severely provoked and reacted in an instant of madness. Or she might have been suffering severe clinical depression. There are so many ways to approach this, Hugh. So many ways to win a jury's understanding.'

'And for manslaughter?'

He was not enjoying this game. He blew out his lips. 'It varies so much, I couldn't give you a figure. It all depends on the circumstances and the judge. Anything from a few years to fifteen, eighteen, with half off for good behaviour. It's such a wide range.'

Significantly less than life, at any rate. For some reason I fastened on to the idea of seven years as a time which seemed survivable, a time which, long though it was, had a foreseeable end. I imagined visiting Ginny in prison year after year, the two of us getting older, nearing fifty before we could start our lives again, in France perhaps, or Italy. Survivable.

A lorry shuddered past in the street outside, filling the room with a low rumble.

'So manslaughter might be the best bet?' I said, groping for reassurance.

'We'll have to wait for Counsel's recommendations, and he won't be able to put anything to Ginny until he has everything in front of him, until he has her story.'

Ginny's story. The great unknown. Part of me longed to hear it, the other part lived in dread of what it might contain. 'She hasn't said anything to you?'

'No. And I haven't pressed her. The only thing I would like to know fairly soon, though, is whether anyone can vouch for her whereabouts on that Saturday afternoon. In my experience alibi witnesses are best caught early, before their memories fade. But she hasn't really been in any state to consider that, so I'll ask her again on Monday.'

'An alibi witness?' I said doubtfully. 'You think that's likely?'

He looked rather disappointed in me, as if I had failed to grasp an essential point. 'What *I* think is neither here nor there,' he stated. 'At this stage we must rule out nothing at all. It would be a terrible mistake to overlook the smallest thing that might help the defence. A case must never be lost for lack of trying.'

He did not remove his energetic gaze from my face

until he was sure I had understood the importance of what he was saying, and in that moment I felt an upsurge of confidence in him, and, with this, a small easing of the burden.

'No stone unturned,' I said.

We got to our feet.

'Not a pebble either.' He endorsed this with a diffident smile. 'You mustn't believe there's nothing that can be done, Hugh. It's very rare that nothing can be done.'

But just then it seemed to me that Ginny's situation was almost hopeless.

A horn tooted and I looked round to see my car move off a yellow line and sweep in to the kerb beside me. Julia lowered the window and one glimpse of her expression told me that there had been no call from Cumberland.

'Want to drive?' she asked.

I shook my head and went round to the passenger side.

'So, no reprieve?' I asked, getting in.

She cast me a scathing glance. 'Was there ever likely to be? All this talk of asking the board to reconsider at the eleventh hour was just Howard playing off both sides against the middle. There was never a chance!'

It was over then. At some point that morning the Cumberland board had formally accepted a bid from another company, a glass manufacturer called Donington. In their explanatory fax to the Hartford team, sent at six last evening after rumours had been circulating all day, the board had cited their responsibility to serve the best interests of the shareholders, a duty they felt would be best fulfilled by accepting the Donington bid.

So it was over, for me at least. Late last night George had talked about fighting the Cumberland board, about writing to every Cumberland shareholder to put the facts before them, to call an extraordinary general meeting and persuade them to oppose the Donington bid and back our own; he had talked about unleashing every trick in the book, using the media, the politicians, all the spoiling tactics we could think of. He talked fiercely, he made a lot of sense, but in my heart I knew my own fight was over. I was ready to let Hartford go, I was no longer bothered by the idea of Howard beating me. In the shadow of Ginny's catastrophe my own battles seemed rather insignificant. The only thing that still had the power to upset me was the thought of Hartford closing, of the people who would never work there again, and the death of the furnaces.

Julia drove along the one-way system, muttering at the lack of road signs, until I pointed her towards the Totnes road.

'George has told everyone, has he?' I asked.

'He will have by now. He warned them yesterday, so they'd be ready for it. And while we're on the subject of staff,' Julia added firmly, 'I'll stay on for as long as you want me, a day or a month, and no redundancy required, thank you very much. I've got another job lined up for when I leave.'

'I wish I could keep you on.'

'That's all right.'

'Won't be able to afford you.'

'That's what my boyfriends say.'

I hadn't faced the money situation yet. Now that the buyout had failed I would have to meet the expenses of the bid, for which I had made myself personally liable – the fees of the venture capitalists, accountants and lawyers – a sum I didn't care to add up quite yet but which would certainly run a long way into six figures. And then, most important of all, I would need to put plenty aside for Ginny's defence, on which no expense was to be spared.

'When did it finally come back?' I said, indicating the car.

'Wednesday.'

I looked for traces of the police examination. Fingerprint powder or whatever they used, but the dashboard was clean and there was nothing to be seen on the doors.

'Mary told me they've finished with Dittisham House as well,' Julia added, 'though it's too late to save the sale, apparently. The people got fed up with waiting.'

Or they didn't like the notoriety that was fast attaching itself to the house, though neither of us remarked on that.

'Mary wanted to know if you were intending to stay the night with them.'

I hadn't got that far. All week I had been choosing a place to sleep almost at random, sometimes driving miles back to London after seeing Tingwall, sometimes travelling the forty minutes to Melton after seeing Ginny at the prison, or one day – it must have been Wednesday – just shutting myself away in Glebe Place, drinking and sleeping, occasionally crying my eyes out, until, waking at two in the morning, I had driven through the night to Dittisham and, going down to the quay, sat on a wall watching the dawn come up. When it was light I had gone to the boat yard and through the fence looked at the draped outline of *Ellie* on the hard standing, and briefly wept again.

I hadn't stayed with Mary and David since the weekend. I hadn't been avoiding them exactly, but at the same time I wasn't ready to discuss the details of Ginny's case with anyone but Tingwall. Julia understood this intuitively, as did David, who, though he had called several times, had been careful to restrict himself to practical matters. Mary was unlikely to be so easily rebuffed, however. When we'd spoken on the phone she'd kept asking the sort of questions that I wasn't ready to answer. While I still valued our friendship, while it had seemed natural to confide in her on the subject of Sylvie, Ginny was an entirely different matter, and, for the moment at least, Mary's curiosity had caused me to pull up my drawbridge.

'I'll decide later,' I said.

'Mary said she could leave supper out for you if you were late. That reminds me.' Julia reached behind her seat and handed me a sandwich. 'It's compulsory,' she said.

I didn't argue. I'd been eating spasmodically, if at

all, and I knew that if I was to be any good to Ginny I had to start pulling myself together.

We reached Hartford under a darkening sky and spitting rain, which cast a gloom over the factory windows and leached the colour from the flowers around the entrance.

Heather, the receptionist, raised puffy eyes and dabbed at them with a handkerchief. 'Oh, Mr Wellesley, I'm so sorry,' she cried, pulling a tragic face.

'I'm very sorry too, Heather.' And for a confusing instant I wondered if we were talking about Hartford or Ginny.

George, Alan and John were waiting in Pa's old office. We shook hands with more than usual energy, the closest we could safely get to emotion.

George declared with a defiant upward thrust of one fist: 'We may have lost the battle, Hugh, but we haven't lost the war! They had the nerve to tell us Donington's bid was worth more than ours? Well, it's not! They're taking some of it in Donington shares – aiming for another merger or whatever – and the market value of the shares is ten pence down on the paper value. I've been on to the lawyers. They say it's good enough for an extraordinary general meeting. We can still get 'em, Hugh! We can still win!' And he gave an excited cry that seemed to intensify the flush of his florid cheeks.

Because I couldn't think of what else to say, I murmured, 'You've been busy then.'

We clustered around the table, ready to sit down. There was a pause while Alan and John looked towards George, waiting for him to make some sort of announcement.

'Yes, uhh . . .' George frowned. 'All of us would like to express our sadness at what has happened to your wife, Hugh. And we'd like you to know that if there's anything we can do you only have to call on us. Anything at all.'

'Thank you.'

'I'd like to second that,' said Alan.

John added a brisk, 'Me too.'

'Thank you. I can only say that . . .' It was hard to compose even these few words. 'I appreciate your thoughts. And if my family problems tipped Cumberland's decision against us, then I regret that very much. For you and for everyone else at Hartford.'

George made an exclamation of denial and Alan followed fast with: 'Listen – Cumberland were out to make our lives difficult from the start, weren't they?'

'Howard was, you mean,' George chipped in. 'One way or another.'

Alan urged, 'Don't blame yourself, Hugh. It was always going to be a battle.'

They were saying what they thought I wanted to hear, but I knew, as they must have known, that the publicity over Ginny, the terrible nature of the crime, and the knowledge that, with all my problems and preoccupations, I couldn't possibly sustain any practical involvement in Hartford, must have counted heavily against us.

There was a slight pause, a moment of mutual sympathy and unease, before we left the subject behind.

Even as we were settling in our seats, George launched his plan of attack. 'The first step,' he said blithely, 'is to get this EGM off the ground. All we need is the backing of ten per cent of the equity. What with your holding, Hugh and your brother's—'

'George—'

Perhaps he knew what was coming, because he frowned at my interruption.

'Are you sure you still have Zircon and the banks behind you?'

I had used 'you' not 'we' and 'us', but if he realised I was excluding myself from this process he didn't comment on it.

'I was coming round to that,' he said rapidly. 'I realise only too well that we'll have to sell them the idea of hanging on. But if we're going to get this EGM off the ground at all, we have to move fast.'

'I think you might have to move fast on the banks too,' I said in my most diplomatic tone. 'I think they'll already have gone cold on you, and the news of the Donington bid will finish them off. I think there's no time to lose.'

This was met by an exchange of glances between George and Alan.

George said, 'In fact, we were hoping you might tackle the banks. We thought it would come best from you.'

'Don't be ridiculous. It would come worst from me. They won't want to know about me.'

'Why not?'

Was this a mistaken show of loyalty or could he really not see the problem? 'George, quite apart from my personal credibility, they'll know I can't possibly have my eye on the ball any more. They'll know I can't possibly give it a hundred per cent, and they'll be dead right.'

'We realise it won't be easy for you, Hugh. We realise your time will be limited. But we've discussed it – and, Hugh, we don't think we can do it without you.'

'I think you could do it without me very well.'

George ignored this. 'You talk the banks' language.'

How to make him realise it was all over? 'I'm out, George.'

'We'll do the rest, all the legwork, all the nitty-gritty. We'll take everything off your back. Just the banks, Hugh,' George pleaded. 'Please – just give it a try.'

I had forgotten how stubborn George could be, and how this quality, so valuable in a production director, could seem less attractive from the receiving end. 'My heart simply wouldn't be in it,' I said, trying to spell it out for him.

'That's the way you feel now, Hugh. And we all understand that. But give it a while. Give it a few days, give it a week.'

'No time,' I argued again. 'I wouldn't have the time.'

'Maybe not just at the moment. But in the future, maybe you'll have more time than you think. Maybe you'll be glad of a project.'

Unexpectedly, this hit a chord. In the months ahead I had been planning to spend my time supporting Ginny, meeting lawyers, doing everything I could.

But now that some of the shock had worn off I could see that I had perhaps been idealising my role, or at least oversimplifying it. Once Ginny got bail she might not want me under her feet the whole time, and I might be glad of some distraction; both of us might be desperate for a semblance of normal life.

Seeing the chink in my armour, George played his last card. 'We owe it to our people, Hugh,' he said in a blatant appeal to my conscience. 'Otherwise they'll be on the scrapheap, claiming benefits, having their skills go to waste. Surely we owe them one last go.'

'I might do more damage than good. With the banks.'

'We'll risk it.'

'Don't say I didn't warn you.'

They were waiting.

'I'll *think* about it,' I sighed, realising that this was as good as a promise and that, somehow or another, I had managed to manoeuvre myself into a corner.

I dropped Julia at the station and drove on to Dartmouth to see David. His surgery, a utilitarian single-storey building which he shared with his two partners, was set on a precipitous slope above the harbour with views across to Kingswear and the marina. Among the sea of yacht masts I found myself looking for the sleek outlines of the customs launch and wondering if the customs men had known of Sylvie's activities before our trip to France. In the next moment I pushed the thought impatiently aside. What did it matter now? It was finished. Sylvie would never be coming back. Except, it seemed, to destroy my life.

The surgery had been refurbished since my last visit. The waiting area had acquired pale wooden chairs with padded seats, potted plants and framed prints, and, on one wall, an electronic announcement board telling patients when their doctor was ready for them.

There were five people waiting, but after ten minutes the receptionist caught my eye and waved me through.

The passage leading to David's room was decorated with photographs and posters of racing cars, pictures which he had accumulated in his early twenties when he'd harboured a passion to become an amateur racing driver. Like most of David's more extravagant ambitions at that time – there had been schemes to fly hot-air balloons and buy into a yacht charter business in the Caribbean – it had fallen victim to the tight financial rein that Pa had kept us on. David had taken this restriction badly, as an unjust denial of his inheritance, yet Pa had always gone out of his way to explain how our trust funds were set up, telling us from a young age that there would be no capital until we were thirty. I could never work out whether David simply hadn't accepted this or had thought he could get round the old man. Either way he had been regularly, and to his mind unfairly, disappointed.

David came round his desk and gripped me awkwardly by both shoulders. I thought for a moment that he was about to embrace me, something that would have startled us both, but he gave me a small shake instead, a sort of rallying jolt. He stepped back, looking slightly cross with himself. 'What a bloody awful business,' he exclaimed finally.

I could only nod.

'Now how's Tingwall shaping up?' he asked, waving me to a seat like a patient. 'He's definitely the best lawyer you'll get locally – I've checked up on him again, asked around.' He pulled up another chair and sat next to me on the patients' side of the desk. 'But being the best around here may not be saying too much.' He rolled a despairing eye at the limitations of the provinces. 'You *are* considering people in London?'

'I'm getting advice on that.'

'Make sure you get the best,' he urged. 'And what about a QC? Tingwall's getting you a QC?'

We had already discussed these things on the phone at least once, maybe twice. Whether David had forgotten or was simply anxious to press his advice home I couldn't tell.

'And the medical side?' he continued systematically, like a chairman working his way through an agenda. 'That's under control, is it?'

'We're getting a letter from her asthma specialist, saying she's got to have bail for health reasons.'

'Anything else you need in that department?' he asked almost fiercely.

'That's what I came about, actually. We need a good psychiatrist. Someone who's prepared to say Ginny's not a suicide risk. Otherwise they might block bail.'

David's expression brightened at the challenge. He tapped his fingertips together while he pondered. 'There's a bloke called Jones. Based in Bristol.'

'He'll be all right, will he?'

'Oh, he'll do the necessary, if that's what you mean.' From the confidence of his tone, Jones and he might have been fellow mafiosi who traded favours in the form of foregone conclusions. 'I'll speak to him this afternoon.' He reached for a pad and made a note.

'Tingwall found a guy called Robertson, but' – it still disturbed me to say it – 'he seemed to think that Ginny might be a risk to herself.' Seeking reassurance, I lifted my brows and turned this into a question.

'Well, anyone would be a bit desperate in her situation, wouldn't they? *Christ!* Facing all *that*.' He grimaced at the thought, and gave a sudden shiver. 'But if she's a bit depressed the right drugs will soon sort her out.'

'You really think so?' I longed for Ginny to be released, but sometimes the prospect of looking after her on my own worried me.

'Oh yes. Jones will know what to prescribe.'

A pause, during which we exchanged a quick glance.

'Nothing else I can do?' he asked.

I shook my head.

Another pause as David prepared himself to say awkwardly, 'Look, it's none of my business, and the last thing I want to do is – *interfere . . .*' He contorted his face, waiting for objections, before continuing gruffly, 'But what have they got in the way of evidence, for Christ's sake? What *can* they have? They must have got something drastically wrong, it's crazy to think that Ginny—' He shut his mouth abruptly as if he'd already said enough.

I would never have foreseen David as an open champion of Ginny's cause, just as I could never have predicted the extent of his concern. I was touched. David had such a long history of detachment, he had always been so wary of gratuitous confidences that he usually steered clear of what he called 'situations'.

'They know Sylvie was killed on the boat,' I told him haltingly. 'And then they have a fingerprint of Ginny's, found on board. And some witness who saw her rowing out to the boat, on the Saturday afternoon.'

David frowned. 'A fingerprint? But what does that mean, for heaven's sake? Ginny's been on the boat often enough.'

'No. No . . . You see, it was in blood. Sylvie's blood.'

'Ah.' He absorbed this grudgingly. '*Ah.*' He stared beyond me in further consideration, then shook his head. 'But couldn't there be some other explanation? Couldn't she have – I don't know . . .' He threw a hand in the air. 'Come into contact with the blood some other way. After the event, or . . .' He ran out of ideas, just as I did whenever I put myself through the same exercise. Catching sight of my face, seeing with alarm that I was close to the edge of my emotions, he added briskly, 'The thing is, there's going to be a way of getting her off, Hugh. There always is. Some fact they haven't checked, some witness who hasn't come forward, some deal to be made with the lawyers. That's why you need the best defence team money can buy. Eh?'

But I wasn't in any mood to be cheered up. 'Ginny's simply not capable of this thing, David. She just couldn't have done it.'

He shifted in his seat. 'No.'

I held on to my voice with difficulty. 'She just couldn't.'

He nodded grimly.

'She . . .' But I couldn't speak, I was clenching my lips too tightly.

Leaning forward, David moved a tentative hand as if to comfort me before thinking better of it and sweeping his hand up towards his chin.

I pulled in my breath with a gasp. 'She has no violence in her. None at all. She couldn't hurt a fly. She just couldn't . . .'

'No.' Swinging to his feet, David fetched water and Kleenex, and, thrusting them at me, waited while I blew my nose and generally pulled myself together.

'I'm keeping your patients waiting,' I said at last.

'Oh, they're used to it,' he declared airily. 'Now what about you? Need anything to make you sleep? Anything to cheer you up?'

'Oh, I'm all right.' I rearranged my expression into something a little less morbid.

'Shall I give you something anyway, just in case?'

I stood up and gave my nose a final blow. 'David, they don't make pills for what I need.'

'You'd be amazed what Prozac can do.' He lifted a satanic eyebrow.

'I'd rather not find out just at the moment.'

'My patients live on the stuff,' he announced, poker-faced. 'High doses – keeps 'em nice and quiet.'

As so often, I wasn't quite sure whether David was spinning one of his darker jokes.

He walked me to the waiting room door then, resuming some of his old manner, gave an evasive almost irritated smile before turning quickly away.

I was unlocking my car when a horn tooted and I looked up to see Mary's car swooping in through the entrance. Parking untidily, she came striding over.

'I caught you! David told me you were popping in. I'm so *glad* I caught you!' She gave me a firm kiss on the cheek and, gripping my arm, surveyed me with fond concern. 'How are you?'

I pulled a so-so expression.

'Now you *are* staying tonight, aren't you?'

'Wish I could, but . . .' I gestured difficulties.

'Oh, come on. Come and stay!'

'I really can't.'

She made a face. 'Why on earth not? Where will you go, for goodness sake?'

'Oh, Melton. I have to go and see to the place.'

She shook her head at me. 'Well, come back for a quick coffee then!'

'Mary, I wish I could, but I have to rush.'

'But I so want to talk to you!' She gave a rapid smile to soften the rebuke in her voice. 'I've got important things to tell you.'

'What sort of important things?'

'I'll explain, but come and have a coffee. It'll be easier over a coffee.'

I couldn't hide my exasperation as I said: 'But what's it about, Mary?'

She sighed at me. 'Why, the case, of course!'

A flutter of hope. 'You've heard something? What is it?'

'It's hard to explain just like that.'

'Mary, just tell me! Tell me, please!'

She gave me a look of mock anger that wasn't entirely light-hearted. 'I can't see what's so difficult about coming home for a minute!' Her good humour had developed a sharp edge to it, and it occurred to me that she too must have been feeling the strain of our family's instant notoriety. 'All right! All right!' she declared suddenly, as though giving in to the whim of a child. 'Let's get out of the wind at any rate.'

We got into my car. Mary pushed her hair back from her face and I dimly noticed that she'd done something new and not entirely successful with the style. She had eye makeup on, too, a shade of blue that contrasted strongly with her pink cheeks and dark eyebrows.

'Right!' she declared forcefully. '*What* I wanted to tell you was that I've been doing some research. I went through my old legal tomes – the ones I still have, at any rate – *and* I went and looked through a friend's legal library which is more up-to-date. *And* I spoke to a friend of a friend in London who's a real ace on case law and precedent. Now it seems there have been some very significant cases in recent years.' She spoke fast and emphatically. 'There was one case where a wife killed her husband's lover and pleaded manslaughter on the grounds of diminished responsibility and only got *eight* years. Which means she served four. And *that* was a case where there were definite overtones of premeditation – the wife went round to the other woman's house with a hammer. *Said* she only intended to break the windows, *but . . .'* She made a knowing face before racing on. '*Then* there was another case. A wife discovered her husband in bed with another woman. She rushed down to the kitchen and got a knife and went up and stabbed him. Said it was PMT that drove her to it, temporary insanity. She virtually walked free—'

'Mary, what are you trying to tell me exactly?' I interrupted in a calm voice.

I had broken her flow. 'What I was *trying* to say was that in these types of cases the jury can often overlook the odd bit of premeditation—'

'I meant, your point. What is your point?'

'If you'd let me explain—'

'Mary . . .' I held up both hands. 'I'm grateful, but I don't think I'm quite ready for this.'

She gave a rapid empty smile. '*All* I'm trying to tell you is that if there's diminished responsibility and not too much premeditation then the sentence could be almost nothing! A few years!'

'I see,' I said tightly. 'I see. Well, thank you for going to the trouble.' Not trusting myself to say any more, I scrambled out of the car and stood looking down at the harbour.

I heard Mary's door slam. 'Hugh,' she cried, coming up behind me. 'Hugh! I just wanted you to realise that it needn't be that bad. I mean – a few years! It's not so much, is it?'

It was suddenly a great deal to me, much more than it had seemed in Tingwall's office. And I was terribly hurt by Mary's presumption of Ginny's guilt, the way she seemed to be offering a few years' prison as some sort of consolation prize. In my mood of desolation it struck me that beneath David's show of concern he might also believe that Ginny was guilty. Perhaps everyone thought she was guilty.

But then perhaps I was reacting so strongly because, deep down, against all my wishes, it was what I believed too.

Ginny appeared at last, and, seeing me, cast her eyes down and wove her way slowly between the crowded tables. She was wearing something nice, I noticed, a flowing ankle-length skirt and matching top, and her hair was newly washed and combed so that it gleamed ochre and amber in the light.

We embraced briefly and sat facing each other across the formica table.

I searched her face. 'How are you?'

'Oh . . .' She pondered this. 'They gave me something. Tranquillisers, I think. They seem to even things out a bit.'

This was more than she had said to me during both of my previous visits put together, and I smiled, 'You look better.' This wasn't true: she looked thinner, her eyes appeared larger in her face and the skin of her cheeks seemed to cling more tightly to the bones. But the empty look that had disturbed me so much on my last visit had faded, and I recognised something of the old Ginny in her eyes.

'How's the room? Did they move you?'

She gave the faintest nod. 'I'm on my own. Not everyone's on their own.'

'Well, that's something!'

'It has sun.'

'That's nice!' I replied rather too brightly. 'Health all right? You've got enough inhalers? You've seen a doctor?'

She was slow to concentrate. 'More than one,' she said. 'Two ... three. Psychiatrists, mainly.'

'I'm afraid that you might have to see another,' I ventured gently. 'A man called Jones. Did Tingwall tell you? It's to make sure we get this bail application through.'

She looked uncertain, as though her memory were playing tricks.

'We need someone to say that you're fit and well to come home. Tingwall should have told you.'

'I didn't know what to say,' she murmured. 'He kept asking me how I felt about the future.'

'Who? Robertson?'

'What was I meant to say?' She cast me a baffled look. 'I didn't know what to say.'

I reached for her hand. 'Darling, don't worry about it. Just leave it to Jones when he comes. He'll make sure it's all right.'

There was a commotion at the next table as a child started to scream.

When the child had quietened down a little Ginny asked dully, 'Will I get bail?'

I hesitated. 'Tingwall thinks there's an excellent chance.' I explained about the QC, and how Tingwall was aiming to pre-empt any objections the police or prosecution might have. But she had seen my hesitation and understood it; she realised it would be a mistake to count too firmly on her freedom.

'But listen,' I said, pushing optimism into my voice, 'I had a long session with Tingwall. We started mapping things out. We've got six months, maybe more, before the trial. That gives him plenty of time to prepare the best possible defence. Now I want you to be quite clear, darling – we're going to have the very best team, the best lawyers, the best experts and doctors – whatever it takes. There won't be a single thing that won't be covered. Not a thing!'

She thought about this but did not seem to draw much comfort from it.

I ploughed on. 'And as for tactics – approaches – there are all sorts of options. Tingwall went through them with me . . . Ginny?'

She had sucked in her lips, she was blinking rapidly: the signs.

'Darling,' I pleaded helplessly.

Pulling her hand away, she stared down at the table and shook her head. It was both an appeal and a warning. She did not want to discuss it.

Retreating, I cast around for safer ground. After a long pause I offered half-heartedly, 'Things at Hartford are still frantic. Everyone racing around . . .'

She nodded to show she was listening.

'But I've backed off for a while. Left them to it. Quite nice, being out of it.' I added for light relief: 'Might try it on a permanent basis.'

There was no flicker of an answering smile. 'And the buyout?'

'Oh, more off than on at the moment.' I shrugged: 'There was always a risk.'

'Sorry.'

'One of those things.' Another pause during which I became increasingly lost. 'Oh . . . The estate agent says there might be some people interested in Melton.'

'That would be good,' she said with visible effort. 'Before they next go over the place get Mrs Hoskins to put plenty of flowers everywhere, won't you? It makes such a difference.'

A couple of young children roared past. We lapsed into silence again.

I said, 'Nothing from the agents in France, though.'

She gave a long jagged sigh. 'I'm sorry,' she gasped, and I realised we weren't talking about houses any more. 'I know you were only trying to help.'

'Doesn't matter.'

'I find it so hard . . . You see' – she raised her eyes at last – 'whenever I think about it, I can't see any way out, and it frightens me to death.'

A spark of dread passed between us.

'Ginny, there *will* be a way out. Wait until you talk it through with Tingwall. He'll explain all the options. I promise – there *will* be a way out! Just tell him what he needs to know. I promise!'

She swung her head slowly from side to side. 'But what can I tell him?'

Aware that she might be on the brink of some irreversible revelation, feeling a terrifying blend of fear and curiosity, I led her slowly forward. 'You must tell him anything that could help. Like where you were on that Saturday afternoon, at exactly what time, and who might have seen you ... Someone *must* have seen you, darling. At Glebe Place, or on the motorway, or ...'

'But I was there.' This comment slipped into the pool of silence, a small ripple which grew and grew. 'I can't say I wasn't there. That's why they're never going to believe me.' She gave a ragged laugh, near tears. 'Never.'

My breath was tight in my chest. 'When you say *there*, you mean ... you mean in Dittisham?'

She nodded bitterly.

'You ...' I could hardly ask it. 'You weren't near the boat, though?'

'I thought you were on board, I went to find you.'

A cold horror settled in my stomach. I felt sick. 'And then?' I whispered.

I thought for a moment that she wasn't going to answer. Her eyes glistened with unshed tears. 'I found her.'

I could hardly speak. 'Found her?'

She put a hand to her head, as though it was causing her pain.

'Ginny, Ginny ...' I tried to keep the shock out of my voice. 'What are you saying? Are you saying she was dead?'

She was silent.

'*Ginny?*' I pleaded. 'What are you saying?'

She rubbed her temples. 'It doesn't matter.'

'But is that what you're saying? For God's sake, *tell me.*'

She looked me straight in the eye then, and it was a look which contained resignation and defeat, and finally, a small but unmistakable flicker of confirmation.

My mind went racing off in several directions, most of them startling, all of them confusing. 'But, Ginny . . . why didn't you tell anyone this? Why didn't you report it?'

She shook her head slowly, and kept shaking it for a long time.

I leant across the table, I seized her hands roughly in mine. 'But you must tell them now! You must!'

'It wouldn't do any good.'

'Why not, for God's sake?'

'Oh Hugh . . .' And she gave me a pitying look.

'I don't understand.'

But she closed herself off from me then. Her face emptied, she dropped her eyes.

I struggled to make sense of it, I tried to grasp what she was telling me, but I was hurt and confused by her lack of faith in me, it was all a jumble, and for a while I felt as though I too were going mad.

Ten

IN ENGLISH courts there are two kinds of magistrate, Tingwall enlightened me. There are the stipendiaries, known colloquially as 'stipes', trained lawyers who sit alone on the bench as full-time professionals, and there are the lay magistrates, part-time justices of the peace who sit for a few days a month in a triumvirate with two fellow JPs.

Exeter had no stipendiaries, only JPs. I wouldn't have given this any thought, I certainly wouldn't have seen it as any kind of disadvantage if Grainger, our QC, hadn't commented to Tingwall within my hearing, 'Oh for a stipe.' Seeing I had picked up on this, Grainger elaborated derisively in his affected drawl, 'JPs can be dreadful old women. Paralysed by the fear of doing the wrong thing. And, as a consequence, of course, frequently doing precisely that.'

I did not fret about this for too long. Partly because I saw Grainger's concern as a way of covering his back. Partly because, by the time we had waited in the hall outside the court for an hour, I was beginning to think that Grainger himself might be a far greater liability. His arrogant overbearing London style seemed destined to rub the JPs up the wrong way, as it had so thoroughly irritated me. I tried to talk myself out of disliking the man, but the way he strutted about, his bombastic voice and imperious manner made me so angry that I had to take myself for a walk around the block. Tingwall reassured me that Grainger was one of the top criminal barristers in the country and that he hadn't won this reputation by chance, but by the time we filed into court I had convinced myself that Grainger was in every respect a terrible mistake.

I recognised one of the male JPs from a previous remand, but the second man and the woman were new. Both men were sixtyish, one a successful business type, the other, the chairman, a tweedy country-man, a landowner or professional man. The woman was younger, about forty, and stylish. They were the sort of people Ginny and I had occasionally met on Wiltshire weekends, though I couldn't decide whether to take encouragement from that.

Stairs led straight up into the dock from the cells below, and to the accompaniment of clanging subter-ranean doors and shuffling feet, Ginny appeared with officers ahead and behind. This sight disturbed me, it seemed grotesque, as though Ginny were the victim of some hideous identity switch.

She did not glance in my direction as she went to the front of the dock and sat down. The business quickly began. Grainger announced that he repre-sented Ginny and made the application for bail.

The prosecution objected to bail due to the serious-ness of the crime and the prison psychiatrist's report, which indicated that Ginny was in a frail state of mind and might be a danger to herself.

Rising, Grainger began his plea. I had to strain to hear him. At first I thought he was simply getting into his stride, working his voice up to a theatrical pitch, but then it dawned on me that this quiet unassuming tone was the one he had deliberately selected for the occasion. The actor-lawyer, appearing for this performance only as the sincere advocate without pretensions. As he pleaded Ginny's previous good character, her exemplary life, her charitable work, her poor health which, the doctors agreed, would suffer dramatically unless she were allowed home, I was forced to hand it to him, grudgingly at first, then with increasing admiration. It was a masterly show of moderation and restraint, with just the right dash of humility. If I hadn't met him beforehand, I would have thought he was an extremely nice man.

Without giving the slightest hint as to the way Ginny intended to plead, he managed to suggest that she was incapable of hurting a fly, and suddenly the idea of her innocence was floating gently and inoffensively on the air. He emphasised that Ginny would be returning to the bosom of her family, that she had the full support of her husband, family and close friends.

Calmly Grainger referred the bench to the report of the eminent psychiatrist Dr Jones, which granted that Ginny had been in a state of shock and depression for the first week after she had been charged, but declared that, with the commencement of treatment, she was now in a robust and sensible frame of mind, and constituted no danger to herself. Mrs Wellesley's mental health would continue to be closely monitored by Dr Jones, whom she would be seeing at least once a week. No good would be served by keeping Ginny in custody, he summarised, and no harm could possibly be done by allowing her out on bail. He offered the surrender of Ginny's passport, residence at Melton, and surety at the court's discretion.

Tingwall had warned me that the JPs would withdraw to consider their decision, so I was taken off-guard when, after a short discussion between themselves, and a brief consultation with the clerk, the chairman promptly announced that bail was granted, subject to residence at Melton, surrender of passport and surety of fifty thousand pounds.

Tingwall had the papers ready, the surety was approved, and with that the court rose for lunch.

I pushed my way out of the public gallery, past the usher and into the court. Ginny turned and met my clumsy all-enveloping embrace with impassivity. 'We're going home,' I said with considerable emotion, 'I'm taking you home.'

'You'll be there?' she said.

I wasn't sure what she meant. 'Of course. Where else would I be?'

Grainger came up and I shook his hand.

'Thank you. You were superb.'

He gave a faint smile, as though he was aware of what I had thought of him and took amusement from having proved me wrong. 'You might want to leave by the back way,' he commented, turning his eyes towards some reporters in a gaggle by the door. 'They can't bother you inside the building, but they'll try for a photograph outside. I wouldn't recommend draping anything over the head, it makes a very unfortunate impression. Dark glasses are not ideal, either. But the head averted, the hair hiding the features? Family on either side and in front?'

I had not been prepared for this. Automatically I looked to Tingwall. 'I'll go and find out,' he said doubtfully, and I realised that he hadn't been prepared for this either.

David's voice came from behind. 'Put me in the vanguard. I'm good barging material.'

'I didn't know you were here,' I laughed.

'Crept in late. Sat at the back.' He kissed Ginny fleetingly on the cheek. 'Why don't I go and get my car and bring it round to the side or wherever it is?'

Tingwall arranged for us to leave through the court office. David, with great seriousness, synchronised his watch with mine and went off to do a recce. Tingwall then took Ginny and me to the court office, as though to do more paperwork. Two sharp-faced reporters followed us across the hall and hung around the office door, making no attempt to conceal their purpose. Someone fetched Ginny's bag from the cells, we found reasons to open the door regularly so the reporters could see we were still in there, then, on the appointed minute, we ran for the side exit and jumped into David's Mercedes.

We would probably have escaped the worst of the press if the automatic barrier hadn't been slow in lifting. Forced to pause in full view of the front of the building, we were soon surrounded by photographers. As they lifted their cameras I called a warning to Ginny and raised my hand to shield her face. And so it was that the photograph that featured regularly in the newspapers over the days and months that followed showed Ginny's head largely obscured by my splayed hand, and, in the foreground, made prominent by the flashlights, my face wearing an ugly aggressive expression, teeth bared, eyes popping, like a dangerous maniac on licence from Broadmoor.

After seeing this photograph for the first time I stopped reading the newspapers.

From superstition or lack of forethought or a mixture of both, I had made no preparations for our arrival at Melton. I hadn't phoned Mrs Hoskins to ask her to turn up the heating, and I hadn't bought any food. So it was that we arrived to a cold dark house with nothing in the fridge but a few eggs, a half-empty carton of milk and some tinned pâté which had been open a dangerously long time.

Leaving Ginny in the kitchen with a cup of tea, I went through the place turning up thermostats, lighting fires, drawing curtains. Returning, I found Ginny sitting in the same position at the kitchen table, staring out of the window into the dusk.

'There's hot water,' I told her.

'I'll go and unpack.'

I carried her bag upstairs. In my pleasure and anxiety at having her home, I talked nervously about anything that came into my head: the food I would buy in the morning, the book I wanted her to read, the latest developments at Hartford, much of which

I had already told her during the journey from Exeter. I joked that unemployment was making me lazy, that I was enjoying not having to get up in the mornings, none of which was true, but which seemed to form a necessary part of the charade of normality.

One by one she took her clothes from the bag and dropped them into the laundry basket, except for two sweaters which she laid on the bed and folded neatly, following the inviolable pattern she always used. Placing the sweaters symmetrically on the shelf she regarded them for a moment before changing her mind and relegating them to the laundry basket with the rest. 'So dirty,' she murmured. 'I felt so dirty in there. I don't think I'll ever feel clean again.'

'Have a long bath,' I cried rousingly, like some ghastly team leader. 'I'll run it for you.'

She seemed to focus on me for the first time since we had got back. 'You're very good to me,' she said.

'Don't be silly,' I laughed awkwardly.

'I can't tell you how much it means, that you . . . that you're here.'

'Of course I'm here. Where else would I be?' I said lightly.

There was a pause. We both looked away.

'Would you like a drink while you're in the bath?' I asked in the same jovial tone. 'A glass of wine?'

It occurred to me that she had wanted to talk and that, in my present state of inadequacy, I had missed the opportunity, or avoided it.

Attempting to be useful, I took the laundry basket down to the utility room and, not sure what else to do with the clothes, emptied them onto the top of the washing machine.

Staring at the pile, unwanted thoughts rushed into my mind, thoughts of what Ginny had been wearing on the weekend that Sylvie had died. I dreaded these invasions, but I couldn't stop them, I couldn't stop trawling my memory for clues – denials or confirmations.

I tried to picture her in the doorway when she'd made her unexpected appearance at Dittisham that Saturday night. She'd been wearing trousers of some sort, not jeans exactly, more like tight slacks, off-white or cream, a pale shirt, and her favourite raspberry-coloured jacket. A long scarf had been jammed untidily into one pocket. But what I was really trying to see, of course, was the blood. Could I have missed it? Even at my least observant could I have failed to notice stains or spatterings of blood?

I threw the laundry basket down and, calling to Ginny to tell her where I was going, drove to the local pub and ordered chicken and chips to take away. The woman behind the bar, whom I recognised from my occasional visits, told me that strictly speaking they didn't do takeaway, but, casting me a collusive smile, said she would manage something if I didn't mind having it wrapped in newspaper. Waiting in a corner of the bar, I felt the scrutiny of the other occupants, and it struck me with renewed force that whatever happened, even if Ginny walked free, we would never be able to live our lives in the same way again. This realisation, though harsh, no longer intimidated me: there were worse things, for Ginny at least.

Returning with my hot newspaper bundle, I found Ginny curled up on the bed, sleeping the deathly sleep of the exhausted. I put the quilt over her and, though I checked her regularly and kept the meal hot in the oven, she didn't wake again, and at midnight I turned off the oven and crept in beside her. When I put my arm around her waist, she gave a small fearful cry like someone caught in a night terror, then, still without waking, gripped my arm and pulled me close against her back and did not let me move away until morning. It was strange to be together in our bed again, in the security of our large comfortable house, to possess the security we had always taken for granted, yet to have lost all certainty of the future. It was like an illusion, a giant exercise in double-thinking whereby nothing was what it seemed.

Listening to Ginny's soft breathing, an image stole around the edges of my mind, the one scene which I had until then managed to block from my thoughts: the vision of Ginny in confrontation with Sylvie. I could see fierce pride in Ginny's face, I could see jealousy and anger, even fury, but the deed itself – that eluded me completely. I could not picture the knife, nor the hand that drove it into Sylvie's flesh; I could not envisage the person who, having committed this cataclysmic act, coolly wrapped the body and bound it and slipped it over the side into the black water. I tried to give the scene substance and action and dialogue, but while it contained Ginny it remained dark and unformed. Maybe I simply lacked the courage for it.

During the first days after Ginny's arrest I had

latched on to the idea of her innocence as an essential survival mechanism which would enable us to get through the long months ahead. But since her declaration in the prison I had been forced to confront the fact that, though I longed to believe her, persistent doubts had settled painfully in my mind.

As I breathed the scent of Ginny's hair, and felt in the touch of our bodies the history of our long years together, one thing was certain. We would stay together in this, we would stick it out through thick and thin. I couldn't abandon her, and I certainly couldn't judge her. It seemed to me that my guilt was inseparable from hers, that, in terms of blame, my selfishness was indivisible from her desperation.

I woke early and made a shopping list: what Ginny would have called a man's list, heavy on luxuries, short on essentials. But then Ginny had always organised the food, the cooking, the staff, the maintenance. From the earliest days of our marriage she had actively discouraged me from involvement in anything remotely domestic. She had not wanted a liberated man, and she had not got one.

In town it took time to discover the best shops. Eventually I found olive oil, sun-dried tomatoes and endives to go with the wild salmon and fresh pasta. I bought a few bottles of Ginny's favourite Pouilly-Fumé, I remembered herbs and flowers, and it was only as I arrived home that I realised I had forgotten butter and fruit juice.

I found the house silent, the bedroom and bathroom empty. Suppressing a dart of panic, I hurried through the ground floor calling Ginny's name before emerging breathlessly onto the terrace.

She was standing looking out over the garden, wearing a Japanese wrap with a woollen coat thrown over the top. She said absently, 'I'm here.'

My relief was so conspicuous that she must have guessed what had been going through my mind.

'The roses haven't been dead-headed,' she commented in the same flat voice. 'Oh, and the agent called. The people want to have another look round the house this afternoon at three. They're going to make an offer, he says.'

'That's good.'

'If they do decide to buy, I was going to ask you . . .' She turned towards me, and I noticed how puffy her eyes looked, and how her skin, always so luminous, had lost its clarity and transparence. 'Could we move straight away?'

'Well . . . If that's what you want.'

'If you wouldn't mind.' Her politeness was almost formal.

'The upheaval . . .'

'It won't be so bad. And it'd give me something to do.'

Though she spoke dully, I was encouraged by the normality of our conversation and the re-emergence of her interest in practical matters, which had always been so important to her. As for moving, I didn't need to be persuaded of the benefits of living full-time in London. Quite apart from the cost of running more than one home, I was forever leaving clothes in the wrong place, not to mention documents and, once, an airline ticket.

'And would you mind . . .' The odd formality again. 'Could we rent something? A cottage?'

Hiding my surprise, I said levelly, 'You don't want to live in London?'

'I'd rather not,' she said. 'If you don't mind.'

'Well—'

'Just a cottage, something really small. Near London if you want. Or . . . near Hartford. It doesn't matter.'

Looking out over the long lawns and spiralling leaves, I began to warm to the idea of a cosy cottage without gardeners and housekeepers, a place where we could live anonymously, in every sense of the word. 'Yes, why not?'

'Wish we could get rid of Provence as well,' she said with a glimmer of her old agitation.

'Well, there's no hurry about that. We don't need to decide for the moment. Not until—' I was going to say, *until things are clearer,* but tried to make a small joke of it instead. 'Until I know whether I'm going to be gainfully employed or not.'

'But all that bother. You won't want the bother of running it.'

I noticed the 'you', the assumption that she wasn't going to be around to organise things any more.

'Let's cross that bridge if and when . . . Anyway, we might want to retire there. I was thinking about it – before all this, I mean. It might be something to plan for, don't you think?'

'Retire?' She looked at me as if I were talking gibberish.

'I mean, when the time comes. In ten years. Who knows? Lots of people retire at fifty. It might be rather nice down there,' I rambled on. 'No rat-race. Uncluttered days. Good people. Food and drink. Friends to stay.'

'Ten years.' She was blinking rapidly. 'Is that what Charles thinks I'll get?'

'*What?* No, *no.*'

'What does he say then?'

'Ginny, when I said ten years it was nothing to do with you and the – *case.*'

'But he must have some idea what I might get.'

'He can't make *any* predictions, Ginny. None at all! Anyway, we're going to get you off! Good Lord, Charles and I haven't even discussed anything else!'

Ignoring this, or accepting it, she looked away and said, 'I'm sorry if it's a nuisance, renting a cottage.'

'Don't be ridiculous!'

'The thing is, I feel that . . . if we can have a few months in a quiet place – just us – I think I'll be able to stand it, the idea of not coming back.'

'Ginny, you mustn't—'

'Otherwise I'm not absolutely sure I'll be able to cope,' she said gravely. 'Dr Jones has given me all these pills. He says I must be sure to take them, otherwise – well, he doesn't give me an otherwise. I think he thinks I'm half gone already. Sometimes I think I am too.' She gave an unhappy laugh. 'There've been times when it's been so hard just to keep going. It's as though . . . as though I can't take it all in. As though everything's too much for my head. And then I get frightened . . .' She was struggling to express it. 'Because if it's going to be like that, then I'm not sure I'll be able to hold on.'

I put an arm round her and pulled her against me. 'Darling, if you're feeling bad, you must talk to me. Promise you'll talk to me?' I kissed the top of her head, but my heart was plummeting at the realisation of how close to the edge she was, and how fearsome was the responsibility I faced in taking care of her. I wondered if it would ever be safe to leave her alone.

As if reading my mind, Ginny said, 'Oh, I'll be all right while I'm here. Honestly. It's after . . . It's the idea of being put away in that awful place.'

'You talk as though it were inevitable. It's not! Once Charles begins on your defence, once he gets your story—'

She moved away. 'My story? There is no story.'

'Ginny, you've got to tell Charles what happened.'

'There is no story,' she repeated with emotion.

I stepped cautiously. 'What about what you told me – about finding Sylvie dead.'

I always forgot how acute she was, how finely attuned to nuance and omission. She heard the doubt lurking at the back of my words and said ironically, 'But if you don't believe me, why should Charles?'

'I do believe you,' I said. 'I do! I just don't understand why you won't talk about it. I can't see why you have to make a secret of it. What possible point can there be?'

'It was a mistake. I made a mistake.'

Inside the house the phone began to ring.

'A *mistake*?' I exclaimed, as mystified as I was exasperated. 'What do you mean?'

Her lids drooped. 'I feel so tired. The drugs probably . . .' She turned and walked into the house.

I called angrily, 'Ginny!' but she didn't stop.

Crossing the hall, she seemed to hear the phone for the first time and, altering direction to pick it up, lifted the receiver almost to her mouth before changing her mind and holding it out to me.

It was George. Watching Ginny climb the stairs, I didn't at first gather what he was saying.

'. . . in the post. Should be with you today.'

'What's that, George?'

'Something from everyone here at Hartford, something that will speak for itself,' he said enigmatically. 'They feel very strongly, Hugh. Also – and I hardly like to mention it, I know how busy you are – there's a meeting with the Chartered Bank tomorrow. I don't want to press you, but it would make all the difference if you could make it.'

It was hard to focus on Hartford matters again. I had already spent a lot of the previous week persuading Zircon and the banks to hold their loans, and George had somehow talked me into attending several strategy meetings.

'Ten o'clock, in Cheapside,' George urged. 'Just an hour. Hugh – I know it's out of your way, I realise you'll have to come up specially, but it's critical.'

'What's happened?'

'They're threatening to turn us down. This will be our one chance to change their minds.'

'But they were okay last week.'

'Something's made them think again. It's really critical, Hugh.'

With George every meeting was critical, every plea for help the very last he would make. While part of me resented the relentlessness of this pressure, I knew that in his position I would do exactly the same thing, that if it weren't for my personal crisis I would be right there beside him, fighting from the front.

'I'm not sure I'll be able to get away,' I told him, already feeling torn. 'Can I let you know?'

'Of course. But Hugh – it would make all the difference.'

I went into the study where I could be more certain of not being overheard before calling Jones. His secretary said he was doing his hospital rounds but should be able to phone me back later.

Even as I rang off I realised I could have saved myself the call. Whatever the psychiatrist might say, however safe he might rate Ginny's mental health, I wouldn't be able to leave her on her own. It wasn't simply a question of watching over her, though that would be a factor for as long as she continued to talk in such disturbing terms; it was also a matter of trust. I had not forgotten the promise I had made to her on the night when we'd searched for the petrol receipt. I had promised that I would never leave her alone again, and though at the time neither of us would have interpreted this as a round-the-clock commitment, I felt I owed her as much now.

I called Dr Jones's secretary and cancelled the message.

The decision was straightforward, the implementation harder. Who would watch over Ginny when I wasn't around? While she had been away I had been opening her mail, and though there had been cards and messages from two or three of her London girlfriends, there was nothing that amounted to a wild rush of unconditional support. And the people who lived around Melton, the people who had been glad to dine at our table, had, whether from reticence or disapproval, been conspicuously silent.

But then friends might not be such a good idea anyway. The few I had seen in recent weeks had expressed the sort of embarrassed sympathy people normally reserve for those who are bankrupt or caught up in a messy divorce. So anxious were they not to seem in the slightest bit curious that they had been breezily distant, almost offhand. Such encounters were not likely to get any easier.

Our families offered even less choice. Ginny was an only child, her father long dead, her mother living abroad. On my side there were only David and Mary, both of whom had heavy commitments and couldn't get away at short notice.

It occurred to me then that Ginny and I had no one but each other, which was, perhaps, all that we had ever had. Despite the frantic pace of our socialising and travelling, neither of us had ever been deeply gregarious at heart. We had gone about our business, we had been surrounded with people much of the time, but at the end of the day we had been glad to retreat to the safety of our own company. Until things had gone wrong between us and we had lost our one

314

safe haven. Then, it seemed to me now, we had both begun to drift.

I called Julia and asked her if she wouldn't mind coming down to work at Melton the next day. Julia, who was staying on until the buyout was resolved, not only had the benefit of being instantly available, but was loyal and discreet. While she wasn't someone Ginny would be able to talk to, she wouldn't intrude either.

The post brought the mysterious missive that George had hinted at. It was a giant greeting card packed with the signatures of the Hartford staff. Above the printed best wishes message had been written: *We're still backing the buyout all the way.* I was touched. At the same time I couldn't help wondering if this gesture of support and encouragement was entirely spontaneous, or something a little more Machiavellian, engineered by George who, in my absence, seemed to have developed unsuspected tactical skills.

I stood the card on my desk, a reminder, if I needed one, that life roared on in the world outside.

I went upstairs to check on Ginny, but she was asleep again, curled up in bed, her mouth slightly open, a faint frown showing above the mask. I glanced at the bottles of pills on the bedside table, but didn't recognise the names of any of the drugs. Taking the extension off the hook, I stole out and closed the door.

Tingwall was in court all morning, his office told me, and it wasn't until after noon that he returned my call.

'How is she?' he asked.

'Very tired.'

'When do you think she'll be up to seeing me?'

'I don't know. But Charles – she won't talk to me. She won't talk about what happened. And I have the feeling she won't talk to you, either.'

'Well . . . it's early days yet. And, Hugh, sometimes people tell their solicitors things they don't tell their own families. Sometimes it's easier to talk to a stranger, particularly when that person is duty-bound not to tell anyone else.' He didn't say: even the husband, though that was what he meant.

'I hope you're right.'

We arranged for me to bring Ginny down to see him in two days' time.

'Dr Bagnall's preliminary report came through.'

The pathologist. The post-mortem. Sylvie's body cut up on a slab. The stench of formalin, like the lab at school. 'And?'

'Nothing very startling, I'm afraid. He agrees with the cause of death, and there's nothing to suggest that the attack couldn't have been carried out by a woman of average height.'

I saw a flash of it then, an image so violent and graphic that it caught me like a panic. Ginny thrusting a knife up under Sylvie's ribs, forcing it home.

To drive the picture out I said quickly, 'But it doesn't prove anything?'

'It certainly doesn't prove that any particular person did or didn't commit the crime.'

'It could have been a man then?'

'Well . . . yes.' That caution had come into his voice again.

'What about the rest of the forensic stuff?'

'I've tracked down a DNA expert, and there's a top fingerprint lab in Wolverhampton. The DNA man isn't free for a couple of weeks, but the fingerprint people can get onto it straight away.'

'And if they don't find anything?'

'Then I think we have to accept there's nothing to be found.'

'We don't have to say that in court?'

'What? No, no. Our barrister will decide what evidence to use, and he'll only use what will actively *help* our case. What did you think of Grainger, by the way?'

'I thought he was pompous and conceited and overbearing,' I said without hesitation.

'Oh.'

'And surprisingly effective.'

'Well, we don't have to commit ourselves to him yet. When the prosecution serve their evidence we could ask him for an opinion, and take it from there.' A pause. 'While we're on the subject – have you come to any decisions about me?'

'You?' I said, knowing perfectly well what he meant.

'Do you want to retain me?'

'You'd better ask Ginny that.'

'Yes, of course. It's just that the real work's about to start and I thought . . .'

'As far as I'm concerned, you'll do, Charles.'

And he laughed, because it was in his nature to take this as a compliment.

I had put out some feelers about Tingwall among my barrister friends but even before the word came back that he was considered competent I had made up my mind to keep him. As a lawyer Tingwall had a rare advantage: he was prepared to become emotionally involved. Let the QC be the bleak professional; for this stage of the case Ginny needed someone who was prepared to go the extra mile.

'Are you married, Charles?' I asked.

'What? Yes. Six years now. Twin boys of two and a half. A real handful.'

I thought: Then you understand. You understand the need to believe that there is going to be a way out.

'I must tell you,' he said, resuming his lawyer's voice. 'The strangest thing. A witness has come forward to corroborate your story.'

'*My* story?'

'He saw you just outside Totnes, driving south, at about six-forty on the Saturday evening of the murder. He was away on holiday when you were arrested. He only heard about it when he got back. Contacted me through your brother last night. His name is Horrocks. An assistant harbour master, I believe.'

I remembered Horrocks. He was one of the men I had stood a drink in the pub when I was trawling for information about *Samphire*.

'He was absolutely adamant about the identification. Knew your car, recognised you. Even waved to you, he said. And – the dream witness – he was in no doubt about the time, because he was due at his sister's silver wedding party and was already ten minutes late. Anyway . . . there we are. Just thought you might be interested.'

'Does Henderson know?'

'I doubt it. But I wouldn't be in a hurry to tell him. Best not to offer information unless it's needed.'

'Ginny could do with a witness like Horrocks.'

'Yes,' he said, as though considering this afresh. 'It would help a lot.'

I woke Ginny for lunch and came down to prepare pâté and smoked salmon and salad. I hadn't tackled a french dressing in years, but I made a passable effort with a combination of the balsamic vinegar and olive oil that Ginny always used, and a dash of mustard.

Ginny appeared and sat down obediently at the kitchen table, like a guest in someone else's house. She looked no less exhausted than she had done that morning. While I cajoled her into eating, we discussed her health. Or I talked about the importance of taking care of herself while Ginny agreed in a vague placatory way. When this subject lapsed I led us on to the practicalities of selling Melton and we discussed it for the rest of the meal. The disposal of the furniture seemed to be the one topic that roused a spark of interest in Ginny, as though she were eager to rid herself of non-essential possessions.

To avoid meeting the prospective purchasers we arranged for Mrs Hoskins to let them in, and drove up onto the downs for a walk. The wind wasn't cold but it was blustery, and Ginny took my arm as we climbed slowly up the rabbit-tracked hill.

'Do you remember that holiday in Brittany?' I asked, resorting to the comfort of nostalgia. 'When we got caught in that downpour?'

She gave a single nod.

'God – the weather!' It had been overcast and rainy for all but two days of our stay. But then La Baule with its long sands and *belle époque* hotels had not really suited either of us. I'd found myself hankering after the craggy coast of North Brittany which had been the scene of so many childhood holidays on *Ellie Miller*, while Ginny had missed the warmth of the Mediterranean and having friends to dine with.

'Not the most successful holiday in the world,' I smiled.

'You wanted to be sailing.'

'Oh, I don't know,' I said with half a laugh. 'Did I?'

'I think so.' She corrected herself: 'I know so.'

'But I still enjoyed the holiday.'

'No, you didn't,' she said with a directness that was quite new to her. 'The holiday was the worst of both worlds. Trying to please each other and ending up doing what neither of us wanted. You should have said, you know. What you wanted. So should I. Perhaps that's where we went wrong.'

She had never spoken like this before. While I welcomed the opening of these dusty attics, I was faintly apprehensive as to what might emerge next.

'But you didn't like sailing,' I ventured.

'Not the long trips, no. But I could have flown across the Channel and joined you in France. I wouldn't have minded going from harbour to harbour.'

'I felt it was too much to ask.'

'But I would have fitted in, I was desperate to fit in,' she said almost to herself. 'I felt it was a necessary part of loving someone, to fit in.'

This thought settled over me uneasily as we climbed the last few yards to the ridge of the hill and paused to look out over the prairie of ploughed fields below.

I said, 'But we were happy in Provence, weren't we?'

'Oh yes,' she agreed without hesitation. 'It was the one place where you were free of it all. The business. And your family.'

'My family?'

She cast me a glance, gearing herself up to voice something that I wouldn't like. 'Your family,' she confirmed. 'Your father mainly. But David and Mary too.'

'But I didn't need to be *free* of them.' Even as I said it, the idea lodged in my mind as a startling and disturbing possibility, made all the more real by the realisation that I had never allowed myself to consider it before. 'Why do you say that?'

'Because you were the one they expected things from. The business. The tradition. All the rest.'

'But my father never interfered. My father never asked anything of me.'

'No?' Her tone betrayed her doubts. Then, attempting to close this unsatisfactory argument: 'But Provence – yes, we were happy there.'

'Hang on,' I said, not ready to let go. 'Are you

saying my family put pressure on me? Because you'd be quite wrong, you know.'

The wind spun her hair across her face and she pushed it back and held it against her head. 'Not pressure like that. Not . . . *open* pressure. But it was still there, wasn't it?' She looked at me with a touch of her old uncertainty. 'You having been groomed to take over. Being your father's favourite. The way he made the business into this great and holy thing. This sacred inheritance. I always felt' – the thought emerged bitterly – 'that you were doing it for him.'

'For him? But it was for us too! Always for us! I don't know how you can think that.'

She gave up the argument with a submissive twist of both hands and walked on. But as we tramped along the undulating ridge her words still rankled.

'How could you think I wasn't doing it for us?' I asked hotly.

She came to a slow halt, as though in her tiredness she could not concentrate and walk at the same time. 'Because you went on and on pushing yourself, spending more and more time away, hardly being at home. Not choosing to be with me. It didn't look to me as though you were doing it for us.'

'It was only because it was all going wrong, Ginny. The business, I mean. I was desperate to save it. I thought if I just kept trying harder . . . And then I seemed to get *overwhelmed*.'

She absorbed this silently and looked away into the wind. 'And all that time I was feeling useless, you see. As though I had nothing to offer you any more.'

'That's ridiculous.'

322

'No!' she argued, a harsh edge to her voice. 'It's not ridiculous. You always say things like that, you always brush things off as if that'll make the subject go away. But I'm telling you – that was how I *felt*. I felt I had nothing to offer you any more.' She stated this with exasperation, as though I had never made any real effort to understand her. 'Oh, it took me ages to work out that I wasn't getting it right, that you hated the people and the parties and the social scene. It took me ages to realise it wasn't what you wanted. I was as bad as you were, you see – I clung on. When things began to go wrong, I just kept trying harder. Because it was the only thing I was good at, organising things, making things happen. I didn't know any other way.' She gave a small shudder. 'But I got there in the end. That weekend when you rushed off to Dittisham, I finally got the message. But by then . . . it was too late.'

'Oh Ginny.' All the accumulated misunderstandings of the years seemed to hang over us like so many missed opportunities. 'What a pair.'

Something in this brought her emotions to the surface and, turning swiftly away, she made a move for home.

'It wasn't too late, you know,' I said after we had walked in silence for a time. 'Not for me.'

But she wouldn't answer that because we were talking about the summer, and the summer was Sylvie.

When we got back she went into the sitting room and dozed off in front of an old film. As I scrubbed the potatoes for supper, her comments rolled round my mind. I accepted that I might not be able to judge my family too objectively – who could? – yet had I really understood so little about myself all these years? Had I really been driven by my obligations to them rather than my own needs, or Ginny's? I had always striven to please my father, certainly, and that had never diminished. And given the choice I had preferred David's approval to his annoyance, which could be fearsome. But had I really been driven by the fear of letting them down? It was a dispiriting thought.

I overcooked the salmon and undercooked the potatoes. Ginny assured me that she wasn't very hungry and wouldn't have eaten much anyway. She drank some Pouilly-Fumé though, two full glasses, and was halfway through a third before she slowed down.

'Tingwall – Charles – needs to see you some time this week,' I told her. 'I have to go down to Hartford on Thursday so I could drop you in Exeter on the way. Will that be all right?'

She took a long troubled breath.

'You have to see him, darling. You have to trust him.'

She nodded stiffly.

'He's really thorough, you know. In fact, I'm pretty impressed with him. I think he's well up to the job.' I added tentatively: 'So long as we give him all the help he needs, of course.'

She was staring out beyond the window, focused on some inner world, and gave no indication of having heard.

Suppressing a creep of frustration, I said, 'You will talk to him, won't you, darling? You can talk to him in confidence, you know. I mean, he won't tell *me* anything you don't want him to.'

I found it impossible to read what was going on in her mind. She gave me nothing back. After the revelations of the walk, the sudden burst of communication, she had put up the shutters again.

'He's been busy,' I said in an effort at conversation. 'Getting hold of experts to check the evidence . . .' Lumbering on, searching for points of interest, I added, 'Oh, and would you believe it, a witness has come forward, confirming my arrival time in Dittisham that day. Ironic, really. Henderson was always so transfixed by that missing journey time. Thought he could catch me out, like some Agatha Christie detective.'

I had her attention at last. 'A witness?'

'A man called Horrocks. An assistant harbour master. Saw me just outside Totnes.'

Her eyes burned brightly, urging me on.

'Saw me at twenty to seven, apparently. Absolutely positive it was me. Knew the car and so on. Even waved at me, though I didn't see him.'

'So . . . So . . .' She was blinking rapidly. 'Does that mean you're in the clear?'

A long confused pause followed.

'Did you think I wasn't?'

'I was worried in case . . . You know, I thought . . . They'd think that we'd . . . together. That you were involved . . .' She dismissed the rest of this thought with an agitated shake of her head before repeating more forcefully, 'Does that mean you're in the clear?'

Conflicting thoughts raced uncomfortably round my brain. 'I would think so, yes.'

'What about afterwards? After you arrived? They won't think you could have got down to the boat then and helped me?'

I was struggling to catch up, to fill the gaps in this startling new scenario. 'No. David saw me in town, remember.'

'And after that?'

'Well, you were there. And David dropped in.'

'That's right, that's right. Yes . . . You had no time, did you?' Without warning she began to blink back tears and laugh at the same time. 'I was so worried. I thought . . .' Now she was laughing more than she was crying, an odd overwrought sound. 'Thank God.'

I went round the table and sat next to her.

She kept repeating, 'Thank God.' Then, with a flash of doubt, 'But can we be sure? Can we really be sure? That it'll be enough?'

'Charles can find out, I imagine.'

'Can he?' She seized on this. 'If he can . . .'

I tried to make light of my next question. 'You thought Henderson might come back for me then?'

'What?' From a state of near-apathy she had become taut as a wire, as though hit by the effects of some fast-working drug, and I wondered if the pills she was taking had interacted with the wine. 'Yes. *Yes*,' she insisted. 'There was always a risk, wasn't there?'

Maintaining my tone, I smiled, 'Was there?'

Caught up in her frantic relief, she was barely listening again.

'Ginny?' I prompted. 'There was a risk that he'd charge me?'

'Yes. *God*. It was my nightmare. My worst nightmare. I thought they'd come back for you. That we'd both end up in prison.' And she half winced, half laughed at the thought.

I was missing something fundamental here, something which both alarmed and electrified me. 'So . . .' I felt my way cautiously, aware of how quickly the shutters might close again. 'If this chap hadn't seen me, if I'd had the time to' – I searched for innocuous words – 'get down to the river . . . then Henderson might have suggested that I'd . . . that I'd . . .?'

'Oh, that you'd killed Sylvie, of course. And that I helped you to get rid of her afterwards.' She went on: 'You *see* . . . That's what *I* thought too. That you'd killed her.'

I was very still now. I was hovering on the brink of understanding, but I still needed to hear it from her mouth.

'But I didn't kill her,' I prompted softly.

'I know that now. But by the time I realised . . . it was too late.' She shook her head again.

'Why was it too late, Ginny?'

Through her tears, she gave me a beautiful lost smile. 'Because by then I'd got rid of her. I'd put her over the side.'

327

Eleven

'OH, I knew the theory. I knew I should sit tight and let it blow over,' Ginny began in a brittle voice. 'Let you get bored with her, get her out of your system. I knew that's what clever women did. But I wasn't feeling clever, not about that sort of thing anyway. And you see – I wasn't at all sure it *would* blow over. In fact the longer it went on, the more convinced I became that I was losing you for ever, that you'd never come back. And I couldn't quite . . . *deal* with that.'

We had come to the smallest of the three living rooms at Melton, the room we called the sitting room, a low-lit room with book-lined walls, soft sofas and a fireplace which threw out plenty of heat. We sat side by side on the smaller sofa, staring into the fire, wine on the low table in front of us.

'It was one thing to suspect that something was going on. But actually knowing, seeing . . . That was *awful*.' And her voice rose to a gasp. 'When I saw you together that weekend, watched you go off in the boat – well, I thought that was it. I could see she was younger. Prettier. And she knew how to sail. Well . . . I couldn't see what possible reason you could have for staying with me. And I didn't need to ask you how you felt about her. I could read the signs. I could see you were completely smitten.'

I forced myself not to say anything, not to offer the kind of instant denials which Ginny seemed to find so meaningless.

'So there I was,' she declared harshly. 'Another weekend on my own, another weekend knowing you were with her. I simply couldn't sit there any more like some animal to the slaughter. The more I thought about it, the more I felt I had absolutely nothing to lose by following you down and making a fool of myself. I'd have gone mad if I'd stayed at home a moment longer. Literally mad.' She stole a nervous glance at me before reaching for her wine and taking a gulp. 'I went through this great debate as I drove down – trying to decide on confrontation versus the oh-so civilised discussion. You know – do you love her, Hugh? Do you intend to leave me? Oh well, in that case, good luck old thing. I knew I'd never be able to carry that one off. Never have been able to deal with things in that way. *Coolly*. Not when I'm . . .' She wrestled with this thought only to leave it unfinished. 'So it was going to have to be the great confrontation. Burst in, have a scene, give you an ultimatum. I knew I'd probably end up behaving . . . *pathetically*. Crying. Making a fool of myself. I knew you'd probably hate me for it, I knew I risked losing you altogether – the hysterical wife, no humiliation untapped – but I couldn't see any other way. At least the whole thing would be out in the open. At least I wouldn't have this feeling that I wanted to die the whole time.'

Catching my expression, she said, 'Oh, please don't think I'm saying all this just to make you feel bad, Hugh. I'm not. Really. I just wanted you to understand how I was feeling, how desperate I was.'

I nodded rapidly, determined not to speak.

She pushed her head back against the sofa before starting off again in a voice that was increasingly unsteady. 'I thought you'd gone straight down to Dittisham that Saturday. When you said you were going into the office for a few hours I thought you were just saying that – you know, to discourage me from joining you, to keep me away. So as soon as I thought you were well on your way I set off. And all the time I was planning what I'd say when I caught you together. I was going to wait until I did catch you together, you see. Awful, I know. Awful to set out to make a scene. But I was hurt. Angry. Off my head with worry. I felt like *killing* you.' She flung me a fierce look. 'Or myself. More likely myself. Anyway . . . You weren't at the house, of course. I didn't drive up. I parked in the village and took the path through the garden. I crept round the house, looking in through the windows like some awful nutter, and then I saw that your car wasn't there, and immediately thought of the boat. I went to the terrace and looked across, and I saw it – the dinghy. Tied up to *Ellie Miller*. To me that meant only one thing, of course. That you must be there with *her*. That if I was quick I'd catch you in the act. Well – I'm not sure I actually wanted to find you in bed with her – I wasn't that masochistic. But together, anyway. I wanted to have a good look at her, you see. I wanted to know just how pretty she was. And I wanted to confront both of you, to make you feel – I don't know – *bad, guilty. Something.* Stupid, of course.' She gave me a scornful sigh. 'Never does any good, that sort of thing, does it? Never makes people change their minds.'

I couldn't let this pass. 'My mind never needed changing. I wanted to finish it. I knew there was no future in it.'

'But I didn't know that, did I?' she argued with a spark of resentment. 'I thought you were mad about her. I thought you were about to leave me. Oh, I tried to tell myself it mightn't be that bad, I tried to be . . . *sensible.* But it never did any good. I couldn't think of any reason why you should stay with me, you see. No confidence. Never have had. Hopeless.'

A pause while she dealt with this thought and put it behind her.

'Anyway . . .' Her voice was flagging. 'I couldn't get out to *Ellie* fast enough. I couldn't bear the thought of missing the two of you together. I rushed down to the quay. I hadn't thought about transport, of course. But there were quite a few people about. A load of people were just getting into a rubber dinghy and I was about to ask them for a lift when I saw *Ellie*'s dinghy, sitting there at the pontoon. The name and everything: *Tender to Ellie Miller.* Well, that drew me up short for a second. I wondered if I'd got it all wrong. I wondered if someone else was on the boat – a repair man or whatever. Then I thought: On a Saturday afternoon? They never work on Saturday afternoons, do they? So I got going again. I hadn't forgotten how to row. You taught me too well. In the days when I pretended to love boats.' Her voice softened a little. 'Well, I loved being with you, doing what you enjoyed, so in a way I did love it, while it lasted.'

Reaching for her wine she cradled it in both hands as if it might warm her. 'By the time I reached the boat I was shaking like a jelly. I could barely tie the dinghy up. And of course I was trying not to make any noise. My heart was hammering so hard I could scarcely breathe. And then I remembered that I'd left my inhaler in the car. God!' She rolled her eyes at the memory. 'So I stayed in the dinghy for a while, trying to catch my breath, trying to prevent an attack. Sat there like a dummy doing my breathing exercises, listening, half expecting to be discovered at any second. Nothing happened, of course, no sounds from the boat.' This thought created its own silence. 'When I'd finally calmed down a bit . . . I climbed aboard. I—' The horror was revisited on her face. 'I went into the cockpit. I looked into the cabin. I . . .' She could barely speak. '. . . *saw her.*'

I waited for a long moment. Finally I murmured, 'And she was dead?'

Her face contorted. 'Yes.' And she turned her gaze onto me, searching my expression, desperate for some sort of reassurance.

I nodded, urging her on.

'She *was* dead.'

'Yes,' I said hastily. 'Yes, of course she was.'

'But they're not going to believe me, are they? They're never going to believe me.' And the despair sounded in her voice.

'Of course they will! Why shouldn't they?'

She was drawing great gulps of air. 'You believe me, though?'

'Of course!'

'Really?'

'*Yes*, Ginny. Really. I wouldn't say so if I didn't!'

But for Ginny no amount of reassurance could ever be enough, and she continued to scrutinise my face before she drew sufficient confidence to go on. Even then she kept casting rapid glances at me, never quite satisfied, never entirely convinced.

'I had a terrible attack, of course,' she sighed, picking up the story again. 'Thought I was going to die. Lay in the cockpit. One of the worst ever. I almost blacked out at one stage. I've no idea how I managed to keep breathing. Thought it would never end. God, I really thought I was going to die! I even said my goodbyes. But then – well, it began to ease. And when it was finally over I lay there for a long time, not daring to move – not wanting to move. Sort of hoping I could put the moment off, hoping I could keep lying there and not have to face up to what was in the boat. Then through it all – the shock and everything – I began to think about what I was going to do. Was I going to row ashore and report it? Was I going to shout and wave from the boat until someone saw me on the bank? Then suddenly ... *suddenly* ... it came to me. I mean, like a bolt from the blue. That I couldn't report it. I *mustn't*. Because ...' She made a statement of this: 'Because.'

'I had killed her.'

Her mouth seesawed, she lifted one hand, the

beginning of a plea. 'Don't think too badly of me, don't . . . But I couldn't think what else – *who* else – it could have been.'

'No.'

'The way you'd been behaving. Frantic. Off your head. I couldn't think . . .' Again she put it to me, 'Who else could it have been?'

'No, I can see . . . I would have thought the same thing.'

She grasped at this. 'Would you? Would you really?'

'Definitely.' Again I tried to give her the reassurance she craved. 'Finding her there on the boat. You thinking I'd been aboard . . . I was the obvious person.'

'Yes!' she affirmed fiercely. 'You *were*, you *were*!' She jerked her arm so violently that she spilt her wine. I took her glass and, putting it on the table, went to the cloakroom to find a cloth and dampen it with water.

She dabbed at her sweater, breathing heavily, clenching her lips. I fetched a glass of water which she drank greedily.

When we had been quiet for some time, she repeated reproachfully, 'It had to be you. It had to be.'

Her eyes flicked towards me, and I quickly agreed, 'Yes. It had to be me.'

Gathering some comfort at last, she prepared to go on. 'I fell apart for a while,' she said shakily. 'The whole thing seemed so ghastly, so totally un—' the word eluded her 'so un-*saveable*. You know how something can happen which is so ghastly that there's nothing you can do to make it right again. Once it's happened, it's happened. However much you may wish it different, there's no *un*doing it, ever, *ever*. Except this was twice as ghastly as anything I could ever have imagined. But then I thought— Then I thought—' She straightened up in her seat and some of the life came back into her voice. 'Perhaps I *can* undo some of this. Usually I pretend that difficult things aren't happening, don't I? I just push them out of my mind.' She held up a staying hand as if I were about to disagree. 'Oh, I do, I know I do! All my life . . . always. But this time – well, I *could* make things right again, couldn't I? Oh, not totally, of course. But almost right. For *you* anyway. For us. And Hugh—' She opened her eyes wide. 'It thrilled me. I mean – I felt glad. Glad that I had thought of it. Glad I was going to do it. I was absolutely determined, you see. Determined not to be weak and pathetic. Determined to carry it through to the very end.'

The phone was ringing but neither of us made a move to answer it and eventually it stopped.

Ginny was still lost in her story. 'I imagined you'd rushed off in a state of shock. Rushed back to London. It seemed to me that I had plenty of time – time to do the thing properly. So I planned it! I thought it through! I sat in the bottom of the cockpit where no one could see me, and I thought about every detail. I was determined, you see, not to forget anything.' Her mouth fell. 'It wasn't possible, of course – not to make any mistakes. But I didn't realise that then.' Suddenly her control deserted her and she clamped a hand to her eyes. Just as abruptly she pulled her hand away again and went on, as though any loss of momentum might sabotage her chances of finishing.

'I knew there was blood – I'd seen it,' she began at speed. 'I knew I'd need something to wrap her up in, to stop the blood and keep it from— So I looked in the cockpit lockers and found some plastic sheeting and a rope. Then I braced myself to go below. The strange thing was that it wasn't as bad as I thought it would be. Partly because I'd geared myself up for it. Partly because I'd made up my mind that I wasn't going to *let* it bother me. Mind over matter,' she exclaimed with a hint of pride, 'like doctors and operations.' She paused for breath before racing on. 'I didn't look at her, though. I half shut my eyes. And I kept talking to myself, blabbering away, which seemed to help, God only knows why. The hardest thing was getting the plastic all the way round her. Not getting any blood on the *outside*—' She jerked to a halt and cried in sudden anguish, 'God, you don't want to hear all this, do you! You don't want all the ghastly details!'

Part of me wanted to hear everything, but it was a part of me I didn't trust. 'Don't tell me anything you don't want to,' I said.

'Nothing I don't want to,' she repeated with irony, blinking back the hovering tears. 'The awful thing was – half of me was proud of what I was doing! So methodical. So efficient. Not forgetting a single thing!' And she gave a sad empty laugh. Blowing her nose, she continued with attempted toughness, 'So! I put her in the plastic, I wrapped the rope round several times, I knotted it. Then I cleaned up as best I could. I was already planning to come back the next day and scrub the floor, scrub every inch of the boat. With bleach – I knew bleach was the only thing. But there wasn't anything more I could do that night, not until dark, so I sat in the companionway and waited. That was the worst, waiting. The darkness seemed to take for ever.' The pretended toughness had vanished. Large splashy tears dropped silently onto her sweater and dripped off her nose. She had run out of tissues so I went and fetched some more. She blew her nose and wiped her eyes ferociously, as though this might be enough to stem the flood.

'It was hard. Moving her.' The effort of speaking was very great and between gasps her voice was all over the place. 'I used a rope – a halyard or something – to hoist her up. I tried using a winch but the rope got into a terrible mess. It took me ages to unravel it. So in the end I just put the rope over the boom and hauled that way. God, it was hard – *hard*. But somehow, *somehow* . . . I got her up. I got her onto the deck and . . .' She trailed off and with a low moan leant forward and sank her head into her hands.

I put an arm round her shoulders, I murmured vague words of comfort, but I hardly knew what I was saying, the images that crowded my mind were so overpowering. I saw Ginny pulling the body onto the side deck and forcing it under the guardrails, I saw it hanging out over the edge of the boat before it finally broke free and slid into the blackness, I heard it hit the water with a low splash, I saw it bobbing up and floating away on the tide. I saw all this and began to realise what a massive undertaking it must have been for Ginny. I felt astonished at her strength of mind, at the sheer force of her determination.

Not trusting myself to say anything useful quite yet, I resorted to offering tea. Ginny nodded from the depths of her hands. When I came back with the mugs she was sitting up again, blowing her nose.

'Sometimes in the night I dream that it didn't happen,' she breathed. 'I dream that it was just – well, a dream. And then I wake . . .' She took the tea and her hands were trembling.

'You'll tell Charles the whole story, won't you?'

She gave a tight shake of her head.

'*Ginny* – for God's sake.'

'Oh, I *suppose*,' she surrendered wearily. 'For what it's worth. But it's not going to do any good, is it?'

'Ginny, don't be—' I caught myself on the brink of saying *ridiculous*. 'There must be a way of proving what happened. But we can't expect him to even *begin* to help us until he knows the truth.'

'But everyone's going to think I'm making it up, aren't they? They're going to think I'm lying. I mean, who's going to believe that I did what I did if it wasn't to cover up for you? I mean, why would I bother, if *you* hadn't killed her? Or if *I* hadn't killed her? If neither . . . then why . . .' In her weariness she was confused by her own argument and put a hand to her head. Emerging from her daze, she said simply, 'It's no good – I've thought it through, I've thought it through a million times. And Hugh—' Her gaze was like a baffled animal's. 'I can't see any way out. And it frightens me to death.'

I tried to keep my own fear out of my face as I pulled her against my shoulder and murmured reassurances which sounded empty even to my own ears.

We lapsed into the silence of exhaustion, and when I finally spoke again I realised Ginny was beyond further talk. I took her up to bed and watched her count out her tablets and wash them down. As we lay in the darkness she grasped my arm and whispered apprehensively, 'Thank you for believing me.'

Knowing what she wanted to hear, knowing she wouldn't sleep until she heard it, I said, 'I never doubted you for a moment, darling. Not for a moment.'

Later as I lay awake with no chance of sleep, I found myself believing almost too much of what she had said: I found myself believing that there was no way out.

'That's right, isn't it?'

I wasn't sure what George had just said, but I gave an authoritative nod.

We were sitting in one of those conference rooms that looks identical to every other conference room in the City, with vertical slatted blinds at the picture windows, neutral walls and an ostentatious elliptical table that stretched almost the length of the room. Our small band was scattered round one end of the table. There was George and Alan and myself, one of our lawyers, and three Chartered Bank people. Significantly – or otherwise – the Chartered party did not include either of the two grey-suited executives who had smiled their way round Hartford on the conducted tour. Instead we had graduated to two full directors.

Now that I was listening properly I realised that George was labouring a point that he had already made twice that morning. The bankers had not been impressed by his argument the first two times around and, hearing it a third time, were looking distinctly po-faced. George was asking them to knock a point off the interest rate they were demanding. He couldn't see why we should pay over the going business rate. He couldn't see that we were in a poor negotiating position, and that the bankers, having let themselves be talked into granting us the loan virtually against their better judgment, were in no mood to do us any more favours. The meeting had gone on too long, we were losing ground. Risking George's wrath, I interrupted him in mid-stream. 'Suppose we agreed to carry this premium for a period of one year?'

They didn't commit themselves, but they didn't turn it down either. They'd probably offer four years, and we'd settle on three, two if we were lucky, which wouldn't be bad under the circumstances. They said they'd come back to us the next day.

I could feel George looking daggers at me as we went down in the lift. He managed to restrain himself until we reached the street.

'It would be nice not to have the ground cut from

under my feet,' he said with barely concealed indignation.

'We were never going to win that one, George.'

'Maybe not, but it would have been nice to discuss it, feel we had a *strategy*.'

'We had to concede something.'

'Why the hell should we pay over the odds?'

'Because we have no choice, that's why.'

'It's another twenty grand a year!'

'We'll have to live with it.'

'I'm not sure we can!'

'In that case we shouldn't be here at all.'

He retorted acidly, 'Well, that's a thought!' Then, sighing hard, he shuffled his unwieldy feet and made an apologetic face. 'It gets me, that's all, the way they squeeze us dry.'

'I know.'

He cast a scornful eye over the glass canyons. 'It's not as if they actually *make* anything, is it? Apart from fat salaries. You know, I'm never bothered by anything the factory throws at me. Employees' problems, suppliers, later deliveries – you name it. No trouble. But this lot! They'd screw their own grandmothers, wouldn't they? And then ask for another meeting to renegotiate the terms. You just never know where you bloody are with the slippery buggers. That's what I can't take!'

'Won't be long now, George.'

'Ha! That's true enough! Death or glory.' He rolled his eyes, then, with a conciliatory expression, asked cautiously, 'Look, Hugh . . . can you spare a couple of hours? I wouldn't bother you, but Cumberland's lawyers are trying to throw a whole new set of spanners in the works. And that's only a half of our problems.'

I hesitated, and in hesitating it came to me that a great deal hung on this small and apparently insignificant decision. A couple of hours would undoubtedly stretch into three, and then the whole afternoon would be gone and I wouldn't get back to Melton until nine or even ten. Tomorrow I was due at Hartford for a late-morning meeting which, given half a chance, would run into the afternoon. Before very long I'd be back on twelve-hour days and fast-evaporating weekends. And Ginny would be on her own with time to think and brood.

'No,' I said. 'I'm sorry.'

George stuck out his chin. 'Tomorrow then, after the meeting?'

'It won't be possible, George. I can't give you any more time at the moment.'

'Just for the next two weeks, until after the EGM? Until we sort out the lawyers?'

'I'm sorry.'

'If I came to Wiltshire?'

I knew I was sounding unreasonable. 'No.'

He exclaimed, 'This is our one chance, Hugh!'

'Don't think I don't know it.' If we didn't win the backing of the Cumberland shareholders at the EGM then the buyout would finally be dead and buried.

George clamped his mouth shut and looked away. Then, with a sigh that seemed to settle in his stomach and swell his considerable girth, he said in an alto-

gether softer tone, 'I didn't mean to be, you know –
unsympathetic. You've got your priorities.'

'I'm sorry I can't do more.'

'You *will* put the motion at the EGM though?'

'Oh, I'll put the motion.'

'See you tomorrow then.' He touched my arm as
he left.

Walking to the car, I wondered how I would feel
if the buyout failed at the eleventh hour through some
avoidable error, if I discovered too late that George
had missed some obvious move. It would exasperate
me, it would hurt me, but it wouldn't kill me. Responsibility had its limits, and I had reached mine. In
making the decision to distance myself from Hartford,
I was wrenching my life out by the roots and shifting
it to new ground. But it was my own choice, made
on my own terms. Perhaps, if Ginny were right, the
first independent choice I had ever made.

Setting off homeward, I called Melton. Julia told
me Ginny was having a short sleep and seemed fine.
This news took the edge off my concern, but like an
ache temporarily suppressed by an analgesic, the
throb of apprehension soon returned. I couldn't
entirely rid myself of the idea that the prison psychiatrist might have got it right and Ginny might be
close to some act of desperation.

The answering machine at Furze Lodge referred
calls for Mary to a mobile number which didn't
answer the first few times I tried it.

'I didn't know you had a mobile,' I remarked
when I finally got through to her.

'Ah, well, you don't know everything about me,'

she teased. 'A girl's got to stay in touch, hasn't she?' She was speaking from some quiet place with no background noise. 'Let me guess,' she said. 'You're on the M4 somewhere. Heading west.'

I laughed, 'How did you know?'

'I cheated. I spoke to Ginny at lunchtime.'

'Mary – thanks for doing that. *Thanks*. How did she sound?'

'Oh . . . fairly shattered. But then, that's not too surprising, is it? She *is* seeing someone good, isn't she, Hugh? The psychiatrist?'

'Yes. Well, David thinks he's good.'

'It's Jones, is it?'

'Yes.'

'He *is* the best. And the drugs – they're really amazing nowadays. Prozac and all that. Ginny tells me you might be looking for a cottage somewhere on the edge of Dartmoor,' Mary continued in some seamless train of thought. 'I could keep an eye out for something, if you'd like me to. I hear of places from time to time.'

'Oh . . . would you? Thanks.'

A pause while we waited for me to come to the point of my call. 'Mary, I want some help.'

'Anything.' Behind the warmth I caught a hint of wariness.

'Blackwell Cottage – do you know who owns it? Or more to the point, who arranged to let it, and who exactly they let it to?'

The silence that followed was aflame with objections. 'Hugh, I don't think that sort of information is going to help anyone.'

'I only want a name, Mary.'

'Yes, but *why* do you want it, Hugh? Contacting witnesses can get misunderstood.'

'I only want to talk to someone.'

'I really don't think it's a good idea.'

Sometimes I forgot that Mary was a lawyer by inclination as well as training, and that in situations like this her caution was liable to come bustling to the fore.

'Fine,' I said, giving in without a fuss.

A sharp pause, and she muttered in a mock head-mistressy voice, 'I suppose that means you'll go and find out anyway, from somebody else?'

I didn't say anything to that. The connection faded as a lorry overtook in the fast lane and she asked: 'Are you still there?'

'I'm still here, Mary.'

'Who do you want to talk to anyway?' she said, trying to maintain a disapproving tone. 'Don't tell me – the long-haired lout?'

'Yes.'

'You realise he's likely to be a prime prosecution witness?'

'I doubt it. He was always completely stoned.'

She gave an admonitory groan. 'All the more reason to stay away. What are you hoping to find out anyway?'

'I'm not sure,' I said, partly playing her at her own game, but also responding to some instinct for caution, a wish to protect Ginny and her story from perfunctory judgments.

'Whoa,' Mary sang. 'If I were to help you – and

I'm not saying I am – then I'd need to know what you were letting yourself – and me – in for.'

Still unwilling to give away too much, I offered a limited version. 'I want to find out about Sylvie's drug-taking, the dealers, the people she mixed with. Joe was around most of the time, he must know.'

'And this is going to help Ginny?' she asked in a voice of concern.

'I think so.'

'How, Hugh?'

I wondered if she meant to sound quite so sceptical. 'By digging out some of the facts the police never considered,' I said doggedly.

'How do you know what they considered?'

'Well – we've got a fair idea,' I bluffed.

'This is something for your solicitor, Hugh. *He's* the person to judge whether something needs investigating, not *you*. And he'll have someone he uses for these things, a retired copper, someone who's used to making these kind of enquiries. Someone,' she added heavily, 'who can speak to witnesses on a professional basis.'

'I don't think Joe's likely to talk to a policeman, retired or otherwise,' I said, for the sake of argument.

'I'm getting signals here,' Mary sighed. 'And the signals are telling me that you're determined to do this your way.'

'Well, I can't leave it, Mary, that's for sure.'

'But where's it going to get you, Hugh? What are you hoping to achieve?'

I felt a swell of resentment at this unrelenting flow of difficulties. 'I'm trying to help Ginny,' I said stiffly.

She didn't speak for so long I began to wonder if she was still there. Finally I heard a long sigh. 'Oh, *Hugh*. The things I do . . . All right, I'll see what I can find out. But on one condition. That if I do find an address for Joe-the-long-haired-loon that you don't go near him yourself. That you pass the address straight on to your solicitor – what's his name – ?'

'Charles Tingwall.'

'Tingwall. And that you leave him to deal with it. Promise me, Hugh?'

I heard myself say, 'Okay.'

'You won't make me regret this, will you?' she murmured as she rang off.

I thought hard before making my next call. I thought of all the objections Mary would make to it if she found out.

David's laconic bark announced that I was interrupting him with a patient.

'Won't keep you,' I promised, 'but could you give me Jean-Paul's address.'

'Jean-who? *Oh*,' he said in the next breath as it came back to him. 'Oh, yes. Hang on . . .' I could imagine him leaning across his desk and flipping open his address book and going down to the 'M's. He gave me an address in the Clifton area of Bristol, and a phone number as well.

'Thanks,' I said. 'And, David, it might be best if you didn't mention this to Mary.'

Whether he simply didn't have time to query this or it would never have occurred to him to discuss it with Mary anyway, he agreed impatiently.

'Anything else?' he asked in a more considerate tone.

'Not at the moment, thanks.'

Then, almost kindly, 'Will we see you soon? On the weekend? I think we should see each other on the weekend. I'll speak to Mary.'

'That would be lovely,' I said automatically, wondering as I rang off how Ginny would feel about the invitation.

I let myself into the house and, hearing laughter, paused uncertainly on the threshold. Following the sound, I found Julia and Ginny at the kitchen table. Ginny was still smiling, her head on one side, her hair falling onto her shoulder in a cinnamon curve.

Seeing me, she stretched out a hand. 'You're home early,' she declared, and the laughter had made her lovely again. She gave me a kiss and didn't let go of my hand. 'We're celebrating,' she said, and something in her tone put me on my guard.

'Why?'

'The people have made an offer for the house.'

I felt a wash of relief. 'That's wonderful.'

As she gave me the details I examined her surreptitiously. She seemed more alert, far less tired. But there was something else, something I couldn't put my finger on.

Julia stood up and looked diplomatically at her watch. 'Better be going. Messages in your study.' She sent me a well-practised eye signal, and I followed her into the hall.

'Howard called,' she said. 'Wanted to speak to you *urgently*. I told him you weren't available. But it was like talking to a rhino, all thick skin and pea brain, so be warned. He may call this evening.'

'Thank you for coming.'

'Any time. I mean that. Just let me know.'

'Maybe a couple of days next week?'

'Of course. I look forward to it.'

Ginny was loading the dishwasher when I got back to the kitchen.

'You seem much brighter,' I said.

'I am.'

'Having Julia wasn't too much trouble then?'

She flashed a glance at me. 'Don't be silly. I know why she was here.'

'Ah.' I made a contrite gesture. 'It was just . . . Jones thought it best. Until we could be sure the medicines were the right ones for you.'

'I've stopped taking them. Except one.'

My anxiety lurched to the surface. I stuttered, 'Is that wise?'

'They made me feel like a zombie.' She began to hunt through the fridge.

'But darling . . .' I came round the table. 'Wouldn't it be best to discuss this with Jones first?'

'I won't change my mind,' she said, her voice rising a notch. 'My head's so much clearer, I feel I can cope. They were doing me no good.'

I watched her long fingers pulling at some cling-film and her movements seemed jerky and uncoordinated.

'If that's what you feel.'

She put the packet of food down and said, 'Nothing's going to stop me feeling desperate, Hugh. Nothing.' And her voice rang nervily. 'But I'd rather feel alive and desperate than half dead all the time. Anyway, I'm still taking a touch of the librium. Well, I think it's librium. It's the other stuff that makes me feel so wretched. Really – I feel so much better.' She must have read the doubt in my face because she said with a touch of indignation, 'I'm not going to kill myself, you know.'

I pulled a stupid smile. 'Promise?'

'I'll give you notice, all right?' she said. 'If I start planning anything.'

I nodded, not encouraged by the knowledge that this was the one bargain a dedicated suicide would never keep.

Ginny insisted on making the supper. I opened a bottle of Chablis for her, what we called cook's rations, and when I wandered back into the kitchen half an hour later I noticed that the bottle was nearly half empty.

Ginny caught my glance and said, 'Yes, I'm drinking. Got to have something to make me sleep.'

'Fine,' I said.

She picked up her glass and, keeping her eyes on mine, took a long defiant gulp. 'You might have to carry me to bed,' and there was both humour and gentle entreaty in her face.

We kissed, and there was stored-up passion in her mouth, and urgency too, as though time for her were already running short. She pressed herself against my body in a way that was for her quite unusual and brazen. 'See what drink does to me,' she said in a low excited voice, and I kissed her again, much harder than before. We stumbled hurriedly upstairs like two teenagers, leaving a scattering of clothes across the bedroom floor. She did not close her eyes as we made love, but watched my face with unwavering intensity. At first I thought she was doing this to bring some greater reality to our lovemaking, to banish whatever demons came to her when her eyes were closed, but in the moment before I was lost in my own sensations it seemed to me that she was searching out something in my face, a truth or a confirmation that she was half afraid to find there. She cried out as she came.

As we lay side by side, panting softly, shoulders touching, I whispered, 'I love you,' and prepared myself for the expressions of doubt that this simple statement had often engendered in the recent past. But she only said, 'It's a long time since we made love before dinner.'

'Lack of time rather than lack of ambition,' I said. My memory searched lazily back. 'We used to quite a lot, though, didn't we? In the old days, at your flat.'

'*God*.' The memory didn't please her. 'I hated that time.'

I made a show of taking offence, twisting my head to give her a mock glare, and laughed accusingly, 'I don't quite know how to take that.'

'Oh, I loved the excitement of it all, of course I did. But I hated loving you so much and not knowing if I was going to keep you. I was so desperate to marry you and I began to think you'd never ask me.'

This was one of those situations where it was going

to be impossible to say the right thing. I ventured, 'Well, you know how I was. Cautious Charlie. One step at a time. Not really appreciating I was on to a good thing.' The truth was that I had hesitated long and hard over making the final leap. There had been a neediness in Ginny which had unsettled me and which instinct had told me would not easily be satisfied. And while she had never been openly possessive she had still managed to make me feel guilty for spending time away from her. I'd known that no marriage was ever perfect, that many of my friends had compromised and settled for a rough measure of contentment, I'd known that Ginny loved me more than was good for her, and probably for me as well; yet I hadn't been able to decide whether my quota of misgivings was normal, whether it formed a suitable basis for a workaday marriage or reasonable grounds for retreat.

'And once we were married?' I asked lightly.

'Then I was terribly happy.'

'So was I.'

'Were you really?' It was a straight question with no apprehensions attached.

'Oh yes,' I replied. 'I felt much more relaxed. I *liked* being married.'

She said in a distant reminiscent tone, 'Then I went and spoilt it all.'

'That's simply not true, darling.'

'Oh, it is, I know it is. I tried too hard, didn't I? Trying to make up for all the things I couldn't do, like have babies. I was always worrying, wasn't I?

Always fussing. And about *things*,' she exclaimed in disgust. 'Really! Such a lot of time wasted on *things*.'

'Really, Ginny, you're being far too hard on yourself. I've had no complaints.'

She turned her head and gazed at me with the same fierce intensity as before. 'I wish we were starting again. I wish it were all different. I wish I could show you how I'd love you now, without all that – *nonsense*.'

Touched by this strange declaration, I said without thinking, 'We've got six months.' Then, in a clumsy attempt to cover my tactlessness: 'I mean, just for a start—'

'No, don't say that!' she interrupted with a shudder. 'Please . . . *don't*. Let's just settle for six months. Don't let's think about anything more.'

And with that she gave me a rough kiss before swinging off the bed and reaching for her clothes. I watched her walk into the bathroom and it struck me that from this crisis Ginny was drawing a measure of, if not confidence, then self-possession. It lent her a strength I had never suspected. I was proud of her for it, and maybe a little in awe of her too.

While Ginny made something exotic with chicken I laid the kitchen table with crystal and candles. As we sat down to eat I thought how far away six months sounded at the moment, and how very quickly it would pass.

Choosing what seemed like a good moment I said gently, 'I won't ask again but . . .' She had already stiffened. 'What happened to the other dinghy? To Sylvie's . . .?'

353

She looked down at the table, she twisted her knife, she brought herself slowly to the subject. 'I took it back to the pontoon, tied it there.' She gave an ironic smile. 'I'd worked *that* one out all right. I just . . .' she raised her head and looked beyond me, lost in memory ' . . . didn't clean enough. *Thought* I had. Scrubbed the floor. And the sides of the bunks. And the seat covers. And the table – the legs, everything. Used a ton of bleach. Didn't want to miss anything, you see. Went over it all again, to be absolutely sure.' She grimaced. 'Wasn't as thorough as I thought, though, was I?' She inhaled sharply as if to put this behind her. 'Then . . . I found her bag. A small shoulder bag. I hadn't noticed it the night before. I couldn't decide what to do with it. I couldn't very well chuck it over the side, in case someone saw me and picked the bag straight up again. So . . . I brought it ashore and put it in a rubbish bin in the village.' Something about this memory made her wince, and I wondered if she had been seen. 'Then I got rid of the cleaning things in a skip. And then I came back. To you.'

At this, we drifted away on our separate thoughts.

'There was nothing else on the boat?' I asked eventually. 'No signs of anyone else?'

'What do you mean – signs?'

'I don't know really. You didn't see anyone rowing near *Ellie*?'

She shook her head.

'On either day?'

'No.'

'Not on your way out that first time, before you

found the body?' I heard myself say 'the body' as though it had never been Sylvie.

'No.'

Hearing the strain in her voice, I said placatingly, 'It was just a thought. That was all.'

She nodded, then, eyelids fluttering nervously, she braced herself to ask, 'Was Sylvie looking for you? Was that why she was there?'

This was the question I had asked myself countless times since her death. 'I don't think so. We hadn't spoken in ages. Two weeks, in fact. We had – broken off communications.' Ginny flinched a little and fiddled with the knife again. 'I can only think . . .' I paused to examine the idea again, to test it against my knowledge of Sylvie. 'I can only think that she'd stashed some drugs on the boat and gone out to pick them up. Or to leave some more. She knew where the key was kept, she knew how to get into the boat.'

'But why would she do that?'

'Because she was dealing in drugs, or running them, or both. I think she and her friends brought them over from France and sold them on. I think she didn't dare keep them at her place. She was incredibly organised where drugs were concerned. She planned her life around them.' I thought of the parcel tape she had used to bind the package to her back, and the waterproof material she had wrapped it in. 'She used every opportunity, every person she met. Including me. Well – *especially* me. That trip to France,' I admitted with an undimmed sense of shame, 'it was all about drugs.'

Ginny looked away and, following some logic of her own, said, 'As soon as I got back to the house

355

that night and found you there, saw you so normal, so un- . . . un-*bothered*, I *knew*! Deep down somewhere, I knew it couldn't be you! But I couldn't bring myself to face it. I couldn't face up to the ghastly thought that I'd done all that – that I'd done everything I'd done – for nothing. *Nothing!*' Reliving this thought she contorted her face as if in pain. 'But then, of course, I realised! I *realised* . . .'

'Realised?'

'That it made no difference.'

And still I didn't get it.

'They would still *think* it was you. Whatever I said, whatever you might say – they'd never believe it, would they? Why should they, after all? So I realised I'd still done the right thing. The only thing.'

I stared at her.

Locked in her memory, she rushed on, 'I still had to finish the job the next day, didn't I? I still had to go and clean the boat out. The floor – the floor was the worst. Bleach was the only thing. Lots of bleach. And the bunks too. It was a nightmare, trying to find every spot—'

She was still in full spate as I reached across and took her hands. 'It's all over,' I soothed her. 'All over now.'

She came to a halt with a final indignant echo: 'It was still the right thing to do.'

The right thing? I didn't know what to say. She had done all this for me. She had succeeded in protecting me – if protection was the word – but at what cost? Could it be worth all this?

'I think I should go to bed now,' Ginny breathed at

last. 'Too much wine.' And she gave a single uncertain laugh.

Clasping her hand, I tucked her arm ceremoniously under mine and, leaving the dinner uncleared, we turned off the lights and headed across the hall. The phone began to ring. We paused and looked at it.

'Might be Tingwall,' I said.

Howard's voice said, 'Hugh! There you are. You're really very difficult to get hold of, you know.' He gave a humourless chuckle to show that he was prepared to forgive me this lapse.

I mouthed 'Howard' to Ginny and cast my eyes heavenward.

'Now listen – this EGM business,' Howard said without pause. 'It's a waste of everyone's time, you know. You should pull your hounds off and save yourself a lot of trouble. Really, Hugh, it's not going to get you *anywhere*.' He was using his this-hurts-me-more-than-it-hurts-you voice. 'We've done a straw poll of the institutional shareholders. And I have to tell you that they're going to back the board all the way. I think you'll find this'll do your little consortium a lot of harm, you know. And the publicity. Well, it's bound to be bad, isn't it' – he hesitated for dramatic effect – 'what with one thing and another . . .'

A mixture of anger and exultation stormed through my veins: for once I knew exactly what I was going to say to Howard.

'Aren't you forgetting something?' I began quietly. 'One small detail? Aren't you forgetting that I don't have to listen to you any more, Howard? That I don't have to take any more of your claptrap? The

357

delights of working with you are now behind me. The Cumberland board now have that pleasure – and good bloody luck to them! You have no rights over me, Howard, and the sooner you realise that, the sooner you might also realise that nothing you say is going to make the blindest difference to what I choose to do. *Since* you mention the EGM, thanks to the terms *you* negotiated for all of us, both David and I have shares in Cumberland, so we have every right to call an EGM if we so wish. And we *do* so wish. Along with all the other shareholders who don't like what's going on.' My heart was pounding with savage excitement. 'I also take exception to your gratuitous and insulting attempt at intimidation. Don't talk to me about publicity or any other of your bully-boy tactics. Your threats don't hold any water with me, Howard. And finally – while we're talking about what I take exception to – I take exception to your calling me at home late in the evening. I have a perfectly good office and daytime phone number, and I don't want my evenings interrupted by you, on the telephone or in any other form—'

The line buzzed in my ear.

'Damn – he's rung off,' I said.

Ginny was laughing gently. 'Well, you told him all right!'

'You think so?'

'Great stuff!'

'There's one thing I wish I'd said.'

'What was that?'

'I wish I'd told him to fuck off.'

But I was pleased all the same.

Twelve

TINGWALL'S SECRETARY looked up from her work. 'Are you sure you don't want him to know that you're here?'

'No. I'll wait, thanks.'

Ginny's meeting with Tingwall had overrun by almost half an hour, but I didn't want to interrupt them, I didn't want Ginny to feel I was looking over her shoulder.

Flicking inattentively through *Country Life* I came across a full-page advertisement for Melton. The photograph had been taken in early summer, with the wistaria and lilac in full bloom, a last flush of blue-bells under the trees and razor-sharp mowing tracks striping the lawns. The house looked idyllic with its wide bays, mellow brickwork and comforting Georgian symmetry, the sort of place that features in glossy picture-books peddling quintessential dreams of English rural life. Nobody is immune to dreams, and being a workaholic I'd probably been more suscept-ible than most, beguiled as I was by visions of instant tranquillity. Yet for all the ambitions Ginny and I had attached to Melton, the dream hadn't been impossible, just a little too wearing perhaps, just an inch or two beyond the grasp of our busy lives.

Tingwall put his head round his door and called, 'Come in, Hugh.'

I met Ginny on the threshold, on her way out. 'Back in a moment,' she murmured. I couldn't read anything in her face as she passed.

Tingwall's expression was more transparent, a blend of gravity and apprehension.

'She's told you what happened,' I said when he had closed the door.

'Yes.'

'Well? What do you think?'

He considered for a long moment before saying, 'Not for Ginny's ears, Hugh, but I have to say that as a defence it would worry me a great deal. You mustn't go entirely by what I say, of course, you must take Grainger's advice, but for what it's worth I can't help thinking it'll be an extremely difficult defence to pull off. Far more difficult than – well, the other alternatives.'

'What are you saying then?' I said in alarm. 'You're not suggesting she should plead guilty?'

'No,' he replied carefully, perching himself on the edge of his desk. 'No, I would never do that. But pleading not guilty has certain risks – a harsher verdict, a heavier sentence. And if on top of that you're asking the jury to believe that an unknown third party committed the crime – well, it's going to present some serious problems, Hugh. To plead that sort of defence successfully one needs hard evidence, you see. Something to back up one's story. Now Ginny might come over well in the witness box – in fact, I've no doubt she'd come over very well indeed. But that in itself –

well, it's not likely to be enough. Not when the opposition have what seems like unassailable forensic evidence.' Glancing towards the door, he lowered his voice. 'And then – who is this third party? Are we saying it's someone completely unknown? If so, why didn't Ginny report the murder straight away? What was to stop her? That's what really bothers me,' he declared unhappily. 'If she tells the jury that she thought *you'd* killed Sylvie and was trying to cover up for you – well, that's not going to look too good, is it? To put it mildly. In the eyes of the world you'd be branded guilty without ever standing trial. It's a Catch-22 situation for Ginny.' He didn't attempt to conceal his dismay. 'She'll be damned if she tells the truth, and damned if she doesn't.'

'But if we could show that someone else had been there? The killer.'

Tingwall lifted his hands and raised his eyes heavenward: if only.

'What evidence would it take?'

He blew out his lips. He began to speak, he paused glumly, he folded his arms only to unfold them again. 'I'll have to think about that,' he said finally. 'A witness, I suppose. Someone who saw a third party going to the yacht before Ginny got there. Or . . . some forensic evidence, something to show that this third party was aboard at the time of the murder.' His tone was not abounding with confidence. 'I'll have to think about it.'

Faced by Tingwall's loss of heart, I found myself faltering. 'What about hiring an investigator?' I asked. 'Someone who can find witnesses the police might have missed? Who can search out Sylvie's druggy friends – the ones the police never bothered with?'

Whether he suddenly appreciated my argument or, faced by the inadequacies of Ginny's story, was all too ready to grasp at straws, Tingwall showed his first real interest in the idea of a drug connection. 'We can give it a try,' he agreed, talking himself into it by the moment. 'There's a chap I use occasionally, here in Exeter. And another in Bristol, ex-CID man. In fact he'd probably be a better bet for this sort of thing. Rather more high-powered. His name's Pike. Not cheap, I'm afraid.' Catching my expression, he said, 'I'll get on to him straight away then.' He added, 'Of course, the prosecution might be lining these people up as witnesses against us. You do realise that?'

I made a show of absorbing this.

'Mind you,' he said with some of his old spark, 'even if they're with the other side it'll be no bad thing to sound them out. At least we'll get a better idea of what we're up against, won't we? So . . . Any thoughts on where Pike might start?'

'There's a man called Hayden. He owns the boat Sylvie used to go sailing on. *Samphire*. Moored on the river. According to the local grapevine Hayden's a professional yacht skipper who lives, or used to live, near Totnes.' Tingwall was making notes. 'And then of course there was Joe who shared the cottage with Sylvie. Or just dossed there. Probably known to the police. Well, I'd imagine so, the way he dosed himself with drugs. Out of his mind most of the time. I'm trying to get his surname and an address.' If Tingwall thought I was overstepping the mark with my amateur detective work he didn't say so. And if he was wondering at the number of facts I hadn't previously disclosed to him or the police, he didn't remark on that either.

'There was another girl who sailed on *Samphire*, but I don't know who she is.'

He was waiting for more, so I told him about the drug running. 'I don't know how regularly they brought drugs across the Channel, but Sylvie had a contact in Cherbourg. He supplied her with a large packet containing some sort of powder. Heroin or cocaine, I imagine.' Tingwall shot me a dart of surprise and what might have been disapproval.

'I have no idea what she did with the drugs once she got them to England. But I have a theory – I think she may have kept them on *Ellie Miller*. I think she may have been using *Ellie* as a – what's the word? – a cache. And *that's* why she went to the boat that day. And that's why she was killed. Maybe she fell out with someone further along the line. Maybe she hadn't paid someone. Maybe she'd been bringing in extra drugs that she hadn't been telling them about.'

Tingwall had stopped writing. 'You've no evidence for this?' he asked quietly.

'No. But I can't think of anything else. She was bright, you see. She knew they were sniffing around.'

'They?'

'The customs.'

Tingwall put his notebook down. 'I wish you'd told me some of this before,' he murmured.

'Didn't think it would look too good on my CV,' I replied flippantly. 'You know – aiding and abetting the smuggling of drugs. And if I were to say that I'd got involved unwittingly, that I didn't know what was going on – the innocent abroad – well, do *you* ever believe that old chestnut when you read it? No, neither do I.'

Tingwall was contemplating this with a dispirited expression when Ginny reappeared. He straightened up, shuffled his feet and smiled boyishly. Which seemed to make two of us who were rather in love with her.

I drove Ginny straight on to Bristol for one of her twice weekly appointments with Dr Jones. During the journey she fell into a listless uncommunicative mood, and I couldn't make out if it was the bad night she'd had or a sudden bout of depression. As we'd got ready for bed she'd become restless and preoccupied, and several times during the night I'd woken to find her gone from the room. Her absences weren't good for my jittery imagination, and twice I'd set off in search of her. The first time I'd found her in the kitchen, staring out of the window into the darkness while the kettle boiled untended on the Aga. An hour later I'd discovered her scrubbing the kitchen table. 'It hasn't been cleaned properly,' she'd complained matter-of-factly. 'Liquid and bleach. You can never get rid of the grease marks without liquid and bleach.' She'd seemed completely unaware of the echoes in this, there was no glint of comprehension, and a warning had begun to tick away in my mind. Feeling out of my depth, I'd remembered the forthcoming visit to Jones with a rush of relief.

The psychiatrist had his consulting rooms in a semi-detached villa in the Kingsdown area of Bristol, not far from the university and the hospitals. Drawing up outside, I said to Ginny, 'If I'm delayed, you won't mind waiting a bit?'

She shook her head and fumbled with the contents of her handbag. I went round and opened the door for her and helped her out. She kissed me absently on the cheek before climbing the few steps to the door and ringing the bell. Watching her pass into the house, I wondered if she would come clean with Jones about the self-appointed reduction in her drug regime, and whether I would be betraying her trust if I contacted him later to find out.

With a street map of Bristol propped against the wheel, I set off in the direction of Clifton. I got lost almost immediately, going down a hill I had climbed just minutes before, but after stopping to get a new perspective on the map managed to put myself back on the right road, and within ten minutes was crawling along the busy street where Jean-Paul lived, squinting at the street numbers. Number nineteen was a flat-fronted terraced house, three storeys high with grimy windows and peeling white stucco and rubbish spinning around the front steps. There were names against three of the bells, none of them Mathieson, so I pressed the fourth, which was labelled Flat 2.

A dog yapped frantically somewhere near by, a succession of heavy vehicles shuddered past on the road behind. I pushed the bell again. I was wondering whether Jean-Paul had changed his mind when the door swung open and he was there, a tall figure standing well back from the threshold. I was surprised at how little he had changed. He was still a string bean of a man with a pinched face, a thatch of dark hair and heavy brows drawn into a permanent frown. He still wore his hair long and his jeans tight, though after fifteen years he had less of the hungry student about him and more of the lean cerebral air of the academic. I saw no resemblance to Sylvie until he stepped back to let me in and then something in his profile, the set of his mouth, gave me a shudder of remembrance.

'Good of you to see me,' I said as he pushed the door shut with a slam that shook the house.

Jerking his head towards the stairs he led the way up to the first floor. His flat consisted of one large room spanning the full width of the house with an open-plan kitchen in one corner, a bed in another, and a door leading to what was presumably the bathroom. Overloaded bookshelves sagged along every wall, and more books were stacked in untidy piles in and around the massive Victorian desk which stood before the windows, its surface almost lost in paper. Mozart was playing softly in quadraphonic sound.

Jean-Paul faced me in the middle of the room. 'So?' he said abruptly.

I hadn't planned this in any detail. 'First, may I say how sorry I am—'

He flicked an impatient hand. 'Think we can skip that bit.'

I understood this, perhaps I had half expected it. I

began again, no more confidently, 'I assure you that my wife did not do this terrible thing. They've got it all wrong. It's the most appalling mistake.'

'So you said on the phone.' His manner was cold.

'The thing is ... I'm trying to find some of the people who knew Sylvie, to see if they can think of anyone ... of any reason ... I was wondering if you could put me on to some of her friends, people who saw her this summer. I thought they might be able to tell me – I don't know – whether anyone had been bothering her in any way ... following her ... That sort of thing.'

He raised a dubious eyebrow and, perching himself on the edge of the desk, said in a voice that was heavy with indifference, 'She didn't tell me much. I didn't see her that often.'

'Anybody you can think of. Anything she told you.'

He exhaled irritably as though he was already regretting having agreed to see me. 'All I knew was that she was living in Dittisham, that she was doing her sculpture or whatever it was.'

'Did she mention Hayden, the person she sailed with?'

'May have. Don't remember.'

'Or Joe, the chap she shared the cottage with?'

'A bit.'

'What was his second name, do you know?'

He gave an exaggerated shrug. 'Wilson. Willis. Wilkins. Something like that.'

'You don't know how I could get in touch with him, do you?'

His eyes glimmered coldly. 'Maybe.'

'You've got a number?'

'He may not want to talk to you.' His tone made it clear he thought this highly likely.

'But could you ask him anyway? Explain how important it is.' Before he could refuse, I pulled out a card and, balancing it on my hand, scribbled my home and mobile numbers on the back. 'I'd be most grateful.'

With the bad grace that seemed to be habitual to him, Jean-Paul dropped the card onto the clutter of papers on the desk behind him, where it sank, a small white rectangle, into a sea of white.

'Did she mention any other people?' I asked. 'Not just in Dittisham, but elsewhere. In London perhaps.'

'Not really. She had friends all over the place.'

'What about business associates?'

'*Business?*' he repeated scornfully. 'What sort of *business?*'

I plunged in. 'Drugs.'

He tossed his head angrily. 'Oh, *please!*'

'They say she was involved in hard drugs.'

'Who says!' he retorted. 'That's crap. She was into hash, a bit of speed maybe. Nothing more. Who says?'

'The police.'

'Rubbish. They never told you that. Who told you that?'

'The hash,' I said, avoiding the question, 'where would she have got it from?'

'Where anyone gets their stuff from.' He was talking to me as if I were a complete imbecile. 'Everywhere.'

'I wondered if perhaps she could have fallen out with the dealer.'

He gave a harsh contemptuous laugh. 'You've been watching too many bad films. People don't get killed by their hash suppliers, otherwise half the university would be decimated. What were you thinking – that she owed somebody money and they killed her for it? Listen, hash costs nothing, and everyone pays up front anyway. Or if they do get credit, it's never for very long or for very much, believe me.' He gave his derisive laugh again. 'Christ, what a pathetic idea.'

I hesitated, remembering the feel of the package around Sylvie's waist the night she dived into the water. 'Once she had something else. A powder.'

His eyes flashed with hostility. He was trying to gauge whether I'd sprung this on him on purpose. 'So?' he said tightly.

'I thought she might have got mixed up with the dealing side.'

He buttoned down his mouth and glared at me by way of a reply. The Mozart came to an end, and there was only the faint rumble of traffic and the tick of a central-heating pipe.

'Her friends,' I said, bringing us back to less contentious ground. 'Was there anyone she was particularly close to?'

'I expect so.'

'Who, do you know?'

'I told you – she had friends all over the place.'

'What about boyfriends?' I asked, holding my expression.

'She told me about one, yes.'

Concealing my leap of curiosity, I said, 'Oh? Who was that?'

'You.' He had enjoyed that moment, he had enjoyed catching me out.

I gave a slow nod which he could take as a tribute to his little coup if he wanted to.

'Well, I *assumed* it was you,' Jean-Paul said, milking the moment a little longer. 'Sylvie said she had a lover, and he was in *glass*. I didn't know what a lover in *glass* was. So she told me. She said the family *made* glass. I asked if it was you – I remembered something about the glass.'

'Was there anyone else? Any other lover?'

'Should there be?' he asked with a spark of sarcasm, and I realised that while Jean-Paul might be tolerant of his sister's hash smoking, he wasn't quite so relaxed about her love life.

I looked away through misty windows to threadbare trees and spotting rain. 'Did she say anything else about me?' I asked, not quite sure why I wanted to know.

'No,' he said dismissively. Then, tiring of his own animosity, he gave the question some consideration. 'She said you had a boat. She said she was going on it. What else?' He blew out his lips. 'It was a long time ago. I really don't remember.'

'When was this?'

'Oh, April, I suppose. Early May. Thereabouts. Oh yeah,' he said as something else came back to him, 'she talked about some trip you were going to make.'

'To France?'

He frowned at me. 'Maybe. I can't remember.' For

no obvious reason he became cross again. He straightened up and folded his arms meaningfully; the interview was over.

'Well, thanks for your help,' I said. 'If you could speak to Joe?'

He made a gesture that was intentionally ambiguous.

'Perhaps I could call you in a day or so?'

'No thanks,' he said bluntly.

'I meant—'

'If Joe feels like making contact, I'll get him to call you direct.'

At the door I said, 'A while ago my brother told me you wanted to see me.'

'That was then.'

'I just wondered . . .'

'I had very little to say to you then,' he declared with a rancour that was all the stronger for having been temporarily forgotten, 'and I've got even less to say to you now.'

The door closed sharply behind me and reaching the ground floor I heard the muffled clamour of strident orchestral music drifting down the stairs after me. As Jean-Paul's last remarks reverberated caustically in my mind, I had the feeling I would not be hearing from Joe.

'I'm glad you were able to come,' Jones smiled, gesturing vaguely towards a chair. He began to search for some errant object, patting his outer pockets several times before swinging open a jacket front and starting on the inner realms, only to return once again to the outer pockets, dipping his hands into the same slots time and again like some bemused rap dancer. He spread a palm and smiled in benign defeat, 'My glasses . . .'

He was a man of indeterminate age, somewhere in his fifties or sixties, short and balding. I couldn't work out if this absentmindedness was genuine or part of some stratagem for putting patients at their ease.

With an exclamation of victory, Jones scooped up his glasses from under some papers and, settling himself behind his desk, cast me a diffident smile.

'I hope it wasn't inconvenient,' he said with a strong Welsh lilt, 'but I felt a chat would be useful.' He had called me late the previous evening after Ginny's visit, to ask if I might be able to come and 'discuss a few things', a request which had sent profound and irrational fears shivering through my heart.

'You worried me,' I told him now. 'You made it sound serious.'

'Did I? Well, I don't think it's anything to be too concerned about,' he said with a caution that managed to convey precisely the opposite impression. 'I just felt there were certain problems which you should be aware of.'

'I know she's not taking all her drugs.'

'Ah.' His eyebrows flew up.

'She didn't tell you?'

'No,' he said with the lack of surprise of a doctor who is used to his patients following their own ideas about what is good for them.

'She's still taking the tranquilliser, I think, but not the Prozac. She said it made her feel worse.'

'I'll have a word with her next time,' he said, making a quick note. 'See if I can find her something that suits her better.' There was a pause in which he gathered himself to tell me what was on his mind. 'Yes, the thing is . . . We had a useful session yesterday, Virginia and I. On the face of it she seems to be coping. She doesn't appear to be too overwhelmed by her situation. She seems to be able to contemplate the future – even the idea of prison – with some degree of composure. But at the same time I'm not absolutely sure that her view of the future, or indeed of the past, is based on reality. I'm not sure she's able to determine what is real and what is not, or to separate what is true from what she would like to be true. Sometimes people evade the truth as a way of managing their fears – evade it, but deep down never lose sight of it. In Virginia's case, however, I think she *has* lost sight of reality. I think fact and fantasy have become profoundly muddled in her mind.'

This was an alien sea, and I was floundering. 'But she's been perfectly – *clear* with me. She's never been confused about anything.'

'Oh, she expresses herself articulately, certainly,' he agreed with alacrity. 'But she's clear on an interpretation of events that deep down she's really quite confused about – if you appreciate the distinction. She would like certain things to be true, but she's not sure whether they are or not. It's not simply a matter of blotting things out, of suppressing unpleasant events, but of having painted herself an alternative

373

picture of events and being unable to distinguish this version from the real thing.'

I was still struggling. 'Are you saying she's not telling the truth?'

'I'm saying she's telling the truth as she sees it, which, as I'm sure you'll appreciate, is rather a different thing. It may well *be* the truth, there's nothing to say it isn't, but she has no way of determining whether it is or not, no way of sorting it out in her mind, you see. And in the end that's what might disturb her.'

I felt as though I had stumbled into an emotional bog, a murky impenetrable place with no points of reference. 'She's told you, then, about Sylvie's death?' I asked, half afraid of what he might say.

'She's told me something,' he said guardedly.

'She's told you she's innocent?'

He made an apologetic gesture. 'I'm sorry, Mr Wellesley, I would be breaking her confidence if I were to discuss that.'

I suppressed a bubble of frustration. 'But what I'm trying to understand is how you've arrived at this view of her? How do you *know* she's getting things muddled?'

'There are certain procedures one can use to determine a patient's state of mind, to establish his or her grasp of reality. These techniques involve discussions of all sorts of existing situations – relationships, family, work, whatever. Now in the course of these discussions Virginia has consistently revealed a confused grasp of existing realities, even of everyday truths. And if someone loses their grasp on mundane matters in this way it's invariably symptomatic of a general and pervasive loss of reality. The delusions they show in small matters extend *to*, and stem *from*, the original trauma and its attendant delusions.'

Delusions. One of those terms like paranoia or psychosis which belong to other people, to strangers with real problems, not to someone you know and love. Fighting my own sense of confusion, I asked fretfully, 'But what sort of things does she get wrong?'

'Wrong is too strong a word,' he commented in his measured Welsh tones. 'But let me think . . . Well, to give you an example, she told me she was an expert sailor, that she'd sailed a lot with you, gone over the Channel many times. But that's not quite accurate, is it?'

He read the answer in my stricken silence.

'I guessed it wasn't, from something she'd said earlier. Now I never dispute her on these matters – I'm very anxious not to undermine her confidence in any way – but if I should inadvertently question something she gets very disturbed. She cannot deal with the idea of being challenged, even on the smallest things. She becomes quite agitated.'

I looked into his bland benevolent face and felt as Ginny must have been feeling, caught between several baffling truths, each distinct, each so fatally blurred that there was no way of knowing which to believe. A man I had only just met was telling me that my wife was mentally unwell and, in trying to gauge the validity of this, all I had to go on was the fact that he had a clutch of qualifications and seemed reasonably well-intentioned.

'Okay,' I sighed. 'Okay. So Ginny wants to pretend. So what does it matter? What's the harm?'

'There's no harm for the moment,' Jones said kindly. 'But if the situation is allowed to continue she will start to find the strain unbearable. Delusions may seem like an excellent self-defence mechanism, but they carry an enormous burden of guilt and confusion. And the real risk comes when and if she is forced to confront her delusions before she is ready, before she's able to come to terms with them in her own way.'

'Risk? What do you mean?'

Jones said in a voice that was suddenly very professional, 'She could become seriously ill.'

The room seemed to crowd in on me and, clambering to my feet, I went to the window and stared unseeing into the back yard. 'So I mustn't say anything to upset her?'

'That's one thing, certainly.'

I turned back. 'What else?'

The light was in his eyes and he blinked up at me from his desk like a dazzled owl. 'It would help if she could get to see me more often. Three times a week if that's possible.'

'But what can I do?'

'You could look for signs of distress. Obsessive behaviour. Worrying excessively and continuously about insignificant problems, like whether the windows are properly closed or an object is correctly placed on a shelf. And repetitive behaviour. Going back to the same task time and again. Frequent hand washing, showering, skin scrubbing.'

I thought: Or table scrubbing, and wished the idea hadn't flown quite so smoothly into my head.

I thanked him before he could come up with any more unsettling thoughts.

As I was leaving I asked: 'She will get better, won't she?' and saw from his face that this was the one question he could not answer.

'Hello, darling.' Ginny planted a kiss somewhere close to my left cheek. 'You're early.'

It was four, precisely the time I'd said I'd get back. 'The meeting went well,' I murmured. Taking on a life of their own, my eyes strayed inexorably to the kitchen table, examining the bare pine surface for signs of recent scouring. I couldn't see anything, no patches of damp, and, though this proved nothing, it seemed to postpone the moment of reckoning.

'Julia had to leave half an hour ago,' Ginny reported as she slid the kettle onto the Aga. 'There were lots of messages. George called at least twice. And several business people – lawyers and accountants, so Julia said. Oh – and *Mary*. She wants us to go down on Sunday to have lunch with them and look at a cottage.' Ginny turned to face me and said in a voice sharp with some emotion I couldn't read, 'You've been plotting behind my back.'

'What – the cottage? Mary offered to keep an eye open, that was all.'

'I'd rather you hadn't asked her,' she said tightly. 'I'd rather you didn't involve Mary in anything to do with us.'

'But she volunteered.'

'She would. She enjoys interfering.' I'd never heard Ginny voice such strong criticism of Mary before. Her eyes narrowed with sudden suspicion. 'You haven't talked to her about *us*, have you?'

'No,' I said unconvincingly.

'My God, if you *have* . . .'

'No, I told her about Sylvie, that was all. Nothing else.'

'About *Sylvie*,' she gasped. 'What did you tell her, for God's sake?'

'Ginny, does it matter?'

'*Yes*, it matters!'

I sat wearily on a chair. 'I told her about the summer. I told her what happened.'

Ginny's chest started heaving. 'What – *everything?*'

'More or less.'

Ginny clamped her lips together and, holding on to her self-control with an effort which distorted her face, she shook her head at me. 'How could you!'

I lifted my hands helplessly. 'Mary's a friend. She was *there*. I needed someone to talk to.'

'But – God, you just don't see it, do you?' she cried through the pull of her breathing. 'You think Mary's so *special*. You think she's such a *friend*. Well, let me tell you, she's no friend of ours and she *never* has been!'

'Oh, *Ginny*—'

'No, *no!*' And suddenly she was in a fury. 'I tell you, she gives this great impression of being so – so – *saint*-like, so sympathetic, but it's all a big act. It's all a front! Oh, she seems like the great Lady Bountiful all right, she seems so caring – but only while it suits her! She's not Howard's sister for nothing, oh *no*. It runs in the family – all this getting people where she wants them, all this playing one off against the other.' She gave a gasp of frustration. 'Oh, you can't see it, I know you can't! For you she can do no wrong. For you she's this perfect person. But let me tell you, she *uses* people, she worms her way into people's confidence as a way of keeping a hold over them. It's *all* about control.' She glared at me. 'You look at me as though I'm mad, but it's true! You just can't see it. Good old Mary! Generous kind Mary! All that charity stuff, up on her high horse. But there's only one thing Mary really cares about in the whole world, only one thing she even *thinks* about – and that's her beloved David, and how she's going to hang on to him. Everything after that – well, it's all a front.' She waved a fierce hand at me. 'Oh, I can see what you're thinking. You think I'm just jealous of her or something. You think I just hate her! But it's not that – it's . . .' She seemed to pull the thought out of the air: 'It's that I'm *frightened* of her. I'm frightened of her little schemes. She'll go behind your back without a second thought, she'll use anyone and anything to keep herself up there as the great and good Mrs Wellesley. She'll—' Words and breath failed her simultaneously, and striding to a drawer she opened it with a bang, pulled out an inhaler and drew on it.

After a long pause I said quietly, 'I have to say I don't agree, I think Mary's always been a good friend to us. But if that's the way you feel . . .' I stood up. 'I assume you don't want to see them on Sunday?'

'All I want,' Ginny laboured, 'is for you to stop telling her about *us* and our private life. That's all. I don't *mind* going to see them, I haven't *minded* all these years, have I? I can deal with her so long as she doesn't start interfering. And I certainly don't want to get the blame for stopping *you* from seeing them.'

I rubbed my face ferociously and said nothing.

She came back to the table. 'Perhaps I should have said all that a long time ago.' She gave me a redeeming look, subdued and penitent.

'Perhaps.'

'It's what I feel.'

'Yes, I can see that.'

Her lids began to flutter, she twisted her fingers into a knot. 'It would be nice . . . if you felt you could tell *me* all those things.'

'I would. I do. Really.'

A silence, during which her eyelids continued their feather-dance. 'Will you tell me what Dr Jones said then?' Catching my expression, she said, 'Oh, I guessed that's where you'd gone. He phoned last night, didn't he?'

I didn't attempt to deny it. 'Oh, he didn't say a lot really,' I began. 'He just wants me to keep an eye on you, that's all.'

'He doesn't think I'm going barmy?'

I smiled. 'No.'

'What *does* he think, then?'

'He thinks . . .' I shrugged while I struggled to find something approaching the truth. '. . . that the strain might get to you.'

Her expression softened. 'You know one of the

380

things I love about you, Hugh? You always try to protect me, don't you?' She cast me a crooked smile that managed to contain affection and rebuke in equal measure. 'Oh, I know what Dr Jones thinks,' she stated robustly. 'Dr Jones thinks I'm a total case. He thinks I'm making it all up. He thinks that I won't face up to what I've done. He thinks I killed Sylvie but I'm suppressing it all, or whatever you do when you're a basket case. He made up his mind right at the beginning. I *knew* it, I sensed it, and now when I see him it's like talking to a brick wall.' She gave a ragged sigh. 'Nice to have your shrink believe in you.'

'He wants to see you three times a week.'

'Oh, does he?' Her voice wobbled. 'Yes, I bet he does.'

'You don't have to. The bail condition is only for twice.'

'But twice a week is quite enough for what he wants!' she exclaimed darkly. 'That's all he needs to wear me down.'

'Can we let you know about Sunday?' I asked Mary when I called her. 'It might be rather last minute.'

'Of *course*,' she cried. 'Don't even think about it. I've booked a restaurant but it can easily be cancelled. But you just *have* to see this house some time! It's absolutely sweet. Beautifully furnished, wonderful view, gorgeous garden, and only a few miles from the motorway.'

'Well, if not Sunday . . .'

'I heard about it through a friend, someone who

381

owes me a favour. The owners want some people who're going to take good care of it while they're abroad. They won't expect much rent.'

'Sounds good.'

She gave a knowing murmur. 'But you're doubtful.'

'Well, it'll be up to Ginny.'

'Of course.' And her tone managed to convey both sympathy and pity.

'Any luck with that address?' I asked.

'Address?' She knew perfectly what I was after. 'Oh, the long-haired creature, you mean? Look, I did try, Hugh. As much as I could without getting into trouble anyway. I found the people who own the cottage. Live in Somerset somewhere. Phoned them, but all they did was put me on to the letting agents and – well, it was *difficult*, Hugh. I mean, I couldn't very well say what it was really about, could I? So I waffled on a bit about the last tenants owing me money and could they let me have an address for the chap, Joe whatever-his-name-was, and they told me they didn't know anything about him, that the place had been let to the lady who was now deceased. That's how they put it – *deceased*. So there we are. Sorry.'

'Thanks for trying.'

'Will you try another way?'

'Tingwall's got a private investigator on it.'

'Ah, that sounds better,' she said approvingly. 'Best to keep your distance, Hugh. Best to keep well clear.' She added brightly, 'What's his name, this chappy?'

'Umm, Pike. Based in Bristol.'

'*Pike*.' She made thinking noises. 'Don't know the

name. But keep me posted, won't you? Let me know how he gets on. You never know, I might be able to help somewhere else along the line. You *will* keep me posted, won't you?'

'Yes, Mary.'

'And Hugh? I think you're amazing, you know that? Absolutely totally amazing.'

I said goodbye before she could explain what she meant by that.

George sat with his back to the study window. Even allowing for the gloom of the rain-swept day, his complexion had an unhealthy grey cast, the pallor of exhaustion and worry, and watching him talk his way through the latest sales figures it occurred to me that with his straining belly, exercise-free lifestyle and rocketing stress levels he was prime heart attack material. Even now he was wading into the chocolate biscuits, washed down by a second cup of Ginny's powerful French coffee.

I interrupted him in mid-sentence. 'What will you do if we find ourselves out of a job, George?'

'Do?' He tried to look surprised at the question, but I could see he'd given it some thought. 'Well, Dorothy fancies a cruise. The *Oriana*, she's keen on the *Oriana*. And me, I fancy some golf. After that . . .' He made a wry face. 'Fifty-five isn't the sort of age when they beat on your door, is it?'

'Retirement, then?'

'I suppose. But I might do the odd thing. I thought – a small garden ornament business.'

'Ornaments?' I couldn't suppress a smile. 'Not gnomes, George?'

'Yes,' he said with perfect seriousness. 'But mainly birdbaths, larger statuary. They've developed this composite that looks like the finest stone but comes in at half the weight. I think there's a market. At the right price.' And we exchanged a smile. 'At the right price' had been a catchphrase of my father's.

'And you?' George asked.

'Me? Ahh. Well, I used to paint. I wouldn't mind having another go at it. Oh, I don't mean profession-ally – too late for that – but for my own amusement. Watercolours, I expect. Landscapes, like every other amateur.'

'And work?'

In the garden a rain squall was flailing the leaves from the rose bushes and ripping the petals from the last spindly blooms. Grasping at a half-considered thought, I said, 'Something hands-on. Something *impractical*. A vineyard. A small farm.'

'Abroad?'

'Probably.' I let the thought expand and settle. 'Won't make me rich, of course.'

'You wouldn't want something more challenging?'

'More challenging? You mean, more stressful, more time-consuming? No.' And I was surprised and reassured by my own certainty. 'No, I wouldn't want all that again. I've been on the roller coaster too long, George. I want out for a while. I want time to dawdle a bit. To remember each day. To notice its passing.'

George considered this with slight puzzlement

before returning his weary gaze to the sales figures. 'Not off the roller coaster yet.'

I almost said: More's the pity.

As we came to the monthly financial summary the phone buzzed and Ginny said, 'There's someone on the direct line. Joe somebody. You asked him to call you, so he says.'

My stomach clenched. I said with false calm, 'Put him on, would you?' I took the phone across the room to the length of its cord.

'Joe?'

A curt 'Yeah'.

'Thanks for calling. I was wondering if I could come and see you.' Silence. I felt a momentary panic. 'Joe?' I said into the silence.

'Yeah.'

I repeated, 'I need to see you.'

'Gimme one good reason.'

'Jean-Paul must have told you—' Aware of George, I lowered my voice still further. 'They've got it all wrong. My wife is not the person.'

'Yeah, well. You would say that, wouldn't you?'

'Maybe,' I said carefully. 'But that doesn't stop it being true. And I can tell you why.'

'Yeah?' The scorn again. 'And why should I listen?'

I sighed, 'Because we both want the same thing. I assume. We want the person who killed Sylvie.'

He exhaled grudgingly into the phone. 'Yeah, well . . . But if you're windin' me up, I'll fuckin' kill you. Okay?'

*

Heavy rain and Saturday night theatre traffic had reduced the western approach roads to a crawl, and by the time I had battled my way along the Marylebone Road and into the dripping labyrinths of Camden Town I was half an hour late. In the glimmer of the tawdry shop lights the *A to Z* offered obscure advice, and after negotiating the one-way system twice, I worked my way onto the Camden Road and, more by chance than design, found the right street.

Joe's place stood at the end of a terrace of identical Victorian houses with blackened brickwork and sullen windows with unshaded light bulbs and drooping curtains. The porch was unlit and if there were names against the cluster of bells I couldn't see them in the feeble glow of the streetlamps. I began to press each bell in turn and, reaching the third, the door sprang open with a loud buzz.

The hall smelled of old frying and new damp and mouldering carpet. Unclaimed letters and circulars littered the floor and a scribbled message on one wall informed the world that Jake and Janey had moved to another address.

I made my way up to the top of the house but no doors opened. Turning back, I followed loud music to a door on the first floor and knocked. A Rastafarian with a knitted hat gave a wide shrug at the name of Joe and waved me doubtfully up the house again. Climbing the last flight of stairs once more, I looked up and saw Joe standing on the landing above.

Through the crack of the open door behind him I glimpsed shabby wallpaper and a Monet exhibition poster, but he didn't invite me inside. Instead he leant against the doorframe with one arm folded and a cigarette held dart fashion in the other. His hair fell in lank waves over his shoulders while a dark stubble crawled unevenly over a thin jowl and scraggy neck. He didn't give the impression of having washed too recently.

'I wanted to ask you about the people Sylvie knew,' I began haltingly. 'Whether there was anyone who might have had reason to harm her.'

'You goin' to crack the case all on yer own, are yer?' he scoffed with an ugly laugh.

'Maybe not,' I admitted. 'But at least I'll have tried.'

'The fuzz been through all this a thousand times, asked loadsa questions. So why should they be wrong all of a sudden?'

'Well, they damn well are,' I said. 'My wife just . . . Well, she found the body, that was all.'

He pitched me a do-me-a-favour look and, drawing on his cigarette, funnelled the smoke expertly out of the side of his mouth. 'And I suppose you don't know nothing about it either.'

'I'd hardly be here otherwise.'

'You'd hardly be here,' he echoed in a mocking imitation of my accent.

Ignoring this, I said, 'I wondered about the drugs. Who Sylvie dealt with, whether she'd got on the wrong side of anyone. A dealer, perhaps.'

Suddenly he was still, his eyes wary behind the wafting smoke. 'A *dealer*?' He shook his head. 'She never got on the wrong side of any dealer. She hadn't been near a dealer.'

'Who did she get it from then?' I added: 'And who did she pass it on to?'

He searched my face as though he suspected me of laying some elaborate trap. 'Pass it on?'

'She collected some stuff in France. Enough for an army.'

He took a last drag of his cigarette before dropping it onto the pockmarked carpet and grinding it in with his heel. 'That wasn't any big deal.'

'It was a large packet.'

'So she got stuff for everyone. So.'

'Everyone?'

'People. Friends. We all forked out for it. It was like a co-op. She made the collection.'

I took a long breath and tried another tack. 'The man she got it from, the man in Cherbourg, was he a regular – *supplier*?'

'Nah. Friend. Doing us a favour.' Now he was watching me with lazy curiosity, wondering how far I would take this, and perhaps also wondering how far he would let me go.

'What about Hayden?'

'What about him?'

'Do you know where I can find him?'

'Why d'yer wanna know?'

I mustered my patience. 'To ask him the same questions.'

'Yeah?' he shrugged. 'Well, he's abroad some place, isn't 'e? Greece. Turkey. On some fat-cat yacht.' Taking some pity on me he added, 'Listen, he can't tell you anything.' I noticed that Joe's grammar, like his accent, came and went, that occasionally the politically correct yoof mumble slipped to reveal the unmistakable education beneath. Minor public school, I guessed. Home counties upbringing.

I said with a small gesture of defeat, 'So if he can't help me, who can?'

Through bleary eyes he gazed at me appraisingly and, with a long lumbering sigh, seemed to come to some kind of decision. 'Look . . . We got stuff in France, okay. Elk knew this geezer in Cherbourg—'

'Elk?'

'Charlie Hayden – Elk. The stuff came from Paris. But it was only, like, twice. A favour, that was all. No big deal.'

Putting a casual note into my voice, I asked, 'What was it, the stuff?'

He looked away crossly, he wasn't certain he wanted to answer that. 'Coke,' he admitted finally. 'And some junk, too.'

Some instinct told me. 'Sylvie was on heroin.'

He raised his eyebrows slightly in agreement. 'She was clean when she went down to Dittisham, she'd done the treatment, the full bit. NA, therapy sessions. But then . . .' He raised a dismissive shoulder and pulled a battered pack of Lucky Strikes from his shirt pocket. I waited silently while he found a light and coughed over his first pull. He tucked one arm under the other and settled into his bird-like stance. 'Then someone started giving her stuff again.'

'Who?'

'Dunno. I wasn't around then. But whoever it was kept it coming.'

'A *dealer*, then?'

He shook his head. 'Nah. Not a dealer. A friend.'

'What sort of friend?' But perhaps that was a stupid question. 'A lover?'

'Maybe.'

'She had a lover?' And the thought sent a sudden tension into my belly.

'I guess. But like I said, I wasn't around then.'

'When did you get down there?'

He blew out his cheeks with the effort of memory. 'Jeese . . . Umm, June? Yeah, some time then.'

I wasn't sure where this was leading, or how best to pursue it. 'Who would know?' I asked eventually. 'Who was around before you got down there?'

He chased something round his teeth with his tongue while he thought about that. 'Yeah – Elk. Elk might know. Yeah. He was around then.'

'But Elk wasn't the guy?'

'What? Nah. Not Elk. Elk never did junk.'

'Was he her lover, though?'

He guffawed, a coarse braying sound. 'Nah. He and Sylvie, they didn't get on. I mean, like they hung out together but they fought. Nah,' he said adamantly, 'not Elk.'

'What about the woman who worked in the pottery shop? Would she have known about Sylvie's friends?'

'Doubt it.'

'What was her name?'

'Liz.' He waved his cigarette vaguely. 'Never knew 'er second name.'

I was drained of ideas. I murmured, 'And there was no one else you can think of . . .'

'What, that mighta killed her? Nah.' His expression grew sly. 'Only you.'

'Don't be bloody stupid,' I said in sudden anger. 'You know it wasn't me.'

He snorted, 'I dunno that! Why should I know that?'

'Because I hadn't seen her in weeks. Because she wasn't coming to see me that afternoon.'

'She said she was goin' out to the boat.'

So that was what he had told the police. 'Not quite the same thing,' I pointed out.

Suddenly he was in no mood to concede this or anything else. 'Yeah, well, you would say that, wouldn't you?'

The place was lovely, a sturdy farmhouse in grey stone with a sheltered garden and views of Dartmoor. It wasn't too large, hardly more than a substantial cottage, and it had a tranquil comforting air, the sort of place where you could imagine yourself hidden from the world.

It seemed promising to me. Mary thought so too because she kept extolling its virtues in ever more extravagant terms, but as David and I followed the women into the garden a certain futility seemed to settle over the expedition. I sensed that Ginny had taken a dislike to the place and that nothing any of us could say was likely to change her mind.

'How do you think she looks?' I asked David quietly.

'Ginny? Oh . . . Surprisingly well, really. Getting on with Jones all right, is she?'

We paused by a weathered sundial. I hesitated, caught between loyalty and a painful need for reassurance. 'He thinks she's suffering from some sort of delusion.'

'Christ, aren't we all?'

'You don't think it's serious then?'

'Look, I'm not the right person to ask,' he protested. 'Doctors know damn-all about psychiatry. We just shove patients towards the men in white coats and breathe a sigh of relief when they're willing to take them on. And then again, most of us are a bit worried about being found lacking in the mental department ourselves.' He gave a dry bark of a laugh. 'You know how the statistics go – doctors sky-high in the suicide league, not to mention the alcohol stakes.'

'It's just that I find it hard to judge how good he is.'

'You and me both. There's not one of them that ever agrees. They argue like crazy between themselves. I can only say that Jones seems to be the best around.'

'He thinks she might find the strain too much.'

'Well, I *would* take notice of that. Psychiatric clap-trap aside, it's the one thing he's likely to get right.'

Absorbing this as best I could, we strolled on through an arch into a paved herb garden. The women were a long way ahead, disappearing around the back of the house.

'How's the case coming along?' David asked with sudden awkwardness. 'Anything I can help with?'

'Not really. Everything's on hold until the prosecution present their evidence.' We came to a halt again. 'There was something though . . .' I framed the question with care. 'I know you said that you only saw Sylvie a couple of times, and there was no way of telling she was on drugs, but what about heroin? Can't you tell with that?'

David looked away towards the rise of the moor. 'In women they say the skin gets a luminous look – quite beautiful, apparently – but unless you know the person . . .' A dismissive lift of the shoulders. 'Otherwise needle marks, of course. But you would have to *see* them.'

'So no one would have known?'

'Not by looking at her, no. Why?'

I wasn't terribly sure why I was asking. 'Just wondered, that was all.'

David grunted, 'She was definitely on heroin, was she?'

'Yes.' We both studied the view again. 'Where would she have got her drugs from if it wasn't from a dealer?'

David threw me a sharp quizzical look. '*Not* from a dealer? Well . . .' He did a mental double-take. 'You know it wasn't a dealer?'

'Apparently not.'

He went through the motions of thinking about this. 'Well, it could have been legally, from a doctor. So long as she was a registered addict. But she wasn't registered with me. Though . . .' He frowned. 'She could have been registered with another doctor, I suppose. When she signed on with me her notes were forwarded from some private doctor off Sloane Square, but she could easily have had a second doctor somewhere else. One she'd persuaded to give her a long-term repeat script. There are some doctors who specialise in signing up drug addicts to boost their lists, and then go and hand out scripts like confetti from a gravy train, with no intention of weaning them off anything.'

'If she had prescriptions she must have used them locally then?'

David missed the question. 'Otherwise another registered addict,' he mused. But he didn't sound convinced. 'Someone who was willing to share their quota. I've got four or five addicts on my books, but they're all on methadone.' He gave a sardonic grunt. 'I will persist in this crazy idea that they'll get off drugs one day, you see. I go through the motions.'

'A local chemist would notice a prescription for heroin then?'

'For diamorphine – that's the name – well, he *might*. Normally it's only used for terminal cases – cancer. Largely dispensed through hospitals and homes.' He cast me a sidelong glance. 'You think this could be important?'

I gave a wide shrug. 'Who knows? But yes. Yes, I do.'

'You think . . .' He wore the irritated expression that always overtook him when he was forced to voice something that might make him look foolish. 'You think the drugs are something to do with her death?'

'Well, it has to be as good as anything the police have come up with, doesn't it?'

David eyed me thoughtfully, as if appreciating for the first time that I had not given up on the idea of Ginny's innocence. He pushed out his lips and nodded sagely. 'I'll see what I can find out.'

The offer surprised me. 'Would you?'

'Sure. There aren't that many chemists in the area. They're always calling me up.' He grunted disdainfully, '*Say* they can't read my handwriting.'

'Thanks, David.' Then, as if I needed to justify myself further: 'I feel I have to try.'

'Of course.' And I recognised the tone in his voice that signalled fast-waning interest.

The women reappeared at the far end of the garden. Ginny was hugging her arms to her stomach, looking cold.

'This EGM,' David said in a voice that was so remote and abrupt I could only wonder at his ability to switch mood. 'Is it going to come off?'

'Yes. You should have been notified. Next Friday.'

'Isn't it all a waste of time, Hugh? I mean, wouldn't we do better to just take the money and run? Or rather, *keep* our money and run?'

'We have very little to lose, David, and an awful lot to gain.'

'*Do* we? You could have fooled me. It seems to me that Cumberland must know what they're doing. They've made their decision and we should accept it.'

From across the flowerbeds Ginny caught my eye as she listened inattentively to something Mary was saying, and it was a plea for rescue.

'They'll close the factory, David. They'll put a lot of people out of work. Isn't that reason enough to give it a try?'

'No.' Warming to his indignation, he protested, 'No, it damn well isn't. That's the way *bad* decisions are made.'

'Look, it's not long to wait now,' I said appeasingly. 'It'll all be settled on Friday.'

He growled uncompromisingly, 'Once a ship's sinking . . .'

Mary and Ginny were moving towards us again.

I touched David's arm. 'One last thing – when did Sylvie join your list?'

'*What?*' He was thoroughly incensed now. 'What's that got to do with anything?'

'I wanted to know when she arrived in Dittisham.'

'Oh.' He allowed himself to be slightly mollified. 'March. Beginning of March.'

Ginny came up and fastened herself to my side.

'You're cold,' I said and, taking off my jacket, put it round her shoulders.

'Well, what do you think?' I asked as we followed David and Mary back to the cars.

She whispered, 'I don't like it.'

'Fine.'

'And it's *not* because Mary's so crazy about it, if that's what you're thinking.'

'No, no – I wasn't. No, don't worry about it. We'll find somewhere else.'

'It's got something spooky about it,' she shivered. 'I feel as though someone died here.'

Suppressing faint alarm, I squeezed her hand. 'In that case . . .'

She stopped suddenly and looked up at me, her eyes burning fiercely, and said for no apparent reason, 'I do love you, you know. Sometimes I don't know what I did to deserve you.'

I kissed her softly on the lips. 'It's me that's the lucky one,' I said.

I glanced up and saw Mary at the corner of the house, looking back at us. Instantly, she gave a broad smile and called, 'David and I both know the way to the restaurant. Why don't we split up in case we get separated?' She put on a comically doubtful expression and laughed, 'If that makes any sense!'

I turned to ask Ginny but she was already shrugging her agreement.

David led the way in his Mercedes, and as I fell in line behind I saw him turn his head to Ginny, asking her something, or replying.

'Ginny didn't like the house,' said Mary, fixing her seat belt.

'I'm afraid not.'

'Oh well. Worth a try.' She didn't seem in the least perturbed. 'How's everything else going?'

'Not a lot of progress at the moment.'

'How's the investigator doing – Mr *Pike*. I must say, it's a rather unfortunate name. Aren't pikes terrible predators, gobbling up everything in sight?'

'No word yet. It's only been a few days.'

'So he hasn't tracked down the dreaded Joe yet?'

I answered the question truthfully. 'No.'

She cast me a sidelong glance. 'Awfully glad you

didn't get involved, Hugh. It really wouldn't have done, you know.'

'I can see that.'

We drove on in silence for a time.

'Tell me,' I asked casually, 'do you know the woman who worked in the pottery shop with Sylvie? Liz something? I tried to phone the place but it must have closed down. The number was discontinued anyway.'

'Haven't a clue! Don't even know which shop it was! But *Hugh!*' she exclaimed, attempting to moderate her disbelief and exasperation with a laugh. 'Same warning applies, for God's sake. Could be a prosecution witness!' She sighed at me as if I was beyond redemption. 'Why do you want to know anyway?'

'I thought she might know who Sylvie's lover was. The one before me.'

'The *one?*' she questioned drily. 'I thought she never had less than a *bevy* on the go.'

'There was one in particular.'

'Well – who knows then? Any red-blooded male in the area, presumably.'

'This one supplied her with drugs.'

Mary gave me an abrupt glance. 'Oh really? *Really.* Well, there you are then. She was always on to the main chance, wasn't she? Addicts are all the same. Dragging people down into their own little cesspool. Polluting everything in their path. They commit most crime nowadays – did you know that? Muggings and burglary. The new scum of the earth.'

I had nothing to say to that.

'You think you'll find this *lover?*' Mary asked.

'No idea.'

'If you ask me you should try your Mr Pike. He'll know all about that little world. He'll know all about the rot at the bottom of the muckheap.'

Thirteen

TINGWALL'S OFFICE lights blazed in the darkened building. A hastily departing staff member let me in and I made my way down the passage and through the dimmed outer office to Tingwall's door, which was open. Catching sight of me, Tingwall stood up in the act of swallowing a hot drink and promptly choked. Spluttering, he put his cup hastily down and waved a voiceless welcome.

'I'm sorry I couldn't make it earlier,' I said. 'A crisis at Hartford.' It would have been truer to say, another crisis in a succession of emergencies. This time it had been a last-minute panic over the documentation for the EGM.

Still speechless, Tingwall clutched his throat and gestured me to my customary chair. I perched on the edge of my seat and, making no attempt to hide my restlessness, looked straight at the clock. Catching this, Tingwall gestured remorse for the delay and, coughing heartily, went to the side and poured himself a glass of water which he downed rapidly and refilled.

'It's just that Ginny will be waiting,' I explained.

'I wouldn't have bothered you ...' Tingwall gasped. 'If it hadn't been ... important.' He drew up a chair and, clearing his throat, sat on the very edge of his seat, arms on knees, hands clasped, eyes grave. 'Look, what I'm about to tell you – well, I think we *must* treat it with caution until everything is confirmed and clarified, until we can get a third opinion and be really sure of our ground, *but* – well, it's possible we may have something on the forensic front.'

'What sort of thing?'

He held up a hand as though to pre-empt some excessive reaction from me. 'I really do think it would be a mistake to get too excited about this,' he warned. Yet behind his calm veneer I realised it was Tingwall himself who was quietly excited. 'It's the fingerprint expert – chap called Armstrong—'

'Our expert?'

'Oh, yes – *our* man. He's looked at the fingerprint that the police took from the boat and he's found two things. First, that it's a pretty poor print – a fragment from an index finger, and lifted off natural wood with a strong grain, which means the print is fairly broken up. Well, I'm not sure if that's the correct technical term, but you can imagine – wood isn't the smoothest of surfaces. *But* even more importantly, he's found only fourteen points of similarity between this print and Ginny's, which is two short of the number which is needed for a positive identification in an English court of law.' He paused to let me absorb the full significance of this. 'What it all boils down to, Hugh, is that in his opinion this print cannot be positively identified as Ginny's. If he's right – and he *is* a top man – then the implications are absolutely—' Losing the word, he wheeled an impatient hand before settling on: 'Crucial.'

Many different thoughts jostled in my mind as I heard myself ask, 'But these points of similarity – fourteen, was it? Isn't that rather a lot?'

'Sixteen is the absolute minimum required in law for a positive ID,' Tingwall repeated, weighing each word authoritatively as though he were in court.' Armstrong explained it all to me – we'll have to wait for his report, of course – but his conclusion was unequivocal, Hugh. He says that in his opinion it would be unsafe to say these prints were from the same person.'

At some point in the last few weeks I had lost the capacity for hope or joy, and, while part of me recognised the importance of this news, my emotions failed to respond. 'Where do we go from here then?'

'We get another expert. I've tracked down a chap called Benyon in London. Meant to be the best independent. He can get back to us in a few days, though he said it could be longer if it's a complex job.'

'And what happens if he doesn't agree? What happens if he thinks the print is Ginny's?'

Tingwall wasn't ready to allow such negative thoughts. 'Armstrong seems sure, Hugh. And a man of his experience doesn't offer an opinion like that without very careful consideration.'

But part of me wanted to deflate his optimism, if only to protect myself from disappointment. 'What about the police expert – why should he be wrong and our people right?'

'Ah!' Tingwall declared, flipping open one palm

like a flashy magician about to produce his best trick. 'We're dealing in reasonable doubt, Hugh. If we manage to cast reasonable doubt on the reliability of the evidence, if we have two top experts saying that they think a match would be unsafe, then the police evidence will be fatally undermined. Reasonable doubt, Hugh. In a case of murder the judge will bend over backwards to make sure that reasonable doubt is understood and acted on by the jury.'

I said ironically, 'But I'm not to get excited?'

Tingwall, whose excitement had become increasingly apparent, had the grace to smile. 'Perhaps I shouldn't have told you at this stage. I'm sorry if you would have preferred me not to. But Hugh, the thing is that if Armstrong is right, and Benyon agrees with him, it will alter our position significantly. The prosecution will be left with nothing but the eyewitness sighting, and eyewitness evidence is always the weakest part of any case. However impressive this eyewitness may be – and we know nothing about him yet – we're back to reasonable doubt. It only needs one small inconsistency, one small hesitation, and a good defence counsel will expose the flaw and rip the evidence apart. Grainger has a reputation for that, you know – demolishing star witnesses.'

Instinct told me that it couldn't be as simple as that. And by way of endorsement, a troubling thought hovered at the edge of my mind and swooped home. 'She cleaned up the boat, Charles. They'll still have that. Why would she want to clean up the boat? Or,' I suggested heavily, 'are we going back to the idea that she was covering up for me?'

'The boat cleaning, that's circumstantial. Not enough in itself, Hugh. And as for Ginny thinking you were the murderer, hopefully we won't have to use that, and certainly not if the case never even gets to trial.'

'Don't tell me they're likely to drop it!' I said, by now so thoroughly unsettled that I took a harsh satisfaction in arguing against my own interests.

'No, but . . .' An inner debate flickered over Tingwall's face. Finally he ventured, 'We'd have to take advice, of course – *plenty* of advice – but it's *possible* we might want to go for an old-style committal in front of a stipendiary, and try to get the case thrown out altogether. But, look,' he cautioned hastily, 'don't take it from me. I mean, I may be way off the mark!'

Two things struck me: that while Tingwall might be meeting the challenge of the case, he was also feeling the full responsibility of it, and that, for all his dedication and tenacity, he was not as confident as he made himself out to be.

Tingwall hurried on, 'I thought that as soon as we have Benyon's fingerprint report and the prosecution's statements, which should come through any day now, we should have a conference with Grainger, sound him out, see if he thinks an old-style committal's a starter. What do you think?'

I looked out into the black November night, aware of how long Ginny had been alone and the time it would take me to get back to her. 'Can I phone my wife?'

Tingwall looked dubious. 'Do you think it's wise to tell her?'

'I'm not going to tell her over the phone, Charles, if that's what you mean.' It wasn't what he meant, of course. He meant that it might not be wise or fair to tell her anything at all. But it occurred to me as I went to make the call in the outer office that raising her hopes might be no bad thing, that hope was a fairly harmless commodity when you didn't have much else to hold on to.

I could never speak to Ginny on the phone these days without listening for sounds of strain in her voice, for some sign that her self-control was wearing thin, and hearing her now I knew with a small lurch of alarm that something had happened. 'What is it?' I asked.

'Nothing.'

'You're upset. Was it Jones?'

She exhaled fiercely into the phone. 'He *refuses* to believe me. He just won't *listen*. He's treating me like an idiot!'

I cursed my weakness for staying at the Hartford meeting for longer than I had meant to. 'Okay,' I said soothingly, 'we'll sort it out. Somehow we'll sort it out, I promise.'

'He's trying to wear me down, just like I said he would. He undermines everything I say – *everything*. Even you and me – he tries to make me say that I'm angry with you, that I was out for some sort of revenge, that I was really trying to get my own back at you and – oh, I don't know – lunatic things!'

'I'll tell him to lay off.'

'Will you?'

'Of course. I'll tell him to lay off or we'll take our business elsewhere.'

'Oh, will you? Will you really? He makes me feel so dreadful. He makes me want to crawl under a stone.'

'Ginny – rise above it, ignore it. Believe in yourself.'

'But I'm so angry, Hugh, I'm so *angry*.'

I searched for words that might have some meaning for her but could only plead impotently: 'I promise I'll sort it out, darling. Just hold on. Please – don't get upset. *Please*.'

'I'm all right,' she said in a calmer voice. 'I'm always better after I've talked to you.'

Tingwall walked me out to my car. 'It must be a hard time for Ginny,' he said as though he had divined something of my conversation. 'It's always so much harder for innocent people. They feel they're battling against the assumption of guilt. I had one chap up on a rape charge and even when he got off he never stopped feeling hounded. It's an awful lot easier being guilty.'

'I'll take your word for it.'

Climbing into the car, I remembered what I had meant to tell him and opened the door again. 'I forgot – your man Pike needn't bother with Sylvie's friend Joe. I found him.'

'Don't we want to talk to him?' Tingwall asked.

'No.'

'No?' Catching some hint of what had been going on behind his back, he shot me a look in which curiosity, disapproval and the sense to ask no more were neatly fused.

'Has Pike made any progress with Hayden?' I asked.

'Nothing yet.'

'Could you let me know the moment he finds anything?'

'Sure.'

He was still giving me a speculative narrow-eyed look as I drove away.

I had a picture of what I would find on my arrival home. Rooms in semi-darkness, Ginny by an unlit fire picking the skin at the edges of her nails – she had already made them raw – and an air of anxiety which she would expect me to alleviate; the rest of the evening bolstering her confidence, a tricky chat with Jones and finally to bed, to find peace of a sort for a few hours. Another day survived.

The lights were on in the drive, the floodlights around the front of the house too. As I parked, Ginny came out to meet me. She was dressed in a simple black dress with a heavy gold necklace and matching earrings. When I kissed her I caught a waft of *Je Reviens*.

'Did I forget something? Are we having a party?'

'Absolutely,' she smiled, taking me into the house.

'Who's coming?'

'Just you and me.'

'Sounds all right to me.'

Passing the kitchen I caught the smell of wonderful things cooking and saw that she had laid the small circular breakfast table with a white cloth and candles and flowers. She led the way into the sitting room and poured me a glass of champagne.

'You look uncertain,' she said.

'No,' I said rather too quickly. 'No, just – surprised.'

'I wanted us to have a jolly evening for a change. You must get fed up with all my moaning.' She flung me a bright smile. 'I want you to feel you've got something to look forward to when you get home. To know that you're going to be spoilt a bit.'

'But I do. I am.'

'Liar,' she smiled. There was a glow in her face which I hadn't seen in a long time. Part of it, I realised, was makeup, a clever mix of colour and shading that lifted her features and intensified her eyes, and which she hadn't bothered to put on for weeks; but there was an inner spark, too, some new resolve.

I gave up with a laugh and raised my drink. 'Here's to jolly evenings.'

As we drank she caught me watching her over my glass. Some of the doubt must have shown in my eyes because she said, 'What *did* Jones tell you? Did he say I was going off my head? Is that what you've been thinking all this time?' Her voice managed to be brittle and fluid at the same time. 'Oh, don't worry, I wouldn't blame you if you had. He's very persuasive. God – sometimes he's had *me* wondering if I'm going barmy. *But*' – she gave me a conspiratorial grin – 'I've finally done what I should have done ages ago. I plucked up all my courage and half an hour ago I called him! I told him what I thought of him!'

I had paused in the act of drinking. 'What did you say to him?' I asked nervously.

'Say?' Her eyes gave a dark triumphant flash. 'I told him that he'd been out of line. That he'd been intimidating me – well, *bullying* me, really. That he'd been making assumptions that weren't his to make. *Undermining* me. That I didn't deserve that. That no one did.' Reliving her own temerity, she gave a strange high-pitched laugh. 'I can be so much braver on the phone – no eye contact, none of those awful silences that he uses to make me feel guilty!'

I was still immobile, the glass just short of my lips. 'And what did he say to that?'

'Well, he didn't want to admit he was wrong, did he? He said he'd never disbelieved anything I'd said, never made up his mind about anything. But he had – he knew he had. He didn't want to admit he'd been . . . *pressuring* me. I made him promise that in future he'd listen without *deciding*, that he'd listen and accept what I had to say. Just *accept*.' And her jaw hardened, she spoke with a sudden vehemence that made her shudder visibly.

I sat down and said, 'Gosh.'

Finding her mood again, she tipped up her chin. 'I felt so much better afterwards, I can't tell you! I felt as though I'd got a little bit of my life back. Oh, I know you would have waded in for me,' she remarked affectionately. 'You always do. But for once I needed to say it for myself, I needed to feel I was fighting my own battles. And I'm glad I did, *glad*. It's done me so much good!' And she sparkled at me, all shaky confidence and new determination.

'There's something else.' She came and knelt on the floor at my feet and rested her arm on my knee. 'I've been thinking that I really must be much more positive! Things are far more likely to go right if one thinks positive, aren't they? And misery's such a bore. So wearing. I should be remembering all the good things and making the most of what I have!' She gave an excited laugh and – a pang of disloyalty – I couldn't help wondering what she'd been taking. 'I want us to plan like mad,' she declared. 'Everything, all the way through to our old age. Every house and holiday and job and – oh, I don't know! But as though I'm going to be around. I need that, I need to believe it's all going to happen.'

'Ginny . . .' I put my drink down. 'Something came up today.' And I told her about the fingerprint expert, how nothing was definite yet, but if all went well and the two experts agreed then her chances would significantly improve.

She listened attentively, she asked a couple of questions then shrugged carelessly, 'There you are. See what a bit of positive thinking can do!' In her sparky optimism I saw the Ginny of years gone by, the Ginny I had fallen in love with, and in apparent awareness of this, she looked up and we exchanged a glance of shared memory.

I was leaning forward to kiss her when the phone rang.

David's voice said, 'Not interrupting dinner?' Without waiting for a reply, he reported, 'The chemists look as though they're going to be a dead loss, I'm afraid. I got four or five to look back through their registers but nothing out of the ordinary in the way of diamorphine scripts. Without asking them for chapter and verse there's not a lot more I can do, I'm afraid.'

'Oh well.'

'Anyway, I was thinking – she's far more likely to have got her stuff on the open market, isn't she? Bristol's seething with drugs. Buy them on every corner. It's not far, after all.'

Bristol made me think of Jean-Paul. Time had not lent him credibility, and I found myself wondering if he had told me anything approaching the truth. 'No, it's not far,' I agreed. 'Thanks anyway.' I hesitated. 'There was one other thing. The woman who worked in the pottery shop with Sylvie. Liz something. Fifty-ish, ethnic clothes, beads. You wouldn't have any idea who she was?'

He made a doubtful sound. 'I know who you might mean. Seen her once or twice. Retired hippy type. Long gypsy skirts. But no – not a patient of mine, not someone I know. Useless again, I'm afraid.'

'Thanks anyway. And thanks for lunch yesterday.'

'Oh, for heaven's sake.' David regarded social niceties as superfluous at the best of times and positively ridiculous within the family. He rang off with a sharp admonitory grunt.

I took the champagne bottle into the kitchen and found Ginny at the table, doing last minute things to some beef that smelled of wine and garlic and herbs. She nodded enthusiastically when I offered to refill her glass. 'Heaven.' And she smiled in such a way that I wasn't quite sure what she was referring to. I was trying another kiss when the phone rang.

'Doomed by the bell,' I muttered.

'Caressus interruptus.'

I snatched the receiver off the hook and was met

411

by the howl of a child. 'Sorry to bother you, Hugh,' Tingwall said over the din, 'but it's Pike. He's found this chap Hayden.'

'Where?'

The screaming reached a terrifying pitch. 'Nothing I can do about this, I'm afraid,' he shouted, sounding harassed. 'In sole charge. Wife at a girls' night. Well, that's what she tells me.' He laughed to show it was a joke. 'No, when I say *found*, it's not quite as good as that. Apparently Hayden's on his way to Heathrow at this moment, heading for the Far East. Pike just missed him in London.'

'Damn. Can he catch him at the airport?' I shouted back.

'He's going to try. He's on his way there now.' Tingwall made some cooing noises off-stage and for a moment the screaming subsided to a succession of wails and sobs. 'At best he might only get a few minutes with Hayden. I've given him some questions to ask, but I wanted to check with you to make sure I hadn't missed anything obvious.'

'Can I speak to Pike direct?'

'What? Sure. He's got a mobile.'

I took down the number and repeated it back to him through the renewed caterwauling.

'Won't be a minute,' I called to Ginny as I rang off and disappeared in the direction of the study.

The number didn't answer first time. When I tried again two minutes later an expressionless voice announced itself as Pike. I explained who I was and Pike told me he was on the motorway, just minutes from the airport.

412

'If you do manage to find him,' I said, 'try to stop him leaving, will you? Any way you can.'

'I'm not sure I understand you.'

'Offer him whatever it takes to delay his flight.'

'What's your limit?'

'I don't know – five hundred? Two thousand? Whatever it takes.'

'Some people won't be bought at any price.'

'This one will,' I said, though I couldn't have said what gave me such confidence.

'Right. I'll keep in touch.'

I gave Pike my number and went through to dinner. I tried to enter into the spirit of Ginny's evening but I must have been a poor actor because Ginny's intuition soon caught me out.

'The phone. Something's happened,' she said.

'I may have to go out later. If I do, will you be all right?'

'Of course.' But she didn't sound at all convinced.

'I may be late. Well – very late.'

That unnerved her. She didn't like being alone in the house at night. The animation fell from her face. 'How late?'

'I don't know. I might have to go to the airport to talk to someone. I could try to get Mrs Hoskins to come over if you like.'

'It can't wait, this thing?'

I shook my head. 'It's someone who might have information, you see. About Sylvie.'

She gave me a searching, almost hostile look. 'I thought Charles was dealing with all that.'

'He's tied up, and this man's about to fly off some-where. It's the only chance.'

She was very still. 'Where's all this leading, Hugh?'

'Leading?'

'What's the point of it all?'

I stared at her, baffled by her attitude. 'The *point*?' I heard the impatience in my voice and argued more reasonably, 'Well, someone killed Sylvie, didn't they? So someone has to know *something* about it. The people she mixed with, the dealers . . . If we don't make an effort to find out, then, then—' But mystifi-cation blocked my words.

'I think . . .' She hesitated for a long moment. 'I think it would be a mistake to hope for too much.'

'I'm not hoping for *too much*—'

The phone rang and, pushing my chair back roughly, I got up to answer it.

'Bingo,' said Pike's voice. 'But you'll need to bring some cash.' Five minutes later, armed with a batch of traveller's cheques and credit cards, still smarting a little from my discussion with Ginny, I was heading for the motorway.

Pike had booked Hayden into one of the smarter hotels on the airport periphery, a newish place with a lobby designed in what Ginny would disdainfully dub the mid-Atlantic country-house style, with garish chintzes and hunting scenes and dimpled leather sofas. Pike hadn't stinted on the room either. He let me into a suite with a lobby, three doors leading off it, and a large display of fresh flowers.

Pike was a nondescript man, dead-eyed and stoop-shouldered, with an unhealthy complexion and lugubrious expression. Closing the door behind me, he murmured in the professional undertone of a copper, 'He's friendly enough, but greedy, I'd say. He finally agreed to a grand, cash in hand, plus a replacement air ticket at seven hundred, plus overnight expenses, but I reckon he'll be after more. Shall I sit in?'

'Please.'

Pike led the way into a sitting room with a mirrored bar complete with counter and stools. Hayden was lying back on a sofa watching television, his feet on a low table, drink in hand and a bowl of nuts balanced precariously on his stomach. Removing his eyes unhurriedly from the screen, he disentangled himself from the sofa and rose to a hefty six foot three or four.

'Hi.' His steely handshake was accompanied by a broad lazy smile that was all the more startling for the contrast between his teeth, which were numerous, even and exceptionally white, and the depth of his golden tan. With his springy sun-bleached hair, athletic shoulders and model-boy looks, he might have come straight from a Californian lifestyle commercial. He was the same man I had watched through the binoculars on *Samphire*, but coloured more vividly.

While Pike made the drinks, Hayden grinned some more before sauntering back to the sofa and sinking into the cushions with his eyes fixed on the television again, as though the business session hadn't yet opened and he was still at leisure. When I sat on the chair opposite he didn't hurry to tear himself away from the blaring comedy but waited for some raucous punch line at which he laughed in a loud contrived way before finally operating the remote control.

He turned his smile on me again, and it was a facile smile without warmth. 'Good trip?' he asked as though we were small-talking at a party.

'Fine, thanks.'

'Great.' He nodded a lot, though not as much as he smiled. 'Going straight back?'

'I expect so.'

'Great. I'll be needing cash, did, ah, he tell you?' He indicated Pike with a movement of his head.

'He told me.'

Pike brought the drinks.

Hayden was watching me indolently, like a man with all the time in the world, and I realised he was waiting for the cash to appear on the table.

I produced the traveller's cheques.

He gave an exaggerated theatrical wince, all regretful head-shaking and raised shoulders. 'Ah – *sorry.*' And behind the knowing eyes I recognised someone who was used to getting his own way. I remembered the scene I had witnessed on *Samphire*, the way Sylvie had stood her ground against him.

Pike caught my eye. 'I'll go and see if the management can oblige.' I passed him the cheques and my Amex Gold Card.

'You won't mind if we start?' I asked when Pike had gone.

'Sure.' His tone told me what I already knew, that

416

he wouldn't be telling me anything of real importance until the money arrived.

'I assume Pike's told you what this is about?'

He started picking at the nuts again and popping them expertly into his mouth. 'Sure.'

'Have you spoken to the police at all?'

'I've been away,' he said in a conversational tone. 'Gib, Turkey, Italy, delivering boats. They couldn't've found me if they'd tried.'

'But you were in Devon until – what, August?'

'I was coming and going. I got this dinky little cottage up near Totnes. For my, ah, old age, you know.' And the idea amused him in the way some equally distant prospect like going grey or bald might amuse him. 'Bit of a ruin still. Done the roof. No heating, no light.' He shrugged. 'Next year, I'm hoping.'

'And *Samphire* – you got to do quite a bit of cruising?'

'Sure. Always take the old girl out when I can. Otherwise she rots – you know?' And he smiled his empty affable smile.

Rather than risk questions that he was unlikely to answer, I threw it open. 'Tell me about Sylvie.'

'Sylvie?' He laughed as if I had said something unexpected. '*Yeah* . . . Well, we went back quite a way, Sylvie and me. South of France, Ibiza . . .' He waved a hand, indicating other times, other places. 'Hung out in the same crowd. So when she came around she, ah, got in touch. You know.'

'What brought her to Devon?'

He spread an open palm. 'New start? I guess.'

'She was happy?'

But this question obviously had its price, and his face took on an impenetrable look.

'I saw Joe the other day,' I said, watching for a reaction which I didn't get. 'He told me all about Sylvie's drug—' I almost said 'problems', but amended this to: 'habits. And he told me about the trips to France on *Samphire*, to the dealer there.' Hayden's bland expression did not alter. 'What I need to know – when our business is done' – I offered my own version of a hollow smile – 'is who else she got her stuff from.'

He showed no surprise at the question. Taking a swig of his drink, he creased up his eyes with the effort of some mental calculation and asked, 'When did you come on the scene with Sylvie? I was trying to work it out.'

'Me? What's that got to do with anything?'

'After Easter, was it?'

'June,' I answered reluctantly.

He began his slow nodding again, and did not stop for a long time. 'Yeah,' he said at last, as though he had finally solved the puzzle. 'Yeah.'

Pike reappeared at last with the hotel night manager in tow, and after signing a batch of traveller's cheques and credit card vouchers I took delivery of a thousand pounds in cash.

I plopped the notes onto the table in front of Hayden.

Unhurriedly he leant forward and scooped them up.

'Well?' I demanded.

'Well?' Hayden repeated in the lazy amused manner that appeared to be his stock in trade. 'Where d'you wanna start?'

'The stuff. Where did she get it?'

And still Hayden took his time. 'Can't tell you where she got *everything*. Sylvie had a lot of contacts – you know? But some of the time, back last winter anyway, she had prescriptions. Nicked, I guess. But she never had any trouble with them. Never got thrown out of any chemist or anything. But she was clever about that sort of thing – you know? Used to ring the changes. Sometimes Dartmouth, sometimes Exeter, sometimes Bristol when she was up that way.'

'They were made out to her, the prescriptions?'

'Nah,' he said without hesitation. 'She used to fill in the names herself. She had three of her own to choose from, you know. Mathieson and a couple of married names.' He chuckled, 'Or do I mean divorced names?' Enjoying his own joke for a moment, he finally sauntered on, 'She had two passports anyway, one French, one British, in different names. That way she could always produce ID.' While I was absorbing this he added, 'The prescriptions, she had plenty last winter. Must have had a whole pad of the things. Cost her, I bet. Well, that's what I thought—'

'Cost her?'

'Sure. Junk isn't my scene, you understand. But – yeah, she'd have bought them.'

I was being slow, but I had to understand this. 'You mean, pads get stolen and sold on?'

Deferring to the expert, Hayden tipped an amused glance at Pike.

'They get stolen all the time,' Pike confirmed in his bleak voice. 'Doctors' cars, surgeries. Though the thieves don't get much joy a lot of the time because the chemists are on the lookout. Lists of stolen pads get circulated. The chemists check up on anything suspect.'

Hayden drained his drink and wiggled his glass hopefully. Pike got grudgingly to his feet and took the glass for a refill.

Hayden yawned.

'So?' I urged.

'Yeah, well . . . the prescriptions, they seemed to run out in . . . I guess it must have been Easter time, and then she, ah, started on at me to go to France all the time, to pick up stuff there. But listen, that wasn't my scene. I mean, the occasional little trip, a bit of hash, that's okay, you know what I mean? But regularly, for junk?' He blew disapprovingly through his lips. 'Well, that's asking for it, isn't it? And I've got my reputation to consider.' He angled his head a little, as if to show his best profile. 'One run-in with the customs and I'd never work again. Like, *never*. So I just told her to jump. I told her that wasn't my game. Then . . . I can't be sure, you know? But I think she got her stuff from Bristol. Well . . . Let's put it this way, she never came back from Bristol without quite a stash. That's all I can tell you, really. That's all I ever knew. Sylvie – she was, like, quite tight about those little things. Protecting her sources, you might say.'

I groped back in search of a loose end. 'You were

going to say something just now,' I reminded him. 'Something about the prescriptions . . .?'

But the thought had gone, and neither Pike nor I managed to prompt his memory.

'What about boyfriends, lovers?' I asked. 'Who was she seeing in the early spring?'

Hayden's face took on an odd gloating look. 'There was some bloke, yeah. She saw him all the way through last winter. That's what our deal was, she used my cottage at weekends, like as a retreat, in exchange for, you know, keeping an eye. She came down from Bristol every weekend, hacked wood, built fires, put buckets out to catch the leaks.'

'She was living in Bristol?'

'Sure. Her brother was there.'

'And the lover, who was he?'

'She never told me. No names, no pack drill,' he smirked. '*But* . .' He paused for dramatic effect. 'I did see him once. He bowled up at the cottage when I was there. Made off smartish when he realised his mistake. Good dresser, smart car – spanking new Mercedes. Money, definitely.'

It wasn't what I had expected.

'Was he local?'

He said with heavy irony, 'That would have been difficult to say, wouldn't it, seeing him like that.'

'What did he look like?'

He made a face. 'Affluent. Oldish. Your average Mercedes owner.' It was hard to tell if he was being deliberately evasive, but in the silence that followed I began to think I had wasted my time and money.

Hayden let me fret a little longer before announcing lightly, 'Saw him again, though.'

I didn't like being strung along, especially by the likes of Hayden. 'Oh yes?' I said harshly.

'Might even be able to place him for you.' He spread his hands like a market trader producing the best goods from the back of the barrow.

'Place him then.'

A look of sly calculation came over Hayden's face, I spotted the light of avarice in his eyes, and with a stab of cold anger I barked, 'Don't even think about it.'

With an expression of injury, Hayden looked around as if to plead his innocence to a wider audience, but behind this extravagant show he was using the time to gauge his position. 'I wasn't thinking about a *thing*,' he protested, laughing to cover his retreat. 'I'm just trying to tell you, that's all.'

'Tell me then.'

'The guy had a boat on the river. I saw him launching a dinghy from the pontoon.'

A small warning sounded in my brain.

Hayden was watching me closely now. 'The dinghy was the tender to a boat called *Ellie Miller*.'

My heart gave a single beat, a thump against my chest. I held on to my expression, I showed nothing in my face, but Hayden, with all the perception of a habitual dissembler had picked something up. 'Someone you know?' he enquired.

'You're sure it was the same man?' I asked, revealing some of my turmoil.

'*Yeah*. It was him all right. And then I went and

asked someone at the yacht charter place who he was, and they said he was the local doctor. Seemed pretty sure. Like I said, you should be able to place him, right?'

The blood seemed to burst in my veins, I was filled with a terrible heat. I held tight to my drink to stop it from spilling. Then a miraculous liberating thought struck me, and it was so obvious that I almost laughed. 'Sylvie was his patient. He was probably making a call when he came to the cottage!' And the relief was already rushing through me.

'His patient. Yeah, that would make sense, wouldn't it?' he said knowingly. 'With the prescriptions, I mean. That was what I was going to say before – right at the end something she said made me think she was getting those prescriptions on tap. Like, on request.'

'You're not hearing what I'm saying,' I said, holding on to my temper with difficulty. 'I'm saying he must have gone to the cottage to see Sylvie as a patient. She must have been ill.'

He reflected on this. 'Could be,' he conceded. 'Just one problem.' And he grinned abruptly; he was enjoying himself. 'The doctor had a key.'

I didn't attempt to sleep when I got back to Melton. After going up to check on Ginny I shut myself in the study to sit out the remains of the night in silence and darkness, with a brandy at my elbow and misery in my heart.

The more I tried to make sense of the thoughts that

bumped and veered around my mind, the more the few remaining certainties of my uncertain life seemed to trickle away, and I had the sensation of slipping headlong towards more appalling upheavals and calamities. On leaving Hayden I had been dazed by disbelief and a smarting sense of betrayal, as though on the subject of duplicity I had anything to be proud of. But now in the long quiet hours of the night the incredulity had begun to fade and, coming to terms with Hayden's revelations, I was left with the most terrifying uncertainty of all: What had I really stumbled across? David had been Sylvie's lover, David had deceived me and, it would appear, everyone else: this much seemed inescapable. But what did it mean? It might mean nothing; it might mean everything. It could be nothing more than an extramarital affair, or something so frightening that I couldn't begin to imagine where it might lead without pulling up in an agony of doubt.

Out of long habit part of me rose to David's defence. David, who had suffered my father's disapproval for so much of his life, who had increasingly felt the bitter dissatisfaction of his own failures; David, the eldest but second son, who had somehow never quite managed to pull his life together. Pa had always judged him harshly, and I did not want to do the same. I told myself that nothing terrible had happened, that, like me, he had simply snatched at temptation; that, like me, he had been used and discarded by Sylvie. These were not heinous crimes, yet for David with his thorny pride, they would be enough to account for his silence. I told myself that this was all there was to it. Now and again I even managed to convince myself. But I couldn't entirely rid myself of hideous black thoughts which came screeching at me out of the darkness, like birds out of the night, and then I was seized by such a combination of misery and dread that it was all I could do not to pick up the phone and call David there and then.

At about six I showered and changed and, leaving a note for Ginny, set off into the gloomy dawn.

The road was clear, I was through Totnes just before eight. I did not stop at Furze Lodge but went straight on to Dartmouth. David's car was not in its place outside the surgery, but the receptionist told me he was due in at nine and had a steady stream of appointments until eleven. I left him a curt note, saying I needed to see him urgently, and drove slowly to Dittisham to wait.

Drawing up outside the house I sat in the car, absorbing the silence, wishing it would last. At nine my mobile began to ring: George on his first call of the day. As soon as he had given up I phoned Julia and told her to keep everyone at bay for the morning.

'Do you want me down at Melton?' she asked.

'I think Ginny's all right.'

'Shall I check?'

'No, I'll call her myself.'

'If you're sure.'

Ginny didn't answer the first time I tried, nor the second, and then the line was engaged for a while, and then it didn't answer again. Reading more into this than was good for me, I called Julia back and asked her if she wouldn't mind going down after all.

For a time I sat in the quiet again, then, breaking free of my trance, got out of the car and, taking the key from its ledge in the porch, let myself into the musty hall. I made my way slowly through the house, examining each room with a new and jaundiced eye, as though it might contain traces of the past which I had not previously had the wit to see.

If David had brought Sylvie here, then it must have been soon after Pa's death. No qualms about that then.

Pausing outside the kitchen I remembered how Sylvie had made her way here unhesitatingly, how she had known where to find everything. Had they drunk coffee here together, kissed, made love? I saw them making love everywhere, on floors, on sofas, upright, naked, clothed.

And the study: I remembered the way she had appeared at the french windows, as though she were used to coming through the garden and arriving unannounced.

These fragments of proof gave me great bursts of misery but also a kind of masochistic satisfaction and, unable to stop myself, I trudged up the stairs and stood on the landing, taking mental measurements of the distances to the various doors. Had Sylvie pulled me into David's room because it was fractionally the closest, or out of some perverse desire to take a second brother to the same bed?

I glanced over the shelves by the bed, I opened the drawers of the bedside table and angrily closed them again, not even wanting to think of what I had expected to find there. I stood at the window and looked down the river to where *Samphire* lay at her mooring, and felt an unexpected gratitude to Hayden. At the end of the day, knowledge, however bitter, gives you some sort of grip on the future.

Returning to the study, I remembered the night when Sylvie and I had made love with the curtains undrawn, and the sound I had heard from the terrace, a memory which until last night I had pushed from my mind. Trying to give the sound substance now, it seemed to me that it was a garden chair being accidentally bumped across stone. In a trick of the imagination I saw not Ginny but David stumbling across the chair in the dark.

hearing a car in the drive, I opened the front door and watched David get out and walk towards me. Looking up, his face darkened and he paused in front of me as if to demand what was going on before changing his mind and passing silently into the house. Automatically he made for the study, the room which he, more than anyone, associated with inquisitions and retribution.

I sat at Pa's desk while David pulled a chair away from the wall and, placing it by the french windows, settled himself warily. 'What's up then?'

Now that the moment had come I could only say, 'You and Sylvie.'

In the pause that followed his mouth twitched but his eyes were steady. 'Yes,' he exhaled abruptly. 'So.'

'You don't think you should tell me about it?'

'What do you want to know?'

'Everything.'

'I don't think you mean that.'

'Don't bloody tell me what I mean!' I blazed with sudden anger. 'Don't bloody talk *down* to me, David. For once, for *once*' – I splayed a furious hand at him – 'just tell me the bloody truth!'

If my anger had taken me by surprise, David met it impassively. Looking away towards the river, he began in a dispassionate voice, 'I met her about a year ago, down on the quay. Pa wasn't too well, I'd been out to look at *Ellie*. I was stacking the dinghy when Sylvie walked up and said, "You're David." That was it, really. We went for a drink. It started from there. We met at weekends. She was living in Bristol. She'd borrowed this cottage near Totnes – Hayden's cottage. Then in March she moved down to Dittisham, rented a place—' He glanced towards me, 'Well, you know about that. Then she broke it off in, oh . . . about May, I suppose. We got together again briefly, but . . .' His shrug indicated that it hadn't worked out. 'I didn't know about you, I promise. Well, not for a long time. Not until I saw you together on *Ellie*. Can't remember when that was – August some time? But until then I had no idea. Really.' He gave a caustic smile. 'Otherwise I would have warned you.'

Another pause, like darkness. David lifted a shoulder as if to say: Well, that's it.

'Haven't you left rather a lot out?' I said.

He examined my face in the sombre light, searching for my meaning. 'Ahh,' he said heavily. 'You mean, our arrangement?'

'The prescriptions.'

He nodded stoically. 'This was Hayden, was it?' Immediately he dismissed the question as of no importance. 'Yes,' he said with a long sigh, 'it's amazing what one does when one's – how shall I put it? – not thinking too cleverly. Enough to get me struck off ten times over, and then some. At first it was just to *help* her, you understand. One last fix, and then she was going to take the cure. She'd been on a cure just that summer, but it hadn't lasted long. She thought she could control it, you see. Take a hit now and again. You can't, of course – control it. Also she had no real will to stop. She never believed it was doing her any harm. They never do. She didn't think about the future. She thought she could just go on—' He broke off suddenly and his mouth turned down. 'Anyway . . . one thing led to another. She kept asking for more. And I kept handing out. The risk was ludicrous. I got calls from chemists a couple of times, thought there'd be trouble, but somehow nothing ever came of it. Sheer luck. I knew it was madness.'

'So why didn't you stop?'

He raised an eyebrow, and his expression seemed to say: Are you sure you really want to hear this? Reading my determination, he announced bluntly, 'Because I wanted her. It wasn't that I couldn't stop – it was that I didn't want to.' His eyes glittered at the memory. Catching an echo of some powerful and voracious emotion, I felt a tremor of jealousy.

I said sharply, 'And Mary?'

'What about Mary?'

'For God's sake – did she know?'

'If she did, she never mentioned it to me.' He added casually, 'She's never said anything to you?'

'No.' And now I had the feeling he was trying to deflect me. 'You got together again, you said, Sylvie and you?'

'What? Oh yes . . . June. July. She wanted some more scripts. But by then it was what you might call a business arrangement.'

'Business?' And suddenly I was having trouble with my patience again. 'Spell it out for me, David.'

Once more he gave me the do-you-really-want-this look, the raised eyebrow and the down-turned mouth. 'She wanted some drugs, I wanted a good lay. I think that more or less sums it up.'

I couldn't work out if this harsh judgment was designed to punish me or himself. Whatever, there was something in his manner that rang false, and I thought I caught a hint of bitterness.

I asked, 'And this was all the way through June and July?'

'No, no,' he exclaimed, irritated at my dull-wittedness. 'We managed without each other very well, believe me. Sometimes I didn't see her for weeks.' He retorted, 'Really.'

I recognised this display. He was using the blend of intimidation and defiance that he had always employed as a child to try to bluff his way out of trouble. I suspected him then. I suspected that he was lying.

I said tersely, 'You were still seeing her when she died.'

There was a pause while we stared at each other across the expanse of the window. 'No, Hugh,' he said very deliberately. 'And I didn't kill her either.'

'Come on,' I argued with a semblance of control. 'She was going to the boat to meet someone. It wasn't me, so it seems fairly obvious that it must have been you. Because when you think about it, there wasn't anyone else it could have been. You couldn't use the house any more, could you, because I was always turning up there. You couldn't go to her cottage – too many people to see your car outside and Joe hanging about all the time. Too far to Hayden's place. So it had to be the boat, didn't it?'

He watched me gravely without attempting a reply.

'Well? Have I got this wrong?' I demanded stiffly. 'I mean, where did you meet? *Tell* me.'

He looked away again, and still he was silent.

'The boat. *The boat*,' I chanted back at him. And for a moment my throat seized, I couldn't speak. And still he said nothing. '*Christ* . . .' My eyes had misted up, my lips were trembling. 'What happened – did Sylvie try to blackmail you or something? Did she get nasty? Did she go mad? Did *you* go mad? Tell me!'

He was looking out at the river, his eyes screwed up against the light. 'It wasn't like that,' he murmured.

'Well? Tell me what it *was* like, for Christ's sake. Tell me something – *anything*.'

He made a mildly dismissive movement of his head, as though any comment would be a waste of time.

I shot to my feet and stood over him, and now I was shaking with rage. 'Tell me why the hell I shouldn't go to the police! Give me one good reason! Just *one*, you bastard.'

He considered this with an air of great weariness. 'For one thing it would be a mistake, because I didn't kill her. For another, it would destroy my career.' He added ironically, 'For what that's worth.'

'I don't give a stuff about your career,' I exploded again. 'What's your goddamned career compared to *Ginny!*'

He looked up at me. 'I'm sorry it's got this far with Ginny, I really am.'

I gave an ugly shout. 'Well, I tell you something – Ginny's not going to prison to save your miserable neck.'

He stood up with an air of infinite dejection. 'I didn't kill her, Hugh.'

'And I'm meant to believe you?'

He gave a distracted nod. 'Yes.'

'Jesus.' I sank back on my seat.

'But listen, Hugh – I'm not sure yet, but I think there's something I might be able to do to help Ginny.'

'Excuse me,' I jeered, '*something you can do?*'

'Yes. But I'll need a bit more time.'

I was momentarily incapable of speech. In his more imperious moments David had always had this ability to reduce me to a state of mute frustration.

'Just give me a bit more time,' he repeated solemnly.

'More time – for *what?*' I burst out at last. 'The only *help* she needs is to get off, for Christ's sake.'

'That's what I meant.'

'Oh, for God's sake get out of here!' I cried, overtaken by a new wave of anger. 'Just bloody get out of my sight.'

Fourteen

To JUDGE by the seating arrangements, the Cumberland board were not expecting a massive turnout. No more than two hundred chairs had been set out in short rows at the far end of one of the hotel's larger conference rooms, giving the effect of emptiness and insignificance, while stacks of spare seats stood idly at the periphery, in the unlikely event of a sudden rush.

George, aided by Julia, was setting up shop outside the door, with piles of Hartford brochures and information sheets for any shareholders who for some reason had not received them through the post. There were also copies of the resolution that I had drafted and formally tabled for the meeting, requiring the Cumberland board to explain why they had not accepted the highest bid.

George looked harassed and downcast, and I guessed that our final tally of proxies hadn't exceeded the discouraging eighteen per cent we had logged last night.

'Press coverage.' George passed me a folder of cuttings.

Most of it was small stuff, paragraphs tucked away on business pages, but one of the tabloids had run a longer piece just that morning, an emotional David and Goliath story in which Cumberland was portrayed as a heartless monolith, needlessly and cruelly consigning a skilled workforce to the scrapheap.

George commented gruffly, 'Every little helps – so they say.'

But we both knew that publicity wouldn't be enough to win us our resolution, let alone the vote of confidence. Nor would the support of the private shareholders who were beginning to trickle in through the doors. The real control lay in the hands of the institutional shareholders, the pension funds and unit trusts whose vast blocks of equity gave them dominant voting power. Knowing George and Alan had spent the whole of the previous day phoning around some of the institutions, I asked, 'Any luck yesterday?'

'A lot said they'd given their proxies to Cumberland.' He shrugged.

'But some might still be uncommitted?'

George gave me a look that said: If only.

Julia handed me an envelope and began to tell us about a pension fund manager she had been in touch with, but recognising the handwriting on the letter I moved to one side and opened it. *Dearest Hugh, I've got all my fingers and toes crossed for you!* Mary had written. *But look – if it's simply a question of more money, please count me in! Probably too late for all that, but if you do need any more, then I'd really like to help. Went to my trustees – yes, I've still got trustees – and found I have bags more to spare than I thought. Up to half a million. I really mean it, Hugh. If it'll make any difference to winning, it would be the proudest moment of my life.* <u>*Really!*</u> *With tons and tons of love, Mary.*

My first reaction was profound gratitude; my next sharp suspicion, made all the more mortifying by the affection that had come before. Where had Mary suddenly found such an enormous sum of money? Why had she left the offer so late? In fact what had prompted her to offer it at all? Giving my darkest thoughts full rein, it seemed to me that this could only have come from David, that only David could possibly have this sort of money lying around. Following on from this came a further rush of unwelcome thoughts: that David was trying to buy me off in some way, and that, being him, he was confident of succeeding; alternatively, that in his proud inarticulate way he was simply trying to help and did not like to do it in person. I wasn't sure which idea made me most uncomfortable. Either way, it was shabby to use Mary.

And then again, perhaps the demons in this were all of my own making. Perhaps this offer was exactly what it seemed. Perhaps Mary in her generosity was simply trying to help and had told David nothing. Perhaps I was simply becoming paranoid, like Ginny. Two frightened people, reacting badly. It was an oddly heartening thought.

Thrusting the note into my pocket, I headed back towards the doors to be intercepted by Julia, brandishing her mobile phone. She hissed under her breath, '*Howard.*'

I moved out of earshot.

'Hugh?' came the smooth tones. 'Listen, can you spare a few minutes?'

'Is this business or social, Howard?'

'Something we might want to discuss. Something that might be helpful to both of us.'

'You're sure about that?'

'Would I bother you otherwise? I'm upstairs. Suite 223.'

'I'll need to bring George with me.'

'Fine.' Ever the orchestrator, he was already sounding pleased with himself.

George pulled an astonished face when I told him. 'What, *now*? We've only got twenty minutes.'

'That's probably the whole point.'

As we headed for the stairs, George said, 'But what can he want?'

'It'll be an offer of some sort, I imagine.'

'God,' he chuckled nervously. 'A *deal*?'

'A softener, more like. A consolation prize, Howard-style. Which means,' I said caustically, 'that there won't be much in it for us.'

Howard was waiting at the door of the suite. 'Welcome,' he smiled, at his most gracious. He appeared to harbour no animosity towards me over my telephone tirade, but then Howard had always regarded people who got angry with him as having a personality defect.

He waved us to a seat. 'Coffee? No? Are you sure?'

As he went and poured himself a cup at a pace that was deliberately unhurried I could see George beginning to fret over the time, but I knew that

Howard would have calculated it down to the last minute and there was no point in rushing him.

Sinking elegantly into a chair, Howard smiled, 'Well, I must say, you've mounted a most impressive campaign. Very thorough. The shareholders, the press and so on. Excellent stuff.'

George, taking this at face value, said, 'Thanks.'

'Pity it had no hope of success. From your point of view, I mean. But, well – it was hardly to be expected, was it?'

'You've got your fifty per cent, have you?' I asked: the proxies he needed to carry the day.

'Of course,' Howard smiled as though it had always been a foregone conclusion.

I wanted to say: Then why are we here? But I knew better than to ask such an obvious question.

'However . . .' Howard sipped at his coffee and gave us a beneficent gaze. 'The situation has changed somewhat. New considerations have come to light. And, without wanting to go into detail – without being *free* to – suffice it to say that events have shifted to the extent that the board might be prepared to review your bid in a more favourable light.'

Startled, I tried to imagine what could possibly have changed. Donington's share value? As far as I knew it hadn't dropped significantly. Or maybe Cumberland's lawyers had uncovered something they didn't like, some fancy footwork in the small print of Donington's offer.

I could see George sparking with excitement but, deliberately failing to catch his eye, I asked Howard, 'What are the terms?'

'Terms?' Howard echoed with the air of cool surprise he assumed when someone spoiled his timing. 'Oh . . . as before,' he stated as though this should have been obvious. 'As before. With an adjustment for the differential between the two bids, of course. To make good our shortfall. You know how it is,' he beamed. 'Duty to the shareholders.'

I had known there would be a catch. 'But our bid was as good as Donington's,' I pointed out. 'If not better.'

'Ah, but you have to allow for the appreciation of the Donington shares. A steady-growth company. We were banking on an annual stock appreciation of at least seven per cent.'

This was rubbish. No one could bank on steady growth at the moment, particularly in china and glass, which had always been a volatile performer in times of economic uncertainty. It was a load of nonsense, but then Howard knew this as well as I did.

'This *notional* differential,' I said. 'What did you have in mind, *allowing* for the fact that our offer is already pitched at, and maybe even beyond, the maximum value of the company? *Allowing* for the fact that we couldn't justify going to our backers and asking them to invest a penny more? *Allowing* for the fact that we have precisely ten minutes to sort this out? *Allowing* for the fact that brinkmanship goes both ways?'

Howard grinned quietly. He liked nothing better than a good fight. 'Well, we're prepared to compromise, to forego some of this *notional* gain, as you put it. We're prepared to settle for half a million.'

I felt a pull in my stomach, a chill of disbelief. I told myself that it was a coincidence. I told myself that stranger things had happened. I tried to keep calm, to conceal the resentment and suspicion that had rushed into my face.

'Can't be done,' I said.

'Oh?' Howard affected surprise. 'We'd give you two weeks to arrange the funding.'

'Not at that price.'

Howard looked pained. 'Couldn't square any less with the board. Or indeed the shareholders. The figure's been agreed, you see, as the most generous we could possibly offer. It's not open to negotiation.'

'There's no more money.' And the violence in my tone made them stare at me.

George ventured at last, 'Perhaps we could have a few minutes?'

'Surely.' Howard finished his coffee and pulled himself lazily to his feet. 'I'll be next door.' Scooping up his mobile, he disappeared through a connecting door.

'It's extortion,' I protested before George could say a word. 'Blackmail. And we're not going to pay a single penny.'

George began to make hasty calculations on his notepad. 'But all this publicity might make it easier to raise the money—'

'It's not the money, George, it's the principle!'

George threw me a baffled look, then another, as if he really couldn't work out what I was talking about. 'Maybe they'll come down a bit.'

'But we'd still be paying over the odds, damn it!'

'Yes, but not much. And this is going to be the end of it, isn't it? They won't be able to go back on their word a second time, will they? We'll be home and dry.'

He was right, but I wasn't in any mood to hear the truth, and while he continued to play with numbers I paced up and down the room, nursing a sense of betrayal and impotence, made all the worse for knowing that my feelings were irrelevant.

'The additional interest wouldn't kill us,' George announced. 'But look, we should grab Alan and get him to go through this—'

'No time. That's the whole point, for heaven's sake. We have no time.' I stopped by the window and stared out into the featureless London street, and in that moment the last of my resentment trickled away like so much useless energy, and I gave in to the inevitable. Yet if I had been outmanoeuvred somewhere along the line, if I had been set up, I told myself that I had not yet been bought, and if anyone thought otherwise they would quickly discover the difference.

'We've got the money,' I admitted.

'*What?*'

'We have the promise of the money. A private investor.'

'*Good God!* You mean— Then—'

As if on cue a soft knock announced Howard's return. 'Don't mean to hurry you,' he said in his most honeyed tones.

'Just supposing we were able to reach an

agreement now,' I said immediately, 'what would happen downstairs?'

'Ah . . . The board would announce that we were reconsidering your bid in every expectation of reaching a favourable outcome.'

'And Donington?'

'By implication, that bid would have run into difficulties, wouldn't it?'

'And our resolution?'

'You'd want to withdraw it, I imagine.'

I turned on my heel and headed for the door. I waited at the top of the stairs for Howard to catch up. 'Half a million is a ludicrous sum,' I said as we started down.

He gave a small laugh. 'That was our valuation, Hugh.'

'Don't give me that crap, Howard. It's just a face-saver, isn't it? A way for your board to go back to the shareholders and say they're getting them a better deal. Anything less than half a million would make you look stupid, wouldn't it? Isn't that more like it? So what's happened to Donington, Howard? Have they pulled out altogether? Have they discovered they can't do business with you?'

'Nothing like that,' he asserted confidently. 'They still have their hat very much in the ring.' Howard was such an excellent liar that it was impossible to tell if this statement bore any relation to the truth.

We halted short of the conference room, and still I was bothered by the fact that I didn't understand what the hell was really going on.

Howard lifted both palms questioningly. 'Are we agreed?'

'No going back,' I warned.

'*Hardly*,' he exclaimed with a look of injury.

I held out my hand. 'You take my hand at your peril, you shit.'

Grasping it, he smiled with something like affection. 'I knew we could do business, Hugh.'

Watching him walk away, I had the sensation of having travelled a long way only to return to the same point. Howard's deviousness did at least have a comforting familiarity.

Julia caught me on the way into the meeting. 'Two unit trust managers have turned up!' she whispered excitedly. 'One I've been talking to all week. He introduced himself just now and pointed out another one. If two have actually bothered to turn up, they can't have given their proxies! And there might be more. Maybe some pension fund managers. I contacted all the unions, you know, every single one. There might be a whole *slab* of votes going begging.'

Maybe that was it. Maybe Howard had lied to me. Maybe the Cumberland board hadn't got the vote in the bag. Maybe we could have won the day on the no-confidence vote and saved ourselves half a million pounds.

'Maybe a lot of things,' I murmured to Julia.

Going into the meeting, I touched the note in my pocket and Ginny's words floated reproachfully into my mind. *Mary isn't Howard's sister for nothing.*

*

443

Grainger's chambers were situated in a dark building overlooking a secretive courtyard of the Inner Temple, just beyond the soot-stained buttresses of the church. The recessed doorway with its ladder of names reminded me of my old staircase at Trinity, but once inside all resemblance to college was dispelled by the lavish carpets and speckling of spotlights, the rag-rolled walls and confident glow of the reproduction furniture.

Grainger's room had extravagantly draped curtains over matching roman blinds, large Impressionist prints, a scattering of bulbous table lamps with pale silk shades, and a large gas log fire. The effect was of a drawing room seconded for office use, and only the wall of legal tomes behind us and the oversize desk ahead of us with its stacks of papers and box-files gave the lie to the mood of elegant inactivity.

Tingwall was already there and kissed Ginny warmly on both cheeks.

'Mrs Wellesley.' Grainger bowed over Ginny's hand and showed her to a chair at a narrow table which abutted the giant desk in a T-shape. Tingwall and I found seats opposite her, while Grainger ostentatiously took his place behind the desk, like a lecturer facing his students.

As soon as the coffee had been poured Grainger fastened his eyes on Ginny and said without preamble, 'We're faced with a difficult decision, Mrs Wellesley. I expect Mr Tingwall has explained something of it to you?'

'Yes,' Ginny replied in a voice so low it was barely audible. She had been looking tired for some days, despite – or possibly because of – the sleeping pills she had been taking with increasing regularity.

'Well, I would like to explain it to you again, if that meets with your approval.' The formality of Grainger's address, the charcoal pinstripe three-piece with the gold watch chain, the calmly intertwined hands, the neat greying hair and patrician features, all served to create an air of effortless authority which was entirely intentional, and, according to Tingwall, entirely appropriated. Apparently Grainger's grand style and Eton drawl obscured a childhood of poverty and deprivation as the son of an unemployed York-shire coal-miner. I didn't care for his chosen persona, but I couldn't blame him for it either. He depended for his living on impressing his clients and intimidat-ing his opponents, although I suspected that he didn't always achieve them in that order.

'Mrs Wellesley,' he began fluidly, 'the decision is a difficult one because it involves risk, and however clear-sighted we try to be, however critically we approach the facts, it will be impossible to assess those risks with any degree of accuracy. All I can do is set out the situation as I see it, explain what is involved in the two principal strategies which are open to you, and give you my opinion as to your best course. After that, the decision must be yours. I cannot make it for you.' In the seclusion of his chambers Grainger's voice, while maintaining the affectation which had so annoyed me at the bail hear-ing, had lost its hunting-field stridency and taken on an intimate almost melodic tone.

Ginny nodded, 'I understand.'

Grainger assumed an expression of exaggerated concentration. 'Now, our *first* option is to offer *no* defence at the committal stage and let the case go unopposed to crown court. This means a wait of perhaps six months and a full hearing before a judge and jury. Of course, in those six months circumstances could change and cause the prosecution to alter its stance, or indeed for us to alter our position in some way, but let's assume for the moment that we will be pleading not guilty to the charge as it stands – that is, to a charge of murder. The first thing to understand is that this is an extremely serious charge and that if you are found guilty you will go to prison for a long time.' His face took on a suitably grave aspect, his voice resonated sympathetically, and I couldn't help thinking what a performer he was, how he relished every moment.

'The second thing to know is that a jury is a thoroughly unpredictable body, and there is no determining in advance how they may or may not be swayed by any particular piece or body of evidence. The only sure thing about a jury is their ability to surprise.' A pause to allow us to absorb what he intended to be a daunting truth. 'Now, for us the *advantage* of letting the case go unchallenged to crown court is that the prosecution will not have the chance to test our defence in advance, nor indeed to appreciate and shore up the weaknesses in their own case. We will, so to speak, have kept our cards close to our chest. That way we can hope to spring a few surprises on the opposition' – his eyes glinted at the thought – 'to discredit a witness or two, to work away at the flaws in their case, without giving them too much warning of our strategy. For the defence advocate this is an important weapon and one he is loath to give away without good reason.'

Ginny broke the short silence that followed. 'I was wondering . . .'

When she failed to continue Grainger prompted briskly, 'Yes, Mrs Wellesley?'

'Would I give evidence?'

'That is something we would not decide until much nearer the time. It is something which would require very careful consideration. Though it is possible, just possible, that we might decide against it.'

'Against . . .' Ginny echoed with what might have been a touch of relief. Blinking rapidly, she said, 'Sorry – I interrupted.'

Grainger smiled faintly and rearranged his hands into an elegant display of interlaced fingertips. 'Now, for the *second* option,' he drawled. 'The second option is to defend the case at committal stage with the object of getting the case thrown out before it ever gets to crown court. This means going for what is termed an old-style committal. Here all the evidence is brought before, usually, a stipendiary magistrate sitting alone, the important witnesses appear in person, the evidence is open to challenge under cross-examination. Clearly the *only* reason for choosing this option is if you think you have a good chance of persuading the magistrate that there is no case to answer – *no case at all*. He must be persuaded that the prosecution's evidence is so insubstantial or unreliable that at crown court no reasonable jury, properly directed, would be likely to return a verdict of guilty. Lack of reliable evidence is *sufficient* in itself for the case to be stopped, *but*' – he raised a finger – 'if the bench can also be persuaded that we have a valid defence then clearly our chances become that much stronger.'

He raised his eyebrows at Tingwall. 'Now, what we have, do we not, are some promising developments.'

Taking his cue eagerly, Tingwall's eyes darted back and forth. 'I took a bit of a gamble. Armstrong – our fingerprint expert – asked if he could talk to the prosecution's expert. Apparently it's quite common when experts of this calibre disagree for them to what they quaintly call "compare notes". Armstrong said it's done to avoid wasting court time, but – well, perhaps they prefer to avoid looking incompetent as well. Anyway, I told him to go ahead, and the upshot of it was that Armstrong gave the prosecution's man chapter and verse on where he thought he'd gone wrong, and the chap went back and had another look at his opinion' – he paused for effect – 'and he's *conceded* on one of the points of similarity.' He tightened his lips as though he didn't trust himself not to break into a grin and give too much away. 'Which means that the prosecution won't be able to use him as a witness because fifteen points of similarity between two prints are not enough!'

Grainger said smoothly, 'We can't of course rule out the possibility that the prosecution will find another expert or two to back them up.'

Tingwall allowed this reluctantly. 'It's *possible*.'

'But let us assume for the *moment* that the Crown is unable to present any fingerprint evidence whatsoever.' Grainger lifted his head to the thought. 'Then we have a situation where the prosecution would be left without any forensic evidence to link us to the scene of the crime. None at all. I need hardly say that this would improve our situation considerably. *However . . .'* He slid his elbows onto the desk and clasped his hands under his chin: his cautionary look. 'Cases can and do get sent up to the crown court on non-forensic evidence alone. That's the first point. Second, the prosecution will still have this eyewitness of theirs.' He picked up a batch of stapled papers and, hooking some half-moon glasses onto his nose, leafed through them. 'It is impossible to tell from a witness statement how a witness will perform in court, how convincing he will be, but if we are to take this statement at face value it would seem that the witness is confident in his identification of Mrs Wellesley. He is saying' – Grainger skimmed the lines – 'that he was by the river on the Saturday afternoon of the weekend in question, at about five, and that he saw this woman get into a dinghy and set off across the water, and that he recognised that woman as Virginia Wellesley. He recognised her because apparently . . .' His eyes darted over the pages again. 'Apparently he had worked at Dittisham House as a gardener some years ago and knows all the family by sight.'

Astonished, I tried to think who it could be. 'Old Gordon?'

Grainger flipped back to the first page. 'His name is . . . Gordon Latimer.'

'Old Gordon,' I affirmed. 'He must be seventy-five, eighty, if he's a day.'

'Age is not yet a barrier to providing evidence,' Grainger commented drily.

'But surely his eyesight can't be too good—'

'It would be pointless to conject on that until we have the opportunity for cross-examination,' Grainger argued firmly. 'For the moment we must look at this statement as it stands, and I have to say that in my *opinion*, unless the witness is manifestly unreliable, it is likely that his evidence will be sufficient to send the case to trial. You see—' He removed his spectacles in a deft movement that was so reminiscent of David that for an instant I had the strange sensation of facing my brother. 'In your statement to the police, Mrs Wellesley, you said that you went to the boat only once during the weekend – on the *Sunday*. There is no mention of going on the Saturday. So we are left with two options. Either we deny the eyewitness's version of events, which will leave us in a his-word-against-ours situation. Or we accept his evidence and offer an explanation as to *why* we went to the boat on the *Saturday* and *why* we failed to tell the police about it.' He made a neat gesture, a small overturning of the hand. 'You appreciate the problem?'

'I explained,' Ginny said. 'I told . . .' And she indicated Tingwall.

'Indeed,' Grainger said smoothly. 'I have read your account of events, Mrs Wellesley. I have read it very carefully indeed. However, if we are going to say that we went out to the boat on the day of the murder and found the body and disposed of it into the water

450

then we face great difficulties. *One*,' he began remorselessly, 'why didn't we report the finding of the body at the time? Two: if we are going to admit to the disposing of the body, then this is going to cast us in an extremely unfortunate light which will undoubtedly do us very great damage. After all, what motive could we have for committing this deliberate and dangerous act if it wasn't to protect ourself or someone extremely close to us?' He left this thought in the air for a second. 'Three: if we say we were trying to protect our husband, only to discover that he was miles away at the time and couldn't have done it, then what suspects are the jury left with? Who are they meant to cast as the murderer?' This, too, hung in the silence for a moment. 'Four: not to put too fine a point on it, Mrs Wellesley, are we likely to be believed?'

Ginny flinched slightly and looked down at her hands before nodding readily. 'Yes, I see the problem . . .'

'If there was a reasonable explanation for your presence on the river on the Saturday,' Grainger reflected, 'and a reasonable explanation for your having failed to mention it to the police, then we *might* think about putting that forward. But I fear that to put forward your account of events as it stands without any evidence to back it up is . . .' He inhaled delicately. 'Well, it is not likely to be the most rewarding approach. You understand what I'm saying, Mrs Wellesley? You see the difficulties?'

If I had been harbouring any hopes of a way out for Ginny they evaporated then. With a stab of alarm

451

I realised that her situation was bleak, that, even without the fingerprint, the evidence was still stacked against her.

I asked Grainger, 'What *is* our defence then?'

The eyes dropped languidly but when they came up again they were very sharp. 'From what we have so far it would seem to me that our most effective defence would be character-led. The impossibility of someone as respectable, virtuous and fragile as Mrs Wellesley committing such a heinous crime; how her life has been exemplary, etcetera etcetera; how it would have been completely out of character for her to hurt a fly; how she, a chronic asthmatic, was seen to suffer no anxiety or nerves or other ill-effects at the time of the crime, and indeed appeared perfectly normal in every respect. Your brother, Mr Wellesley, will be an excellent witness in that regard, having seen both of you that Saturday evening. Then, on the practical side, if Mrs Wellesley had committed this terrible crime, why was she not covered in blood? Indeed, how could she have appeared later that evening without so much as a bloodstain on her? You will attest, Mr Wellesley, as to how normal and indeed immaculate she looked. And so on, and so on. In this way we would hope to appeal to both the hearts and the minds of the jury, we would hope to cast some doubt on the evidence of the eyewitness. We would *chip* away. We would be going for the reasonable doubt. And don't forget – that's all we need: reasonable doubt.'

Tingwall piped up, 'The old-style committal, are you ruling that out then?'

'We have to balance the likely benefits against the more certain costs,' Grainger ventured with an air of great sagacity. 'It all hinges on this eyewitness. If we want to gamble on his unreliability – and I use the word "gamble" advisedly – then we should go for the old-style committal. The stakes would be high. If he turned out to be an uncertain witness, we stand to gain everything – the total collapse of the Crown's case. But if he turned out to be an unassailable witness then we would gain very little – at the great expense of having revealed much of our defence. A risky business indeed. The *alternative* is to play safe. To keep our cards close to our chest, to hope to catch the prosecution off-guard, and to go for the hearts and minds of a jury in the way I described – in which case we should wait.'

'So what's your advice?' I asked.

He tapped his fingers together while he thought about it. 'It's hard to give such a thing as *advice* when one is dealing with a key eyewitness who is by definition an unknown quantity. However, going by the witness statement . . .' He looked upwards as though searching for a last drop of inspiration. '. . . my instinct – and that's another word I use advisedly – my *instinct* would be to let it go to trial. Trust to the twelve good men and women, and maintain our element of surprise.'

I asked, 'When do we have to make up our minds?'

Grainger addressed Tingwall. 'Perhaps you would like to discuss the matter further with Mrs Wellesley, come back to me with any questions, and perhaps we can make a decision in the next week or so?'

We all stood up and Grainger moved fluidly to open the door. Ginny paused beside Grainger and said in an undertone, 'I have one question.' She frowned over the thought. 'If Old Gordon is a good witness, if he's going to be absolutely certain that he saw me, then . . . wouldn't I do better to plead guilty?'

'Absolutely not,' I protested over the taut silence which followed.

Grainger observed Ginny for a long moment. 'In some cases a guilty plea to a lesser charge can prove the best course. But, Mrs Wellesley' – he fixed her with cold eyes – 'only *you* can decide if this option is open to us.'

'Why on earth did you say that?' I demanded, taking an aggressive weave through the traffic.

Ginny looked ahead, her profile unreadable. 'Because in the end it might be best.'

'But you can't plead guilty to something you didn't do. It's ridiculous.'

'It could be the least bad thing to do. You heard what he said.' And there was a nervy finality in her voice, an attempt to shut me out.

'The least bad thing. For Christ's sake, Ginny – how can you even *think* of it?' I kept glancing across at her but she didn't reply. 'Promise me you won't even think of it.'

'But Old Gordon was there,' she argued finally. 'He saw me all right. He even nodded to me. We were just feet apart. He's not going to be mistaken in court.'

'Ginny, for *heaven's sake* – it's still early days yet.

Anything could happen. All sorts of things might turn up. I don't know – witnesses, somebody who . . . somebody who . . .' I broke off in sudden misery, knowing I couldn't put the problem of David off any longer. I had spent most of the last two days persuading myself that there was no point in dragging him into our nightmare, that he had nothing to contribute to Ginny's case. Yet his story had left out too much, the gaps and evasions had left me with the wretched suspicion that he had given me something less than the truth.

Grasping some of my turmoil, Ginny had turned to look at me. I hadn't told her about David, partly because I'd been coming to terms with it, partly because the implications of what he'd told me had frightened me too much. 'Listen, something's come up,' I began unhappily. 'I didn't have the chance to tell you before. Well – I *did*,' I admitted, 'but I couldn't, I was feeling too bloody sick about it, too . . . The thing is' – and my throat tightened, I could hardly say it – 'I wasn't the only one having an affair with Sylvie.' I felt a fresh surge of incredulity. '*David* was. David was having a great big affair with Sylvie. All the way through last winter and most of the summer too. They used to meet on the boat – some of the time, anyway. And I think—' I had to force the words out: 'I think he was on the boat that day. At least he didn't deny it, for Christ's sake! I think he was there, and I think – oh *shit!*' And suddenly all my emotions shot to the surface and I couldn't see the road, it had become so blurred.

'Stop,' Ginny begged, casting nervous glances at the speeding traffic. 'Stop, *please*.'

I drew into the kerb amid a storm of protesting horns. I pulled out a handkerchief and rubbed it furiously across my eyes.

'*David?*' Ginny echoed as though she'd only just understood what I was saying. 'All through the winter?'

'The summer too.'

She digested this. 'It was serious then.'

'Serious? Well,' I scoffed, 'I don't think it was *love* exactly. From what he told me, more like lust. Lust and drugs. He used to supply her with drugs.' I had made it sound sordid, but then maybe I had intended to. 'He swears there was no more to it, he swears it was just an affair, he says it fizzled out. All I bloody know is that they met on the boat regularly and he didn't bloody deny he was there that day. He didn't – *Christ*, I don't know!' I suppressed a fresh burst of emotion. 'If he's lied to me I'll bloody kill him.' And even as I said it I felt the old ache of responsibility, the old instinct to defend him.

Ginny was looking blankly ahead. 'Tell me,' she murmured in a reminiscent tone, 'what was so special about her? What was it that made you both forget everything – everybody – else?'

I blew my nose savagely, I took my time but in the end I could only say, 'I don't know.' I added, 'But perhaps that was it, perhaps it was the very fact that she was impossible to know, that she was anything you wanted her to be. She gave this great impression of freedom, of anything being possible.'

Ginny gave an ironic murmur as if to say: And I didn't, I suppose; I was the one who held you back.

'And the sex?' she asked calmly. 'Was that especially terrific?'

There are some truths that must never be told. Bracing myself for the lie, I replied, 'I think it was like they say – it's the secretiveness of these things that gives them an edge, the danger of discovery. So, in that way – yes, it was exciting, I suppose.'

'She didn't do anything amazing that I didn't do?'

'No,' I said, trying to push pictures of Sylvie at her most adventurous and uninhibited from my mind. 'Nothing like that.'

'*David.*' Turning the idea over in her mind again, she shook her head. 'He always seemed so – immune. So unemotional. Well – she must have had something.'

I thought: What she had was allure without conscience.

Ginny took a puff on her inhaler and coughed a few times. A new phalanx of traffic roared past and the noise seemed to invade the car. I restarted the engine and pulled out.

Ginny asked unsteadily, 'So you think that . . .?'

'I don't know what to think!'

She kept looking at me. 'What will you do?'

Making up my mind, I said, 'I'll go and see him.'

'And then?'

'And then I have no idea!' I answered sharply, not wanting to imagine what would happen to David's life if he were interviewed by the police.

She was quiet for a time, then: 'Don't assume too much, will you?'

Jerking my head round, I almost jumped a red light. 'What do you mean?'

'Don't think the worst.'

'I'm not thinking anything!' I exclaimed, feeling a dart of indignation because she had touched on the truth.

As we came up the drive in the twilight the figure of Julia appeared at the front door with three brilliantly coloured helium balloons in one hand and a bottle of champagne in the other. She waved them energetically and called out to us, 'The deal's been done!' Then with upstretched arms, in loud theatrical tones as if announcing it to the whole county: 'Hartford is yours!'

'Good God,' I laughed uncertainly.

'The most deserved event of the year!' And she hugged me enthusiastically, champagne, balloons and all. 'George just called. It's in the bag!' She went to embrace Ginny. '*And . . .*' She made another grandiose gesture, a flourish of both arms. 'You have exchanged contracts on the house. It was sold at three this afternoon. I tell you – it's all happening!'

I smiled because everyone else was smiling, and because deep down I did feel glad: glad for George and everyone else at Hartford, glad for Ginny because she could finally get to grips with the move, and, if I thought about it, glad for myself, though, in the shadow of everything else that was going on, the pleasure emerged as a rather pale and inconsequential emotion.

David's surgery said he was out on a call, so I left a message on his pager, and then, with some hesitation, tried Furze Lodge.

Mary answered. 'I gather hearty congratulations are in order!' she cried. 'I'm *so* delighted, Hugh! What a triumph! You must be thrilled!'

'I am. All thanks to you, Mary.'

'Well . . . I'm proud to be part of it all, Hugh. *Proud.* And I know you'll make a success of it. I never had any doubts.'

'I'll do my best.'

'You must be over the moon!'

'Yes.'

Her tone shifted. 'You don't *sound* very happy.'

'I'm just incredibly tired, that's all. Hasn't sunk in yet.' I tried to relax my voice as I said, 'Is David around tonight?'

'Tonight? Hang on . . . The diary, the diary.' She made searching noises. 'Here we are . . . He's in after seven-thirty. In theory anyway.'

'If you speak to him, can you tell him I need to see him?'

'What – tonight?'

'I should be with you about eight.'

A short pause. 'Can I say what it's about?' And her voice was taut with curiosity.

'Oh – just—' I said the first thing that came into my head. 'A legal thing.'

'To do with the buyout?'

Feeling cornered, I said, 'Pa's estate, actually.'

'Pa's *estate?*' She didn't try to hide her surprise. 'And it's urgent?'

'I want to get it out of the way.'

'But you sound so grim, Hugh. Is there something the matter? Not Ginny, I hope?'

'No. No, really.'

'Well, if you don't want to tell me . . .'

'Nothing to tell,' I said stubbornly.

Her reproach hung in the air. 'You'll have some supper at least?' she said.

'No, Mary.'

'I'll tell David you're coming then.' And when she rang off her tone contained a note of faint injury.

I stayed long enough to make a quick congratulatory call to George, who from the sound of it was holding a party for the entire Hartford staff, and to glance through the mail and messages, which Julia had laid out in order of importance. I skimmed the letters until I came to an unopened envelope marked Strictly Private. It was from Jones. I sat down and read it quickly, then again more carefully. '. . . *nothing has happened to change my original opinion . . . she has developed severe paranoid delusions with marked persecutory tendencies . . . increasingly retreating into unreality . . . convincing herself of plots, including the notion that I am opposed to her and scheming to give evidence against her. I am concerned that if she continues to refuse medication she may suffer a major crisis . . .*'

With a chill in my heart, I read the letter a third time before locking it away in a drawer.

Charged with a new sense of urgency, I went through to the sitting room to find Ginny.

She looked up from her conversation with Julia. 'You're going now? It wouldn't be better to wait until tomorrow?'

'No. No, I must go now.'

She tilted her head to be kissed.

I asked, 'You'll be all right?' Feeling traitorous, I examined her expression for signs of impending crisis.

Sensing this or something close to it, Ginny frowned, 'I'll be fine.'

'I'll bag a bed for the night, if that's all right,' Julia announced from the far side of the room. 'Not safe on the roads.' She raised her glass and cast me a meaningful look.

Ginny got up suddenly and followed me into the hall. 'You won't forget,' she breathed nervously.

'What about?'

'About keeping an open mind.'

'You make me feel that I'm being unreasonable,' I said accusingly. 'For Christ's sake, Ginny, somebody killed Sylvie!'

She dropped her eyes. 'Yes.' She kissed me again and her lips were cold against my cheek.

'He's been delayed. Some emergency.' Mary closed the door behind me. 'Come and have a large drink. You must be exhausted.'

She led the way into the drawing room and threw open the drinks cupboard.

'Whisky,' I said. 'Please.'

She poured a glass and, bringing it over, came up

very close and smiled up into my face. 'Now what on earth's this about?' she asked. 'What's the matter?'

'The matter?'

'Why you're here.'

'I told you.'

'Come on.' She cast me a reproving smile that suggested I could do better than that.

I exhaled unhappily. 'It's rather complicated, Mary.'

'You can tell me, surely,' she said coaxingly. 'David and I have no secrets.'

I felt like saying: Everyone has secrets. Instead I murmured, 'In that case he can tell you himself, can't he?' I hadn't meant to sound dismissive, I raised my hand as if to take it back, but a purposeful expression had already settled over Mary's face. Taking my hand, she led me to a chair by the fireside and, pulling up a stool, sat facing me, knee to knee, as she had done all those weeks ago at Dittisham House. Recalling my uninhibited outpourings about Sylvie, I felt an abrupt and belated vulnerability, a sense of having disclosed too much.

'Hugh...' She flashed me one of her warmest smiles. 'You're very dear to me, you know. After David and the children... well, you're probably the most *precious* person in the whole world to me. I want you to be all right, I want you to be happy, I want you and Ginny to be over this whole ghastly business.' The smile again, which somehow failed to illuminate her heavy features. 'But Hugh darling' – a dipping of the voice – 'it would be quite wrong of you to think that David has the answer to your problems.' Her avid eyes searched my face to see if I had grasped her message.

She had caught me totally off-balance. 'My problems? I don't understand,' I stammered, having a suspicion that I might understand rather too well.

She gave me an appraising look and began again. 'Hugh darling – I believe you have ideas about David that are quite mistaken.'

'Do I?'

'*Indeed* you do,' she said firmly. Then, disdainfully: 'Oh, he got waylaid by that woman' – she gave a scornful laugh – 'if that's the right expression. He had his head turned – but then I don't need to tell *you* about that. But that's *all*, Hugh.' She shook her head emphatically. 'That's *all*.'

I stared at her. 'You knew?'

'Of course,' she declared with a touch of pride. 'All that stuff about a wife being the last to know? Well, I knew immediately. I may be many things, but I'm not stupid. There were a thousand things.' She gave a tiny snort. 'I knew.'

'You never said anything?'

'Oh *no*. The thing was bound to burn itself out quickly enough. She was such a user, wasn't she? Off to the next man, off to the next meal ticket. I knew she'd disappear sooner or later.' She gave a dismissive shrug. 'And I was right. She ditched him, didn't she? Oh, he was upset for a while, went around looking like a whipped dog, but it was just his pride, wasn't it? Feeling his age, needing to know he could still *pull the chicks*' – she used the expression derisively, with a roll of the eyes – 'all that stuff. He was over it in no time. I knew he would be. But Hugh—' she leant forward, arms on knees, eyes locked on mine '—that's all it was. He doesn't deserve to have his career ruined, his life wrecked. He doesn't.'

I felt a terrible tension, a warring of instincts and loyalties. I screwed up my face and managed to say, 'But *someone* was on the boat that day.'

She gave me a soft pitying look. 'Not David, Hugh. Couldn't have been. He was seeing patients all morning, and then he had lunch with me, and then he went to a partners' meeting which lasted most of the afternoon.' She was very gentle with me now. 'There wasn't a moment of his day which wasn't accounted for.'

Part of me tried to accept this, but another confused part of me wanted to shout: But you're bound to say that, aren't you?

'I know the way it must look to you,' Mary conceded with the same patient note of understanding, 'but I *promise* you – he wasn't there. He couldn't have been there.'

I can't have looked terribly convinced because a spark of exasperation passed over her face and she argued with more determination, 'You would be ruining his life, Hugh! And for what? For an *affair*. With someone like *that*. It's too ghastly. Too – unfair. Don't repay me this way, Hugh – *please*.'

I felt a sudden coldness. 'Repay you?'

She dropped her eyes and fanned her fingers as if to withdraw the remark. 'Just promise me,' she said, returning her gaze to mine. 'Promise me you won't ruin his life – *our* lives – for *nothing*.'

I thought of Ginny, I thought of everything we had been through, and I hardened my heart. 'I can't promise that, Mary. I just can't.'

A succession of violent emotions passed over Mary's face, her features seemed to swell. Finally she said in a voice that trembled with feeling, 'I've gone out on a limb for you, Hugh. I've protected you, supported you, *lied* for you. Don't do this to me. Don't repay me this way.'

'If it's a question of repayment,' I said tightly. 'You can keep the money. I don't care about the money.'

She threw me a furious look. 'It's not the *money*, for God's sake.'

We glared at each other, separated by the depth of our misunderstanding.

'*Lied*,' I echoed as her words came back to me. 'I'm sorry you feel you had to *lie* for me as well.'

'Not for *you*.'

'Who for then?'

She shook her head, as though she had already said too much. 'Leave it. Please. Let's just leave it.'

But something in her manner drew me forward, a suggestion of momentous revelations, and I was filled with a strange beating fear. 'You can't say something like that and expect me to ignore it.'

She kept shaking her head. 'If only you could understand that David wasn't involved. If only you could *believe* me, then—' Her eyes sparkled with unshed tears. I had never seen her upset before.

'Mary, don't.'

'I'm sorry,' she said, pulling herself together with an effort. 'I didn't mean to . . .' She fumbled in her sleeve for a handkerchief. 'But Hugh – promise me, please.'

'I can't do that, Mary. I can't promise something like that.'

She gave a shudder that shook her whole body. 'How I wish I didn't have to do this!' she cried. 'I never wanted to have to *say* anything – ever! Ever! I wanted to *save* you that at least. Oh Hugh, how I wish—' She sniffed hard and wiped her eyes, and when she looked up again her makeup had run, a streak of blue that leached down one cheek. 'And, believe me, you *must* believe me, it's *not* an either-or thing – I would *hate* you to think that! It's not as if I'd *ever* go to the police! I'd rather die! I'd rather die than tell them! But Hugh – you *have* to understand that it wasn't David! You *have* to realise!'

As she made her circuitous way towards the point, my sense of foreboding grew.

Mary said again, 'I'd never tell! Never!' Calming herself visibly, she dabbed her eyes again. 'In fact, I'd lie to them again. I'd lie to them every time.' She took a sharp breath. 'I did lie, you see. I lied to them straight away. When David and I gave our finger-prints to the police, they asked me about the day the woman died, whether I knew anything, whether I'd seen anything. And I said I hadn't. But – it wasn't true.' She paused and looked at me in anguish, as if we might yet escape this moment of truth. 'I saw Ginny, you see. I was at Dittisham House with Mrs Perry, and I saw Ginny.'

466

I kept staring at her.

'I was up in David's old room,' she began slowly. 'I looked out at the river and I saw a dinghy tied up to *Ellie*. I knew it couldn't be David – he was at the partners' meeting. I thought maybe it was someone from the yard. There were some binoculars there by the window. I was looking through them when I saw someone come up on deck.' She gave a tiny shudder. 'It was the woman. There was no mistaking her – the long hair, the tight clothes. It was definitely her. I thought – well, you can imagine. I thought she was hanging around in the hope of seeing David. I thought she was trying to get him back or something. I was ready to get hopping mad. But then – *then* – oh, *Hugh*.' Mary's face crumpled, she clenched her lips together, when she finally spoke her tone rose in despair. 'Ginny . . . came. In a dinghy. She . . . rowed up to the boat. She rowed up to the boat and . . . they talked, she and . . . *her*. For a minute or so. Then—' Her mouth moved but no words came.

'Then?'

She forced herself on. 'Then . . . Ginny climbed on board. And . . . they talked some more. I think they were— No,' she suppressed some unspoken thought, 'no, I couldn't tell from that distance. No – they *talked*. And then . . .' Each word was dragged from her with terrible effort. 'Then . . . they both . . . went down below. Into the cabin.'

My mind was cold and clear, but my imagination was blurry. I saw the two figures climbing down the companionway, but they remained a long way off, I

467

couldn't bring them into focus. I said, 'You're sure it was Ginny?'

Mary nodded sadly.

'From so far away?'

'Hugh, believe me, she was the *last* person I was expecting to see. I couldn't believe it at first, I kept looking. But that hair – no one else has hair like Ginny's, no one. And she was wearing that jacket of hers, the dark pink one – sort of raspberry-coloured. I'd remembered it, it was such a lovely jacket. And she had the same long floaty scarf she'd worn with it before, sort of cream and raspberry mixed. She wasn't really dressed for the water. So smart. And then she turned towards me.' She exhaled sharply. 'It was her.'

I didn't say anything for a while. 'Go on,' I murmured at last.

She continued in a flat voice, 'Oh . . , I waited a while, but Mrs Perry needed to get home and I had to get on. It was after five. I kept going back to the window, looking, but there was no sign of anybody. I thought – well, I didn't know what to think. Maybe that Ginny knew her, that they had arranged to . . .' Suddenly dissatisfied with this idea, she abandoned it with a small movement of her head. 'I had a last look before I left, but I couldn't see anything.' Her final words emerged as a murmur: 'Just the two dinghies.'

The silence that followed was broken only by the sound of Mary's sighs. 'Oh, Hugh,' she said at last, 'I'm so sorry you had to know.'

I pictured Ginny as she had appeared at Dittisham House that night, I saw the raspberry jacket and the long floaty scarf jammed halfway into one pocket, and a strange calm spread through me, and it was the calm that comes at the end of a long and troubled journey.

Fifteen

LIKE AN icy hand the cold had stolen in off the blackness of the moor. Climbing out of bed I caught the glint of frost on the window panes. The freeze had begun two weeks after Christmas and, ten bitter days later, was showing no sign of a thaw. I felt my way to the bathroom and, turning on a light, peered blindly at my watch. Not yet seven. Pulling on a robe I went down the narrow cottage stairs to the boiler to see if I could entice it into action. I twisted the thermostat to and fro, checked the setting on the time controller and gave the pump a solid whack. With a shudder of complaint, the ancient furnace roared capriciously back into life.

The boiler wasn't the only primitive contraption in the rented cottage – the cooker was slow, the fridge antique – and in this weather the steep track leading up from the road was icy and treacherous, but Ginny liked the place, she felt safe here, and it was only twenty minutes from Hartford, so, all said, it still had a lot to recommend it. We wouldn't be here for very much longer anyway. With Melton gone and Glebe Place virtually sold and the various loans and mortgages almost settled, we could think about buying a new place in the spring. I spent a lot of my time on such practicalities nowadays, I positively over-whelmed myself with details of every kind. That way I maintained an illusion of usefulness.

Making myself some coffee in the still-unfamiliar kitchen, I heard creaking floorboards above and set out a tea tray for Ginny, with some fruit and a couple of Ryvita, which was about all she ate these days. I found her running a bath. Her nakedness alarmed me, she had grown so very thin, and I had to make an effort not to say anything. She greeted me with a pale smile.

'Would you like your tea here?' I asked.

'Please.'

The morning tea tray was one of our little rituals, along with Ginny's pretence at eating. Normally I was first in the bathroom so as to be ready to leave the house by eight, but since the committal proceedings had begun we had altered our timetable and now Ginny bathed first while I drank my coffee in front of the breakfast news.

'I'm out,' she announced ten minutes later, going past me to the wardrobe. 'I'm not sure what to wear. What do you think?'

We stood before the rail of clothes. We had already decided against anything too bright, and she had worn grey for the first day and navy blue for the second.

'The black?' I suggested.

'Mmm. But it needs something to soften it up a bit.' She pulled out a scarf in muted blues. 'What do you think?'

'Perfect.' But then Ginny always looked perfect. I

thought of the stipendiary magistrate who had been sent down from London to hear the case, and, while he was doubtless the most scrupulous of men, I couldn't believe that he would be immune to appearances and that Ginny, with her frail understated femininity, wouldn't make a favourable impression.

When we had dressed we got ready to leave for Exeter. After two days these departures had also developed a certain ritual. I asked Ginny to check that she had two full inhalers with her; she asked me if I had my briefcase. I was certain she wouldn't be warm enough; she told me I worried too much. By such solicitous concern did we conduct our relationship, by such scrupulous consideration did we maintain a veneer of composure.

The track had been gritted but a fresh sprinkling of snow had formed an ice sheet in the night, and, though I took the slope very gingerly, I felt the wheels slip at the last turn. The next instant the back of the car thumped into the earth wall and we began to slither crabwise towards the road. At the last moment the brakes gripped and the car slid to a halt a couple of feet into the road. I reversed back onto the track just as a car sped past, blowing its horn.

'I'll get it gritted again,' I said when my nerves had quietened down a little.

Ginny had her head pressed against the back of the seat, eyes screwed up, breathing sharply.

'Are you all right?'

'Yup,' she rasped.

'Breathe,' I said. 'Keep it slow. Calm thoughts. Plenty of time. No hurry.' I made her unclench her fisted hands, I pressed her shoulders gently down, I lifted her coat collar higher around her neck.

She gave a small gasping laugh. 'What would I do without you?' Taking long steady draughts of air, she opened her eyes and turned her head towards me. 'I really don't know, you know – what I'd do without you. I certainly couldn't have gone ahead with the court thing. Not if you hadn't believed in me.' She lifted my hand and pressed it against her cheek. 'Sometimes I get the feeling that Grainger doesn't. Believe in me, I mean. Oh, he doesn't actually say anything of course, but ever since I asked him if I'd do better pleading guilty he's never quite looked me in the eye again. I think he thinks I *did it!*' She vamped the words and gave an ironic little laugh that didn't quite come off. 'And Charles,' she added with sudden bewilderment, 'sometimes I think he has his doubts as well.'

'That's just not true,' I argued, 'Charles has no doubts at all. Honestly.'

She frowned, not entirely sure whether she could take this protestation of honesty at face value. 'Anyway,' she said with forced brightness, 'you're the only person who matters. So long as you believe in me, then the rest of the world can—' She dismissed the rest of the world with a shake of her head.

I maintained my gaze as best I could. I couldn't think of anything to say.

She brought her face close to mine. 'Thank you, darling. Thank you for giving me the most important thing of all.'

I saw the need in her eyes, and the vulnerability,

and my mouth jerked into a smile, I gave an indeterminate shrug. 'Dear heart,' I murmured, gripped by
emotions so disturbing that it was all I could do to
keep them out of my face.

'Love you,' she said fiercely.

'Love you too.'

Her eyes didn't leave my face but took on a glint
of faint puzzlement, as though she had caught something in my expression which confused her.

I said quickly, 'It'll be all right, darling. I have a
feeling about it.'

Her lids fluttered, she nodded jerkily, then, hugging her arms against her body, settled back in her
seat.

I fumbled with the heating controls and we set off
again. Worried about ice, I concentrated hard on my
driving, but the road had been salted, it seemed safe
enough, and when we had been silent for some time
I offered, 'I'm sure you're wrong about Grainger, you
know. I think he's right with you.'

She thought about this. 'Oh, he may be with me.
But that's not quite the same as believing in me, is
it?'

'Well, he seems optimistic enough. I think he's glad
you decided on the committal.'

'Oh he just likes the gamble, whatever he may say,'
Ginny remarked, loosing one of her perceptive darts.
'He enjoys the risk.'

I had been careful to take a back seat in the decision
over the full committal. I had left Ginny to talk the
whole thing through with Tingwall and said almost
nothing during a second conference with Grainger. I

had listened to Ginny's agonised deliberations, I had commiserated with her dilemma, but I had managed to offer no firm opinion. I felt the loneliness of the priest who has heard too much and must now remain silent.

Once the decision to go for the full committal had been taken and the date set, Ginny had started to show signs of strain, as if she had only just appreciated what lay ahead. She had spent the intervening weeks fighting asthma and other obscure nervous attacks which frequently sent her to bed for hours at a time. The weight had continued to drop off her, and the fluttering of her eyelids had become more pronounced. Often she cried out during the night, sudden shouts that had me waking with a racing heart.

Yet as we walked into Tingwall's office none of this was apparent. She assumed her public mask, a look of serenity and quiet acceptance, and I could only wonder at her extraordinary self-control.

Tingwall was also showing his nerves. As we sat down for our daily recap, he didn't so much smile as expose his teeth, and his eyes danced excitedly. 'So, all the police evidence is out of the way now. I thought Grainger made some good points off Inspector Henderson yesterday. Getting him to admit that you had been totally consistent in everything you'd said, Ginny. That you'd never made a single admission in all those hours of questioning. And asking him how he thought a woman of your build might have lifted a body up a steep ladder – well, it all adds up.' He bared his teeth again in the semblance of a smile.

'But the main thing, of course, is the lack of forensic evidence. That will hardly have gone unnoticed. So!' He clasped his hands together, a troop leader boosting morale. 'It's just the eyewitness now.'

The *just* lingered uncomfortably in the air, and Tingwall quickly corrected himself. 'It's Gordon Latimer now.'

I asked, 'Will his evidence take long?'

'Impossible to say. And then there'll be Grainger's cross-examination. Really impossible to say. But I can try to get the occasional message out to you.'

I made my usual face. 'Thanks.' As a defence witness I was not permitted to sit in court, so rather than hang around the door in a state of anxiety I had spent much of the last two days at a nearby hotel, doing business on the phone and waiting for occasional calls from Tingwall's assistant.

At twenty to ten Tingwall drove us to the court. As the building came into sight Ginny delved into her bag and took a puff of her inhalant. She had not forgotten the mass of press who had greeted our first appearance on Monday morning, thrusting their lenses against the car windows and jostling us as we entered the building. Ginny hadn't attempted to hide her face. We had decided that, as someone with nothing to hide, she should hold her head high. But the aggressiveness of their behaviour had shaken her and once inside she'd suffered a massive asthma attack.

There was only one photographer today, a down-at-heel man in a faded anorak who waited until we had got out of the car before taking a few desultory pictures. Inside the building we were left alone: for this hearing reporting restrictions were in place, and no word of the proceedings nor comment of any sort was permitted to be published.

In the hall was a motley gathering: defendants and their supporters destined for other courts – according to Tingwall mainly traffic offenders and TV licence evaders, with a sprinkling of shoplifters and drunks; and then, to one side, Henderson and his henchmen in their best suits, watching us with their unblinking policemen's eyes; and, far to the other side, visible in an adjacent lobby, Grainger, holding court with his junior and Tingwall's assistant.

Grainger greeted us with his usual air of melancholic authority. 'The Crown present their Mr *Latimer* today. Now, Mrs Wellesley, my cross-examination could be long and detailed, but don't be surprised if it is rather less comprehensive, covering only a few major points. Much will depend on how the witness appears, and the strength of his evidence. You appreciate?' He cast a peremptory glance over us all, looking for questions but expecting none. 'All must be decided as the situation reveals itself . . .'

My attention was diverted by the sight of a figure making his way perilously across the hall, a man who was both familiar and strange, someone I knew but couldn't place. It was another moment before I realised with a slight shock that the emaciated bow-backed figure was Old Gordon. His tweeds may have fitted him in younger sturdier days, but now they hung on him like sacking. He walked unsteadily, with a marked shuffle, and leant heavily on his companion, a middle-aged woman whom I dimly recognised as his daughter. It was hard to believe it was the same man I had last seen a year ago at my father's funeral. He seemed to have aged twenty years. His narrow skull was exceptionally bony and his sparse lifeless hair floated above it like down. The skin hung heavily on his cadaverous face and his pouchy eyes had the watery look of advanced sickness.

Grainger must have caught some of my astonishment because when I looked back at him he raised a mildly inquisitive eyebrow.

I said in an undertone, 'Gordon Latimer.'

He followed my gaze. 'The one leaning on the woman?'

'Yes.'

He watched while Old Gordon took a seat, and when he turned back to me a closed uncommunicative expression had settled over his face. 'You're sure?'

'Yes. Though he looks absolutely terrible, poor chap. I can't believe it.'

Grainger murmured as though to himself but pitched for my hearing too, 'Nothing is certain in this life but uncertainty.'

Without explaining this, he summoned his team and moved towards the court. Ginny and I embraced briefly. Watching Tingwall lead her away I couldn't rid myself of a creeping unease, an irrational sense of approaching doom.

A familiar voice said, 'Hi there,' and Julia swooped up to peck my cheek.

'What are you doing here? I thought you had a decent job to go to.'

'Decent jobs – curse of the upwardly mobile. No, I thought I'd come and see if I could be useful.'

'Not a lot to be done,' I said flatly. Then: 'Have you been fired or something?' She'd only started her new job two months before.

'Not that I know of,' she said airily. 'No – I'm on sick leave. I've got flu.'

I peered at her. 'I'm sorry.'

She touched my arm. 'Hugh – not really.'

'Oh. *Oh*. Sorry, I'm a bit slow today.'

'Come and have a coffee.'

There was a trolley selling drinks and snacks, and we carried two cups of watery coffee to a corner.

'How are things at Hartford?' Julia asked.

'Umm . . .' It was an effort to think of Hartford. 'Pretty good. No – *more* than good. Orders up twenty per cent. Packenhams have re-listed us – did I tell you?' She nodded. 'They even gave us a window display at Christmas. And . . . well, the staff have been wonderful. Productivity up. Costs down . . .' I trailed off, easily distracted.

'So ya-boo to Howard!' Julia crowed.

But I was hardly listening. I was watching Old Gordon, and my disquiet returned, a niggling worry that I couldn't quite name. 'Would you do something for me, Julia? Would you go and sit in the court when it starts and come and tell me what's happening?'

'You'll be here?'

In saying yes I realised I had taken the decision not to go and work from the hotel.

'Do you want full notes or—'

'No – just the gist of it.'

She gestured towards the people accumulating around the entrance to the court. 'Never mind about later,' she growled. 'I'd better go now if I'm to get a seat.' She hurried away and, sweeping past the queue, spoke to the usher and, without seeming to incur any objections, stationed herself at the head of the line.

I was about to go and find a quiet corner when I glanced back and paused. Julia had turned to talk to another woman just behind her, and the woman was Mary. I kept looking, I waited until the woman turned her head again, but there was no doubt about it. For an instant I felt put out, even a little indignant, that she should have turned up without telling us. In the next instant I was ashamed of such uncharitable thoughts. Mary would be here out of the best of motives, to support us, and as if to confirm it she turned and, catching sight of me, clasped her hands together in a gesture of encouragement and solidarity. I waved back.

When the hall was almost deserted I chose a seat not far from Old Gordon. The old man was hunched in his chair, staring vacantly at the floor. When his daughter spoke to him he lifted his rheumy eyes and peered vacantly about him. His gaze passed over me without focus or recognition.

An usher called his name. His daughter roused him and helped him to his feet. Watching him walk arthritically into the court, my disquiet took new shape, bringing regular beats of alarm that had me on my feet, then sitting again, then pacing restlessly up and down until Julia finally emerged twenty minutes later.

'He's very doddery,' she whispered, 'and a bit vague. I wouldn't say he was doing too well.'

'Where are you sitting?'

She gave me a sharp look. 'Me? At this end, in the back row, by the door. Why?'

'Who's next to you?'

'No one special.' Reading my mind only too well, she hissed, 'Look, is this a good idea?'

'Choose a moment when there's something going on. Some distraction.'

'I really don't think this is a good idea,' she muttered as she went back into the court. Two minutes later she reappeared and waved me hastily past her and through a second door, which led into the public gallery.

My arrival went unnoticed amid some general movement in the court. Only one head turned as I sat down. Some sixth sense had made Mary glance round from her place in the front row of the gallery. Her eyes widened slightly at the sight of me, then with a quick bright smile she looked away again.

I slid down in my seat and shaded my eyes with one hand. In the witness box to one side of the room Old Gordon was settling himself on a chair and being offered a glass of water. Ginny was sitting in the dock with her back to me. Ahead of her were the lawyers, also with their backs to me. Only the magistrate was facing the gallery.

The magistrate leant forward. 'Are you well enough to continue, Mr Latimer?'

The old man's eyes swivelled nervously. 'Aye.'

The magistrate, an owl-faced man with pebble glasses and thick grey hair, nodded to the prosecuting counsel, who rose to his feet.

'Mr Latimer, could you once again cast your mind back to the thirtieth of September last year?' the prosecutor began. 'You were telling us where you were in the afternoon at approximately five o'clock. You said you were down by the ferry, is that right?'

Old Gordon appeared to concentrate hard. 'By the ferry, aye.' His voice was thin and reedy and breathless.

'When you say the ferry, Mr Latimer, you mean the ferry that crosses the River Dart from Dittisham village?'

The old man's mouth moved several times before murmuring: 'Aye.'

'Mr Latimer, what were you doing there by the ferry that day?'

Gordon's hooded lids blinked heavily and his jaw slackened, and it seemed to me that he was having difficulty in comprehending even the most basic question.

'Sitting,' he muttered at last.

'You were sitting where exactly?'

Gordon's eyes wandered anxiously. 'By the pub.' Then after another pause: 'Always sit by the pub.'

'This is the pub called the Ferry Boat Inn?'

Another pause. 'Aye.'

'You were sitting on a bench, were you?'

He nodded distractedly.

'If you could say yes or no, Mr Latimer,' the prosecutor reminded him gently.

Gordon hesitated for a long moment, as though he had forgotten the question. 'Aye,' he said finally.

'Thank you. And this bench overlooks the ferry pontoon?'

The old man seemed beset by a growing air of apprehension, as if each question were leading him further on to perilous ground. 'Aye.'

'While you were sitting on the bench that day, could you please tell us what you saw?'

'Saw . . . Mrs Wellesley,' he whispered, and his eyes were agitated.

'You mean Mrs Virginia Wellesley?'

The pause stretched out.

'Mr Latimer? This person was Mrs Virginia Wellesley?'

'Mrs Hugh,' Gordon said at last.

'By that you mean Mrs Hugh Wellesley? Virginia Wellesley?'

This seemed to confuse him for a moment. 'Mrs Hugh,' he repeated in a voice that was increasingly quavery and fearful.

'Quite. Mrs Hugh Wellesley. Do you see her in court, Mr Latimer?'

The rheumy eyes registered something like bafflement, the mouth began a gasping fish-like motion.

'Mr Latimer, do you see Mrs Wellesley in court?'

A measure of understanding dawned. He began to cast about uncertainly. His glance came past the gallery, stopped momentarily before drifting away and roaming the room. Screwing up his eyes, leaning forward slightly as if to focus better, his gaze finally settled on the dock. 'Aye.'

'You can see Mrs Wellesley? Could you point her out to us, please, Mr Latimer?'

Gordon raised a hooked finger at Ginny.

'Let it be shown that Mr Latimer was indicating the defendant. Now, Mr Latimer, could you tell us what Mrs Wellesley was doing when you saw her that day?'

The jaw sagged again. The effort of memory seemed almost beyond him. 'A boat. Took a boat.'

'Did you see her go to this boat?'

Pause. 'Aye.'

'Where was she when you first saw her?'

His brows pulled down, he seemed to glower.

The prosecutor tried again. 'Did she pass close by you?'

Gordon gave a slight nod. With the bent shoulders and gaping mouth, with the bony head hanging forward on the scrawny neck, he had the look of an ancient bird.

'Was that a yes, Mr Latimer? If you wouldn't mind speaking out . . .' Getting no response, the prosecutor urged, 'Did she pass close to you, Mr Latimer? If you could say yes or no?'

'Yes.'

'How close would you say?'

This question troubled him. 'Close,' he offered tentatively.

'As far as she is from you now, in this courtroom? Further? Nearer?'

'Same.'

'So, two yards at the most. And did you get a good look at her?'

'Aye – Mrs Hugh.'

'You were sure it was her?'

The eyes were fearful again. 'Aye.'

'Now this boat she went to, what kind of a boat was it?'

He thought for a long moment. 'Small boat.'

'A rowing boat perhaps?'

He nodded vaguely.

'Was it a rowing boat? If you could just say yes or no, Mr Latimer?'

'Aye . . . yes.'

'And Mrs Wellesley went off in it, you said?'

Another pause: 'Aye.' The old man reached out for the glass of water. The prosecutor waited while he grasped it with clawed hands and brought the rim unsteadily to his lips. As he drank, water spilled down his chin and fell onto his jacket. An usher came forward and took the glass from him and placed it back on one side. Old Gordon made no attempt to mop up the spilt water and it formed a darkening stain on his lapel.

The prosecutor continued, 'So she rowed off, did she, Mr Latimer?'

Old Gordon's concentration seemed to have drifted again, and the question had to be put to him a second time. 'Aye,' he said at last.

The magistrate, who had been making notes much of the time, was now watching Gordon intently.

'Which direction did she row off in?' asked the prosecutor.

Silence.

'Was it up river, or down river, or across river?'

Gordon frowned a great deal before breathing, 'Up.'

'Up. She rowed off *up* river.' The prosecutor glanced down at his papers and, coming to what looked like an abrupt decision, said, 'Thank you, Mr Latimer,' and, nodding to the bench, sat down.

Grainger rose to his feet. 'Mr Latimer,' he began in a kind unhurried tone, 'you are fond of sitting there by the pub, are you?'

Pause. 'Aye.'

'You like to watch the world go by?'

The empty colourless eyes seemed to focus momentarily. 'Aye.'

'And there's quite a bit to see, is there? The ferry, the pleasure boats coming and going, and so on?'

A whisper. 'Aye.'

'You go there regularly?'

Grimacing, Gordon sucked in his thin lips. 'Not so much.'

'Not so much now. What about last autumn, Mr Latimer, in September at the time you say you saw Mrs Wellesley on the pontoon – did you go there regularly then?'

Much thought again. 'Some.'

'How often did you go in a week, Mr Latimer?'

The troubled look again, the groping for words. 'Sundays. Other times. When it were fine.'

'You would invariably go on a Sunday?'

'When it were fine.'

'So last autumn, if it was fine, you would go on a Sunday. And other days too, if it was fine?'

The old boy was flagging. His shoulders bowed further, his chin descended almost to his chest. 'Aye.' And it was little more than a gasp.

'I'm so sorry – did you say yes, Mr Latimer?'

'Aye – yes.'

'So how often might you go and sit by the pub then, Mr Latimer? As often as three times a week? Four? If it was fine.'

He had to think about that for a long time. 'Sundays. Tuesdays sometimes. An' Fridays.'

'As many as three days a week then? What about Saturdays?'

Gordon seemed uncertain about that.

'Did you go there on Saturdays at all?'

'At my daughter Saturdays.'

'Ah. So you generally visited your daughter on Saturdays?' A pause. 'Have I got that right?'

Gordon's mouth began to work in increasing agitation. 'Aye, to my daughter.'

'Where does your daughter live, Mr Latimer?'

Another long pause. 'Primrose Cottage.'

'That's in Dittisham village, is it?' When he had his reply Grainger said in a pleasant almost reminiscent tone, 'So on a day when you went to visit her, you would stay until what time?'

'Teatime. Leave after tea.'

'*After* tea? And what time did tea finish?'

This was the one answer which came without hesitation. 'Half past six.'

'So on the days you visited your daughter you wouldn't leave until after six-thirty?'

'Aye.'

'Now on a day you went to see your daughter, would you also find the time to go and sit by the pub?'

The old man looked thoroughly bemused at this. His pale eyes cast anxiously about, his mouth drooped at the corners and his lower jaw reverted to its strange gasping motion.

Grainger repeated the question carefully.

No one moved. The court seemed to hold its collective breath.

Finally the thin voice rasped, 'At my daughter Saturdays.'

'Forgive me,' Grainger said, selecting a compassionate tone, 'I just need to be clear. Last September you were in the habit of visiting your daughter every Saturday until seven. So are we to understand that you never went and sat by the pub on a Saturday?'

The old man's face crumpled further, he seemed thoroughly confused. Eventually he gave an odd movement of his head.

'Can I take that as a yes, Mr Latimer?'

Another indeterminate movement.

Grainger turned towards the bench, as though for assistance. The magistrate leant forward and said in the ringing tones that people usually reserve for the deaf, 'Mr Latimer, do you understand the question?'

Old Gordon's mouth went through its frantic motions.

'I'll ask Mr Grainger to put it to you one more time, shall I? Mr Grainger, if you please.'

Grainger repeated, 'Last September you were in the habit of visiting your daughter every Saturday until seven. Can we take it, then, that you never went and sat by the Ferry Boat Inn on a Saturday?'

Old Gordon closed his mouth and nodded distinctly. 'Aye.'

'Thank you.' And Grainger's tone left no doubt that he had made his point. 'Now, Mr Latimer, if I may I'd like to take you back to the occasion when you saw Mrs Wellesley setting off in the boat. Which day of the week was that?'

It was as though the old man suddenly appreciated his predicament. He became increasingly distressed, his face contorted into a grimace of woe and confusion, his mouth wobbled. Finally he shook his head.

The tension was like an electric charge. My mind told me that it was all over, logic insisted that we had won, but the consequences of this thought were so overwhelming that for the moment my emotions refused to follow.

Grainger was driving his advantage home. 'You can't say?' he repeated. 'So it could have been a Sunday?'

The old man lifted a bent hand to his chest as if his breathing were giving him trouble.

'So it might have been a Sunday?' Grainger pressed with the urgency of a man who senses he is running out of time. 'Mr Latimer?'

'Can't say.'

The magistrate leant forward. 'Mr Latimer, are you feeling unwell?'

'Can't say,' Gordon echoed miserably.

'Mr Latimer.' The magistrate raised his voice again. 'Are you feeling all right?'

'Can't remember like I used to,' Gordon cried plaintively.

'Is it your memory that's troubling you, Mr Latimer, or are you feeling unwell?'

'Memory . . . bad.'

'So apart from your memory you're feeling all right?'

Old Gordon nodded despairingly, and he seemed close to tears.

'In order that the court can be absolutely clear,' the magistrate continued with great deliberation, 'you are saying, Mr Latimer, that you cannot be sure which day of the week it was when you saw Mrs Wellesley go off in the boat?'

The old man's mouth turned down almost to his chin, he blinked rapidly and shook his head. 'Memory . . . it's terrible.'

The magistrate took his time writing his notes before looking towards Grainger. 'Any more questions, Mr Grainger?'

'No, sir.'

There was a pause as the usher helped Gordon from the witness box. The old man's corrugated cheeks were streaked with tears, and his eyes held the terrors of bewilderment.

The prosecutor stood up briefly and said disconsolately, 'Sir, that completes the case for the prosecution.'

The magistrate looked expectantly at Grainger, who rose and announced in a firm voice, 'Sir, I would like to move that there is absolutely no case to answer. The Crown has offered no forensic evidence *whatsoever* that links my client to the scene of the crime. Nor has it produced a *single* piece of forensic evidence to link her to the victim. Indeed, its case relies solely on Mr Latimer's eyewitness evidence, and Mr Latimer *cannot remember* which day it was that he saw my client rowing off "up river". Now we do not dispute the fact that my client took a dinghy from the pontoon and rowed out to the yacht *Ellie Miller* on the day *after* the murder, on the *Sunday*. My client herself volunteered this information to the police at her first interview, and was happy to repeat it in her subsequent statement. What we dispute utterly is that she was anywhere near the water on the day before, on the *Saturday*, and indeed the prosecution have entirely failed to prove that she was *anywhere* in the vicinity on that day. Thus, sir, I submit that there is simply no case to answer and that it would be unsafe in every respect to allow this case to proceed any further.'

Grainger sat down. The magistrate studied his notes before bending forward to have a word with the clerk. Looking out over the court, he said with a long sigh of exasperation, 'I agree with you entirely, Mr Grainger, for all the reasons you have stated—'

There was a startled cry, and a banging of doors as some people hurried from the gallery.

491

'The prosecution have failed to produce any reliable evidence to connect Mrs Wellesley to this crime—'

I buried my head in my hands.

'. . . In my view it would be unsafe in the extreme to allow this case to proceed to the crown court. I find that there is no case to answer, and the defendant is therefore discharged.'

He addressed Ginny then – something about being free to go – but I couldn't hear his words for the violence of my own emotions. Julia's voice sounded in my ear and her arm came round my shoulders, and she may have been crying too.

Even before the magistrate had left the court, the place erupted into noise and movement. Someone close by began shouting, a man pushed roughly past me. Julia led me out of the gallery and into the well of the court. In the midst of the people congratulating her, Ginny looked small and dazed. Reaching her, we embraced uncertainly as if neither of us could quite absorb what had happened, and then her arms tightened around my waist and she was gasping, and laughing a little too.

Tingwall was hovering, grinning all over his squinty-eyed face.

'Not too late to fire me,' he chuckled.

'I always said you were too young for the job.' And I embraced him.

I heard Mary's voice. 'Ginny!' she cried, and, sweeping past me, enveloped Ginny in a large hug. 'I'm so, *so* glad!' she declared. 'I'm so pleased! Oh, Ginny! I'm going to phone David this minute! We're so thrilled!' Throwing up her arms as though lost for further words, she laughed in an odd overexcited way and enveloped Ginny again.

I went over to Grainger who was packing his papers away. 'Thank you,' I said simply, and shook his hand.

'It would have been hard to lose,' he said with a sigh of disappointment, like a prize fighter cheated of a good bout. 'That old man . . . In the circumstances it was a lucky thing that your wife is something of a gambler.'

'You still handled it brilliantly.'

His eyes narrowed. 'Did I? You were in court?'

I smiled at how easily I had been caught out. 'Just at the end,' I admitted.

'Oh, Mr Wellesley.' He shook his head with an ironic show of disapproval. 'If we had gone to trial, that little escapade could have made our lives very difficult.'

'Perhaps I'm a gambler too.'

He thought about that. 'Yes,' he drawled in his unfathomable accent, 'I think you probably are.'

Before I could ask him what he meant by that Tingwall came bustling up with something he wanted me to read.

'I prepared this for the press last night. A statement.' Waving the paper in the air, he giggled like a child. 'I knew, you see. I knew!' Waiting for my grin of acknowledgement, accepting it with a small swagger, he read from the handwritten sheet. 'Mrs Wellesley has protested her innocence most vigorously ever since she was charged, and with the throwing out of the case her position has been entirely vindicated. There was never the slightest evidence against Mrs Wellesley, yet she has been forced to suffer months of needless distress as a result of a charge that from every point of view should never have been brought. Her family would now ask that she be left in peace.' He looked up. 'I would have liked more time on it, but what do you think?'

'I think it's fine.'

I turned to find Mary at my elbow. She drew me aside and whispered fervently, 'Hugh – you've no idea what this means to me. *No* idea. I've been *praying* for this from the very beginning.' Her eyes with their garish blue lids looked fiercely into mine. '*Praying!*'

'I know.'

'What we need to do now is forget,' she said in a confidential tone. '*Forget* we ever had that talk. *Forget* what I said.'

I stared at her in open astonishment, wondering how she could possibly imagine I could forget something so devastating, something which was going to darken my life for ever. '*Forget?*'

She grasped my arm. 'As far as we can, of course.'

I shook my head.

'All in the past now, Hugh,' she insisted. 'The *past*.' She laughed suddenly, the same odd laugh again. 'Well – I must go and phone David! He'll be so thrilled.' With a jolly wave, she hurried off.

The next few hours were a confusion of down-ward-floating emotions. Tingwall went to the front of the court building and read his statement to the horde of waiting press who had materialised, as always, out of nowhere. Then when Tingwall's assistant had brought his car round to the front we left the shelter of the building and launched ourselves at the jostling photographers and shouting reporters for what I fervently hoped would be the last time. Ginny ignored their questions until, on reaching the car, a BBC reporter put a microphone under her nose and asked how she felt. 'I feel immensely glad that it's all over,' she replied.

Back at Tingwall's office we drank champagne, made a few calls to spread the news and took the congratulations of the firm's partners before going to lunch at a nearby restaurant. Tingwall and Julia chattered excitedly, but Ginny and I were rather more subdued, too drained of feeling for such straightforward emotions as joy or relief. I drank too much wine and compounded the error with two brandies, so that when we set off for home it was Ginny who had to drive through the gathering dusk.

The cottage was icy. I thumped the boiler to no avail while Ginny answered a steady stream of calls from friends and well-wishers. Finally, at nine, we took the phone off the hook and huddled side by side in front of the fire with a sandwich and a glass of wine.

'I think back to last winter,' Ginny murmured reminiscently. 'I think of everything we had then and how unhappy we were. And then I think of what we have now, and – well, I wouldn't change all this for anything, not for *anything*. I wouldn't be anywhere else but in this freezing little dump of a cottage with you. I feel so lucky, Hugh. The luckiest person in the world.

Most of all' – and her voice was rough and low – 'I feel so terribly lucky to have you.'

'Darling.'

She pulled back a little and looked into my face. She asked softly, 'I do have you, don't I?'

'Of course.' I added a smile. 'Of course you do.' And something in my heart felt infinitely weary.

'It's all I've ever wanted, you see. You and me. For us to be happy.'

I put my wine down, then hers, and we wrapped our arms around each other. I saw the future stretching out before us, and it seemed to go on for ever. I saw Hartford growing steadily, I saw us in a pretty house near by, I saw summers in France and, when Hartford didn't need me any more, I saw us going to live there amid the vineyards: I saw all these things, and none of them could assuage my loneliness.

Ginny moved against me, her lips travelled across my cheek, she opened her soft mouth to mine. Soon we went upstairs to the warmth of our bed and, as Ginny's passionate body pressed itself against mine, I felt a surge of love, and a chasm of emptiness.

Sixteen

Entering the silent house, breathing the musty blend of furniture polish and wood smoke that took me lurching back to my childhood, I thought: This is the last time I will stand here, this is the last time I will feel so close to my past.

The remains of the furniture had been removed during the week, organised, like everything else to do with the sale, by Mary. Two geometric patches of deeper colour marked the spot on the study carpet where Pa's desk had stood, and ancient scorchmarks long hidden by a well-placed rug fanned out from the grate, from the days when Pa had favoured blazing open fires. The shadowy outlines of pictures lined the stairs, and in my old room the dusty curtains framed unwashed windows clouded with the grime of the long winter.

The bed had gone, the side table too, but, as Mary had forewarned me, everything that neither she nor Ginny had claimed and which was otherwise destined for jumble sales had been stored here, an accumulation of old lamps, rickety chairs and cardboard boxes stacked high with kitchen utensils, chipped china and battered paperbacks: the family detritus of fifty years.

I found my old paintings in a cardboard box half crushed by a pile of *Eagles* dating back to the sixties. The Winsor & Newton watercolours, the set of sable brushes which at fourteen I had saved up for so carefully were not with them however, and, though I hunted desultorily through a few of the neighbouring boxes, I soon realised the search was hopeless. My old lamp with its parchment shade lay on a chair but when I picked it up the top lurched over and I saw that the shade had acquired a second split.

Shutting the door, I carried the paintings down to the car and, after one last look around the hall, locked up the house. Touched by a last bout of nostalgia, I took a wander round the side of the house to the terrace. Dark shadows dotted the flagstones where the flower urns had stood, and one of the flowerbeds showed signs of fresh digging where a plant had been removed. That would be Mary, who was always on the lookout for additions to her garden.

The river was grey under a cold March sky, and an exceptionally high tide had lifted the water almost to the branches of the trees overhanging the opposite bank. Another boat lay at *Ellie Miller*'s mooring, a modern tub with its name displayed garishly down the side. *Ellie* had been taken to Plymouth to be refitted, renamed and, in due course, we hoped, sold. There would be no buyers for her here.

I went down the steps to the middle terrace and on to the lower garden. Under the bare trees the last of the crocuses lay flat like fallen warriors, and in the rough grass the daffodil shoots stood stiff and tall, awaiting their moment.

I glanced up and saw beyond the summerhouse a bowed figure standing among the apple trees, head canted upward in contemplation of something above his head. He had his back to me but as I made my way towards him I recognised the bony head and the bent shoulders under the baggy tweed jacket.

'Hello there,' I called.

Old Gordon turned. 'Mr Hugh!' he exclaimed amiably.' 'Day to you.' He raised a gnarled hand in salute and gestured on upwards at the trees. 'Need a good prune. Won't get much fruit without a good prune.'

'Aha.' I inspected the branches dutifully. 'I'm afraid everything's been rather neglected.'

'Not too late, if it's done quick.' He nodded and hummed a little. 'Mrs Bennett – she's keen on her fruit. Likes makin' apple pies, she does. Does 'em for the fête.' He chortled, 'Dozens o' the blessed things.'

'Ahh.' The Bennetts, who had lived on the other side of the village for some years, were the new owners of Dittisham House. 'You'll be working here then? I thought you were retired, Gordon.'

'Ah, yes and no, yes and no. Still do bits and pieces. Can't risk the prunin' meself, o' course. I'd be no sooner up a ladder than sailin' off it again.' He cackled at the thought, showing a fine set of false teeth. 'But I don' mind a bit o' diggin' and weedin'. Keeps me goin'.'

'You're feeling pretty fit then?'

'Can' complain, Mr Hugh. Can' complain at all. Good to be back on me feet again, I can tell yer.'

'I, er . . . I'd heard you hadn't been too well.'

He made an exaggerated grimace. 'Bad winter. Bad.

Rheumatics. Heart. *Angina*. Felt somethin' terrible. *Terrible*.' He blew out his sunken cheeks at the memory, before brightening suddenly. 'But I'm all set now.'

'I'm so glad.'

The old man's face puckered again, and he cast me a troubled glance. 'Sorry about the court business, Mr Hugh.'

'It doesn't matter, Gordon. Really.'

'They kept askin', the police. Never stopped askin'. Dates, times. Dates, times. On and on. What a palaver.' He rolled his drooping eyes and jerked a clawed hand in a gesture of disbelief. 'Then they got me makin' this statement. Puttin' me name to it. And all the time I thought maybe I was helpin' out, yer see. Thought I was doin' good. An' then, next thing I know, they says they want me in court, and, I tell you, Mr Hugh, if I'd 'a' realised . . .'

'I understand, Gordon, really.'

'I didn' know I was sayin' things against Mrs Hugh. They never told me that.'

'No, I'm sure they didn't.'

'If I'd 'a' known, well . . . I'd 'a' kept me mouth shut.'

'But you couldn't have known. Honestly – we didn't blame you, Gordon. Not for a moment.'

He was lost in his reminiscences again. 'They kept sayin' ter me – just say it like you said it before, in the statement. But comes to it, comes to the day, an' I couldn' get a darn' thing straight in me head. I was feelin' so bad with me heart. Been bad for weeks.

Between you and me, Mr Hugh, thought I was on the way out. Thought me number was well and truly up.'

'Gordon, don't worry about it. After all, everything worked out fine in the end.'

He grunted, 'Gets so you can't be sure of anythin'.'

Nodding solemnly, I contemplated the truth of that remark. I looked up at the trees. 'Hope you get a good harvest.'

'Better, hadn' I? All those pies to fill!' The cadaverous face split into a quiet grin.

'Take care, Gordon.'

He laughed, 'That's one thing you may be sure of, Mr Hugh.'

I drove away at a crawl while my thoughts circled restlessly, stirring up long-suppressed ideas that I had almost persuaded myself to forget, converging on a single unhappy notion which proceeded to worry at me like a cracked tooth. Absorbing the idea, allowing it houseroom, it seemed to me that truth was a terribly overrated objective, that in going after it you ended up not with the hoped-for sense of resolution but with yet another bout of turmoil and unhappiness.

But there was one thing more unsettling than an unhappy truth, and that was the kind of uncertainty which was eating away at me now. Accelerating to the next junction, I took the turning for Furze Lodge.

The house was open. No one answered my calls and I wandered from room to room until, coming into the kitchen, I spotted David through the window, digging a hole in the lawn.

Coming closer, I saw it was a long shallow trench.

'Drainage?' I asked.

He spun around, looking startled, and flashed me a reproachful look. Calming down just as rapidly, he offered, 'Electricity cable.'

'Floodlighting?'

'Mary wants a summerhouse in the far corner there, and maybe one day a swimming pool, though I think they're a total waste of time myself.' In a movement that was almost violent, he plunged the spade into the ground and shovelled some earth. 'How's Ginny?'

'She's fine.'

'And the new house?'

'Oh, dust and mess. We're camping at the builders' convenience – you know.'

'And Hartford?'

'Fingers crossed, going better than I ever dared hope.'

David said drily, 'That must please Howard no end.'

He shifted a few more feet of earth before resting on his spade. 'I should have hired a digger.'

'I'd help if . . .' I gestured as though for a second spade.

David swung his gaze on me and I could see that he was in a prickly mood. 'So what brings you here after all this time? I was beginning to think the Cold War had set in.'

'I was just picking up some stuff from Dittisham. I thought I'd pop in.'

He raised a sceptical eyebrow and waited for me to tell him something nearer the truth.

'I wanted to ask you something,' I confessed. 'I wanted to ask if Old Gordon was a patient of yours.'

'Of course.' He gave a small snort. 'How else do you think I fixed him? And to answer your next question, it was a mixture of codeine, antihistamine and a tranquilliser called thioridazine. Guaranteed to addle the brain in the right doses.' He snapped irritably, 'And you don't need to look so bloody disapproving. It wasn't going to kill him. He's perfectly all right now.'

There is an instant after a truth is confirmed when, though you've known what was coming, the facts still seem bald and shocking.

David growled, 'Besides, his memory had been dodgy for years. He'd probably got the whole thing wrong anyway. The wrong day, the wrong person – who knows? So it wasn't as if I was perpetrating a great miscarriage of justice, was it?'

I didn't say anything.

David cast me a scathing look. 'You didn't realise?' he asked, working himself up into some kind of fury.

'I half guessed. When I saw him at the court . . .'

'Come on, you must have known! I'd promised, hadn't I?'

'Promised?'

'I said I'd help.' He repeated almost crossly: '*I said I'd help*. You must have realised!'

'I suppose I didn't want to think about it. I didn't want to . . .' I shrugged, 'deal with it. But now . . . well, I can only say thank you. *God* – that's totally inadequate, isn't it? What I mean is – I'll never be able to thank you enough, David. Never.'

'Stuff your gratitude, Hugh,' David said with sudden vehemence. 'I may be an adulterer and a liar and a few other things besides, but I wasn't going to let Ginny go to prison for something she didn't do. Even *I* thought that was a bit much. You know – something I might *just* have difficulty in living with for the rest of my life. I may be a shit, but not *that* much of a shit.'

'It's all right,' I said quietly. 'I know what really happened. Mary told me.'

I had caught him by surprise. He stared at me in dismay or alarm or both. 'What did Mary tell you?'

'Oh . . .' I still found it hard to say. 'That she saw Ginny go out to the boat and talk to Sylvie and go aboard and—' I cut myself short with a sharp gesture.

'She said *that*? My God.' He shook his head incredulously. 'God.' He gave an unsteady laugh that was suddenly quite devoid of assurance. 'You should know better than to believe anything that Mary tells you.'

I felt a momentary disconnection from the conversation, as though it were happening at some other time in my own past or future. 'She'd seen Ginny,' I argued hoarsely. 'She must have. She described what she was wearing. She . . .' But I was silenced by the look on David's face.

'You poor sod,' he murmured pityingly. 'You thought . . . all this time . . .'

Doubts roared through my mind. I felt a tug in my chest, a sudden heat, followed by the first stirrings of a fearsome anger. 'What the hell are you saying?'

'Hugh – I'm saying that Mary was lying.'

504

'She never saw Ginny?'

'She never saw Ginny,' he sighed. 'Not then anyway. Ginny arrived a lot later. I'm sorry. I'm really sorry.' He sounded genuinely shaken. 'When was this? When did Mary tell you this? Were you about to go to the police? Was that what it was? She'd have done anything, I'm afraid, to stop you doing that. Was it the police?'

I didn't trust myself to speak.

'I'm really sorry, Hugh.' He raised both shoulders in an exaggerated appeal for understanding.

'*You bastard!* She was protecting *you!*' I exploded at last.

He flinched, he was halfway to making a contrite face when my anger burst over me in a hot wave and I lunged for him. Grabbing him by his shirt, I twisted it tight under his chin. 'You bastard! *You bastard!*' My rage was huge and ugly and inconsolable. I was overcome by the lust for revenge. I wanted to inflict the most terrible pain and suffering on him, as he had done on me, and at that moment no punishment could possibly have been too terrible. I pushed my fists higher and higher under his chin, driving his head back until he was forced to twist away. As he straightened up, I aimed a punch at his face but my swing was wild and hopelessly wide and, seeing it coming, he lashed out with an arm and deflected my blow. I came in with a weak left hook but he ducked under that and my fist swished uselessly through the air. In my rage and frustration, I became more cunning. I dropped my arms to my sides as if in surrender and the moment he relaxed I sent a sharp little jab

505

into his stomach which doubled him over. As his head came up for air I splayed my feet, dug in my heels, and put all my weight into a low upward swing that whistled up under his chin. Even before my knuckles made contact I knew it was going to be a powerful blow. There was a loud crack, the impact sent a sharp jabbing pain into my hand, David cried out and jerked back before falling slowly onto one knee. Clasping a hand to his chin, panting hard, he looked up at me with what might have been a plea for truce, but if he thought I was finished he had another think coming.

He staggered to his feet and we faced each other warily. He tried to say something but I wasn't listening and I went for him again with a tight swing of my left fist, a feint which I intended to follow with another solid blow from the right. But he caught my first arm and held onto it and tried to twist me off-balance. I shoved my shoulder under his arm in a half-remembered wrestling manoeuvre but he hooked his foot behind my ankle and the next moment we fell untidily to the ground. For a few seconds we grappled ineffectually. I became aware of a frenzied barking and growling from one of David's dogs. Perhaps it was the fear of being bitten that gave me new strength but I managed to push David over onto his back and land a quick knuckle on his face. I didn't think I'd hit him very hard until I saw his nose spout a stream of blood. While I stared at the blood spreading down his face, his fist came out of nowhere and caught me high on the cheek, just under one eye. I felt my head snap back, I saw stars and, falling sideways, rolled slowly onto my back.

There was a silence broken only by the sound of our panting. After a second or two I heard a different sort of panting and felt a wet nose snuffling at my face. I pushed the dog away and it went to inspect David, who murmured, 'Piss off, Bodger,' so I knew he couldn't be too badly hurt.

My face was throbbing painfully, and my hand too. I touched them gingerly, but as far as I could tell nothing was broken. I'd only ever got into one serious fight, at school, and that had ended in defeat after one blow. I was rather surprised that I had managed to land any sort of a punch on David, let alone a couple which had found their target. But I felt no sense of satisfaction, far less triumph, only a depressing futility.

Pressing a hand to my burning cheek, I sat up cautiously and looked across at David. He was still lying flat on his back. Opening one eye a crack he peered blearily at me before closing it again. The dog stood nearby, wagging its tail sporadically.

'Couldn't let her go,' David said without warning.

My breath caught high in my chest. I kept very still, as if by ignoring him he might leave the subject alone.

'Just couldn't do without her.'

'For Christ's sake shut up!' I retorted furiously. 'I don't bloody want to hear.'

'Please,' he asked simply. When I didn't reply he continued with a gasp, 'Never thought anyone would ever get such a hold on me. I'd never . . . in all my life . . . Never been so – *taken*. So – *mesmerised*. Or perhaps I mean obsessed,' he said in the bemused tone of someone who still hasn't quite worked things out. 'Hardly knew what to do with myself. Got so I couldn't even *think* when I was away from her. Couldn't function. She was so – *different*. So – *crazy*. Made me laugh. Made me feel— *Okay*,' he conceded as though I'd put up some sort of argument, 'Okay, it was sex to begin with. I mean, I hadn't strayed for a long time, I'd forgotten how . . . well, how bloody fantastic it could be.' His voice shuddered at the memory. 'But then . . . then it was more than that. Much more. I always felt so good when I was with her. For the first time in my life – good, *good*. I thought, so *this* is what it's all about, this is what people go on about. She made me feel alive, Hugh. That was the thing –' the gasp again ' – *alive*.' His tone dropped. 'I thought we had a future. I thought I could cure her, you see. I thought I could get her off the drugs. I thought she would do it for *me*. That's the worst thing, thinking that someone's going to change because you want them to. But I really believed—'

He broke off suddenly. I looked across at him and his blood-smeared face was so contorted with grief that I quickly looked away again.

'I believed she'd do it for me,' he whispered at last in a raw voice. 'But I was wrong. She was never going to change. I didn't give up trying though. I never gave up trying. I had this plan. I was going to take her away. We were going to make a new start, somewhere completely different. America. Italy. Somewhere

where she wouldn't know people in the drug world. Somewhere she could do a sculpting course and study her New Age stuff. We made plans. Lots of plans.' He made a harsh sound, a sigh that was also an expression of despair. 'Right up until the end, until the last day. More plans.'

The dog, who had been sitting down, got up and, whining softly, tried to lick David's face. Holding it at bay with one hand, he went on, 'I stopped her drugs when I realised she was making no effort to cut down on them. Well, that was the reason I gave for stopping them – because she wouldn't cut down – but really I was trying to force her into coming away with me. I couldn't think of any other way. She'd never agree on a date, she was always wriggling out of it for some reason or another. It had got so she wouldn't even talk about it any more. I began to imagine the worst – imagine that she was going to finish the whole thing. I was terrified she'd just up and off one day and I'd never see her again. I thought that if I cut off the drugs she'd come crawling back.' He grunted at the idea. 'Of course, crawling back wasn't Sylvie's style. She just found other ways of getting what she wanted. Her brother in Bristol. That chap Hayden and the excursions to France.'

And me, I thought. Don't forget me.

As if reading my thoughts, David said matter-of-factly, 'I didn't cotton on to you for a long time, honestly. Amazing what you miss when you're not looking. I thought you were simply having troubles with Ginny. When you kept coming down to the boat I thought you were just trying to get away from it all. I didn't realise until the very end, really. Until just before . . .'

Cautiously, patting his nose gingerly, he pushed himself up onto one elbow. Then, just as slowly, he sat up and, pulling his feet towards him, rested his forearms on his knees and stared out across the garden. Our breath formed puffs of vapour in the cold, the ground was very damp, but neither of us thought of moving.

'She was furious with me,' David went on. 'When I stopped the drugs. I saw the wild side of her then, and how. But it didn't change anything. It didn't stop me wanting her,' he said gruffly. 'Nothing could do that. She was my drug, you see. I could never get enough of her, even after all those months. Could never *imagine* getting enough of her.' His voice cracked, he shook his head as though he himself scarcely believed the power she had exerted over him. 'Part of me knew what she was like, knew she wasn't too good at commitment, that she'd never stayed with anything for very long. But I thought it would all be different once we got away, once she was off that bloody poison.'

He raised a weary hand and rubbed his eyelids. 'She always came back,' he said dully. 'Always. Oh, sometimes it was to wrangle a script out of me, sure. *Sure*. But most of the time she came back because she needed to see me, just like I needed to see her. Because we couldn't stay away from each other. Underneath it all we had something, you see. Something *strong*. We were two of a kind. She always said so. Two of a kind.' His voice rose and he stalled momentarily. 'I think we could have made it together, you know. I think we could have been happy. I think – I think—' He could hardly say it. 'I think I loved her. I think I really loved her.' He dropped his head into his hands and snatched at his breath.

I looked away and watched a magpie prowling through the trees. After a while I said, 'What about Mary?'

He brought his head up heavily, dragging his hands down his face as he did so. 'Mary,' he sighed. '*Mary*. At the beginning – well, what she didn't know wouldn't hurt her and all that. But then – yes, I would have left her, I would have left her like a shot if Sylvie had ever got her act together, if she'd ever committed herself.' A slight shrug. 'I can't say our marriage was bad exactly, but it was pretty mechanical. It had never been much else, really. In those days I thought you just settled for a nice efficient person who shared some of your interests and who'd do a good job with the children. That sounds pretty unfeeling, I suppose, but that was what I thought it was all about. I never minded the fact that Mary wasn't a great beauty – I never thought that mattered. I wanted someone who'd be a good wife, who'd fit in with my life, back me up.'

When he showed no sign of continuing, I said, 'She found out.' It was half a statement, half a question.

'I guess so,' he breathed distractedly. 'I guess so.'

He turned away, and we sat in silence for a time. Only the dog stirred, cocking its ears to some far-off sound and lifting its nose to the air.

My anger had evaporated; only the sour aftertaste

511

of violence remained. I had no feelings left for David, except perhaps pity. And, for the moment at least, gratitude for having told me his story and set me free. I almost left then, I almost got up and walked away to start the miraculous new existence which unexpectedly stretched before me, the new life with a Ginny whose only crime was to have tried to save her worthless husband. I almost got up and walked away, but something made me hesitate.

'I had no idea. No idea at all,' David murmured at last, giving voice to some thought of his own. When he next spoke, it was with new emotion. 'I'd arranged to meet Sylvie on the boat that day. Most of the summer we'd been meeting at someone's house, a chap who'd gone away for a few months. But that day we decided to meet on the boat.' He paused, and it was only with a visible effort that he forced himself on. 'I got delayed – a stupid meeting – then they paged me – a heart attack. By the time I got down to the river I was almost an hour late. But I knew she'd wait. When she'd called she'd sounded really happy, really keen to see me. I knew she'd wait.' He rubbed his head, close to misery again. 'But when I got down there I couldn't find the dinghy oars. Then I couldn't find the *dinghy*. Thought someone must have pinched it. I was about to borrow someone else's when' – he inhaled sharply – 'when I looked up and saw someone rowing the dinghy towards me. I thought it must be Sylvie, that for some reason she'd taken my dinghy instead of *Samphire*'s. I almost called out to her. It took me ages to realise that it was Mary. She was wearing this baggy old oilskin, one of Pa's relics, with the hood up. As soon as I realised it was her, I knew she could only have been to *Ellie* – I mean, there was nowhere else she could have been. At first I persuaded myself that Sylvie would have made herself scarce in some way, that she would have seen Mary coming. That's what I wanted to believe anyway, that's what I told myself . . .' He screwed up his eyes, his mouth turned down, he said bleakly, 'Although deep down . . . deep down I had an awful feeling, even then.'

I had been avoiding the moment of confrontation, I had been shutting it out, but there was no escaping it now. Feeling emotionally sick, I gave the thought life. *Mary*.

'Mary never went out to *Ellie* normally,' David was saying, 'she could hardly row a dinghy. There had to be a *reason*, and the only reason . . .' But he couldn't cope with this thought and pushed it aside. 'So there I was . . . I couldn't face a scene there on the river, so I went up the road and round a corner where Mary wouldn't see me. As soon as she'd landed, she rushed off, went straight past me. I couldn't decide what to do then. I looked for Sylvie, of course. I'd bought her a mobile phone but she never remembered to take it with her, she was always leaving it in the wrong place, so I wasn't surprised when it didn't answer. And then I looked for her dinghy. I couldn't see it at *Ellie*. I couldn't see it at *Samphire*.' Quite suddenly he began to cry, awkwardly, with great contortions of his face. A trickle of tears mixed with the drying blood and dripped in a pink stream off the end of his chin. 'It must have been there, of course, at *Ellie* – I just didn't see it. I can't stop thinking that if only I'd gone out there, *if only I'd gone and had a look* then maybe I could have saved her.' And he gave a loud sob, a howl of irretrievable loss that made the dog recoil and whimper uneasily.

I stared at him, this brother I hardly knew. I reached out and gripped his arm. 'You mustn't think about that—'

'I can't help it!' he cried helplessly. 'It's all I ever think about! If only I hadn't been late, if only I hadn't been called out, if only— Oh God, oh *God*,' he wailed, 'it's all I ever think about!'

I shifted closer and put an arm round his shoulders. In my mind's eye I pictured the shadowy figure spying on Sylvie and me from the terrace at Dittisham House, and I saw Mary there in the darkness, I saw Mary creeping up to the window and bumping the metal chair across the stone flags, and I wondered how often she had crept up on David and Sylvie, how often she had seen them together.

'Afterwards I couldn't get rid of this – this *feeling*,' David said despairingly. 'I knew . . . I just *knew* something was wrong. I drove around most of the evening. I went to her cottage, I went to Dittisham House and found you and Ginny. And I couldn't find her, I couldn't find her anywhere. And then, next day when they found her . . . When they found her . . . *Christ* . . .' Weeping again, he shook his head and kept shaking it. 'But I needed to know, you see. I needed to know for sure, so before Mary went out I went and looked at her car. And the oilskin was there in the boot, in a plastic bag. With some clothes. And the clothes, they were . . . covered, absolutely covered . . . '

A wind had sprung up, intensifying the cold. My hands were frozen and I thought I felt David shiver. 'Come inside,' I said.

'I wouldn't have let Ginny go to prison,' David said as I helped him to his feet. 'I swear it.' He faced me for the first time since I had hit him, and I saw that one eye was swelling badly. 'I swear it,' he repeated.

'I know that.'

He nodded emotionally.

We walked towards the house.

'Does Mary realise?' I asked.

'That I know? That I saw her? No. We've never spoken of it, or anything to do with it. I don't think she has any idea. But I'll be leaving quite soon,' he said firmly. 'I thought it wouldn't be safe to leave before, in case the police thought – well, whatever they might think. But I'll leave quite soon now. In a week or so. I'll miss the children, of course . . .' He made a hopeless gesture.

We went into the kitchen and David reached a hand into the serving hatch and pulled out a bottle of cognac. He poured two measures and we knocked them back.

'You'd better go and clean yourself up,' I told him as he refilled our glasses.

He ran exploratory fingers over his face, and raised a critical eyebrow. 'You too. You're going to have a real shiner, I'm afraid.'

I drained the last of my drink. 'I'll wash on the way out.'

We faced each other.

'Don't think too badly of her,' David said with a bitter ring to his voice. 'She worked very hard on Howard, you know, to get him to bring the Cumberland board round. In fact, I'm pretty sure she swung it for you.'

'Swung it? But how?'

'Oh, I think she knew things about Howard that he didn't want the world to know.'

Ginny's words came to me again: *She's not Howard's sister for nothing*, and the sick feeling crept back into my stomach.

We heard the car at the same time.

I touched his arm and hurried towards the downstairs cloakroom to splash water over my face. Glancing back, I saw David pouring himself another drink. Looking up, he raised his glass in an ironic salute and his battle-scarred face took on its habitual mask of sardonic indifference.

I emerged from the cloakroom as the children burst noisily into the house. They gave me a happy unsurprised wave before roaring on towards the kitchen.

'Hugh! How lovely!' Mary advanced rapidly on me. 'Good God!' she laughed. 'What *have* you done to yourself!'

'I walked into something,' I said.

And mustering a smile, fixing an expression of pleasure on my face, I bent down to kiss her.

Living up to their reputation for maximum disruption, the builders had left a pile of gravel just inside the gates. Forced to abandon the car, I loaded the box of pictures under my arm and strode up the drive. Fumbling with the door handle, I sent the half-painted door against its stop with a bang.

'Is that you?' Ginny called, appearing round the kitchen door.

I dropped the box on a chair and faced her.

'Oh!' she cried, clamping a hand to her mouth. 'Good God! Whatever happened to you?' She came and raised gentle fingertips to my face.

'I've been stupid.'

'*Have* you?' She had a wonderful way of making it sound the most unlikely thing in the world.

'I can't believe how stupid I've been.'

Looking alarmed, she took a fearful breath. 'Not the car? You haven't had an accident?'

'No. Nothing like that.'

Her worst fears allayed, she pressed a hand to her chest, she took a series of sharp breaths. 'What then?'

'I walked into something.'

'Into *something*?'

'A large man in a pub?'

But her anxiety wasn't going to be bought off by thin jokes. 'Oh yes?' she said sternly.

'Okay,' I laughed, preparing to parade my stupidity. 'It *was* the car – but not while it was going any-where. I opened the door to put something inside and I turned round too quickly – I just wasn't looking – and the door swung back in my face and the corner got me right here.' Pointing at the swelling, I put on a gormless expression: the complete idiot.

She frowned, not entirely satisfied with this, I could

see the questions hovering, then with an obvious effort she put her doubts behind her, and a smile bubbled to her lips. 'A large man in a pub is going to get you far more sympathy.'

'In that case, the large man has it.'

She raised herself on tiptoe and kissed my bruised cheek.

'Was that the sympathy?' I asked.

She slipped an arm round me. 'You might get a raw steak for the eye if you're lucky.'

I would have said I loved her then, but just at that moment my heart was too full.

CLARE FRANCIS

Requiem

£6.99

Glen Ashard – Scottish home of ex-rock star Nick Mackenzie and his beautiful wife Alusha. A haven of peace and security after all the years on the road.

Until the day a small plane flies off course and sprays a death-laden chemical down on their lives . . .

And Daisy Field, environmental campaigner, picks up the trail. A woman determined to fight the profits-over-safety attitude of the agro-chemical multinationals.

From the wilds of Scotland to the air-conditioned offices of Chicago and Virginia, from Madison Square Gardens to a seedy security firm in South London, *Requiem* pulls Daisy into a chilling search for answers – struggling against apathy, sabotage and impossible odds . . .

'She writes with passion . . . undoubtedly her most
ambitious novel to date'
Sunday Express

'The effect is moving and the story great'
Mail on Sunday

'Pacy . . . intriguing'
The Times

Clare Francis
Red Crystal £5.99

THE ANGER IS THERE, THE INJUSTICE, THE REPRESSION, THE
SITUATION JUST NEEDS TO BE POLARISED –
CRYSTALLISED . . .

Out of the savagery of the Paris barricades there was born the
most sinister of all the terrorist groups of the 1960s. Secretly
funded by Moscow, trained in subversion and assassination in
Italy, the Crystal Faction came to England. To wage war . . .

For Nick Ryder of Special Branch, finding and infiltrating the cell
presented a daunting challenge. Hampered by the deviousness
of his own superiors and lack of cooperation from MI5, he was
drawn slowly but inexorably into a tangled web of sex, drugs,
murder, intrigue and lost innocence.

And at the centre, the beautiful Gabriele Schroeder, leader of the
Crystal Faction. A tough, daring, utterly ruthless woman for
whom killing had become a pleasure . . .

'The climax is agonising, and made only too horribly likely by the
author's careful groundwork and ability to maintain suspense'
Books & Bookmen

'A sexy as well as a fast-paced thriller'
Daily Express

All Pan Books are available at your local bookshop or newsagent, or can be ordered direct from the publisher. Indicate the number of copies required and fill in the form below.

Send to: Macmillan General Books C.S.
                Book Service By Post
                PO Box 29, Douglas I-O-M
                IM99 1BQ

or phone: 01624 675137, quoting title, author and credit card number.

or fax: 01624 670923, quoting title, author, and credit card number.

or Internet: http://www.bookpost.co.uk

Please enclose a remittance* to the value of the cover price plus 75 pence per book for post and packing. Overseas customers please allow £1.00 per copy for post and packing.

*Payment may be made in sterling by UK personal cheque, Eurocheque, postal order, sterling draft or international money order, made payable to Book Service By Post.

Alternatively by Access/Visa/MasterCard

Card No. ☐☐☐☐ ☐☐☐☐ ☐☐☐☐ ☐☐☐☐ ☐☐☐☐ ☐☐

Expiry Date ☐☐☐☐ ☐☐☐☐ ☐☐☐☐ ☐☐☐☐ ☐☐☐☐ ☐☐

Signature _____

Applicable only in the UK and BFPO addresses.

While every effort is made to keep prices low, it is sometimes necessary to increase prices at short notice. Pan Books reserve the right to show on covers and charge new retail prices which may differ from those advertised in the text or elsewhere.

NAME AND ADDRESS IN BLOCK CAPITAL LETTERS PLEASE

Name _____

Address _____

_____

_____

_____

8/95

Please allow 28 days for delivery.
Please tick box if you do not wish to receive any additional information. ☐